TALES OF THE
TIME SCOUTS

VICTORVILLE CITY LIBRARY
15011 Circle Dr
Victorville, CA 92395
760-245-4222

BAEN BOOKS BY ROBERT ASPRIN

The Time Scout series with Linda Evans

Time Scout
Wagers of Sin
Ripping Time
The House That Jack Built
Tales of the Time Scouts (Omnibus)
Tales of the Time Scouts: II (Omnibus, forthcoming)

For King and Country with Linda Evans

License Invoked with Jody Lynn Nye

E. Godz with Esther Friesner

Myth-Interpretations: The Worlds of Robert Asprin

ALSO BY LINDA EVANS

Far Edge of Darkness
Sleipnir

Road to Damascus with John Ringo

Hell's Gate with David Weber
Hell Hath No Fury with David Weber

TALES OF THE TIME SCOUTS

ROBERT ASPRIN
LINDA EVANS

This is a work of fiction. All the characters and events portrayed in this book are fictional, and any resemblance to real people or incidents is purely coincidental.

A Baen Books Original

Baen Publishing Enterprises
P.O. Box 1403
Riverdale, NY 10471
www.baen.com

ISBN: 978-1-4767-8097-9

Cover art by Adam Burn

First Baen printing, December 2015

Distributed by Simon & Schuster
1230 Avenue of the Americas
New York, NY 10020

Printed in the United States of America

10 9 8 7 6 5 4 3 2 1

Contents

TIME SCOUT

Robert Asprin and
Linda Evans

Chapter 1

It wasn't difficult to tell visitors from 'eighty-sixers. Visitors were the ones with the round mouths and rounder eyes and steadily decreasing bankrolls. Like refugees from Grandma's attic, they were decked out in whatever the Outfitters had decreed the current "look of the century." Invariable struggles with unfamiliar bits of clothing, awkward baggage arrangements, and foreign money marked them even faster than an up-tilted head on a New York City sidewalk.

'Eighty-sixers, by contrast, stood out by virtue of omission. They neither gawked nor engaged in that most offensive of tourist behaviors, the "I-know-it-all-and-will-share-it-with-you" bravado that masks someone who wouldn't know a drachma from a sesterce, even if his life depended on it.

Which, in TT-86, it might.

Nope, the 'eighty-sixers were the ones who hauled luggage, snagged stray children back from the brink of disaster, and calmed flaring tempers in three different languages in as many minutes, all without loosening a fold of those impossible-to-wrap Roman togas or bumping into a single person with those equally impossible-to-manage Victorian bustles.

'Eighty-sixers were right at home in La-La Land.

Frankly, Malcolm Moore couldn't imagine living anywhere else.

Which was why he was currently threading his way through the Commons of Shangri-la Station, decked out in his most threadbare woolen tunic (the one with the artistic wine and dung stains), his dirtiest cheap sandals, and his very finest bronze collar (the one that read MALCOLUM SERVUS ______).

The blank spot waited for the name of any person offering him a job. Adding the customer's name would take only seconds with his battery-powered engraver, and he had a grinder in his room to smooth out the name again for the next trip. The metal was currently as shiny as his hopes and as empty as his belly.

Occasionally, Malcolm felt the pun inherent in his name had become a harbinger of plain bad luck.

"Well, my luck's gotta change sometime," he muttered, girding metaphorical loins for battle.

His destination, of course, was Gate Six. Tourists were already beginning to converge on its waiting area, milling about in animated groups and smiling clusters. Hangers-on thronged the vast Commons just to watch the show. A departure at Gate Six was an Event, worth watching even for those not making the trip. Tables at little cafes and bars, especially those in the "Roman City" section of the terminal, were filling up fast.

In "Urbs Romae" hot-dog stands took the form of ancient sausage-and-wine-vendor shops visible on the streets of ancient Rome, complete with vats of hot oil in which the hot dogs sizzled. Countersunk amphorae in the countertops brimmed with higher quality wine than anything down time. Better cafes were designed like temples, private courtyards, even colonnaded gardens complete with fountains and flowerbeds. The clink of glassware and the rich scents of coffee, warm pastries, and expensive liquor caressed Malcolm's nostrils like a lover's fingertips. His belly rumbled. God, he was hungry. . . .

He nodded to a few friends already seated at cafe tables. They waved and were kind enough not to offer him a seat, since he was clearly dressed for business. As he approached the Down Time's narrow, dim storefront, half-hidden under the crossbeams of a support for a second-story catwalk (cleverly disguised as "marble" columns and balcony), he spotted Marcus and waved. His young friend was busy setting out shot glasses at one of the window-seat tables the bar boasted. A three-foot porthole affair, it gave the impression of peeping out through the side of an ancient sailing ship.

"Bona fortuna," the bartender mouthed through the glass; then he touched his temple and winked. Malcolm grinned. Marcus—who possessed no last name—had once expressed a private opinion that anyone who wanted to visit the genuine Urbs Romae was slightly off in the head.

"Go back?" he'd said the one time Malcolm had suggested they combine their respective talents as partners in the freelance guide business. Startlement in his young eyes had given way almost immediately to a glint akin to fear. "You do me honor, friend. But no. Shangri-la is more fun." The strain around his smile prompted Malcolm to change the subject with a mental note never to raise it again.

Urbs Romae was Malcolm's favorite part of Shangri-la Station, probably because ancient Rome was his specialty. Beyond the entrance to the Down Time Bar & Grill, the Commons stretched away like the inside of a shopping mall designed by Escher. Two hundred yards across and nearly three times that length, the Commons was a multi-level monstrosity of girders, broad catwalks, ramps, balconies, and cantilevered platforms disguised as an astonishing number of items. Many of them led absolutely nowhere.

Pleasant fountains and pools splashed under the perpetual glow of the Commons' lights. The occasional ash of color against blue-tiled fountains betrayed the presence of exotic fish kept to graze the algae. Urbs Romae's floor was a colorful patchwork of mosaics in the ancient style, most of them put together by the enterprising merchants whose shops bordered them. Signs shrouded the walls at random intervals, while staircases stretched upward past storefronts and hotel windows to unpredictable levels along the walls.

Some ramps and catwalks were still under construction or at least seemed to be. A number ended in blank stretches of concrete wall, while others reached islands that floated four and five stories above the main floor, supported by open strutwork like scaffolding around a cathedral under reconstruction. A few ramps and stairways stretched from scattered spots to end in thin air, leaving one to wonder whether they led up to something invisible or down from a hole out of nothing.

Malcolm grinned. First impressions of Shangri-la left most visitors convinced that the time terminal's nickname, La-La Land, came from the lunatic walks to nowhere.

Large signs bordered several blank stretches, where balconies and catwalks had been screened off with chain-link fencing that made no pretense of blending in with the rest of Urbs Romae. The signs, in multiple languages, warned of the dangers of unexplored gates. The fencing wasn't so much to keep things from wandering *in* as to keep other things from wandering *out.* The signs, of course, were a legal precaution. Most tourists weren't stupid enough to wander through an open portal without a guide. But there had been casualties at other stations and lawsuits had occasionally been filed by bereaved families. Residents of TT-86 were grateful for their own station manager's precautions.

Nobody wanted the time terminal shut down for slipshod management.

Nobody.

Today's batch of tourists and guides looked like refugees from *Spartacus.* Most of the men tugged uncomfortably at dress-like tunics and expended considerable effort avoiding one another's eyes. Knobby knees and hairy legs were very much in evidence. Malcolm chuckled. *Ah, Gate Six. . . .* Malcolm wore his own threadbare tunic with the ease of long practice. He barely registered the difference between his business costumes and what he normally wore, although he did note that his sandal strap needed repairing again.

Women in elegant *stolas* chatted animatedly in groups, comparing jewelry, embroidered borders, and elegant coiffeurs. Others wandered into the gate's waiting area, where they relaxed in comfortable chairs, sipped from paper cups, and watched the show. Those, Malcolm knew, were rich enough they'd been down time before. First-time tourists were too excited to sit down. Malcolm pushed past the periphery of the growing crowd in search of likely employers.

"Morning, Malcolm."

He turned to find Skeeter Jackson, clad elegantly in a Greek-style chiton. He held back a groan and forced a smile. "Morning, Skeeter." After the brief handclasp, he counted his fingernails.

Skeeter nodded to Malcolm's tunic. "I see you're trying the slave-guide routine." Brown eyes sparkled. "Great stains. I'll have to get your recipe sometime." Skeeter's wide smile, which was, as far as anyone had ever been able to tell, the only genuine thing about him, was infectious.

"Sure," Malcolm laughed. "One quart liquefied mare's dung, two quarts sour Roman wine, and three pints Tiberian mud. Spread carefully with an artist's brush, let dry for two weeks, then launder in cold water. Works wonders on raw wool."

Skeeter's eyes had widened. "Gad. You're serious." His own garments, as always, were fastidiously neat and apparently new. Where he'd obtained them, Malcolm didn't want to know. "Well, good luck." Skeeter offered. "I have an appointment to keep." He winked. "See you around."

The slim young man grinned like an imp counting damned souls and slipped off into the growing crowd. Malcolm surreptitiously checked his belt pouch to be sure the battery-powered engraver and business cards were still there.

"Well," he told himself, "at least he never seems to roll one of us 'eighty-sixers." He glanced at one of several dozen chronometers which depended from the distant ceiling and checked the countdown on Gate Six.

Time to get to work.

The crowd was growing denser. The noise volume increased exponentially. Hired baggage handlers worked to balance awkward loads comprised of odd-sized parcels and sacks and leather satchels, while Time Tours guides double-checked their customer lists and gave last-minute instructions. Ticket takers at the entrance to Gate Six's main ramp waved through a couple of company executives on their way to check the upper platform. Already Malcolm estimated the crowd at some seventy-five people.

"Too big for a tour group," he muttered. Time Tours, Inc., was getting greedy. The noise of tourist voices and baggage handlers grunting at their work bounced off girders high overhead and reverberated, creating a roar of confused echoes. At least with a group this size, he ought to be able to find something. He plastered a hopeful smile on his face, fished into the leather pouch at his waist for business cards, and got busy.

"Hello," he introduced himself to the first prospect, extending a hand to a tall, robust man whose tan and fair hair said "California tycoon." "Please allow me to introduce myself. Malcolm Moore, freelance guide."

The man shook his hand warily, then glanced at the business card he'd proffered. It read:

Malcolm Moore, Time Guide
Rome AD 47% London 1888 1 Denver 1885
Other Destinations Available upon Request
Experience Adventure without the Hassle of a Tour Schedule!
Private Side Tours and In-Depth Guide Services for
Individuals, Families, Students, Business Groups
Best Rates In Shangri-la Contact: TT-86 Room 503

The tycoon scanned his card and glanced back up. "You're a freelancer?" The tone was more dubious than ever.

"My specialty is ancient Rome," Malcolm said with a warm, sincere smile. "I hold a Ph.D. in Classics and Anthropology and have nearly seven years experience as a guide. The formal tour," he nodded toward uniformed Time Tours employees taking tickets and answering questions, "includes the Circus Maximus chariot races and gladiatorial combats, but Time Tours is bypassing the extraordinary experience of the . . ."

"Thank you," the man handed back the card, "but I'm not interested."

Malcolm forced the smile to remain. "Of course. Some other time, perhaps."

He moved on to the next potential customer. "Please allow me to introduce myself . . ."

Begging never got any easier.

Given the chill of this crowd, Time Tours had been poisoning their customers against freelancers. Skeeter Jackson, drat the boy, seemed to be doing fine, whatever he was up to in that far corner. His smile glowed brighter than the overhead lights.

By the time the countdown clock read T-minus-ten minutes, Malcolm had begun to consider offering his services as a baggage handler just to pick up enough cash for a few meals, but a man had his pride. Malcolm was a guide and a damned good one. If he lost what was left of his reputation as a professional, his life here would be over. He scanned the crowd from one edge, counting heads and costumes, and decided glumly that he had, in fact, talked to everyone.

Well . . . damn.

A desperate attempt to hold onto the shreds of his dignity sent Malcolm to retreat. He retired from the immediate vicinity of Gate Six, accompanied by a return of nagging worries about how he might pay for his room and the next few meals. Overriding that, Malcolm suffered a keen disappointment that had very little to do with money or the loss of his old, full-time job. Malcolm Moore had no idea how guides for the big outfits like Time Tours felt; but for him, stepping through a portal into another century was a thrill better than eating regularly, almost better than sex.

It was that thrill which kept him at TT-86, working every departure, no matter the destination, for the chance to try it again.

Malcolm headed for the shadows of a vine-draped portico, close enough to Gate Six to watch the fun, but far enough away to avoid attracting attention from friends who would want to sympathize. Montgomery Wilkes, looking very out of place in his dark, up-time uniform, strode through the crowd with the singular intensity of a charging rhino. Even tourists scuttled out of his way. Malcolm frowned. What was Wilkes doing out of his inner sanctum? La-La Lands' head ATF agent never attended a Gate opening. He glanced again at the nearest overhead chronometer board and found the answer.

Ah . . .

Primary, too, was due to cycle. He'd forgotten in the hustle of trying to line up a job that a new batch of tourists would be arriving today from up time. Malcolm rubbed the tip of his nose and smiled. A double-gate day. . . . Maybe there was hope, after all. Even without a job, it ought to be fun.

Down at Gate Six, last-minute purchases were in full swing. Strolling vendors worked the crowd efficiently, burdened down with everything from ropes of "safe" sausages to extra leather satchels for souvenirs, the latest "must-have" survival junk, and local coinage for those stupid enough to leave money exchanges to the last minute.

Malcolm wondered if he should consider a career as a vendor? They always seemed to do well and it would be steady work. Connie, maybe, would give him a job. He shook his head absently as he watched everything from last-minute mugs of coffee to tawdry bits of jewelry exchange hands. Nah, he'd get bored too quickly trying to hold down a mundane job, even here. Setting up his own shop was out of the question. Besides the higher rent for business space and all that hideous government paperwork to cope with, there was the question of where he would get the capital to buy inventory? Investors weren't interested in ex-guides; they wanted shrewd business acumen and plenty of sales management experience.

Of course, he could always go back to time scouting.

Malcolm glanced involuntarily toward the nearest barricades. The area had been fenced off because the gate hadn't yet been explored or was inherently unstable. Malcolm had risked down-time explorations into unknown gates as a freelance time scout only twice. A stray shiver crawled up his spine. Kit Carson, the first—and best—of all the time scouts, was famous all over the world. And damned lucky to be alive. Malcolm wasn't exactly a coward, but time scouting was not Malcolm's idea of a sane career. He was more than happy to settle for rubbing shoulders with giants and sharing war stories with the real heroes of TT-86 over beer and pretzels.

A strident klaxon sounded, echoing five stories above the terminal floor. Conversation cut off mid-sentence. As abruptly as it had sounded, the klaxon died away, replaced by an amplified voice. Long-time residents leaned forward in chairs, absently twirling half-empty glasses or drawing designs in the condensate on table tops with idle fingertips. The throng in the waiting area paused expectantly.

"Your attention, please. Gate Six is due to open in three minutes. Returning parties will have gate priority. All departures, please remain in the holding area until guides are notified that the gate is clear."

The message repeated in three other languages.

Malcolm wished his tunic had pockets so he could thrust his hands into them. Instead he crossed his arms and waited. Another ear-splitting klaxon sounded.

"Your attention, please. Gate One is due to open in ten minutes. All departures, be advised that if you have not cleared Station Medical, you will not be permitted to pass Primary. Please have your baggage ready for customs . . ."

Malcolm stopped listening. He'd memorized the up-time departure litany years ago. Besides, departures down-time were always more entertaining than watching a bunch of government agents search luggage. The real fun at Primary wouldn't begin until the new arrivals started coming through. Malcolm's gaze found the countdown for Gate Six. Any second now . . .

A hum of sub-harmonics rumbled through the time terminal as Gate Six, the biggest of TT-86's active gates, came to life. Outside the range of audible sound, yet detectable through the vibration of bones at the base of one's skull, the sound that wasn't a sound intensified. Across the Commons, tourists pressed behind their ears with the heels of hands in an attempt to relieve the unpleasant sensation. Malcolm traced his gaze up a pair of broad ramps—one of which descended toward the waiting area from a wide catwalk, the other of which would handle departures—and waited eagerly.

Up at the edge of the catwalk an utterly blank section of wall began to shimmer. Like a heat haze over a stretch of noonday highway, the air rippled. Colors dopplered through the spectrum in odd, distorted patterns. Gasps rose from the waiting area, distinctly audible in the hush. Then a black spot appeared in the dead center of the blank wall.

Tourists gaped and pointed. For most, it was only the second time in their lives they'd seen a temporal gate up-close and personal—their first, of course, being Primary on the down-time trip to Shangri-la.

Conversation, which had begun to pick up again in the wake of the first shimmer, died off sharply. Baggage handlers finished tying off their loads. Last-minute transactions led to more money changing hands. More than one guide gulped down the last scalding coffee they'd taste in two weeks.

The spot on the wall dilated, spreading outward like a growth of bread mold viewed on high-speed film. In the center of the darkness, as though viewed through the wrong end of a telescope, Malcolm made out the shape of dim shelves and tiny amphorae stacked neatly in rows at the back of a long, deep room. Then light flared like a twinkling star as someone on the other side lit a lamp.

Tourists on the floor exclaimed, then laughed in nervous delight as a man dressed as a Roman slave, but moving with the purpose and authority of a Time Tours organizer, stepped through. He rushed at them like a hurled baseball, growing in apparent height from a few inches to full size in the blink of an eyelash, then calmly stepped through onto the metal grating. He landed barking orders.

Tourists, some looking dazed and ill, others talking animatedly, all of them visibly tired, spilled through the open gate onto the catwalk and down the ramp. Most clutched souvenirs. Some clutched each other. Guides had to remind most of them to slide credit-card-sized timecards through the encoder at the bottom of the ramp. Malcolm grinned again. The ritual never varied. The ones who remembered to "dock out" of Porta Romae were experienced temporal travelers. The ones clutching each other had discovered a deep-seated, unexpected fear of temporal travel, either because it was too dirty and violent for their taste or because they'd spent the trip terrified of making a mistake the guides couldn't fix.

The ones that looked dazed and ill either hadn't enjoyed the gladiatorial games as much as they'd thought or were still attempting to overcome the effects of too much boozing and not enough attention to proper diet and rest. Malcolm's clients never returned up time looking like they needed the nearest hospital bed. Of course, people with the sense to hire a private guide, even for a package deal like Time Tours offered, rarely had the poor judgment to get hung over after a two-week-long binge on lead-laced Roman wine.

Not for the first time, Malcolm permitted himself a moment's bitter resentment of Time Tours and their whole slick, money-milling operation. If not for their shady, underhanded tricks . . .

"Penny for 'em," someone said at Malcolm's elbow.

He started and glanced around to find Ann Vinh Mulhaney gazing up at him. He relaxed with a smile. She must have come straight from the weapons range when the klaxon sounded. She hadn't bothered to unholster the pistols at her belt or loosen her hair from its confining elastic tie. At five feet, five inches, Ann was a little shorter than Malcolm, but evenly matched with Sven Bailey, who strolled up behind her. He, too, was dressed for the weapons range.

They must've just released a new class, probably the one scheduled for London. Sven, who out-massed dainty little Ann by at least two to one despite their matched heights, nodded politely toward Malcolm, then watched the departing tourists with a despairing shake of his head.

"What a miserable bunch they were," he commented to no one in particular. "Stupid, too, if you're still here." He glanced briefly toward Malcolm.

He shrugged, acknowledging the well-meant compliment, and answered Ann's question. "I'm just watching the fun, same as everyone. How are you two?"

Sven, TT-86's recognized master of bladed weapons, grunted once and didn't deign to answer. Ann laughed. She was one of the few residents who felt comfortable laughing *at* Sven Bailey. She tossed her ponytail and rested slim hands on her hips. "He lost his last bet. Five shots out of six, loser picks up the tab at Down Time."

Malcolm smiled. "Sven, haven't you learned yet not to shoot against her?"

Sven Bailey regarded his fingernails studiously. "Yep." Then he glanced up with a sardonic twist of the lips. 'Trouble is, the students keep trying to lose *their* money. What's a guy to do?"

Malcolm grinned. "The way I hear it, you two split the take."

Sven only looked hurt. Ann laughed aloud. "What a horrid rumor." She winked. "Care to join us? We're heading over to the Down Time to cool out and grab a bite to eat."

Malcolm was well beyond the stage of flushing with embarrassment every time he had to turn down an invitation from lack of funds. 'Thanks, but no. I think I'll see the departure through, then head up toward Primary and try to line up some prospects from the new arrivals. And I've got to fix this blasted sandal again. It keeps coming loose at the sole."

Sven nodded, accepting his face-saving excuses without comment. Ann started to protest, then glanced at Sven. She sighed. "If you change your mind, I'll spot you for a drink. Or better yet Sven can pick up the tab from my winnings." She winked at Malcolm. Sven just crossed his arms and snorted, reminding Malcolm of a burly bulldog humoring an upstart chickadee. "By the way," she smiled, "Kevin and I were thinking about inviting some people over for dinner tomorrow night. If you're free at, on, say about sixish, stop by. The kids love it when you visit."

"Sure," he said, without really meaning it. "Thanks."

Fortunately, they moved off before noticing the dull flush that crept up Malcolm's neck into his cheeks. If Ann Vinh Mulhaney had pre-planned a dinner party for tomorrow night, he'd eat his sandal, broken strap and all. Her gesture warmed him, though, even as he rubbed the back of his neck and muttered, "I've got to get a full-time job with *someone.*" But not with Time Tours.

Never with Time Tours.

He'd starve first.

Tourists over at Gate Six had started to climb the ramp, each one in turn presenting his or her Timecard to have the departure logged properly. Excited women could be heard clear across the Commons, shrieking and giggling as they plucked up the nerve to step through the open portal. That ritual never varied, either. Scuttlebutt had it that Time Tours had sound-proofed the exits on the other side of *all* their gates, rather than hush the tourists. He had to chuckle. He couldn't really blame them. Stepping through that first time was an unnerving experience.

Inevitably—this time about three quarters of the way through the departure—someone fumbled a load of poorly tied baggage. Parcels scattered across the catwalk, creating a major hitch in the traffic flow.

Three separate guides, glancing wildly at the overhead chronometer, converged on the mess and snatched up baggage willy nilly. A fourth guide all but shoved the remaining tourists through the open gate. The edges of the gate had begun to shrink slowly back toward the center.

Malcolm shook his head. With years of experience behind them, Time Tours really ought to manage better than that. He grunted aloud. *That's what comes of exploiting stranded down-timers to haul baggage.* Somebody really should do something about the poor souls who wandered in through open gates and found themselves lost in an alien world. His old outfit had never used them as grunt labor.

Of course, his old outfit had quietly gone bankrupt, too.

The guides who'd snatched up the spilled parcels lunged through and vanished. Moments later, Gate Six winked closed for another two weeks. Malcolm sighed and turned his attention to Primary. He checked the chronometer and swore under his breath. He just had time, if he hustled. He left Urbs Romae behind and half jogged through Frontier Town, with its saloons and strolling "cowboys," then picked up speed through Victoria Station's "cobbled" streets, lined with shops whose windows boasted graceful Victorian gowns and masculine deerstalkers. The klaxon sounded, an ear-splitting noise that caused Malcolm to swear under his breath.

"Your attention, please. Gate One is due to open in two minutes. All departures, be advised that if you have not cleared Station Medical, you will not be permitted to pass Primary. Please have your baggage ready for customs . . ."

Malcolm cut across one edge of Edo Castletown, with its extraordinary gardens, sixteenth-century Japanese architecture, and swaggering tourists dressed as samurai warriors. He jogged past the Neo Edo Hotel, skirting a group of kimono-clad women who had paused to admire the mural inside the lobby. The desk clerk grinned and waved as he shot past.

Primary, less than a hundred feet beyond the farthest edge of Castletown, consisted of an imposing set of barriers, armed guards, ramps, fences, metal detectors, and X-ray equipment, plus dual medical stations, all clustered at the bottom of a broad ramp that led fifteen feet into thin air then simply stopped. Malcolm had once wondered why the station hadn't simply been constructed so that the floor was dead-level even with Gate One, or Primary, as everyone in residence called it.

Upon subsequent interaction with officials from the Bureau of Access Time Functions, Malcolm had decided ATF must have insisted on the arrangement for its unsettling psychological impact Montgomery Wilkes, inspecting everything like a prowling leopard, stood out simply by the sweating hush which followed his rounds.

Malcolm found a good vantage point and leaned his shoulder against the station wall, extremely glad he didn't work for the ATF agent. He glanced at the nearest chronometer and sighed. *Whew . . .* Seconds to spare. The line of returning tourists and businessmen had already formed, snaking past Malcolm's position through a series of roped-off switchbacks. Customs agents were rubbing metaphorical hands in anticipation.

Malcolm's skull bones warned him moments before the main gate into Shangri-la dilated open. Then up-timers streamed through the open portal into the terminal, while departures cleared customs in the usual inefficient dribble. New arrivals stopped at the medical station set up on the inbound side of the gate to have their medical records checked, logged, and mass-scanned into TT-86's medical database. The usual clusters of wide-eyed tourists, grey-suited business types, liveried tour guides, and uniformed government officials—including TT-86's up-time postman with the usual load of letters, laser disks, and parcels—edged clear of Medical and entered the controlled chaos of La-La Land.

"Okay," Malcolm muttered, "let's see what Father Christmas brought us this time." Once a time-guide, always a time-guide. The occupation was addictive.

He double-checked the big chronometer board. The next departure was set for three days hence, London. Denver followed that by twelve hours and Edo a day after that. One of the quarterly departures to twelfth-century Mongolia would be leaving in six days. He shook his head. Mongolia was out of the question. None of that incoming group looked hardy enough for three months in deadly country inhabited by even deadlier people.

Gate Five didn't get much traffic, even when it *was* open.

He eyed the inbound crowd. London, Denver, or ancient Tokyo . . . Most of the tourists to Edo were Japanese businessmen. They tended to stick with Japanese tour guides. The only time Malcolm had been to sixteenth-century Edo had been on a scheduled tour for his old company and he'd been in *heavy* disguise. The Tokugawa shoguns had developed a nasty habit of executing any *gaijin* unfortunate enough even to be shipwrecked on Japanese shores. After that first visit, Malcolm had firmly decided he'd acquired a good knowledge of sixteenth-century Japanese, Portuguese, and Dutch for nothing.

London or Denver, then . . . He'd have three days, minimum, to work on a client. His gaze rested on a likely-looking prospect, a middle-aged woman who had paused to gape in open confusion while the three small children clustered at her side shoved fists into their mouths and clutched luggage covered with Cowboys and Indians. The smallest boy wore a plastic ten-gallon hat and a toy six-gun rig. Mom glanced from side to side, up and down, stared at the chronometer, and appeared ready to burst into tears.

"Bingo." Tourist in need of help.

He hadn't taken more than three steps, however, when a redheaded gamine clad in a black leather miniskirt, black stretch-lace body suit, and black thigh-high leather boots, hauling a compact suitcase that looked like it weighed as much as she did, bore down on him with the apparent homing instinct of a striking hawk: "Hi! I'm looking for Kit Carson—any idea where I might find him?"

"Uh . . ." Malcolm said intelligently as every drop of blood in his brain transmuted instantaneously to the nether regions of his anatomy. Not only did Malcolm have no idea where the retired time scout might be lurking this time of day . . .

God . . . it *ought to be* illegal *to look like that!*

Clearly, it'd been far too long since Malcolm had—

He gave himself an irritable mental kick. Just where *might* she find Kit? He probably wasn't at his hotel, not this late in the morning;

but it was a little early for drinking. Of course, he enjoyed watching departures as much as any other 'eighty-sixer.

The delightful little minx who'd accosted him was tapping one leather-clad foot in an excess of energy. With her short auburn hair, freckles, and clear green eyes, she gave the impression of an Irish alley-cat, intent on her own business and impatient with anything that got in her way. She was the darned cutest thing Malcolm had seen come through Primary in months. He kept his gaze on her face with studied care.

"Try the Down Time Bar and Grill. If anyone knows, the regulars there might. Or you could . . ."

He trailed off. She was already gone, like a bullet from the barrel of a smoking gun. That damned leather miniskirt did evil things to Malcolm's breath control.

"Well." He rested hands on hips. "If that doesn't . . ." He couldn't imagine why a girl that age—and in a tearing hurry, besides—would be looking for Kit Carson of all people. "Huh." He tried to put her out of his mind and turned to find his bewildered tourist with the cute kids. He needed a job worse than he needed a mystery.

"Oh, bloody hell . . ." Skeeter Jackson, the louse, had already collared the scared family and was hard at work playing with the youngest kid. Mom was beaming. God help them.

He considered warning her, then glanced down at his artistically filthy tunic and swore again. Compared with Skeeter Jackson's groomed appearance, he didn't stand a chance. Maybe he could get her aside later and explain the difference between reliable guides and the Skeeter Jacksons of this world. Malcolm sighed. The way his luck had been running lately, she'd slap him for maligning that "nice young man."

He decided maybe it wouldn't hurt to take Ann up on her offer, after all. Malcolm strolled down the Commons on a reverse course through Castletown, Victoria Station, and Frontier Town. He entered Urbs Romae just as the klaxon for closure of Primary sounded, warning everyone that TT-86 was about to be sealed in again for another couple of days, at least. Up ahead, the pert little up-timer looking for Kit sailed straight past the Down Time without spotting it. He grinned and decided to see how long it took her to holler for help.

Just what *did* she want with Kit Carson?

Whatever it was, Malcolm had a feeling the next few days were going to prove most entertaining.

Margo thumped down the long, cluttered concourse, berating herself as she went. "Honestly," she fumed, "the first person you ask is a guy in a Roman tunic and slave collar? He's probably some poor down-timer who wandered through an unstable gate, like the articles warned about. Stupid, greenhorn idiot . . ."

Margo did not enjoy looking like a fool.

"No wonder he took so long answering. Probably had to translate everything I said first. At least he spoke *some* English. And I've got the right station, that's something to celebrate," she added under her breath, glancing in restrained awe at the sprawling complex which stretched away in a maze of catwalks, shops, waiting areas, and cross-corridors that led only God knew where. The care she'd taken to research a time terminal's layout didn't begin to convey the reality of the place. It was enormous, bewildering. And none of the information she'd found described the private sections of a terminal, visible in tantalizing glimpses off the Commons. She found herself wanting to explore . . .

"First," she told herself sternly, "I find Kit Carson. Everything else is secondary. That Roman guy said he might be at some bar, so all I have to do now is find him. I can talk anybody into anything. All I have to do is find him. . . ."

Unfortunately, she didn't find the Down Time on the main concourse or any of the balconies connected to it. Margo set down her heavy suitcase, panting slightly, and scowled at an empty set of chairs clustered around a closed gate.

"*What* Down Time Bar and Grill?" Grimly, Margo picked up her case again, regretting the decision to stuff everything into one piece of luggage. She looked for a terminal directory, something like she'd always found at ordinary shopping malls, but saw nothing remotely resembling one. She didn't want to betray complete ignorance by *asking* someone. Margo was desperate to give the impression that she was worldly, well-traveled, able to take care of herself.

But the Down Time Bar and Grill was apparently close kin to the Flying Dutchman, because it didn't appear to exist. Maybe it *was* down time? *Don't be ridiculous. Nobody'd put a bar on the other side of a time gate.* Finally she started hunting down the maze of cross-linked, interconnecting corridors that formed the private portion of TT-86. Stairways led to corridors on other levels, some of them brightly lit, others dim and deserted Within minutes, she was hopelessly lost and fuming.

She set the case down again and rubbed her aching palm. Margo glared at a receding stretch of corridor broken occasionally by more corridors and locked doors. "Don't these people believe in posting a directory somewhere?"

"May I help you?"

The voice was polite, male, and almost directly behind her.

She spun around.

The guy in the tunic. Oh, shit. . . . Ever since New York, she'd been so careful—and this was a down-timer, God knew what he'd try to pull—

"Are you following me?" she demanded, furious that her voice came out breathy and scared instead of calm and assured.

He scratched the back of his neck under the thick bronze collar. "Well, I couldn't help but notice you passed the Down Time, then took a really wrong turn off the Commons. It's easy to get lost, back here."

Margo's heart pounded so hard her chest hurt. She backed away a step. "I ought to warn you," she said in a tone meant to be forbidding, "I know martial arts."

"As a matter of fact, so do I."

Oh, God . . .

He grinned disarmingly, reminding Margo quite suddenly of her high school history teacher. "Most temporal guides do, you know."

Temporal guide?

He held out a business card neatly clasped between two fingers. "Malcolm Moore, freelance time guide."

Margo felt her face flame. "I . . . uh . . ." Clearly he knew exactly what she'd been thinking—and seemed to find it amusing. She took the card hesitantly and risked glancing at it. The card seemed genuine enough. "Uh, hi. I'm Margo."

If he was offended that she'd withheld her last name, he didn't show it. He said only, "Nice to meet you, Margo," and shook her hand formally.

"If you like, I'll take you back to the Down Time."

She hesitated.

He grinned. "No charge. I only charge for tours on the *other* side of time gates."

"Oh. Okay." Then, grudgingly, because she was embarrassed she hadn't said it sooner, "Thanks."

"Don't mention it."

He had a nice smile. Maybe she could trust him, just a little. *Should'a worn something else, though.* His glance slid across her with inevitable—she almost might have said involuntary—interest. Most guys looked at her that way, thinking she was at least the eighteen she tried to appear rather than the almost-seventeen she was. Yes, she should have worn something else. But the boots were too bulky to pack in her case and she'd wanted to use every possible advantage she possessed when she finally came face to face with Kit Carson. . . . *Well you made this bed. Lie in it.* Margo picked up her case and followed him back toward a corridor she was certain led in the wrong direction, only to emerge in a cross-corridor she recognized as the one she'd taken off the Commons. Margo sighed and relegated herself to having to overcome yet another handicap on her quest: a reputation for stupidity. Maybe Mr. Moore wouldn't say anything about having to lead her out by the hand; but she wouldn't bet on it. And she certainly didn't have enough money to bribe him.

They regained the Commons in silence, for which she was grateful. As they approached an enormous area caged to prevent tourist access, Margo frowned. She'd noticed it before, but only peripherally. Inside the cage was an irregular-shaped hole in the concrete.

"What's that?" she asked hesitantly, afraid she knew the answer already. *Unstable gate . . .*

Malcolm Moore glanced around. "What's what? Oh, the unstable gate."

"I know about those."

"Yes. Well, the floor collapsed when this one opened under it. A coffee stand fell through."

She edged closer for a better look and paled. The sight was unnerving. Air at the bottom seemed to ripple oddly. Every few seconds, she heard the splash of water. The bones behind her ears buzzed uncomfortably. "Fell through into where?"

"We think it's the Bermuda Triangle." His voice was flat, completely deadpan.

"The *Bermuda Triangle?* Don't jerk me around!"

"Hey," he held out both hands, "who declared war? Honest, we think it's the Bermuda Triangle. Katie and Jack Sherman almost drowned when the gate opened up the first time. Their coffee shop went straight to the bottom. I was on the rescue team that went through for them. Not only is it an unstable gate, the darned thing leads to a whole nexus of other gates popping open and closed. Picking the right one back to La-La Land was murder. Took us five wrong tries. We almost didn't get back."

"Oh." *Great. Unstable nexus gates, yet.* "I know about unstable nexus gates," Margo muttered, wondering why none of her research had turned up that little tidbit. Maybe the government didn't want to scare people? "I've been on time terminals before."

He appeared to accept the lie. She'd sooner have died than admit she'd sold almost everything she owned—and very nearly a good bit more—to raise the price of a down-time ticket onto TT-86. Margo eyed the hole in the floor with a slight chill of misgiving. Well, adventure was what she was here for, wasn't it?

"So where's this bar?" she demanded, turning her back on the watery chasm. "I have business with Mr. Carson."

Malcolm Moore eyed her for one heartbeat longer than he should have—did he suspect anything? ATF had accepted her faked ID without a second glance—then he shrugged and jerked his head. "It's down this way, in Urbs Romae. The Roman City," he translated, assuming she wouldn't know the meaning of "urbs."

Margo muttered, "I know where the word urban comes from." It was very nearly the only Latin she knew, but she knew *that.*

The corners of his eyes crinkled nicely when he smiled. Margo decided Malcolm Moore didn't remind her of any of the men she'd known, after all. "Come on. I'll show you where it is. It's a little tricky to spot."

She followed, hauling a suitcase that weighed more by the moment. When she had trouble keeping up, he glanced around and slowed his pace slightly to match hers.

"Are you by any chance planning to visit London? Or Denver?"

"Why?"

He grimaced expressively. "Just hoping. I'm looking for a client for one of the upcoming tours. We freelancers have to hustle for a job."

"Oh. No, I wasn't planning a tour. Sorry."

"Don't mention it." His eyes, however, remained bright with unspoken curiosity. Just how often did Kit Carson get visitors? If the world's most famous time scout turned out to be a cranky recluse . . . Given the difficulty she'd had ferreting out recent information on him, he probably was. Well, coping with her father ought to have been training enough to deal with any ill-tempered male ego. That training had gotten her out of New York alive, hadn't it?

Malcolm Moore led her at least halfway down the Commons, through areas that reminded Margo of history-book pictures. She knew where the various gates led, having researched TT-86 as thoroughly as possible before taking the plunge. This portion of the terminal led to ancient Athens, while the section over there was designed like a city in the High Andes. They passed shops that fascinated with glimpses of exotic interiors. One restaurant was shaped like a South American pyramid; its doorway was a replica of the Sun Gate at Teotihuacan.

Beyond that, Margo spotted intricate knotted patterns and interwoven mythical beasts carved around shop doorways. One restaurant had been built into a dragon-prowed ship, with signs painted to look like Viking runes. The scents wafting out of the restaurants made her empty belly rumble in complaint.

Should've eaten lunch before I came down time. I bet the prices here are sky-high. At least in New York, she'd been able to buy cheap hot dogs from street vendors. They passed into an area of mosaic floors and Roman-style shop fronts, then her guide ducked under a span of fake columns and steel supports and indicated a dim doorway. The clink of glasses and the unmistakable scent of beer wafted out from the interior. There was no shop sign visible anywhere. No wonder she'd missed it. *Must be a hangout for residents only, if they don't advertise.*

"*Voila,*" Malcolm Moore said with a courtly flourish and a smile. "The Down Time Bar and Grill."

"Thanks." She flashed him a quick smile of gratitude, then headed for the dim-lit entrance, leaving him to follow or wander off on his own, whichever he preferred. Her attention was already focused on what she was going to say to the legendary Kenneth "Kit" Carson, the man on whom her entire future—and more—depended. Mouth dry, palms wet, Margo gripped her suitcase in one hand and her courage in the other, then charged across the threshold.

". . . so anyway," Ann laughed above the sharp crack of billiard balls from the back room, "he learned a valuable lesson about concentrating on the front-sight post. Marcus, hello, yes, I'll have another."

Across the table, Sven groaned theatrically. Rachel Eisenstein's musical laughter provided a comical counterpoint to Sven Bailey's gloom.

"Oh, hush up and finish your beer," Ann told him. "I won fair and square."

"I know. That's what's so damn depressing." Ann winked at Marcus while Rachel sipped from her wineglass and continued to laugh silently. Sven took another pull from his beer mug and sighed. The young bartender grinned and went in search of refills.

Granville Baxter wandered in, having to duck under the doorway, and paused to allow his eyes to adjust to the dim interior. His grey business suit was still crisp and neat, but the man who wore it had a wilted look that said, "I need a drink. Now." Rachel waved and indicated an empty chair. Baxter's maternal Masai heritage coupled with a few paternal ancestors who'd been NBA stars gave him a height advantage over every single 'eighty-sixer in La-La Land. Granville Baxter, however, had no earthly interest in sports, other than occasionally sponsoring special Time Tours package deals for rich franchises.

Time Tours considered Baxter a marketing genius. "Mind if I join you?" he asked, ever polite even at the Down Time.

Sven gestured to one of several empty chairs. "Park 'em."

The Time Tours executive sank back with a sigh, fished in a pocket for a handkerchief, and blotted his dark brow.

"Double-gate day," he said, providing all the explanation any 'eighty-sixer needed.

Ann waved at Marcus and nodded toward Baxter. The bartender nodded back and drew a stein of Bax's favorite brew.

"How'd it go?" Sven asked, with a long pull at his own beer.

Bax—who had occasionally said dire things about his parents' decision to name him "Granville"—grimaced. "Baggage troubles again. Other than that, pretty smooth. Oh, we had the typical three or four who decide they want to switch tours after they get to the terminal and we had one woman who threw up all over a whole family on the other side, but nothing too rough. Forgot her scopolamine patch. I'll tell you, though, if my new baggage manager doesn't get his act together by the London departure, he's going to go begging a job somewhere else—Oh, Marcus, bless you."

Half the beer vanished in one long gulp.

Ann sympathized. One transfer, one promotion, and one family crisis had led to four new baggage managers for Time Tours at TT-86 in the past six months. Bax's own job might be on the line if baggage handlers screwed up again. Rich tourists tolerated very little in the way of mistakes from hired underlings. Even geniuses were expendable if the right tourist pitched a loud-enough fit.

Marcus set out the rest of the drinks.

"So," Bax asked, "any problems at Medical with the new arrivals?"

Rachel had just begun to reply when a startling young woman clad entirely in black leather and lace, with short, auburn hair and a suitcase gripped like a set of nunchucks, charged through the doorway on a direct course for their table.

"Hello," she said, from halfway across the room. "I'm looking for Kit Carson. I was told he might be here."

Ann and Rachel exchanged glances. Even Bax lifted one brow. "No," he said in a friendly fashion. "I'm afraid he isn't, unless he's in back playing billiards."

The young woman swung around, clearly ready to interrupt the game in progress. Every male eye in the room followed the swing of her short skirt.

"No, he isn't back there," Ann said, forestalling her. "That's Skeeter and Goldie, trying to outscam one another."

The crack of billiard balls underscored the statement. The red-haired girl all but scowled. "Any idea how I can find him? It's important."

"Well," Bax scratched the back of his head, "you could pull up a chair and wet your throat until he gets here." He looked hopeful. "He'll be here, probably sooner than later. Kit always stops by, especially on gate days." Whoever she was, this girl didn't look in the mood to hang around and wait. Marcus, in his delightfully accented English, volunteered, "He has the hotel. He is there?"

Her eyes brightened. "Hotel? Which hotel?" Sven set his mug on the table with a faint click of glass on wood. "The Neo Edo. It's right on the Commons, down by the big fish pond, with an entrance that looks like—"

She was gone before he could finish.

"Well," he said into the astonished silence.

Before anyone else could speak, Malcolm Moore stepped into the bar. He was still dressed for business and wore a wicked grin. "I see by the open mouths you've all met Margo. Anybody find out why she's looking for Kit?"

"Margo? You *know* her?" Bax demanded. "Who is she?" Malcolm dragged over an empty chair. Ann high-signed Marcus for another beer. "No," he admitted with a chagrined air, "I don't know her. She came barreling through Primary and collared me right off, asking about Kit, then promptly got lost back in Residential looking for the Down Time. I was hoping maybe she'd told you guys why she wants to find Kit. Prickly little cactus blossom, isn't she?"

Sven laughed at the look on Granville Baxter's face. "Bax, she'd put you in an early grave. Stick to Time Tours if you want to die young."

Bax shot him a look of utter disgust and studied his beer.

"Well," Malcolm nodded thanks when Marcus brought him a chilled mug, "I get the feeling things are going to be lively for a while." He saluted the group with his beer and grinned.

"You," Sven Bailey muttered, "just said a freakin' mouthful. The sixty-four-thousand-dollar question is, do we warn Kit?"

Ann and Rachel exchanged glances, Bax choked on his beer, and across the bar even Marcus started to laugh. Malcolm chuckled "Poor Kit. Well, let's put it to a vote, shall we? All in favor?"

Solemnly, but with eyes twinkling, Kit's friends cast their votes with upraised hands. Malcolm plucked a few threads from the raveling hem of his tunic. "Short thread does the honors."

Malcolm, of course, came up short. As always. He sighed, took the inevitable ribbing with a long drag at his beer, and headed for the phone

Chapter 2

Government paperwork was only one of many things about running a time-terminal hotel which Kit Carson hated. A laundry list of his favorite complaints, carefully filed away in one corner of his mind where they wouldn't distract, included laundry bills; the price of food brought in past customs; the cost of replacing towels, ashtrays, and plumbing fixtures carted off by the guests; a work force likely to vanish at a moment's notice; crushing boredom interspersed with ulcer-generating crises; and—near the top of the list—*tourists.*

Paperwork, however, was the thing he despised most.

He'd almost rather have returned to academia.

The Neo Edo's executive office, larger than some modern, up-time homes, was one of the features of his current career that made it tolerable. His office boasted a video wall with panoramic real-time views of the Commons and equally panoramic taped views of multiple down-time vistas. A wet bar stocked with illegal bottles of liquid ambrosia (which both Kit and his predecessor, the builder of Neo Edo, had brought back up time) was available any time the job grew too hairy.

Priceless paintings and art treasures rescued from palaces destroyed by the Onin Wars in fifteenth-century Kyoto graced Kit's office, which also boasted pristine *tatami* rice mats on the floor and the clean, uncluttered look of sliding paper-screen walls and delicately carved woodwork.

The office's best feature, however, was a recessed light well which cast realistic-looking "daylight" over a miniature Japanese dry landscape garden. The serene arrangement of raked white sand, upright stones, and elegantly clipped topiary which filled an entire corner of the office rested the eyes and soothed the soul.

It was Kit's salvation on paperwork days. He would periodically sit back in his chair, nurse a good bourbon, and contemplate the symbolic "islands" the rock formations represented, floating in their withered "sea" of sand. It gave Kit intense pleasure to symbolically consign the drafters of the requisite government forms to a long life marooned on one of those miniature desert islands, without hope of rescue.

Talk about the perfect Zen hell. . . .

The phone call interrupted him halfway through a form that required an entire battery of expensive lawyers to decipher. Kit grinned despite the fact that the call had come through on the "Panic Button." He tucked the receiver between shoulder and ear, allowed his gaze to stray to the corner garden, and said, "Yeah, Jimmy?"

Jimmy Okuda, at the front desk, was the only person with direct access to that particular intercom line. A call on the Panic Button usually meant another jump in Kit's blood pressure; today, the distraction was more than welcome.

"Call from Malcolm Moore, Kit."

"Malcolm?" What was Jimmy doing, buzzing him on the Panic Button for a call from Malcolm Moore? "Uh . . . put him through."

An outside line flashed as Jimmy transferred the call. What on earth could Malcolm Moore want? Kit had offered him a job more than once, only to be refused politely but firmly. Kit pressed the button. "Malcolm? Hello, what can I do for you?"

"Kit, sorry to interrupt whatever you're doing, but you're going to have a visitor in about five minutes."

"Oh?" Malcolm's tone invited all sorts of speculation. From the background noise, Malcolm was calling from the Down Time. That could mean *anything* might be on its way. Just as Kit had started reviewing lethal potentialities from his down-time adventures—and wondering where he'd left the soft body armor he'd used in his scouting days—Malcolm said, "An up-timer's looking for you."

"Up-timer?"

Malcolm chuckled thinly. "Some day, Kit, I will get you to tell me about that deal in Bangkok. Yeah, an up-timer. Real impatient, too. We took a vote and decided you deserved a warning before this one collared you." Malcolm was laughing at some inside joke to which Kit was clearly not privy.

"Uh-huh. Thanks, I think."

"Don't mention it. What're friends for? Relieve our curiosity, would you? Sven says he'll buy, if you'll tell."

Kit raised a brow. If Sven Bailey was that curious, something decidedly odd was up. "I'll let you know. Thanks for the warning."

Malcolm hung up. Kit shoved back his chair. Whoever was on his way, meeting the guy face to face, cold, was not Kit's idea of good strategy. He paused at the doorway to slip on his shoes, thought about his attire and hastily exchanged his comfortable kimono for a business jacket and slacks, then headed down to Neo Edo's main desk. "Jimmy, Malcolm says an up-time visitor is headed this way. Tell 'em I'm out, would you? I want to be scarce for a few minutes. Lay a false trail or something."

Jimmy, also a retired time scout, winked and nodded. "Sure thing, Kit."

Time scouts could never be too careful.

Particularly world-famous ones.

Kit damned all reporters everywhere and made tracks through a gathering crowd. The Neo Edo's lobby was a modern re-interpretation of the receiving hall of the shoguns at Edo Castle, as it had appeared before Ieyasu Tokugawa's famous shogunate headquarters had burned to the ground in the Long-Sleeves Fire of 1657. The lobby's showpiece was the mural-sized reproduction of Miyamoto Musashi's famous, lost painting of sunrise over Edo Castle, commissioned from the master warrior-poet-painter by none other than Japan's third Shogun, Iemitsu Tokugawa. The painting drew the eye even from the Commons, which meant tourists who wandered in to admire the artwork often stayed to become customers.

Homako Tani had been a shrewd hotelier.

La-La Land scuttlebutt had it that the Neo Edo's builder had liberated the original during the 1657 conflagration which had destroyed Edo Castle; but Kit had never found any trace of it, not even in Homako's private safe. Of course, scuttlebutt also had it that Homako Tani had been murdered by the irascible Musashi, himself, during a down-time visit to feudal Japan, for some minor insult the *ronin* samurai hadn't been willing to overlook. Other rumors had him last seen stepping through an unstable gate into Tang Dynasty China; and others that he'd gone into permanent retirement in Tibet as the Dalai Lama.

The point was, nobody knew what had become of Homako, not even the named partners in the law firm of Chase, Carstedt, and Syvertsen, who had delivered the impressive envelope deeding him ownership of the Neo Edo for "payment of debts." The only debt Homako Tani had ever owed Kit Carson was having his backside hauled out of that incendiary fiasco in Silver Plume, Colorado. So far as Kit knew, Homako never had gone back to the Old West. The stink of burnt saloons, banks, and cathouses had lingered in Kit's lungs for weeks afterward. He still mourned that sweet little four-inch "Wesson Favorite" he'd lost during the confusion. Only a thousand of the S&W Model .44 cal. DA revolvers were ever made, and his had gone up in smoke.

Kit sighed. Whatever the true fate of Homako Tani, the "inheritance" had come just as Kit was being forced into retirement. He'd needed a job, more to justify hanging around La-La Land than anything, since he didn't really need money. The Neo Edo had seemed a gift from the gods. After three years of managing the hotel, Kit had begun to suspect Homako Tani had simply come to hate government paperwork and tourists so desperately he'd bailed out before his sanity snapped. Kit shouldered his way politely past incoming arrivals from Primary, nodding and smiling to customers whose loud voices grated on his nerves, and headed past the pebble-lined fish pond just outside his lobby. He glanced both ways down the Commons, but saw nothing out of the ordinary. Just the usual batch of new tourists gawking and lugging heavy suitcases while trying to decide which hotel they could best afford.

Kit wandered over toward a free-standing souvenir-and-information stall with a nonchalance born of long practice and pretended to study the trinkets. The stall's owner, Nyoko Aoki, raised a brow, but she said nothing, tending her genuine customers with studied diligence. Nyoko's stand provided a perfect view of the Neo Edo's main lobby. The hotel's graceful facade towered three stories above the Commons floor, rising to a peak two stories below the ceiling. The name was painted tastefully in gilt English script and Japanese characters. The tourists provided perfect cover as they busily bought up station maps, guidebooks, and T-shirts or wandered into the hotel lobby to admire Musashi's mural.

Kit didn't have to wait long, although the visitor's appearance startled him considerably. The minute Kit spotted her, he knew that *this* was the up-timer Malcolm had called about. She was young, redheaded, and apparently operated on full throttle as her natural mode.

Unlike any normal tourist, she was not gawking, window-shopping, or looking for a station guidebook. The way she was dressed—and the way she moved inside all that black lace and leather—got attention from ninety percent of the men on the Commons and not a few of the women.

Kit found it suddenly difficult to control his breathing properly. *Good God, she's easy on the eyes.* Hard on the pulse, though. . . . A man could get himself into serious trouble with that girl, just by smiling at her. She charged into the Neo Edo like a runaway bullet train and cornered poor Jimmy behind the desk. His eyes had bugged. Kit couldn't quite hear what was being said over the tourist babble, but he could see her impatient frown and Jimmy's shrug and uplifted hands. He could also read Jimmy's lips: 'Try the Time Tripper."

Good. Wild-goose-chase time. She shot out of the Neo Edo's lobby at full tilt. Who in God's name was this kid? He'd expected . . . Well, Kit wasn't sure who, or what, he'd actually expected. But it wasn't a redheaded speed demon with an Irish wildcat manner and motives as inscrutable as a mandarin's. Malcolm, drat the man, hadn't given him even a hint. Of course, with Sven offering to buy drinks in exchange for information, maybe no one else really knew, either.

Kit followed her thoughtfully. He was certain he'd never run across her down time. *Her,* he'd have remembered. Vividly. He was equally certain he'd never met her up time, either. Hell, he hadn't *been* up time in years, probably not since that sexy little kitten had been wrapped in diapers. If that girl was past eighteen, it wasn't by more than a few days.

So who was she and why was she looking for him?

Probably a journalist, he thought gloomily, trying to make a name for herself. She had that supercharged "I'm going to get this story if it kills you" look of someone out for a first Pulitzer.

God . . .

Her skin was delightfully flushed, either from carrying that suitcase—which looked heavy—or from sheer pique. Kit grinned. Good. If she were sufficiently off-balance when they finally met, so much the better for him.

Kit bought a tourist map for camouflage and followed her at a respectable distance. She certainly didn't dawdle. Whoever she was, she headed straight for the Time Tripper, a modestly priced hostelry catering to families on tight budgets. Middle-aged fathers, respectable in their Hawaiian shirts and jeans, ogled her from over their wives' heads and ignored whining kids.

She cornered the hapless desk clerk, who shrugged, looked thoroughly irritated, and gestured vaguely toward the next hotel. When she stooped to retrieve her suitcase, Kit's viscera reacted mindlessly. The man standing next to him groaned, "Oh, *yes,* there is a God. . . ." Kit grinned. The guy pulled himself out of a trance when the woman next to him hit him on the shoulder. "Hey! Quit drooling!"

Another man said, "Five minutes with her would probably kill a horse."

"Yeah," his companion moaned, "but what a way to go. . . ."

They were undoubtedly right on all counts. That girl spelled T-R-O-U-B-L-E—and her trouble had his name over it. He sighed. When the redheaded whirlwind headed for the Tempus Fugit, Kit decided to let her continue the hunt alone. If Jimmy had laid his groundwork properly, she'd spend the next several minutes going from hotel to hotel. That would give Kit time to dig up what he could on her. He watched her eye-catching retreat toward the Fugit, then hastily backtracked toward the Down Time.

Margo rapidly received the impression that people were jerking her around, apparently for the fun of it. None of the desk clerks had seen Kit Carson, despite what that grinning idiot at the Neo Edo had told her. If Kit Carson had "stepped out for a meeting with the other hotel managers, sorry, I'm not sure which hotel," Margo would eat her luggage, suitcase and all.

"This is ridiculous!" she fumed, heading for yet another hotel. "He's got to be here somewhere!"

The desk clerk at the Hotel Acropolis looked at her like she'd taken leave of her senses. "Meeting? What meeting? I *am* the manager." The middle-aged woman patted the back of Margo's hand. "Honey, Jimmy probably called Kit, wherever he was, and warned him you were coming. Kit doesn't much care for unannounced visitors. If I were you, I'd settle into a room someplace, call for an appointment, and meet him at his office."

Margo thanked her for the advice and left in a hurry, more determined than ever to track him down. If she simply called for an appointment, he'd find some excuse or other to delay meeting her, probably permanently. Margo might be a nobody, but she wasn't going to remain one and she wasn't going to let a little thing like impossible-to-get appointments stand in her way. Working as she was against a ticking clock—with a six-month countdown not even God could delay—she simply didn't have time for failure.

"If I were Kit Carson," she muttered half-aloud, "and I were trying to find out who was looking for me, where would I go?"

Someplace where he could talk to the people who'd already talked to her.

"Right. Back to the Down Time."

She transferred the hateful suitcase to her other hand, eyed the vast stretch of Commons she had to re-cross, and groaned aloud.

"Consider it training in physical endurance," she told herself. The scent of food wafting out into the Commons from various restaurants was nearly more than Margo could bear. She was sorely tempted to stop for a good hot meal, but didn't want the trail to grow any colder than it already had.

You'll see, she told a host of nay-sayers, beginning with that pig of a high-school guidance counselor, moving on to Billy "The Rat" Pandropolous and ending—inevitably—with her father. Hateful, hurtful words rang in her ears, retaining the power to injure long after the bruises had healed. *Just you watch. You'll see.* Margo's eyes burned. She blinked back the tears. Small towns were terrible places to grow up with world-sized dreams—especially when those dreams were the only things you had left to hold onto. She was scared to death of Kit Carson already—had clung to this dream so long she was afraid to have it shattered, too. But the clock was ticking and Margo wasn't a quitter. No, by God, she wasn't. Just standing here was proof of that. Margo narrowed her eyes. *All right, Kit Carson. Ready or not, here I come.*

She closed in on the Down Time Bar and Grill.

Kit ducked under the girders and stepped across the Down Time's threshold. "Hey!" Malcolm called from a crowded, jovial table.

"Did you meet her?"

"Not exactly," Kit said drily. "I'll get with you in a minute."

Malcolm only grinned at the threat in his voice. Sven Bailey chuckled and popped a handful of peanuts into his mouth, washing them down with a sweating beer. Ann Mulhaney and, oh God, Rachel Eisenstein, leaned expectantly on their elbows, grinning in his direction. Rachel's eyes twinkled. Kit knew one helluva ribbing was coming, for sure—Rachel was the one person in La-La Land whose wit he could never top. Granville Baxter grinned and lifted his beer in a silent salute.

Kit stepped behind the bar and borrowed the phone.

A voice at the other end said, "Time Tripper, may I help you?"

"Yeah, Orva, this is Kit. What can you tell me about the girl who's been asking for me?"

Kit was tempted to hold the receiver away from his ear as Orva vented considerable irritation. She was just starting to say, "I have no idea why . . ." when the subject of their conversation stalked through the Down Time's door and dropped her suitcase with a bang. Kit held back a groan and tried to blend in with the wall. Sven grinned like the evil gnome he was. Rachel hid her eyes and shook with silent laughter. The redheaded wonder of the hour glared at Malcolm, who shrugged and nodded toward Kit.

Thanks, buddy, Kit thought sourly. *I owe you.*

Malcolm was grinning expectantly.

"Uh, gotta go," Kit muttered.

The line clicked dead. The outrageous little redhead cornered Kit behind the bar. "Mr. Carson? Kit Carson?"

She was standing directly in the center of the only narrow egress from this end of the bar, arms akimbo, hands on her hips, eyes flashing with barely suppressed irritation. Kit didn't think he'd ever seen a sight quite like her. She stood glaring up at him like an enraged scarlet parakeet.

Kit hung up the phone and said cautiously, "And you are . . .?"

"Margo."

Uh-huh. He surveyed her silently, waiting for the rest. When she didn't offer it, he prompted, "Margo . . ."

She still didn't offer a last name. Instead, she said, "I have a business proposition for you, Mr. Carson."

Oh, God, here it comes. The story of your life, major news feature, blockbuster motion picture . . .

In that getup, she *looked* like a Hollywood wannabe. Who knew, maybe she did have studio connections. For all he knew, she was somebody's kid, looking for a thrill.

"Lady," he said, with as patient a sigh as he could manage, "I never discuss business on my feet and I never, ever discuss business with someone who has backed me into a corner."

Her eyes widened. She had the decency to color an unbecoming shade of pink. Margo No-Name backed off sufficiently for Kit to edge out from behind the bar. Once he'd escaped, he leaned against the comfortably worn wooden bumper. "Now, if you want to talk business, kid, I suggest you buy me a drink."

From the way her mouth dropped open, one would've thought

he'd suggested they get naked and mud-wrestle. He revised his estimate from Hollywood to Smallville. She closed her mouth and said primly, "Of course."

She moved one hand surreptitiously toward a small belt pouch, giving away her insecurity and lack of funds in one greenhorn motion. Kit sighed. Journalism student, he revised his mental estimation, and not overly bright at that.

He said, "Marcus, how about my usual—no, make it a bourbon—and whatever the lad wants. She's buying." Marcus, who by this time was accustomed to the oddities of up-timers, only nodded. "House bourbon? Or the Special?" He glanced from Kit to the kid then back, smiling far back in his dark eyes. Marcus had seen it all, even *before* his arrival in La-La Land. The "Special" was a particular bottle Kit had brought back on one of his last trips. The Down Time kept it in a private cabinet for special occasions. Two matching bottles sat in Kit's private liquor cabinet. Getting through an interview with a journalism student called for more fortitude than a lone bottle of Kirin (his usual) could provide, but this was not a celebration. "House will be fine."

Marcus nodded. Kit reluctantly led his mystery pursuer to a table. He chose a spot as far toward the back of the Down Time as he could get, in the dimmest corner of the dark room, far enough from his friends to prevent casual eavesdropping and dark enough to make it hard to read his face. If he had to endure this, by God, she was going to *work* for the story. The darker the corner, the better.

Wordlessly, Margo picked up her suitcase and followed.

Chapter 3

Nothing was working out as she had planned.

Nothing.

Margo cursed her bad timing, bad temper, and bad luck and followed the retired time scout into the dingiest corner of what had to be the darkest, most miserable bar in Shangri-la Station. The atmosphere matched her mood: gloomy as a wet cat and just about as friendly. Even the carved wooden masks which dominated the bar's primitive decor seemed to be scowling at her.

As for Kit Carson, internationally famous time scout . . .

She glared at his retreating back. He looked nothing like the famous photos *Time* magazine had published a decade previously, or the even older photos from his days as one of Georgetown's brightest young faculty members. For one thing, he'd been smiling in those pictures. For another, he'd aged; or maybe "weathered" was a better term for it. Clearly, time-scouting was hard on the health. Moreover, he wasn't in "uniform." She wasn't sure what she'd expected him to be wearing, but that drab suit and wilted tie were a considerable letdown. The *Time* pictorial, the one which had fired her childhood imagination and had given her the courage to get through the last few years, had shown the pioneer of all time scouts in full regalia, armed to the teeth and ready for the Roman arena. The man whose current scowl boded ill things for Margo's future, the man who had "pushed" the famous Roman Gate—the one right here in

Shangri-la Station which Time Tours ran so profitably—was a real disappointment in the hero department.

If legend were accurate, he had nearly died pushing that gate. Margo didn't put much stock in the legend, now. Kenneth "Kit" Carson didn't look a thing like a man who'd survived gladiatorial combat. Long, thin, and wiry, he wore that rumpled business suit the way a convict might wear his uniform and sported a bristly mustache as thin and scraggly as the rest of him. His hair—too long and combed back from a high, craggy forehead—was going grey. He slouched when he walked, looking several inches shorter than the six-foot-two she knew him to be. He darted his gaze around the dim room like a man searching for enemies, rather than someone looking for a private table in a perfectly ordinary bar.

He didn't look like a retired hero *or* a retired history professor. He looked like a thoroughly irritated, dangerous old man, past sixty at least. Margo, at sixteen and forty-some weeks, swallowed hard and told herself, *Get a grip. Remember the speech you rehearsed.* Unfortunately, not only had the body of her speech fled, so had the carefully prepared intro, leaving her floundering for words as she set down her case and scooted into the booth her life's hero had chosen. He'd already taken a seat at the very back. The booth reeked of beer and cheap smoke.

The bartender, a good-looking young man with a great smile, arrived with a tumblerful of bourbon and an expectant air. He slid the bourbon unerringly across the dimly lit table toward Kit Carson, then turned to her.

"Uh . . ." She tried to think what she ought to order. *Make a good impression . . .* Margo vacillated between her favorite—a raspberry daiquiri—and something that might rescue the shreds of her reputation with this man. She hadn't seen prices listed anywhere and tried to estimate how much this interview was going to cost. *Oh, hell . . .* Margo threw caution to the winds, figuring decisiveness was better than looking like a dithering idiot. "Bourbon. Same as Mr. Carson's."

The waiter, a dim shape at best in this hell-hole of a corner, bowed in a curiously ancient fashion and disappeared. Kit Carson only grunted, an enigmatic sound that might have been admiration or thinly veiled disgust. At least he hadn't asked if she were old enough to drink. The bourbon arrived. She knocked back half of it in one gulp, then sat blinking involuntary tears and blessing the darkness.

*Gah. . . .*Where had they distilled this stuff?

"So . . ." She sensed more than saw movement across the table. "You said you had a business proposition?" The voice emanating from the dark was about as warm as a Minneapolis January. "I might remind you, young lady, I'm taking time out of a busy schedule at the Neo Edo. I already have a business to run." This wasn't going well at all.

I'm not going to give up! Not that easily! Margo cleared her throat, thought about taking another sip of her drink, then thought better. No sense strangling again and cementing her doom. Her hands were trembling against the nearly invisible bourbon glass. She cleared her throat again, afraid her voice would come out a scared squeak. "I've been looking for you, Mr. Carson, because everyone agrees you're the very best time scout in the business."

"I'm retired," he said drily.

She wished she could see his face and decided he'd chosen this spot deliberately to put her off balance.

Cranky old . . .

"Yes, I know. I understand that. But . . ." *Oh, God, I sound like an idiot.* "I want to become a time scout. I've come to you for training." She blurted it out before she could lose her nerve.

A choked sound in the darkness hinted that she'd caught him mid-sip. He gave out a strangled wheeze, coughed once, then set his drink down with a sharp click. A match flared, revealing a thin, strong hand and a stubby candle in a glass holder. Carson lit the candle, fanned out the match, then just stared at her. His eyes in the golden candle glow were frankly disbelieving.

"You what?"

The question came out flat as a Minnesota wheatfield. He hadn't moved and didn't blink.

"I want to be a time scout." She held his gaze steadily.

"Uh-huh." He held her gaze until *she* blinked. His eyes narrowed to slits, while his lips thinned to the merest white line under the bristly mustache. *Oh, God, don't think about your father; you aren't facing* him *so just hang onto your nerve . . .*

Abruptly he downed the rest of the bourbon in one gulp and bellowed, "Marcus! Bring me the whole damned bottle!"

Marcus arrived hastily. "You are all right, Kit?"

Kit, no less. The bartender was on first-name basis with the most famous time scout in the world and she was left feeling like a little girl begging her father for a candy bar.

Kit flashed the young man that world-famous smile and said, "Yeah, I'm fine. Just leave the bottle, would you? And get a glass of white wine for the lady. I think she damn near choked on that bourbon."

Margo felt her cheeks grow hot. "I like bourbon."

"Uh-huh." It was remarkable, how much meaning Kit Carson could work into that two-syllable catch-phrase.

"Well, I do! Look, I'm serious—"

He held up a hand. "No. Not until I've had another drink."

Margo narrowed her eyes. He wasn't an alcoholic, was he? She'd had enough of dealing with *that* for several lifetimes.

The bartender returned with the requested bottle and a surprisingly elegant glass of wine. Kit poured for himself and sipped judiciously, then leaned back against worn leather upholstery. Margo ignored the wine. She hadn't ordered it and would neither drink it nor pay for it.

"Now," Carson said. His face had closed into an unreadable mask. "You're serious about time scouting, are you? Who jilted you, little girl?"

"*Huh?* What do you mean, who jilted me?" Her bewildered question opened the door to as scathing an insult as Margo had ever received. "Well, clearly you're bent on suicide." Margo opened her mouth several times, aghast that nothing suitable would come out in the way of a retort. Kit Carson grinned—nastily. "Honey, whoever he was—or she was—they weren't worth it. My advice is get over the broken heart, go back home, and get a safe little job as a finance banker or a construction worker or something. Forget time-scouting."

Margo knocked back the bourbon angrily. *How dare he . . .*

She sucked air and coughed. *Damn, damn, damn. . . .*"I wasn't jilted by anybody," she gritted. "And I'm not suicidal."

"Uh-huh. Then you're crazy. Or just plain stupid."

Margo bit dawn on her temper. "Why? I *know* it's a dangerous profession. Wanting to scout doesn't make me a loon or a fool. Lots of people do it and I'm not the first woman to take on a dangerous job."

Carson poured a refill for himself. "You're not drinking your wine."

"No," she grated. "I'm not" She held out the empty bourbon glass. He held her gaze for a moment, then splashed liquid fire and waited until she'd choked it down.

"Okay," Carson said, in the manner of a history teacher warming to a lecture, "for the moment, let's rule out stupid. After all, you did have the sense to look for an experienced teacher."

Margo was sure she was being subtly insulted, but couldn't nail down why. Something in the glint of those cynical eyes . . .

"So . . . that leaves us with crazy, which is a word that clearly sets your pearly white teeth on edge."

"Well, wouldn't you be insulted?"

That world-famous grin came and went, like an evil jack o'-lantern in the dim candle glow. "In your situation? No. But clearly you are, so an explanation is in order. You want to know why you are crazy? Fine. Because you've got about as much chance of time-scouting as Marcus, there, has of becoming an astronaut. Kid, you're flogging a dead horse."

She turned involuntarily and found the gorgeous young Marcus near the front of the bar. Smiling and waiting on new customers, he looked like a perfectly ordinary college-age guy in jeans and a T-shirt. Margo glared at the retired time scout. "That's a pretty big insult, don't you think? It's clear he's a friend of yours." Then she twigged to the name, the not-quite-Italian accent, the curious bow he'd given Kit. Marcus was still a popular modern name, but it had been a popular name in ancient Rome, too. "Oh. Down-timer?"

Carson nodded. "Roman Gate. Some asshole tourist decided it would be fun to buy a slave and brought him through to La-La Land, then dumped him and vanished up time before the ATF could arrest him. Not only does Marcus have no legal standing whatsoever, he literally could never overcome the handicap he's carrying in terms of education, ingrained superstitions, what have you. He's an ancient Roman slave. And if you don't know what that means, not only here," he tapped his temple, "but also here," he tapped his heart, "then you have no business even trying to become a time scout."

"I'm not an uneducated slave dumped up time to cope with alien technology," Margo countered. "It's a helluva lot easier to understand ancient superstitions than it is to comprehend physics and math. And I got brilliant grades in dramatics, even had a chance to work off-Broadway." The half-truth sounded convincing enough; at least her voice had held steady. "I came here, instead. Frankly, I don't see how your argument holds water."

Carson sighed. "Look. First of all, there is no way I'm going to shepherd some greenhorn scout, regardless of who they are or how brilliant at dramatics they think they are, through the toughest training you've ever imagined, any more than I'm going to try to hammer some sense into that empty little head of yours." She bristled silently. "Second, you're a woman."

Congratulations, she fumed silently. An MCP, *on top of everything else.* You *and my father should start a club.* "I know all the arguments—"

"Do you?" Brown eyes narrowed into an intricate ladder of lines and gullies put there by too much sun and too many years of hard living. "Then you should've had the sense not to waste my time. Women can't be time scouts."

Margo's temper flared. "You're supposed to be the best there is! Why don't you stop quoting all the doom-sayers and find a way! From what I've gathered, you had to retire but didn't much like it. Think what a challenge it'd be, training the first woman time scout in the business."

His eyes glinted briefly. *Interest? Or acknowledgement of spunk? Impossible to tell. . . .* He knocked back his bourbon and gave her a long, clear-eyed stare. Margo, determined to match him, knocked back her own. This was getting easier. Either that or her throat was numb. The edges of Carson's face had begun to waver a bit, though. Bad sign. *Definitely should've had lunch.*

Carson, evidently sober as a stone, tipped more bourbon into his tumbler. Gamely she held out her glass. Very gently, he closed his hand around it and pushed it to the table.

"Point one: you're drunk and don't have the sense to quit. I will not ride herd on a greenhorn trying to prove a point to the whole world." Margo flushed. "Point two: the role of women down time, just about anywhere or anywhen you might land, is . . . less than what we'd consider socially respected. And women's mobility in many societies was severely limited. Then there's the problem of fashion."

Margo had thought all this through and had a counterargument ready, but Carson wasn't slowing down long enough to voice it. She sat and listened helplessly while the man whose accomplishments had given her the courage to keep going nailed down the coffin lid on her dreams.

"Women's fashions change radically from locale to locale, often from year to year. What happens if you go scouting through an unknown gate and show up a couple of centuries off in clothing style? Or maybe a whole continent off? Any idea how ridiculous you'd look in 200 B.C. China, wearing an eighteenth-century British ball gown? You'd stick out like the proverbial sore thumb. Maybe—*probably*, even—you'd end up dead. Quite a few societies weren't real tolerant of witches."

"—But—"

"At best, you'd end up in prison for life. Or even more fun, in some asshole's private harem. Just how fond of rape are you, Margo?"

She felt like he'd punched her. Painful memory threatened to break her control. Margo was shaking down to her fingertips and Carson, damn him, wasn't done yet. In fact, the look in his eyes was one of growing satisfaction as he noticed the tremor in her hand.

He leaned forward, closing in on the kill. "Point three: I will not train a nice kid and turn her over to the likes of some of the brutes I've encountered. Even the nicest down-time men often have a nasty habit of beating their favorite women for cardinal sins like talking too much. Whatever your reasons, Margo, forget 'em. Go home."

The interview was clearly over.

Kit Carson didn't quite condescend to pat her head on the way out. He left her sitting in the candle-lit booth, fighting tears of rage—and worse—of crushing disappointment. Margo downed a big glass of bourbon and vowed, *One day you're* gonna *eat those words. Cold and raw, you'll eat "em.* She couldn't bear to glance in the direction of his friends. *Margo* flinched inwardly at the spate of laughter from a crowded table across the room. She closed her hand around the bourbon bottle, gripping until he fingers ached She was not a quitter. She intended to become the world's first woman time scout. She didn't care what it took.

The bill, when Marcus the displaced slave presented it, represented a third of everything Margo possessed in the world, even minus the glass of white wine. She was being charged only for the bottle of bourbon. Margo groaned inwardly and dug into her belt pouch for money. How she was going to pay for a room now . . .

"Well," she told herself, "time to put Plan B into operation."

Find a job and settle in for a long, hard battle to find someone willing to train her. If Kit Carson wouldn't do it, maybe someone else would. Malcolm Moore, maybe. Freelance time guide wasn't what she had in mind, but it was a start. If, of course, he could be convinced to help train his own competition . . .

Margo poured another shot of bourbon. As long as she was paying for it . . .

Clearly, this would be a long, long day.

Chapter 4

The klaxon marking the re-opening of Primary sounded just as Kit settled down for breakfast in Frontier Town's Bronco Billy Cafe. He smiled to himself, wishing a mental *bon voyage* to the redheaded Margo of No Last Name. The computerized register of incoming tourists had shown only Margo Smith, who held a transfer ID stamp from New York. In New York City, anyone could get any sort of credentials and could have any fake name tacked onto one's mandatory medical records, which had to match a person's retinal scans and fingerprints to get past ATF Security.

After the orbital blowup, which had created the time strings that made temporal travel possible, so many records had been damaged and destroyed, New York's underworld had cleaned up issuing new identities. Scuttlebutt had it that new IDs were cheaper than downtime tickets to a temporal station.

If Smith were Margo's real last name, Kit would eat his shoes.

He hadn't seen her since her arrival—thank God—although he'd heard from several people that she was asking everywhere for a teacher. So far as he knew, everyone had turned her down flat. Now she'd be departing for home where she belonged. It was with a sense of profound relief that Kit banished all thought of Margo Smith. He smiled at the waitress, clad primly in a high-collared dress with a striped, floor-length skirt.

"Morning, Kit," she dimpled "The usual?"

"Good morning, Bertie. Yes, please, with a side of hash browns."

Bertie poured coffee and produced a copy of this morning's *Shangri-la Gazette.* Kit was halfway through the "Scout Reports" section—which comprised at least a third of the small newspaper—when the klaxon announcing the closure of Primary sounded. Kit grinned. "Bye, Margo. Have a nice, safe life." He settled deeper into his chair, sipped coffee, and continued reading the latest reports from young time scouts who were busy continuing his work into all manner of unlikely places and times.

"Well, what do you know about that?" Some lucky scout over at TT-73 had pushed a gate into the middle of the Russian palace built by Catherine the Great and had inadvertently caught her *in flagrante delicto* with one of those infamous Russian boars. . . .

Kit chuckled, then raised a brow at the purported offers generated in a bidding war between up-time porno outfits. The clever scout had brought back a videotape. Another scout, over at TT-13, had returned from a hair-raising trip into the European Wurm glaciation with an anthropologist's ransom in documentation on Cro-Magnon lifestyles.

Sometimes, Kit really missed his old life.

Bertie returned with his breakfast and a smile. She glanced at the open newspaper. "I see you found the story on Catherine's palace."

Kit chuckled. "Yep. Lucky mutt."

Bertie rolled her eyes. "Personally, I think it's disgusting what the porno outfits are offering him. And who'd want to sleep with a giant hog? Now, the scout who took the video is another matter." She winked. "Any lonely time scout needs a room for the night. . . ."

Kit grinned, knowing Bertie's offer was only a tease, at least where he was concerned. Kit had a far-flung reputation as the world's straightest-laced time scout. It made most of the women on TT-86 treat him like a favorite uncle of a third grandfather. That had its advantages, but sometimes . . .

He sighed and pushed away thoughts of Sarah. *Ancient history, Kit.* But he still couldn't help wondering something if he might have found a way to make it work. *Yeah. Right. You weren't good enough for her, Georgia Boy.* Despite the years, their last fight still had the power to hurt him. And when he'd gone looking for her, what her father and uncle had said . . .

Kit gave a deliberate mental shrug. She'd made her choices and he'd made his. He'd been through every conceivable argument over the years, trying to figure a way it might have gone differently, and he'd never found one. So Kit picked up his fork, carefully not allowing himself to wonder what had become of Sarah—or if she ever thought about him when she read the newspapers or watched the idiotic docudramas . . .

Really, Kit told himself sourly, *after all this time, there is no point crying about it.* He smoothed the paper, turned to a fresh page, and dug into the heaping plate of Denver-style steak and eggs, with a bird's-nest side of golden-brown hashed potatoes drenched with melted cheese and liberally mixed with fried onions and green-pepper chunks. *Ahh. . . .*Bronco Billy's knew how to make breakfast.

Kit was halfway through the steak, cooked rare just the way he liked it, when a shadow fell across his table. He glanced up—and nearly choked on a bite of half-swallowed beef.

Margo.

She was dressed conservatively enough in jeans and a semi-see-through sweater, but wore a look of determined sweetness that didn't fit the tilt of her chin. "Hello, Mr. Carson. May I join you?"

Kit coughed, still half-choked on the bite in his throat. He grabbed the coffee cup and gulped, scalding the roof of his mouth and his tongue. Kit burned the back of his throat, too; but the steaming liquid dislodged the bite of steak. He wheezed, swallowing while he blinked involuntary tears. He finally sat back and glared at her. This was the second time she'd nearly strangled him, catching him off-guard like that. *Christ, I'm losing my touch if a half-grown kid can damn near kill me twice in two days.*

"Still here, I see," he growled, still sounding half strangled. "I was hoping you'd gone home."

Margo's smile was chilly. "I told you, Mr. Carson. I have no intention of going home. I'm going to be a time scout and I don't care what it takes."

He thought about Catherine the Great and her Russian boar and wondered what this green lad would've done in that situation. Gone all schoolgirl incensed, or burst in protesting cruelty to animals?

"Uh-huh. Just how much money have you got, kid?"

Her face flushed unbecomingly. "Enough. And I've applied for a job."

"Doing what?" Kit blurted. "Serving drinks in that damned leather miniskirt of yours?"

Margo's eyes narrowed. "Listen, Mr. Carson, I will stay on this terminal, no matter how long it takes or who I have to find to teach me. But I'm going to be a time scout. I was hoping I could persuade you to change your mind. I'm not stupid and I have some pretty good ideas about overcoming the handicap of my gender. But I'm not going to stand here and be insulted like some truant schoolkid, because I am *not* a child."

You damn near are, Kit groused to himself, impressed with her tenacity and appalled that she was so determined to die. Kit sat back in his chair and ran one hand through his greying hair. "Look, Margo, I admire your determination. Really, I do."

The look in her eyes, sudden and unexpected, disturbed Kit *Good God, is she going to cry?* Kit cleared his throat.

"But I won't be a party to your death, which is likely to be messy and very painful. Did you bother to read any of the scouting reports in this?" He held up the *Gazette.* "Or the obituaries section?"

Time scouts' obituaries took up a whole page of the *Shangri-la Gazette.* The details were often gruesome. She shrugged. "People die all the time."

"Yes, they do. So do time scouts. Let me tell you *how* time scouts die, kid. Sam One-Eagle over at TT-37 was killed by the Inquisition. They burned him alive, Margo, after taking all the skin off his back with whips and breaking all his major bones on the rack. His partner crawled back through with burns over most of his body from trying to rescue him. David lived for a month. The nurses said he spent most of it screaming."

Margo had blanched. But her chin came up. "So what? I could get run over by a bus, too, and plane crash victims get toasted just as thoroughly."

Kit tossed his hands heavenward. "Good God, Margo. The Inquisition is nothing to be flippant about. You haven't seen one of their torture rooms. I have. And I have the scars to prove it. Would you like to see them?"

Slim jaw muscles tightened. She didn't say a word.

"And do you have any idea, kid, what gave me away? What got me arrested by those bastards?"

She shook her head.

"A mispronounced word, Margo. That was all. A mispronounced word. And I speak fluent medieval Spanish." She swallowed; but she had a comeback. "You lived through it."

Kit sighed and pushed his plate away. He wasn't hungry any longer. "Fine. You want to get *killed,* feel free. Just don't ask me to help you do it. Now scram, before I lose my temper."

Margo didn't say another word. She just stalked out of Bronco Billy's and vanished into the bustle of Frontier Town. Kit muttered under his breath and glared at the passing crowds. Just what was it about this kid that needled him so thoroughly? She was every damned bit as stubborn as Sarah and made him very nearly as crazy.

Maybe it was genetic. He never had been able to resist petite women with heart-shaped faces and freckles.

"Huh. Women."

He shook out his newspaper irritably and folded it over to a new section.

"Mr. Carson?"

"What?" he snapped, glaring up at a middle-aged man he'd never laid eyes on. *Good God, can't a man eat his breakfast in peace?*

"I'm sorry to interrupt . . ." The man's voice trailed off. "Er, I, that is—Excuse me. I'll come back later."

He was already in the process of stepping away from the table. Kit focused on the slim portfolio he carried, the carefully pressed suit, the expensive shoes . . .

"Don't run away," Kit said with a lingering growl in his voice. "Sorry I snapped at you. I just finished a very unpleasant conversation, is all. Please, sit down."

And if you're a reporter, mister, you'll end up wearing what's left of my breakfast . . .

"My name is Fisk, Harry Fisk." He offered a business card, which gave Kit no real clues other than that his office was in Miami. "I represent the management of TT-27, located in the Caribbean Basin. We're looking for a consultant . . ."

Kit heard him out. The job sounded intriguing. A lucrative, full-time consultant ship, unlimited trips to a time he was pretty sure he'd never visited, as primary consultant to the Time Tours agent looking to develop a new gate destination. Paid apartments at TT-27's finest luxury hotel . . .

It was a magnificent chance to escape Neo Edo's paperwork and the endless stream of raucous, thieving tourists. Kit scratched his chin and thought about it. Leaving TT-86 meant leaving friends. And he did owe it to Jimmy and the other retired time scouts in his employment to look after them. He wouldn't sell out to just anyone.

"No," he decided, "I don't think so, Mr. Fisk. I have a hotel to run."

"We would be more than happy to install a full-time manager for the duration of your consultantship, Mr. Carson. Time Tours wants the best for this project."

Huh. Now there was a fat offer. Paradise for as long as he wanted and he would keep his steady income, too. And somebody *else* did the paperwork. The image of Margo, her face pinched and white as she stood over his table staring him down, flashed through his mind.

Dammit, kid, stay out of my head.

Kit toyed with his cold eggs, scooting them back and forth on the plate with the tines of his fork. He'd been waiting for something like this for a long time.

"No," he found himself saying. "I appreciate the offer, really, but not just now."

Mr. Fisk's face fell—ludicrously. "I really wish you would reconsider, Mr. Carson."

Kit shrugged. "Ask me again in a week or so. We time scouts are a changeable lot."

Fisk tightened his lips imperceptibly. "Yes, so I've discovered.

Well, you have my card, but my employers are most anxious to press ahead with this project and there are other retired time scouts on my list."

Kit nodded. "I expect there are. And I'm sure most of them need the job more than I do." He held out his hand. Fisk shook it, betraying grudging respect in his eyes.

"If you reconsider your position in the next two days, please let me know."

He had until Primary cycled to change his mind.

Kit didn't foresee that happening.

Mr. Fisk left him with his cold eggs.

"Huh. It was probably a scam, anyway," Kit muttered. "Too good to be true equals dubious in my book. Besides, who wants to live in the Bermuda Triangle?" He could do that by jumping down La-La Land's unstable gate. He shoved Fisk's business card into his pocket and tackled his cold breakfast, telling himself his decision had nothing to do with keeping track of that stupid little imp, Margo.

Sure it doesn't, Kit. And a toadie frog's got wings.

He muttered into his scraggly mustache and finished his morning paper, determined not to think about Margo or her suicide mission. *Why was it,* Kit mourned silently, *that all the* real *trouble in his life inevitably came skipping in on the coattails of some irresistibly pretty girl?*

If word of this got around . . .

Well, he'd just take his lumps and deal with the snickers. What Kit Carson did, or didn't do, was his own damned business. *Yeah. Mine and the rest of La-La Land's.* He signaled Bertie for a fresh cup of coffee and promptly fell to worrying about where Margo was going to find someone reputable enough to trust with her life. Maybe he could talk to Sergei or Leon or . . .

No, he told himself, *if you won't teach her yourself, do* not *try and line up somebody else for the job.* Frankly, he couldn't think of a single time scout who'd be willing to try it, anyway.

Vastly relieved by that observation, Kit put Margo firmly out of mind.

⁂

Why, Margo wailed silently, *does he have to be so beastly?* She'd found a quiet spot under a vine-covered portico in Urbs Romae where she could sit with knees tucked under chin and indulge in a good, long cry.

Mom warned me . . .

That only brought fresh misery and a new flood of angry tears. She wiped her cheek with the back of one fist and sniffed hugely. "I won't give up. Damn him, I won't. There just has to be someone else on this miserable station who'll teach me."

So far, she had struck out with everyone she'd approached, even the freelance guides like Malcolm Moore. At least most of them had been nicer about it than Kit Carson. Even a brusque, "Get lost, brat," was kinder than gruesome images of people being tortured to death.

"I'll bet he doesn't have any lousy scars," she sniffed. "And Sam One-Eagle probably isn't any more real than these stupid fake columns. He doesn't want me to be a scout, is all, so he's trying to scare me."

The thought of returning to Minnesota and the jeers . . .

Never mind her father . . .

Margo shivered and hugged her knees more tightly.

"Hell will freeze over first."

"Hell will freeze over before what?"

Margo jumped nearly out of her skin. The voice had spoken almost in her ear. She swung around and found a face peering at her through the vines. A male face. A *gorgeous* male face. Margo's personal-defense radar surged onto full-power alert. She'd had all she wanted of gorgeous men. But his winning smile was the friendliest thing she'd seen in two and a half days and after that miserable, gawdawful interview with Kit Carson . . .

"Hey, what's wrong?" He'd noticed the tears. Whoever he was, he ducked under the vines and dug for a handkerchief. "Here, use mine."

Margo eyed him suspiciously, then accepted the hanky. "Thanks." She dried her face and blew her nose, then wadded up the handkerchief and offered it back.

"No, keep it. You look like you need it more than I do." He sat down cross-legged on the floor. "You're still a little drippy," he added with an attempt at a laugh.

Margo grimaced and blotted her cheeks. "Sorry. I'm not normally so weepy. But it's been a bad week."

"What's wrong? You look half starved."

Margo sniffed. She was. "Well . . . it's been a couple of days since I ate."

"A couple *of days?* Good grief, what happened? Some con artist steal all your money?"

Margo laughed, surprising herself. "No. I didn't have much to steal in the first place. And what there was, I've used up. All I have left is my suitcase and a hotel bill I can't pay tonight."

He tipped his head to one side. "Are you the girl everyone's talking about? The one who wants to become a time scout?"

"Oh, God . . ." *Insult on top of injury.*

"Hey, no, don't cry again. Honest, it's okay. I've been looking for you."

Margo blinked and stared at him. "Why?"

"I'm a scout. I've been looking for a partner."

"Honest?" Her voice came out all watery and breathy. It couldn't be true—but oh, Lord, how she wanted it to be . . .

He grinned. "Honest. My name's Jackson. Skeeter Jackson. I just got back from a quick run up time and heard you were looking for a teacher. I've been thinking I needed a partner for a while—that's why I was up time, actually—then I come back and what do I find? The challenge of a lifetime, right in my own backyard!" He grinned and held out a hand.

Margo couldn't believe it. A week of her precious six months gone and all she'd had to show for it was a collection of insults, and now . . . maybe there was a God, after all. She'd be careful—Billy Pandropolous, who was enough heartbreak for any lifetime, had taught her nothing, if not that. But Skeeter Jackson didn't appear to be hustling her. At least, not yet. She shook his hand. "Mr. Jackson, if you're for real—well, you'll be a lifesaver. I mean it. And I promise, I will work as hard as I have to. I'll make you proud." She ventured a tentative smile, appealing directly to what men seemed to value most. "I'll even try to make you rich."

Skeeter Jackson's eyes were warm, friendly. "I'm sure you will. Come on, let me buy you some breakfast."

He gave her a hand up. Margo dried her cheeks again and gave him a brave smile. "Thanks. I'll pay you back. . . ."

He laughed and gallantly offered his arm. "Don't mention it. I'll take it out of your wages."

Margo found herself grinning as she took Mr. Jackson's arm. Maybe, finally, her luck had changed for the better. Just wait until Kit Carson heard about this! He'd choke on his eggs again. And after the way he'd treated her, he deserved it! Dreaming of thrills, adventure, and plates of heaped bacon and pancakes, Margo accompanied her new teacher out into the bright, busy Commons of Shangri-la Station.

Chapter 5

The Down Time's pool room was a snoop's paradise. Thanks to the acoustics, it was possible to hear snatches of several conversations at once. Kit had always wondered if the place had been purpose-built. He lined up a shot, called it, and put the two ball neatly in a side pocket. Out in the bar proper, somebody was laughing about an invasion of grasshoppers at TT-37.

"Came right through a random gate into Commons. Tourists screaming, Station Pest Control tearing hair and swearing. Must've killed a million of 'em, minimum. Took days to sweep 'em all up."

In another corner, Robert Li's unmistakable bass voice rumbled, ". . . so when Wilkes said that, Bull told him all ATF courtesy passes were canceled, effective immediately. . . ."

Kit grinned. Another wrinkle in the continuing saga. The station manager's battle to keep ATF's nose where it belonged—out of everybody else's business—had spawned an entertainment form unique to La-La Land. Known as "Bull Watching," it involved avid betting on the outcome of any random encounter between Bull Morgan and Montgomery Wilkes.

Kit called and sank another ball, then lined up his next shot. Over in the corner, Goldie Morran frowned, looking every inch the disapproving dowager one might see on the Paris Opera House's grand marble staircase opening night, dressed to the nines and staring down that long, thin nose of hers like a Russian aristocrat

Even the hair—a particularly precise shade of purple Kit still associated with seventh-grade English teachers and aging duchesses—contributed to the overall impression.

Goldie eyed the line of Kit's cue stick and sniffed. "I knew I would regret this game. You're too lucky."

Kit chuckled. "Luck, dear Goldie, is what we make it." The next ball he called rattled musically into the far corner pocket. "As you, of all people, should know."

She only smiled, a thin hawkish smile that spoke volumes to those who knew her well. Kit suppressed the urge to look for the knife about to plunge into his back. He lined up his next shot and was just about set when Robert Li's voice interrupted from the doorway.

"Ah, Kit, there you are."

La-La Land's antiquarian, a long-time friend, *knew* that interrupting a game for anything less than catastrophic emergency was considered a hanging offense. Particularly when the opponent was Goldie Morran. Playing Goldie took concentration if you wanted to leave the room wearing the shirt you'd come in with. Kit had momentary visions of Tokugawa samurai pouring through the Nippon Gate into the Neo Edo's main lobby, demanding room service.

"What is it?" he asked warily.

Robert lounged against the door frame and idly inspected his fingernails. "Seen the Wunderkind lately?"

The Wunderkind could refer to only one person: Margo.

Oh, great. Now what's she done?

In her four days at La-La Land, she had managed to set more tongues wagging than Byron and his sister had in four months of Sundays.

"Uh, no." He lined up his shot again. "Don't much care if I ever do, either." He began the shot.

"Well, she's been hanging around with Skeeter Jackson. Says he's going to teach her to time scout."

The shot went wild. Kit's cue actually raked the felt table, leaving an ugly mar in its smooth surface. He swore and glared at his so-called friend, then at Goldie. She widened her eyes and shrugged innocence, reminding Kit unpleasantly of Lucrezia Borgia that night he'd accidentally surprised her in the infamous walled garden. . . .

"Huh."

Kit surrendered the table with as much grace as he could muster and said goodbye to the game. Robert Li, whose maternal Scandinavian heritage—fair skin and rosy cheeks—was overshadowed by a Hong Kong Chinese grandfather's legacy, only grinned. A completely scrutable scoundrel, he settled his shoulder more comfortably against the doorframe to watch. During the next two minutes, Goldie ran the table, hardly pausing for breath between shots. She spun the final shot off Kit's scratch, giving the ball just enough English off that long mar in the felt to sink it with a rattle like doom.

"Tough luck," she smiled, holding out one thin-boned hand.

Kit dug into his pocket and came up with the cash, paying her off wordlessly. Robert, still standing in the doorway, grinned sheepishly as she passed him on the way out.

"Sorry, Kit."

"Oh, don't mention it. I just love ruining a perfectly good pool table and losing a week's profits."

'Well, gosh, Kit, I just thought you'd laugh. How was I to know you'd take the news so personally? Don't tell me the famous Kit Carson has fallen for that redheaded imp?"

Wisely, Robert made himself scarce. But the antiquarian chuckled all the way out to Commons. Kit muttered impolite words under his breath. *With such friends* . . . He unscrewed the sections of his cue stick and slipped them into their leather case, then settled up the damages with Samir Adin, the night manager. "You what?" Samir asked in gaping disbelief.

"I scratched. Here, this ought to cover the cost of refelting it."

"You scratched. Unbelievable. Did I miss the earthquake or something?"

Kit scowled. "Very funny. Frankly, I'd say it hit at least 7.5 on the Richter. Had Goldie's name all over it. Give me a Kirin, would you?"

Samir chuckled and dug for a cold bottle. "I keep telling you, Kit. If you want to beat Goldie Morran, play her when she's unconscious."

Kit downed the Kirin in five long swallows and felt better immediately. "Well, a man can dream, can't he? Hillary had Everest, Peary had the Pole, and I cling to the dream of beating Goldie Morran at pool."

Samir, a deeply sympathetic soul, broke into song, giving him a stirring rendition of "To Dream the Impossible Dream".

"Oh, you're no help," Kit grinned. "Why do I come in here, anyway?"

Samir chuckled. "That one's easy. All time scouts are gluttons for punishment. It's in the job description."

Kit laughed. "You've got me there. I *wrote* the damned thing."

Samir thumped him on the back by way of condolences and sent him on his way. Kit shoved hands into pockets, cue case tucked under one arm. *Well, that story ought to be a nine-day wonder. It'll be all over La-La Land by bedtime.* He strolled glumly through Urbs Romae, going nowhere in particular, then sniffed appreciatively at the scents wafting from the Epicurean Delight. *Dinner sounds good, after that beer. Hmm . . .*

He wondered what Arley Eisenstein had written on the Special Board for tonight. Arley's restaurant was *the* place to eat in La-La Land. Other restaurants boasted more posh in their decor, but Arley had discovered the secret of enticing the world's best chefs to take turns in his kitchen. Down-time agents on his payroll obtained recipes in exchange for a slice of the Epicurean Delights profits. Some of what they brought back, of course, made haggis sound appetizing. But he came up with enough "lost" winners to make a tidy profit.

Chefs who wanted access to Arley's culinary secrets paid through supervising Arley's kitchen for a stipulated number of days per year. Since most tourists couldn't identify ingredients in what they ate, never mind figure out procedure . . . From the rumors, the arrangement was wildly profitable in up-time restaurants.

It certainly was for Arley. Unless you were a resident, you booked reservations two months in advance. 'Eighty-sixers, on the other hand, sampled the Delight whenever they liked. Arley made it a policy always to hold back at least three tables for station residents. Any given night, all three would be full.

Kit's mouth was already watering.

He cut around a column to head for the restaurant and very nearly ran down Connie Logan. She emitted a tiny screech and teetered. Kit grabbed her arm and steadied her.

"Sorry," they said simultaneously.

Kit blinked. She was about a foot too tall.

"Good God."

Connie was clad in a silk kimono held together by sewing pins and basting threads. Peeping out from under the pinned hem were "shoes" that resembled beach thongs, except they were made of wood and the soles were at least eleven inches thick.

Connie blinked, owl-like, from behind her glasses. "Hi, Kit. What do you think?" She held out both arms to display the half-finished work to its best prickly advantage.

"Let me guess," Kit said drolly. "Your customer wants to join the semi-annual grand procession of harlots through Yoshiwara?"

Connie rolled her eyes. "No. He wants to give his favorite down-time mistress a present. I'm trying it out, to be sure it *can* be worn. Now I understand why those old woodcuts show guys walking on either side of those poor girls, balancing them. These shoes are murder."

Kit grinned and offered his hand. "Shall we dance?"

Connie stuck out her tongue, but accepted the offer with alacrity. "Just help me over to the bench and I'll get rid of these lousy clogs. I was afraid to kick them off. Didn't want to lurch off balance and break an ankle."

Kit glanced around and guided her toward the targeted seat. Even in La-La Land, Connie was attracting stares. The shoes thunked with every step. "So who is this customer?"

Connie shuddered. "Don't ask. He's about seventy-five and covered with tattoos." *Yakuza.* Japanese mob . . .

Sixteenth-century Edo's Yoshiwara district had become a popular spot for Japanese businessmen's tours. Japan's recovery from the tsunamis, volcanic eruptions, and economic disasters left behind in the aftermath of *The Accident,* as that fateful orbital blowup had come to be called, had astonished most of the world. For the survivors, it was back to business as usual and most of the businesses were rich and getting richer. Japanese corporate tours were mostly organized by Yakuza gangs—which had *really* cleaned up in the reconstruction, since they apparently controlled the lion's share of the Japanese construction industry.

Kit wondered how Time Tours guides enjoyed rubbing shoulders with Japanese gangsters. He knew Granville Baxter hated them, but business, as they say . . . Grant didn't make corporate decisions. He just dealt with the field problems and gritted his teeth while making the home office a ton of money.

Kit eased Connie down to the bench. "There," he smiled. "All safe and sound."

She winced and wriggled to avoid pins, then sighed. "Thanks a million. Computer design may be my forte, but it just doesn't take the place of field testing. Sometimes," she grimaced at her feet, "it's a little rough on body and soul."

Kit stooped and eased off her shoes, earning a deep sigh. Connie's feet, clad in tabi socks, were visibly swollen even through the cotton. He rubbed gently. She collapsed bonelessly against the backrest.

"Oh, God . . . I love you, Kit Carson."

Kit chuckled. "That's what all the ladies say. Had dinner yet?"

She peeled one eyelid. "No, but I don't have time. Still have a special order for the London run to finish designing and after that I have a new batch of sketches from Rome and some samples that you just wouldn't believe, how gorgeous they are. . . ."

Kit grinned. "I'll take a rain check, then. Don't forget to order pizza or something."

"Scout's honor." Connie melted another few inches down the bench while Kit finished her feet, then sighed and stood up. She wriggled cotton-clad toes against the concrete. "Blessings on your soul, Kit. I may be able to limp back, now."

"Mind if I ask a stupid question?"

"Shoot."

"How come you tortured yourself into walking halfway down the Commons in those things?"

Connie grinned. "I paced it out beforehand, to the exact distance of the harlots' processions through Yoshiwara. If I can go the distance in those infernal shoes, anyone can."

Connie Logan wasn't exactly sickly, but she was fragile. Kit scratched the side of his jaw. "Well, I guess you have a point. Still seems a helluva way to design costumes."

Connie laughed. "This, from the man who pioneered masochism into a new art form. Just why *did* you become a time scout?"

"I cannot tell a lie." He leaned closer and whispered, "Because it's fun."

"There you have it. *I* get to play dress-up, every day." She stooped for the hideous shoes, then gave him a quick hug full of pins. "Thanks, hon. Gotta go. Oh . . . I saw that kid the other day, with Skeeter Jackson."

Kit groaned.

Connie's brows twitched down. "Good grief, Kit, she really got to you, didn't she? You ought to say something to her. She worships you, and Skeeter's going to get her killed. You wouldn't believe what he had her wearing."

"Great. Since when did I get promoted to greenhorn-daddy?"

Connie flashed him a grin. "You don't fool me, Kenneth Carson. You care. It's why we like you. Gotta run."

Kit was still grumbling under his breath long after Connie had vanished back toward her outfitters' shop. "Sometimes," he groused, "this Mr. Nice Guy rep is more trouble than it's worth." He sighed. "Well, hell." He really couldn't countenance allowing Skeeter Jackson to pass himself off as an instructor of time scouts.

Normally residents didn't interfere in other residents' business dealings. But there was a difference between fleecing obnoxious tourists out of a few dollars and perpetrating negligent homicide. Skeeter, never having been a scout—having rarely even been down time—probably didn't realize just how deadly his current scam was. Kit swore under his breath. He probably wouldn't earn any thanks, but he had to try.

Kit dropped by the Neo Edo just long enough to put away his cue case and be sure Jimmy had the business well in hand, then started asking around for Skeeter. Typically, nobody recalled seeing him. Kit knew some of his favorite haunts, but the rascal wasn't in any of them. Skeeter generally avoided Castletown, since even he didn't care to risk fleecing the wrong person and end up someplace really nasty, minus several fingers. Kit checked all of Skeeter's favorite watering holes in Frontier Town, then hit the pubs in Victoria Station. Nothing. Skeeter Jackson was making himself mighty scarce.

"Well, he's got to be someplace."

With no gates currently open, Shangri-la Station was closed up tight. The only exits were hermetically sealed airlocks leading—if the main chronometers and Kit's own equipment were correct—into the heart of the Tibetan Himalayas, circa late April of 1910. The only reason those airlocks would ever be opened would be to escape a catastrophic station fire. And since Halon systems had been built into every cranny of La-La Land . . .

Skeeter hadn't left the station, not unless he'd fallen through an unstable gate somewhere.

"We should be so lucky," Kit muttered. "Well, genius, now what?" He planted hands on hips and surveyed the breadth of Victoria Station, which wound from one side of Commons to the other in a maze of pseudo-cobbled streets, wrought-iron "street lamps," park-like waiting areas, picturesque shop fronts, and the inevitable cob-webbing of catwalks and ramps which led up to the Britannia Gate near the ceiling.

A tourist in a garish bar-girl costume left the Prince Albert Pub and fumbled in a small purse that would have been more appropriate for an American frontier matron. Slim white shoulders rose above a shocking neckline. Kit couldn't see her face. A drooping bunch of black feathers from a hat that should have been paired with a tea gown hid her features. The hemline of her dress was cut rakishly high enough to reveal shoes that were completely out of period.

"Huh. She went to a lousy outfitter."

The tourist closed her purse, then turned on an emphatic stilt heel. Kit groaned. *It figured.*

Margo . . .

"Well, Connie did warn me." He squared metaphorical shoulders and moved to intercept her, stepping out from behind a "street lamp" into her path. "Hi."

Margo glanced up, badly startled, and teetered on high heels. Kit let her regain her balance.

"Oh. It's you." Belatedly, she said, "Hi." Then her chin came up. "I found a teacher."

"Yes, I know. That's why I want to talk to you."

Margo's eyes widened. "You do?" Almost instantly, suspicion flared. "Why?"

Kit sighed. "Look, can we just declare a truce for about fifteen minutes?"

She eyed him narrowly, then shrugged. "Sure." She tossed her head slightly to bounce feathers out of her eyes.

Kit started to say, "That hat's on backwards," then bit his tongue. He didn't want to antagonize her. He wanted to save her life. So he suggested, "Let's go over to the library. It's quiet. We shouldn't be interrupted."

Margo eyed him curiously. "Why are you taking the trouble? I thought you hated me."

"Hated you? I don't hate anybody, Margo. Time scouts can't afford the luxury of hate."

Or love . . .

Margo's eyes had gone curiously wide and vulnerable, "Oh. Well, I'm glad."

Kit recalled what Connie had said—"she worships you"—and sighed. He wasn't cut out to be anybody's personal hero.

"Come on, Margo. The sooner I get this said, the sooner you can tell me where to jump off, then we can both call it quits." He eyed her unhappily. "And contrary to what you clearly believe, I don't enjoy hurting people's feelings."

For once, she didn't come back with a sharp remark. She just followed him wordlessly toward the library.

Margo knew time terminals had libraries. Tourists, guides, and time scouts all used them, to one degree or another. Her original legwork had revealed that time terminal libraries were among the most sophisticated research facilities in the world. But Skeeter Jackson hadn't suggested they go there and she hadn't given it much thought. Margo had never been fond of books. She preferred direct, dramatic action and firsthand experience. Poring through dusty, musty pages nobody had cracked open in fifty years only made her crazy. Besides, all those experts disagreed anyway, and a time scout's job was to go places and find out what the truth was.

Still . . .

La-La Land's library overawed.

Margo repressed a delicate shudder and didn't even try to calculate the number of books contained in this . . . the word "room" seemed inadequate. And computer terminals, too, with recognizable CD-ROM and video drives, all voice-activated. Judging from the snippets of soft-voiced commands she heard from a dozen busy users, they were programmed for multiple-language recognition. The computers drew Margo's attention more thoroughly than any of the books.

Mr. Carson—she had trouble thinking of him as "Kit"—spoke briefly with a slim, dark-skinned man in his mid-thirties, then steered her toward the back.

Several private cubicles had been built into the back wall, complete with computer and sound-board hookups.

"What are these for?"

"Language labs." Carson said quietly. "I take it you haven't been here yet?"

Margo detected no particular edge to his voice, but the question irritated her. "No. Skeeter has me busy doing important things." *Like earning a living to pay for the equipment I'm going to need.*

"Uh-huh. This one's empty." He pushed open a door and held it for her.

Margo fluffed inside and took the only chair. Her nemesis closed the door with a quiet click of the latch.

"Now. About this teacher of yours . . ."

"I suppose you're going to tell me how he's charging more than I can afford and what a fool I am and how I'll starve before I get my first big contract with Time Tours or some other outfit. Well guess again. He's not charging me anything but an advance on expenses and most of what I need I'm earning with the job he helped me find. *He* wants a partner."

Kit Carson just looked at her. He leaned against the door, crossed his ankles comfortably, and looked at her like she was the most recalcitrant, lame-brained child he'd ever encountered. It made her mad. "Don't smirk at me, you egotistical—!"

"Margo," he formed a classic "T" shape with his hands, "time out, remember? No insults, no temper tantrums. And I'm not smirking."

"Huh. Could'a fooled me." But she subsided. He was trying to be nice for a change; the least she could do was listen. "Okay, go on."

"Skeeter Jackson has told you he's a time scout, looking for a partner. True or false?"

"True." She bit one fingernail, then folded her arms and tried not to fidget. "What of it?"

"He's not a time scout. Never has been, never will be. Frankly, he's neither crazy nor stupid and he knows his limits."

Oh, no . . .

"Are you calling Mr. Jackson a liar?" she asked quietly.

His smile held a certain strained quality. "Yes. And before you say anything, I'd like to point out that liar's not the worst thing he's been called. Backstabbing cheat comes a little closer."

"How *dare* you—"

"Shut up and listen!"

The indolent pose had vanished. Margo shut up. She'd never heard such cold authority in *anyone's* voice. He wasn't angry—just relentless. And Margo was scared. After Billy Pandropolous . . .

"Skeeter Jackson is a *con artist.* A two-bit operator who makes his living fleecing tourists. If there's a scam on the books, he's used it. Currency exchange scams, luggage theft, pick-pocketing, black-marketeering, you name it."

Margo didn't want to hear any more. Every word he clipped off reduced her closer to the status of gullible fool—again.

"Skeeter doesn't touch 'eighty-sixers, which is the only reason Station Security tolerates him. He's probably wanted in half the sovereign nations in the world on various charges. Nothing violent, nothing dangerous . . . until now."

"What do you mean?" Even Margo realized how petulant she sounded.

"If I thought all you'd lose was the shirt off your pretty back, I'd let you have all the rope you want to hang yourself. But if you keep 'studying' with Skeeter Jackson, then walk through an unexplored gate thinking you're a time scout, you won't come back."

"Well, you didn't leave me much choice, did you? I *did* come to you first, if you'll recall."

He nodded. "Yep. And I gave you a fair assessment of your chances. I just thought you deserved to know how deadly this little game of yours is. Walking in with eyes wide open is a little different from being conned. Like I said before, I don't want your death on my conscience."

"Thanks for caring!" Margo snapped. "I can do without your advice, if that's all you've got to say!" He sighed and didn't offer to move. "Well? Are you leaving or what?"

"Just what is he teaching you?" Margo crossed her arms again.

"None of your business. If you won't teach me, why should I bother answering questions you'll just charge me money to answer?"

His eyes narrowed. "Don't be insulting. Who picked out that ensemble you're wearing?"

She just glared at him. Clearly, she'd made some mistakes—and vowed she'd die a torturous death before she admitted it.

"Okay," he muttered, "the kid gloves come off. Let's say Skeeter sends you through the 'safest' tourist gate there is, just for practice. If you walk through the Britannia Gate wearing that getup, the first thing that's going to happen is some well-bred lady on the other side will either scream or faint. Whores don't generally stroll through Battersea Park."

Margo paled, then flushed bright red. "I'm not a whore! And I'm not wearing this dress in London, you'll notice! I'm wearing it for a bunch of drunken tourists in Victoria Station! Besides, what's wrong with it? Skeeter showed me photos—"

"Margo, you look like a two-bit trollop in that thing. Skeeter likes skin and he doesn't have the faintest idea what decently bred Victorian women wore. If he had a photo, it was of a Denver saloon trollop. Denver cathouses are among the few down-time attractions Skeeter Jackson *has* visited."

Margo wanted to hide. At least she'd had the sense to tell Skeeter no the couple of times he'd suggested . . .

"Margo, you've just illustrated my point for me. You don't know what you're doing and neither does Skeeter. If you'd have walked through the Britannia Gate in that dress, here's what would've happened: After some poor, shocked matron had a fit of vapors, her outraged gentleman companion would have called for a constable. You'd either have ended up in the Old Bailey for peddling your wares in the wrong part of town or landed in an asylum. Street walkers who went mad from syphilis weren't handled particularly gently."

Margo didn't want to hear any more. Rose-colored balloons of hope broke with every word, but Kit Carson showed no inclination to stop. "Let's even suppose you didn't get nailed by the law. That by some miracle you actually found the slums where that getup might look more appropriate. Do you know what they were called? Never mind where they were? If you stumbled into them by sheer chance, you'd still be in trouble. Because some whore would carve you up for encroaching on her territory or some tough would decide to make you his meal ticket—after trying out the wares for himself first. Unless, of course, you were *really* lucky and the Ripper decided you were a likely looking target."

Margo went cold all over. *Jack the Ripper?* She couldn't help glancing at her dress, any more than she could hide an involuntary shudder. Carson, to give him his due, didn't crack a smile. He just nailed home the point like a vampire hunter pounding in the stake.

"The Ripper liked his victims helpless. Most psychopaths do. Step through the Britannia Gate without training or a guide, and you'll end up looking more helpless than any other walker on the street. Believe me, it won't be long before Red Jack starts having a bloody good time gutting you like a market fish—"

"STOP!" Margo had covered her ears. He stopped.

Margo was breathing as hard as she did after a sparring session in the *dojo.* Kit Carson, curse him, might have been sipping tea at a garden social for all the emotion he betrayed. *I won't give up! I can't!*

Margo literally had nowhere else to go. And she was running out of time. Her six months were nearly one-sixth gone already. "I can take care of myself," she said stubbornly. "Skeeter's all I've got left. Any teacher's better than none and you won't help me."

He straightened up from the door. "That's right, kid. I won't. And if I let you stick with Skeeter, he'll get you killed. Not even he realizes what he's setting you up for. Believe me, when I catch up to that young fool, I'll roast his ears good."

"*What?*" She came to her feet, shaking to her pinched toes as panic set in. She was out of money, out of hope, out of everything. If Kit forced Skeeter to kick her out . . .

"You *can't!* If you bully him off the job . . . You just *can't!*"

Blue eyes glinted like hard sapphires. "Oh, yes I can."

"Dammit—!"

"Don't you have any brains in that decorative little head of yours?" He took a step forward, evidently intent on opening her skull to look.

She held her ground. "I will not give up! And you don't have any right to interfere! It's my life, not yours. I'll risk it as I please, Mr. Hot-Shot Retiree!"

He flushed. "Look, you stubborn little—"

"Stubborn?" Margo laughed shrilly. Then, before she could quite believe she'd said it, Margo heard herself say, "Well, if I'm stubborn, I come by it honestly! With you for a grandfather, what else could you . . ."

Kit Carson halted mid-stride. His face collapsed into a tangle of weathered lines, aging him ten years in an instant. Despite the tan, he had blanched the color of dirty snow.

A knot of panic condensed in Margo's belly, the germ of a glacier. *Shit . . . oh, shit, me and my big mouth . . .*

For at least ten thudding heartbeats, he just stood there, looking like a stray word might knock him to the ground. Piercing blue eyes had lost their focus. Margo groped uncertainly for the chair and shoved it aside, anxious to put room between herself and the forceful man who would be coming out of shock any second.

Empty blue eyes focused slowly on her face. His brows came

together. He studied her for another thudding stretch of heartbeats. Margo didn't know what to say or do to fix this. When he drew a halting sip of air, she braced for the worst, but he didn't say anything. He seemed incapable of speech. After a moment, he shut his eyes. Then, without a single word spoken, he turned and opened the door. He left her standing behind the chair, feeling like she wanted to die and get the hurting over with, rather than face what she'd just done.

Kit didn't hear or see much of anything. He navigated the library on autopilot and found Brian Hendrickson behind the main reference desk. He located the desk by bumping into it.

"Good afternoon, Kit. What can I—dear God, what's wrong?"

The librarian's face swam into focus. Kit gripped the edge of the reference desk until his knuckles hurt. "Am I awake?"

"Are you *what?*"

"Am I awake?"

Brian blinked. "Uh—yes?"

Kit swore. His belly did another drop into oblivion. He wished for the tiniest of moments he could follow it. "I was afraid of that." He left Hendrickson gaping after him and literally ran into Margo halfway back to the cubicle. She staggered, blinking tears, then made to cut around him.

"Oh, no you don't!" He sidestepped quickly, blocking her path. "Back where you came from!" He pointed imperiously.

Her face was blotched and red. *"Leave me alone!"* She tried to bolt. He cut her off neatly and resisted the urge to seize her wrists. The last thing he wanted her to do was scream. But when she shoved him hard enough to stagger him off balance, he reacted before his brain could catch up—which wasn't very difficult in his current state of mind. Kit snatched her off balance, swearing under his breath, and forcibly pulled her toward the back of the library. Predictably, she resisted.

Kit swung her around hard enough to jounce her teeth together. "Do you really want me to turn you over Grandpa's knee, *little girl?"*

Margo worked her mouth like a drowning fish. "You—you wouldn't—" She halted mid-protest. "You would." For a moment, they stalemated in the center of La-La Land's library. Then she wrenched free of his grip, with an against-the-thumb movement that spoke of some martial arts training, but she didn't try to leave. She stood glaring at him, chest heaving against the plunging neckline of her dress in a fashion that made him want to throw a flour sack over her torso. Then she broke and fled toward the language lab. Kit drew a deep, shaky breath.

Dear God. . . .

He needed time to absorb this, time to figure out when and how . . .

Sarah, why didn't you ever tell me?

The hurt in his chest made his whole soul ache.

Kit lifted a shaking hand to his eyes. *Gotta think. Sarah and I broke up in . . . if she was pregnant then, and had a child before . . . Sarah's child would've had to be about seventeen when Margo was . . .* "Dear God. She could be."

Teenage pregnancies had very nearly become the rule, rather than the exception, during the years Margo's mother would have been a teenager. Margo had reminded Kit all along of someone. Now he knew. She didn't look much like Sarah, but that temper, not to mention the pride . . . even the determination to get what she wanted and everything be damned that stood in her way. Margo was Sarah van Wyyck all over again.

He didn't know whether to laugh or cry or swear aloud.

Meanwhile, his *granddaughter* had to be faced.

"Christ, and she's still set on being a time scout."

His viscera did another swan dive into a bottomless chasm. I *can't let her do this. . . .*Hard on the heels of that thought came another. *And just how do you propose to stop her?*

The whole library wavered in his vision for a moment as he superimposed Margo's face over some of the sights that still gave him nightmares. *She doesn't understand . . . thinks it's high adventure and she'll live forever . . . and I can't even insist on partnering her, can't even go along and watch her back . . .*

If Kit stepped through another unknown gate, odds were extremely high the attempt would kill him.

"What am I going to do? She wants this . . ." And was it any wonder? What must the kid have grown up thinking and dreaming every time she heard about her famous granddaddy?

"Dammit, Kit, pull it together. . . ."

Walking back into the language lab was possibly the hardest thing Kit had ever done.

Margo had pulled the chair into the far corner, but she wasn't sitting in it. She'd taken up a stance *behind* it, gripping the back as though he were a savage lion in need of taming. He recalled some of the ugly things he'd said to her and swallowed. *Damn* . . . Kit closed the door softly and faced her. Tear streaks ran down her face in jagged paths. But her chin was still up, still defiant, despite visible fear in her eyes.

"I'm not an ogre," Kit muttered. "You can put down the chair."

Very slowly, Margo let go her death grip. The front legs settled with a quiet thump. She swallowed a couple of times. "I didn't mean—I mean, I didn't plan to—"

"It's said," Kit interrupted brusquely. "And yes, you do come by it honestly."

For some reason, that brought a fresh flood of tears. Kit felt as though he'd just hit her and couldn't for the life of him figure out how to repair the damage. The sense of helplessness which paralyzed him reminded Kit unpleasantly of the times Sarah had dissolved into tears.

"I—Skeeter, he—and you—" Margo's voice control was gone.

Kit finally thought to hunt for a handkerchief and found a rumpled one in a back pocket. "Here."

She all but snatched it out of his hand, then turned her back and struggled visibly to regain the shreds of her dignity. Kit waited quietly, aware that a woman's pride was a far more serious matter than a man's—and men had been known to do murder when theirs was injured. She hiccoughed a few times and blotted her face, then blew her nose.

"Sorry," she muttered. "I ruined Skeeter's hanky, too." Kit winced. He decided he did *not* want to know how Skeeter Jackson had comforted his granddaughter. If he'd hurt her . . . *I'll toss him through the next unstable gate that opens.* She finally faced him, a watery-eyed waif in a bedraggled strumpet's gown. *No wonder she paid somebody to change the name on her ID card to* Smith. *Didn't want anyone to know who she really was, desperate to do this on her own merits . . .*

Kit knew only too well how that felt. He cleared his throat, more to gain time than anything. "You're dead set on this time-scouting business."

She swallowed. Her eyes, red and angry as bee stings, still brimmed with unshed tears. "I've wanted it all my life."

Once again he cleared his throat. "Things as they are, I can't say I blame you. . . ." Then he eyed her critically, studying her for the first time as a potential scout. He shook his head over the visible cleavage. "Best thing to do would be disguise you as a boy, but you're not really built for it."

Her eyes widened. "You mean—" Then, hastily, "It's not real. I mean, they're *real,* but I'm wearing stays. A corset. Skeeter bought them for me at an outfitter's. They really make me look . . . well, more voluptuous." Kit, thoroughly familiar with the bio-mechanical effect of a woman's corset stays, flushed. *I'm talking to my granddaughter about the size of her breasts . . .*

Margo was still talking as fast as possible. "I could wear baggy shirts, you know, to hide things, and my hips aren't really that wide, it's just I have a narrow waist. . . ."

Kit shook his head. The kid really did want this. *God help us both . . .*

Her face fell. He realized she must have misinterpreted that head shake. Kit sighed. "All right, Margo. I'll do it. But under conditions—"

"Really?" Her voice squealed into the soprano register. Her bedraggled face lit up like Christmas.

"Under conditions!" Kit repeated sharply. She gulped and heard him out. "First, I decide when—or if—you're ready. Second, you agree to do everything I tell you, exactly as I tell you. Understand? And you *don't* do anything I don't specifically tell you to do. If, after we're into training, I decide you don't have what it takes, you agree to switch to something else, time guiding, maybe.

There's a world of difference between the two professions. Guiding's fun. Sometimes dangerous, but mostly not. Scouting's deadly. If you thought convincing me to train you was hard, you don't even know the meaning yet. By the time I've put you through training, you will. Any time you want to quit, holler."

"I won't quit."

Kit managed a wan smile. "I expected you'd say that. But I mean it. Remember the bourbon. Knowing when to quit can be just as important as fighting for what you want."

A flush of pink crept into her cheeks. She rubbed her nose with the back of one hand and sniffed hugely. "Okay."

"Any questions?" She shook her head.

"Okay." He had about a million of his own—but now wasn't the right time to broach them. He took a deep breath and struggled against the cold in the pit of his belly. "Let's get started."

Chapter 6

A rattle of glassware punctuated the low buzz of voices like frog-song through the hum of mosquitoes. Familiar and comforting, the sounds rose in a welcoming chorus from the Down Time's open doorway. Kit ushered Margo in first, aware that speculative glances were levied in their direction. Several glances lingered, some on Margo, some on the scouting equipment he conspicuously carried in the trademark leather satchel he'd been the first to construct. Dirt-stained and battered, it nevertheless remained sturdy and functional. At one time, Kit wouldn't have felt fully dressed without it.

Behind the bar, a young woman with a long-boned face the British royals would've been proud to claim wiped up a spill and nodded. "Evenin', luv."

"Hello, Molly. Any seats left?"

In answer, she jerked her head toward a small table at the side of the room, missing all but two of its chairs. The Down Time was jam-packed, of course. *Too much to ask for a quiet night, tonight of all nights.* Kit recognized nearly everyone. Laughter punctuated a dozen conversations. "Thanks, Molly. How about a couple of ice waters?"

Molly's long, clear-eyed gaze followed Margo as she made her way toward the indicated table, but the barmaid withheld comment, as she generally did. She filled a couple of glasses with ice cubes and water and handed them over. "Anythin' else?"

Kit shook his head. "No, not just now. Maybe later."

"Luv . . ."

Kit paused mid-step, causing the ice cubes to clink faintly. The chill of condensate sank into his hands, echoing the coldness which still gripped the rest of him. "Yeah?"

Molly's brow had furrowed the tiniest bit, betraying intense worry. "Keep 'em open, Kit. She's a sharper, she is."

Kit glanced over to the table. Margo had taken up residence in the outer chair, which would leave Kit with his back against the wall. Margo's cheeks were visibly flushed despite the low-light conditions which prevailed this time of night in the Down Time. She was all but quivering with excitement.

"I suspect she's had reason," Kit said quietly. "I'm just trying to keep her alive."

Molly nodded. "'At's awright, but keep 'em open, luv. Tike care she don't steal yer bees an' 'oney while yer's back's turned."

Her concern that he might lose money to Margo surprised Kit—and touched him. "I'll do that."

She nodded briskly and turned to cater to another customer's needs. Kit eased his way between tables, greeting friends as he went and parrying curious questions with a smile and off-hand jokes. Margo watched the ritual with wide eyes. He finally set the water glasses down and took the other chair. Margo sipped—then shot him a startled glance.

"*Water?* I'm not a baby!"

"You're drinking what I am. Pay attention."

Kit didn't think he'd ever seen a more skillful disgruntled female flounce—stationary, no less, in a straight-backed bar chair—but she didn't argue. "I'm listening."

Given the rapt attention on her face, she *was,* too. "All right, Margo. Phase One: Equipment lecture."

Kit rummaged in the satchel for his personal log and ATLS. Margo would need her own set. Kit made a quick note on his mental to-do list, then set both items out for inspection. "These two pieces of hardware are your lifeline."

Margo peered at them without offering to touch. "What are they? I read that scouts used microcomputers and some gizmo to determine absolute time and Skee—I mean," she flushed, "I was saving money from my job to buy whatever I'd need. Is that what these are?"

"Yes." Kit picked up the personal log. A compact unit, smaller than an average letter-sized sheet of paper, it weighed more than it looked. "This is a time scout's personal log." He opened the case, pressed a latch, and lifted the tiny screen, revealing a keypad and the mesh grid of a microphone. "The casing is waterproof, shockproof, just about everything we can protect it from, except maybe immersion in strong acid or molten metal—or molten rock. It can be used in either voice or key mode. Scanners and digitizing micro-cameras can be attached. The personal log operates on a solar-powered system backed up with batteries that last about twenty-four hours between charges. It writes automatically to a micro-layer space-grown crystal matrix for storage, so there's no chance of losing data even if you do experience catastrophic power failure. They're expensive, but you don't set foot through a gate without one."

"So, they're like a trip diary, for recording notes and stuff?"

Kit shook his head. "Much more important and much more detailed. This," he tapped his log, "is quite literally what keeps me from killing myself."

A tiny vertical line appeared between Margo's brows. The uncertainty in her eyes mirrored a chain of thought that was almost comical.

"No," Kit smiled, "I'm not suicidal. Although a large percentage of the population would argue any time scout is. How much reading have you done? Do you know what Shadowing is?"

Margo hesitated, clearly caught between answers. "Don't be embarrassed to say no."

"Well, no. I mean, I know there's something weird about the gates and time scouts have to retire early because you can't ever be in the same time twice, but I never read the word 'shadowing' or heard it used."

As though to underscore her admission, a shadow falling across the table interrupted them. Kit glanced up—and held back a groan. Malcolm Moore had pulled up a chair. "Mind if I join you? This looks interesting." He glanced from the scouting equipment to Kit to Margo and back to Kit, then grinned expectantly.

Kit considered telling him to buzz off, then thought better. Malcolm's assistance might actually be useful. He'd scouted a couple of times and had given it up for guiding,

"Sure. Park it."

Malcolm turned the chair around and sat down. "Hello, Margo. You look, um . . ."

"Ridiculous," Kit said drily.

Margo flushed. "I didn't have time to change." She snatched the hat into her lap and ruffled her short hair. Kit winced at the movement of cleavage—and at Malcolm's interested attention.

"Malcolm," he said under his breath, "as you are a friend, don't do that again."

Malcolm's brows soared. "Good Lord, Kit, what's eating you? Can't a man even pay a lady the compliment of noticing?"

"No."

Margo just put her hands over her face.

"She's, uh . . ." *Oh, hell* . . . "She's my grandkid."

Malcolm rocked back on his chair and stared. "Margo's your *granddaughter?*"

Conversation cut short throughout the bar. Kit felt the flush start in his neck and work its way up into his hairline. Margo risked a peek, then groaned and hid her face again.

"Well, I'll be . . . suckered." Malcolm Moore was grinning like the proverbial village idiot. "Miss Margo, you can't imagine what a wonderful surprise this is."

The buzz of conversation picked up again, livelier than ever.

"I, uh," Margo floundered for words. She shot a stricken glance at Kit, then settled for a faint, "Thanks."

Kit glowered at Malcolm. "What I'm trying to do, here, is keep her alive. She wants to scout."

Malcolm's grin widened, which Kit would've bet was physically impossible. "Really? What was it you said the other day—"

"Never mind what I said the other day. I'm training her. Maybe. If—" he turned a severe glare on Margo "—she listens and learns."

"I'm listening! So show me, already!"

"Good." Kit drew a breath and downed half his water in one gulp, wishing it were something stronger. "Malcolm, here, has scouted a couple of times."

Malcolm nodded. "Exactly twice. Then I switched to guiding."

Margo rested her chin on her hands. "Why?"

Malcolm chuckled. "Because I wanted to live to see thirty."

"Why does everyone keep saying scouting's so dangerous?"

Malcolm glanced over. Kit just shrugged, leaving Malcolm on his own—and Kit was sure any answer the guide provided would be more than effective.

"Well," Malcolm said quietly, "because it is. My first time out, I beat the witch-finders to the gate by about four minutes. One of them actually got through on sheer momentum and had to be tossed back through just as the gate was closing. If the gate hadn't opened up, I'd have . . . Well, never mind. The second time, I missed Shadowing myself by about half an hour. Promised myself I'd never set foot through an unknown gate again."

Then he chuckled and rubbed the back of his neck. "Well, I did risk it just once more, when we rescued the folks who fell through that unstable gate in the floor, but I didn't stop to think, then, I just jumped. I was lucky. Someone, thank God, had their log and ATLS with them, so at least I have a record of which gates we stumbled through trying to get home again."

"Okay, so it's dangerous. What's this Shadowing stuff all about, exactly?"

Kit tapped the personal log absently with one fingernail. "It means you can't cross your own shadow. Not and survive. If you step through a gate into, say, Rome on A.D. 100, March twenty-fourth, 2:00 p.m. sun time, you log into this machine exactly when and where you are. How you determine when and where you are, I'll explain in a minute. The point is, you note down exactly when you arrived, where you arrived, how long you stayed, and when you left. You keep track of when and where you've been. Okay, let's say somebody else pushes a gate into Meso-America, A.D. 100, March twenty-third. If you step through that gate, and stay past March twenty-fourth 2:00 p.m.

Italian time, one of you disappears. The current you. The Roman you is alive in the past, but the real-time you just died. You cannot cross your own shadow. Paradox doesn't happen, because you vanish completely, forever."

Margo shrugged. "Sounds easy enough to avoid. You just don't try to watch Julius Caesar murdered twice."

Malcolm said, "You couldn't do that, anyway. The two ends of the time strings that form gates are connected. They move at the same pace. If a week goes by here, a week goes by there. Once you miss an opportunity to see something, it's gone forever, unless another time string opens up to the same point in time.

Of course, if you tried to go back, you'd cross your shadow and end up not seeing it—or anything else—ever again."

"The point is," Kit nodded, "the more down-time trips you make, the greater the odds that when you step through a gate into some unknown time, you'll already exist somewhere and somewhen else. Eventually the odds catch up and you die."

Margo chewed her lower lip in a thoughtful fashion. "So . . . you take this gamble every time you walk through an open gate, because you never know when—to what time—it leads? Why bother to keep records at all, if you could just vanish anyway? Seems like a lot of fuss, when you could blip out before you knew what hit you, no matter what you put in this thing. I mean, you don't know when you're going, so what does it matter that you know when you've been?"

Kit told himself that Margo was very young. "A couple of reasons. First, it's your job, as scout, to keep meticulous records. Scholars and tour companies will want to review any data you bring back. Second, if you don't keep records, you could accidentally kill yourself just trying to take a vacation or by trying to visit another station, or even the wrong gate in the same station."

"Huh?" She leveled an incredulous stare in Kit's direction. Clearly, she hadn't done enough research. Margo damned small-town libraries, high schools controlled by school boards opposed to things like "Evil-lution" and a father who'd drunk every penny she might have saved toward a computer to hook into the big information nets.

Malcolm nodded. "He's right. Even guides have to be careful about that. Every station is built at least as far back as 1910, to get around the problem of people stepping into a time after they were born. That's why up-time lobbies have warning signs. Surely you saw the one on the other side of our Primary? IF YOU WERE BORN ON OR BEFORE APRIL 28, 1910, DO NOT STEP THROUGH THIS GATE. YOU WILL DIE IF YOU ATTEMPT TO ENTER THE TIME TERMINAL! The date on that sign changes every day, to match Shangri-la's relative temporal location. They had to beef up security about ten years ago when a few desperate senior citizens committed suicide by stepping through, rather than face starvation or terminal cancer."

"Well, I understand that danger," Margo sniffed, "and I remember seeing TV shows about those poor old people who killed themselves. But what's this stuff about dying if you visit some other terminal or the wrong gate on the same terminal?"

"We're not just trying to scare you off," Kit said quietly. "The temporal position of any station, in its relation to absolute time, is different from any other station's temporal position. Terminals 17 and 56 are absolutely deadly to *anyone* on Shangri-la. If I tried to visit TT-56, I'd accidentally emerge into last week, when I was very much present at Shangri-la Station, which is currently . . ."

He checked the chronometer built into his personal log. "Which is currently April 28,1910, 22:01:17, local—i.e. Tibetan—time zone. Time guides have to be careful, too."

Malcolm nodded. "It's why we guides tend to specialize in tours through just a handful of gates leading out of one terminal. I could go to one of the other terminals and look for a scouting job, but I'd have to do careful homework first to be sure which terminals and which tours were safe for me. The Denver and London gates here in La-La Land can be just as deadly. The Denver gate is currently opening into 1885, the London gate into 1888. If I try to take a tourist to Denver during the same week I'd already taken someone else to London three years previously . . ." He shrugged. "I'd accidentally kill myself. So we keep damned good records of where and when we've been. That little credit card you were issued when you bought your Primary Gate ticket? The one they encoded for you before you came down time? When tourists use the gates, their Timecards are encoded in both directions—going down time and coming back—so they have a record of when they've been. If the computer catches an overlap, it sounds an alarm."

Margo's eyes were beginning to take on a glazed look.

"Careful as the precautions are," Kit added grimly, "there are still accidents, even with the tourists. Time scouts have to be paranoid about it. For instance, I could only visit TT-17 if I went up time and stayed for at least a year. TT-17's always twelve months and six hours behind this one, same geographical zone, about a thousand miles north of here. If I went through TT-17's Primary without letting it 'catch up' and pass by my last exit from TT-86, I'd never live to see the other side."

Malcolm said, "There have even been organized-crime murders committed that way, particularly *yakuza* killings. They select a victim, get them to take out a huge insurance policy naming a gang member as beneficiary, treat them to an Edo Castletown tour out of Shangri-la on a false ID, then some other gang member takes them to Terminal 56 on their *own* ID, so they shadow themselves in front of witnesses. Instant profit."

Margo shivered. "Okay. I think I get it."

"Now that you've been here, you'll have the same problem. The longer you stay, the greater the chance of overlap. The more gates you step through, the more complicated the whole mess becomes. That's why the log is essential."

Margo rested her elbows on the table. "Okay, point taken. We have to be careful. But I still say you can get run over by a bus, not paying attention. What's the other thing for?"

Kit sat back in his chair. Was she being flippant to hide fear? Or was she just that silly? Or that stubborn? He wondered how often she'd gotten what she wanted just by smiling that enchanting smile or by coming back with a wisecrack that set people to chuckling. Just what sort of life had Margo known before hunting him up? Given her prickly defenses and that over-sharp tongue, Kit wasn't too sure he wanted an answer.

"It's an ATLS. Absolute Time Locator System. That 'gizmo' you mentioned reading about. It works on a combination of geo-magnetic sensors and star-charting systems. The ATLS places you more or less exactly in time and geographic location, relative to absolute Greenwich time."

"More or less?" Margo echoed. "Isn't it precise?"

"Scouts always fudge by at least twenty-four hours in both directions when using the ATLS, just to be sure. Most of us build an even larger safety margin in, because as good as the ATLS is, it isn't absolutely precise. It can't be. Our lives are riding on how closely we cut it. Without it—and the personal log—we couldn't function at all. Even time touring would be impossible, because the tour companies need scouts to push new tour routes. The ATLS's casing gives it the same land of protection your personal log has."

Margo was frowning at the ATLS. "If it's so dangerous to step through, why not just put the ATLS on a long pole and shove that through, then let it do its thing? That way nobody'd ever have to risk going 'poof.'"

Kit shook his head. "It isn't that simple. For one, you have only a fifty-fifty chancc of a gate opening at night. If it opens during the day, you can't take a star-fix, so the long pole idea would be useless. Or it might be a cloudy night—no stars. We *could* roboticize the whole thing, I suppose, and send it through to take the proper magnetic and star-fix readings, but it would cost a ton of money for each robot and there are thousands of unexplored gates with new ones opening all the time. Anything could still go wrong and recovering the robot might prove impossible. Frankly, human scouts are cheaper, more reliable, and have the advantage of being able to gather detailed social data no robot could. That's important particularly when scholarly research or potential time touring is involved.

"We," he tapped his breast bone, "are expendable. We're independent businessmen, on nobody's payroll. No insurance company in the world will touch us, not even Lloyd's of London. That's another downside to scouting. No health coverage, no life insurance, no disability policies. You sign on for this job, you take your chances. There is a guild, if you care to pay the dues, but the treasury's almost always empty. Time scouts tend to suffer catastrophic illnesses and injuries with depressing frequency. I hope," he added grimly, "that you have a high pain threshold and don't faint at the sight of blood—yours or anyone else's."

Margo didn't answer. But her chin came up a stubborn notch, despite sudden pallor beneath already fair skin.

Kit sat back. "Huh. I'll give you credit for guts, girl. All right, let me show you how these operate."

He and Malcolm took her step by step through the operation of both machines, although they couldn't shoot a star-fix from inside La-La Land. The personal log she caught onto fairly quickly. The ATLS's geo-magnetic sensors gave her trouble.

"No, you're plotting that reading backwards, Margo. You've just put yourself half a continent off target, which means you've just calculated the time zone completely wrong, as well. Run it again."

"I hate math!" Margo snapped. "How was I supposed to know I'd need all this crap?"

Malcolm visibly suppressed a wince. Very gently, Kit took the ATLS from her. "All right. We'll begin by having you hone up on basic skills. I'll schedule study times for you in the library. And not just for remedial math. You'll need language skills, historical studies, costuming and customs, sociological structures . . .

Margo was looking at him in wide-eyed horror.

"Let me guess," Kit said drolly. "You thought time scouting was a way to avoid college?"

She didn't answer, but he could read it in her eyes.

"Kid, if you want to be a time scout, the first thing you have to become is a *scholar*. Scouts are a rough and ready bunch—we have to be—but most of us started life as historians or classics professors or philosophers or anthropologists. We're the best-educated bunch of roughnecks this side of eternity."

Malcolm laughed "I have a Ph.D. in Roman antiquities."

Margo sat back and crossed her arms. "This is maddening. If I'd wanted a Ph.D., I've have gone to school. All I want to do is explore neat places!"

Kit started to say something that would have been entirely too heartfelt, but Malcolm beat him to the punch.

"Fame and fortune and adventure?" he asked in a voice dry as fine wine.

She flushed.

Kit felt like cheering. "That's fine," he told her. "But you have to pay the dues. And we have an agreement, Margo. You do what I tell you, when I tell you, or you don't set that first pretty pink toe across the threshold of agate."

She pouted at the ATLS. Then sighed. "All right. I'll go to the library. Isn't there anything to this job besides studying?"

"Sure." Kit sat back. "Plenty, in fact. How much martial arts training have you had?"

She shrugged. "High school stuff. I have a belt."

"What kind, which discipline?"

"Brown belt, Tai Kwan Do."

Kit grunted. All flying lacks and damn near no full-contact sparring, not compared to what she'd need. Tai Kwan Do spent too much time "pulling" its punches short to give a student a taste of what it was like to hit—or be hit. He saw the chance for an object lesson that might just sink home.

"All right. Let's go."

"Go? Go where?"

Kit returned the log and ATLS to their leather satchel.

"To the gym. I want to test how much you know."

"You . . . *now?*"

Kit grinned. "Yep. What's the matter, Margo? Afraid an old man will whip you?"

Slim jaw muscles took on a marble hardness. She came to her feet and planted hands on hips. "No. I'm not afraid of anybody or anything. Where's the damned gym?"

"Watch your language," he said mildly "The gym is in the basement, next to the weapons ranges."

Her eyes widened "Weapons ranges?" Her expression hovered somewhere between excitement and dismay. "You mean, like guns and stuff?"

Kit exchanged glances with Malcolm, who rolled his eyes. Kit forcibly held back a sigh. "Yes, Margo. I mean exactly like guns and stuff. If it can be shot, slashed with, or jabbed into someone, you're going to learn how to use it."

"Oh."

Clearly, this was another aspect of time scouting his granddaughter had not considered. She looked like she'd rather have picked up a live cobra than picked up a weapon. Good. Maybe this would convince her to quit. Given the set of her jaw, Kit rather doubted that, but it made for a pleasant fantasy. He had a sinking feeling *nothing* he did or said would dissuade her.

Margo said primly, "If we're going to spar, I'll need to visit the lady's room first."

Malcolm shot to his feet and hovered at the back of her chair, but didn't quite offer to take her hand to assist her. Kit glowered. Margo gave Malcolm a sweet smile that left Kit's glower even darker. Malcolm had the good grace to look sheepish as Margo made her way through the crowded bar. Very nearly every eye in the place followed her progress. Kit shook his head. The dress had to go. Preferably into the trash. Or maybe over Skeeter Jackson's head.

"How about you, Malcolm? You coming to the gym, too?"

The freelance guide chuckled. "Just try and get rid of me. I wouldn't miss this for a full-time job."

"You," Kit muttered, "are a pain in the neck."

"Hey, don't blame me," Malcolm laughed. "You're the one who agreed to teach her."

"Yeah, I did. I figure it's either teach her or bury her."

Malcolm's laughter vanished. "Yeah. I know. You need help, you let me know."

Kit gave him a pained smile. "I'll do that. I figure I owe you."

Malcolm groaned. "How come I have a bad feeling about this?"

"Because," Kit punched his shoulder, "your luck stinks."

The younger man chuckled. 'Well, I won't argue that. All right, here she comes. Smile, Grandpa."

Kit muttered, "You'd better salute when you say that, mister." Malcolm just laughed. Kit said forlornly, "I will never live this down.

Never." He pasted on what he hoped passed for a smile. "Okay, Margo, let's go."

Phase One underway.

And a lifetime's worth of worrying yet to come.

Chapter 7

News travels fast in a small town.

And despite its enormous size for a complex under one roof, TT-86 was, in fact, a very small town, as isolated in some ways as a medieval village. There was no live television, no live radio, no satellite hookups to talk to relatives left behind. Electronic recreation was available, of course, for a price. Most private quarters had televisions and laser-disk players and nearly every resident owned some kind of computer.

But in order to satisfy the craving for live entertainment, 'eighty-sixers resorted to a time-honored form of recreation first invented by bored cave-dwellers who found themselves stuck in cramped quarters with nowhere to go. 'Eighty-sixers gossiped. About everything. Tourists, other stations, down-time mishaps and adventures, each other . . .

Someone had once laughingly suggested that station management install "backyard fences" in the residential sections. The jokester had immediately initiated a six-month wrangle over where, what color, who would pay for them, wood vs. chain-link, and installation vs. maintenance logistics, until Bull Morgan had finally put his authoritative foot down in the middle of the ruckus and quashed it with a succinct. "No fences!"

Long-time 'eighty-sixers still occasionally grumbled over it.

Kit had no more than opened the gym door than someone called out, "Hey, Grandpa! How's the arthritis?"

Kit shot back a time-honored response and told Margo, "That way. You'll find clean gym shorts and T-shirts at the window. Tell 'em to put it on my bill."

"Okay."

At least nobody wolf-whistled at Margo's stilt-heeled progress toward the women's shower room. Kit changed and emerged to find Malcolm against one wall. Margo had not yet put in an appearance.

"Aren't you going to spar with us?" Kit asked with a wolfish grin.

Malcolm feigned surprise. "Me? End up wrestling around on the floor with your grandkid? Kit, stupid I ain't."

"You're twenty years younger than I, dammit. Dress out. If you're short of pocket cash, I'll pay for the rental. Hell, I'll pay for the sparring session. If we knock her flat enough, maybe she'll give up."

"Well, okay. It's your party. But I wouldn't count on it. She does remind me a little of you."

Kit tossed his towel at Malcolm's head. The younger man grinned, caught it, and tossed it right back, then headed for the shower room. Margo emerged decently clad in shorts, a loose T-shirt, and rented cotton-soled shoes. She moved well, but that might just have been youth and an unfortunate tendency toward exhibitionism. Clearly, she was perfectly well aware that every male eye in the room was on her.

Huh. It's not bad enough she's my granddaughter, but she has to be sexy as a minx, too. And legally old enough to make her own decisions if the age on her ID were accurate. She *looked* eighteen, anyway. He'd tackle her about her exact age later. Kit tried to adjust himself to the uncomfortable new mindset as she crossed the last couple of yards and came to a halt. She balanced lightly on the balls of her feet. "Well, are you ready?"

Kit shook his head. "Malcolm's joining us. I want to watch you two spar first. Then you and I will pair off."

She didn't look happy about that.

Malcolm finally arrived "Okay, boss. Shoot."

"Let's see what the two of you can do, shall we?"

Malcolm nodded and gave Margo a formal bow. She returned it in classic sportsman-like fashion—and Malcolm charged. Half a second later, Margo grunted sharply. Her back connected with the mat. Kit shook his head and tsk-tsked.

"Margo, didn't your instructor ever teach you to keep your eyes on your opponent?"

She glared up at him from an extremely indelicate position with Malcolm between her knees. He'd pinned her wrists to the floor. "How was I supposed to know he'd cheat?"

Malcolm grinned. "This isn't a *dojo,* Miss Margo."

"And it sure as hell ain't a high school match," Kit added drily. "We're here to see how you can fight. If you want to discuss customs and courtesies in the competitive arena, go talk to an etiquette master."

Malcolm rose easily. Margo scrambled to her feet, mastering a huffy glare on the way up. "All right," she muttered. "Let's see you try that again. This time, I'll be watching."

Malcolm moved in fast and grappled her, using classic Greco-Roman grappling styles. The unexpected move completely flummoxed Margo. She staggered backward, trying to extricate herself from wrestling holds she didn't have the strength or technique to break.

"Hey! What is this?" She tried stamping on Malcolm's instep. He picked her up, leading to chuckles from across the gym. Interested spectators had halted all pretense of continuing any workouts.

Kit suppressed a grin, wisely deciding that laughing at her would be a mistake. Wordlessly, he separated them. Margo stood glaring and huffing for breath. Malcolm offered a polite bow which she ignored icily. "All right," Kit said, stepping off the mat once more, "let's see what else you can do."

She turned that alley-cat glare on him—and Malcolm came in fast. But this time he didn't catch her off guard. Margo snapped out a beautifully executed snap kick, lifting her knee and extending her leg so fast it was difficult to follow the motion. Her foot brushed Malcolm's cheek. That kick would've scored wonderfully on the sporting circuit. If she'd kicked him in the nose or forehead, she might even have rendered him unconscious.

Unfortunately for Margo, neither Malcolm's nose nor his forehead were in the right spot. He kept coming. Margo's heel sailed straight over his shoulder. Before she could snap back from the unexpected move, she found herself on the floor, in exactly the same position as before with Malcolm between her knees.

"It's not fair!" she wailed. "That would've knocked him out!"

Kit nodded. "Yep, if you'd actually kicked him, it probably would've. But you didn't."

"Look, I don't want to break your friend's face!"

Malcolm chuckled. "I appreciate your concern, Miss Margo." He let her up, and she rubbed her wrists, then eased a strained muscle in her thigh.

Kit said, "Take five."

He went back to the equipment room and found sparring helmets, gloves, and padded shoes, then returned to find Margo glowering silently at Malcolm. "Okay, this should be pretty much like what you used in karate competitions."

She eyed the equipment dubiously.

Oh, great. "Let me guess? You never did any full-contact competitions?"

"Well, no," she admitted. "We always pulled the punches short and made sure the kicks didn't connect. Our high school didn't have money for this kind of stuff."

Kit thought dark thoughts about any school administration that would allow kids to risk injury in a "sport" that was designed to cripple and kill. Pushing these thoughts aside, he showed her how the padded helmet worked. Similar to the leather helmets boxers wore, it was made of soft plastic, with a big pad across the forehead and down the sides of the face, straps under the jaw, and a pad that extended around the sides of the head a bit. Malcolm strapped on his own helmet, then slipped into shoes and gloves while Margo struggled with hers.

When she was ready, she said uncertainly, "I still don't want to cripple him or anything."

Kit nodded. "Just make him go oof and I'll be happy."

"Okay."

Once again, Malcolm charged in, giving her almost no time to react. Margo executed a side check kick and hit him right across the pelvis. He said "oof!" and stopped abruptly. As he folded over, Margo hit him just above his right ear with her left fist. Another sharp "oof!" accompanied the punch. Margo struck with her right fist across the back of the skull on his way down. A third ludicrous "oof!" tore loose. When his face hit the mat, a final, muffled *"oof . . ."* prompted grins all across the gym.

Margo said sweetly, "You mean, like those four?"

Kit just looked at her. "Aren't you going to finish him off?"

From near Margo's feet, Malcolm muttered into the mat, "Oh, God, don't encourage her."

Kit chuckled and nudged him with an unsympathetic toe. "C'mon, Malcolm, get up and do it again. This doesn't prove she's any good, it just proves you've gotten overconfident."

Margo huffed and crossed her arms.

Malcolm scraped himself off the mat and stood up, moving a little awkwardly. Kit grinned. "What's the matter, Malcolm? A little slow on the rebound?"

"You," Malcolm muttered, "are a pain."

"Every chance I get."

Malcolm charged without warning. Margo threw up another check kick, but Malcolm stopped short, leaving the kick whistling through empty air. By the time she'd finished executing it, she was turned away from him. Malcolm rushed in gleefully. Kit winced and braced himself for Margo's wail of protest. Her back was toward him as Malcolm rushed forward—

Then she astonished them both.

Margo stepped *toward* Malcolm. When he hit her, Margo brought her elbow straight back with the forearm parallel to floor, fist clenched, palm up. She leaned into it and hit him in the solar plexus. He snapped forward with an ugly sound that caused Kit to grimace in sympathy. Margo dropped as he did, then grabbed him around the neck with both arms and jerked him forward. Poor Malcolm landed dead on his backside with Margo balanced lightly on her feet behind him. She grabbed his hair in her gloved fist and punched him in the base of the skull with her right hand, pulling the punch so that it just popped him.

While Malcolm's eyes and nose streamed wetness, Margo said even more sweetly, "You mean finish him off like that?"

Kit crossed his arms to hide his amusement. He didn't want Margo getting cocky. Poor Malcolm was blinking and struggling manfully to dry his face with his gloves. "Well, that's one," Kit drawled, "but in a real situation, you always need to kill or cripple at least twice."

"Twice?" Margo echoed. "Oh, so he doesn't surprise you when you think he's down."

When she made to finish Malcolm off again, Kit waved her back.

"No, Malcolm is clearly finished. This time."

The freelance guide glared at Kit as though to say, "Malcolm does not want to play anymore. Malcolm is in pain and will pay you back for this, good buddy."

Kit shrugged as though to say, "Who knew?"

Malcolm had struggled to his feet. "You . . ." he wheezed at Kit, ". . . should be damned glad Bull doesn't allow litigation lawyers in La-La Land."

"So I should," Kit said mildly. "And so should you. Go one more time."

"Gripes, Kit, what're you trying to do? Give Rachel Eisenstein more business?"

Margo was literally preening.

Kit's grin was entirely unsympathetic. "The day Margo puts you in the hospital is the day I'll eat your shoes. C'mon, buddy. Brace up."

Margo gave him a mocking bow, carefully keeping her eyes on him. Malcolm groaned and settled himself. "All right," he muttered. "We'll just see."

Malcolm, forced into the role of attacker by the requirements of the sparring session, came in again—but this time, he surprised her. Malcolm came at her like a trained Tai Kwan Do fighter, throwing a beautiful front snap kick of his own. It knocked her back with an unladylike sound. Malcolm charged in flailing, punching with both fists, one-two, one-two. Margo staggered back, moving away, bringing her arms up as he tried to hit her. Then she threw up a hook kick, sweeping his arms down out of the way with her foot. Before he could recover, she punched him twice in the face, using the momentum of her forward motion. As he backed away from her, Margo threw her shoulder into his gut, knocking him backwards. Then she really surprised Kit—not to mention Malcolm. She grabbed the back of his leading knee and snatched it up past her own hip while continuing to push with her shoulder. Malcolm smacked the mat flat on his back and gave out an ugly, "whoof!"

Margo landed between his knees in a parody of his early pins. She said, "Your turn!" and raked his face with one gloved hand, then popped him in the Adam's apple with the other.

"Gak!" Malcolm's eyes bulged and crossed, simultaneously.

Margo jumped up, grinning impishly, then actually curtsied to Kit. Laughter erupted across the gym, along with sporadic applause. Margo curtsied again to the audience, drawing greater applause. Malcolm rolled over onto his hands and knees, coughed, and wheezed in Kit's general direction. "Stuff it, Kit. Mamma always taught me never fight with girls. Mamma was usually right."

Kit managed to return Margo's triumphant grin with a bored expression. "Thought you were trained in Tai Kwan Do," he observed drily. "What was that little flip at the end of Malcolm's second fall?"

Margo's grin widened. "Well, my freshman year in high school, I took Judo until I found out they weren't going to let us roll around on the floor like that with boys."

"Don't be nasty, little girl," he said mildly.

Margo just laughed. "Next?" she challenged.

He privately conceded her the right to be pleased with herself, but cocky was dangerous. Time for a reality check. He stepped out onto the mat.

Malcolm wheezed, "Wait a sec. Lemme get out of the way,"

All across the gym, spectators pressed a little closer. Someone gave Malcolm a cup of water, which he gulped down. He took the ribbing surprisingly well, grinning and unfastening the gloves, pulling off the helmet and rubbing at the base of his skull.

Margo watched him with a glow of satisfaction warming her all the way through. She'd scored big time and she knew it. She saw grudging respect in Malcolm's eyes and open interest in several faces as they appraised her. *Finally,* she thought, *finally, I do something right around here!* Maybe now Kenneth "Kit" Carson would start showing her a little respect!

Flying high, Margo playfully lunged straight toward him.

Afterward, she wasn't sure what he'd done, except that he turned and raised one hand while the other came down. She was never sure if she touched him or he touched her, but she was abruptly sitting on her butt clear off the edge of the mat on a cold, hard floor. The ache jolted all the way up her spine.

When Margo recovered from shock, all she could find to say was a wailing, "Ow!" Then she turned to glare at Kit. "You threw me off the mat!"

"No," he disagreed with a tiny smile, "you threw you off the mat."

"HUH?"

"Okay," he said kindly, "ready to do a little serious sparring now?"

That was more than Margo's bruised ego could bear. She charged in, launching another nice high front snap kick—only Kit's head wasn't there. It was down around her belt level and the left foot she was using for support was suddenly up a little higher than her left ankle used to be, and at least a foot forward, while her backside traveled rapidly straight toward the floor.

This time, Margo was the one who blinked involuntary tears. *Owww. . . .*Malcolm was in her line of sight, grinning insufferably.

Kit Carson, damn him, said, "Well, don't just sit there, kid. Come on, I thought you wanted to fight."

She scrambled up and launched herself forward with a flurry of fists, as fast and furious as the punches Malcolm had thrown at her. Margo saw his open palms come up between her blows, but her fists never hit quite where she expected. Then, quite suddenly—due to a light pressure on her right wrist and elbow—she found it necessary to throw herself at top speed straight toward the floor. She landed hard, face first. At least this time she'd landed *on* the mat. Margo saw red. She regained all fours while he just stood there, smiling down at her. She lunged straight for his crotch, determined to grab whatever she could.

He grasped her wrist. Lightly. With nothing but his thumb and center finger. Adding insult to injury, he even left his index finger lightly extended. Before she could recover, he backed up enough to straighten her arm, then turned slightly. Her elbow straightened painfully across the front of his knee. He continued his turn, in slow motion to emphasize the point. Margo gasped—then gasped again as that lazy turn forced her to attempt crawling around him in a circle, just to prevent her elbow from being popped out of joint. Howls of amusement erupted throughout the gym. *Oh, God, they're laughing at me . . .*

While she continued crawling around in a state of growing panic and embarrassment, Kit told her, "That's enough for today, I think. Get showered and we'll talk about this."

He finally let her go. Margo stuffed a wail back inside before it could burst loose, but she couldn't stop the impulse to rub her wrist. All around men were chuckling and returning to their own workouts. She bit back a scathing comment, realizing even through a haze of humiliation that she had a lot to learn. *He set me up, dammit, he set me up . . .* Well, she'd asked for it, hadn't she? That thought got Margo through a long, miserable shower. Hot water pounded against bruises and relaxed knots of muscle from her neck to her toes. When she emerged, wrapped in a towel, she found the locker room attendant and tried to reclaim her clothes. The woman smiled and handed her another set of clean workout clothes.

Margo groaned. "Oh, God, not another torture session?"

"No," the attendant smiled, "just something a little less, um, I think Kit said *scandalous* than your dress." She handed that over, too, along with the stilt heels, bedraggled hat, and corset. "Keep the gym shoes, too."

"Thanks," Margo muttered, earning a sympathetic laugh.

Margo considered putting her own clothes back on, Kit Carson be damned, but she was so muscle-sore, just the *thought* of cinching herself into that corset was unendurable. Besides, she'd had enough humiliation for one day. She didn't want any reminders of her own poor judgment where Skeeter Jackson was concerned. She hoped that rat made himself *scarce.* She never wanted to see him again, let alone talk to him. Margo wadded the dress, corset, and shoes into a ball and balanced the hat on top.

"Well," she sighed, "chalk one up to experience, Margo. It's going to be a longer day than you thought."

She lifted her chin, refusing to acknowledge utter defeat. She'd bested Malcolm Moore and convinced Kit to train her. That was worth a great deal. With those moderately cheering thoughts, Margo headed toward her next confrontation with the maddening man she'd chosen as teacher. *Surely,* she told herself by way of a pep talk, *it'll get better soon.* And if it didn't? Or if he decided she didn't have what it took?

Well, he could toss her out, but by God she wasn't going to quit!

While Margo showered and changed, Kit sent Malcolm off with enough pocket change for a good, solid meal, then phoned to transfer funds into Malcolm's account to cover the sparring session and damages sustained. He had further plans for the guide concerning his granddaughter's training, which meant he didn't want Malcolm quitting for good before Margo's lessons had even begun. Malcolm didn't know it yet, but he was about to become substantially richer—and probably a little bit greyer. Kit shook his head. Who'd have guessed the kid would work him over so thoroughly?

He took advantage of Margo's tardiness in the shower to hunt up the next of Margo's instructors. The weapons ranges were nearly empty. Ann Vinh Mulhaney was seated cross-legged on the floor next to an empty shooting bench, cleaning several break-action revolvers. "Hi, Kit," she smiled. "I hear Margo gave Malcolm a working over."

"News travels fast," he chuckled. "Poor Malcolm. He'll get over it, though. Especially when I offer him the chance to get even." Ann laughed. "Poor Margo. Where is the Wunderkind, by the way?"

"Showering. I think she's in there sulking, actually. She, er, didn't do so well against Aikido."

"So I heard. What's up? Rumors are flying that you plan to teach her to scout, but I didn't put much stock in them."

Kit scratched the back of his head. "Well, actually . . . I want you to teach her to shoot."

"You want me to what?" Ann Vinh Mulhaney's eyes widened. TT-86's resident firearms instructor planted hands on slender hips, ignoring smears of carbon residue and solvent on her hands. "Don't tell me those rumors are true?"

Kit cleared his throat.

Ann stared at him in dawning horror. "Oh, God, you *are* teaching her, aren't you? Any particular reason? I mean other than you've clearly lost what brains you ever had?"

Kit flushed. "Dammit, Ann, she'll do this on her own if I don't. You know how stubborn I am. She's just as bad, and just turned eighteen, and convinced the world's hers for the plucking. She doesn't give a hoot about the risks, she just wants to follow in my goddamned footsteps. . . ."

Ann's demeanor changed at once. "Oh, Kit. You poor thing." She rested a hand on his arm. He relaxed slowly, letting the anger and worry go muscle by muscle. When he could breathe without hurting his chest again, Ann said, "All right, Kit. I'll teach her. But if I pass judgment and it's bad . . ."

He met her eyes. "Maybe she'll listen to another woman."

"Maybe. I've got a lesson starting in a few minutes or I'd offer to take her on right now. Go talk to Sven and see what he has to say; then come back tomorrow morning and we can get started."

"Thanks, Ann." He squeezed her arm in heartfelt gratitude.

She smiled. "Don't thank me. This is going to cost, Kenneth Carson." But she winked to remove the sting.

Kit just groaned. "What do you want?"

"How about the honeymoon suite for a week?"

"A *week?* Do you have any idea what I could get for . . ." He trailed off. "Okay. A week."

"And my normal fees, plus fifty percent for private tutoring."

Grandkids were expensive. "Anything else? My signature in blood?"

Ann chuckled. "You think I'm expensive, wait until you tackle Sven."

"Great. Thanks. What does *he* want?"

"Out of the whole deal. I can hardly wait to see what you offer him that changes his mind."

Kit decided to kiss an entire quarter's worth of profits goodbye and went looking for Sven. Kit found him in the armory sharpening a *Radius.*

"Hi, Sven."

"Hi, yourself. The answer's no."

The scream of naked steel on the whetstone didn't encourage argument. Kit found a chair and plopped down. "Bull hockey."

Sven glanced up. "No way. She gets killed, you come hunting me, I have to break your neck. . . . Nope. No thanks."

"Would you rather have her go down time without lessons?"

"Huh. You'd rope her down, first."

"Yeah, but she'd have to go to the bathroom sometime and that's one determined kid. I mean it, Sven. I need you on this one. Ann can teach her everything she needs to know about projectile weapons, but she needs blades, too, and more martial arts than she's got. She needs lessons. Good lessons. Your lessons."

Sven put a finer edge on the *gladius,* then turned it and started working the other side. "You won't interfere?"

"Nope."

"Or get pissed off if she gets hurt?"

"Not a bit. The rougher it gets, the more likely she is to wake up and pick another career."

Sven snorted. "You're all heart, Grandpa. Well, the answer's still no. She's cute. She'll come to her senses."

Kit counted ten. Searched for some other argument. "I've got a Musashi sword-guard."

Sven halted mid-stroke, then swore and reshaped the ruined edge. "Bastard. Is it signed?"

Gotcha. "Yep."

Sven glared at him. "Where the hell did you get an original Musashi *tsuba?*"

"Found it in the Neo Edo's safe. There's some amazing stuff in that safe."

Sven laughed darkly. "I'll just bet there is." He set the *gladius* aside and leaned back "If it was just the *tsuba,* Kit, I'd tell you to get the hell out of here." He held Kit's gaze. "You really want to teach the kid that bad?"

"Yes, I do," Kit said quietly. "If I thought there was a way out of it . . . but I haven't found one yet. I want her to have a fighting chance."

Sven shook his head. "A woman scout. And a raw kid, at that. My friend, you're crazy." He gave Kit a lopsided smile. "But then, we always knew that. All right. I'll do it. And Kit—keep the Musashi. God knows, I owe you a couple of favors here and there. Just let me look at it now and again and we'll call it even."

Kit, who couldn't have taken the priceless Musashi sword-guard back up time in any case, decided he'd just found Sven's next birthday present. 'Thanks, buddy."

"Sure. Any time you want to go off the deep end, you just let me know. When do you want her to start?"

"Any time you're ready."

Sven sighed. "Well, hell I guess that's now. Have you eaten dinner?"

Kit shook his head "No, and I suspect Margo's half starved. Why don't I call and see if the Delight has a table open?"

"Sounds good to me. I'll meet you upstairs as soon as I finish locking up down here."

The Epicurean Delight's decor reflected its location in Urbs Romae: mosaic floors, frescoed walls (some of them painted by a muralist who'd spent a year down time studying with ancient master artists), and tables interspersed with genuine Roman-style dinner couches for those with the desire to eat lying down. Live music was provided by an accomplished lyrist dressed in Greek slave's robes. The waiting staff, too, dressed as well-liveried slaves. The evening's clientele boasted six instantly recognizable millionaires, one anonymous Japanese billionaire and his current mistress, a member of Great Britain's House of Lords and *his* current mistress, and three world-famous actresses who chatted animatedly about the down-time research they planned to do in London for their next film.

All in all, it was another typical night at the Delight. Kit noted Margo's eyes widen when the head waiter seated them next to the actresses. "That's—"

"Yep," Kit said, cutting her off. "Get used to it, Margo," he grinned. "'IT-86 is a magnet for the jet set, miserable lot of deadbeats that they are. Just don't plan on joining their ranks and you'll live a happier life. Now, while we wait for Sven to join us . . ."

Margo's face took on a shuttered, wary look. "Yeah?"

"Relax, kid, I don't bite. Those three," he nodded toward the actresses, "are here doing role research. You said you wanted to be on stage, right?" She nodded.

"Good." Kit leaned forward and interlaced his fingers comfortably. "I want you to think of scouting as role research for the most challenging stage play you've ever been cast as lead actress in."

Margo grinned. "That's dead easy."

"No, it isn't. If you flub your lines, there won't be any prompters backstage. You won't have a director to yell, 'CUT! Take it from page six. . . . You'll be on your own. Your performance won't be judged by a critic, it'll be judged by survival. Your audience will be the down-time people you encounter Fool them and maybe you'll get back in once piece. Now . . . about your performance in the gym."

Her eyes flashed. "I'll get better!"

"I'm sure you will. I want you to answer one question for me, but I want you to think about it before you answer."

"I'm listening."

Kit nodded. "I want you to tell me what the goals of a time scout are. Ah, hello, Arley, how are you?"

Arley Eisenstein greeted Margo warmly, welcoming her to TT-86, then recommended the House Special. "It's a new recipe, Egyptian, wonderful. You're my guinea pigs."

Kit smiled. "I'm game. Margo?"

With a combative look in her eye, Margo said, "Anything he's having, I'll have."

"Anything?" Arley said with an up-tilted eyebrow.

"Anything."

Arley rubbed his palms together in gleeful anticipation. "Oh, good. This ought to be fun. I'll tell Jacque to get started. Is anyone else joining you?"

"Just Sven, far as I know, but I don't mind company if somebody wants a chair."

"Good, good. The more the merrier," Arley laughed "Wine? Appetizers?"

Kit glanced at Margo, who was clearly tired but still on edge. "Is this Special of yours poultry, fish, pork, or beef? Or something else altogether?"

Arley winked. "Seafood. Mostly."

"All right, why don't we start with a half-carafe of Piesporter Michelsburg and some fresh fruit and bread and I'll let you choose the wine for the main course?"

Arley flashed a delighted smile. "Mead. Egyptian mead. I'll send Julie out with the appetizers," Arley promised. He smiled warmly again at Margo, then threaded his way through the Delight, pausing now and again to speak with other clients. Sven Bailey arrived.

"So this is the one, huh?" he said without preamble. His long, shuttered stare brought an uncomfortable flood of color to Margo's cheeks—and a glitter of irritation to her eyes.

"I'm the one what?" she asked coldly.

Sven just grunted and ignored her. He plopped into a chair. "You're sure about this?"

Kit shrugged. "Yep."

"Huh."

Margo glanced from Sven to Kit, then back. She clearly wanted to ask a question and just as clearly wasn't sure she wanted to risk the answer yet. Kit took pity on her.

"Margo, this is Sven Bailey, acknowledged far and wide as the most dangerous man on TT-86."

Margo's eyes widened. Sven just snorted. "Damned right I am. Last man who tried to prove otherwise ended up dead." He guffawed, leaving Margo to stare uneasily anywhere but at him. Kit didn't bother to explain that the gentleman in question had been a mad tourist who'd insisted on using the Biddle style of formal knife-fighting, despite Sven's solemn warnings that it would get him killed (which it had, in some filthy little Soho alley, where he'd found out that knife-fencing and street fighting were not the same animal, after all).

Sven high-signed Julie, who beamed in their direction while balancing a wine carafe and glasses on a silver tray. "Hi, guys," she said brightly, setting down glasses and a perfectly chilled carafe of Piesporter, along with tumblers of ice water. "What'll your poison be, Sven?"

He sniffed at the wine. "Not that. How about a Sam Adams?"

"Any thoughts on dinner? We have a wonderful seafood special tonight, a new dish from ancient Egypt . . ."

"Hell, no. Let Arley experiment on somebody else. You still doing that beef thing you had in here last week?"

Julie dimpled. "We sure are. Rare?"

"Make it moo."

Margo looked like she was about to lose her appetite—or worse.

Kit grinned. "What's wrong, kid? No stomach for blood?"

Margo compressed her lips. "I'm fine."

Sven eyed her. "You sure act squeamish for a kid about to try time scouting."

She fidgeted in her chair, but refrained from comment. "Speaking of time scouting," Kit said, rubbing the side of his nose, "any thoughts about the answer to that question I posed?"

Margo glanced at Sven. She looked suddenly very young and uncertain. Then her chin came up. "Well . . . A time scouts job is to find out where a gate leads."

Kit shook his head. "I didn't ask what a scout's job was, I asked what a scout's goals are. That's a little different proposition."

For a second, she looked so tired and hungry and miserable and confused, Kit thought she might cry. He prompted, "Just tell me what pops into your head. What's a scout's primary goal?"

'To make money."

Sven let loose an astonishing guffaw that startled diners in a circle three tables deep, then pounded Margo's back with friendly affection. She nearly came adrift from her chair, but managed a sheepish smile. Kit grinned. "Money, eh? Well, yes, if you're lucky. If the gate you push doesn't lead to the Russian steppes in the middle of the last ice age. A few scientists might want a peek, but there's not much commercial potential in a mile-high glacier. What else?"

"To stay alive," she said, with a tiny toss of her short hair.

"Absolutely," Kit agreed.

"You're gettin' there, girl. What else?" Sven asked, taking the burden of grilling her off Kit's hands.

She chewed her lower lip thoughtfully. "Learn stuff about where you are, of course. Do you take a camera?"

Kit thought about Catherine the Great and her Russian boar and winked at Sven. He'd clearly read the same article, judging by the sudden twinkle in his eyes. "Sometimes. Usually not. Cameras aren't essential equipment."

"What else ought to be my goal, then?"

Kit nodded. "Good. You're asking questions." He leaned forward. "Point number one: the kind of karate you've learned in high school might be great for a soldier attacking someone else, but soldiering—fighting battles—isn't the primary goal of a scout."

"Hell, no," Sven muttered. "You want a battle, go live in Serbia or anywhere from Istanbul down to Cairo. Last I heard, Israel was threatening to pop a nuke or two if the Moslem states didn't stop recruiting *jihad* fighters from down time and I can't say as I blame either side. Gad, what a mess."

Even Margo had the sense to shiver. What the time strings had done to the incendiary Middle East didn't bear thinking about. A coalition of Moslem and Jewish women had come together to try and stop the fighting, but so far neither side was listening to the voice of sanity. The whole region had been declared off limits after TT-66 had been bombed into oblivion. Kit, like most 'eighty-sixers, had lost good friends during the death of the station.

Kit cleared his throat and defused the sudden chill by pouring wine for Margo and himself. "All right, then," Kit said, "a scout's goal isn't to engage in battle. It's to go someplace, to learn whatever he can, *then get away clean,* doing the least amount of damage to the local environment—including the denizens of that environment."

"Especially the denizens," Sven said, by way of emphasis. "Anything else is borrowing trouble. Big trouble. If you piss off somebody who can't be killed and you end up in a life-or-death situation with them, you'll be the one kissing your backside goodbye."

"Wait a second," Margo said with a frown. "What do you mean, somebody who can't be killed? Anybody can be killed."

"Not exactly," Kit said quietly. "If someone's death would alter history, then that person can't be killed. At least, not by an up-timer. Paradox will not happen. History won't change. People have tried. It never works.

"Never. Let's say you try to assassinate somebody famous, like George Washington. Your gun will jam or misfire, or you'll trip at the last second so the knife doesn't hit a vital spot. *Something* will happen to prevent you from changing anything critical. The tricky part here is, it can happen when you least expect it."

"Like if you get into a fatal fight with somebody who seems unimportant," Sven said quietly. "If their death would affect history, then they won't die. That doesn't mean *you* won't."

For once, Margo looked worried instead of flippant. She glanced at Sven, then back to Kit. "Okay." It came out surprisingly subdued. "What else?"

"Another point to remember is that we're the outsiders, down time. Even if somebody is unimportant enough that their death wouldn't matter to history, we don't have a moral right to go barging in with a macho attitude that we'll just smash anything that puts us in danger, without taking precautions to avoid problems in the first place."

"The best way to win a fight," Sven put in, "is to avoid fighting in the first place. The real kicker, of course, is learning how to avoid the fight."

Margo chewed one thumbnail. "And if you can't? I mean, what if some psychopathic kook jumps you?"

His cruel comments about Jack the Ripper had clearly made an impression. Kit refilled her wineglass. "That's always possible, of course, and sometimes there may be nothing for it but to break a neck or shatter a kneecap, but most of the time your goal is to be invisible. If you can't be, then your goal is to keep someone from breaking *your* neck or shattering *your* kneecap. And, of course, to get the hell back to the terminal in one piece. When it comes to scouts, heroes are just people who confuse cowardice with common sense."

Sven gestured lazily with one thick hand. "Anybody knows that, Kit does. A real running expert on smash and skedaddle. And the only man on the station I can't throw five out of five times, sparring."

Kit chuckled thinly, drawing little circles in the condensate on the tabletop. "Only before I retired, buddy. I wouldn't go near you, right now."

"Only proves you should," Sven came back with a grin. "Keep you on your toes. Keep you young."

"Don't rub it in too deep," Kit laughed. "You're not that far behind me. Let's see, how old will you be come June?"

"Old enough," Sven said with a mock glower that fooled no one.

Margo was staring, oogle-eyed, from one to the other. Then quite suddenly she relaxed, as though she'd finally decided Sven didn't plan to pick up his steak knife and do her in between the salad and the main course.

"Now, that's not to say," Kit said with a smile, drawing the discussion back to the topic at hand, "that there's anything inherently wrong with good karate. I've got a black in Sho Shin Ri and another in . . . Well, I have several and they're all useful now and again. But Aikido—which is what happened to you, by the way—is probably the perfect defensive art."

Margo did another beautifully executed stationary female flounce and glared at him—although less murderously than in the gym. "That was humiliating."

"So's dying," Sven said laconically.

Margo flushed. "Okay, so I have a lot to learn. That's why I came looking for a teacher. At least it'll be more interesting than *math!*"

Sven grinned. "You don't know math, you'll kill yourself just as dead as a back-street punk with a dirk would. Now, if you really want to kill, Korean Hap Ki Do or Hwarangdo are interesting forms to get into. If you have six or eight years. Of course," Sven rubbed his hands together and grinned, "Kit will tell you the years spent studying Hap Ki Do's art of invisibility would be far more useful to a scout than its fighting style."

Kit ignored the gambit to reopen a favorite discussion. "Unfortunately," Kit told Margo, "you don't have years because you'll be spending most of your time studying, not sparring. So what we'll do is set you up with an Aikido instructor to give you a good grounding in basics and a few specific moves, things that maybe could get you out of tight spots."

Sven punched Margo good naturedly in the shoulder, causing her to wince. "That's right. Stuff to let you use those damned attractive legs of yours to run like hell."

Margo scowled at Sven. "My legs are none of your business!"

"Oh, yes they are," he grinned, an evil, thickset imp who leaned back and cracked his knuckles while staring her down.

Margo turned a dismayed look on Kit. "He isn't . . ."

Kit nodded.

"Oh, no . . ." She sat back in stunned horror. "My *teacher?*"

"Yep," Sven said as his beer arrived with the bread and fruit plate. "Tomorrow morning, 7:00 a.m. Dress out and be prompt. Because if you're late, I am going to wipe up the mat with you." Then he laughed. "Hell, I'm going to wipe up the mat with you either way, but if you're late, I'll be irritated when I do it." He held up his glass in a toast. "Enjoy your dinner."

The look of stricken horror Margo tried to hide was comical.

Kit grinned and refilled her wine glass. "Drink up, kid. Tomorrow you go into training, which means no more alcohol." The stricken look deepened.

"None? Not even wine?"

"None," Kit and Sven said simultaneously.

"A muddle-headed scout—" Kit began.

"I know, I know," Margo groaned. "Doesn't live long."

Thus proving she can learn, if she hears it often enough. "After you finish up with Sven, Ann Vinh Mulhaney will be ready for you."

"What does *she* do?" Margo wailed.

"She shoots the pants off me," Sven chuckled.

Margo just covered her face. "I'm doomed."

Kit tousled her hair, earning a fierce glare. "You could always quit and go home."

"Never!" The alley-cat snarl prompted a grin of anticipation from Sven Bailey.

"Well, then," Kit smiled, "eat your dinner and pay attention. Uncle Sven and I are about to start your first lesson in survival theory."

She gave them both a dubious glance. "That being?" Sven guffawed. "When the fight starts, be someplace else. And always remember, nobody watches your butt for you when it's You versus the Universe—and Margo, the universe just don't give a damn. Death's a high price to pay for stupidity or carelessness, but they'll get you eventually if you don't do your job. And that job," he took another sip of his Sam Adams and warmed to the subject, "ain't pushing gates to get rich and famous. Now. The underlying principle of Aikido is real simple. There's you," he dropped a couple of droplets of water into the bowl of his spoon, "and there's the universe." He dropped another couple of drops nearby, carefully balancing the spoon so they remained separated.

"The trick with Aikido is to become one with the universe," he allowed the droplets to run together, "so that nothing catches you by surprise. Master that and you can offer an enemy reconciliation instead of battle. The rest is just vigilance and practice."

Margo was staring dubiously at the water droplets. "You're kidding."

"Nope."

She sighed. "Okay. What do I have to do to snuggle up to the universe? Chant 'om' a couple thousand times an hour?"

Sven and Kit exchanged glances. Sven's questioning look clearly said, "Are you *sure* about this?"

Kit's grimace said "Yeah, dammit, wish I could say otherwise."

'Well," Sven said almost tiredly, "no, you don't chant 'om.' There isn't a secret key, some trick that will do it. Either it happens or it doesn't. The way you begin in Aikido is to start by doing wrist exercises." He demonstrated as Julie made her way toward their table with a heaping tray on which their dinner plates had been cast in the starring role. Sven shook out his napkin. "Why don't you practice that while Miss Julie puts that plate of eels and steamed octopus in front of you?"

Margo swung around in her chair. "*What?*"

Julie dutifully conjured a dish of baby octopus—tentacles artistically arranged around the eels—swimming in a garlic sauce that brimmed with unidentifiable spices and grated vegetables.

"Oh, my God . . ."

Kit couldn't help it. He started laughing. Sven was already wiping tears.

"C'mon, Margo," Kit teased, "what happened to your brave challenge? I thought you'd try anything I was game to try."

"But . . . but . . ."

"Let me guess," Kit said drily, "they didn't serve octopus in whatever little town you grew up in?"

Margo was still transfixed by the sight in front of her. The eels, which had been gutted and de-boned, still had their heads, producing the indelible impression that the plateful of slippery food was staring back. She swallowed convulsively. "I, uh . . ." She picked up her fork with an air of grim determination. "All right. *How* does one eat them?"

"That's the spirit," Sven laughed. "The eels, you cut into pieces. The octopi, you eat whole."

She shut her eyes and swallowed again, then tried a bite. She widened her eyes. "Hey, that's good!"

Kit chuckled. "Of course it is. Arley Eisenstein wouldn't serve it otherwise. *Bon appetit.*"

He dug in with gusto.

True to her word, Margo matched him bite for bite—and enjoyed every last morsel.

The best thing Margo could say about her first lesson with Sven Bailey was that she didn't have to pay for it. The worst thing was, Malcolm Moore showed up to watch. After the first five minutes, she seriously regretted the previous day's sparring session. He enjoyed her utter trouncing far too thoroughly to outlast the brief satisfaction it had given her to show him up. After the first seven minutes, she had more bruises than she'd given Malcolm—and Sven Bailey was just getting warmed up. She gritted her teeth and stood it. After fifteen minutes of hell, which proved beyond any doubt that Margo was in over her head, Sven Bailey stepped back and said, "Okay.

What've you learned?" Margo rubbed the freshest set of bruises and said, "That I have a lot to learn. I knew *that* last night."

"That's it? That's all you've figured out?" His tone relegated her to the realm of idiots, worms, and cockroaches.

Margo bit her tongue with difficulty.

Sven rested hands on hips and studied her. "I was under the impression you were here to *learn* something."

"So show me something to learn! All you've done so far is throw me around like a sack of flour!"

"Sit down."

"What?"

He jabbed an emphatic middle finger toward the mat.

"Sit!"

She sat.

"Close your eyes."

She did so.

"Now, breathe."

Margo felt like an idiot, sitting in the middle of the gym with people staring at her while she did nothing out breathe.

"Forget Malcolm, forget the other people. Concentrate on your center. Breathe. Down to the bottom. Hold it. Hold it. . . . Exhale. Again."

Grudgingly, her body began to relax. Tension made itself known in burning muscles from neck to hips. She shifted slightly for a more comfortable position.

"What are you feeling?"

"My neck is tight. My shoulders, too. My back hurts."

"Good, that's where you're fighting yourself. That's what I'm talking about when I ask what you've learned. You're fighting yourself as hard as you were fighting me. Keep breathing."

For half an hour, all Sven Bailey let her do was breathe and listen to her body's multiple complaints. When he finally allowed her to stand up again she felt looser, but restless.

"Now," Sven said, circling her slowly, "let's practice wrist exercises. The strength in your wrists is pathetic. To study Aikido, that has to change. Like this . . ."

For another half-hour, Margo exercised her wrists until her arms trembled and her wrist bones ached.

"Very good. Now, let's practice standing."

"Standing?"

Sven crossed his arms. "Are you going to question everything I tell you or do you want to learn something?"

"Yes! I'd just like to learn it before I'm eighty!"

Sven's appraising stare was about as warm as last winter's icicles. "You can't even crawl yet and you want to run the marathon?"

Margo clamped her lips shut. If she antagonized her teacher, Kit would yank her right out of training. Her mother's voice came back to her: *Margo, you're too impatient for your own good. Slow down. You'll get it all done.* Yes, she would—but would she get it done in *time?* She was still fighting a relentless deadline, but if she hoped to succeed, she *had* to do things their way. *If only you hadn't gotten sick, you bastard. . . .* But he had. And like Sven Bailey's relentless personality, there was nothing she could do to change that. She could only adapt and incorporate the fact into her plans.

Margo drew several deep breaths. "Okay. All right. I'm sorry. Mom always told me I was in a tearing rush to do everything, even when I was learning to crawl. I'll do better. I promise." She tried a sweet smile and knew she'd succeeded when a little of the darkness left his scowl. "Okay, Mr. Bailey, how am I supposed to stand? Show me."

Sven put her in position, then began to talk—surprisingly enough, about something besides breathing and strengthening her wrists.

"The idea we have in mind is to give you a broad foundation in unarmed combat before we move to armed combat. No, Margo, sink down a little further, that's right, hold it. If you rely on the weapon alone, without backup layers of self-defense, you risk being caught helpless if you lose use of the weapon. Whether you're carrying a firearm, a knife, some kind of chemical, or a club, you need to have other layers of protection in your defenses. One layer is alertness. If you don't notice an attacker, he'll take you by surprise. And once that happens, you're in trouble. For the next twenty-four hours, I want you to practice a little game. Tomorrow, tell me how well you do. See how many times you notice someone before they're aware of you and how many times they notice you first. Keep a record and we'll talk more about alertness tomorrow."

For once, Margo could see the immediate usefulness of the lesson. She vowed to score one hundred percent on this particular test. Nobody would catch her napping.

"All right, shift your stance like this. Good. Now . . . one reason to stay alert. Suppose you have a gun."

Margo nodded. "Okay."

Sven backed up at least twenty feet. "I've got a knife." He brandished a closed hand as though holding a knife in a fencing grip. "Lady, I'm gonna cut your throat. Draw from your holster and shoot me."

He rushed at her. Margo grabbed for her hip, pretending to go for a gun—

And landed hard on her back. Sven's hand slashed her throat.

She widened her eyes. "Hey! No fair!"

"There's no such thing as fair, girl." He let her up. "Get back into your stance. Remember, a man armed with a knife can cover twenty feet faster than you can draw a gun. Keep your distance from potential threats and stay alert."

Quite suddenly, the game wasn't so funny.

Margo reassumed her stance. "What else?"

"Forget everything you've ever seen in movies. I'm talking martial arts, knives, fistfights, *or* guns. Movies are crap. They'll get you killed. A knife fight is likelier to leave you dead than a gunfight—dead or crippled—if you don't know exactly what you're doing. Know how to use your weapon. Ann will teach you projectile weapons: firearms, archery, even blowguns. I'll teach you the rest. Getting tired? Good. Next, you fall."

And she did, too. Repeatedly. Sven taught her a better way to fall than her karate instructors had ever shown her. By the time Sven was satisfied that Margo had at least learned how to fall down, she was shaking with exhaustion and covered with sweat.

"Okay," Sven finally told her, "shower and change into fresh clothes. Ann's waiting for you on the range."

Margo held back a groan and scraped herself off the mat. Malcolm Moore abandoned a *kata* of his own and intercepted her hallway across the gym.

"Please," Margo said, holding out both hands to ward him off, "don't rub it in."

"No hard feelings." He smiled, surprising her with the friendliness in his eyes, and held out one hand. She shook it warily. "Really, Margo," he said with a self-conscious laugh, "you pointed out how badly I need to practice. I've been lax lately. Thanks for reminding me to get back in shape."

"Oh. Well, you're welcome."

"Sven gave you a hard time." It wasn't a question. His friendly smile prompted a heartfelt response. "All he let me do was breathe, stand in one place, and fall down!"

Malcolm grinned. "I can think of worse things he might have made you do."

Much to her surprise, Margo found herself laughing. "Well, yeah, I guess that's true." She nodded toward the shower. "I, uh, have to get cleaned up. I'm supposed to learn how to shoot."

Her lack of enthusiasm must have communicated itself to Malcolm Moore, because he chuckled. "I'll make a wager with you. An hour from now, you'll be singing a different tune. In fact, I'll bet you enjoy it so much by the end of the week, you'll be sneaking in to practice when you're supposed to be studying math."

Margo rose to the challenge with glee. "That's a bet! What'll you wager?"

Malcolm grinned again. "Me? Hell, Margo, I'm broke."

She laughed. "Me, too."

"Okay, how about something besides money?"

"Like what?" She was abruptly wary.

Malcolm blinked, clearly taken aback for a moment by her tone. Margo gave herself a mental kick. Malcolm wasn't Billy Pandropolous or even Skeeter Jackson. Kit Carson wouldn't trust him if he were, for one thing, and he wasn't like any guy Margo had ever met, for another.

"Well," he said slowly, "about the only thing I have to offer is guide services. I could take you down time to London—if Kit agreed to pay for the tickets," he added hastily.

Margo's pulse started to pound. *Down time to London? Oh, please* . . . But what to wager in return? And would Kit Carson say yes even if she won the bet?

"All right, one down-time trip with all the trimmings against . . ." She swallowed and risked it. "What do you want?"

Malcolm eyed her thoughtfully. Margo braced herself for the worst. But Malcolm Moore didn't say, "An hour in my bedroom" or anything even remotely close to that. "How about your life story?"

"Huh?"

"Well . . ." That nice smile of his made her feel warm and funny inside. "How else do people get to be friends, if they don't know anything about one another?"

But . . .

Her life story? She turned away. "There's not much to tell." To her horror, her voice wobbled.

He touched her arm gently. "Margo, I'm sorry. I didn't mean to pry. I just thought it might be nice to get to know you."

She wrapped both arms around herself and wondered about that. Was she a person worth getting to know? Her father had certainly never thought so. Billy Pandropolous had—for reasons of his own, involving sex and cold, hard cash and a booming market for pretty Minnesota. But Malcolm wasn't like that. Was he? Billy had seemed nice at first, too. Or maybe Malcolm was just looking for a chink in the armor, to get even? It was silly of her, perhaps, but she didn't think so.

But tell Malcolm about her father's drunken rages? Or finding her mother and a stranger she'd never seen beaten to death on the kitchen and living room floors? Or running for New York the second she turned sixteen to try and earn the cash to find her grandfather, only to land in Billy Pandropolous' loving hands?

She blinked back tears. Well, she could always lie. "Okay," she said reluctantly. "I guess it wouldn't be much of a bet if I didn't have an incentive to win?" He smiled. "True enough. Do we have a deal?" She shook his hand. "Deal. And now I really do have to go. I don't want to keep a teacher waiting."

"Mind if I watch? Or would I make you nervous?" Margo thought about it and decided she really didn't mind. "No, I think maybe I'd feel a little less nervous if I had a friendly face around."

"Scared of guns?" he asked sympathetically.

"Well, wouldn't you be?"

Malcolm chuckled. "You've been watching the evening news too much. Get showered. I'll tell Ann it's my fault you're late."

"Thanks."

"Don't mention it."

Irrationally, Margo felt better as she headed for the showers. Maybe—just maybe—she'd found her first real friend.

Hearing protectors and range glasses were mandatory on TT-86's firing line. The range was indoors, of necessity. One lane was a hundred yards long, designed for high-power rifles as well as rimfire rifles, shotguns, and pistols, but most of the lanes were ten yards long, about the right distance for most personal defense training. La-La Land's weapons trainers dreamed of a three-hundred-yard lane, but the cost for that much space was just too high. There were no clay pigeons to shoot at, no cute little metal animals or numbered bull's-eyes. All targets were either blank sheets of paper, human silhouettes, or plain, circular steel plates. Other time terminals which boasted safari tours included animal-shaped targets marked with kill zones.

Ann Vinh Mulhaney's targets were marked with loll zones, too: centered around the human torso and braincase.

Margo looked a little green already. Malcolm, lounging comfortably on a bench nearby, felt sorry for her.

"Get used to it," Ann told her. "Time scouting is not a picnic."

"So everybody keeps telling me," Margo said with a shaky little laugh that didn't fool anyone.

"Did anyone talk about the dangers of tangling with people who can't be killed down time?"

Margo nodded. "Last night, yes."

"Good. People who are critical to history can often be . . . dissuaded . . . even if they can't be killed. Self-defense is a dangerous proposition at best, but self-defense down time is really tricky, because you never know if what you try will actually work. So it's good to have a variety of options—fast legs, the ability to ride horses or drive a harnessed team, a good grounding in martial arts. Remember, the first lesson of self-defense is—"

"Avoid the situation in the first place," Margo sighed. "That's what Sven said."

'Then you'd better remember it. All right. A gun is only one layer of your defense. But if you're going down time, it's useful to know how to use one. You won't carry one with you, because you'll never know whether or not a firearm will be an anachronism there. But once you get where you're going, you may need to pick one up in a hurry, if they exist. Firearms have changed a lot since their invention in the 1300s. So we're going to start with something simple and fairly modern, something easy to shoot, just to get you used to marksmanship principles. Once I'm convinced you can hit what you're shooting at, I'll start teaching you historical firearms all the way back to the early pole guns. You're going to have homework, too."

Margo groaned and looked to Malcolm for support.

He grinned and shrugged. "Can't learn without studying. Remember, I already have my Ph.D. and I spend my spare time studying everything I can get my hands on."

Margo managed a smile that looked a little strained.

"All right. *What* will I be studying?"

"Principles of safety. Types of mechanical actions. Types of ammunition. How to load and unload. How various specific firearms function and differ from one another."

'Yuck."

"You could always find another career," Ann said sweetly.

"So show me!"

To Margo's horror, her "shooting lesson" began with a three-hour NRA course on basic safety. Granted, her teacher covered several basic types of modern guns, too, but she was required to pay attention while Ann Mulhaney just stood there and talked, showed her photographs and models, and repeated, "Keep the muzzle pointed in a safe direction; keep your finger off the trigger until you're ready to shoot; and keep the action open and the gun unloaded until it's ready for use" so many times Margo thought she'd go mad.

"All right, what's the first safety principle?"

"Keep the damned thing pointed in a safe direction!"

'That being?"

"Away from what I don't want to shoot. My foot. The neighbor's window. Not up, if there's a second floor to the building I'm in, or down if I'm upstairs somewhere." Margo crossed her arms. "When do I get to shoot?"

"Later. Let me see you de-cock that single-action revolver again."

Margo fumbled the job three times before she got it right She grinned in proud relief when she finally managed it correctly.

"Remember, a lot of these older-style guns and some of the modern ones have no mechanical hammer blocks, Margo. Screw this up with a loaded single-action that *doesn't* have a way to block the hammer from striking the firing pin, and you'll have an accidental discharge. If it's pointed at your stomach—" Ann forcibly moved the muzzle away from Margo's middle "—you'll end up gut-shot."

Margo's sense of accomplishment dissolved. She felt like crying. First Kit had roughed her up, then Sven had hurt her, and now Ann Mulhaney was making her look like a dangerous fool. "I'm sorry! I'm tired and hungry. . . ."

Ann said shortly, "Get used to it, Margo. You won't have the luxury of choosing the time and place for a gunfight to save your life."

She wanted to scream. Instead she tried to reason with her tormentor. "Yes, but I could choose the time and place for the lessons! How am I supposed to learn this stuff when I'm beat on my feet? Don't you people ever *eat?*'"

Her tummy rumbled in echo. Malcolm Moore must've heard it, too, because he chuckled.

Ann sighed and smiled ruefully, then retrieved the Colt Army single-action pistol. "All right, Margo, point taken. Eight o'clock tomorrow morning and don't be late this time. I have other lessons tomorrow besides yours."

Margo wanted to collapse right where she was. "I'll be here."

Where she'd find food, Margo had no idea. She didn't have

enough money even for a hotdog.

"Well," Malcolm said on their way out of the gym, "what do you think?"

"You haven't won your bet yet," Margo said sourly. He laughed easily. "I have until the end of the week, remember? That gives me a couple of days. How about lunch?"

"I'm broke. I mean really, truly broke. I think I have ten cents to my name."

"Where are you staying?"

"On a couch in Kit's living room."

The chagrin in her voice caused Malcolm to chuckle. "How come you never call him 'Grandpa' or 'Grandfather'?" He watched curiously for her reaction. She looked uncomfortable. It took her a moment to answer. "Well . . . he's not exactly the kind of person it's easy to call that."

Malcolm drew his own conclusions. "He scares you."

She glanced up swiftly. The little-girl vulnerability in her eyes shocked Malcolm nearly speechless. Then the moment passed and the flippant "who cares" look was back. "Nothing scares me."

Malcolm stopped several feet short of the elevator, causing Margo to stop short as well.

"What?" she wailed. "What'd I do now?"

"Margo," he said gently, "if nothing scares you, then I may not have very long to get to know you. And that's sad. Sadder than you can know."

A tiny vertical line appeared between manicured brows the color of bright new flames. She studied him with frank curiosity, head tip-tilted to one side like a canary faced with an unknown beast beyond its wire cage. It occurred to Malcolm that she was very, very young and trying desperately to hide it. Hard on the heels of that thought was another: *She's been roughed up by life already. Dammit, she's too young to look like that. What the hell happened to this kid before she found Kit?* The interest he felt turned suddenly protective.

Margo sighed, which prevented him from saying anything he might have later regretted. "You're odd, Malcolm," she said slowly.

"Am I?"

"Yes. You . . ." She didn't finish.

I don't hit on you like the other boys? Is that it?

Or maybe, considering the wary tension in her body, it wasn't just boys her own age who'd . . .

Malcolm forced his thoughts into less private realms of speculation. "How about some lunch? I have sandwich fixings in my fridge. We could meet somewhere for a picnic on the Commons. Unless you have another lesson?"

Margo relaxed fractionally. "Not that I know of," she said a trifle ruefully. "A picnic on the Commons sounds nice. I . . ." She broke off abruptly.

"What?"

She mumbled something that sounded like, "Never mind," and avoided his gaze.

Malcolm touched her shoulder very gently. "Hey. It's me, remember? The guy you wiped up the mat with?"

Almost as though disobeying a stern command to stay downturned, a corner of her lips quirked upward. She sniffed once. "Huh. I gotta beat up a guy before he'll ask me out?"

Malcolm laughed. "No, but it ought to give you a little peace of mind, knowing you can."

She gave him an odd look, then both corners of her lips twitched upwards.

'That's better," he smiled. "Why don't you find a nice spot somewhere in Castletown, maybe by one of the garden pools. We'll have a quiet lunch."

Her smile brightened. "All right. You know, that sounds wonderful. Thanks, Malcolm."

"My pleasure."

He held the elevator door with a courtly flourish that brought sparkling laughter to her eyes. *That* brought a sense of dismay to Malcolm's determination to remain an utter gentleman. He could fall for this kid—hard—without much trouble at all. Margo got off at the Commons level with a cheery smile and headed toward Castletown. Malcolm watched her go, then punched the button for his floor.

Whatever that little girl was hiding inside, it was hurting her. He'd started out the week feeling sorry for Kit. Now he felt sorry for them both.

"Well," he told himself philosophically as the elevator rose with an efficient whir, "looks like another job for Mr. Fix-It." He just hoped Kit's granddaughter didn't get them all into a jam they couldn't untangle. Given what he'd seen so far, she could wreak havoc just by breathing.

She could also break Kit's heart without even trying.

The insight left him with a chill chasing itself down his back. Malcolm made himself a promise, then and there: *I'll do whatever I can—whatever Margo and Kit will let me—to keep that from happening.*

Where that promise might lead him, Malcolm didn't even want to consider.

Chapter 8

Kit was looking for ways to avoid finishing a stack of bills when he spotted Margo on one of the real-time screens on his office video wall. She was sitting beside a pebbled fishpond in Edo Castletown, staring into the water and looking so vulnerable and alone, Kit felt his heart thump.

He shoved back his chair and headed downstairs, pausing only long enough to slip on shoes. He didn't even change out of the vintage kimono he habitually wore while working. Kit wasn't sure what he'd say to her, but maybe the excuse of just getting to know her better would suffice. She was trailing one fingertip in the clear water when he arrived.

"Hi."

She glanced up. Her eyes widened slightly. "Good Lord. You're wearing a kimono?"

Kit grinned. "I'm running away from paperwork. I, uh, usually try and wear the most comfortable thing I own when I have to tackle stacks of bills or government forms. Mind if I join you?"

"Oh. Sure."

"Such enthusiasm," he tut-tutted, settling down beside her.

She tucked knees under chin and stared at the colorful fish. "I'm tired," she admitted, "and hungry. Malcolm thought it might be nice to eat a couple of sandwiches on the Commons. So I picked a spot."

"Malcolm?"

She grimaced. "He watched my lessons today."

Ahh . . .

They fell silent for a few moments, just watching the fish make lazy circles above artistically arranged slate-blue pebbles. Finally Margo glanced up sidewise. "You don't like paperwork much?"

Kit rubbed his nose. "No. Tops a whole list of things I loathe."

She smiled. "I guess everybody's got their own list, huh?"

"What's on yours?"

She rested chin on knees again. "Oh, stuff."

"Like for instance?"

"I dunno. Snow, for one. Minnesota winters suck. Snow gets old real fast. Especially when you're too old to make snow angels in it. All that's left is cussing because the roads are closed and you're late to wherever it is you need to be."

Kit smiled. "You sound like eighteen going on forty-two." She stuck out her tongue, prompting a chuckle. "I was twenty, you know, before I saw more than a quarter inch all at one time."

"You're from Georgia. Doesn't snow much."

"Just what do you know about me? I mean, besides what's in all the tabloids?"

Margo grinned. "They're awful, aren't they? I think my favorite was the one where you were abducted by mad scientists from way, way up time and they altered your sex and you got pregnant and then they changed your sex back and sent you home after you had the baby."

"Oh, good God, you're kidding?"

Her eyes twinkled. "Nope. They even had a picture; you were out to here." She indicated a very pregnant stomach. "I love what they can do with computer graphics programs, don't you? The little old ladies that buy those things in the grocery stores actually believed it."

Kit just groaned. "I knew there was a reason I didn't go up time much these days."

Margo chuckled.

Kit decided the time was right, but he hesitated anyway, reluctant to destroy their fragile rapport. "Margo . . ."

She looked up again. "Yeah?"

"Would you tell me about my . . . I don't even know if I have a son or a daughter."

The sparkle vanished from Margo's green eyes. She swallowed and turned her face away. "Daughter. You had a daughter."

"Had?"

Margo wouldn't look at him. "Mom died. A few years ago."

The ache of losing something he'd never had a chance to cherish left Kit struggling against sudden tightness in his chest. He blinked rapidly several times, fighting a salty sting behind his eyelids. *How* had Kit's only child died? His daughter . . . She couldn't have been very old, if she'd died several years ago. An auto accident? Catastrophic illness?

"What was her name?" Kit whispered, trying to keep his voice steady. "What did she look like?"

Margo didn't answer for a moment. Then, in a low voice, "Mom's name was Kitty."

Quicksilver pain flashed through him. Sarah had actually named their child *Kitty*—

"She had hazel eyes. Kind of sandy-colored hair. When I was a little girl she laughed a lot. Look, I know . . . I know you want to hear about this and I want to tell you, but—" She blinked rapidly. Kit realized quite abruptly his grandchild, too, was on the verge of tears.

"Margo?"

She turned away again. "I was the one who found her. Can we talk about something else? Please?"

How old had Margo been when her mother died?

Kit wanted to ask a thousand questions, but Margo wasn't ready to answer them.

"What about your grandmother?" Kit tried, remembering with cutting clarity the last time he'd seen Sarah.

Margo sniffed. "I've never seen her. Mom ran away with Dad when she was seventeen. I'm not sure Grandma van Wyyck even knew where Mom was or that we existed. I . . . I had a picture. But everything I had was stolen. In New York. I even had to buy new shoes."

Kit, too, mourned that photograph's loss. "What was the picture like? How did she look? Did she seem happy?"

Margo seemed to come back from someplace even farther away than Kit had been. She studied him for a long moment. "You're still in love with her. Aren't you?"

Kit managed a pained smile. "Does it show?"

"Well, you're crying."

"Am I?" He swiped at his cheeks. "Damn . . ."

Margo dug in a pocket and held out his hanky. She'd laundered it somewhere. "Here."

Kit managed a shaky laugh. "Thanks, imp. You've rescued my reputation as an unflappable time scout."

She started to say something, then stopped.

"What? Whatever it is, say it. Or ask it."

Margo frowned. "It's nothing much. Just . . . Everything I ever heard or read . . . Mom used to say you grew up a dirt-poor Georgia boy, had to scrap and fight for everything you had. I used to think about that, sometimes. It made me proud, knowing you'd made it, but . . . I always thought . . ."

"You thought I ran out on Sarah van Wyyck? Because she stood in the way of my plans?"

She flushed, but her silence answered the question.

"I loved your grandmother very much, Margo. But sometimes even when people love one another, they have different dreams, different goals. Your grandmother's life and mine . . . it didn't work. Probably never would have worked. But I still loved her, even when she left me."

Margo's eyes widened. "*She* left *you?*"

Kit cleared his throat. "At the risk of sounding like my granddaughter, mind if we talk about something else?"

Margo blinked. Then she said, "I guess we all have stuff it hurts too much to talk about, huh?"

"Yeah. I guess we do."

She gave him a funny little smile. "Did you ever go back to Georgia?"

"No. I didn't really see much point. You plan on going back someday? To Minnesota?"

Her face hardened. "Yeah. I do. But not for very long."

"Unfinished business?"

She sniffed. "Something like that." She shook herself slightly. "Anyway, that's about it for my life's history. I had a twin brother, but he was killed in the big quakes caused by *The Accident*. That's when my folks left California and moved to Minnesota. I don't really remember it. I was just a baby." She shrugged. "I grew up, left home, came here. The rest isn't worth telling."

Kit thought it would have been, but didn't want to press the issue. He'd already learned more than he'd dared hope. A daughter, a grandson—both lost to him—and a granddaughter who didn't like snow and thought tabloids were stupid and was the kind of person who'd go back and settle old scores. Or maybe debts. Just what sort of unfinished business did she have and with whom? She was hardly old enough to have made the kind of enemies Kit had occasionally made.

An affair of the heart, maybe, despite her protestations that she hadn't been jilted. A man didn't have to jilt a girl to make her want to come back and settle affairs. Sometimes all he had to do was fail to notice. Or fail to act. Or maybe it was simply that she needed to repay someone who'd helped her buy that ticket to New York.

Or . . . Maybe someday she'd trust him enough to tell the rest.

Kit spotted Malcolm heading their way from Residential, an honest-to-goodness picnic basket slung over one arm, and decided to let his granddaughter have her picnic without Grandpa hanging around. "Well, here comes your lunch date. I guess I'd better tackle that paperwork. Just do the fish a favor and don't flip Malcolm into the pond between the sandwiches and the desserts?"

The sparkle came back to Margo's eyes. "Okay. Although after what Sven did to me, I don't think I could flip a soda straw into the fish pond."

Kit rumpled her hair affectionately. "Good. Proves you're doing it right. See you at dinner, imp." Her smile brightened his whole mood. "Okay." Kit returned Malcolm's wave, then headed back up to his office. Very deliberately, Kit switched the camera view on one particular video screen, leaving his grandkid her privacy. Besides, with Malcolm Moore as chaperon he didn't really have anything to worry about. Kit chuckled, recalling the full-blown panic in Skeeter Jackson's eyes when he'd cornered *that* worthy and made matters crystal clear, then settled down to the bills in a better frame of mind than he'd enjoyed in days.

Two days into Margo's weapons training, Kit started getting bad news. First came the altercation on Commons when a drunken tourist accosted her. She flipped him straight into a fishpond, almost as though deliberately recalling his advice not to toss Malcolm into one. Bull Morgan had not been amused when the drunken idiot turned out to be a billionaire who threatened to sue. Fortunately, Margo'd had plenty of witnesses for Kit to counter-threaten with sexual assault charges. The billionaire had slunk away down time on his tour, muttering into his expensively manicured beard.

Kit told Margo, "Next time, try not to dislocate shoulders or drown importunate perverts. Nothing excuses his behavior, but there's such a thing as overreaction."

She had sulked for hours. He supposed he couldn't blame her. Frankly, if he'd been there, the jerk might I've suffered more than a wrenched shoulder and a publicly humiliating dunking into a goldfish pond. But as a scout-in-training, she had to learn self-control and alternative methods of extricating herself from sticky situations.

Then he checked in with Ann and Sven.

"She has the attention span of a two-year-old," Ann Vinh Mulhaney complained. "Either she doesn't want to learn or she's afraid of the guns."

"She wants to learn, all right," Kit said grimly. "But she wouldn't admit to fear of a live cobra in her shower stall if she thought I'd halt her training over it."

Ann frowned. "That's not good."

"I know."

Kit ran a hand through his hair. After their heart-to-heart by the fishpond, Kit knew it would be doubly—triply—difficult if he had to tell Margo her dreams weren't going to come true. His heart was still in his throat just thinking about letting her scout. He didn't know what he'd do if he lost her, too. But he wanted as much as any other grandfather on the planet to make his grandchild happy. If he had to tell her two days into training that it was hopeless . . .

"Is there any hope?"

The tiny firearms instructor hesitated. "Well . . . maybe. Her hand is very steady and she has a good eye. When she's actually shooting, she scores well. But she won't apply herself to the *learning.* Has she been doing her homework?"

Kit frowned. "Homework? Not unless she's doing it in the library. She drags in like a half-dead cat, gulps supper, then collapses for the night. I didn't think it was possible to wear out an eighteen-year-old."

Ann didn't smile. "She needs to study. She keeps forgetting basics, like working the pump on the pump shotgun. Then she gets angry with herself when it won't function like a semiautomatic. The double-action revolver isn't a problem, but the self-loading pistols . . ." Ann just shuddered. "I haven't even tried historical firearms yet. I don't dare."

"Great. I'll start working her on basic firearms mechanical actions while she eats."

"Good. She needs it."

The story was much the same from Sven. The stocky martial arts instructor saw him coming from across the weapons range, clearly considered ducking out the nearest exit, then visibly braced himself.

'That bad?" Kit asked without preamble.

"Kit," Sven growled, "you got a big problem in that kid."

"You don't need to tell me that. All I get these days is trouble. Let me guess. She won't apply herself to the learning."

"Oh, no," Sven shook his shaggy head. "She's nuts to absorb the stuff, fast as I can teach her. And she's good, for a novice. Problem is, her attitude stinks."

"What about her attitude?" Kit asked tiredly. "In a thousand words or less."

Sven's evil grin came and went. "Rough, is it? *Teenagers.* If they weren't so cute, we'd drown 'em."

"The cuter they are, the bigger the occasional desire to hold their heads underwater. So what *is* Margo's problem?"

"No patience, *no feel* for Aikido. She just wants to make the moves like an automaton and hurry on to something else. Kit, that kid is in one damned big hurry to do *something* and I'm not sure it'll be healthy once she does it."

Great. Sven was waxing philosophical about his only grandkid, who was in a tearing *hurry* to die. He wondered if her impatience were part of her general personality, part of that mysterious unfinished business she'd mentioned, or just eagerness to get past the lessons and into something she could consider an adventure?

"Maybe she just wants to get down time," Kit sighed. "In her place, I would. Here she is on TT-86 watching the tourists go places she can't and all I let her do is read books and take lumps from you and Ann."

Sven pursed his lips, looking faintly like a thoughtful bulldog. "Could be, I guess. She's young, wants an adventure. Maybe you should give it to her. Settle her down."

"Give her an adventure?" Kit echoed "You mean send her down time? Before she's ready?"

Sven shrugged. "Sure. Why not? I'm not talking about a scouting trip. Send her on a tour. The Britannia Gate is due to open soon. Outfit her for a tourist jaunt and send the kid to London for a few days. Might take the itch out of her trousers, give her a taste of what it is she's letting herself in for."

"I can't go with her," Kit pointed out unhappily.

Sven's sympathetic glance didn't help much. "Stinks," he agreed. "So send Malcolm. He owes her a guided tour, anyway."

Kit sharpened his gaze. "He what?"

Sven widened his eyes innocently, then chuckled. "Well, now, so Grandpa *doesn't* know all. I'm disappointed—and surprised you hadn't heard. They a bet. Malcolm thought she'd end up liking the shooting; she said she wouldn't. They bet on it."

"What in God's name did they bet? Margo's broke. I know. I won't give her an allowance until she's earned one.

Kit trusted Malcolm as far as any man would with a granddaughter who looked and behaved the way Margo did; but he couldn't imagine what she might have wagered—and given the effect she had on men, he knew the male libido well enough to imagine the worst, even from Malcolm.

Sven patted his shoulder. "Not to worry. Scuttlebutt has it she bet her life story against a guided tour."

"Her life story? Huh." The rest of Margo's life story was something *Kit* would have paid a ransom to hear. "Too bad Malcolm lost."

Sven grinned. "You said it. There'll be other bets. I'll start her on bladed weapons next, but I'd like her to settle down before then. Think about the Britannia Gate. Might do her some good."

"Yeah," Kit said glumly, thinking about that billionaire and the fishpond "But will it do the rest of us any good?" Sven just laughed at him. "Your grey's showing, Grandpa. How about a sparring session?"

Kit considered it, then shook his head. "No, I think I'll take your advice. Which means I'd better hunt up Malcolm before he accepts a job to Mongolia or someplace equally improbable. Thanks, Sven."

"Don't mention it."

Kit found the freelance guide working the newcomers who planned to do the London trip. He waited until a curvaceous young thing had turned him down, then approached while Malcolm was looking bluer than a well-aged round of Roquefort cheese. "Any luck?"

Malcolm grimaced. "Nope. Time Tours is getting nasty about sharing business with freelancers."

Kit made a mental note to "lean" a little on Granville Baxter. There was enough money to be made for everyone. Malcolm's freelance business didn't hurt Time Tours' profits in the slightest. "Tell you what. I'd like to hire you."

Malcolm just stared. "You? For Pete's sake, why?"

Kit laughed. "Let's wet our throats someplace and talk business."

"Well, sure," Malcolm agreed readily. "Anytime you want to pick up the tab, Kit, you just holler."

The Prince Albert Pub was the handiest place to sit down and cool their thirst. The interior was a good bit cleaner than most genuine Victorian-era pubs, the prices were moderate for La-La Land, and the place was virtually empty in the post-lunch-hour vacuum. They found a table near the front windows and sat down.

"Have you eaten yet?" Kit asked, glancing at the menu. "I worked through lunch." Then he grinned sheepishly. "You're a good excuse. I'm playing hooky from paperwork day."

"Oh, ho," Malcolm chuckled, picking up his own menu. "Better not let Big Brother find out."

Kit grimaced. "Paperwork sucks," he said eloquently, half quoting Margo. "Hmm . . . I haven't had kippers in years."

"Never could abide them."

"A Victorian time guide *and* a born Brit and you can't abide kippers? What's the world coming to?"

"A better sense of what's edible, hopefully."

Kit laughed. "Then for God's sake, don't order lunch in medieval Edo."

Malcolm shuddered. "Once was enough to convince me, thank you. I'll stick to steak and kidneys, any day of the week."

"Beats some of what I've eaten," Kit agreed. He set his menu down and flagged a waitress. They ordered lunch and started emptying glasses of dark ale.

"So, what's on your mind?" Malcolm asked.

"Margo. What else?"

The younger man just grinned. "Anything in particular or everything in general? Or both?"

"Both, actually," Kit admitted, "but her lack of progress in her studies, particularly."

Malcolm's smile vanished. "She isn't stupid, Kit. What's the problem?"

"Sven thinks she's too hyped on going down time to concentrate."

The time guide sat back and fiddled with his glass, leaving a series of wet rings on the wooden tabletop. "He could be right," Malcolm said slowly. "That probably isn't all of it, but he could have something, there. Going down time is all she talks about."

"How much time are you spending with her?"

Malcolm flushed. "Not enough to warrant that tone, Kit. But I worry about her. I figure if she's with me, she's not falling prey to someone like Skeeter. And you know we get sharks through here every time Primary opens."

Kit knew. He relaxed. "Yeah, don't we just? Any feel for how she's coming with her lessons? Ann and Sven are under-whelmed."

Malcolm shook his head. "No, we don't talk much about her studies, not the bookwork part of them. Mostly she asks questions about my experiences down time or what I know about *yours.* She's . . ." He hesitated.

"She's what?"

"I don't know. Guarded, I guess. She doesn't let the thorns down long, if you catch my drift."

"Tell me about it. She sleeps on my couch, eats my food, showers in my bathroom, and about the only thing I can get her to relax and talk about is how much fun it is living in La-La Land. Do you have any idea how many obscure television celebrities that girl knows by sight?"

Malcolm chuckled. "Really? Well, she did want to be an actress. But then, what little girl didn't at some point in life? As I recall, my sisters went through the 'I'll die if I'm not an actress' phase shortly after the 'I'll die if I don't have a horse phase and the 'I'll die if I'm not an Olympic figure skater' phase."

Kit grinned. "I didn't have any sisters. Sounds like I missed out on all the fun. But seriously, Margo and I have had only one real heart-to-heart since she's been here and what I found out then . . ." He shook his head. "She's so full of hurt, she doesn't want to talk about any of the million or so silly little details I'd give the Neo Edo to know."

Malcolm sighed. "I figured as much. What are—" He paused, visible startlement passing over his mobile features, then pressed a hand to the back of his ear. "There's no gate due to cycle—is there?"

Kit felt it too: that sub-harmonic sensation which heralded a gate opening nearby. Whatever it was, it was out of phase—and from the feel of it, this was one *big* gate.

"New gate!"

"Right!"

They scrambled for the door and all but collided with the Prince

Albert's owner. "Where is it?" Peg Ames demanded breathlessly. She was holding her head. "Mother Bear, that's going to be a big gate. That *hurts.*"

It did, too, much worse than the Porta Romae—which was La-La Land's biggest active gate. 'Eighty-sixers converged on the Commons at a dead run from storefronts, even from residential corridors. Several carried scanners designed to search for the unstable fields that heralded a gate's arrival in the temporal-spatial continuum. Tourists looked bewildered. They huddled in groups, holding their ears. A klaxon's strident *SKRONNK!* echoed off girders and concrete walls in a mad rhythm. Someone had sounded the special alert siren activated only during station emergencies. The last time that siren had sounded, the semi-permanent unstable gate under the Sherman's coffee shop had endangered the lives of more than a dozen rescue workers.

Station Security converged from various points around the Commons. Several men and women in innocuous grey uniforms arrived in their wake, carrying everything from capture nets to tranquilizer rifles and riot shotguns. Discreet black lettering across grey uniform pockets read *Pest Control.* Their stalwart corps had risen considerably in status ever since an outbreak of Black Death on TT-13—and that wooly rhinoceros fiasco on TT-51—had been traced to station managers' refusals to pay for adequate pest control services. *Nobody* argued now with anything a Pest Control officer requisitioned.

Bull Morgan, a stocky man who wore his suit like a casino pit boss wore a scowl, shouldered his way through the crowd, a fireplug on legs. Worry had creased his brow above a nose broken in one too many fist fights. Mike Benson, head of La-La Land's security, followed in the Station Manager's wake, blue eyes narrowed as he scanned the air for the first telltale sign of the new gate's location. He spoke urgently into a walkie-talkie.

Bull high-signed someone with a scanner. "Has anybody—?"

"Oh, shit!"

A dozen scanners were pointed straight upward.

Then the ceiling opened up. A chronometer board vanished into blackness. The air dopplered through the whole visible spectrum in a chaotic display. Kit clamped hands over his ears in reflex action, even though the gesture did nothing to damp out the sound that wasn't a sound. Everyone—tourists and 'eighty-sixers alike—backed away from the area, leaving wrought-iron benches empty near the center of Victoria Station. The gate widened, ragged and pulsating unsteadily near the edges. It shrank visibly, then expanded with a rush like an oncoming freight train, only to collapse back toward its center again just as fast.

It didn't take a sophisticated scanner to determine this gate's condition. It was *visible* to the naked eye.

"Unstable!" Malcolm shouted.

Kit just nodded and hoped to hell nothing fell through it from a height of five stories. Even the floor pulsed angrily in the backlash of sub-harmonics. The gate widened savagely once more. Blackness swallowed more and more of the ceiling, crept outward and engulfed the upper level of the nearest wall, taking catwalks with it. *Biggest damned gate I've ever seen . . .*

Ragged light flared: lightning bolts against a backdrop of black storm clouds, seen in miniature through the gate's distortion. For a split second, Kit glimpsed what looked for all the world like a rain-lashed seacoast. Then driving rain spilled into TT-86. Tourists broke and ran for cover under the nearest storefronts. Kit narrowed his eyes against the sudden deluge. Another wild gust of rain burst through, soaking them to the skin. He lifted a hand to protect his eyes—

Something enormous crashed through.

"LOOK OUT!"

Whatever it was, it let out a scream like a frightened schoolgirl then plunged five stories toward the floor. Kit threw himself backward as it dropped straight toward them. A long, sinuous body impacted messily less than three feet away.

A gout of blood and entrails spattered Malcolm. "Aw, bloody *damn!*"

Another drenching gust of rain blasted through the gate, washing spattered onlookers clean. A trail of gore and broken bone stretched twenty feet across cracked cobblestones and smashed benches. Before Kit could cast more than a cursory glance at it, another dark shape dove through. This one was winged.

"Holy—"

A defiant scream like bending metal echoed through the Commons. A smaller winged shape darted through the black madness, then another and another, until a whole seething flock of wildly gyrating winged things darted frantically amongst the girders, lightning sizzled through and struck a catwalk near the fourth floor. Blue fire danced across steel gridwork. Thunder smashed through the station, shattering upper-level windows. Glass tinkled in sharp slivers on the cobbles. Then the gate collapsed,

It vanished, almost in the blink of a stunned eyelash. A final drizzle of rain drifted down in a bewildered sort of mist to settle into forlorn puddles. Silence—profound and complete—reigned for a full heartbeat. Then someone pointed and someone else screamed. An enormous shape with leathery wings skimmed low above the crowd. Kit dove instinctively for the floor. *My God . . .*

Its wingspan was nearly the size of a Learjet's. It snapped a long, sharp beak with a clacking sound like striking two-by-fours and passed less than a foot above the nearest "streetlamp."

This time, 'eighty-sixers broke and ran. A silver underbelly caught the lights as it winged around toward the ceiling. Dark markings in black and grey mottled its back and wings. An enormous, broad vertical crest was patterned like moth's wings, with huge eyespots and scarlet streaks. It snapped at a tourist on the third floor and narrowly missed her head. The woman screamed and hugged the catwalk. Pest Control tracked it with shotguns.

"DONT SHOOT IT!" Bull yelled. "TAKE IT ALIVE!" Half a dozen Pest Control officers swore, but dropped shotguns in favor of big capture nets. Kit scrambled up and grabbed the edge of the nearest net. Malcolm latched onto another section and lifted it in readiness for the beast's next pass.

"What is that thing?" a nearby Time Tours employee gasped.

The enormous animal soared toward the ceiling on thirty-foot wings, scraping a catwalk with one wingtip.

Sue Fritchey said calmly, "Looks like a *Pteranodon sternbergi* to me. Damned near as big as a Quetzalecoatlus—and that's the biggest pterodactyl we know about. That gate opened right into the Upper Cretaceous. Here it comes! Ready . . . wait . . . wait . . ."

Kit hung onto his nerve and faced down a lethally sharp beak as the giant pterosaur swooped directly toward them. The head and neck alone were longer than Sven Bailey was tall. Kit's lizard-brain, that portion of the human cranium that controls fight-or-flight reactions, was screaming "RUN!" at the top of its lungs.

Kit ignored it.

Sue was still cautioning them, "Wait . . . almost . . . almost . . . NOW!"

A dozen men heaved the big net. It tangled in leathery wings. Another net hit it, settling over the sharp beak and soaring crest. The huge pterodactyl came down hard in a mass of screaming, struggling beak, wings, and claws. Someone fired tranquilizers into it, three shots in rapid succession. Bull Morgan darted over to help hold the nets. A powerful wing lifted Kit off the ground and tried to fling him back toward the shattered cobbles, but he hung onto the rope. Malcolm came loose and vanished from Kit's immediate awareness. Kit thought he heard a cry of pain and an explosive curse, but he was abruptly confronted by a baleful scarlet eye and a snapping, up-curved beak that severed half-inch hemp fibers like spaghetti strings.

One of the Pest Control officers darted in with a coil of rope and risked hands in order to rope the sharp beak shut. A twist of the pterosaur's neck lifted him off the floor and sent him flying, but the ropes around its beak held. The tiny crimson eye rolled murderously; then, slowly, that wicked little eye began to close. By the time the tranquilizers had taken effect, Kit was bruised and battered, but La-La Land had quite a zoological prize. "Good work," Bull said, panting slightly. "What're those?"

He pointed toward the ceiling. Sue Fritchey was studying the smaller winged figures—perched now amongst the rafters—through her field glasses. "Those over there are *Ichthyornis*, looks like. Little primitive birds, beaks full of teeth, about the size of a seagull. Fish eaters. They'd be about the right time period and ecosystem to come through with a *sternbergi*. Must be twenty of 'em up there. And over there," she swung the glasses around, "we've got about fifteen little pterosaurs the size of crows. Hell, I have *no* idea what those are. Those, either." She'd swung the glasses around toward a pair sitting by themselves near the rafters. "They look like predators of some sort, but I'm not sure. *Could* be fish eaters, but the beaks look wrong. Far as I know, there's nothing in the fossil record anything like what I'm seeing."

"Are there enough of any of those things for a breeding colony?" Bull asked sharply.

"Maybe. Those two by themselves, probably not. Those pterosaurs, though, and the *Ichthyornis* flock . . . Close to critical failure of the gene pool, of course, but we've rescued species from that close to the brink. Depends on the number of breeding—or gravid—females up there. It's hard to sex birds without plumage differences to go by and I'm not seeing any. And I have no idea how to sex pterosaurs."

Nobody cracked the obvious jokes.

"Any danger to the tourists?" Bull asked, glancing unhappily at the damage and the white-faced tourists still cowering in storefronts.

"Dunno. Probably not, unless the animals feel threatened. I doubt they would unless somebody went after 'em. Birds, anyway, aren't as violently reactive as, say, killer bees, although the pterosaurs may be. Not as likely, but we just don't know."

"Then we don't disturb them until we get additional expert advice," Bull decided. "Next time Primary cycles, send for whoever you need. Those things eat fish? Okay, stock all the fishponds in the station and keep 'em stocked. Watch the little buggers and let me know if they put anybody in danger. Well, more danger than being spattered with dinosaur droppings."

The Pest Control crews chuckled. Sue Fritchey said, "They're not dinosaurs, they're pterosaurs and proto-birds. But don't worry, we'll handle it."

Bull nodded, then glanced at Malcolm and Kit. "Thanks for the help, boys."

"Glad to pitch in," Kit smiled. "It's not every day even I get to wrestle a giant pterodactyl to the ground."

Bull chuckled. "Point taken. You all right, Malcolm?"

Kit looked around. The young guide was nursing his wrist. "Yeah, just bloody bruised."

Bull peered closely at the wrist, which was visibly swelling. "Have Rachel look at it and don't argue. My tab. I'll call her."

Malcolm sighed. "Thanks, Bull. Me and my lousy luck."

Kit grinned. "Don't think you get out of this job so easily."

Malcolm gave him a sour glance. "*What* job? You haven't even told me what it is, yet."

Kit formed a sling from Malcolm's shirt and suspended his wrist at chest height. "What I had in mind was nursemaiding Margo through the Britannia Gate."

Malcolm stared, then eased the sling into a more comfortable position. His eyes had already begun to glow. "Are you serious?"

"Dead serious. Speaking of dead, what the devil was that thing?" He jabbed a thumb at the creature which had fallen through the ceiling. Judging from the remains, it had been all teeth, tail, and claws. Several tourists had crowded closer already.

Sue Fritchey waded in. "Sickle-claw killer of some kind, about the size of Utah-raptor, but a different species from the look of it. We didn't know they'd survived that late into the Cretaceous. Just be real glad it's dead."

Malcolm shivered absently. "Am I *ever.* Say, that thing is warm!" He leaned over for a better look.

Sure enough, heat was rising from the dead sickle-claw.

"Yep," Sue said, moving back after a cursory glance. "Get back, please."

"But, it's *warm!* Surely *you* can appreciate what this means for the scientific debate over ornithischian endothermy!"

Sue glared at him. "Yes, I do! I also appreciate that it's a cooling corpse. Its parasites are going to start leaving in droves—and I don't want *anyone* finding a tick the size of their own pinkie or a pinworm the size of a ballpoint pen! Jimmy, scour and disinfect this whole area!"

Malcolm moved hastily away. Tourists abandoned attempts to see the dead 'raptor and crowded around the netted pterodactyl instead. Pest Control was bringing up a forklift hoist and a large wooden pallet to transport it.

"C'mon, hero," Kit said, taking Malcolm's elbow. "Let's clean you up and look at that wrist." He steered Malcolm through the crowd and hustled him off to Rachel Eisenstein's infirmary. She fussed over the wrist, told him he'd sprained it heroically and warned him, "Don't tackle anything more strenuous than dinner for a couple of days, okay?" She suspended his injured wrist in a real sling. His shirt, retired from sling duty, had begun to dry, revealing tears and gore stains. The rest of him, however, was squeaky clean; Rachel had given him a *bath* in disinfectant and new clothes.

"Yes, ma'am." He saluted her with his unbandaged hand.

"Good," Rachel smiled. "Now, scoot. I have work to do. Some of the tourists were hurt during the ruckus and others are having hysterics. Unstable gates," she grimaced, "are not conducive to integrated psyches. Wish I'd been there to see it. Just my luck I was stuck on call and couldn't leave."

Kit sympathized, then they left Rachel to the demands of her profession. Once in the corridor, Kit said, "You never did answer. Are you game for the Britannia Gate?"

Malcolm chuckled thinly. "You should know without having to ask. Where shall I take her? A night at the opera? Or maybe a stay in the East End to discourage girlish romantic fantasies?"

"I leave that to your discretion and wisdom. I would suggest we collect my granddaughter, though, and head over to Connie Logan's. Kid'll need a good down-time kit."

Malcolm nodded. "Are we playing tourist for this trip or am I getting her ready for her role as disguised boy?"

Kit considered. "Again, use your discretion, but I'm inclined to think a little of both."

"So am I. I'll, uh, meet you at Connie's," he said. "In, say, fifteen or twenty? These pants Rachel gave me, uh, pinch."

"Make it the Prince Albert and we'll finish lunch before we collar her."

Malcolm grinned. "Whatever you say, boss! You may shower me with free food and money all you like."

Kit just snorted. "I'd tell you to go soak your head, but you already did. See you at the Albert."

Connie Logan's establishment was—in keeping with La-La Land's reputation—one of the true first-class Outfitters in the business. Connie was young for it, barely twenty-six, but she'd started with an advantage. A theatrical aunt who'd owned a small touring company had raised her in the business of historical costuming, then died and left her with an inventory, a room full of cloth waiting to be turned into historically accurate clothing, considerable skill as a seamstress and designer, and enough money to attract venture capital.

Connie Logan was sharp, creative, and a delight to 'eighty-sixers. They often laid wagers on what she'd be seen wearing next. The sign over her doorway was short but effective: Clothes and Stuff. A few tourists were stupid enough to prefer shops with fancier names, but not many. On their way across the Commons, Margo admitted that she hadn't been inside yet.

"I hate to shop when I'm too broke to buy anything," she admitted. "It's depressing."

"What about that barmaid's dress?" Her cheeks colored. "Skeeter gave me money for that. He told me to buy it in Costumes Forever because the prices were better. I, uh, haven't been shopping since."

"Well, you're in for a treat, then." Kit smiled, but he wondered privately if this scheme would help or only exacerbate matters. When he steered her through Clothes and Stuff's doorway, Margo spent a full minute in the center of the main aisle just staring. Then she gave a low sound of utter ecstasy, turned in a complete circle to gape at shelves, display racks, and glass cases, then ended with a wide-eyed, "Shoppers freaking *paradise!*" She thereupon bolted for the nearest dress racks. Malcolm took one look at Kit's face and convulsed with silent laughter.

"Oh, shut up," Kit groused. "Some help you are."

"Kit, you have to admit, there's a pretty darned funny side to this. She's eighteen. She's female. She's just been given an expense account in heaven."

"Oh, great. Make me feel better." Malcolm's long face creased in a wide grin.

"I suspect the Neo Edo can support it."

"Huh. *Your* taxes aren't due next time Primary cycles."

Malcolm's eyes twinkled. "Oh, yes they are. I just don't have enough income for it to matter."

Kit thumped his shoulder. "Just wait. I'll take care of that little problem."

"Thanks," Malcolm drawled. "I'll go from owing zip to owing a third of whatever you pay me."

"Well, I could just pay you two thirds of what we agreed on. . . ."

"Fat chance. A man's got his pride, after all. Hey, look, Connie has a new line ready for the London season."

He wandered off to do his own window shopping. Intrigued as always by the contents of Clothes and Stuff, Kit cruised the aisles as well, just to get a feel for what they'd need. Neat racks displayed costumes appropriate to La-La Land's resident gates. Costumes were situated in carefully arranged groupings, neatly labeled as to geographic location, exact time period, and appropriate occupation or social occasion. Items could be either rented (for those on a budget) or purchased (for those with essentially skys-the-limit funds).

Shelving units and glass cases held every manner of accessory, including an astonishing variety of footgear, belts, undergarments, gloves, fans, hosiery, hats, coats and cloaks, appropriate equivalents of the modern handbag, jewelry, timepieces, even items designed to conceal weapons: shoulder holsters for guns and knives, belt holsters and sheaths, ankle rigs, even garter-belt sheaths and holsters. One entire case was devoted to wigs and false hairpieces in every conceivable shade, most attached to hairpins or combs to be added as necessary to elegant coiffures. Every one of them was styled after authentic period hairpieces.

Another section of the shop included appropriately designed luggage, lighting equipment from candle lanterns to oil lamps, sanitary and survival gear, tools, weapons, even historically appropriate eyeglasses. One employee on Connie's payroll did nothing but grind prescription glasses and long-wear contact lenses to order for those who needed them.

If it had existed down time and people had used it, or if it was necessary to survival and it could be disguised, Clothes and Stuff stocked it or was prepared to manufacture it.

Connie herself, in direct contrast to her shop, was anything but neat and organized. She emerged from the back where she kept her office and design studio, noticed Kit, and waved. Kit chuckled. Beneath a hand-basted kimono that gaped open because she hadn't tied on an *obi* to hold it closed, she was clad in bits and pieces of Victorian undergarments. She wore hobnailed Roman "boots" on her feet and an ancient Meso-American feathered headdress appropriate for a jaguar priest over long, glossy black hair. Her eyes, a startling Irish blue, sparkled as she came across the shop, clomping every step of the way in her ancient footgear. "Hi, Kit! What brings you in?" He met her beside a glass case containing lace-and-lawn caps, feathered and plain fans, plus silk, leather, and cloth gloves while Margo emitted the most outlandish sounds he'd ever heard a female make off a mattress.

"What do you think?" he smiled, nodding toward the enraptured figure pawing through a rack of ball gowns. "Margo, of course. I'm sending her down the Britannia Gate with Malcolm. Sort of a trial run just to get her feet wet, give her a taste for time travel."

"Good idea. Hang on a sec, would you? These feathers itch."

She lifted off the headdress. The glossy black hair came with it. She shook out her own hair, then vanished into the back. When she returned, the kimono had gone as well, replaced by a set of cowboy-style leather chaps, worn over woolen drawers and a boned corset. Occasionally Kit had known her to change clothing five times during the course of a twenty-minute conversation as she tried out various new creations. Across the room, Margo noticed. She stared for a full thirty seconds, round-eyed, then returned to her window shopping with another silly squeal as her attention rested on something else utterly wonderful.

"Very becoming," Kit drawled.

Connie laughed. "They're hideous and the corset is cutting me in half, but I had to be sure the busks and side steels were bent to the right shape before I had William stitch the cover closed."

"And the chaps?"

"The customer said they chafed him. I'm testing them out to see what the problem is."

"Uh-huh."

Kit, like most 'eighty-sixers, had eventually realized that when she was working, Connie Logan was completely unconcerned about her appearance. And since she worked most of the hours she was awake—"What do you mean, do something fun for a change? I *love* designing clothes!"—Connie Logan was at first glance the most eccentric loon in a time station crammed full of them.

Kit thought she was the most charming nut he'd ever known.

Even he deferred to her encyclopedic knowledge.

"London, is it?" Connie asked, peering toward Margo, who had discovered the Roman *stolas* with their richly embroidered hems. "What's the program? Simple tour? Teaching experience? Test-run scouting trip?"

"All of the above. I leave the outfitting choices to you and Malcolm."

"But not to Margo?" Connie smiled.

He rolled his eyes. "Let's see what she picks on her own and judge from that."

"Fair enough. Rent or buy?"

"Rent what's rescuable when they get back. I'll buy what's ruined."

"Okay." Her glance traveled beyond Kit's shoulder to a group of tourists selecting accessories for the dresses they carried, "Oh, damn . . ." She bolted past Kit's shoulder. "No, no, no, not that fan, that's an evening fan for the opera, what you have there is a morning dress for strolling and paying calls. You'd stick out like an idiot, carrying that around London. Here, what you need is this, or this, or maybe this . . . And that pair of slippers is completely wrong, what you need are these side-button boots. Size six? Hmm . . . a little narrow, I think. Try this six-and-a-half."

The astonished tourists gaped at the figure Connie made, her girlish pudginess stuffed into a lawn shift, woolen combinations peeking out from under several layers of petticoats, the tightly laced corset which created unsightly bulges both above and below, topped off with the leather chaps—tied on *over* the petticoats. The Roman "boots" were icing on the cake. "Uh . . . thank you . . ."

They accepted Connie's choices a bit reluctantly, but obediently sat down to try on the boots.

Connie came back shaking her head "If they'd just read the signs . . . You have to watch 'em like hawks. Let's check on Margo. Oh, Lord, she's already in trouble. . . ."

And Connie was off again, before Kit could open his mouth to add a single comment.

"No, no, Margo, not that; you've got a charity schoolgirl's cap paired with a lady's tea gown. . . ."

"Malcolm," Kit waved to get the guide's attention, "get over here! Connie's on the warpath and we need some decisions!"

Malcolm, looking for all the world like a truant schoolboy caught in a candy store, hastened over. "Sorry. Just catching up on the newest down-time styles.

"There've been changes in top hats since last season—they're more tapered from crown to brim—and the new dress lounge coats are magnificent, with that new rolled collar. But did you see those hideous woolen jersey Jaeger suits?" Malcolm shuddered. "They wore those things in July and August, even while exercising. No wonder people died of heatstroke."

"Malcolm, I didn't know you were a clothes horse," Kit teased.

The guide—currently dressed in faded jeans and a cheap T-shirt—grinned. "Me? Never. But I'd better update my wardrobe before I step through the Britannia Gate or I'll look like an old fuddy-duddy."

"You *are* an old fuddy-duddy," Kit laughed, "and so am I. Let's get this over with. Gad, but I hate shopping."

"Only when you're not stepping through the gate," Malcolm smiled.

"Too true. Now, about what she'll need—"

An animal scream lifted from Commons, high and piercing, followed an instant later by a woman's shriek of terror. Kit and Malcolm jerked around, then ran for the door. Surely another new gate hadn't opened? The warning klaxon hadn't sounded and Kit hadn't felt the telltale buzz in his skull bones. Someone started cursing. Then Kit rounded an ornamental garden plot and found a woman in medieval regalia staring at the ceiling and sobbing in rage.

"They killed her! Goddamn them, they killed her!"

The men with her, also dressed in medieval garb, were struggling to soothe terrified, hooded falcons on their arms. One bird had already sprained a wing trying to escape its jesses.

"Who killed whom?" Malcolm blurted.

A few spots of blood on the concrete and a couple of feathers gave Kit the clue. "I'd say those two bird-things Sue couldn't identify made lunch of this lady's falcon."

The lady in question affirmed Kit's guess in most unladylike language. Malcolm coughed and turned aside to hide a grin. Pest Control came running, Sue Fritchey in the lead.

"What happened?"

The woman whose valuable hunting falcon had just become a paleo-hawk's dinner told her—scathingly.

"Uh-oh. I was afraid of something like this. Where are they now? Ah . . . there. Okay. Jimmy, Bill, Alice, we need capture nets and tranks, stat. We let those things keep feeding, we won't have any pterosaurs or *Ichthyornises* to study. And maybe a tourist will get hurt."

That last had clearly been an afterthought. Kit hid a grin. The tourist who'd lost her falcon began demanding reimbursement. Someone called Bull Morgan to mediate.

"C'mon, Malcolm. Looks like the fun's over. We have a trip down time to plan."

Margo, not surprisingly, hadn't even heard the ruckus. She was still flitting from rack to rack, cooing and all but drooling on the clothes. Even Connie was laughing at her. Kit shook his head. An unlimited expense account in heaven . . .

"Well, let's see what our prodigy's chosen, shall we?"

"Don't I get an opinion?" Margo demanded. The three faces ranged against her grimaced simultaneously. If Margo hadn't been so flaming angry, it would've been comical. "Well, don't I? I'm going to be the one wearing these!"

She held out the ridiculous embroidered smock, the baggy pants with their hideous flap front that fell open if the buttons popped loose—never mind the rags she was supposed to tie around her knees to hold the pants off the ground—then kicked at the scuffed, wide-toed leather boots. The shapeless felt hat was so pitiful she couldn't even bring herself to look at it.

"This is only one of the outfits you'll be wearing," Malcolm Moore told her, sounding infuriatingly patient.

"But they're *ugly!*"

"You're not in training to be a fashion model," Kit said sternly.

Margo subsided, but not happily. "I know."

"Now, about the choices you made," he continued, "Connie has a few words."

"Starting with the ball gown," the outlandish outfitter said, hanging it back on its rack. "The first word is 'No.' Your job isn't to go down time and party it up. It's to learn scouting. If you want to revisit London later for a vacation, on your own time and money, fine. Until then, the party dresses stay here."

Margo sighed, "All right I'm supposed to go down time and be miserable."

"Not at all!" Connie said, somewhat sharply. "You have a remarkably negative attitude, Margo, for someone who's been given the chance to go down time for free. Britannia Gate tours cost several thousand dollars each."

Margo felt her cheeks burn. She hadn't thought of it quite like that. "I'm sorry. It's just I got so excited when you said I could go and that we could pick out clothes . . ." She turned an appeal for forgiveness on Kit. "I'm sorry, really I am. I was just so disappointed after I saw those," she pointed to the glittering silks, velvets, and satins, "then you said what I would get to wear was these."

The humble farm clothing—men's farm clothing—lacked only mud to make the hideousness complete.

"Apology accepted," Kit said quietly. "Once you learn your trade, Margo—and you have a great deal yet to learn—you can play dress-up as often as you like. But not while you're on the job. *Never* while you're on the job."

Margo felt like crying. She'd been rude and ungrateful—her temper *always* got her into trouble—and they were being desperately nice to her. It wasn't a situation she was accustomed to. She felt lost as to how she ought to respond.

Connie Logan said more kindly, "Here, let's see what else we can find. Malcolm, what about having her pose as a charity girl?"

"We'd need a chaperon for that," Malcolm said slowly, "but I like the charity girl idea. Her hair's short and that'll either have to be disguised or explained. Charity-girl is the perfect cover. As for a chaperon, I could hire someone from an agency and rent a flat for the week we'll be there."

"I don't understand," Margo said. "What's a charity girl? Why would that make a good cover story for my hair?"

"Poverty-stricken children—orphans, children with destitute parents—were sometimes taken in by charitable institutions," Malcolm explained. "There were dozens of schools supported by patrons and patronesses. Children wore uniforms and numbered badges to identify them. Because sanitation was a problem and head lice were common, even girls' hair was cut short."

"*Head lice?*" Margo grabbed the sides of her head, instinctively trying to protect her scalp from an invasion of vermin.

Kit cleared his throat. "Sanitation in Victorian London was quite a bit better than many places you'll end up as a scout. Head lice—and other nasties—can be eliminated once you get back."

Margo just stared, overcome with an intense desire to be ill. She hadn't thought about *lice.* The more she studied for this job, the clearer it became there was a great deal she hadn't thought about.

"Well, I'm not quitting," she said stubbornly, straightening her spine. "Nobody ever died from being dirty."

Malcolm exchanged glances with Kit, who said repressively, "Millions have done just that. The point is, you keep yourself as clean as you can and deal with medical problems when you return. If you return. Why do you think you're required to receive so many inoculations before coming to a time terminal? Up time, we don't even vaccinate for smallpox any longer. It's an extinct disease. However, in someplace as relatively sanitary as Denver in the 1890s you could still contract it. Not to mention lockjaw or blood poisoning from a simple cut or scrape. So you take your medicine, keep yourself clean, and hope you don't come back with anything Medical can't handle.

"Now, I think this charity-girl idea's a good one, but that leaves us with another question, Malcolm. Namely, how to explain your association with her. You're known in London."

"Fairly well, in certain circles," Malcolm agreed.

"So people will know you wouldn't have a reason to associate with a charity girl of eighteen. And her accents all wrong, anyway, to pose as a British orphan."

"The few people I know down time believe me to be an eccentric gentleman from British Honduras—which helps explain away the occasional wobble or two in my accent."

Margo blinked. He'd sounded astonishingly British during that sentence, which he hadn't before. In fact, given the small amount of stage training she'd had, she'd have bet everything she owned it had been genuine, not affected.

"How did you do that?"

"Do what?" He sounded American again, as American as Minnesota winters.

"Sound British? I thought you were American."

Malcolm grinned. "Good. I've studied hard to sound like that. Heading down time to Denver with an English accent isn't a good idea. Fortunately I have a quick ear and years of practice. But I was born in England." He cleared his throat and glanced away. "I survived The Flood, actually."

Mar go said breathlessly, "The Flood? From *The Accident?*"

Malcolm rubbed the back of one ear. "Well, yes. I was just a kid. We lived in Brighton, you see, near the seaside. We ran a little tourist hostel during the summers.

My family was lucky. We only lost my elder brother when the house caved in."

Margo didn't know what to say. The English coast had been wiped out by tidal waves. All the coastlines of the world had been hit hard. Several dozen cities had been reduced to rubble and the ensuing chaos, rampant epidemics, and starvation had reshaped world politics forever. Margo hadn't been old enough to remember it. She forgot, sometimes, that most of the people on this time terminal *did* remember the world before the time gates and the accident which had caused them.

She wondered quite suddenly if that was why her father had been the way he was. Had he blamed himself all those years ago for her brother's death, then found himself unable to cope with the changed world? She shivered, not wanting to sympathize with him, but something in Malcolm's voice had triggered memories of her father during his more sober moments. The look in her father's eyes during those times echoed the desperate struggle not to remember she saw now in Malcolm's dark eyes.

"I'm sorry, Malcolm. I didn't know."

He managed a smile. "How could you? Don't dwell on it. I don't. Now, what were we saying? Oh yeah, my background. The people I know down time think I'm a gentleman from British Honduras, with no visible means of support and no daily job to distract me from gentlemanly pursuits. I just happen to have a lot of wealthy, scatterbrained friends who pay me visits from the other side of the water, particularly America." He grinned. "That way it's natural for my tourists to gawk at the sights. Londoners in the 1880s considered Americans boorish provincials just this side of savagery."

Margo sniffed. "How rude."

Connie laughed. "Honey, you don't know the half of it. Victorian Londoners took class consciousness to new extremes." She gestured to the Britannia section of her shop. "It's why I carry such a varied line of costumes for the Britannia Gate. Clothes said *everything* about your station in life. Wear the wrong thing and you become a laughingstock—"

"Or worse," Kit put in.

"—or you just blend into the background and become invisible."

Malcolm nodded. "Yes. But you have to be careful. The wrong clothing could get you hauled off to jail or Bedlam Hospital to be locked in with the other madwomen."

Margo shivered. "What about this charity girl stuff, then?"

"Well," Malcolm said, glancing at Kit, "given my reputation as something of an eccentric, it wouldn't be out of character for me to sponsor a young girl who'd been orphaned in a cholera epidemic, say, or by one of the tropical fevers that laid so many Europeans low in Honduras. You could be the child of some deceased friend or even a relative. A niece, maybe, brought back to England for schooling."

Kit was nodding. "I like it. All right, choose something appropriate. Connie, why don't you fit her out while Malcolm and I update his wardrobe? If he's going to keep up his reputation in London, I suspect he'll need a new item or two. And you'll need a couple of 'incognito' getups as well, I think, so your down-time friends don't recognize you when you two go slumming."

Connie beamed. "Help yourselves. Gosh, I love it when scouts and guides put their heads together and go shopping!"

Kit groaned. Malcolm laughed. "Don't worry, Kit. I'll try to be gentle with your budget."

"Pray do, sir," Kit drolled. "It isn't unlimited, you know."

They strolled off in the direction of the men's clothing. Margo watched them go. "They're . . ." She paused, suddenly embarrassed.

"They're what?" Connie asked curiously.

"Nothing," Margo mumbled. She'd been about to say, "They're really sweet, aren't they?" but had stopped herself just in time. She'd gotten where she was by being tough and uncaring. Now wasn't the time to let down her guard, not with her dreams within grasp. But she couldn't help thinking it. They *were* sweet. Even Kit, when he wasn't glowering at her for whatever she'd done wrong most recently. A flash of insight told Margo he glowered because he didn't really know how to talk to her.

That was all right. She didn't really know how to talk to him, either, not without a whole retinue of defenses in place. A smart mouth and a lifelong habit of sarcasm—skillfully combined with pouting frowns and winning smiles—weren't exactly the most useful skills if she wanted to learn more about this man as a human being, rather than a legend.

Get real, Margo. Remember the fishpond. Try to get better acquainted with him—with either of them—and you'll have to talk about yourself. The less said on that subject, the better. For everyone concerned.

Margo sighed unhappily, earning a long, curious look from Connie, then she shook herself free of the mood and said brightly, "Okay, about this charity-girl costume. Show me!"

Chapter 9

Brian Hendrickson had come from a family whose older sons enlisted for life in the Royal Navy. Brian—a third son born in the islands—had become a historian rather than a sailor. But his military upbringing lingered in a meticulous personality and a tendency to run his library with martial efficiency. His accent, a delightfully odd one, was right at home in La-La Land.

Kit, taking advantage of Margo's mood after the shopping trip, escorted her from Clothes and Stuff directly to the reference desk in La-La Land's library. It was high time she started learning more than remedial math, firearms history, and martial arts.

"Brian, this is Margo, my granddaughter. Margo, Brian Hendrickson, TT-86's resident librarian."

He smiled pleasantly and kissed the air above her hand, Continental-style. "Most pleased to meet you, Miss Margo."

She blinked, clearly startled. Brian Hendrickson startled most newcomers to TT-86.

"Where are you *from?*" Margo blurted.

A dazzling smile came and went. "It is more a matter of where I am *not* from, actually. I was born in the British Virgins, spent the first three years of my life in Glasgow, then my father was posted to Hong Kong. Let's see . . . I've nearly forgotten the Falklands, haven't I? I took my university degrees from Cambridge."

"Oh." She looked a little round-eyed.

Kit grinned. "Which brings us to the reason we're here. She needs advanced lessons."

"Hmm, yes, I should think so, if rumors are true."

"They're true," Kit sighed. "Detailed histories, languages, the works."

The librarian tapped well-manicured fingertips against the desktop. "Yes. I should think Latin to start, followed by French—modern, middle, and old—to cover all bets. And Italian and Greek. And we'd better throw in the main Chinese dialects—"

"You're not serious?" Margo broke in, her voice echoing the panic in her eyes. *"Latin?* And . . . and Chinese and all those Frenches . . . and . . ."

Brian blinked. "Well, yes, I am serious. Goodness, Miss Margo, you can't expect to scout if you don't speak at least ten languages fluently."

"Ten?" She glanced wildly at Kit. *"TEN?"*

Kit only rubbed the side of his nose. "Well, that's a fairly limited beginning, but yes, ten might prove just barely adequate. I speak twenty fluently and can make myself understood in considerably more than that. I did warn you, Margo. Scouting is a scholarly business, above all else. When you're not down time exploring a gate, you're studying. Constantly."

"But—"

"I don't make up these rules just to upset you."

"I know, I know," she wailed, "I understand that, but . . ."

"He's right, Miss Margo," the librarian said quietly. "My steadiest customers are never the tourists. They're the guides and the scouts. Particularly the scouts. They spend hours here every day, learning and learning. In fact, if you'll examine the gentlemen at the computers over there or back in the language labs, you'll discover half the scouts who work out of TT-86 on a regular basis. Excuse me, please."

Kit glanced around. John Merylbone, a fairly new scout despite his age—he was pushing fifty—had come up to the desk.

"Brian, sorry to interrupt, but I need help. I'm looking for information on early British scholars' costumes. I'd heard there was a good general reference by Cunnington and Lucas from 1978."

Brian stared at the scout for long, unblinking moments, giving the distinct impression that John's request was utterly beneath his notice. Margo whispered, "Isn't that a little rude?"

Kit smiled. "No, actually he's thinking. Watch."

Brian started talking. "Well, yes, that's a very good general reference, but it contains a good bit more than you'll need. Covers all manner of charity costumes, through several centuries, actually. I'd recommend Rymer's *Foedera,* vol. VII, or *Statutes of the Colleges of Oxford for the Royal Commission*—that's translated from the Latin, which is useful—or perhaps Gibson's *Statua Antiqua Universitatis Oxoniensis.* Loggan also did some excellent work in *Cantabrigia Illustrata* and *Oxonia Illustrata.*"

The librarian was busy jotting down names and titles while he spoke.

"Good grief! He didn't even use the computer!"

Kit only smiled. "Don't look so horrified. Nobody's asking you to learn as much as Brian knows. *Nobody* knows as much as Brian Hendrickson. He has a photographic memory. Useful for a research librarian on a time terminal."

"Oh. I was beginning to worry."

"You do that," Kit laughed. "I like it better when you're worried. Proves you're thinking."

She put out a pink tongue. "You're mean and horrible. Why does everybody else like you?"

Kit scratched his head. "Search me. Guess it's my good looks and charm."

Margo actually laughed. When she relaxed, his granddaughter was a remarkably pretty girl, with no trace of that Irish alley-cat glare. He sighed, feeling old before he was ready for it.

"What's wrong?" Margo asked.

"Nothing," Kit said, forcing a smile. "Let's set up your study schedule."

Brian returned from helping the other scout and they got down to business. He assigned Margo a language lab, where she was to spend four hours every other day learning the first of the languages on her list. The next four hours of her library days (after lunch, which

Kit agreed to have delivered to her from the Neo Edo so she wouldn't need to leave the library) were to be devoted to detailed historical studies.

"Let's start her with American history, since that's what she's likeliest to absorb readily," Brian suggested. "Then we'll put her on European history, working backwards from the twentieth century. We'll tackle Africa, Asia, South America, India, and the Middle East a little later in the program, after she's settled down into the study routine and is capable of absorbing cultural detail significantly different from her own."

Kit and Brian agreed she'd be better off leaving the library during the evenings to eat dinner and do homework, and to alternate library days with continued weapons training. With any luck, the physical exercise would leave her tired enough to sleep after homework sessions.

By the time they were done setting up her schedule, Margo was visibly horrified and trying hard not to show it. She gave him a brave smile as they left the library. "One thing's for sure, life'll never be the same around you. Latin, Chinese, and French, oh my . . ."

"Better that than lions, tigers, *or* bears," Kit chuckled. "Just remember, you can never truly understand a nation or its people until you can speak its language."

"Right," she sighed, giving him another brave smile. "I just hope scouting is worth all this agony."

Kit resisted the urge to ruffle her short hair. "I doubt you'll be disappointed. Surprised, probably—almost undoubtedly. But disappointed? No, I don't think so. Time travel is *never* what people expect it to be. And that," he smiled, "is half the fun."

"Well, goodness, I hope so. My head already hurts and I haven't even started yet!"

Kit laughed. "That's because you're stretching your brain, possibly for the first time. Cheer up. By the time you're done, not only will you have the equivalent of several Ph.D.s you didn't have to pay some university to earn, you'll have the ability to do field research most Ph.D.s still can't afford to do. Education," he smiled, "is *never* a waste of time."

She gave him an odd look, but said nothing. Kit found himself fervently hoping that the trip to London would convince Margo she needed every bit of the "brain work" he and Brian had outlined. Margo loose for a week in London, even with Malcolm Moore along to protect her . . . Kit was so apprehensive, that before he went to bed that night, he found himself standing in the living room doorway, just watching her sleep.

Young, vulnerable . . .

He turned away silently and went to bed.

But not to sleep.

Malcolm came for Margo early in the morning the day the Britannia Gate was due to open.

"Hi!" The world was wonderful this morning. Today was the day she would finally step through a gate into history.

"Sleep well?" Malcolm asked.

Margo laughed. "I was so excited I hardly closed my eyes all night."

"Thought as much," he chuckled. "Kit up yet?"

"In the shower."

"All packed?"

"Yes!"

"Good. We have one last appointment before we go."

Uh-oh. Margo regarded him suspiciously. "What is it?"

A pained smile came and went. "You're not going to like it, but I think it's vital."

"What?"

"We need to visit Paula Booker." Margo wondered who the devil that was. "For?"

"Your hair."

Margo touched her short, flame-colored hair. "What's wrong with my hair?"

"Nothing—for here and now. Everything for down time. That color stands out. We want to be inconspicuous. The less noticed you are, the better."

"What are you going to do about it? Dye it?" Margo asked sarcastically.

"Yep."

She stared. "Oh, no."

Malcolm sighed. "I knew this wouldn't be well received. That's why I wanted Kit's opinion."

"On what?" Kit asked, emerging from the bathroom. He was—uncharacteristically—clad only in a towel. His hair was still wet and he hadn't shaved yet. Margo stared, knowing it was rude, but she couldn't help it.

There *were* scars. Terrible ones.

"Margo's hair," Malcolm said. "I think Paula should dye it."

Margo managed to drag her stare from Kit's whip-scarred torso and met his gaze. He ignored her stricken look and merely studied her critically. "Yes," he said slowly, "I didn't think it was too important yet, but you're probably right. She's awfully noticeable."

"Thanks for the compliment," Margo muttered. The last thing she wanted to be was "noticeable" if attracting attention earned her scars like Kit's, but the timing was *rotten*. She'd spent the last twenty-four hours trying hopelessly to memorize Latin declensions and conjugations and whatever else all those verb and noun forms were called. All those fickle, changeable word endings left her head spinning. She'd tried—really tried—and now as a reward they wanted to dye her best feature some hideous, drab color to match the clothes they'd picked for her to wear.

Margo wanted to cry or scream at something or wail about how monstrously unfair it was. Instead, she swallowed it raw. Time was ticking away and she was still not much closer to scouting than the day she'd stepped through Primary into La-La Land with a heart full of bright hopes and no notion how murderously difficult it was going to be.

You'll see, she promised. *When we get to London, you'll see. I'll prove to you both I can do this.*

"Okay," she said finally. "I guess I go down time looking like a mud hen. Sven keeps telling me, be invisible. I should've seen this coming, huh?" Then, in a bright tone that turned a bitter complaint into a cheery joke, she said, "Let's get this over with and get down time before I'm too old to enjoy it!"

Kit laughed and even Malcolm chuckled. Margo swept out of the apartment before she gave it all away by crying. Malcolm caught up and fell into step.

"You know, Margo," he said conversationally, "it might help to think of this as the biggest game of dress-up you ever played."

She glanced up, startled. *"Dress-up?* Oh, good grief, Malcolm, I haven't played dress-up since—" She broke off abruptly, recalling the beating her father had given her for liberating her mother's makeup. "Well, not in a long time," she temporized, covering the stumble she'd made with a bright smile. "It's just you caught me off guard and . . . well . . . nothing's like I expected it to be. Nothing."

"Very little in life usually is," Malcolm said, without the trace of a smile.

"I suppose so. But I don't have to like it." Malcolm's glance was keen. "No one said you had to, Margo. Do you think I enjoy groveling for a job every day of my life, living on rice and dried beans, and swallowing my pride when people are rude, callous, or downright cruel? But I do it and smile because that's the price of living my dream."

Margo chewed that over as they left Residential behind and emerged into the throng crowding Frontier Town. A lad sporting an oversized cowboy hat and an undersized leather gun-belt drew and fired his pretend six-shooter at a diving pterosaur. It splashed into a nearby fishpond. "Got him!" the lad crowed.

Unperturbed, the pterosaur emerged with a wriggling goldfish nearly as large as it was. The kid's father laughed and called him over. He practically swaggered back.

Margo smiled. "I'd say *he*'s living his dream, huh?" Then more seriously, "Not too many people ever get the chance to try that, do they? I think you're the first person I ever met who *was* doing it." Except, maybe, Billy Pandropolous, and his dream was more akin to nightmare for everyone who came close to him. "I envy you."

"You know," Malcolm said quietly, "you may be the first person ever to do *that.*"

"Huh. You got lousy friends, then. They can't see what's right in front of 'em. Moneys not everything." She flushed suddenly, realizing she'd just insulted Malcolm's friends—at least one of whom was Kit Carson.

"How right you are," Malcolm said with a smile. "I'm glad you're beginning to see that. Some people never figure it out. This way." He nodded toward Urbs Romae. "Better hustle or we'll be late."

Paula Booker's establishment was tucked away in one corner of the Commons. Margo was expecting a hair-styling salon. What they entered looked more like the waiting room of an upscale medical clinic. Just as they entered, two men emerged from an inner sanctum. One assisted the other, who shuffled awkwardly as though his groin hurt. The first one said sympathetically, "You think that's bad, you should see what she did to mine."

"Yeah," the second man said through clenched teeth, "but a whole new foreskin? God, I hurt. . . ."

Margo stared until they had passed through the outer door and vanished down the Commons.

"What was *that* all about?"

"Zipper Jockeys." Astonishingly, Malcolm Moore wore the blackest scowl she'd ever seen.

"Zipper Jockeys?" she echoed.

"They're here for one of the sex tours. Bastards go down time and spend the whole trip brothel hopping. Paula takes revenge on 'em, though. Does corrective surgery more than they deserve, so their modern circumcisions won't arouse suspicion in most places that TT-86's gates lead to, circumcisions were practiced only by the Jewish. Anti-Semitism being the ugly thing it was in many down-time cultures . . ."

"Oh. That's lousy. The anti-Semitism, I mean."

"Yes. Bigotry is. But Zipper Jockeys deserve what they get. Paula ranks them down around the level of flatworms, which personally I think is too high on the evolutionary scale. She makes sure they hurt good and hard before they head out to rape women. If she could get away with it, she'd castrate them."

Margo glared after the departing men. "Someone should do something! Someone should stop it!"

"Yes," Malcolm said tightly. "Someone should. Time Tours won't.

They make money off the trade. So does the government. A *lot* of money. Half the Zipper Jockeys that go down time have to be quarantined when they come back, until Medical can deal with the venereal diseases they pick up."

"That's disgusting!"

"Personally, I think they should be marooned down time to die from whatever they catch."

No compromise softened Malcolm Moore's voice. All at once, Margo realized how very much she liked this time guide. "Thanks, Malcolm."

He shot her a startled look. "For what?"

"Nothing. Just thanks. What about my hair?"

He shook himself visibly and gave her one last penetrating look, then stepped over to a reception window. "Malcolm Moore, for the 8:15 appointment."

"Have a seat, please."

They didn't have to wait long. The inner door opened to reveal the most astonishing individual Margo had ever laid eyes on. She knew her mouth had fallen open, but she couldn't help it. "Hi, Paula," Malcolm said, rising to his feet.

"Hello, Malcolm." Paula Booker was . . . Cadaverous.

That was the only word to describe the cosmetologist's appearance. Tall—she topped out at six feet in flat, surgical-style shoes—and gaunt. Paula's face had hollows like a skull's. White hair wisped around a face the color of a bloodless corpse. But she wasn't old. If Paula Booker were a day over thirty-five, Margo would eat her own shoes.

With those pale eyes and that funereal expression, TT-86's cosmetologist looked very much like a female Lurch from an unknown branch of the Addams Family Tree.

"How are you this morning?" Paula asked as Malcolm shook her hand.

Even Paula's *voice* was soft and creepy.

Margo realized how intensely she was staring when both Malcolm and Paula turned and stared back.

"I—uh—"

To Margo's astonishment, Paula started laughing. The sight was so disturbing, Margo actually had trouble getting to her feet. She tripped over her own shoe and stumbled.

"Malcolm," Paula Booker winked, "let's show this young lady my photographs, shall we?"

Margo followed uneasily as Paula Booker escorted them into a private office. One wall was covered—literally covered—with photos of one of the most beautiful women Margo had ever seen. Ash-blonde hair, sparkling blue eyes, fine bone structure above hollowed cheeks—

"My God! It's you!" Margo blurted.

Paula laughed again. "Aren't I a great walking advertisement?"

"You . . ." Margo stared from the photos to the apparition before her and back again. "You did *that* to yourself?"

Paula's grin was a terrifying vision. "Indeed I did. Every morning I put on the finishing touches with makeup."

"But you could've been a movie star! A world-famous model!"

"Oh, I was. A model, that is. It was dead boring." Paula's eyes twinkled. "This is much more fun. And I get to do such interesting plastic surgery, too. I have a medical degree just for that. Somebody Caucasian wants to go to Edo, I doctor them a little and presto, they're virtually indistinguishable from a native-born Japanese. I can alter skin tone, hair color, whatever's required."

Margo thought about the man limping out of Paula's clinic and grinned. "That's terrific!" She fluffed her own hair. "What can we do about this? Everyone says I have to dye it."

Paula studied Margo for several moments. "Yes, but we won't want to go too dark, unless you want her looking as funereal as I do?" She glanced at Malcolm. "Black hair with that skin tone will look terrible. Even dark brown is going to make her look anemic."

"Can't be helped. Use your judgment on how dark, but she can't go scouting looking like that."

"No," Paula agreed. "Definitely not. Red hair was associated with witches throughout most of the Middle Ages. Probably one reason red hair is relatively rare today—the gene pool was reduced through burning at the stake. All right, Margo, let's get started. Malcolm, you're welcome to sit in the waiting room. This will take a while."

How long could it take to dye one head of very short hair brown? Margo's answer came when Paula revealed her intention to dye every *bit* of Margo's hair: body-wide.

"You can't be serious!"

"Dead serious. And you'll need to touch up the roots every four weeks."

"But—but—" That seemed to have become virtually the only thing Margo was capable of saying, lately.

Three hours later, Margo emerged, forlorn as a wet cat. She took one look into the waiting room's mirror and burst into tears—again.

"Hey," Malcolm said, rising hastily to his feet, "you look great!"

"No, I don't!" Margo wailed. "I look . . . I look *awful.*"

The mirror revealed a pinched, pale face like an orphan someone had beaten and left for dead in some unspeakable sewer. She'd have died before revealing the ignominy of having hair dye applied elsewhere with a cotton swab.

"Hey, shh. Let's grab a bite of lunch somewhere then change into our costumes and pick up your luggage. We only have a couple of hours before the Britannia Gate opens."

Not even that prospect had the power to dispel the gloom that had settled over Margo. Just one other little consideration she hadn't foreseen in becoming a time scout. To get what she wanted, Margo had to give up being pretty.

That blow, after all the other battles she'd fought through nearly seventeen miserable years of being made to feel stupid, unwanted, unloved, and a burden to everyone who knew her was nearly more than Margo could bear. The solitary, single thing that kept her from breaking down into hysterical tears was the knowledge that such a childish display would destroy her chances of scouting forever.

Her chin quivered despite her best efforts to keep it still, but she held it high. She was *going* to do this. No matter what it took, no matter how many obstacles Kit Carson threw in her path. She was going to scout or die trying.

And nothing was going to stand in her way.

Nothing.

Chapter 10

Victoria Station hadn't yet recovered from the damage of the unstable gate, but the worst debris had been hauled away and repairs had begun. Margo, palms sweating, clutched the handle of her frayed carpet bag. Malcolm smiled down at her, causing a sudden trip-hammer lurch under her breastbone. Malcolm Moore, dressed as a wealthy Victorian gentleman, was enough to set Margo's pulse racing.

He grinned suddenly. "You look nervous."

"I *am* nervous. This is real. It isn't a stage play, it's *real.* Do you get used to it?"

Malcolm's eyes took on a faraway look as his gaze focused on something Margo couldn't see. "No," he said softly. "You don't. At least, I don't. I could've found any number of teaching positions up time, particularly with my scouting-and-time guiding credentials in addition to my degrees. But I don't want to go back. Stepping through a gate . . ." He grinned again. "You'll see."

The air began to buzz. Margo pressed a hand to the bones of her skull. "Ow."

"Any moment, now."

Malcolm sounded even more excited than Margo felt, which was saying quite a lot. She checked her "uniform" again to be sure everything was in place. Under a heavy walking cloak, Margo's deep azure dress and starched white pinafore were immaculate. A pretty white cap and an enormous straw hat mercifully covered her hideous brown hair. Thick-knitted stockings, ankle-length boots, and fingerless mittens completed the ensemble, topped off by a beautiful badge in which a crown and the letters R.M.I.G. enclosed a setsquare and compasses.

'This," Connie Logan had told her with a smile, "is a particularly prestigious school uniform."

'What does R.M.I.G. stand for?"

"Royal Masonic Institution for Girls."

Malcolm, it turned out, was a Freemason, both in real life and in his down-time persona.

"I've found it helps enormously," he'd told her. "If you're in trouble—and it's very easy to fall into trouble, even for an experienced guide—having a network of sworn brothers dedicated to a creed of helping those in need can literally be a lifesaver."

"Are all guides and scouts Masons?" Margo asked, wondering with a sinking sensation if this would be yet another barrier to be overcome.

"No, but quite a few are. Don't worry about it, Margo. Membership isn't required."

At the time, Margo had felt relieved, but now, reviewing the details of her costume again, she wondered if anyone down time would expect her to know secret rituals or anything. Maybe this uncertainty had been part of Kit's plan? To impress upon her how much she had to learn? Margo shifted the carpet bag to her other hand and stiffened her back—although slouching was all but impossible, anyway, what with the horrid undergarments that were already pinching and chafing.

Doubtless physical discomfort was just another part of Kit Carson's plan to discourage her. Well, it wasn't going to work.

The air began to shimmer up near the ceiling. Well-dressed men and women stirred excitedly. Then the gate began to cycle. Rather than opening out of the wall, darkness grew out of thin air right off the end of the high, grid-work platform, a ragged hole, a widening maw . . .

Margo gasped. Through it, she could make out the colors of

twilight, the twinkle of a high, lonely star. Nearer at hand, a breeze stirred barren, low-hanging branches. She could see—but not hear—dead leaves which gusted into view. A warm, golden glow appeared, then a dark shape occluded the lantern light—

Titters of laughter ran through the crowd when a figure in a tall hat and opera cape stepped through, rushing at them like an oncoming train. The gentleman doffed his hat politely to the waiting crowd below. "Your patience, please, ladies and gentlemen."

Tourists had begun to emerge from the Britannia Gate. Women in smart dresses, men in evening suits, ragged servants hauling steamer trunks, carpet bags, and leather cases, young women dressed as housemaids, all poured through onto the platform and made their way down the ramp to the Commons floor. Many were smiling and chatting. Others looked grim. Still others staggered with assistance from Time Tours employees.

"Never fails," Malcolm murmured. "Always, a few come back sick as dogs."

"I won't," Margo vowed.

"No." Malcolm agreed drily. "You won't. That's what I'm here for."

She suppressed a huff, wanting to point out that she didn't need a nursemaid, but even she realized she *did* need a reliable guide. And then, before she expected it, their turn came.

"Oh," Margo said excitedly, "here we go!" Malcolm gallantly offered his arm. Margo laughed and accepted it, then laughed again when he insisted on carrying her carpet bag. Their "porter," a husky young man named John, took charge of their hefty steamer trunk. Margo slid her Timecard through the encoder, then hurried up the long ramp at Malcolm's side while John waited with the other baggage handlers. Margo paused at the very threshold of nothingness, mortified that her hindbrain whispered, "If I step off, there's nothing there but a five-story drop to the floor."

She screwed both eyes shut and followed Malcolm off the edge of the platform. For an instant she thought she *was* falling.

"Open your eyes!" Malcolm said urgently. She opened them—and gasped. The ground was rushing at her—Malcolm steadied her through. "That's a girl," he said encouragingly.

Margo shuddered with sudden cold. "Are you quite all right, my dear?" Margo blinked. The smiling, relaxed Malcolm with the easy American voice had gone completely. In his place stood a distinguished British gentleman peering anxiously down at her. "Uh—yeah."

Very gently, Malcolm drew her to one side, making room for other tourists. "Margo, the proper response to such a question is not 'Uh, yeah.' That's terribly anachronistic here."

Margo felt her cheeks burn. "All right," she said in a low voice. "What should I have said?"

"You should have said, 'Yes, sir, thank you kindly, it was just a passing dizziness. Might I have your arm for a moment more, please?' To which I would naturally respond by offering to escort you to some place of rest where I might fetch you a glass of water or stronger spirits if such might be required."

Margo was so fascinated by the archaic speech patterns and the wonderful sound of his voice, she almost forgot to pay attention to what he'd actually said. "All right. I mean, very well. I'll . . . I'll try, Malcolm, really I will."

"Ah-ah," he said with a smile. "Here, I am Mr. Moore. You are Miss Margo Smythe, my ward. Never fail to call me Mr. Moore. Anything else would be seen as unforgivably forward."

Behind them, the gate had begun to shrink. Porters rushed through with the last of the luggage, then the gate into La-La Land vanished into a tangle of brown vines and a high stone wall. For a terrible instant, Margo experienced complete panic. *We're cut off*. . .

Then Malcolm high-signed John, who joined them and set the trunk down with a sigh. "'At's good, Mister Moore, sir."

Malcolm grinned. "Good show, John. Your Cockneys coming along nicely."

"I been doin a study on it, sir." John's eyes twinkled. Malcolm had introduced him as a graduate student who planned to stay down time for several months working on his doctoral dissertation on the London underclass. He and Kit had come to an agreement: John would "work" as a manservant for Malcolm and Margo during their week in London, doing whatever was required of him. In return, Kit would front him the money for the initial gate ticket. He'd provided for his own living expenses and gear.

"Where are we?" Margo asked quietly. She stamped her feet to keep them warm.

"In the private garden of a house near Battersea Park at Chelsea Reach."

"Chelsea Reach?"

"A stretch of the Thames. We're across the river from where we shall need to be for most of our stay."

Gas lights illuminated a garden where the tourists now milled excitedly. Time Tours guides dressed as liveried servants organized sixty-some people into a double line, gentlemen escorting ladies, while the porters struggled with heavy trunks. They carried luggage into a three-story, graceful house where gas lights burned warmly. The interior seemed warm and inviting compared with the damp, frigid garden.

"It's cold," Margo complained.

"Well, it *is* late February. We shall have a hard frost tonight or I'm no judge of weather."

She tucked her hands inside the cape. "Now what?"

"First, fetch out your ATLS and log, please." He glanced toward the darkening sky. "We'll need to take readings and start our trip chronometers running. Remember, Miss Smythe, it is essential that you start your trip chronometer running very quickly after passing a gate. And shoot an ATLS and star-fix as soon as possible. And as I suspect we'll have fog soon, do hurry with it. London generally does in the early evenings."

"But we already know exactly when we are," Margo pointed out.

"On a tour, yes. As a scout, you won't. You'll have to determine that as the opportunity arises. Just because your Timecard was logged in for the Britannia Gate, doesn't mean you may skip this ritual. Most gates you'll step through as a scout won't *have* an encoder available yet, for the simple reason that you'll be the first one stepping through it. And when you come through in broad daylight, you'll have to wait until nightfall to update your exact geo-temporal reading."

Margo dug out her equipment and took the ATLS reading. Malcolm checked her and made a small correction, then showed her how to take a star-fix. She mastered the knack after three tries and proudly entered the readings in her log.

"There! How did I do?"

"Your ATLS reading was off far enough that you'd have placed yourself in the Irish Sea, but not too bad for a first attempt under field conditions. We'll take readings each night we're here, to give you the practice."

Malcolm finished entering data into his own log, made certain Margo had properly initiated the chronometer sequence, then put away their equipment.

"Now what?"

The tourists had lined up along a garden path and were filing slowly into the house.

"Time Tours will have made arrangements for cabriolet carriages to take us to various good hotels for the evening."

"I thought carriages were called hansoms."

Malcolm smiled. "Hansom cabs are very popular just now, but they're small, two-wheeled affairs. Hansoms cannot carry any significant amount of luggage. Hence the need for something a bit sturdier."

They joined the line and moved steadily toward the house. Margo wanted to rush forward and explore. She found it increasingly difficult to stand still.

"Patience," Malcolm laughed. "We've an entire week ahead of us."

"When will our cab be here?"

"Our hosts," Malcolm said, glancing a little coldly at the liveried Time Tours guides, "will serve refreshments while carriages are summoned. We'll be departing in small groups at least fifteen minutes apart, to reduce the chance that anyone will notice the numbers of people coming and going from this house."

"How did Time Tours get hold of this place?"

Malcolm said quietly, "I'm told the spinster lady who owned it had a fit of the vapors the first time the Britannia Gate opened in her garden. When it happened several weeks in a row, she sold the place cheaply to a scout and retired permanently to Scotland. Time Tours bought it from the scout."

Margo hadn't considered what people *down* time must think when a gate opened right in front of them. "Who was the scout?"

Malcolm shrugged. "Your grandfather."

Oh.

"I would suggest," Malcolm said as they moved across the threshold into a surprisingly chilly drawing room, "that we refrain from discussing up-time affairs for the week as much as possible. You are here to learn, certainly, but discussing anything from up time is very dangerous within earshot of people who understand the language you're speaking. If you must ask a question, keep your voice down and try to ask it where others can't hear you. I'll pass along my advice under the same set of strictures."

Again, Margo was trying to get the rhythm of Malcolm's new speech patterns. "Very well, Mal—Mr. Moore."

He patted her hand. "Very good, Miss Smythe. And now, if you would be so kind as to permit me, I will introduce you to London."

He led her toward a warm coal fire and beckoned to a "servant" who brought steaming cups of tea.

"My dear, warm yourself while I see about our luggage and transportation."

He signaled to John, who carried their steamer trunk toward a long front hall where other porters waited. Margo sipped astringent tea, grateful for the warmth; the room's lingering chill surprised her. Other tourists were talking excitedly, admiring the furnishings, the rugs, the draperies, the view out the windows. Margo was a little envious of the women's dresses. One elegantly attired lady smiled and approached her.

"That's a charming costume," she said. "What is it?"

Feeling vastly superior, Margo said, "It's one of the most prestigious school uniforms in London, from the Royal Masonic Institution for Girls." She dredged up Connie Logan's lecture and added, "It was founded in Somers Town, London, by a chevalier in 1788."

"It's delightful. Could I see the whole costume?"

Margo dimpled and set down her teacup, then slipped off the cape and pirouetted.

"Oh, look!" exclaimed another tourist. "It's darling!"

"Where did you get it?"

"Connie Logan, Clothes and Stuff."

"I wish I'd thought to dress Louisa like that," one lady laughed. Her daughter, looking dowdy in a plain grey morning dress, was pouting under a stylish hat decorated rather hideously with dead birds.

"And look at that brooch. What an intriguing design. Is that the school's crest?"

"Yes. It's a badge. All the charity schools issued them to identify their pupils."

"Ladies," Malcolm smiled, bowing slightly, "if I might rescue my ward, our cabriolet is waiting. Here, let me help you on with that cape, my dear. The night is dreadfully chilly and John neglected to bring along our lap rug."

A flutter of excited laughter ran through the room.

"Who *is* that gentleman?"

"Oh, I wish our guide sounded like that!"

"Or looked like him . . ."

"I don't care what Time Tours says, the next time I come here, I'm going to hire him. I don't care *what* it costs!"

Malcolm smiled, murmured, "A moment, my dear," and handed around business cards with a polite bow and smile to each lady. He then offered Margo his arm. "A moment's attention to business works wonders, don't you agree?"

Margo laughed, waved goodbye to her brief acquaintances, then strolled out into the London night on Malcolm's capable arm.

By the time their cab had swayed through five dark streets, thick fog had left them blind. Swirling, foul yellow drifts blanketed the streets. Even the horse vanished from view. Only the soft clip-clop of its hooves assured Margo they weren't drifting along by magic.

"London stinks," Margo whispered. "like a barnyard. And that fog smells awful."

"London is full of horses," Malcolm whispered back. "Some hundred tons of manure fall on London streets every day."

"Every *day?*"

"Daily," Malcolm affirmed. "And the fogs have been known to kill hundreds in a single day. If you find it difficult to breathe, you must tell me at once and we'll take a train for the country until the worst of it clears."

"I can breathe," Margo whispered, "it just isn't pleasant. Are we going to a hotel?"

"Actually, no. We'll stay at a boarding house near Victoria Station for the night, then rent a flat on the morrow. That will give us privacy to come and go without undue notice. John, here, will be staying on at the flat once we've gone."

"Mr. Carson be terrible gen'rous, Mr. Moore," John said in the darkness.

Margo giggled. "You sound so funny."

"He sounds exactly as he should," Malcolm said sternly. "You do not. Charity-school girls are demure and silent, not giggling, brash things given to rude comments."

"Well, excuse me," Margo muttered.

"Certainly not. Study your part, young lady. That is an order."

Margo sighed. Another domineering male . . . She almost looked forward to trading the schoolgirl getup for the rough clothes of a country farmer or the even rougher getup of a costermonger. Masquerading as a boy, she wouldn't need to worry so much about observing all these confining social conventions. She began to catch a glimmer of what Kit had meant when he'd insisted women would have a rough go of it trying to scout.

The sound of water lapping against stone and a hollow change in the sound of the horse's hooves told Margo they were very near the river. The occasional complaining grumble of a steam whistle drifted on the evil yellow fog like the distant cries of dying hounds. "Where are we? I can't see a thing."

"Crossing Lambeth Bridge."

A few rents in the murk revealed a distant, dark wall.

"And that?"

"Millbank Penitentiary. New Bridewell's not far from here, either."

"New Bridewell?"

"A rather notorious prison, my dear. You do ask the most shocking questions."

Fog closed in again the moment they left the open bridge with its fitful breeze. Margo heard the heavy, muted rumbling of not-too-distant trains. A shrill whistle shivered through the foul, wet air, so close Margo jumped.

"Don't be alarmed, Miss Smythe. It is merely a train arriving at Victoria Station."

"Will we hear that all night?" Malcolm's chuckle reached her. "Indeed."

Fiend. He'd done this on purpose, to leave her groggy and off balance tomorrow. He *knew* she was already running on virtually no sleep. *Well, when you start scouting, you may be short of sleep, too. Consider it part of the lesson.* At length, their driver halted. Malcolm left her shivering inside the cold carriage. He made arrangements with the lady who ran the boarding house, then offered his hand and assisted her from the cab.

"Oh, you poor dear, you must be tired," the plump lady smiled, ushering them up a long, dark staircase. A gaslight at the landing threw feeble light down the stairwell. Margo had to watch the hem of her dress to keep from tripping in the shadows. "Your guardian said you'd come all the way from Honduras and then by train, poor thing, orphaned by them terrible fevers, and now he's enrolled you in the School, but can't bear to part company wi' you yet. Such a nice gentleman, your guardian, watch your step, dear, that's good, and here's your room. Mr. Moore's is directly along the hall, there, second on your right. I'll have hot water sent up. And here's your bag, dearie," she said, taking the carpet bag from John and setting it on a heavy piece of furniture that evidently was meant as a dry sink, judging from the basin and pitcher her hostess took from its lower recesses.

"I'll leave you now to rest and see you at breakfast, dearie. Pull the bell if you need anything."

And that—Margo gaped as the landlady left in a rustle of petticoats and firmly closed the door—was that.

And she died more than a hundred years ago. . . .

Margo shivered, momentarily overcome by the unreality of it. It wasn't at all like watching an old film or even like participating in a stage play. It was like stepping into someone else's life, complete with sounds and smells and the sensation that if she blinked it would all vanish like a soap bubble. But it didn't. She sank down slowly on the edge of a feather tick. Bed ropes creaked. The room smelled musty. Gaslight burned softly behind a frosted globe on the wall. Margo wondered how in the world to turn it off. She untied her hat and took it off then removed the cap and the heavy woolen cape. The once-white cap was grey from coal smoke. She shivered absently. The room was freezing and damp. No central heat.

"Now what?" she wondered aloud.

A soft tap on the door brought her to her feet. Margo clutched the cap in knotted fingers. "*Who is it?*" Her voice came out shaky and thin.

"It's Mr. Moore, Miss Smythe. Might I speak with you for a moment?"

Margo all but flew across the room. She snatched the door open.

He smiled widely at her expression, then nodded toward the gaslight. "See that little chain on the side?"

Margo peered toward the light. "Yes."

"Pull it once to turn off the lamp. Don't blow out the flame or your room will fill up with gas and we'll all die rather messily."

Oh. "Thank you. I—I was wondering about that."

"Very good. Any other questions before I retire for the evening?"

Margo had about a million of them, but the only thing that popped into her head was, "How do I get warm? It's freezing in here."

Malcolm glanced around the room. "No fireplace. No stove, either. The landlady is doubtless afraid of fires and rightly so. But there should be plenty of quilts in that linen press." He pointed to a heavy piece of furniture across the room. "Pile them on and snuggle in. Anything else?"

Margo didn't dare admit that she wanted—desperately—to say "I'm scared." So she shook her head and gave him a bright smile.

"Very good, then. I shall see you at breakfast." He bent and kissed her forehead. "Good night, my dear. Lock your door."

Then he stepped down the hall and entered his room. His door clicked softly shut. A key turned in the lock. Margo stood gazing down the dimly lit corridor for several moments while her brow tingled under the remembered feel of Malcolm Moore's lips.

Oh, don't be ridiculous! All you need is to pull some stupid schoolgirl stunt like falling for a poverty-stricken time guide. He's too old for you, anyway, and thinks youre silly into the bargain. Besides, you had enough heartache from Billy Pandropolous to swear off men for all time.

She closed her door and locked it, experiencing a swift prickle of tears behind her eyelids. She didn't want Malcolm Moore to think she was silly. She wanted to prove to him—and everyone else—that she could do this job. Do it and be good at it.

She lay awake far into the night, listening to the rumble of carriages and wagons through London's filthy streets and wincing at the shriek of steam locomotives. And the whole time she lay there, Margo wondered miserably what that kiss would have felt like against her lips.

Workaday London enthralled.

Malcolm made arrangements for a small flat in western London, several streets east of Grosvenor Square, which was itself just east of the ultrafashionable Hyde Park in Mayfair. The West End was where—according to Malcolm—Britain's ten thousand or so members of "Society" (some fifteen hundred families) made their London homes. The houses were splendid, but their construction surprised Margo. Most of them were more like condos than individual houses. Immensely long stone and brick facades took up entire city blocks, subdivided into individual "houses" that each wealthy family owned.

"It's a law," Malcolm explained, "passed after the Great Fire of 1666. Not only fewer combustible materials, but this construction plan was adopted to help combat the spread of another disastrous fire."

"How bad was it?"

Malcolm said quietly, "Most of London burned. Only a tiny corner of the city was spared. One of its blessings, of course, was that the fire evidently destroyed the plague, since there haven't been any outbreaks since then. Cholera, on the other hand, remains a serious difficulty."

Margo gazed in rapt fascination at the long, mellow facades, the immaculately clean walks, the ladies being assisted by liveried footmen into carriages for their round of "morning calls." They were gorgeous in heavy silks, furs, and luxuriant feathered hats. Margo sighed, acutely conscious of her charity-school costume and short, dyed hair; but she didn't let that spoil the fun of watching the "quality" pass by.

"We're far enough from the heart of Mayfair," Malcolm told her once they had settled into the six-room flat, "to go unnoticed in our seedier disguises, but close enough to avoid the filth and crime of the East End and allow me to continue my persona as independent gentleman."

"Have you been here before?"

"Not this particular flat, no; but this general area, yes. I bring my tourists here rather than to a hotel, unless they insist otherwise. Living in a flat and buying vegetables and fish from the markets gives one rather a better feel for life here. Unpack your things, Miss Smythe, and we'll begin our work."

He had John hire a carriage and horses for the week while they unpacked. Malcolm arranged with the landlady for deliveries to be made from a reputable chandler to victual them with staples. Once the food arrived, he showed Margo how to prepare a British-style luncheon for a country outing. "A country outing?" Margo asked excitedly. "Really?"

Malcolm smiled. "I doubt it's what you have in mind. Pack that set of tweeds for me, would you? That's a dear. And bring along that loose shirt, those trousers, and that pair of boots for yourself. Yes, those. As a scout, one of the most important things you'll need to know is how to handle horses. I'm going to teach you to ride."

The closest thing to a horse Margo had ever ridden was a carousel at the state fair. And only then because her neighbors had taken her with their kids, pitying a child whose father spent most of what he had on liquor—and, eventually, worse. "I don't know anything about horses," she said dubiously.

"You will." Malcolm's cheerful smile removed the hint of threat. The horses John hired—four altogether—came in two distinct pairs. As John shook out the reins over the carriage horses, Malcolm explained.

"Those are cobs, sturdy draft horses used for pulling loads. This isn't the fanciest carriage available, although it's smart and very up-to-date in keeping with my persona here."

"What's it called?"

"It's a four-wheeled brougham, with a hard top," he rapped the ceiling with his knuckles, "which will make it easier for you to change your attire without being noticed. This is the family vehicle of the 1880s, very respectable."

"And the horses tied behind?" They were much sleeker than the stocky carriage horses.

"Hacks. General riding animals, not nearly as expensive or handsome as hunters, but much easier to manage and cheaper to rent for those who don't care to feed a horse year-round, pay for its stabling, a groomsman, a blacksmith . . ."

"Expensive, huh?"

"Very. That's why livery stables do such a brisk business hiring animals and carriages."

Margo thought about what Connie had said on the subject of class distinction and decided to risk a question. "What do the really rich people think about people who hire carriages and horses?"

Malcolm's mobile features lit up. "Very good, Miss Smythe! Generally, we're snubbed, of course. Anyone with pretensions to society keeps a carriage and horses of his own. I am absolved through the eccentricity of my comings and goings from Honduras. Providing I ever acquire the capital, I intend to take out a long-term lease on a small house where I might entertain guests. All my down-time acquaintances urge me to do so, in order to keep a permanent staff rather than relying on the vagaries of agency people."

Margo wondered how much that would cost, but didn't quite dare ask. That seemed like an awfully personal question and she was still feeling very uncertain in the aftermath of that harmless kiss last night.

"Speaking of money, do you remember my lecture on currency?"

Oh, no . . .

"I, uh . . ." Margo tried frantically to recall what Malcolm had taught her during their visit to Goldie Morran, one of TT-86's money changers. "The basic unit's the pound. It's abbreviated with that little 'U' thing."

"And a pound is made up of . . ."

She cast back through the confusion of foreign terms. "Twenty shillings."

"Twenty-one shillings being called?"

Oh, God, it was some sort of bird . . . "A hen?"

Malcolm sat back and covered his eyes, stricken with helpless laughter. "The association," he wheezed, "is flawlessly logical, I'll have to credit you that much. A *guinea,* Margo. A guinea."

"A guinea," she repeated grimly. "Twenty-one shillings is a guinea."

"Now, what else do we call twenty shillings, other than a pound?"

Margo screwed shut her eyes and tried to remember. Not a king, there was a queen on the throne. "A sovereign."

"Or quid, in slang terms. What's it made of?"

"Gold. So's a half-sovereign!" she finished triumphantly.

"And half of that?"

Something else to do with royalty. But what, she couldn't remember. She lifted her hands helplessly.

"A crown. Five shillings is a crown, or a 'bull' in slang usage."

Margo took a deep breath. "A crown. A quarter-sovereign is a crown. Then there's the half-crown, or two-and-a-half shillings." Her head hurt.

"Two shillings is . . ."

"I don't know," Margo wailed. "My head aches!" Malcolm produced a card from his waistcoat pocket, hand-written with what was clearly a period ink-pen. "Study this. If you forget and must refer to this, please explain that you're a recently orphaned American with a British benefactor and you just can't keep all this straight, then bat your eyelashes and look helpless and the shopkeepers will probably fall over themselves trying to assist you." Margo couldn't help it. She burst out laughing at the ludicrous face Malcolm presented. He grinned and handed over the card. Margo settled herself to study the rest of the currency—florins, pence, groats, pennies, farthings, and all the rest—with a much-improved frame of mind.

Horses, Margo learned, were tricky beasts.

Changing clothes in the cramped carriage was easy compared to managing an animal that weighed half a ton and scared her to death every time it blew quietly at the front of her shirt.

"All right," Malcolm said patiently when she succeeded in bridling the hack without losing a thumb or fingers, "do it again."

She shut her eyes, summoned up every erg of patience she possessed, and unbuckled the bridle. Then performed the whole terrifying procedure again. They'd been at this an hour and she still hadn't even *saddled* the horse, much less gotten on its back. The "riding" lesson had begun with a bewildering new set of terms to learn: withers, fetlocks, gaits, snaffles, cinches, leathers, headstalls . . .

Oh, God, why did I ever think time scouting would be easier than college?

But even she could see the practical necessity of learning to control *the* mode of transportation from prehistory right down to the invention of the mass-produced automobile.

Margo finally mastered haltering and bridling, moved on to saddling, then spent twenty minutes exercising her hack on a lunge line to learn the difference in its gaits and to judge what it took to control a horse from the ground. By the time she passed muster, she was exhausted. Her toes, fingertips, and nose were numb with cold.

"Shall we break for lunch," Malcolm suggested, "then try our first ride afterward?"

Oh, thank God.

"Cool out your horse by walking him up and down the lane for about five minutes while John spreads out a blanket. Then we'll water him and rest a bit ourselves." At least Malcolm accompanied her on the walk. The horse's hooves clopped softly behind them. Margo had begun to feel less nervous asking questions. "Why do we have to cool him out? It's freezing out here!"

"Any time you work a horse, cool him out. Particularly in cold weather. An overheated horse can catch a fatal chill if he's not properly cooled down afterward. Horses are remarkably delicate creatures, prone to all sorts of illness and accident. Your life literally depends on the care you give your horse. Treat him with better care than you treat yourself. Your horse is fed and watered before you even think of resting or eating your own meal. Otherwise, you may not have a horse afterward." It made sense. It also sounded remarkably similar to Ann Vinh Mulhaney's lecture on caring for one's firearms: "Keep them clean. Particularly if you're using a black-powder weapon. Clean it every time you use it. Black powder and early priming compounds are corrosive. Clean your gun thoroughly or it'll be useless—and that can happen fast. Don't ever bet your life on a dirty weapon."

"Mal—Mr. Moore," she amended hastily, "are you carrying a firearm?"

He glanced swiftly at her. "Whatever brought on that question?"

"You just sounded like Ms. Mulhaney, about keeping firearms clean or losing the use of them. So then I wondered."

"One generally doesn't ask a gentlemen, 'Sir, are you armed?' As it happens, I am. I never travel to London, never mind outside it, without a good revolver on my person."

"Isn't that illegal?"

His lips twitched faintly. "Not yet."

Oh.

"There are a few things about down-time cultures," Malcolm said with a sigh, "that are vastly preferable to up-time nonsense. Self-defense attitudes being one of them. Let's turn about, shall we? I believe he's cooling out nicely."

Margo turned the horse and they returned to the hired carriage, where she tied the reins and draped a warm blanket over his back. She then watered the animal from a pail John produced.

"Thank you, John," she smiled.

"Me pleasure, miss."

Margo grinned, but refrained from comment, since they were supposed to stay "in character" as much as possible to avoid slip-ups.

Lunch was simple but good: slices of beef and cheese on crusted rolls and red wine in sturdy mugs. John had built a warm fire and spread out a blanket for them. Margo relaxed, draping her heavy cape around her shoulders and leaning close to the fire to keep from catching a chill. Clouds raced past through a lacing of barren branches above their little fire. She couldn't identify the tall tree but sunlight filtering down through the spider-work of twigs and branches was wonderful. "Nice."

Birdsong twittered through the silence. One of the horses blew quietly and let a hind leg go slack as it dozed. Tired as she was, it would have been incredibly easy just to close her eyes and fall asleep to the hush of birdsong and the profound silence behind it. Far, far away Margo heard voices, the words indistinguishable with distance. And beyond the voices, the faint hoot of a train.

Margo hadn't realized the world before automobiles and jet aircraft could be so quiet. "Ready for that riding lesson?" Margo opened her eyes and found Malcolm smiling down at her.

"Yes, Mr. Moore, I believe I am."

"Good." He offered her a hand up. Margo scrambled to her feet, refreshed and ready to tackle anything. *Today,* she told herself, *I become a horsewoman.*

The horse—of course—had other ideas. Margo learned the first critical lesson about horseback riding within five minutes. When you fall off, you get back on. Heart in her mouth, she tried again. This time, she rechecked the cinch first, as Malcolm had told her before lunch—and which she'd forgotten in the interim—then clambered back aboard.

This time, the saddle held. She started breathing again and relaxed her death grip on the mane. "Okay, I'm on. Now what?"

Malcolm was busy mounting his own horse. Margo discovered an intense envy of the ease with which he floated into the saddle and found a seat. "Follow me and copy what I do."

He set off by thumping heels sharply against the horse's belly. Margo tried it. Her hack moved off sedately with a placid "I have a novice on my back" air about him.

"It works!"

"Well, of course it works," Malcolm laughed. He reined in to let her pass. "Heels down, toes in."

"Ow! That hurts!"

"And don't forget to grip with your thighs. But leave your hands relaxed. You don't want to bruise his mouth with the bit."

What about my *bruises?*

Concentrating on heels, toes, thighs, and hands all at the same time while steering and not falling off was nerve-racking. For the first ten minutes, Margo sweat into her clothes and was thoroughly miserable. The horse didn't seem to mind, however.

"Keep right on," Malcolm said over his shoulder. "I'll follow you for a bit."

He reined around behind her. Margo's horse tried to follow. She hauled on the reins, overcorrected, and sent her horse straight toward a hedgerow. She straightened him out after wandering back and forth across the lane several times. Eventually she mastered the knack of keeping a fairly steady course.

"You're doing fine," Malcolm said from behind her. "Sit up a little straighten. That's good. Toes *in.* Heels *down.* Better. Elbows relaxed, wrists relaxed. Good. Gather up the reins slightly. If he bolts now, he'll have the bit in his teeth and there'll be no stopping him. Firm but relaxed."

"If he *bolts?*" Margo asked. "Why would he do that?"

"Horses just do. It's called shying. Anything can scare a horse. A leaf rustling the wrong way. A noise. An unexpected movement or color. Or a particular item. A parasol. A train. A lawn chair."

"Great. I'm stuck way up here on something likely to jump at a shadow?"

"Precisely. Tighten your thighs. Heels *down*"

Ow . . .

After half an hour, Malcolm let her trot. That was worse. The gait jolted her from top to bottom. Learning to *post* a trot put cramps in her thigh muscles. He brought her back down to a walk again to let her rest.

"I hate this!"

"That's because we haven't tried the canter yet," Malcolm smiled.

"And when we get to do that? Next week?"

Malcolm laughed. "Patience, Miss Smythe. Patience. You can't fly until you've learned to flap your wings properly. Now, the post again."

Margo held back a groan and kicked her horse into the posting trot that jolted everything that *could* be jolted. She missed her timing, rising on the wrong swing of the horse's withers, and discovered that was worse. She jolted along for a couple of paces before she got it right again. Eventually, Margo mastered it.

"All right," Malcolm said, drawing up beside her, "let's see if the nag will canter."

Malcolm clucked once and urged his horse forward with thighs, knees, and heels. He leaned forward—And shot away in a thunder of hoof-beats. Belatedly Margo kicked her own horse to greater speed. One moment they were jolting through a horrendous trot. The next, Margo was flying. *"Oh!"*

It was wonderful.

She found herself grinning like an idiot as her horse caught up with Malcolm's. "Hi!"

He glanced over and grinned. "Better?"

"Wow!"

"Thought you'd like that!"

"It's . . . it's terrific!" She felt alive all over, even down to her toes. The horse moved under her in a smoothly bunched rhythm, while hedgerows whipped past to a glorious, stinging wind in her face.

"Better pull up," Malcolm warned, "before we come to the crossroad."

Margo didn't want to pull up and go back. Greatly daring, she kicked her horse to greater speed. He burst into a gallop that tore the breath from her lungs and left her ecstatic. Eyes shining, she tore down the country lane and shot into the crossroad—And nearly ran down a heavy coach and four sweating horses. Margo screamed. Her own horse shied, nearly tossing her out of the saddle. Then the nag plunged into a watery meadow at full gallop. Margo hauled on the reins. The horse didn't slow down. She pulled harder, still to no avail. Freezing spray from the wet meadow soaked her legs. Patches of ice shattered under her horse's flying hooves. Then Malcolm thundered up and leaned over. He seized the reins in an iron grip. Her horse tossed its head, trying to rear, then settled down to a trot. They finally halted.

Malcolm sat panting on his own horse, literally white with rage. "OUT OF THE SADDLE! Walk him back!"

Margo slid to the ground. Rubbery legs nearly dumped her headlong into muddy, half-frozen water. She wanted to cry. Instead she snatched the reins and led the horse back toward the crossroad. Malcolm sent his own mount back at a hard gallop, spattering her with mud from head to foot. That did it. She started crying, silently. She was furious and miserable and consumed with embarrassment. Malcolm had stopped far ahead, where he was talking with the driver of the coach. The carriage had careered off the road.

"Oh, no," she wailed. What if someone had been hurt? *I'm an idiot . . .*

She couldn't bear even to look at the coach as she slunk past, leading the horse back down the lane. When Malcolm passed her, back in the saddle, he was moving at a slow walk, but he didn't even acknowledge her presence. When she finally regained the carriage, Malcolm was waiting.

"Fortunately," he said in a tone as icy as the water in her shoes, "no one was injured. Now get back on that horse and do as I tell you this time."

She scrubbed mud and tears with the back of one hand. "M-my feet are wet. And freezing."

Malcolm produced dry stockings. She changed, then wearily hauled herself back into the saddle. The rest of the afternoon passed in frigid silence, broken only by Malcolm's barked instructions. Margo learned to control her horse at the canter and the gallop. By twilight she was able to stay with him when Malcolm deliberately spooked the hack into rearing, shying, and bolting with her.

It was a hard-won accomplishment and she should have been proud of it. All she felt was miserable, bruised, and exhausted. Whatever wasn't numb from the cold ached mercilessly. John solicitously filled a basin for her to wash off the mud. He'd heated the water over the fire. Her fingers stung like fire when she dunked them into the hot water. She finally struggled back into the hateful undergarments, the charity gown and pinafore. Then she had to take another ATLS and star-fix reading and update her personal log. When Malcolm finally allowed her to climb into the carriage for the return to town, she hid her face in the side cushions and pretended to sleep.

Malcolm settled beside her while John loaded the luggage and lit the carriage lanterns, then they set out through the dark. As a first-day down time, it had been a mixed success at best. They rattled along in utter silence for nearly half an hour. Then Malcolm said quietly, "Miss—Margo. Are you awake?"

She made some strangled sound that was meant to be a "Yes" and came out sounding more like a cat caught in a vacuum cleaner.

Malcolm hesitated in the dark, then settled an arm around her shoulders. She turned toward him and gave in, wetting his tweed coat thoroughly between hiccoughs.

"Shh . . ."

With the release of tension—and the sure knowledge that he'd forgiven her—crushing exhaustion overtook Margo. She fell asleep to the jolt of carriage wheels on the rutted lane, the warmth of Malcolm's arm around her, and the thump of his heartbeat under her ear. The last, whispery sensation to come to her in the darkness was the scent of his skin as he bent and softly kissed her hair.

Nothing in Margo's experience prepared her for the East End.

Not an abusive father, not the crime and violence of New York City, not even the barrage of televised images of starving, ragged third worlders, brandished like meat cleavers by charities desperately trying to stave off global disaster.

"My God," Margo kept whispering. "My God . . ."

They set out very early in the morning. Malcolm thrust a pistol into a holster under his jacket and pocketed a tin wrapped with waxed cord, then asked John to drive them to Lower Thames Street, near the famous London Docks.

The docks had been cut out of the earth in Wapping to form a deep, rectangular "harbor" filled with river water. The city surrounded it on all sides. Steamers and sailing ships were literally parked at the end of narrow, filthy streets.

They picked up an empty pushcart cart John had procured and began walking through the pre-dawn chill. Margo's old boots and woolen, uncreased trousers chafed. Her ragged shirt and threadbare pea jacket barely kept out the chill. Swing docks afforded occasional glimpses of the river as they passed the stinking, bow-windowed taverns of Wapping. Sailors accosted everything female with such gusto Margo huddled more deeply into her boy's garments, desperately grateful for the disguise. *Okay, so they were right.* She didn't have to be happy about it, but she could disguise herself. Fortunately, none of the sailors so much as glanced at her twice. Malcolm steered them toward the riverbank, where the stench of tidal mudflats was overwhelming. They watched young kids, mostly barefooted, picking through the freezing mud.

"Mudlarks," he explained quietly. 'They scavenge bits of iron or coal, anything they can sell for a few pence. Most children are supposed to be in school, but the poorest often dodge it, as you see. There used to be much fiercer competition down there, before mandatory schooling laws were passed. On Saturdays, the riverbanks are alive with starving mudlarks."

One romantic illusion after another shattered into slivers on the cold road.

"What are those?" she asked, pointing to a boat mid-river with large nets out. "Fishermen?"

"No. Draggers. They look for dropped valuables, including bodies they can loot for money and other sellable items."

"Corpses." Margo gasped. "My God, Malcolm—" She bit her tongue. "Sorry."

"Dressed as a boy, it's not such a grave error, but I'd still prefer you said Mr. Moore. People will take you for my apprentice. You've seen enough here. We have to get to Billingsgate before the worst of the crowds do."

"Billingsgate?"

"Billingsgate Market," Malcolm explained as they neared a

maelstrom of carts, wagons, barrels, boats, and human beings. "Royal Charter gives Billingsgate a monopoly oil fish."

The stench and noise were unbelievable. Margo wanted to cover her ears and hold her breath. They shoved in cheek-to-jowl with hundreds of other costermongers buying their day's wares to peddle. Liveried servants from fine houses, ordinary lower-class wives, and buyers for restaurants as well as shippers who would take loads of fish inland for sale, all fought one another for the day's catch.

"Salmon for Belgravia," Malcolm shouted above the roar, "and herrings for Whitechapel!"

"What do we want?"

"Eels!"

Eels?

After that dinner at the Epicurean Delight, Billingsgate's eels came as another rude shock. Malcolm filled their cart with the most repugnant, slithery mess Margo had ever seen. Jellied eels went from huge enameled bowls into stoneware pots. From another vendor they procured hot "pie-and-mash" pies, plus a supply of hideous green stuff the screaming fishwife called "liquor." Malcolm bargained the prices lower in an ear bending accent. The language the fishwives used put to shame anything Margo had heard on the streets of New York—when she understood it at all. Malcolm stacked the pies in their cart, layered them on boards and wrapped them in worn woolen cloth to keep them warm. Margo—under instructions to pay attention to details—tried to keep track of what she witnessed, but there was so much to take in she found it all running together in a screaming blur.

They finally escaped Billingsgate's scaly stench and set out. Malcolm did a surprisingly brisk business selling eels and pies as they entered the cramped streets of Wapping. Of Malcolm's colorful patter, however, Margo didn't understand one word in four.

"Give yer plates of meat a treat," he called out, "rest a bit, I've eels to eat!" Then, another block onward, "Yer trouble and strife givin' you worries? Tike 'ome 'ot eels, thankee and tip o' the titfer t' you, mate." Then, to a hollow-cheeked lad who eyed the cart longingly, "Wot, no bees 'n' 'oney? Rough days but I gots mouths ter feed meself." And finally, in a completely incomprehensible exchange with a sailor, "Aye, let's 'ope ain't no pleasure an' pain t'day. A penny, an' enjoy."

When they moved out of earshot, Margo could no longer contain burning curiosity. "What in the world are you *saying?*"

Malcolm grinned. "It's Cockney speech. Cockney's more than an accent, it's a way of speaking. Rhyming sales patter and no real attention to grammar."

"But what does it *mean?*"

He chuckled and eased the cart over to one side of the narrow street. "All right. I'll try to translate what I've been saying." He glanced upward, evidently casting back through his patter of the previous few minutes. "Plates of meat—those are your feet. Essentially I said, 'Give your feet a treat. Sit down and rest a while, have some delicious eels.' Then let's see, what did I say next?"

"Something about trouble and strife giving you worries. That made sense, at least."

"Did it?" His mobile mouth quirked upward at the corners. "Trouble and strife means your wife."

"Your wife?"

Malcolm laughed. "That phrase meant 'Is your wife giving you problems?' Take home some hot eels.' Hinting of course, that a warm breakfast might soothe her ragged temper."

"What's a titfer?" His eyes twinkled. "Tit for tat means hat. Cockney loves to abbreviate as much as any other language. A tip of the titfer—"

"Is a tip of the hat," Margo finished.

"Right. Bees and honey is money—and without it, you're sunk if you want breakfast from this cart."

"What about the pleasure and pain bit?"

Malcolm chuckled. "I told him I hoped it didn't rain."

Margo rolled her eyes, "Good grief. How is anyone supposed to learn all this? And what's that horrible stuff made of, anyway?" Margo asked, pointing to the green "liquor" in the cart.

"Parsley sauce."

"Parsley sauce? Oh. I couldn't imagine what it was." She'd had visions of some Cockney fishwife growing mold in vats and adding gelatin.

"Actually, it's quite good. Want to sample the wares?"

Margo was starving. "Uh, no. Thanks."

Malcolm cut up one of the pies anyway and spread parsley sauce on it. "You need to eat. The days cold and it'll be long."

She shut her eyes and bit into it. Then glanced up, startled. "Hey, not bad!"

Malcolm grinned and wolfed his own down. "You look too healthy. Suck in your cheeks a little. Better . . ." He scooped up a handful of filth and smeared mud across one cheek. "Yes, that's it."

Margo tried to hold her breath. The mud stank.

He smeared his clothes artistically then washed his hands from a bottle in the bottom of the cart. "Next stop, Whitechapel. Watch your step—this is a rough area."

Whitechapel's main roads were surprisingly wide—and every last inch of roadway was jammed with wagons and ox-carts. Behind the main streets, however . . .

London's deadly slum was a sunless maze of narrow alleyways, winding, dangerous streets, and courtyards where nothing green found purchase in the filthy soil. Crowded conditions left some people living on ramshackle staircases. Mud and filth reeked underfoot. Everywhere Margo looked were ragged, filthy people: sleeping on stairs, in puddles of filth, in rooms whose doors sagged so far open she could see drunken men and women snoring in piles of decaying refuse. The stench was overwhelming. Here and there, men and women urinated openly in the streets.

Margo whispered, "Isn't this where Jack—"

He hushed her. "Not until later in the year. August."

Margo shivered and eyed ill-kept women, wondering which of them might fall victim to the notorious serial murderer. It was an unsettling thought. Kit Carson's brutal assessment of her chances in this slum rang in her ears. All *right,* she grudged him, *you've got a point.* Malcolm sold a few eels, mostly to sleepy women whose clothing still reeked of their previous night's customers. Everywhere the stench of human waste, cheap gin, and rot rose like a miasma from the ground.

"Are *all* the women in Whitechapel prostitutes?" Margo whispered.

Malcolm shook his head "Not all." Then in a cautious whisper, "There are some eighty-thousand whores in London, most trying to stave off starvation." Margo understood that statement now in a way that would have been impossible two hours previously.

"Do they stay prostitutes?"

"Some yes, many no. Many take to the 'gay' life, as prostitution was known, only long enough to find a better-paying job. Northwest of here, up in Spitalfields for instance, a woman can get work in the garment district sweat shops. If she doesn't have too many mouths to feed, she might eke out a living without going back on the streets."

They glanced at a yawning fourteen-year-old who eyed Margo speculatively, appraising the "young man" for potential business even this early in the day. She switched her attention to Malcolm and smiled. "Tumble for a pie?"

Malcolm just shook his head, leaving the girl hurling curses at them.

Margo was fascinated and repulsed at the same time. She felt as though she'd stepped into a living play whose author had no real ending in mind. *Study your part, study the background.* That was what Kit and Malcolm had brought her here to learn.

"With so many women in the business," Margo asked slowly, trying hard to understand, "isn't competition fierce?"

"Ye-esss . . . in a manner of speaking. Officially, you understand, sex was considered extremely bad for one's health. Led to a breakdown of one's physical constitution and mental faculties. Privately, our straight-laced Victorian gentleman considered sex his natural right—and any woman born lower than his station was fair game. London had several million souls, recall, not to mention seafaring crews. Remind yourself to look up an eleven-volume personal memoir called *My Secret Life* when we return to the station library. It's available on computer now. You'll find it . . . revealing of Victorian social attitudes."

"What happens to all these women? When they're too old or ill to work?"

"Some go to the Magdalen for help."

"Magdalen?"

"South of the Thames," Malcolm murmured as they trundled their cart along, "you will find four kinds of 'charity' institutions, if one can call them that. Bedlam—Bethlehem Hospital—is for mental patients. Old Bridewell was originally a school to train apprentices, but it turned into a brutal prison. Eventually a new school was attached to the prison grounds to house legitimate apprentices. Bridewell apprentices are notorious delinquents, the terror of the city. Then there are protected girls in the purple uniforms of the Lambeth Asylum for Female Orphans, and of course the grey of the Magdalen Hospital for seduced girls and prostitutes. A number of the girls rescued by Magdalen go mad anyway from incurable syphilis."

Margo shuddered. She'd grown up taking medical miracles for granted. How long did it take the "social disease" to deteriorate a person's brain into insanity? While she tried to take it all in, they sold eels and pies and moved steadily westward. Then, astonishing her with the abruptness of the transition, the dome of St. Paul's Cathedral loomed up over the dreary skyline. They found themselves abruptly in the heart of the bright, sunlit "City" where London's Lord Mayor ruled from Mansion House. Margo gaped at the wealthy carriages which jostled for space on the narrow streets.

"It's amazing," she said, staring back the way they'd come. "I can hardly believe the change."

"Yes. It is startling, isn't it?"

The respite didn't last long, though. Past Lincoln Inn Fields, they plunged once more into a realm of dark, sagging rooflines which overhung one another. The bright sunlight they'd left behind seemed centuries as well as miles away.

"How can they live and work so close to this misery and not *care?*"

Malcolm gave her a long, penetrating look. "They haven't wanted to see it. An effort is eventually made, particularly after Red Jack ensures that conditions in Whitechapel are widely reported upon. And the Salvation Army got its start here a few years ago, so there is some—" He broke off and swore under his breath. "Damn, I hadn't noticed we'd left Charing Cross Road. Heads up, now. We've wandered into St. Giles."

They'd entered a "traffic circle" marked "Seven Dials" but there was no traffic, pedestrian or otherwise. At the center of the circle stood a dilapidated clock tower with seven faces. Running outward from the tower like mangled spokes from a wheel were seven sunless alleyways and wretched, filthy courtyards. They vanished into a slum that made Whitechapel seem luxurious. A noxious vapor rose from the houses, hanging like fog over sagging rooftops. Broken gin bottles littered the filthy ground. Under layers of filth and dirty ice might have been paved streets.

"Malcolm . . ." She felt as though the blank windows—many of them without glass—were staring at her like malicious eyes.

"These seven streets are the most dangerous place in all of London. Watch our backs until we're well out of here."

From out of the gloom in the dank alleyways, rough men in tattered clothing watched through narrowed eyes. Margo kept a sharp lookout and wished they could break into a run. *You'll cope with this on your own as a scout. This is the career you asked Kit Carson to give you.*

At the moment, Margo would almost have traded this for another beating at her father's hands.

Almost.

Then she saw furtive movement in the shadows, the glint of steel—

The man who grabbed her from behind laid a straight razor at her throat. She froze, a scream dying in her throat. Two other toughs materialized in front of Malcolm. Margo realized with a shock, *They're younger than I am!*

The feel of sharp steel at her throat left her trembling. Margo's attacker tightened his arm around her waist. "Look it, 'ee don' even shave yet." The boy's breath was foul. " 'ow bouts I teach 'im?"

The other boys grinned. Their straight razors glinted evilly. Malcolm had gone very still, trapped between them.

" 'and over the tike, mate, an' mibey we let 'im shave 'is own self?"

While Margo tried to sort out what, exactly, he'd demanded, Malcolm reached for the money pouch at his waist.

"Quick, now," the boldest said. He dropped his gaze from Margo to watch Malcolm pluck at his purse strings.

Margo moved instantly. She grabbed her assailant's wrist, twisting toward him as she shoved the wicked straight razor away from her throat—then grabbed a handful of his crotch and *crushed.*

The boy screamed. She continued the turn, dragging his arm up behind him, then kicked the back of his knee. He went down with a gurgling sound and writhed on the ground, holding himself.

She whirled—Malcolm had gone absolutely *white.* "You little *idiot—*"

Before either of the other boys could strike, an enormous bull of a man stepped out from the alleyway and shoved them aside.

"You 'urt me boy," he said, staring at Margo. The bludgeon he held was as thick as Margo's thigh. His shoulders were twice the size of Malcolm's. He wore a thick woolen coat that covered him almost to the knees. Rough work pants and low, broken shoes completed the picture of the quintessential murderous lout. He grinned at Margo. "First I cracks your skull." He licked dirty lips. "Then me nephews cuts up wot's left."

Margo was suddenly conscious of other grimy faces in the shadows, watching with inhuman detachment. Malcolm swore and backed away from the trio, turning so they couldn't see him draw his revolver from concealment. The moose in the center hefted his cudgel. He charged so fast, Margo didn't even have time to scream.

Malcolm fired three shots and dove to one side. One of the shots hit the man's right ankle. The would-be killer screamed, lurched, and sprawled into the filth. The teenagers ran clattering down an alley. Malcolm whipped around like a cat and grabbed Margo's wrist, dragging her in the opposite direction. They dashed the length of a filthy, stinking alleyway and emerged into St. Giles-in-the-Field. Malcolm dodged into a rank, overgrown churchyard and dragged her behind a crumbling gravestone, then pressed a hard hand over her mouth. They waited, hearts thudding, but Margo heard no immediate sound of pursuit.

"Reload this," Malcolm said brusquely, thrusting his pistol and the tin from his pocket into her hands. He crept out of the graveyard and eased his way to the edge of the churchyard, peering back the way they'd come.

Margo stared stupidly at the gun. The tin was heavy. It rattled. She had no idea how to reload this revolver. It wasn't anything like the revolvers Ann Mulhaney had taught her to shoot. She was still staring idiotically at it when Malcolm returned.

He took the pistol—then swore in language she hadn't known he could use. "You didn't reload!"

Tears prickled behind her eyes. "I—"

"First you pull a stupid stunt like fighting that street tough—"

"But he was robbing us!"

Malcolm's pallor turned to marble coldness. "*I was going to give him the goddamned money!* My God, it's just a few pence! You nearly got us both killed—and I 'ad to risk shooting that lout—"

"You didn't even shoot to kill!"

If she'd used that tone with her father, he'd have blacked half her face. Malcolm didn't hit her. Instead, his voice went as icy as the filthy stone against which she huddled.

"We are not at liberty to shoot whomever we please. Getting out of a fatal jam without killing *anyone* is a time scout's job. If the Britannia Gate opened up right now and Kit stepped through, I'd tell him to send you packing back to whatever miserable little town you came from. Give me the goddamned bullets."

She handed over the tin. Her hand shook. Malcolm jerked the cord loose, opened the sliding lid, and dumped three rounds into her hand.

"You're going to reload this gun right now. Pull up on that T-shaped handle."

It blurred through hot tears, but she jerked up on it. The whole top of the revolver swung forward and down, revealing the back of the cylinder. Three empty cases and the two unfired rounds popped up slightly. Her fingers shook but she pulled out the spent cases and reloaded the empty chambers. Then she closed the gun up again.

"You were supposed to know how to do this. Skip your lessons again and . . ."

He left the threat hanging. He'd already destroyed any hope she'd ever entertained of becoming a scout. Her whole chest ached with the need to sob. But she held it all inside, except for the hot, miserable tears she could not quite contain.

Malcolm checked the alleyway again, leaving her to huddle against the wretched gravestone. She slid down into the weeds and fought the tightness in her throat. *I won't give up. I won't. It isn't fair!* She'd only done what Sven Bailey had taught her. Hadn't she? *Know when to quit,* Kit had told her. I *won't quit! Not when I've come so far!* Somehow, she'd find a way to get back into Malcolm's good graces. She *had* to. She'd sooner commit suicide than go back to Minnesota a failure.

During the endless walk up through Spitalfields, Margo listened with everything in her, ruthlessly shoving aside humiliation and terror for the more immediate need to *learn.* She picked up slang, names for items she'd never seen before, tidbits of news and gossip that led her to several startling conclusions about the state of the world in 1888.

"Malcolm?" Her voice quavered only a little.

"Yes?" *His* voice was still icy.

"This isn't an ordinary slum, is it? Spitalfields, I mean. It isn't like Whitechapel or St. Giles."

He glanced back. Some of the chill in his eyes thawed into surprise. "Why do you ask?"

She bit her lower lip, then nodded toward women who spoke in a language that wasn't English, toward men who dressed in dark coats, wore their beards long, and looked at the world through eyes which had seen too much hardship. "These people look and sound like refugees. Who are they?"

Malcolm actually halted. Absently he blew against his fingers to warm them while giving Margo an appraising stare.

"Well, I'll be suckered. . . ." he said softly.

She waited, wondering if she'd get a reprieve.

"Who do you think they are?" He'd given her a challenge.

She studied the older women, who wore shawls over their hair, watched the younger girls with shining black tresses and shy smiles, the old men with wide-brimmed black hats and hand-woven, fringed vests. The younger people looked hopeful, busy. The older ones seemed uncertain and afraid, suspicious of her and of Malcolm. The language sounded like German, sort of. Then the whole picture clicked.

Yiddish.

"They're Jewish refugees," she said slowly. "But from what? Hitler . . . has he even been born yet?"

"Hitler was not the first madman to order pogroms against the Jewish communities of Europe. Just the most sweepingly brutal. Stalin was almost as bad, of course. The bloody pogroms going on all across Europe started about eight years ago, in 1880. Jews are being murdered, driven out of their homes, out of their own countries."

"Then . . . what went on during World War II was a . . . a sort of continuation of this? Only much worse? I never realized that." Margo looked up and down the street, where kosher slaughterhouses and butcher shops fought for space with tailors' establishments and bakeshops. In that moment, echoing down empty places in her mind she hadn't even known existed, Margo saw connections, running forward into the future from this moment and backward from it. In an instant, her narrow Minnesota universe expanded with dizzying explosiveness into an infinitely larger place with more intricately bound pieces of the human puzzle to try and understand than she had ever thought possible.

She understood, in a flash, why Malcolm Moore was willing to endure grueling poverty and the humiliation of a freelance guide's life just to step through one more gate.

He wanted to *understand.*

Margo gazed down those infinite corridors in her mind, filled with endless blank gaps, and knew that she had to fill them in—or at least as many of them as she could before she died trying.

When she came up for air, Malcolm was staring at her in the oddest fashion, as though she'd just suffered a stroke and hadn't yet found the wit to fall down. The only thing she could think to say was, "They must have been . . . I can't even imagine what they must have thought when Hitler started bombing London."

Something far back in his eyes changed, in response to what must have been visible in her own. For a moment, Margo knew he understood exactly what was shining inside her. Sudden, unexpected tears filled his eyes. He turned aside and blew out his breath and cleared his throat. A steaming vapor cloud dissipated in the freezing February air.

"It's half my own fault," he mumbled, "if not more. You were already badly upset and I should have made certain you knew how to operate a top-break revolver before we even set foot through the gate. It's just there's so much to remember, sometimes even experienced guides forget little things like checking up on what your partner knows." A crook of his lips and an embarrassed flush surprised her. "And, well, I'm not really used to *having* a partner along."

Margo found it suddenly impossible to swallow properly. "I'm starting to understand, Malcolm. Really, I am. I'm studying every minute we're here. I'm trying to learn *how* to learn, not just *what* to learn."

Malcolm touched her chin. "That's a good beginning, Margo. We'll give it another go, shall we?"

Her eyes filled in turn. Scouting was about so much more than just adventure and money, that for the first time, Margo wasn't sure she had what it took. She dashed knuckles across her eyes and sniffed hugely. "Thanks, Malcolm. Ever so."

He tousled her short hair. "Well spoken, young Smythe. It's barely gone noon. You have a good stretch of London left to study." His grin took any possible sting out of the words.

Wordlessly, Margo set herself the task of trying to understand what she saw around her, rather than just staring at it like a sun-struck tourist.

Margo studied hard for the duration of their stay. She learned—slowly and painfully—but she learned, nonetheless. Malcolm grilled her endlessly in the evenings with help from John, who was amassing quite a wealth of notes for his own research. Margo recorded observations in her personal log each evening, while they were still fresh in her mind. Even she was surprised by the detail she could recall when she put out the effort.

Then Malcolm told her he'd been in touch with some friends who were in town for the Season. An invitation for dinner had been received and duly accepted. She panicked. "What should I do? What should I *say?*"

"As little as possible," Malcolm said drily.

She managed a smile. *Don't screw this up,* was the message, loud and clear. Of course, a scout wouldn't have to worry about things like formal social evenings with the British peerage very often. . . . She dreaded returning to the book work she knew would be waiting for her on the time terminal. Learning by *doing* was so much more interesting. But she clearly needed some of that tedious cultural and historical reading. She held back a shudder. Margo had learned more about Victorian England in three days than she would have in three *years* cooped up in some stuffy classroom.

"Well," she said philosophically, "everyone keeps telling me charity girls are supposed to be demure and silent. I can always blush and stammer out something silly and let you rescue me."

"That's one solution. In this case, actually not a bad one, since socially you are not yet out. Have you been reading the newspapers as I suggested?"

"They're weird."

"And the magazines?"

"No photographs. Just those dull black-and-white etchings."

"You're supposed to be reading the articles," he said, brows twitching down in exasperation.

"Well, I can't make sense of half of them."

"Ah," was all the comment he made.

"Yeah, yeah, I know. I have a lot to learn."

"Yes," he said, looking down that extremely British nose of his, "you do."

"Well, you don't have to rub it in."

"Mmm, yes, I think I do. We very nearly died in St. Giles and . . . Well, the less said about your first riding lesson, the better. An unprepared scout has a very short career."

If he was aware of the pun, he wasn't smiling.

Margo sighed. "Okay. I'm trying. Really, I am."

"I know. Now, about dinner. Let me explain cutlery. . . ."

Margo's last three days in London were as glorious as the first four had been miserable and terrifying. She mastered the knack of fluttering her eyelashes and deferring questions with naive requests of her own.

"Oh, but I'm so dull, you don't want to hear about an orphan. Please, tell me about riding to hounds. I don't understand anything about it and it seems so exciting. . . ."

In her school-girl mob cap and pinafore, she wasn't taken seriously by anyone. Even the ladies thought she was adorable.

"Mr. Moore, what an absolutely delightful child. Your ward is a charm."

"You really must bring her out in a year or two."

"Oh, no, not back to that dreadful tropical backwater, surely?"

And so the evening went, in a wonderful haze of wine, sparkling conversation, and more food than she could possibly eat, course after course of it, with delicate little desserts between. She floated to bed that night and dreamed of long formal gowns, bright laughter, and an endless round of parties and dinners with Malcolm at her side. . . .

The next day they went riding again, this time in Hyde Park, with Margo sidesaddle in a long riding habit and Malcolm in immaculate morning attire. Some of the women they'd seen last night at dinner smiled and greeted Malcolm, then smiled at her. Margo returned the greetings with what she hoped was a properly humble air, but inside she was bubbling.

Hyde Park was glorious in the early morning sunlight, so glorious she could almost forget the horror of disease, squalor, and violent death such a short distance east. Because she was not yet "out" socially, none of the gentlemen they had dined with noticed her, but that was all right. It meant Margo had been accepted as a temporal native. She'd passed a difficult test with flying colors, as difficult in its way as that lethal little confrontation in St. Giles.

They spent the afternoon window shopping beneath the glass roof of the Royal Arcade on Old Bond Street, which linked the fashionable Brown Hotel to Bond. John trailed along as chaperon. Margo gawked through the windows into Bretell's at #12 where Queen Victoria herself bestowed her considerable patronage. Margo left the Arcade utterly dazzled.

On their final day, Malcolm took her by train down to Brighton, where they wandered along chilly streets and Malcolm pointed out the myriad differences between the city of 1888 and the city where his family had been caught in the great flood of 1998. They paused within sight of the waterfront. Malcolm gazed out at the leaden spray crashing against the shingle and went utterly silent. Margo found she couldn't bear the look in his eyes. She summoned her nerve and took his gloved hand in hers. He glanced down, eyes widening in surprise, then he swallowed hard.

"Thank you, Miss Smythe. I—"

He couldn't continue.

Margo found herself moving on instinct. She guided him down the street to a warm inn and selected a seat in the corner. When the innkeeper bustled over, she smiled and said, "Stout, please, for my guardian and might I have a cup of hot tea?"

"Surely, miss. Is there anything else I can get for the gentleman? He seems a mite poorly."

Malcolm was visibly pulling himself together. "Forgive me, innkeep," he rubbed the bridge of his nose with a gloved hand, "but I lost a dear brother not far from here. Drowned in the sea. I . . . hadn't been back to Brighton since, you see."

The innkeeper shook his head mournfully and hurried away to bring the dark beer and a steaming cup of tea. Margo sipped in silence while Malcolm regained his composure.

"I shouldn't have come back," he said quietly.

"Don't the tourists come here on holiday?"

"Not often in February," he smiled wanly. "If one of my guests desires a holiday at the seaside, I generally recommend the Isle of Wight or even Man. I've avoided Brighton. Particularly during February."

The orbital blowup, Margo knew, had occurred in February, catching Atlantic coastlines in the middle of the night. The loss of life had been devastating even in the relatively sheltered English Channel.

Malcolm sipped his dark stout again. "You did very well just now," he murmured. "I'm not accustomed to being rescued by someone I'm guiding. You kept me from considerable embarrassment out there. This," he lifted the glass in a tiny salute and gestured at the inn, "was just what I needed: the shock of staying in persona to wake me up and the stout to deaden the hurt. Thank you."

"I—It just seemed the right thing to do."

A faint smile creased wan cheeks. "You've a good instinct, then. That's important. More so than you might guess." He drained the last of the stout, then took out his pocket watch. "If we're to make that return train, we'd best be leaving."

When Malcolm squeezed her gloved hand, Margo felt as though she were flying.

By the time the scheduled re-opening of the Britannia Gate forced them to leave London, Margo knew she'd found what she wanted to do for the rest of her life. *I've done it; I've gone through a whole week down time, and I've come out just fine.* She had a lot to learn yet, of course—she'd endured humiliation and learned valuable lessons—but now that she'd done it, she knew this was exactly what she'd wanted all along.

You'll see, she promised an unshaven face in her memory, *you'll see, damn you. I'll do it. This was harder than anything you ever did to me, but I did it. And I'll do it again. Just you wait. I'll* prove *it to you.*

Margo had found where she belonged. All that remained now was to convince Kit Carson. And Malcolm Moore. Margo cast a last, longing glance at the gaslit windows of the Time Tours gatehouse, then stepped boldly through onto the grated platform in La-La Land.

It felt like she'd come home at last.

Chapter 11

"There are," Sven Bailey told her patiently, "three basic grips in knife fighting." He demonstrated. 'The hammer grip is the way most people pick up a knife, even kitchen carving and paring knives. It's a good, solid grip."

Margo practiced on the slim knife he handed her.

"Then comes the fencing grip." He shifted the knife in his hand as though he were holding an envelope out to someone else. His thumb rested on the top of the grip. 'This is a deadly grip in the hands of a trained knife fighter, very difficult to defend against. Learn to use it."

Margo copied the hold on her own knife. It felt odd.

"Third," Sven shifted his blade again, "we have the ice-pick grip." He now held the knife upside down, so that the blade lay flat against the length of his forearm.

"That looks silly," Margo commented. It felt silly, too.

Sven lifted his forearm toward her. "Would you care to hit my arm with that sharp edge in the way?"

"Well, no."

"Right. It guards your arm somewhat. Moreover," he moved with lightning speed, "you can come across your body with a wicked slash and follow up with a powerful stab."

The knifepoint stopped half an inch from Margo's breastbone. She gulped. "Oh."

"Limited, but useful. You'll master all three grips and the moves useful or unique to them."

"All right. Where do we begin?"

"With the types of knife blades and what each is useful for." He retrieved the practice knife he'd loaned her, then rummaged in a case he'd brought out to the practice floor. Sven laid out half a dozen knives, all carefully sheathed.

"All right. There are two very basic blade shapes, with multiple variations. This," he drew a ten-inch, thick-bladed knife, "is a Bowie. The spine is thick for strength. This whole side has been cut away, so the knife isn't symmetrical. The curved upper edge is called a false edge. It's often sharpened, but not always. Sometimes these blades have 'saw teeth' added. Mostly saw teeth are a sales gimmick, based on bad twentieth-century movies. The teeth are too large to be any good for sawing anything. Avoid them. They can get caught on ribs, then you're stuck with no knife."

"No saw teeth," Margo repeated.

'The Bowie is an excellent *survival* knife. It's strong enough to use for camp chores like cutting small branches for firewood if you don't have a hand axe. The blades are thick enough to use as a pry bar without too much risk of snapping the tip off. Unfortunately, it has its drawbacks: sheer size, lack of a second sharp edge all the way back to the guard, and, worst of all, it's anachronistic as hell in most places or times you'd end up. But you'll learn to use one because we're being thorough."

"Okay."

'This," he unsheathed a beautiful, perfectly symmetrical blade some eight inches in length, "is a leaf-point or spear-point dagger. The shape is exactly the same as ancient spearpoints, even the Roman short sword, the *gladius.* Unlike the *gladius,* it's small enough and sharp enough along both edges to make a nearly perfect fighting knife. It'll slash the hell out of anything you cut with it. And it's thin enough and symmetrical enough to make a beautiful stabbing point, although the point isn't strong and it may snap off. A bodkin or stiletto," he drew out a thing like a knitting needle or an ice pick with slim grips, "is a perfect stabbing weapon, designed to penetrate the links of chain-mail armor. Its use is limited, however, to stabbing."

He put away the blades he'd shown her so far.

"Now, something that's neither Bowie nor leaf point is the world-famous Randall #1." He slipped a glittering ten-inch blade from a worn sheathe. "Some people will tell you it's a modified Bowie. Bo Randall, who invented it back before World War II, pointed out rightly that the shape of this second edge is nothing at all like a Bowie. It's straight, not curved. He didn't design it as a Bowie and he took great exception to having his knife classified as a Bowie. This is one of the best all-around fighting knives ever made. Again, the problem you have is the anachronistic shape for most of history."

Margo sighed. "Why am I learning to use knives I won't carry?"

"Because I'm thorough and careful. Don't argue."

"What are these others?"

'This is a skinning knife." It was a relatively flat, wide blade with a thin spine, and very delicate compared to the fighting knives. "It's specialized for skinning an animal. This," the next blade was curved, thick, and shaped nothing like any of the others, "is a hunting knife. Filleting knives," he held up yet another, "are similar to skinners and completely useless for our purposes. Now, this odd-shaped little jewel is a Ghurka knife."

It was a strange, zig-zag shape, with an ornate hilt.

"This," he drew a crescent-moon sword blade, "is called a scimitar. You'll learn to use them, but the chances of your running across them are fairly slim because of relatively limited geographical distribution. Now, this Tanto," he drew a blade shaped something like an Exact-O knife, "was designed to penetrate enamel-style armor in the Orient. It has the same tip shape as some Asian fishing knives. Again, limited usefulness as a fighting knife, but we'll work with it because you may run across one if you end up in the Western Pacific Rim. Japanese samurai swords and halberds had the same blade shape, just longer and heavier. Now, last but not least is this little jewel."

The final knife was a T-handled thing that looked like a corkscrew, but the blade was shaped exactly like the spear-point dagger—except that the whole blade was only three inches long and the inch closest to the handle was little more than a dull-edged, narrow rectangular bar.

"What's that thing?" Margo laughed.

"A push dagger. Far too many instructors ignore them. That's stupid. The push dagger," he demonstrated the hold, with the T-handle clenched in the fist and the short blade extending beyond the knuckles, "is a very deadly weapon. It's next to impossible to dislodge it from your hand. You can slash," he demonstrated rapidly, "or stab with a simple punch, or," he opened his hand, seized her wrist, and without letting go of the knife, said, "you can grab an opponent without cutting them. The push dagger gives you some *nice* options."

Margo widened her eyes and stared at her wrist. "Good God."

Sven Bailey grinned wickedly and let her go. "Yeah. Isn't it great?"

Margo laughed. "I'm just thinking what a karate punch would be like with that thing in your fist."

"Exactly. You," he pointed with the tip of the push dagger, "will learn to use this very well. It's particularly suited to women who don't have much experience knife fighting—but then, that won't apply to you, will it?"

Margo chuckled ruefully. "Not by the time you're done with me."

"Right. Now, as to the tactics of knife fighting, forget *everything* you've ever seen in any movie. Stupid doesn't begin to cover it. Movie knife fighting—like movie gun fighting or fist fighting—will get you killed. Knife fights are dirty, dangerous affairs carried on by people who want to cut your guts open and spill them in the mud. Literally. Unless you're very careful and very good, you'll bleed to death within seconds of losing a knife fight. The idea," he smiled grimly, "is to avoid fighting in the first place. But if you can't, you make damn sure it's the bastard who attacks you who bleeds to death, not you. Knife fighting is, encounter for encounter, far deadlier than any gunfight. If a bad guy shoots you, chances are extremely good you'll live through it."

"What? Are you pulling my leg?" Margo demanded, thinking of a lifetime worth of newspaper, magazine, and television news articles.

"Unless it's a sawed-off shotgun at close range, or the shot hits a vital organ, chances are you'll live given relatively decent medical care. But if you're cut up in a knife fight, shock and blood loss will loll you quick. And I mean *quick.* In seconds, if you're hit in the right places. One good slash," he traced a finger across her lower arm, "will sever muscles to the bone, cut arteries, veins, and may even fracture bone itself. If you're hit across the femoral, the jugular, or the carotids, you're dead. Period. Same with abdominal or chest wounds, most times. You'll bleed out or die of shock before you can get help."

Margo swallowed. "Wonderful. What happens if some guy jumps me by surprise?"

Sven held her regard steadily. "Easy. You never *let* anyone jump you by surprise."

He wasn't kidding.

"Pay attention to your surroundings *constantly.* What's potentially hiding in the shadows of that bush? Behind that tree, around that corner, in that doorway? Is the man behind me just strolling along for a walk or following me? What about the guy lounging around on the steps up ahead? *Pay attention.* Somebody takes you by surprise, you've already lost. Remember that exercise I had you practice before you went tripping off to London. Notice everyone else before they notice you."

Margo flashed back to the attack in St. Giles. If she hadn't been watching so carefully. . . . "All right, point taken."

"Your homework on alertness is simple but effective. You've tried it once, for a day. Now we get serious about it. For the next week, keep track of everyone you encounter. Strangers, people you know, people who know you. As before, keep a count of how many times they notice you before you notice them, and vice versa. Every time someone sees you and reacts before you do is a potentially lethal encounter that you won't walk away from."

"Isn't that a little paranoid?"

Sven shook his head. "This is standard training for self-defense on urban streets, never mind military situations. Your job as scout combines features of both. Learn to notice everything around you. Alertness is half the fight. Being prepared to act on an instant's notice is the other half. No moments of doubt, hesitation, self-questioning. Go for a crippling blow whenever you can, but if it comes down to a lethal fight and you're not prepared to kill the other bastard to stay alive. . . .well, then, you're in the wrong job, kid."

Margo chewed her lip. Would she be able to pull a trigger? Or cut someone's throat? Martial arts was one thing, with its focus on getting the hell out with minimal damage; knifing or shooting someone was something else. Clearly, she had some soul searching to do.

"Problems?" Sven asked quietly.

That question deserved an honest answer. "Maybe. I don't know. I survived St. Giles, but it shook me up. I need to do some heavy thinking tonight."

Sven nodded. "Good. That's critical. Unless you're prepared to use deadly force, and I mean prepared here," he tapped her head, "and here," he tapped her chest, "you *won't* use it when the flag drops on a lethal encounter. You'll be the one carried home. Think it out. Meanwhile, you might as well start learning technique."

Kit finished up at the Neo Edo's office and checked his watch. Time for Margo's next firearms lesson. After the hair-raising conversation he'd shared with Malcolm, Kit intended to watch every single one of Margo's shooting lessons. He slipped on a pair of shoes at the door and headed out to the Commons, then stopped at a little "open-air" stand for a quick lunch.

"Hi, Kit," Keiko smiled. "What'll it be?"

He pored over the selection of soups, sniffed the yaldtori appreciatively, and glanced over at the large fish tank where customers could make their sushi choices—live fish being the best way to ensure freshness in a setting like a time terminal. The tank was five feet deep and eight feet long, filled with salt water and swimming sushi delicacies.

"That young yellowtail," Kit pointed to the fish he wanted, "looks good."

"Hail."

Keiko turned to pick up the dip net—and shrieked.

A leather-winged shape zipped past, skimmed the top of the tank, then flapped off with Kit's lunch. The Japanese didn't precisely have the same corrosive vocabulary available to English speakers, but Keiko had no shortage of colorful curses to heap on the heads of fish thieves and other assorted miscreants.

"They eat all my profits!" she stormed, shaking a fist at the pterodactyl. It had perched in the girders high overhead, busily gulping the profit in question.

"I, uh, think I'll try the yaldtori," Kit hastily amended, trying to suppress a grin. "Talk to Bull Morgan about the problem."

"I have." Keiko said sourly as he fixed Kits' lunch. "He says, let them eat my fish. He will pay me. This does not make my customers happy when they steal my fish and leave messes!"

There was no doubt about the messes. Paper parasols—particularly those with hideous monster faces painted on top—had become all the rage in La-La Land. Kit stole a glance over his shoulder at the pterodactyls and the primitive birds busy swooping and diving on La-La Land's ornamental fish ponds, sidewalk cafes, and open-air food stands and grinned. Half the people in sight carried open parasols.

Across the nearest pond a very elderly Japanese man missing a couple of fingertips (and probably tattooed over his entire body) cursed at one of the *Ichthyornises* when it dove after a goldfish he'd been admiring, not only swallowing it in two gulps but splashing his suit in the process of flapping away again. Its feathers were so waterlogged, the primitive, short-tailed bird made it only as far as the top of a nearby shrub, where it spread wings to dry in the manner of cormorants or anhingas. The singular difference was a beak filled with extremely sharp teeth. That tooth-filled beak—and an angry hiss—changed the elderly gentleman's mind when he advanced, evidently intent on wringing its neck. His subsequent retreat was calculated to look thoughtful and planned. Kit managed not to laugh. He'd never seen a yakuza thug back down from a bird. Kit felt like cheering.

"Thanks," he said when Keiko handed him a plate filled with rice and barbecued chicken chunks on little wooden skewers. "Mmm . . ."

He strolled over to a seat and hurried through his lunch while tourists snapped photos of the *Ichthyornis* drying its wings. Sue Fritchey was sweating it out until Primary cycled again, waiting for a message from colleagues up time about La-La Land's newest residents. The giant pterosaur was supposedly recovering just fine from its adventure and was eating all the fish they could toss into its enormous beak. They'd urgently need a resupply of fish by the time Primary cycled, what with a thirty-foot fish eater and two separate flocks of smaller ones to keep happy.

Bull had given standing orders that station personnel were to secure fish from any down-time gate that opened. What would happen if they couldn't get permission to ship the beasts to an up-time research facility . . . ?

Kit had visions of shopkeepers like Keiko buying shotguns.

Knowing Bull, he'd order an enormous fish tank constructed somewhere in the Commons and stock it with several thousand fish, then sell tickets to the feeding shows and lectures. Kit grinned. Sounded like a good subject for a quiet bet or two.

He finished his lunch and headed downstairs to the weapons ranges. Margo was just getting started with Ann when she glanced up. She flushed when she saw him.

"Hi," he smiled, trying to sound friendly.

"Hi." Her closed expression said, "I resent you checking up on me."

Well, that was exactly what he was doing and he had no intention of backing down.

"Hi, Kit," Ann said with a friendly nod. "Have a seat."

"Thanks." He settled on one of the benches at the back of the range and slipped in foam hearing protectors.

Ann started Margo off with a relatively "modern" top-break revolver, double-action, very similar to the one Malcolm said she'd been unable to use in London. Margo donned eye- and hearing-protection equipment. Ann did the same and ran out a target, then said, "Whenever you're ready."

Margo took her time and placed five of the six on the paper—but nowhere near the center.

"Front sight," Ann said patiently. "Concentrate on the front sight."

Margo opened the action and dumped out the spent brass. "I thought the whole sight picture was important."

"It is, but the front sight is critical. As long as the front sight is placed properly, your rear sight can be slightly off and you'll still hit near what you're shooting. But let that front sight drift off, and it won't matter how perfectly your rear sight is aligned, either with the target or with the front sight. You'll miss, clean."

Margo tried again. She was still flinching, but the shots were a little closer together. "All right, unload the brass and hand me the pistol."

"Why?" Margo asked curiously. Ann took the pistol—offered, Kit noticed approvingly, in the proper manner: action open, muzzle down.

"You've developed a whopping flinch. So we'll do a ball-and-dummy drill. I'll load the pistol for you."

Ann turned away, blocking the gun from Margo's immediate view, then handed it back. "All right. Let's see how bad that flinch is."

Margo fired the first round with a solid bang. The second time, the pistol only went click—and the barrel jerked about an inch anyway.

"Oh!" Margo gasped. "I did that, didn't I?"

"Yes. You're anticipating the noise and the recoil. This drill will help you learn to pull through smoothly without flinching, because you'll never know which chamber might be loaded or empty."

Ann put her through a solid twenty minutes of ball-and-dummy drills. By the end, Margo had developed a much smoother trigger pull and her group size shrank considerably.

"Very good." Ann pulled in the target and ran out a new one. "Now, concentrate on that front sight."

Another fifteen minutes, and the spread of Margo's shots was down to six inches at six yards. Not exactly impressive, but an improvement. Ann drilled her on front sight for another ten minutes, then let her take a short break. Margo pulled off the protective eyeglasses and earmuffs and ruffled her hair. Kit regretted the necessity to dye it. She looked like an abandoned waif with pale skin and dark hair, but it was far safer for her.

The discouragement in her eyes needed dispelling, though.

"You're doing well," Kit said when she glanced his way.

Margo flushed again, but from pleasure this time. "I'm working hard on it."

Kit nodded. "You keep practicing, you'll get much better. Maybe

Malcolm will even win that bet."

Margo's whole face went scarlet. "You heard about that."

Kit laughed. "Margo, everyone in La-La Land heard about it."

"That'll teach me to make bets," she said ruefully.

"All right," Ann said, coming back with another case, "back to work. Now we take a step backwards in time. Muzzle-loading black-powder firearms were more common far longer than metallic-cartridge, breech-loading guns. Metallic cartridges didn't become common until the 1870s. The little, low-powered rim fire and pin-fire cartridges date from the decade before the American Civil War, but they were nowhere nearly as common as percussion-fired, muzzle-loading black-powder guns. Flintlock and matchlock guns in particular had a longer period of use than cartridge guns. You'll need to know how to handle these firearms and they're a bit more complicated to use."

Margo gave Ann a brave smile. "All right. Show me."

"We'll start with a little demonstration."

Ann shook out a thin line of various types of powders: smokeless rifle powders, smokeless pistol powders, then black powder. "Modern, smokeless powders are not explosive. They burn. They don't explode. The priming compound in the base of the cartridge case *is* a chemical explosive, but it's a tiny, tiny amount of it. All the primer does is create the spark of flame needed to start the powder burning. This is modern pistol powder and this is modern rifle powder. Now this," Ann pointed, "is *black* powder. Unlike modern powders, it *is* explosive. It burns far, far faster and is much more dangerous, particularly under compression. Watch."

She lit a long match and touched it to the end of the line of powders. The modern rifle powder flared and burned slowly, the pistol powder burned a good bit faster—then the black powder flashed wildly, gone in a split second.

"Good God!"

"Yes. That's to teach you to respect black powder. Be careful when handling it, especially when you're reloading black-powder weapons. A mistake can injure, potentially even kill you."

"Great."

Ann smiled. "*Just* keep your wits about you and practice. Now, let's start with the components of ammunition for black-powder weapons. In most historical arms, there was no cartridge case, just loose powder, a projectile called a 'ball' and a bit of cloth called a patch, which is greased to help you push the ball down the barrel and to help prevent fouling. During the American Civil War era, a bullet called the minie ball did away with the need for a patch, but it never caught on well with hunters and sportsmen."

Margo said, "Okay, ball and powder and patch. Show me." Ann demonstrated the whole loading process. "There are two important things to remember about black-powder firearms. One, be sure the ball is seated all the way to the bottom. Check the length of the ramrod," she showed Margo how, "to be sure you haven't left a gap at the bottom between the back of the barrel and the ball."

"Okay. But why's that important?"

"Remember what I said about thousands of pounds per square inch of pressure inside the cartridge cases of modern guns when smokeless powder begins to burn? Well, black powder doesn't burn, it explodes. If you leave a gap here," she pointed to the bottom end of the barrel, "what you've done, essentially, is build a miniature bomb."

Margo's eyes widened. "Oh."

"Yes. The gun barrel can blow up in your face. The other thing to remember is that sparks can still be smoldering inside the barrel. There isn't any way to get into this end of it. It's all closed up and solid, no breech to open, so you can't just check it. If you try to dump more powder into a hot barrel without swabbing it out first with a wet swab, you could ignite the powder you're pouring in—which could, in turn, set off the powder from the container you're pouring from. That's why you should always load from a measurer that holds just enough powder for one shot. Of course, under battle conditions, you may not have time to swab out the barrel," Ann said with a grin.

Margo gulped and looked massively uncertain. Ann smiled. "Not to worry. If you hope to use firearms through most of their historical existence, you'll need to master these next lessons, but black-powder firearms aren't dangerous so long as you learn what you're doing and pay attention while you're doing it. Power tools in untrained hands are just as dangerous, if not more so. Any questions before we get started?"

Margo glanced back toward Kit, chewed her lower lip, then shook her head. "No. Just show me what I'm supposed to do."

Ann started her on a simple replica Colt 1860 Army black-powder revolver, showing her how to load, prime with percussion caps, and fire six shots. Reloading took another entire two minutes. After Margo mastered the concepts involved, she asked cheerfully, "What's next? I know about flintlocks."

"Very good. And here is a beautiful Kentucky rifle to practice with."

"Ooh! Daniel Boone and settlers on the Cumberland Gap trail and . . ."

Kit grinned. His granddaughter's romantic notions had finally landed her with a gun she loved. She even did well with it. Malcolm just might win that bet, after all. After the flintlock, Ann took her on to more esoteric types like wheel-locks and even matchlocks.

"How in the world did people keep these things burning?" Margo demanded with a half-hearted laugh the second time her slow-smoldering match went out. "Am I doing something wrong? Or is it really that hard?"

Ann chuckled. "During battles, they'd keep the matches swinging in circles between shots just to be sure. Looked weird as hell during night fighting."

Margo grinned. "I'll bet. Rain must've been a bummer."

"Yes, it did wreak a bit of havoc on a few plans. But then, rain wasn't kind to bow strings, either, or to paper cartridges. Modern guns are nicely weatherproof compared to most projectile weapons. And speaking of other projectile weapons, we need to train you in crossbows and stickbows, recurves . . ."

Margo's eyes widened. Then she grinned wickedly. "What, no blowguns? Or ad-ads?"

"Oh, goodie! One of my students finally wants to learn flint-knapping and spear throwing!"

Kit couldn't help it. He started to chuckle.

Margo turned on him with a hot glare. "What's so funny?"

"I'm sorry, Margo," he said, still laughing. "But you're so transparent. Learning flint-knapping wouldn't exactly be a waste of time. You literally *could* end up someplace where stone weapons are the only ones available. Remember that scout who just came back from the Wurm glaciation, did the work on Cro-Magnon lifestyles?"

"Yeah, I remember reading that. In the *Shangri-la Gazette.*"

"Right. And you did see what fell through the ceiling the other day, didn't you?"

Margo rubbed the back of her neck. "Yeah, well, I *was* thinking about that. What *do* you do if you come face to face with a wooly rhinoceros or something?"

"Look for the nearest tree," Kit advised. "They're mean-tempered brutes. It took a cooperative effort from multiple hunters to bring them down. As for the 'or something,' it depends on what it is. I have a feeling we should add biology and big-game hunting to your curriculum."

She went a little green around the edges.

"Well, there's nothing intrinsically horrible about it," Kit pointed out. "It's useful to know how to kill various species if you're either starving to death or in danger of immediate dismemberment. And I've seen you eat meat, so I know you're not a vegetarian. What *do* they teach in high school these days?"

"Uh, respect for other living creatures?" Ann just rolled her eyes.

"Well," Margo thrust her hands into her pockets, "I'm not a vegan or anything, and I like steaks and chicken and stuff and a neighbor gave us some venison once. I've just never had to hunt anything to get a meal. I know I grew up in Minnesota and all, but I've never even been fishing," she admitted with a slow flush that made Kit wonder again what her upbringing had really been.

Kit nodded, pleased that she was finally able to admit she lacked knowledge or skills she needed. "That's all right. Lots of city kids don't. As for respecting animals, there isn't a hunter alive that doesn't respect hell out of major predators. And most hunters respect game animals, too. It's a different mindset, maybe, from what you're used to, but the respect is genuine. Now . . . if you plan on stepping through unexplored gates, you'd better know how to forage off the land. Not to mention knowing how to keep local four-footed critters from having you as a light snack between meals. So we'll start you on hunting techniques to get you ready for your first attempt at catching your own food."

"Okay."

"Just remember one thing: try to avoid putting four-footed creatures on some moral pedestal that bears no resemblance whatsoever to reality. Misjudging animal behavior and motives does the animal no favors and can be fatal to you. I think," he stood up, "I'll head back upstairs now. You're making good progress," he allowed, "but you still have a lot of work ahead of you. Ann, thanks. I'll see you at dinner, Margo. Meet me at the Delight."

"Really?" Margo's face lit up.

"Yes, really," he grinned. "See you this evening."

As he left the range, he heard Ann saying, "Now, this is a very early type of firearm called a pole gun. . . ."

Chapter 12

Margo was on her way to the Delight when the bones behind her ears began to ache. She frowned and peered toward the nearest chronometer for the scheduled gate postings. "London . . . Primary . . . Rome . . . Denver . . ." She ran down the whole list, but nothing was due to open. The sensation worsened.

"Oh, no, not again . . ."

" 'Eighty-sixers began to converge. Margo decided she'd better skedaddle, post-haste. She put on a burst of speed—and propelled herself straight through a black rent in the air that appeared smack in front of her. She screamed and plunged through the gate before she could halt her forward momentum. She had a brief, tunnel-vision view of a broad, silver river in flood stage, long low banks that sloped gently up to what appeared to be a vast flat plain, and a walled city. A two-part fortified bridge with a tower spanned the river. Standing at the crest of a low, open hill, the city clearly commanded a strategic position overlooking the river. Twin spires of a white stone cathedral were visible above the city walls. *Between* Margo and the walls . . .

It looked like a *battle.*

Then she was through the gate. Margo stumbled right into the thick of it. Men in medieval-looking armor hacked at one another with swords. Horsemen on heavy chargers rode down men on foot. Volleys of arrows fell like black rain, pinioning anything unfortunate enough to be under them. A man right in front of her screamed and clutched at a steel crossbow shaft that appeared from nowhere and embedded itself in his chest armor. He went down with a terrible cry and was trampled by a screaming warhorse. Blood and mud and screams of dying men and wounded horses spattered her from all sides.

Her gaze focused abruptly on a man who'd skidded to a halt right in front of her. Wide, shocked eyes took her measure. *He's younger than I am. . . .* He carried several sheaves of arrows like firewood under his left arm, a bow slung across his back, and a wicked knife in his other hand. He said something and lunged, knife held loosely in an overconfident grip. She whipped around, right side to him, then seized his wrist and yanked forward on it while turning into him. His elbow straightened across her hip. He yelled in pain. Margo kept the elbow forcibly straight and kicked his near ankle with a sweeping blow. She jerked him forward at the same instant. His face slammed into the ground. The knife popped loose.

Thank God. Margo whirled, looking for the gate. And found an older, far stronger man charging right at her, wild-eyed. He swung a massive wooden maul at least four feet long straight over his head, ready to crush her skull. Margo screamed and ran. The gate pulsed unevenly ahead of her. Two men crashed into her path, slashing at one another with long swords. Margo dodged past and hurtled toward the gate. Then risked a glance over her shoulder. The madman with the maul was still back there.

He snarled something that sounded like, *Shown Dark! Shown Dark!* A heavily armored horsemen nearby jerked around at his shout—and charged *him.* The rider's shouts made no sense at all. Margo put on a burst of speed. She could just see the Commons as the gate shivered inward and outward again, a quivering hole in the light. *Don't close—oh, God, don't close yet—*

Margo dove through to safety.

And found herself running down a corridor of shocked spectators, straight for a concrete wall. The wild-eyed soldier was right behind her, chased by a suddenly panic-stricken horse. She heard the animals scream of terror as she turned and flattened against cold concrete.

The soldier charged, wooden maul right over his head, ready to strike. Trapped on either side by milling, confused tourists, Margo saw only one way out. She ran *at* him. Margo lunged with both hands at the butt of the maul handle. Her double-handed blow connected, jarring her to the elbows. The heavy wooden mallet popped loose and clattered on the concrete. The badly startled soldier crashed full-tilt into the concrete wall. He staggered back, dizzy and confused, just as the armored rider came loose from his terrified horse. The animal bucked and shrilled a trumpeting cry. The rider landed with a heavy clang on the concrete floor.

He rolled and came awkwardly to his feet, surprising hell out of Margo. *Good grief, they* could *move around in that armor. . . .* He took one look at the Commons through a slitted visor then broke and ran back through the gate without his horse.

The charger reared again, caught sight of the open gate and shied away. A ten-year-old girl in a Frontier Town long skirt tripped directly in its path. Margo reacted without thinking. She grabbed the charger's trailing reins and dug in and hauled its head around just before it could trample the child. The horse screamed savagely and reared to full height. Margo swore and dodged murderous hooves. Someone else grabbed for the bridle and missed. Margo lunged and grabbed the bridle by the cheek strap—and learned why war horses were so valuable. The bit was a wicked affair, with long, pointed steel shafts on either side. The horse reared with her, hauling her off the floor. Then it gave a nasty toss of its head. Margo lost her grip on the bridle. She came loose, falling backwards and flailing for balance. The horse—eyes gleaming wickedly—raked that damned bit straight down her arm, catching her thigh for good measure on the way down.

She impacted the concrete floor with a muffled cry of pain.

Someone else snatched the trailing reins, forcing it around before it could strike with murderous hooves. "Head it into the gate!" someone yelled. "My God, do you know what that horse would be worth to a guide? Let me try to control him!" In a blur, Margo watched a man leap into the saddle. The horse sunfished, screaming savagely. The rider came adrift with a yell. The warhorse ended facing the pulsing gate. Someone much smarter gave the animal a mighty smack on the hind quarters. It bolted straight through and vanished into the melee beyond. The gate shrank rapidly closed within seconds.

A disturbance somewhere behind them caught Margo's attention. She turned her head to look—*Oh, shit . . .*

That wild-eyed soldier hadn't gone back through. Clad in woolen hose, pointed leather shoes, and a quilted leather tunic to which metal plates had been sewn, he was facing down the crowd with that heavy wooden maul of his. Blood snaked downward from his nose and a cut on his brow. An empty quiver for arrows and a bow at least five-and-a-half feet tall lay on the floor. *"Shawn Dark!"*

He launched straight toward her. Margo, bleeding and whimpering, rolled awkwardly on the floor. Someone tried to tackle him, but was too late. The soldier brought the maul down in a smashing blow. Margo barely rolled out from under it. An iron band around the end of the hammer sparked on concrete a hair's breadth from her ear. He staggered past, off balance—and ran straight into the arms of station security. Four men put him in a headlock, finally immobilizing him.

Another disturbance in the crowd caught the periphery of her attention, then Kit bent over her. He was utterly ashen. "Margo! Margo, you're hurt . . ."

She waved an unsteady hand toward the soldier. "He . . . came through the gate . . ."

Kit was examining her arm, her thigh. "Not deep, thank God," he said with a heartfelt grin that actually wobbled.

He really cares . . .

Margo hadn't realized how much. Kit tore his own shirt for compresses and tied them down. The soldier, still struggling against restraint, snarled something at him. Kit glanced up, looking astonished, then spoke gently in some language Margo had never heard. The man glowered, then slowly stopped struggling. Another few words from Kit and fear began to shine in his eyes. He whispered something to which Kit replied Whatever Kit said, it terrified the soldier.

"Let him go," Kit said quietly.

The men who'd grabbed him looked uncertain, then released him. The soldier stood uncertainly in the midst of the crowd, looking suddenly terrified and utterly alone.

"He'll need to see Buddy for orientation," Kit said. "Has anyone called him yet?"

Someone near the edge of the crowd said, "He's on his way down."

"Anybody tell Bull what happened?"

One of the Pest Control officers, standing sheepishly by with an empty net, said, "Al's already gone for him. Kit, that grandkid of yours saved a little girl's life before you got here. She acted real quick, caught a French charger by the bridle before any of us were in position to act. It raked her with its spiked bit, but she saved the kid's life. Would've trampled her for sure."

Kit glanced sharply at her, then said, "Can you stand on that leg?"

Margo tried. A nauseating wave of pain swept through her. Kit simply picked her up and strode hastily through the crowd, which gave way with astonishing rapidity.

Margo bit her lips, not wanting Kit to know how badly she hurt. "What did that soldier say, when you talked to him?"

He glanced down just long enough to meet her gaze. "He was at the siege of Orleans in medieval France. He was fighting for his life. When you appeared out of nowhere, he thought Jeanne d'Arc had opened the gates of hell. Now he thinks you've sent him through *into* hell."

"Jeanne d'Arc, that's what he called me,"

Kit tightened his lips. "Yes. He thought you *were* Joan of Arc. He said something about you thrashing another archer?"

"He tried to stab me. I disarmed him, that's all. . . ." She didn't want to talk. Margo's stomach was so uneasy it was all she could do to swallow down the nausea that accompanied every throb in her arm and leg.

Kit just nodded. "Well, the English army lost the battle at Orleans, rather badly. This fellow's a Welsh archer, a longbowman. Like the English, he thought Joan was a witch. The Burgundians caught her a couple of years after Orleans and turned her over to the English. They burned her."

Margo shut her eyes. "I . . . I fell through the gate when it opened. I didn't have any equipment, I don't know when it was . . ." She started to cry.

"Hang in there, Margo. I'm taking you to Rachel Eisenstein. They're not serious cuts, I promise."

"Good," she whispered.

Kit tightened his arms around her and shoved open the infirmary door with the point of his shoulder.

"Rachel! Emergency!"

The station doctor appeared at a run. "What happened?"

"Medieval warhorse raked Margo with a spiked bit. Slashes to arm and thigh. Unexpected gate into a fifteenth-century battle."

They eased her onto an examining table and Rachel stripped off Margo's ruined clothes. "It isn't as bad as it feels," Rachel told her gently, swabbing out the long slices. She gave Margo a local anesthetic and cleaned the wounds, then stitched them up. She finished off with bandages.

"Your medical records indicate no allergies to penicillin," Rachel said, consulting a computer screen. "That's correct?"

"Yes," Margo said in a small voice. "That's right. I'm not."

The doctor injected antibiotics and anti-tetanus and gave her a prescription for oral capsules as well. "When you're wounded with a down-time weapon that's been only God knows where and in God knows what, we take no chances."

Margo felt sick again, clear through.

"Not to worry," Rachel said with a smile. "We'll take good care of you. Put her to bed, Kit, and feed her when she feels like eating."

Margo felt like a complete fool when they settled her in a wheelchair. Kit wheeled her back out onto the Commons.

"What happened, exactly?" Kit asked quietly. Margo told him.

"You were lucky," he told her when she'd finished. "Medieval war horses were trained to kill foot soldiers. If the charger hadn't been so spooked by the gate, he'd have crushed you. I'll question the Welshman more closely to see if we can pinpoint more or less when you emerged through that gate."

Don't I even rate a well done for saving that kid? she wondered miserably.

Evidently not, as Kit didn't say another word on the subject. He took her back to his quarters and tucked her in, the only concession being that he put her in his own bed and carried his pillow and blanket to the couch.

"Hungry?" he asked, settling down beside her.

She turned away. "No."

He hesitated, then touched her shoulder. "You did okay, kid. But you have so much to learn. . . ."

"I know," Margo said bitterly. "Everyone keeps telling me."

Kit dropped his hand. "I'll check on you again later. Call me if you need anything."

Margo didn't want anything more from Kit. She was tired and sick and her injuries throbbed and the best he could manage to say to her was, "You did okay."

She muffled her face in the pillow and drowned out all sound of a misery she could hardly bear.

Kit sat in the darkness, nursing a shot glass of bourbon. So close . . . dear God, she'd come so close, and didn't even realize it. His hand was still a little unsteady as he drained the glass and poured again. A knock at the door interrupted an endless stream of graphic images his mind insisted on presenting had the confrontation gone even a little differently.

Kit climbed wearily to his feet and found the door.

"Yeah?"

"It's Bull."

Kit unlocked it. "Come on in."

"Drinking in the dark?" Bull asked with a frown.

"Margo's asleep. I didn't want to disturb her." He flicked on a table lamp.

"I won't stay long then. I've spoken with our newest down timer. He's suspicious and unhappy and protested rather violently when I confiscated his weapons, but I didn't order confinement. He seemed genuinely apologetic that he'd attacked the wrong person. Ordinarily, you know, I'd order strict confinement for a fight with lethal weapons, but under the circumstances . . ."

"Yeah," Kit said heavily.

"I'll confine him if you'd prefer."

Kit glanced up. "No. No, don't do that. He was shaken and scared. Battle does strange things to a man's mind, as it is, never mind falling through a gate into La-La Land. What's his name, anyway?"

"Kynan Rhys Gower."

"Poor bastard."

"Yeah. It's rough on the down timers. Buddy's already had a long session with him. He says it's the usual reaction: he's confused, scared, convinced he's in hell. I wish to God the government would come up with some sane policy regarding them, but chances are it'd be worse for 'em than leaving 'em here."

Kit snorted, "When the government gets involved, things *always* get worse."

Bull smiled wryly. "Ain't it the truth? How's Margo?"

"Rachel set fifteen stitches in her arm, nearly fifty in her leg."

Bull winced. "That serious?"

"No, the slashes were shallow, thank God, just long. She should be fine, so long as massive infection doesn't set in. Rachel's put her on antibiotics."

"Good. I hear she saved a little girl's life."

Kit managed a wan smile. "Yes. She's a hero. She was damn near a *dead* hero."

"If you're going to let her scout, Kit, you'd better get used to the idea."

Kit stared at the wall. "Yeah. I know. Doesn't make it any easier."

"Nope. Never does. Get some sleep, Kit. And put away the booze."

Kit grimaced. "Sure, boss." Then he glanced up. 'Thanks."

"Don't mention it," Bull smiled, squat and square and for the moment, human instead of demi-legend. Human enough to show how much he cared, anyway, which meant a great deal to Kit in that moment. Bull Morgan thumped Kit on the arm. "See you around, Kit. Tell Margo I asked about her."

Kit nodded and let him out, then locked the door and put away the bourbon. But it was a long time before sleep came. He steeled himself to make the decision and finally settled on Rome as the best place for Margo's next down-time testing ground. Stubborn, brash, untrained . . .

And once again, Kit would not be able to go with her.

The silver lining in all this darkness, Kit grumbled to himself as he sought a more comfortable position on the couch, was that Malcolm Moore wouldn't have to worry about rent and meals for months to come. If he'd thought it practical, Kit would have asked Malcolm to consider scouting again, just to be sure Margo had an experienced partner.

Yeah, right. She'd take to that idea with all the enthusiasm of a wet cat.

He sighed and wondered how she'd receive the news that another down-time trip was scheduled? She'd probably see it as her just reward for playing hero. Kit was rapidly discovering that being a grandfather wasn't half the fun it was cracked up to be. When, if ever, did he get to stop being the "mean one" in Margo's life? Every time things seemed to be straightening out between them, something always seemed to happen to muck it up again.

He blinked a few times, remembering how life with Sarah had gone much the same way—and how *that* had ended. He lay quietly in the darkness listening to Margo's steady even breaths in the next room and tried to keep fear at bay by planning out the next phase of her training.

He wasn't terribly successful at either.

Chapter 13

Kynan Rhys Gower was trapped in hell.

Everyone here who could actually talk to him said otherwise, of course, but Kynan knew it was hell nonetheless, even if it didn't resemble anything the priests had ever described. The closest thing to a priest here, a man called "Buddy," had told him he could never escape—not to his home or even back to the accursed battle against the witch woman fighting on the side of the upstart French.

It hurt him, gnawed at him, that he was cut off forever from everything and everyone he knew and loved. A king whose laws forbade it, Kynan might have understood. But he could not understand why, if this infernal land's diabolical passageway that opened out of thin air could be made to open with the regularity of the rising and setting sun, could the wizard or demon or hell-spawned sprite who controlled them not reopen the one passageway that would lead him home? Yet Buddy had told Kynan he would never again see the dark hills of Wales or the laughter in his son's eyes. . . .

At least a hundred times every day, as he struggled to understand devilish things beyond his comprehension, Kynan was tempted to do violence to *something*. But they'd taken away his weapons. Without them, he was less than a man. Less, even, than the commonest Welsh farm girl, who at least carried a small knife for chores.

Kynan swallowed his pain, his confusion, and the demeaning

status in which he found himself—a virtual slave in Satan's dominions—and worked hard to earn the scant coins he needed to pay for his tiny sleeping room and the meals of rice and strange vegetables which kept him alive. He missed meat desperately but was unable to afford it on what he earned.

Several times a day, his hatred of the strange, demon birds which lived here—birds with teeth in their bills—deepened as he watched them eat colorful fish that *he* was forbidden to take for his own meals. If he hadn't been terrified of incurring the king's wrath for killing one of the protected birds, he'd have killed and eaten one of *them.*

So he carried baggage for rich people whose behavior he could scarcely comprehend and whose language he could comprehend not at all, found a second job sweeping floors in the bewildering place in which he was trapped, and quietly hugged his misery and terror and bitterness to himself. Every time he saw the grinning jackanapes who'd first told him what had happened to him, who had *laughed* at him while four strong men held him down . . .

Every time he saw the man called Kit Carson, Kynan wished to do more than violence. He wished to do murder.

But he'd watched that man practice mock fighting in the huge, lighted hall called "gym." He was a cunning, strong warrior as well as a knave. If Kynan wished to purge the stain of disgrace from his honor, it would have to come through sudden, unexpected attack. Kynan once would have sneered at any man who planned such a treacherous approach to an affair of honor, would have rightly called him blackguard. But Kynan was no longer in a land which made sense. He was in hell.

In hell, a man could be forgiven much.

So he pushed his hated broom down the hated floor, sweeping up the hated trash while trying to avoid running into hated, arrogant "tourists" and gradually filled his wheeled trash bin with little bits of refuse. Later he would have to open stationary trash bins along the "Commons" and empty them as well, carrying the "plastic" sacks inside down to the "incinerator" and "recycling center." Even the alien, English words that somehow weren't really English made his head ache. Kynan had never spoken much English—his commander had translated battlefield commands—but the so-called English spoken here . . . even words he thought he knew made little or no sense.

He pushed his broom and wheeled cart into the area of "Commons" called "Victoria Station"—named, someone said, for a *Queen* of England, who had brazenly ruled in her own name despite a perfectly eligible husband who could have sat the throne in her stead—and filled another tray with dust and trash, emptying it into his bin. A spate of laughter made him grit his teeth. They weren't laughing at him, but Kynan was so lost in despair, he could scarcely endure the sound of another person's joy. It only reminded him how cruelly alone he was.

He glanced up, drawn against his will to look. A group of men in strange, long-coated suits and pretty, sweet-faced women in even stranger dresses were playing an odd game, setting out little wire hoops with weighted feet, standing up two wooden sticks painted with bright bands of color, arguing which of them would claim wooden balls banded with a matching stripe of color.

A pang ran through him. He wondered what his wife and son might be doing now. Wondered if the village men would teach the boy to use longbow and maul—or if the French would even leave enough men alive to return to the village. What would become of his family? A sickness wrought of empty, helpless longing threatened him again, as it did many, many times each day.

Kynan straightened his back against it. He was a Welshman, a veteran soldier. He might be lost, abandoned by God and saints alike, but he would not give Satan the satisfaction of watching him buckle under the weight of fear and loss which hourly were heaped on him. Kynan watched the game players dully, wondering what these particular demons were doing.

Then he noticed the mallets.

Made of wood and banded like the balls, they were smaller than the battle mauls he was accustomed to carrying, but they were hefty wooden mallets, nonetheless. Kynan watched with mounting interest as the players began a baffling game which involved hitting the wooden balls through the wire hoops. None of them knew the first thing about using a mallet, but clearly, despite a smallish size, they would prove formidable weapons in the hands of a trained soldier. Now if he only had a proper mallet like that . . .

He counted the number of players: five. Then he spotted a wooden cart on which a sixth ball and mallet rested, forgotten. None of the players paid it the slightest attention. Perhaps God had not entirely abandoned him after all? *If I cannot escape hell,* he thought, staring intently at that mallet, *perhaps I will at least be permitted a way to restore my honor.* He maneuvered his trash cart around the players, sweeping up dust and bits of paper as he went, pausing to clean up the occasional splatter of bird shit, and worked his way around to the abandoned mallet. None of the players or spectators—many of whom carried odd sticks with tautly stretched shades to protect their heads from non-existent sunshine—paid him the slightest attention. Good.

It took half a heartbeat to lift the mallet from its resting place and slip it into his wheeled bin. Only after he had made good his escape did Kynan allow himself a long, shuddering breath. Satan's minions had not noticed the theft. If the Evil One had noticed, either he didn't care or thought it amusing to allow his latest victim a chance at vengeance. Kynan touched the hidden mallet handle with trembling fingertips. *At last,* he breathed silently, eyes closed, *I am a man again.* Soon, the knave who had laughed at him would rue the day his betters had failed to teach him manners.

If a man must die in hell, it were best to die with a weapon in hand, striking down an enemy.

Fortunately for Kit's peace of mind, Margo's injuries healed quickly and cleanly. He made certain the leg would hold the strain of a lethal encounter by sparring with her in the gym while Sven evaluated her performance.

"You're favoring it," Sven pointed out. "Does it hurt?"

"No," she admitted. "Not really. I've just grown used to babying it."

The admission brought a scowl to Sven's lips. Kit wisely stepped aside while Sven Bailey *really* put her through her paces. By the time he'd finished with her, she was a limp mass of sweat and aching muscles.

"You're out of shape," Sven told her brusquely. "More practice."

Margo just nodded, too tired to protest.

"How about that dinner at the Delight?" Kit asked. "We, uh, were interrupted last time we tried."

A wan smile came and went. "Sure. No disgruntled soldiers this time?"

"We'll do our best to avoid them," Kit smiled.

The Welsh bowman had certainly avoided Kit. From what he'd heard, Kynan was busy trying to master the modern technology involved in living on a time terminal while taking on odd jobs to keep body and soul together.

"Just let me shower first," Margo said with a grimace. "I stink."

Kit laughed and headed for the showers himself.

Shortly they were back on the Commons, heading for the Delight. Urbs Romae was nearly deserted, as the major gates opening this week were in other parts of the station. A line had formed, of course, in front of the Epicurean Delight, but when Arley saw Kit and Margo standing outside, he waved them in.

"Hello, don't stand out there, your table's ready. Rachel tells me you're healing well, young lady."

Margo smiled ruefully. "Sven Bailey just proved that."

Arley laughed. "You look tired and hungry. Would you like a menu or the House Specialty?"

"A menu!" Margo said hastily.

Kit grinned "Still upset about those eels?"

Margo managed to affect a wounded dignity despite her youth and state of fatigue.

Arley winked. "I think you'll enjoy the Specialty tonight. Trust me."

"Why do I have a bad feeling about this?" Margo asked as she settled into the chair Arley held for her. "All right, I'll try it, whatever it is."

"Kit?"

"Same for me."

The Delight's owner rubbed his hands. "Good. I'll send out a bottle of something appropriate."

The wine, when it arrived, was a clear red. "Well, at least it won't be eels," Kit remarked as the waiter poured. "Thank God."

"I thought you *liked* that dinner."

He put on his best lecture expression and said, "*Ab uno disce omnes,* Margo."

Margo just looked at him.

Kit frowned. "Margo, didn't you understand that?"

"Uh, no?"

His frown deepened. "Just how well are you doing with your Latin?"

Her face took on a familiar, panic-stricken look. *Oh-oh.*

"I *am* studying!" she said desperately. As though to prove it, she rattled off, "*Abeunt studia in mores!*"

"Quoting Ovid now, eh?" Kit said sourly. "Take that advice to heart. Study harder. Studies *do* turn into habits, but only if you keep up with them."

He made a mental note to check how often she'd actually been to the language lab. She should've been able to translate something as simple as, "From one, learn to judge all," by now.

She tightened her lips. "I will. I am. I'm *trying.* Isn't there any easier way to learn all those words and those awful endings that keep changing?"

"Unfortunately, no. Brian's already installed the best language-learning programs available. But learning languages takes work. Constant, hard work."

She sighed, then tried a winning smile that didn't fool him in the slightest. "I learned an interesting thing from Sven today. There was this guy named Musashi, a Japanese guy from the same time period as the Edo gate. He was so good at dueling, he stopped fighting with real knives. Just used a wooden practice sword whenever he was challenged. Isn't that amazing? I wonder if Sven's good enough to do that?"

"Probably," Kit said drily. "I thought you were studying American history, not Japanese?"

"I am," she said hastily, "but Sven was telling me, you know, during our lesson today. I used to be scared of him, but he's really interesting if you can get him to talk." *Clever little minx. Why does she keep changing the subject?*

"Hmm, yes? I rather imagine Francis Marion was much the same."

Again, Margo drew an utter blank.

Kit unfolded his napkin with a little snap. "Just what period of American history did you say you were reading? It *was* the Revolution, wasn't it?"

Margo's whole face colored. "Well, yes, I did. I was. I am. I mean—"

"Spill it, Margo. You're not studying, are you?"

"I study until I'm sick of studying! I learned more in one week in London than I've learned the whole time I've been stuck in that library!"

"Margo—"

"No! Don't say it! All I hear from you is 'Margo, study this, Margo, do that; Margo, pay attention; Margo, that was barely adequate'!"

He thought she might well burst into tears. "I'm only worried about you, Margo," he said quietly. "You have years of studying ahead of you before you can hope to—"

"*Years?*" Her lips quivered. "But I don't have—" She halted. Her chin came up defiantly. "I don't need years. I'm learning a lot and what I don't know, I can fake."

Kit rocked back. *Fake it?* "You can't be serious."

Her eyes flashed. "Why not? I got along just fine in London, except for not knowing that pistol, and I've fixed that problem. Just ask Ann if I haven't. I can shoot anything she hands me. Even that laser-guided blowgun she made me learn to use! Sven said my job is to avoid being seen, anyway, and I'm good at sneaking around in the dark!"

Kit held onto his temper. "Margo, you can't fake languages."

"No . . . but I can fake being a deaf mute, which is just as good! I've worked so hard, dammit! I deserve a chance to prove myself."

Kit didn't know whether to be angry or scared out of his mind. "You'll get that chance. When I think you're ready."

For a moment she just sat there, breathing hard. Tears welled up and spilled down her cheeks. Then, in a low, hurt voice, she said, "I'm not hungry any more. I'll think I'll go *study!*"

She fled past a whole line of waiting tourists who gaped after her. Kit cursed under his breath and shoved back his chair. Arley met him halfway to the door.

"Trouble?"

Kit nodded tightly. "Cancel our orders, would you? Put it on my bill."

"She's young, Kit."

"That's no excuse. The universe doesn't give a damn when it squashes you."

Arley let him go without further attempts at sympathy. Kit headed for the library. He *had* to make her understand. After London—and St. Giles—he'd hoped . . . But all she saw was the need to study fighting techniques, not the history and languages to help avoid the fight in the first place. She clearly understood the tactical advantage of invisibility but wasn't thinking of *knowledge* as one way to achieve it. Scouting was a career men spent years—sometimes decades—preparing for, only to run into trouble anyway because they slipped up on some tiny, seemingly insignificant detail. He *had* to make her understand that, make her understand she simply *must* take the necessary time to prepare for it. Otherwise, he'd lose her just as surely as he'd lost Sarah.

Kit was barreling around the corner past Li's Antiquities when a sixth sense lifted the hairs on the back of his neck. He jerked his gaze up—and tracked the lethal swing of a heavy wooden croquet mallet straight toward his skull.

Kit swept his right arm upward by instinct, deflecting the blow at the expense of pain like an electric shock straight to the bone. He leaned away even as he swept the mallet aside. The thick wooden head narrowly missed his temple, lifting hair with the wind of its passage. Kit stepped forward with his left foot, turning with the sweep. He shoved the croquet mallet down and pushed his attacker's face straight into the wall. Both the mallet and the attacker's skull went *CRACK* against concrete.

A howl of pain reached him. Kit jumped clear. His arm ached, the ache becoming a relentless throb within seconds. He cradled it to his chest and felt for fractures he hoped he wouldn't find. Then his attacker staggered back from the wall.

Aw, nuts . . .

The Welshman.

"Coward!" Kynan Rhys Gower spat at him. "Filthy dog!"

The Welshman came at him again, mallet raised over his head in a classic attack position. Kit, one arm all but useless, saw no other choice. He threw a sidekick straight into the onrushing Welshman's hips. The blow caught him just above the pubic bone. Kynan Rhys Gower folded up with an ugly sound. The mallet whistled just above Kit's back.

Kit recovered his balance while the Welshman struggled to regain his feet.

"Can't we talk about this?" Kit gasped, using Kynan's native language. *Where in hell did he get a croquet mallet?*

For answer, Kynan swept that damned mallet up and sideways. Kit couldn't get out of the way in time, although he twisted into a pretzel trying. He *felt* ribs crunch. The whole Commons greyed out for a moment while his voice expressed some creative sounds.

Fortunately, Kynan Rhys Gower was still off balance and staggering from that blow to the hips. This allowed Kit to recover while the Welshman was drawing the mallet back for the next try. *Okay, that's it . . .*

Time for a quick *coup de grace* to end this nonsense. Kit attacked first. In one swift motion, he swept the mallet back with one arm then threw a shoulder blow into the Welsh man's ribcage. His whole weight hit just below Kynan's raised arm. He felt ribs crack again, and although they weren't his, a shock of pain jolted through his own broken ribs anyway. Kynan howled and tried to fend him off with the mallet.

Kit grabbed the heavy wooden head and pulled sharply—then slammed Kynan's straightened elbow and shoved back on the mallet.

Kynan gasped in pain. Then, with a circular sweep, push, and snatch, Kit simply jerked the makeshift weapon away.

Kynan was left blinking in pain and surprise, disarmed before he quite knew what had happened.

"Now look," Kit wheezed, "I don't know what your problem is . . . and I'm not a vindictive guy . . ."

Kynan started to spring at him, fingers curved into claws ready to gouge whatever they found. ". . . but this has *got* to stop . . ." Kit swept the croquet mallet around and hit Kynan's ankle on the "funny spot"—just hard enough for the desired effect, but without the force to break it. Kynan gave out a strangled gasp and grabbed for his ankle. Kit shoved gently on his chest. He went down with a sound like a hurt child. "Oww. . . ."

Kit held the mallet in an easy grip, standing near enough to strike a lethal blow if he wanted. Kynan sat on the concrete floor, holding his ankle, trying to hold his ribcage, and met his gaze. Clearly, he knew he was at Kit's mercy.

Equally clearly, he expected to die. Pity swept away Kit's rage. He drew several deep, calming breaths. "Do you yield?" he asked quietly.

Surprise flickered through Kynan's eyes. He blinked uncertainly. But he didn't answer.

"I'd like to know why you tried to murder me." *That* prompted an answer.

"No man laughs at Kynan Rhys Gower and lives! You've taken my honor, my soul. . . . Curse you! Take my life and let this hell end!"

Try as he could, Kit couldn't recall *anything* the Welshman might have construed as being laughed at. "What are you talking about? When did I rob you of your honor? When did I laugh at you?"

Kynan's glance might have sent another man back a step. Kit held his ground, prompting Kynan to drop his gaze.

"You permitted the *woman* to humiliate me," he muttered. "Then you grinned like the gibbering blackguard you are when I was helpless against four!"

Kit was utterly baffled. He'd come in on the very tail end of that fight, how could he have allowed anyone to humiliate this man, when he hadn't even *been* there? In fact, he could identify only one instant

Kynan could possibly be referring to. When realization sank home, Kit very nearly swung the mallet at his thick, medieval skull. If his ribs hadn't ached so fiercely, he might have.

"That *woman,*" he hissed, "is *my grandchild.* You tried to kill her—after she was wounded trying to save a child from that damned French warhorse! I was not laughing at you! I wasn't even *thinking* about you! I was smiling in sheer relief because she would not lose the use of her leg."

Kynan Rhys Gower looked suddenly doubtful, which was small consolation considering how close he'd come to killing Kit.

Kit tapped Kynan's chest with the mallet. "Is it not bad enough you attacked a lady? Now you take offense where none was given and try to murder a man who has been wronged in his own kin by you!

"Shut up and listen! I didn't 'permit' anyone to humiliate you, much less Margo. I wasn't even *there* when you attacked her. You had better get used to a few new ideas, Kynan Rhys Gower. And the first one is this: women here are perfectly capable of protecting themselves when knaves rush at them with war hammers."

Kynan compressed his lips, "Knave, is it?"

Kit swore under his breath. "What would you call a man who attacked a girl barely eighteen, a girl already cut so badly her leg had to be sewn together—then tried to break a man's skull rather than call him out fairly to ask satisfaction—or at least an explanation?"

Kynan didn't answer. Not that Kit actually expected him to, but Kit always tried reasoning with people whenever circumstances permitted. Unfortunately, some people simply wouldn't be reasoned with. Kit was abruptly disgusted with the whole situation, including his own anger. If he'd dared trust the Welshman, he'd have left Kynan sitting on his backside in the middle of the Commons.

Fortunately, Station Security arrived on the scene. Mike Benson took one look and hauled Kynan to his feet. Benson cuffed the Welshman's hands behind him, then, in a quick maneuver that was anything but gentle, put him face down on the floor and hobbled his legs. A strangled sound of pain escaped him.

"Better have someone look at him," Kit sighed. "I think I broke some of his ribs."

Mike Benson grimaced. "Serves him right, I'd say. Where'd this bastard get a weapon?"

"Hell if I know." Kit handed over the croquet mallet "I'd check the outfitters' stores, see if any of 'em are missing part of a set."

Robert Li spoke up from the doorway of his antiquities shop. "I think he stole it from a group of grad students practicing for the spring garden parties in London. I heard a couple of them talking about a mallet missing out of their set the other day." He glanced at Kit. "I'm sorry, Kit. I had no idea the theft would turn out so serious. I just thought it was part of a practical joke or something. You all right?"

Kit nodded curtly. "I'm fine." Hell would freeze before he admitted to broken ribs. He'd bribe Rachel Eisenstein, if necessary, to keep it quiet.

Benson ordered his men to take Kynan to a holding cell. The Welshman looked as though he'd considered struggling, then glanced at Kit and settled down to trudge away in his hobbles.

"You're standing mighty funny, Kit." In his late fifties, Mike Benson was solidly built, with thinning grey hair and cold blue eyes that had seen everything, sometimes twice. "How're *your* ribs?"

Aw, hell . . .

Without asking, Benson peeled back his shirt. "Hmm . . . Better have these x-rayed. I think he broke a few."

"I'll take care of it," Kit grated.

"What was that guff he was giving you when I came up?" Benson asked.

Kit explained.

Mike Benson ran a hand across his short hair and gazed into empty space as though considering the wisdom of speaking. He glanced at Kits ribs and spoke anyway. "Kit, that girl's been nothing but trouble since she got here. No offense, but she's a magnet for disaster."

"Great. What else has she done that I don't know about?"

"Nothing illegal, if that's worrying you. Just . . . well, watch out when she's around. Skeeter Jackson and the occasional drunken billionaire aren't the only hotheads panting over her."

Great. Just wonderful.

A strained smile appeared around the security chief's eyes. "At least it's been more interesting around here since she arrived. Sometimes herding tourists from gate to gate is like dealing with squabbling school kids. If I'd wanted that, I'd have stayed on the force in Chicago when they tried retiring me to crossing guard."

Kit forced a laugh. "You'd have lasted six weeks. You thrive on La-La Land's unique brand of lunacy."

Benson sniffed. "Maybe I do. Maybe I do, at that. Of course, I could say the same. You might've retired up time a couple of years ago. What keeps you hanging around this asylum ?"

Kit let his shoulders relax, which was something of a mistake. He hissed softly and adjusted his stance. "Search me. Sheer meanness, I guess. What'll you do with Kynan?"

A wicked grin came and went. "Bull told me to watch out for that one. Almost confined him when he attacked Margo. I think about a month of restricted environment"—Kit mentally translated *jail*—"and community service for assault with a deadly weapon ought to change his attitude. The garbage pits are short of help just now."

Kit winced. "Poor bastard. Sometimes I think it'd be easier on the down timers if we just drugged them until their gates reopened."

Benson shrugged. "Yeah, but some never do. As you damned well know. Be sure Rachel looks at you."

"Huh. I've gone to ground in hog lots with worse than this and survived. Man'd think I'd turned into a mewling baby since I retired, the way people act . . ."

Benson grinned. "Hog lot, eh? You must tell me that story sometime."

Kit laughed. "Sure. You buy the beer and I'll tell all."

"Deal. Stay out of trouble."

Kit watched him stroll away, then winced. His ribs smarted. "Well," he quoted a very ancient comedy team, "this is another fine mess you've gotten us into, isn't it?"

He didn't feel up to tackling Margo's attitude toward education just now. *Better go crawling to Rachel and deal with my injuries.* With any luck, the promise of another down-time excursion would help repair this latest breach in his relationship with Margo. And the trip itself ought to go a long way toward convincing her she couldn't "fake it" down time.

"What're you coming to, Kit," he muttered on the way across the Commons, "bribing your own grandkid with expensive down-time presents?"

Kit knew—from first-hand experience—that once you gave in and paid Dane-geld, the Dane *never* went away.

Well, it was a little late for that now. And she did need a lesson in coping with down-time languages and customs completely alien from her own. Of La-La Land's major gates which fit that bill, Porta Romae was by far the safest.

Margo loose in Rome was an image of sufficient horror to sober even the most reckless of time guides. And Kit had never, in his entire professional career, been considered reckless. *When,* he wondered a little despairingly, *does the worrying end and the enjoyment begin?* Given the way his luck had been running of late, probably never.

"Must be Malcolm's fault," he decided. "His luck's rubbing off."

And that was the very best Kit could find to say about the whole mess.

Chapter 14

Porta Romae, the Roman Gate, opened into the storage room of a busy wine shop on the Via Appia. Ancient Rome's "Main Street" ran from the Appian Gate to the great Circus Maximus where it turned north past the foot of monumental Palatine Hill, home of gods and emperors.

The hulking Circus rose like a battleship from the valley floor, its bulk silhouetted against a brilliant white sky. In deepest antiquity the Circus had been merely an open sweep of valley where even the Etruscans had run sacred funerary races. Over the intervening centuries the Circus, with its towering monuments and soaring wood-and-stone bleachers, had come to dominate the valley between the Palatine and Aventine Hills, one of the most sacred spots in the city of Rome.

The air of electric excitement which permeated the whole district when a games day approached was apparent the moment one stepped through the Roman gate and heard the screams of caged beasts, the shrill calls of high-strung racing horses, and the roar of Roman voices betting, arguing, laughing, and ordering food.

For Malcolm Moore, the chance to step through Porta Romae, the first of the great time gates to be explored (and subsequently the first owned lock, stock, and barrel by Time Tours) was worth every moment of the heartache, the uncertainty and the misery that accompanied the life of a freelance guide. Whenever he stepped through onto the packed-earth floor in a crowd of excited tourists, something in his soul came back to life again.

Stepping through into the midst of the festival of the Magna Mater of Rome was simply icing on the cake.

Malcolm had guided tourists through the Porta Romae many times, but he'd managed to attend the Hilaria and the Ludi Megalenses only twice—and this was the first year Imperial decree would permit the Procession of Attis in its entirety through the streets of Rome. He could scarcely contain an idiotic grin.

Margo, of course, approached the trip in much the same light she'd approached London. Young Margo had no concept what the next two weeks would entail. Given the glimpses he'd seen in London of a bright and thoughtful young mind struggling to overcome something terrible in her past and make something good and decent of her future, Malcolm found himself looking forward to watching her process of self-discovery in Rome. He hoped she would surprise him.

Before new arrivals had finished clearing the gate, Malcolm reminded Margo to take a reading with her ATLS. He pulled her off to one side and put her through the drill of ATLS readings and log updates, then checked her work. He glanced carefully through her notations, double-checked her ATLS readings, and nodded. "Very good. You're getting the hang of it."

She beamed.

He finished his own notations then put away his equipment in the carefully disguised bag he would carry. Malcolm adjusted his slave's collar and scrutinized the drape of Margo's provincial garb.

"I want her to look like a trader from somewhere really remote," Kit had said in the back room of Connie Logan's Clothes and Stuff. "Ideas?"

"Roman Syria," Malcolm had suggested at once. "Palmyra's perfect."

"Why Palmyra?" Margo asked curiously.

"Palmyrenes were almost unknown in Rome of A.D. 47. No one should question your complete lack of ancient languages—which also means they won't be able to question you about home. And since they can't talk directly with you, I'll be able to 'translate'—and I *do* know the answers. Palmyra was only incorporated as an autonomous part of Roman Syria thirty-seven years before A.D. 47, with very tenuous trading ties to Rome, at best."

The costume Connie had come up with was delightful: draped folds of a Parthian-style tunic with voluminous trousers and leggings embroidered in wine-red designs. Metal "suspenders" supported the leggings, fastening them to the tunics gold-embroidered hem. The trousers and even the long, narrow sleeves fell in a series of soft, U-shaped drapes down arms and legs. Overhanging the draped tunic came a cloak that fell in loose folds down the back. The shoes were elaborately embroidered "Persian" slippers. Capping off the costume came a cloth belt from which hung a scabbard for a long dagger.

When Margo heard the size of the estimated bill, she actually paled. "My God! Why so much?"

Connie grinned. "Any guesses?"

Margo glanced at the half-finished garments strewn everywhere in Connie's design studio. Computer-controlled sewing machines dominated two whole walls. "I have no idea."

"The chain-stitch sewing machine was invented in 1830. The lock-stitch machine came even later. Before that, all clothing was assembled by hand."

"But not all your costumes are this expensive. Not even close. What are you going to do? Hand spin the thread for this thing?"

Connie laughed. "No, although I've done that, too, on occasion, and spent hours at a loom hand weaving. Most costumes can be assembled by machine from the threads up. Even for pre-sewing-machine time periods, we can sometimes fudge. Take this."

She snagged an extraordinary gown from a peg. In three parts, it consisted of a coat-like overdress, a wide, skirt-like affair, and a triangular piece that was evidently meant to go across the front of the bosom, tapering to a point at the waist.

'This is an eighteenth-century English gown. One of our smaller gates opens into colonial Virginia every five years or so. It's due to open in about a month and a couple of researchers are going through for an extended sabbatical in Williamsburg." She chuckled. "Goldie

Morran always makes a killing, exporting China metal to Williamsburg through whoever's going down time. The researchers carry the stuff through to help pay for their research trips."

"China metal?" Margo asked. "What on earth is that?"

"Ordinary nickel-silver," Malcolm grinned. "Not any silver in it, even. It's a base-metal alloy similar to German silver. It's used in cheap costume jewelry, junk trays and candlesticks, that sort of thing."

"Yes," Kit chuckled, "but in Colonial Williamsburg it was worth as much as gold." His eyes twinkled. "Much like Connie's gowns."

Connie grinned. "Speaking of which . . . This gown has seven-hundred eleven inches of seams alone, never mind hems for both skirts and the sleeves or the decorative stitching visible from the surface. I can do an average of ten inches of seam an hour by hand, against a few seconds by machine. If I fudge and set the computers to simulate the slight variations in hand stitching, I can assemble a whole gown in a few hours—except for decorative stitching, any quilting the customer wants, and so on. I can't do that by machine. Someone down time would notice. Fashion has always been closely studied, both by practitioners and by poorer folk who want to ape the newest styles in cheaper versions. So some of it can't be fudged.

"Now, with your Palmyrene costume, I can't fudge *anything.* It'll take hours and hours of work to complete. I won't have to hand spin or weave, but the embroidery alone will be murder. I'll have to pull a couple of assistants off other jobs to finish it in time,"

"Which is expensive," Margo sighed. "I guess," she said, giving Kit and Malcolm a hang-dog look, "I'd better not get it dirty, huh?"

Malcolm, like Kit and Connie, had laughed. But now, the overly cautious way Margo moved told Malcolm she was terrified of ruining Connie Logan's exquisite creation.

"Margo," he said, "one piece of advice." She glanced up, trying to avoid a dusty stack of wine jars.

"What's that?"

"That costume is meant to be lived in. It may have been expensive, but it isn't a museum piece. Keep walking around like that and some Roman snob is going to think you're a *puer delicatus* for sale."

Margo's face registered absolute bafflement. "Pretty boys brought twice as much at the slave markets as pretty girls, whether they were destined for a brothel or a private bed."

Lips and eyes went round with shock.

"This isn't Minnesota. It isn't London, either. Morals here aren't at *all* what they are up time. Not even remotely close. Neither are the laws. So don't go mincing around as if you're afraid to smudge your clothes. You're a wealthy young foreigner, son of a merchant prince in one of the richest caravan states the desert ever produced. Act like it."

She closed her mouth. "Okay, Malcolm."

"Study wealthy Romans on the street for body language. That isn't the same here, either. Neither are common gestures like nodding and shaking your head. To indicate yes, tip your head back. To indicate no, tuck your chin." He demonstrated. "Shake your head side to side and a Roman will wonder what's wrong with your ears."

"What if I screw up?"

"Intelligent question. Romans were notoriously rude about their cultural superiority. If you make any minor errors, they'll put it down to a rank provincialism without the saving graces of intelligence, manners, or culture,"

"Worse than the Victorians?"

"Lots worse," Malcolm said drily.

"Too bad. It's a horrid thing to say about people who invented . . . well, lots of things."

Malcolm sighed. "Margo, you really have to study."

"I know! I *am* studying. I'll study more when we get back! At least I can now tell you everything Francis Marion ever did, said, or thought!"

Still a sore subject. He was sorry, indeed, that she and Kit had fought about it. All La-La Land had buzzed with the gossip when Margo had walked out of the Delight and headed for the library in tears—leaving Kit so rattled a *down timer,* for God's sake, had nearly gotten the better of him in a hand-to-hand fight with a croquet mallet. That was the primary reason Malcolm was here: to convince her how important those studies were. Malcolm took his job seriously.

Then he had to stifle a grin. If the Hilaria and Ludi Megalenses didn't convince Margo she needed to study, nothing would.

A Time Tours guide opened the outside door again to communicate with employees in the wine shop proper. The roar of noise from the Via Appia just beyond caused a wave of excited laughter to ripple its way back through the tourists. The soundproofed door closed and the Time Tours guide stepped onto a crate to command attention.

"As you know, we'll all be staying at the inn we've purchased in the Aventinus district, west of the Baths of Decius and southwest of the Temples of Minerva and Luna. That's very close to the Circus Maximus, in the heart of the sacred district, so we're not far from it now. We'll go there first. It's vital that everyone know how to find it. If you get lost, find the Circus and you can find the inn again. The most important instruction I have for you is simple: *Don't get separated from your guides!* There are more than a million people living in Rome right now, not to mention the thousands more who've crowded in for the Games of the Magna Mater. You don't know the language or the customs. If you lose your guide, you could find yourself in fatal trouble very fast. Our porters will carry your luggage, since neither free-born men nor free-born women carried their own parcels. You've already been warned not to venture out after dark. Rome is a deadly city by night Not even the ruling classes walk the streets after dark. Now . . . are there any questions?"

"What do we do after you show us the hotel?" a man near the center of the group asked.

"You've already been assigned to your tour groups. Each group will follow an itinerary based on the selections you made at the time station. Today is the Sacrifice of Attis, with an historic first procession of the sacred pine, plus the regular annual celebrations and the dedications of new priests. Three days from now the Hilaria begins. The Ludi Megalenses games begin on April fourth and will continue through the tenth, with Circus games and races daily. Chariot races, horse races, and bestiaries are scheduled for the mornings, gladiatorial combats for the afternoons.

"As you know, when the Games open, it will be arena

seating"—another ripple of laughter went through the crowd at the silly pun—"so we'll need to find seats quickly to be assured of places. Be ready to enter the Circus by sunrise. The gate back to the time terminal reopens shortly after midnight on the eleventh. You'll probably be exhausted—so don't arrive late!"

"What about the lottery?"

The speaker was another man, near the edge of the crowd.

"We've already drawn the winners of the Messalina lottery but we won't announce the results until tomorrow. As you know, there will be only three winners and the liaisons have to be carefully arranged by our employee in the Imperial palace. With Claudius in town, these trysts have to be set up with care. The winners, as you know, are not guaranteed a night with the Empress. Messalina has the right to refuse any lover she wants, but her tastes in men are generally broad enough we don't anticipate any problems. After all, she does sleep with Claudius."

A titter of laughter ran around the room. Malcolm didn't join in. Everyone had been shown photographs in advance to prevent the disaster of someone laughing at the disfigured emperor should they accidentally stumble across an Imperial procession. Margo, not knowing any better, laughed too, then turned a puzzled glance toward him.

"What's wrong, Malcolm?" she asked anxiously. "That was funny. Wasn't it?"

"No. It wasn't."

She studied his face for a moment. "Why not? You've seen him, haven't you?"

"Yes. That's precisely why I don't find it funny."

Margo's brows drew together, but she didn't respond flippantly. Good. She was learning. Up near the front of the room, the Time Tours guide said, "All right, everybody ready? Any last questions? Good. Let's have some fun!"

Malcolm said quietly, "When we get to the street, it's okay to stare at the buildings. You're dressed like a provincial; it'll be expected."

Margo nodded eagerly. The shine had returned to her eyes.

The door to the street opened once more to a bedlam of noise. Margo craned her neck to see outside, but was too short to see over the people between them and the door. The line moved forward slowly. The tour was permitted to leave in small groups of no more than three or four plus porters and guides. It always took a while to assemble a group for departure or to disperse a newly arrived tour without raising suspicion about the number of people entering and leaving the wine shop. "Defer to *anyone* wearing a toga," Malcolm went on as soon as the door closed and Margo's attention returned to him. "If you encounter a member of the Praetorian Guard, try to look like the humblest, least important worm on the streets. You *don't* want to catch a Guardsman's attention. If I tell you to do something, do it fast and ask why later."

"Okay. What's the Praetorian Guard look like?"

"Roman soldiers. If you see anyone dressed like the soldiers in *Ben Hur,* get out of the way."

'They look like soldiers? Helmets with plumes, metal breastplates, little skirts, all that?"

"They don't just look like soldiers, Margo, they *are* soldiers. Bloody arrogant ones, at that."

Margo smiled. "Your accent's slipping, Malcolm."

He rubbed the end of his nose. "Well, yes. But the Praetorian Guard is something you don't want to tangle with. A lot of them are *Germans.* They're taller—a lot taller—than Romans. Now, about another important matter, have you studied the money?"

Margo groaned. "A little. Mostly I was trying to cram Latin."

The line moved forward again in a blare of noise from the open door.

"You're dressed as a free man, so you'll be expected to know the use of Roman money. As your slave, all I can do is translate. The more you know about the local money, the less likely you'll be completely rooked. I can tell you fair value for items, but remember we're not here to shop. We're here to learn."

Margo nodded impatiently. They were almost to the door.

"One last thing. I'm dressed as your slave. You're dressed as my *dominus*—my master. That's for public appearances. Don't let the master-slave thing go to your head or I'll turn you over my knee the second we're in private."

Margo shot him a startled glance. "You wouldn't!"

Malcolm grinned. "Oh, yes I would. *I'm* the teacher—the *magister*—and *you're* the pupil. Forget that and I'll remind you."

The door opened in front of them and Margo let out a tiny squeal of excitement. It was their turn to cross the threshold and enter the street. Then Margo got her first good look at genuine imperial Romans.

Her mouth dropped open. "They're . . . they're so *short!*"

The look on her face was so priceless, Malcolm burst out laughing. Margo was a dainty little thing, but very few of the people on the street were even close to her height. Malcolm towered over everyone in sight. Even the wine-shop counter and seats were designed for child-sized bodies.

Margo gaped, staring from one Roman to the next. "They're *tiny!*"

"Among scholars," Malcolm told her with a chuckle, "speculation is rife that Julius Caesar's six-foot height had no little impact on his success as a politician. Everybody had to look up to him."

Margo grinned. "That's funny."

Malcolm laughed. "Yes. *That* is. Ready?"

"And then some! Show me!"

"Okay, hang a sharp right-left-right-left past the end of the Circus Maximus, then follow the Via Ostiensis until it breaks southwest toward the Porta Ostiensa: the Ostian Gate. We'll take side streets around the Aventine Hill to the inn."

Margo cast a worried glance at him. "If I take the wrong turn?"

"I'll be right behind you. Just don't walk too fast. I *am* carrying all the luggage." That was one of the downsides to freelance guiding in Rome.

Margo set out without further delay. Malcolm hoisted the bundles to a more comfortable position on his back and followed. Crowds jostled him as he made his way down the stone sidewalk. He tried, with little success, to avoid being bumped off into the muck in the streets. When Margo reached the first corner, she paused.

"People are staring at me."

"You're dressed like a provincial. They'll probably laugh at your expense. Ignore them."

"Are those stepping stones to the other side?" She pointed at a series of high, squared-off stones set like miniature tank traps in the street.

"Yes."

"The street stinks. Worse than London."

Several people crossed on the stones, with pedestrian traffic flowing first one direction then the other as people took turns. Those who were impatient braved the muck.

'Yuck. This place is filthy!"

"No, actually it's very clean. State-owned slaves periodically clean the streets and the Cloaca Maxima is still in use in Rome even in our time."

"The what?"

"The main sewer of Rome. Just how much reading did you finish?"

"Uh. . . ." She took advantage of a switch in traffic flow to cross the paving stones. Malcolm, caught in a crunch of people, had to resort to wading across at street level just to keep up with her.

"Hsst! Slow down!"

She glanced back and slowed down for all of three minutes, then the lure of more delightful sights down the street caused another lapse. She drew ahead again, paying no attention to Malcolm struggling along with their luggage. Malcolm held his temper and followed, wondering how long it would take her to admit she was in trouble.

She negotiated the dogleg around the end of the Circus just fine, despite the inattention she paid to the directions he'd given her. Malcolm didn't begrudge her the awed stare at the immense arena's facade. A single-story building ran around the outside, crammed with shops selling everything from baskets to hot sausages. Shopkeepers lived on the mezzanine above. Entrances near each shop led directly into the arena-level seats behind the podium wall. Stairs led upward to the second and third tiers where the long stone bleachers of the center sections gave way to wooden bleachers rounding the semicircular end. High overhead, three stories up, rose the colonnade and wooden arches which surmounted the end of the arena.

Margo walked with her neck cricked, staring upward and bumping into Romans who grinned and nudged one another.

"Barbarian's new to town."

"Wonder what god's-forsaken corner that rube's from?"

"Bet his eyes are about to pop!"

"Hey, *meretrix!* Take a look at the barbarian. Could be a good prospect!" This latter was shouted to a nearby woman in a short tunic. She ogled the Palmyrene "boy" hopefully. Margo, oblivious, passed the whore without noticing. Malcolm winked at her. "Maybe later?" he said in Latin.

The woman laughed. "Cheap enough for you? Or expensive enough for him?"

Malcolm grinned. "You look good to me, but who knows what a Palmyrene likes? Sheep, maybe?"

She laughed and passed the joke on to another loitering whore nearby. Several Roman men also laughed, overhearing the exchange.

Margo, oblivious, trailed a wake of good-natured laughter at her expense. She found the Via Ostiensis without difficulty. But she was so busy gawking at the sights, she didn't pay attention to the markings on the buildings when the Via Ostiensis apparently veered southwest. Margo committed the classic folly of taking the wrong fork in the road, wandering enthralled from one shop to the next. Malcolm, sweating under the weight of the luggage, let her walk all the way to the end of the Via Ardeatina. When Porta Ardeatina grew visible in the distance, she paused, then stared uncomprehendingly at her surroundings. She ended with a beseeching look at Malcolm.

"Where are we?"

He caught his breath. "You tell me."

Margo widened pretty green eyes. "*What?* Don't tell me we're lost? I thought you *knew* Rome?"

"I do. *I* know exactly where we are. We're about a hundred yards from the Porta Ardeatina on the southern edge of Rome. Hell and gone, I might add, from the inn.

"Why didn't you say something?"

"Margo, I was under the impression you'd learned something from your experiences in London. Was I wrong?"

Margo had the good grace to flush bright red.

"Pay attention to what you're doing." He said it quietly but with enough force to make her hang her head. "I refuse to believe Sven Bailey has trained you for several weeks, yet neglected to mention that little gem of survival wisdom."

Margo's flush deepened. "No harm done. We weren't mugged or anything."

He could have pointed out that *she* wasn't carrying anything heavy and so wasn't in a fit position to judge harm done, but he'd voluntarily assumed the weight of responsibility when he'd decided to teach her this little object lesson.

"Not yet," he pointed out. "But you still need to pay attention, Margo. There are consequences to everything you do—or don't do. As a scout, you won't have me along to bail you out."

She huffed as only Margo could do. The elegant folds of her costume flounced with the movement, leading Malcolm's attention badly astray from the lesson at hand. When Margo pouted, Malcolm was hard pressed to keep his attention on the job at hand—or anything else, for that matter.

All right, eyes front and center, Malcolm! You were hired to play teacher, not Don Juan. But darn it . . . all that spirit and tenacity and the occasional flashes of warmth and brilliance, glimpsed behind the pert facade and the periodic deep-seated hurt in her eyes, had come gift wrapped in *such* a pretty package . . .

None of which was her fault.

Maybe Kit picked the wrong guide for this job.

"Okay," Margo sighed. "I screwed up again. It's my fault, I admit it. But I *am* here to learn. So *show* me."

He found it increasingly difficult to remain firm with her "All right. This time, follow my directions."

Malcolm was tempted to make her retrace her steps and follow the route he'd given her. Instead, he deliberately took her through a maze of narrow, cramped side streets that wandered in zigzags up and down Rome's hills and valleys, just to underscore the lesson in paying attention. They finally emerged on the Via Ostiensis near the Ostian Gate. He led her back north again, to the place where he'd meant for her to leave the Ostian Way, where they should have circled the Aventine Hill. By the time they reached the inn, Malcolm's shoulders ached.

"You're late," the Time Tours employee said sourly, glancing at Malcolm for an explanation as he checked off their names against his master list.

"Object lesson," Malcolm said shortly, offering no further excuses. He retreated to their assigned room and dropped their luggage to the tiled floor then sat down on a wooden bed frame, not even bothering to locate the rolled-up bedding first. He could feel the pull of tired muscles from his neck to the middle of his back. When Margo came in, she caught him working his shoulders in circles. Her face flamed again.

"Are you hurt?"

Contrite as a child, now that the damage was done. He studied her silently. She was biting her lower lip. Malcolm had forgotten how very young eighteen was, with its mixture of invincible assuredness, fragile emotions, and the desperate need to be taken seriously—even when caught in complete ignorance. Malcolm sighed. "Not much." She glided across the room in a ripple of Parthian folds, then knelt behind him. Before he could protest, she was rubbing his shoulders. Malcolm shut his eyes. *God . . .* She was surprisingly skilled, working hard knots out of aching muscles from his neck to the middle of his back. *Where'd you learn to do that, little girl?* When her touch lightened to the merest whisper across his neck, Malcolm's insides reacted mindlessly. She didn't know what she was doing to him . . . Did she?

Malcolm shot to his feet. "Gotta see about lunch," he mumbled, bolting for the safety of the crowded dining tables. The *last* thing any of them needed was for him to lose control. If Malcolm ever kissed her the way his body demanded she be kissed . . .

He called to mind Kit's blackest glower and held it firmly in place. *Grandpa,* Malcolm warned himself solemnly, *would not be amused.* Not at all.

Margo had never seen anything like the Procession of Attis.

Their inn lay on the southern side of the Aventine Hill near the Tiber. From there, Malcolm led the way around the end of the Circus where the starting gates overlooked a bend in the river and kept going all the way to the Palatine side of the mile-long Circus.

"Hey!" Margo said, pointing to a small, round temple. "I know that one! That's the Temple of Vesta!"

"Mmm . . . Well, it's been misnamed that for years, yes." Margo's spirits fell. "You're in good company." Malcolm grinned. "Hundreds of books still mislabel it that. Actually it was the Temple of Hercules. And that," he pointed to a squarish temple a stone's throw away, "is the Temple of Fortuna Virilis."

"Fortuna Virilis?"

"Temple of Man's Fate. Fate and the Circus games are *very* closely connected."

That made sense. Men *died* in the Circus.

"See up there?" he pointed to the crown of the Palatine Hill. "That's the Imperial residence. And that," he pointed to a magnificent temple which faced the great Circus, "is the Temple of the Magna Mater Deum Idea."

"What's that?" Margo asked breathlessly.

"What does it sound like?"

She considered, dredging up the bits of Latin she'd absorbed. "Magna sounds like magnificent. Mater . . . I'm not sure. Magnificent Material? Matter?"

"No, *mater* means mother. It's one of the words that sound similar in all languages descended from Indo-European: mater, mere, madre, mutter, mother."

"Oh. Magnificent Mother?"

"Close. Great Mother. What about the Deum Idea?"

"Uh . . . Deum is, like, deify?"

"Good guess. Deum translates 'of the gods'." Malcolm explained.

"Great Mother of the Gods of Ideas?" she guessed.

Malcolm grinned. "Not quite, although it's a logical enough guess. Idea in this case, however, refers to a mountain in Phrygia, near Troy.

The Magna Mater is the goddess Cybele, the great mother of the gods from Phrygia. She's an import to Rome, but a very old one. About three hundred years ago, in fact. Her cult's been completely Romanized, of course. The Julian *gens*—Julius and Augustus Caesar's family—claims her as a founding deity. She was sacred to Aeneas, who founded their family. Claudius' family also has ties to her through Claudia Quintas."

Margo stared up the Palatine Hill, wondering what Malcolm saw that she didn't because she didn't know what to look for or what she was looking at. *Okay, I have to study and I will. But if I don't start scouting soon, it'll be too late and I'll never prove anything . . .*

They fought their way through thick crowds until they could see the Via Appia where it turned to round the Palatine Hill. In the distance they could hear the sound of flutes and drums.

"Just in time," Malcolm grinned.

Margo craned to see. She was taller than the waiting crowd, which was a novel experience. She could see movement now in the street. Sunlight glittered against gold. The shrill of trumpets and the sharp sound of tympani drums rose above the noise of the crowd. Then she could see individuals. The person in the lead wore a long gown with folds of cloth pulled up like a hood. Under it Margo could see some kind of crown with three separate disks across the brow.

"Is that a priestess?" she asked excitedly.

"No, that's the *archgalli*—the High Priest of Attis. He just arrived in Rome through the new port Claudius is building. He managed to secure permission for this procession, to carry the sacred tree to Cybele's temple."

Margo blinked. "But he's dressed like a woman. I mean, he isn't dressed like any of the other men I've seen so far. Is it because he's a foreigner?"

"No, you were right the first time. Attis' priests wore women's clothing. For that matter, so did the priests of Hercules."

Hercules? Mr. Macho himself, the guy with all the muscles who'd done all those impossible labors or whatever they were called? Why would Hercules' priests dress like women? It didn't make any sense.

With every maddening snippet of information Malcolm shared, she sensed a vast depth of knowledge he *wasn't* sharing. She glanced up, wanting to ask, but he was so visibly excited by the procession wending its way toward them she decided to hold her question for later. He darted his gaze eagerly, noting details, even mumbling to himself.

The high priest—*archgalli*, Malcolm had called him—neared their position. He moved slowly, wailing in a shrill voice and weeping while beating himself with a long flail. He held a scepter made of reeds in his other hand. Behind him came sweating bearers with a heavy litter. On it rode the gilded statue of a gorgeous young man in a soft, peaked cap. His "shirt" was open to the groin, leaving his chest and belly bare to well below the navel. His trousers were carved with diamond-shaped cutouts like a Harlequin's costume. In one hand he held what looked like a walking cane.

In the other, he held a small tympani drum exactly like the ones carried by wailing priests who trailed behind. They beat their drums with flails, then beat themselves, then sounded the tympanies again. Priests behind them, also wailing at the top of their lungs, carried more of the reed scepters. Behind *them* came another litter carried by sweating priests. On it was a statue of a tree. Sunstruck pine cones glittered with gold leaf.

"A pine tree?" Margo asked doubtfully.

"Shh! Later! Look!"

Margo widened her eyes. "My God . . ."

Half a dozen men each held thick leather leashes which chained a pair of *lions.* The huge cats glared at the crowd with hateful amber eyes. Margo clutched Malcolm's arm. *"They're not even caged!"* The lion handlers were sweating profusely, dragging on the leashes to keep their charges in the center of the street. Behind the stalking lions came another great litter. On it rode a gilded statue of a tall, beautiful woman. She rode a chariot drawn by lions.

"Cybele?" Margo whispered.

Malcolm just nodded. He was listening to the chanting priests. What were they saying? The crowd took up the chant, too, as the Magna Mater passed regally by. Some people tossed coins which weeping priests scooped off the paving stones and dropped into little bowls. Behind the gilded image came two priests who led a great black bull with scarlet robes draped across its back. At the rear of the procession came trumpeters, flute players, and a host of young men who stumbled along with glazed eyes, beating themselves with flails and wailing. They carried no reed scepters.

"Who are *they?*" Margo asked.

"Initiates. They'll dedicate themselves to Attis today. But I rather doubt they'll do it in the traditional Phrygian fashion. Claudius hasn't legalized *that.*"

"They look stoned."

"They probably are."

She stared. "Why?"

"Purification ritual. Come on, if we scramble, I know a way up the hill."

Margo followed his lead as they dodged up the Palatine through narrow alleys that led past the Imperial palace toward the crowning Temple of Magna Mater. Crowds had gathered there, too. In a courtyard at the front of the temple they found space to jam themselves close enough to watch. The shrill of flutes, trumpets, and wailing voices drew nearer as the procession wound its way up the far side of the Palatine.

"They're passing through the Forum," Malcolm explained, "down the Sacra Via. Look, here they come."

Margo stood on tiptoe, anxious not to miss anything. What exactly was going on? She didn't know anything about Attis or Cybele—and Malcolm was so caught up in the moment she didn't want to interrupt to ask for explanations. The High Priest arrived first and took a position near a long, deep trench which had been dug in the courtyard. Planks capped it, arranged so that gaps showed. The images of Attis, Cybele, and the pine tree were carried up the steps to the entrance of the temple. The leashed lions snarled at the crowd. The roar vibrated against Margo's chest, bringing a prickle of unreasoning terror to the back of her neck.

The courtyard filled up. The black bull was led in and paraded around the periphery. Over in front of the temple, priests had lifted the gilded image of Attis off its litter. They were tying it to the gilt pine tree with stout ropes. Other ropes served as guide wires to keep the pine tree from toppling under the weight.

A line of robed priestesses—Margo was sure, this time, that she was looking at women—appeared from inside Cybele's temple and took up positions in a semicircle. The High Priest led the black bull onto the platform, where several attendants held it with strong ropes. A swift glance at Malcolm showed Margo a man completely lost in study. He watched the barbaric scene as though memorizing every baffling detail.

This is his specialty, Margo remembered suddenly, *what he took his degrees in, Classics and Antiquities and stuff. He's forgotten me completely.* She'd seen Malcolm the teacher, Malcolm the guide, Malcolm the sparring partner, even Malcolm the perennially broke friend who made her smile when she felt like curling into a ball and hiding from the world, but she'd never seen Malcolm the scholar enthralled by his life's passion. The intensity of his gaze made her wish suddenly he'd look at *her* that way.

If you want him to do that, you are going to have to meet him on even ground, Margo. And that meant she had to become a scholar. Well, she'd already discovered a burning desire to learn and understand; what better place to start than with something Malcolm, too, found passionately interesting? So *get started already!*

Margo studied the scene before her, trying to look at it as a student of ancient cultures. She wished she hadn't skipped so many Latin lessons or skimped on the cultural reading Kit had assigned her in favor of more time in the gym. Robed initiates stripped naked and descended into the deep trench. The bull lowed piteously. Its eyes rolled white. Someone she couldn't see too well was doing something under the animal's belly. She caught a flash of sunlight on steel as the High Priest shouted something.

The bull screamed and lunged. The men holding it strained at the ropes. The knife flashed again—to the throat, this time—and Margo flinched. *God, they're really killing it . . .* Blood poured through gaps into file trench. The bull fought, screaming and bellowing and bleeding to death at the end of its ropes. Margo covered her ears. She'd never seen an animal die up close like this, hadn't realized they would scream so pitifully. It was terrible, cruel, monstrous. . . . *You're not in Minnesota, Margo.* But the bull's agonizing death shook her, nonetheless. *They don't take so long to die in modern slaughterhouses,* she told herself. But it would be a long time before she wanted to eat beef again. Eventually the bull sank to its knees, dead. The High Priest held up something long and crooked at one end, like the walking cane on Attis' statue.

Then she realized what it was. "My God!" Her shocked expletive was lost in the cheer from the crowd. Trumpets sounded again, wild and shrill in the April sunlight. The young initiates emerged, reeling and covered with blood. They looked like they'd been *drinking* it. They stumbled past the High Priest, each touching the bull's severed member in turn, then vanished into the temple. The priestesses followed. The High Priest, too, entered the temple. Other priests took up a chant that lasted a long time. Then, at some signal from inside the temple, the crowd began to cheer wildly. The high priest of Attis returned, still holding the bull's severed genitals.

Margo's head swam. None of this made any sense. The crowd had taken up its own chant. Malcolm looked like he was trying to memorize every word. Then she realized he'd loosened the flap on the bag which held his personal log. How long had he been recording? She caught a glint in his palm and recognized a miniature digitizing camera, one that worked like a video recorder but fed directly to the computerized log. Surely he'd attended one of these parades and ceremonies before?

No, she remembered suddenly, *this was supposed to be a historic first for Rome.*

No wonder he'd been desperate to get here and see this, record it in its entirety. She wondered how many other scholars had come on this tour? Given the questions about the Messalina lottery, probably none. Perhaps Malcolm *was* the only scholar present to record the Procession of Attis. She felt like a heel that she hadn't thought to turn on *her* recorder, too.

"Malcolm," Margo hissed, "just what *are* Attis and Cybele?"

He hushed her. He seemed to be waiting for something, as though unsure what might happen next. The High Priest bowed low before the great gilded statue of Cybele in her lion chariot. He placed the severed bull's phallus before it and backed away, flailing himself and chanting. Initiates stumbled out, assisted by other priests. Then, at something which completely escaped her, he said, "Ahh" and suddenly relaxed.

The High Priest had obtained a basket filled with reed scepters. He presented one to each reeling initiate. While Margo stared, the new priests broke the reed scepters violently in half, then carried them one by one and tied the broken reeds to the gilded pine tree. The crowd was chanting along with the priests.

"What are they saying?" Margo demanded. "What are they *doing?*"

Once again, Malcolm hushed her. She stood in the midst of an insane crowd and tried hard to figure out the lunacy she'd just witnessed, but didn't come up with anything rational as explanation. *Some scholar I am.* To interpret something, one first had to know something on which to base an interpretation.

Why was it there was never enough time to fulfill one's dreams properly? To be a proper scout would take years. If she took years, the one burning goal that had made the past three years tolerable would never amount to anything more than daydreams. Margo sighed as the priests re-entered the Temple, carrying their sacred images inside. Then it was all over and the crowd broke up. People chattered excitedly, sounding for all the world like sports fans comparing the performances of favorite basketball stars. Malcolm fussed briefly with the bag containing his personal log, sliding the digitizing camera back into it and shutting off everything. Then he stood blinking like a sleepy English spaniel just coming awake in the morning.

"Well . . ." Malcolm's glance rested on her. His face reddened. "Hi. I, uh, think you had a question?" he asked sheepishly.

"Or three, yes." She stood glaring at him, hands on hips, then had to laugh. "You look so funny when you're embarrassed, Malcolm. What the hell was that all about? I tried to make sense of it, but it was pretty weird."

"Today is known as Black Friday, the day of the Sun's death," Malcolm explained as he led the way down from the sacred Palatine Hill. "Attis is a Solar god, castrated and sacrificed to fructify the earth, then reborn again after coupling with his mother consort Cybele. The Taurobolium—the ritual slaughter of the bull—is a purification ritual."

"Did they really drink its blood?"

"Yes, indeed. Then each initiate mated with a priestess of Cybele in the Temple of the Magna Mater. I'm surprised they didn't couple in the courtyard. I believe in some areas, the sacred marriages are done publicly." He smiled. "Roman morals, however, are generally much stricter, despite what you may see in movies. Of course," his eyes twinkled, "all bets are off during Hilaria."

A shiver ran up Margo's back. Hilaria was only a couple of days away. Just exactly what *would* the festival be like? And her seventeenth birthday was going to fall right in the middle of it. She couldn't have asked for a better birthday present.

"Anyway, after going inside to mate with the Goddess, our young initiates symbolically castrated themselves by breaking those reed scepters. I'd wondered how they would get away with the ritual in Rome, Imperial law being what it is."

"What do you mean? What's so terrible about breaking a bundle of reeds in half?"

Malcolm grimaced expressively. "It used to be a requirement of the priesthood of Attis for the initiate to castrate himself and present the severed organ to the Goddess."

Margo halted in the middle of the street. "Yuck!"

"Margo, you're blocking the way."

She started walking again, but her expression caused Malcolm to chuckle. "It's a very, very common myth in this part of the world, actually," Malcolm said as they turned into another narrow side street. "It's already ancient by these peoples' reckoning. The Sun God or Grain God mates the Mother Goddess, sometimes in her incarnation as the Moon, sometimes as Earth. The Solar God reigns as sacred king, is ritually killed, then is reborn again to begin the cycle of seasons and crops all over again. Hercules is another ritually murdered sacred king. But he was burned alive rather than being castrated and hung to bleed to death on a pine. In Carthage, ancient sacred kings were burned alive on pyres as the solar Hercules. Aeneas barely escaped that fate when he ran away from Queen Dido of Carthage. In Egypt, Ra-Osiris was cut into pieces and scattered—"

"Malcolm, that's gross!"

His glance was highly sardonic. "Well, yes, from our perspective it is. But they really believed sacrificial blood was required to fertilize the earth. Crops wouldn't grow without it. And they really believed the god and his severed phallus were regenerated by the blood and by mating with the Goddess. That's why the full-fledged priests in the procession carried reed scepters. They're symbols of the god's phallus reborn as grain. It's the same reason you'll find Herms—phallus symbols—all over Herculaneum, for instance, which has Hercules as its patron deity. They're considered good luck symbols. People put them up by their doorways, touch them for luck."

Margo could understand rubbing a stone penis for luck better than she could a man mutilating himself. "But Malcolm . . . what kind of man would want to do that to himself? Did they do it voluntarily? Or were they prisoners?"

"No, they were volunteers. Look on the bright side: the tradition was modified years ago to kill the bull instead of the castrated priests. And now the tradition's been modified again, substituting broken reed scepters for the real castration. Roman law wouldn't tolerate the cult, otherwise. Of course, the Romans like to pay lip service to civilized notions about human sacrifices, but they have their own darker element to religious practices."

"Like what?"

"The Games."

"Those are *human sacrifices?*" She halted again, blocking the flow of the dispersing crowd behind her. Someone cursed at her in Latin. Hastily she stepped aside. "Malcolm, you're not serious? Nobody in any of my history classes ever said anything about human sacrifices in Rome and I didn't find anything like that in any of the reading I *did* do. I mean . . . the Romans were supposed to be *civilized!*" She stared down the hill toward the hulking facade of the great Circus. "Why would civilized people do something like that? I don't understand. Malcolm, it doesn't make sense and it ought to, if it's true."

Malcolm's eyes glinted. "I seem to have reawakened that curious itch to learn I first glimpsed in London. All right. Let's see if I can shed some light. Centuries ago, probably during Etruscan times, the Circus Maximus began life as a natural amphitheater of ritual sacrifice. The games, mostly races, were part of elaborate funerary rites. When we watch the Ludi Megalenses in a few days, keep that in mind. We are not merely watching spectator sports. The Games are *not* a Roman form of NFL football. We'll be watching a sacred drama.

"It's *exciting* drama and the spectacles help the emperor keep the unemployed masses quiet by giving them something to do, but it's still sacred at its core and most people in this time recognize the ritual for what it is—if not overtly, then at some level of awareness.

"You asked if the priests of Cybele were volunteers or prisoners. The participants in Roman games *are* largely prisoners: criminals and slaves, prisoners of war. It's always easier on the king to substitute slaves for the real thing when the king must die. And in this particular time and this particular place, that is precisely what must happen."

The dust and noise of the bright April morning faded from Margo's awareness. She had difficulty taking in everything Malcolm had said. She understood much more clearly now why he'd said most guides held advanced degrees. They had to, in order to explain to tourists what they were watching. *But I can't spend years at this before my first scouting trip!* What she needed to become was a *generalist*. She could learn a little about a lot of things and fake it whenever she had to.

Meanwhile, she'd learn everything Malcolm would teach her.

"Huh. So now what?"

"Now," Malcolm grinned, "I think it's time to scout out some lunch."

"Now *there's* a plan I like!"

Malcolm laughed and took her back down the sacred Palatine Hill in search of her first genuine Roman meal.

Grey light had barely touched the sky when Malcolm stepped out of the Time Tours inn. Wagons and carts, caught like vampires by the sunrise, had been unharnessed and abandoned where they stood.

Slaves and yeoman farmers carted off the goods by hand.

"The next three days," Malcolm told Margo as she joined him, "are going to be very much a repeat of yesterday."

"More weird parades?"

He shook his head. "No. That's reserved for the day of Attis' sacrifice. But Attis is a popular cult, particularly amongst the poor in the slums and in the port cities. A lot of people will walk around in a festive state of mourning, if that makes any sense, flailing themselves same as the priests yesterday and weeping for the tragic fate of their god."

She wrinkled her nose. Malcolm chuckled. "Get used to weird sights if you want to scout. Now, since the real fun doesn't begin until the Hilaria, and since that doesn't start for three days, I have a different plan of action in mind."

"That being?"

"Ostia."

"What's that? Another sacred ritual where some poor schmuck gets to play king of the hour?"

"No," Malcolm smiled. "Ostia is the port city downriver from Rome."

"Oh. Oh! That means a sightseeing trip outside Rome?"

Malcolm resisted the urge to tousle her hair. "Yes. Claudius has been building new harbor facilities. I want to see them. You should, too, just to get a grasp of Roman engineering." He chuckled. "The engineers told the emperor the harbor would be ruinously expensive, but it *had* to be built because the main harbor is silting in. I can hardly wait to see it, even if it won't be finished in Claudius' lifetime. It's said to be spectacular."

Margo had brightened visibly. "That sounds super! How do we get there?"

"We hire a boat."

She grinned. "Great! Show me!"

Malcolm made arrangements with a local merchant willing to hire out his little *lenunculi* since he was on holiday for the festivals. The boat reeked of fish, but handled beautifully.

"You know how to sail, I guess?" Margo asked.

"Yep. So will you, by the time we get to Ostia." She groaned, but took to the lessons cheerfully once they were on the water. Malcolm taught her the rudiments of terminology while he navigated the heavy traffic in the Tiber. Once they were downstream from Rome and into quieter water, he started the hands-on lessons. She was clumsy at first and nearly put them into the near bank a couple of times but eventually caught on. He let her steer for a while and relaxed in the warm morning sunshine. "You like it here," she said after a while. Malcolm peeled an eyelid and found her watching him pensively. He smiled. "Yes, I do."

"Even though they're barbaric and put people to death in the arena?"

He considered how best to answer. "Every culture's barbaric in some fashion. It's a matter of perspective. The reverse is generally true, as well. Every culture has something fine and useful to offer. It's a matter of how you look at it. The trick in scouting is to figure out what you're looking at, to decide what—if anything—you can gain from that particular culture and time period, then to make off safely with whatever you've found, whether it's scholarly information or something more lucrative. Like, say, a potential new tourist gate or some treasure that's about to be lost through natural or man-made calamity. The more you know about when and where you are when you step through, the likelier you'll be able to identify what's useful."

"You don't care much about the money, do you?"

He chuckled and tucked his hands more comfortably behind his head. "You're beginning to figure me out, young lady. Nope. Not like some scouts and guides, anyway." He winked. "That's not to say I'd be averse to picking up a nice little treasure if I had the chance. But for me, it's the *learning* that's the kick. It's why Kit's rich and I'm broke. He likes to learn, too. Isn't a scout alive who doesn't. But he cares more about the money than I do and truthfully . . . I think he's a lot luckier than I am."

"People make their own luck," Margo said with surprising vehemence.

He glanced into her eyes, then smiled. "Well, yes. Maybe they do.

You're here, after all. And I'd have bet money you'd never get this far."

She flushed. "Thanks. I think."

Malcolm laughed. "Well, considering the first thing you did in La-La Land was get lost in Residential . . . Straighten the rudder, Margo. We're headed for the river bank again."

She put out her tongue and steered for the central current again. It was a glorious day for a sail, perfect weather and perfect company, but as they neared the new port, river traffic grew much thicker. Malcolm took over and steered a course toward the far bank to get the best view possible when they neared what should be the spot for the new harbor facility.

"There are a lot of boats coming up river," Margo commented.

"Ostia's the grain port for Rome. Italian agriculture's in trouble, mostly for economic reasons. Almost all of Rome's food supply, grain in particular, is imported. In fact, Rome imports far more than she exports. Take that, for instance." He pointed to a heavily laded *corbita,* a land of heavy freighter, passing majestically on its way upriver. "Those amphorae probably contain wine or olive oil, I can't see the markings at this distance to be sure. Those bales are Egyptian cotton and imported luxury goods." A barge towed by *scaphae* followed. Huddled on its decks were miserable, half-naked men and women in chains.

Margo's eyes widened. "Those are slaves!"

"Ostia *is* a trading port," Malcolm pointed out "And slaves are big business. Rome has had a slave economy for centuries."

She followed the barge's progress until it passed out of sight beyond a bend, then shivered. They rounded another curve in the river and the new port came into view. Ostia was just visible in the distance, more than two miles away across silty salt marsh. The new port rose from the marshes as though the gods themselves had set the giant stones in place. Margo breathed, "Wow!" For once, Malcolm shared her awe. Two curving breakwaters had been constructed across the entrance to an enormous excavation. The main harbor—some one hundred seventy acres of it—had already been dug and flooded. Between the two breakwaters, Roman engineers had built an artificial island. A tall tower rose toward the bright sky, incomplete as yet. An artificial channel connected the newly dug harbor with the river.

Malcolm dragged over the bag containing his ATLS and log and slung it across his chest, bandolier style, then risked a quick scan with a digitizing camera which hooked into the log like an ordinary scanning mouse. He photographed the entire panorama, then steered for the middle of the Tiber. Now that he'd seen the whole layout, he was dying to get a closer look. Margo leaned over the prow like an excited kid.

"What's that?" Margo asked, pointing to the tower. "A temple of some land?"

"No. Much more important." She glanced around, brow furrowed.

"Like what?"

He grinned. "A lighthouse."

"A lighthouse?" Margo laughed. "I never thought about ancient people building practical things like lighthouses, but I guess they'd need one, wouldn't they? Especially to navigate around that island in the fog."

"Yes. It's almost finished. Claudius will dedicate the new harbor this year, although construction will continue through A.D. 54 under Nero, after Claudiu's death. Get your log. I want you to start recording your impressions. Just open the flap on your bag a little and press voice record."

She did so, draping the bag around her own neck and shoulder much as he had.

"Wow. That's really something, Malcolm." She began describing everything in sight, then started asking questions. "How long must it have taken to dig all that out? Months? Years? And look at those walls. What is that? Stone? Or concrete? And look at those piers. They're solid stone! How'd they get those blocks into place? Say, what's that?"

Malcolm grinned. Witnessing Margo's mind come alive was almost as much fun as studying the new port to satisfy his own scholarly itch. They moved on down river and spent the day in Ostia, prowling the wharves while merchants offloaded cargo for the river voyage up to Rome and manufactured goods arrived for export to the far-flung provinces. Ostia's harbor was so badly silted, the town was already showing the effects of lost business to overland routes. Eventually, even Claudius' fine new harbor would silt in and everything would come overland from Naples—until Trajan would finally build his non-silting, hexagonal-basin harbor. Almost sixty years from now, Ostia would come into her true glory as a port. But even now, Ostia was an impressive little city.

Malcolm took her to the barracks of the *vigiles* and explained the function of the special cohort.

"Firemen?" Margo echoed. "I thought Benjamin Franklin invented fire departments."

"Say, you *have* been doing that American history reading, haven't you? Very good. In a manner of speaking, he did. But the Romans had a special fire-fighting brigade to protect the grain port and there was even a private company in Rome. Of course, *its* main job was to arrive at a fire and convince the owner to sell out cheap before putting out the blaze . . ."

"That's *awful!*"

"Free enterprise in action." Malcolm grinned. "The owner got filthy rich."

Margo huffed. Malcolm's gut response disturbed him to his core. *C'mon, Malcolm, she's your student.* But he couldn't help the fact that Margo was doing seriously troubling things to his bodily chemistry.

"Come on, I'll show you the Mithraeum and the Temple of Vulcan."

Margo giggled. "The guy with the ears?" Malcolm gave her his best disapproving scholar's glare, which reduced her to fits of laughter.

"I'm sorry," she laughed, "but it always tickles me. And you look so funny when you're irritated."

He sighed, feeling suddenly old. *Was* a man old at thirty-six? *Old enough for a bubbly eighteen-year-old to consider funny . . .*

It was just as well. He needed complications in his life the way a flock of turkeys needed Thanksgiving. Malcolm adjusted the fit of his slave's collar and gestured to his "master."

"This way, if you please. The buildings you see here are the *collegia* of the boatmen, professional guilds with considerable clout in Ostia. Down that way are the warehouses and if we look off to the southeast, we can just see the roof of Ostia's Temple of Cybele. . . ."

Margo waited until Malcolm had fallen asleep, then quietly dressed in the darkness and slipped out of their rented room. She wanted to get away by herself to think. What with lessons and downtime adventures, she hadn't really found five whole minutes to just *think* about the enormity of what she was doing. She knew she was taking a risk, going out at night, but Ostia wasn't Rome. *Besides, I need to prove I'm ready to go solo.*

Margo gained the dark street without raising an alarm. She leaned against the wall and let go her breath, then grinned. *So far so good.* When her eyes adjusted, Margo caught her breath. *The sky* . . . Clearer even than a winter Minnesota night. The sky was so filled with stars Margo lost whole minutes just gazing upward *Everybody should see a sky like this just once before they die* . . . Margo had met folks who'd never seen anything but the murky yellow glow that passed for night in places like New York. *Maybe if they saw a sky like that they wouldn't feel so . . . so self-important.*

Feeling keenly her own insignificance, Margo found her way to the docks. Wooden hulls creaked in the night. Wind flapped in loose sails, sang through slack rigging. Where ships rode quietly at anchor, a few braziers burned on high stern decks, marking the presence of night watchmen. Margo found a stone archway near the entrance to one long pier and settled in the shadows. Far away, drifting on the spring wind, she could hear a magical chorus of frogs and insects from vast salt marshes. Margo sighed. *I'm really sitting on a dock two thousand years before I was born.*

She'd planned this moment all her life. So why wasn't she happy? Malcolm Moore's smile flitted into her awareness, causing her pulse to dance like mating butterflies. Malcolm Moore was more than a good teacher. He was becoming a good friend, maybe the best friend she'd ever found. She was grateful for that, but . . .

But what?

But deep down, you're afraid of him, that's what. And she wasn't sure she wanted to be, which scared her even worse.

Starlight silvered the rolling breakers. In her own time, the sea had wiped out some of the world's greatest cities. Margo didn't understand all the science and stuff that had caused *The Accident.* All she knew was a burning need to grasp the opportunity before her. And she *would* grasp it. Come hell, high water . . . or Malcolm Moore. How much time was left? She counted backwards in her head. *Three months.* Margo bit her lip. Was she being foolish, rushing her training just to prove *him* wrong?

"I *have* to! I just have to . . ."

Her father's voice, angry and slurred, slapped her from out of the past. "You'll turn out same's her! Filthy, stinking whore—" *My mother was not a whore!*

All those years ago, Margo had wanted to shout it back at him. *Not* shouting it had probably saved her life. But not saying it—then or now—didn't change facts. Everyone else *had* said it: the cops, the newspeople, the foster parents who took her out of a hospital bed and gave her a home in another town. Even the judge who'd eventually passed sentence on her father had said it. Margo, trying to rebuild her life, had turned a dry-eyed mask to the world to hide the pain.

Leaning against a cold stone pier, Margo thought she finally understood what had driven her mother to prostitution. Since leaving Minnesota, there'd been a moment or two when Margo's hunger and desperation had made *any* source of money seem attractive. How much worse must it have been for her mother, with a young child to raise, mortgage payments, groceries, medical bills . . .

And a husband who drank whatever money he got his hands on—including any he could beat out of her. In that moment, it became doubly critical for Margo to succeed. Not only did she have to prove to her father she could do this . . . *I'll make you proud, Mom. And I'll pay him back for what he did to us. I hate him! I'm glad he's dying, he deserves it . . .* But she wanted him to live just long enough. The only way Margo could find to strike back at him, to really *prove* she wasn't everything he'd ever called her, was to do something no other woman had ever been able to do.

And she had only three months left in which to do it. Three months to convince Kit she was ready to scout, to tackle an unknown gate, to come back with proof of her success. Three months. From where she sat, it seemed as impossible as telling Kit the truth about his only child.

Malcolm Moore's smile, flickering at the edges of memory, seemed nearly as great a threat to Margo's plans as the ticking clock. Men were nothing but trouble. They used you if they could, hurt you when they pleased, shattered your dreams if you didn't run faster than they could punch you to the ground . . .

Malcolm Moore isn't like Billy Pandropolous. Or my father. But it didn't matter. She didn't have time for love. At least Malcolm Moore was too much of a gentleman to hurt her the way Billy Pandropolous had. That was very little comfort when Margo crawled back to their rented room in the wee hours and huddled under her cold blanket for the remainder of the night.

Margo tried to keep up a brave front when they returned to Rome. Malcolm, suspecting none of the turmoil inside her every time his wide mouth curved into a smile, showed her the Campus Martius, where the secular games were held in the Circus Flaminius. The area also boasted gardens where young men could exercise and play, the *Villa Publica* where Romans assembled for the census and to levy troops for the legions, the *Septa* where people came to vote, splendid shops where the wealthy purchased luxury items imported from around the empire, even a place along the Tiber where Romans could swim and splash in the shallows.

They toured the Forum Romanum, with its Comitium, the Forum's political center; the religious Regia with the *real* Temple of Vesta, the House of the Vestals, and the seat of the Pontifex Maximus; and the Forum proper, a marketplace, center of civic activities, public functions, and ceremonies. The Forum's famous *rostrum* or speaker's platform was where a man could address his fellow citizens while running for office or just pass along juicy tidbits of news. Decorated with the prows of ships taken in battle, it was impressive, with its backdrop of the Temple of the Divine Julius (on the spot where his body had been cremated), marble-faced *basilicas* or law courts and other public buildings. Margo was surprised to find women lawyers arguing cases in the *basilicas.*

"Yes, women lawyers were increasingly common from the late Republic on," Malcolm explained. "Women in Imperial Rome weren't confined to the home as they were in early times and other cultures."

Margo liked that. The water clocks used to time the lawyers' speeches fascinated her. Some dripped water from a tank into a bowl, lifting a float with an attached rod whose cogs turned the hour hand. Another kind used water pressure to blow a tiny trumpet every hour.

"An alarm clock," Margo marveled. "They use an alarm clock!"

Malcolm only smiled, which left her insides in turmoil.

They followed the course of the aqueducts through the city, while Malcolm explained how the public fountains worked and how the aqueducts fed the great public baths as well as private homes. He even hired a boat and took her into the immense Cloaca Maxima which drained the city's swampy valleys.

He took her down the fullers' street, showing her how "dry cleaning" was done by slaves who stomped soiled garments into damp fuller's earth. The absorptive clay then dried and was beaten out of the cloth, taking with it oils and dirt. Then he let her watch Roman glass production, following that with a trip to a mosaic artist's studio, a visit to the Porticus Aemelia—the river port of Rome—and its warehouses, called the "Emporia," and another to the slave market. The sights *there* left her with nightmares. She was determined not to show it, however. If he could stomach it, so could she. Then, just when her spirits had reached an all-time low, the Hilaria—and her seventeenth birthday—began. It wasn't at all what Margo had imagined. "Hilaria" had conjured images of comic actors staging street performances or maybe people dressing up in funny costumes and laughing at one another, dancing and singing like Mardi Gras, maybe.

Minnesota had not prepared her for Roman street orgies.

"It's a celebration!" Malcolm shouted above the roar. Nearly a million singing, laughing people had taken to the streets, dancing and guzzling more wine than Margo had seen outside a Mogen David warehouse. "Their sun god just got reincarnated today! By the old reckoning, it's New Year's!"

Times Square had *never* witnessed a party like this. Margo laughed. "Tell you a secret!"

"What?"

"It's my birthday, too!"

"Oh, ho!" Malcolm's grin did seriously dangerous things to her insides. "I can't think of a better way to spend your birthday. Can you?"

She shook her head, grinning like a fool. It occurred to her in that moment, she'd never been so happy in her life.

Someone shoved a wineskin at Margo's mouth. It was drink or drown. She drank—and nearly drowned anyway. Malcolm pounded her back and grinned. "Does Rome know how to throw a bash or what?"

Margo caught her breath and wiped her face. "It's *wilder* than Mardi Gras!" Not that she'd ever *been* to New Orleans. . . .

A girl ran past, shrieking and giggling, while a middle-aged man dashed after in drunken pursuit. When Margo tried to back into an alleyway to avoid being trampled, she literally tripped across a much-occupied couple.

"Oh, my God . . ."

The alley was very much taken. By more than one couple. None of them were vertical. Well, that couple down there was, sort of. She beat a hasty retreat, so embarrassed she hardly knew where to look. Malcolm, the wretch, just waggled his brows. "What's wrong? You're not shocked, are you?"

"Aren't you?" Margo demanded. She didn't know whether to be more embarrassed that she'd seen them, or that her whole body had started to tingle in places Malcolm's grin made hot and fluttery by turns. *Oh, no, Margo, get hold of yourself. This road leads to* trouble. *That's why that Presbyterian preacher the Smiths went to on Sundays always . . .* Quite suddenly she giggled.

"What?" Malcolm asked, leaning close enough to hear over the tumult.

"I just wondered what Reverend Williams would have said if he'd seen that alley!"

Malcolm's eyes widened, then he laughed. "Probably something about fire and brimstone. To a Roman, the Hilaria's a sacred celebration. Casual affairs are *expected.* Of course, the rest of the year women are supposed to be nicely chaste, just like home, and no self-respecting patrician lady would be caught dead out here having the time of her life."

Someone in an outrageous animal mask pranced by, waving a wine jar and singing something that Margo suspected was extremely bawdy.

"I'll bet their husbands and brothers are out in force!"

Malcolm laughed, then snagged a couple of wine cups from a street vendor and bought a whole wineskin. "Too right. Roman gentlemen know how to dissipate with the best of 'em." He hoisted the wineskin with a chuckle. "Come on, let's find something to eat."

Quite unexpectedly, Margo realized she was having a good time. She relaxed. Maybe a little dissipation would be fun. She'd certainly worked hard enough to earn a party. *And if you have to say goodbye to this man someday soon, maybe you should enjoy him while you still have the chance.* So Margo ate sausages that had been cooked in deep vats of olive oil, tried fresh-baked bread hot from the oven and wonderful little cakes made with honey and sesame seeds, and washed it all down with sweet red wine that left her giddy.

Greatly daring, she joined a dance, not caring when people laughed and called her *provincialis, rusticus,* and other probably less flattering names. Malcolm roared with laughter, then cut in line behind her. His hands came to rest on her hips, leaving her flushed from scalp to toes. They snaked their way through crowded streets in a wild line dance that ended in front of a tall marble temple. When the dance broke up, Margo staggered dizzily, then fell laughing against Malcolm. He caught her and set her back on her feet. His face was flushed.

Her heart gave a traitorous thump.

"Where are we?" she asked breathlessly. Over there was the long side of the Circus and over that way was the river, but she didn't know what this temple was.

"That's the Temple of Ceres, Liber, and Libera." It came out oddly husky. His eyes were fever bright.

"Who?"

"Ceres, Goddess of Grain and Agriculture. Liber Pater and Libera, very ancient Italian god and goddess. She and Liber Pater celebrate a sacred marriage."

Margo found herself swallowing hard. "Really?"

"They join during the Ludi Ceriales. That's about twenty-two days from now."

The whole city beyond Malcolm's bright eyes was spinning in her awareness. "Do Roman gods do anything besides make love?"

"Not in the spring." He was very close to her. His smile—and that answer—did wicked things to Margo's insides. The way the corners of his eyes crinkled, the way his hair fell across his forehead in an unruly curl, the way he took her questions seriously even when laughter made his eyes sparkle—even the sharp masculine scent of him—

Everything about Malcolm Moore set her blood pounding. *I don't care if this is all there is, I don't care about scouting, I don't care about anything, oh God, let him kiss me . . .* As though he'd heard her silent prayer, Malcolm bent toward her. April sunlight turned the dark sheen of his hair to the gloss of a raven's wing. Then his mouth covered hers, warm and demanding and gentle all at the same time. Her senses reeled. She found herself clutching the front of his tunic. Margo had never been kissed like this, as though her mouth were a precious jewel which must be handled with exquisite care. Then his hand slipped from her face and touched the side of her breast—

The kiss exploded into a mindless clutching at one another in the bright April sunlight. Afterward Margo was hardly cognizant of stumbling through the streets with his hand on her waist. Was hardly aware of the change when he plunged into a rustling grove of trees and sought a remote, unoccupied corner. Peripherally she noticed low-hanging branches that dipped to screen a tiny glen. A natural spring bubbled up from a rocky basin and poured away through the trees.

Then she was in his arms again and his hands were on her bare skin and the only thing in her awareness was the pounding of his heart against hers as they went to the sweet-scented earth in the tangle of their clothing.

Only afterward did the full enormity of what she'd done sink in. Margo lay in the crook of Malcolm's arm, his body pressed warmly against hers, his breath shuddering against her ear. The fire of their joining still lingered in deep tremors inside her.

Then, like ice water through her veins:

I slept with him.

Dear God, I slept with him.

Panic smote her so hard Malcolm stirred. "Margo? What's wrong?"

She couldn't answer. Couldn't put into words the myriad terrors ripping her apart. *Dad was right. I'm nothing but a two-bit whore. I'll never be anything, never amount to anything. I can't even say no when I* know *it's the wrong thing to do, I could be pregnant . . .*

Oh, God. She could be.

She'd destroyed everything she'd worked for, would never be able to face down that bastard who'd murdered her mother, could never tell him he'd been wrong—

And Kit Carson . . .

If she couldn't even be trusted not to fall into bed with the first man who took her down time . . .

She began to cry. When the dam burst, she couldn't control the flood. Malcolm touched her shoulder.

"Margo? Please, what is it?"

She jerked away, so miserable she wanted to die.

Malcolm's tender concern only made the enormity of her folly worse. Clearly, he'd anticipated a jolly romp in the grass with a woman capable of enjoying the moment. A woman he'd *thought* had just turned nineteen. All she'd managed to give him was a ten-minute quickie with a scared kid. Worse, a scared kid with a past. The fact that it had been the most profoundly shattering experience of her young life . . .

She hid her face in the sweet grass and cried until she thought her heart would burst.

Malcolm listened for a long time, damning himself for several dozen kinds of fool. He finally dared a question.

"Margo, I have to ask. Who was he?"

She strangled on another hiccough and stopped crying long enough to ask, "Who?"

Malcolm wanted to touch the nape of her neck, but she wasn't ready for that yet. "The bastard who hurt you."

She finally rolled over to face him. Tear streaks blotched reddened cheeks. Faint surprise flickered in her eyes. For several moments, he thought she wasn't going to answer. When she did, it still wasn't really an answer.

"You sound angry."

This time he did touch her, very gently. And this time, she didn't flinch away. "I *am* angry, Margo. More than you can know."

She held his gaze for long seconds. Behind her, spring water poured over a lip of stone and meandered through Diana's sacred grove down to the Tiber and the distant sea.

Then she turned away again. "You're wrong. It wasn't what you're thinking. And I was wrong, too. About a lot of things."

Malcolm bit one lip. *God, who* did *this to her? "I'll take him apart. . . .* "Maybe, but so was he. Whoever he was, whatever reason he had for doing it. He was wrong."

"How—how can you be so—so damned nice?" *Meaning you only sleep with boys who are rotten to you?*

He decided to introduce a little levity. "But I'm not nice. I'm a calculating cad, Miss Margo." She went very still in his arms. "Consider: I dragged you two thousand years into the past, plied you with sweet Roman wine, then danced you through half the streets in the city for the express purpose of scaring *myself* half witless. We perverts are like that, you know. Devious fellows. Well do anything to indulge our bent for self-inflicted terror."

His smile, calculated to put her at ease, shattered her fragile self-control. Margo's whole face crumpled, then she turned away from him, shutting him out once again. "Where are my clothes? I'm too naked. If you want to talk, let me get dressed."

"Margo . . ."

She paused, holding the Parthian tunic in front of herself like a shield. "What?"

"You've no idea how sad that makes me feel."

Her brows dove together. "How sad what makes you feel?"

"That you can take your clothes off to sleep with a man, but you can't talk to him afterward. That's what love is all *about.* Touching and talking and caring."

She opened her lips several times, but no sound came out. Then, bitterly, "Who made you the world's expert, anyway? You're a penniless bachelor! You . . . you *are* a bachelor, aren't you?" she asked suddenly, hugging the tunic more tightly to her breasts.

He managed a smile. "Yes. I'm a bachelor, Margo. And I never claimed to be anyone's expert on the subject. But I do think you ought to be at least friends with the people you sleep with. Otherwise, it's the saddest thing in the world, groping after something you can't define with a total stranger who probably can't define it, either."

"*I know exactly what sex is!*" She crouched in the sunlight, fingers dug into the earth, the folds of her tunic forgotten. "It's getting drunk and thinking you're having a good time, then waking up trapped and hurt and scared of everyone you thought you liked! It's miserable and lonely and I'm sorry I ever laid eyes on you! *Damn* you, Malcolm Moore! You *ruined* my seventeenth birthday!"

SEVENTEENTH? Malcolm opened his mouth, but nothing came out. Terror and regret and rage at her lie tore through him so savagely he couldn't even move. *Seventeen? My God, Kit will kill me—*

She flung herself into her Parthian tunic and trousers, then fled. Malcolm swore and hurtled himself into his own clothing, but by the time he gained the street, dodging tree trunks and pleasantly occupied couples, she was gone, swallowed up by the teeming celebration beyond the temple precinct. He stood on the stone sidewalk, shaken so deeply he could scarcely breathe.

Idiot, fool, dolt . . . You knew she'd been hiding from something! Whatever it is, you just drove her right back into the middle of it. In a moment of utter folly, Malcolm had allowed himself to forget that Margo was young and vulnerable, trying to hide something desperately painful behind a pert, sexy exterior. Donning a mask of confidence and challenging the world didn't change the fact that she was a scared little girl hiding in a woman's body. Memory crucified him. The passion, the quivering fire against him and inside him . . .

There wasn't anything he could do now except pick up the pieces and go on, hoping Margo would eventually forgive him.

It was even money Kit Carson never would.

Chapter 15

The rest of Margo's stay in Rome was a nightmare.

After fleeing Malcolm, she lost her way in the tangle of narrow, crooked streets. Margo wandered for hours, seeing hardly anything, scarcely paying attention to where she put her feet, much less where she was going. When the light began to go, Margo came out of her mental fog with an abrupt jolt. She blinked at unfamiliar surroundings, discovering she had no earthly idea where she was or where the Time Tours inn might be.

"Malcolm . . ." she quavered.

But Malcolm wasn't there to bail her out. She was on her own in the growing darkness. The crowds had thinned out, leaving her virtually alone on a grimy little street of four- and five-story Roman tenements. Haphazard, rickety wooden buildings a block long, the tenement "islands" sported cheap shops at street level and increasing poverty the higher one climbed the stairs.

She had to find shelter. Rome's streets were deadly after dark. Margo glanced both ways down the street, then, swallowing hard, she headed back the way she'd come. She walked several blocks without finding a trace of anything remotely resembling a landmark she recognized. She moved faster, heart in her throat, abruptly aware of men loitering in darkened doorways and *zigzag* alleys.

When Margo spotted an inn, she didn't care how dirty it was or how drunk its occupants. She bolted inside, feeling marginally safer in the boisterous, lighted room. She drew immediate attention, but managed to stare down several curious types who shrugged and returned to their wine and dice games. The innkeeper communicated through signs and gestures. She handed over coins and he handed over food and a blanket. The food was hot, the blanket was threadbare, and the corner she eventually chose to bed down in was drafty, but at least she wasn't alone in the dark on dangerous streets.

Tomorrow she would find Malcolm. Find him and offer an apology and try to explain. . . . She had to find him. The prospect of even one night alone was suddenly more daunting than she'd bargained for. She hid her face in the blanket. Then—asserting itself through rising panic—a spark of intelligence or maybe just Sven's training told her to take precautions. Under cover of her threadbare woolen blanket, Margo transferred her money to her ATLS pouch and drew her short knife, gripping it tightly under the covers. That done, she felt marginally safer.

Even so, sleep took a long time coming. And when she did finally nod off, violent dreams woke her every hour.

By the time sunlight streamed into the room, Margo was exhausted. But her ATLS bag and knife remained in her possession. Her belly rumbled audibly. *Later,* she told her stomach. First she had to find Malcolm. Margo set out to locate the Aventinus district and quickly realized that she hadn't absorbed nearly enough of Malcolm's lessons on the layout of Rome. She guessed she was somewhere east of Campus Martius, so she began walking west. That took her into a rat's maze of "islands", private houses, and public buildings strewn haphazardly across Rome's hills.

By mid-day she was light-headed and still hadn't found the Time Tours inn. The high facade of the Circus, so visible from the Aventinus district, was obscured by clusters of temples and great houses of the rich perched on hilltops. She was so hungry she spent some of her precious money on sausage and wine, then set out again. Hilaria was still in full swing, reminding her all too vividly of Malcolm. What must he be thinking? He'd be frantic by now. What could she possibly tell him to explain, to make this right?

Margo was lost in the worry of what she would say when someone plowed into her, running full tilt. Margo had only a split second to notice the slave's collar, the chains at his wrists, the ripped clothing and wild eyes . . . Then she slammed backwards. Margo felt the back of her head connect sickeningly against stone.

An explosion of darkness wiped out everything after that.

When she woke, Margo had no idea where she was. Her head ached—throbbed—so fiercely she was afraid she might be ill. A weight of blankets covered her. Margo managed to open her eyes and found only darkness. For a moment, panic smote her so hard she struggled against the blankets and the pain. Then a glimmering edge of light revealed the position of a door. She was in someone's bed in someone's house—

And somehow, she'd lost several hours.

She hoped it was only hours.

A cautious exploration revealed her own clothing still in place, although the ATLS bag and knife belt were gone. Someone had tied a poultice around her head. That boded well. *If they're taking care of me, I'm probably not in too much danger.* But where was she? And how much time had passed? Margo didn't feel much like getting up in an attempt to find out.

Eventually the door opened. A young woman carrying an oil lamp peered into the room. Worry creased her brow when Margo met her gaze. She said something that sounded anxious and called to someone beyond Margo's view. Then she set the oil lamp down on a table and bent over Margo. "Ow!"

The young woman murmured soothingly and readjusted the poultice. A moment later a thin, balding man entered the room. He wore several tunics and a worried expression. Within three sentences, it became apparent to him that Margo didn't have the faintest idea what he was saying.

He halted, looked even more worried, and said slowly, *"Esne Parthus?"*

Margo struggled to find her voice. *"M-minime non Parthus,* uh, *sed* uh *Palmyrenus sum,"* she quavered, hoping she'd gotten the, "I'm Palmyrene, not Parthian," correct in her shaky Latin.

"Ahh . . . *Paterne tuus Romae es?*"

Something about her father and Rome. Margo tried to remember how to shake her head no, decided that would hurt entirely too much, and tried the Latin again. "*Non Romae est.*"

He looked disappointed and even more worried. "*Tuique servi?*"

Servants? Oh . . . Where were her slaves?

To avoid a struggling explanation, Margo touched her head and moaned. Her host's eyes widened in alarm. He spoke sharply to the young woman, who carefully removed the poultice. She applied a new one, then picked up a basin and set Margo's arm in it. Before Margo knew what they were doing, the woman had sliced open Margo's arm. She yelled and tried to jerk away. The Roman and his servant woman held her down, murmuring anxiously, then forcibly held her arm over the basin and let her bleed into it. By the time they were done, Margo felt light-headed and queasy.

If they keep this up, they'll kill me with kindness . . .

She was required to drink a noxious potion which she didn't have the strength to refuse. The Roman touched her hand and said something that Margo supposed was meant to comfort; then they left her alone to sleep. She made an effort to sit up. Between the pain in her head, the forcible bleeding, and whatever they'd made her drink, she was too woozy. Margo collapsed again with a faint moan.

Tomorrow, she promised. *I'll get the hell out of here tomorrow.*

Margo was a virtual prisoner for the next four solid days. Too ill and light-headed to leave the room, she at least convinced Quintus Flaminius, her "host," to stop cutting her veins open every few hours. He wasn't happy about it, but her recovery sped up significantly—particularly when she insisted on replacing the wine at her meals with as much water as she could drink. She'd learned in basic first aid that recovering from blood loss required replacement of liquids. And alcohol, while liquid, tended to dehydrate, not rehydrate. So she drank water until she thought she would burst and *willed* herself to recover.

Her ATLS bag and knife belt proved to be safely stored in a wooden chest near her bed. Whenever she was alone, Margo updated her log and checked the chronometer to be sure how much time remained before Porta Romae cycled again. According to the log, she had four days remaining in Rome. What Malcolm must think by now . . .

But Margo had no way to get a message to him. The only thing she could do was get well and get the hell out of here. By the fifth day, the headaches had disappeared and Margo was able to walk again without dizziness. Her host was evidently a very wealthy man. The villa she discovered beyond the confines of her sick room was breathtaking with frescoes, mosaic floors, and priceless statuary.

Quintus escorted her into a garden courtyard at the center of his house, guiding her to a marble bench, then clapped his hands. A chained figure Margo vaguely recalled was hauled, weeping and ashen, into the courtyard and thrust to his knees at his master's feet.

Margo stared. *Why, it's just a boy!*

Perhaps thirteen or fourteen, he huddled at Quintus Flaminius' feet and waited. Flaminius spoke harshly to him, pointing at Margo for emphasis. The boy kissed Margo's feet, startling her badly, then huddled almost in a fetal ball beside her toes. Flaminius clapped his hands again. Collared slaves carried out a brazier on poles and set it down near Quintus. Heat shimmered in the spring air. A long iron rod had been thrust into glowing coals.

Flaminius snapped out something to his slave. The boy looked up. . . . A wild cry broke from ashen lips. He started back, trying to scramble to his feet, then flung himself at Flaminius' legs, clinging to his calves and pleading, "*Domine, domine. . . .*"

Was he acknowledging Flaminius as his master? Or just begging mercy with the only word he had wit to retain?

The slaves who'd carried the brazier into the courtyard seized him, holding him immobile. Flaminius picked up the iron rod with great deliberation, then nodded to his men. They stripped the boy's tunic back from his thighs. He whimpered. . . .

The sickening smell of seared flesh and a high, ragged scream jolted Margo. *Oh, God. . . .*

They branded him with a lurid "F" across the thigh. Margo gagged and feared she might pass out. By all rights the boy *should* have. He didn't. He just lay on the ground moaning and clutching at the dirt with thin fingers. Flaminius reheated the branding iron. Slaves held the boy again. This time Flaminius moved the iron toward the boy's *face . . .*

"NO!"

Margo was on her feet, the cry torn from her.

Flaminius halted in surprise, then stared at the tears welling in her eyes. Very slowly, he replaced the branding iron in the brazier. He gestured to his men and they released the trembling boy, who kissed his master's feet—then wept on Margo's. She swayed. . . .

Flaminius eased her back to a seat on the marble bench and called to a slave. A moment later, the rim of a goblet touched her lips. She swallowed strong red wine and fought to regain control of herself. Flaminius was speaking quietly to his slave. Margo recognized very little of what he said, catching only the version of her name she'd given him: Margo Sumitus. When Flaminius escorted her back to her sick room, she didn't argue. What surprised her, however, was the boy who'd been branded. He limped after them, still chained and struggling, then took a seat next to her bed. He remained behind even when Flaminius left, putting himself between her and the door as though he intended to guard Margo's very life.

She wondered what his name was and why he'd run away in the first place. He met her gaze, clearly curious about his foreign benefactor who'd kept him from being branded a second time, then flushed and jerked his gaze down again.

She sat up in bed. Then touched her chest. "Margo," she said. Then she pointed to him.

The boy whispered, *"Domine, sum Achillei."*

Domine?

Surely she'd misunderstood? But Malcolm had been clear about the meaning of that word. *Dominus* meant master.

Young Achilles glanced up. *"Esne Palmyrenus?"* he asked, sounding awestruck.

She shrugged. That wasn't important. *"Et tu?"*

His, *"Graecus sum. . . ."* came out strangled and so tremulous that Margo's heart constricted. How had this boy come to be a slave?

More importantly, how had he come to be *her* slave? And what was she going to do about it?

When her host returned to check up on her, Margo struggled to ask. Her Latin was insufficient for the question, but Flaminius removed all doubt when he put Achilles' chains in her hands and said, "*Achilles tuus est servus.*"

Oh, great. What am I supposed to do with a slave? He handed her an iron key.

Margo stared at it for a moment. Achilles sat on his heels, head bowed. *Maybe he'll run again, but so what? I won't hunt him down if he does.* She unlocked his chains. Achilles caught his breath, then tears welled up in his eyes and he ducked his head. Flaminius grunted softly, a sound of profound surprise, then shrugged as if to say, "Your loss."

At dinner that night, Margo's unexpected new acquisition waited on her hand and foot. He escorted her to bed, made certain she was comfortably covered, and blew out the lamps. Then took up a guard stance again between her bed and the door.

He was still there the next morning, asleep but in the same spot. *Huh.*

By her calculations, she had two days left to find the Time Tours inn, explain and apologize to Malcolm, and go back to La-La Land—a wiser and more cautious trainee scout.

When she tried to leave, Flaminius exclaimed in horror and insisted, by gestures and signs, that she was a guest in his home and he wouldn't think of allowing her to leave while she was still recovering. Desperate to get out of the house, she finally resorted to saying, "Circus, Quintus Flaminius. Ludi Megalenses . . ." figuring if she once made it out into the crowded streets, she'd be able to slip away and break free of his smothering hospitality.

Understanding lit his eyes. Whatever he said, she suspected it ran along the lines of, "Of course, you've come all the way from Palmyra to see the games and here one of my slaves has injured you so you've been too ill to go. . . ."

By gestures and signs, he made it clear that tomorrow they would go to the games. Margo bit down on her frustration and acquiesced.

Meanwhile, there was the problem of Achilles. She didn't *like* having a slave. He *hovered.* Everywhere she turned, there he was. If she'd given permission, he'd have dressed and undressed her, even bathed her. Fortunately, the villa had its own private bath which Margo was able to use in complete privacy, barring the door when Achilles tried to follow her in.

Let 'em think I'm an eccentric provincial, she groused.

Whatever Margo's host and slave thought, the heated bath was extraordinary. She didn't want to leave. *Ooh, a person could get used to this. . . .*

She lazed in the heated pool of water half the day, just soaking away aches and bruises and scrubbing every inch of herself clean. Then she ate an equally lazy lunch in the courtyard garden, listening to the tinkling splash of fountains and wishing Malcolm were here. *Tomorrow,* she told herself. Tomorrow she would find that opportunity to escape her host's clutches.

Unfortunately, her host had other ideas.

Margo didn't *walk* to the Circus.

She was *carried* there, in a sedan chair supported by long poles. Perched on the shoulders of four sweating slaves, the chair carried Margo well above the heads of the surrounding crowd. She felt ridiculous, conspicuous, and foolish. And utterly helpless to climb down and get *away.* Another sedan chair a few paces behind carried Quintus Flaminius.

Achilles, eyes bright despite the limp which he struggled to hide, followed Margo's chair. Outside the Circus Maximus, thick crowds fought toward the entrances. Dozens of stalls marked the locations of shops selling food, wine, even glass bowls and cups with circus-racing scenes molded into them. *Commemorative sports glasses,* Margo marveled. *Who'd have guessed?* Other stalls housed "bookies" who took bets on the outcomes of upcoming races and the combats scheduled for afterward. Crowds of men thronged the betting stalls, shouting for their turn to place bets before the games began, collecting their markers, handing over their coins. She'd read somewhere, in one of those endless books in La-La Land's library, that betting on the games had been illegal in Rome. If that were the case, those charged with enforcing the law apparently didn't mind looking the other way most of the time.

Quintus' slaves set the sedan chairs down near an arched entrance to the great arena. Margo thought seriously about bolting through the crowd, but Quintus took her arm, smiling and chatting, and guided her straight toward the entrance. He paid her admission and collected three red handkerchiefs to cheer on the faction favored by the emperor. At least, she was pretty sure red was the color Claudius favored, since she overheard the words *Imperator* and *Princeps* used in connection with the red handkerchiefs. He handed her one handkerchief and handed the other to Achilles, then dismissed his own slaves.

He gave Achilles some copper coins and dispatched him on some errand; the boy returned sooner than Margo had expected with a basket of food and a jar of wine. Then Quintus escorted Margo into the Circus Maximus. She slowed to stare, overawed. Quintus grinned, then led her to seats midway up a wooden section of the stands, in the second tier near the first turning post. Everyone she saw up in the third tier was either collared as a slave or dressed as a foreigner: no togas. She smiled grimly, pleased she'd understood that all on her own. Doubtless the only reason she was seated here, rather than up there, was because she was the guest of a Roman.

The Circus itself was nothing like she'd imagined. The vast course wasn't an oval. One short end—where the starting gates were located—was essentially straight. Two long straight aways created an oblong ending in a semi circle. Three levels of seats, some wooden and some stone, rose in tiers. Including the seats, the huge arena was by Margo's estimation just short of a full mile from starting gates to the back of the seating.

Sand over packed earth—except for down near the starting gates where the surface was paved—the track caught the sunlight with an unnatural glitter. She noticed slaves carrying baskets down the track, sprinkling something shiny onto the sand. Some kind of glittering mineral, maybe? She'd seen flakes of mica in granite catch the sun like that. *Expensive, but pretty.*

A long barrier wall perhaps six feet high ran down the center of the track, decorated with tall marble columns which held gleaming female statues—some winged, some wingless. Miniature temples held altars to gods Margo couldn't identify. Crossbeams supported stone eggs and dolphins. A gleaming gold statue even she recognized as Cybele riding a lion stood near one end. Next to the Magna Mater rested a cluster of marble trees, but they didn't look like Attis' sacred pine. She wondered what they were.

In the center of the barrier wall rose a towering Egyptian obelisk. *Now who brought that here?* It must have been quite a feat, getting it across the Mediterranean by sailing ship. A golden flame set onto the top caught the morning sunlight like fire. On the long Aventine straightaway rose a magnificent colonnaded temple built right into the stands. Below it rested a platform. *Bet that's the judges' box,* she decided, spotting a white line chalked in the sand just beneath it.

Visible beyond obelisk and statues, another temple gleamed in the morning sunlight. High above it the Imperial palace rose on the Palatine Hill. Whatever it was, this second temple had been built directly into the lower tiers of seats with a series of columns and a beautiful triangular pediment above a broad stone porch. A number of empty couches awaited occupants. I *wonder if that's where Claudius sits.*

Down at the starting gates, grey and red marble columns decorated the arches of the starting stalls. There were twelve, barricaded at the moment with double wooden doors. Metal grills blocked the tops. An elaborate viewing box with a stone balustrade took up the center portion of the marble facade. Low, round pedestals supporting tall, squarish pillars topped with stone heads stood between each gate. White chalk-marked lanes led from the starting gates to another white line that crossed the whole width of the track at the end of the barrier wall. *Wonder what that's for?*

Just below Margo's seat, down on the track itself, stood a small square shrine with columns, resting on circular stone steps. A little tree of some sort grew up from the earth of the track itself beside the shrine. Between the track and the podium wall ran an immense, ten-foot-wide moat filled with water. A high metal grillwork rose from the podium wall in front of the first tier of seats all the way around the elongated horseshoe of the arena.

The turning posts weren't actually part of the central spine, Margo realized. Three tall, tapered stone columns rose from half-moon shaped pedestals. Each tapered column, covered with bronze plaques, ended in an egg-shaped tip. They reminded her uncomfortably of a man's . . .

Huh, the Given Roman preoccupation with sex, I wouldn't be at all surprised.

The stands filled up quickly. Margo was surprised at how fast an enormous crowd could enter the Circus. She tried to estimate the seating capacity, multiplying by the lines scored into the bleachers, and came up with more than a hundred fifty thousand. Surely that was too high? A group of laughing men and women took seats behind her, jabbing her uncomfortably in the back with their knees. Margo had to sit with her own knees tucked almost to her chin to avoid hitting the people in front of her. *Well, maybe I didn't guess too high.* They were cramming people in like sardines. She hoped the wooden bleachers didn't collapse under the weight.

The stands were almost full when a blare of trumpets signaled activity at the far end. Men on foot appeared, bearing tall standards that glittered brightly in the sunlight. Golden eagles surmounted rectangles marked SPQR. A roar rose from a hundred fifty thousand throats. The whole stadium surged to its collective feet. Margo stood up, too.

What? Where?

Quintus Flaminius was pointing down the track.

A man had appeared behind the eagle standards, limping awkwardly onto the track from an entrance down near the starting gates. Robed in gleaming white, with broad purple stripes along the edges of a white woolen toga, he was the instant focus of attention. The crowd had gone wild. Whoever he was, he moved on unsteady legs. *Drunk?* Margo wondered. Surely not?

Then the women behind her babbled something about the *Princeps.* Margo gasped. *Claudius!* She hadn't expected the emperor to *walk* at the head of the procession. She'd pictured him as riding in a gilt chariot or something. Maybe that was reserved for generals who'd won battles. Claudius moved carefully, doggedly, lacking anything like stately grace as he led the procession into the great Circus.

Unexpectedly, Margo's heart constricted. She hadn't realized the twisting of his face, so painfully visible in the Time Tours photograph, had extended to other physical difficulties. No wonder Malcolm had refused to laugh at him. The courage—and pain—that procession must be costing him . . .

Margo gulped and felt her cheeks burn. *She* had run away from her problem rather than face it head on the way Claudius faced his illness. Look where that had led her. She bit her lip. *Tonight,* she promised herself. *I'll find him tonight after the games, when I can get away from Flaminius.*

Behind Claudius came musicians: drummers and pipers filled the arena with rolling thunder and skirling music while brassy horns sang out in voices so wild Margo's back shivered. Behind the musicians came carriages and hand-carried litters on which rode the Roman gods and goddesses. She had no idea who they all were, but their statues caught the morning sun in as splendid a pageant as Margo had ever seen.

The procession made its way around the mica-glittered track in a complete circuit, ending at the marble temple on the Palatine side. Claudius ascended a staircase slowly, followed by bearers who carried the images of the deities up to the platform to "watch" the games. Claudius himself took a backless stone chair near the front of the platform. He lifted his hand and the crowd went insane. *Popular guy.*

Margo discovered unexpectedly that she was glad. A hush fell across the great Circus. In the sudden quiet she could hear the scream of high-strung horses, the thud of hooves against wooden doors. The smell of sweat and adrenaline drifted on the wind along with the distant snarls of wild beasts. Margo leaned forward.

A well-dressed official of some sort had appeared in the balustraded box above the starting gates. Other figures were visible as well, fussing over some sort of machinery. A white cloth fluttered from the official's hand. She wished irritably for a lowly pair of binoculars. It looked very much like someone was turning a barrel on a spit and drawing something out of it, but she couldn't see what. *We should've found seats closer to the start.*

Other men had climbed onto the barrier wall, some of them dressed well, others clad in simple tunics. Ladders were run up to the crossbeams holding the eggs and dolphins. Several moments passed while the tension mounted. Men who could only be field judges took their positions. Then, before she was ready for it, the white cloth dropped.

A snapping sound cracked through the breathless arena. The crash of wooden doors flung wide reached her even at the far end of the Circus. Then twelve chariots dashed into view, horses flying four abreast as they raced down the chalked-out lanes. Margo was on her feet with the rest of the crowd. The chariots tore across the pavement toward the first white line in the sand. Trumpets sang out as they flashed past. Then twelve racing chariots like dolls teacups on wheels broke position and flung inward toward the barrier wall.

They tore down the track in a thunder of hooves. Drivers whipped their teams to greater speed. Their short capes snapped in the wind. They'd wrapped long reins completely around their waists, crouched over the tiny platforms like jockeys on skateboards. Green tunics, red tunics, blue and white ones . . . The four racing factions of the Circus stampeded for the best position as they swept toward the first turn. Margo held her breath.

The leader, a green driver, swept around the turn. The second chariot sped around in his wake. The third chariot brushed its wheels against a stone curb. The chariot lurched. The pole snapped. Margo screamed. The delicate chariot, little more than a wooden shell with a latticework floor, disintegrated into flinders. Galloping horses dragged their driver out of the wreckage. He fought to draw a knife at his belt. Other chariots swung wide to miss the wreckage.

The driver sliced through the reins and rolled heavily across the track. The other chariots left him lying on the sand. Slaves raced out to pull the driver and the wreckage off the track. Others caught the runaway team and led the horses out of the arena. The remaining chariots swept back toward the first turn for their second lap. Men on ladders had taken down one egg and one dolphin from the crossbeams.

Margo drank in details, determined to think like a scout for a change. The horses wore collars around their necks instead of harnesses like she'd seen in London. *How can they breathe, pulling against their windpipes like that?* The horses' manes had been tied up so they couldn't stream in the wind. Their tails had been bobbed short, like a Manx cat's, Wickerwork on the lightweight racing chariots bore the teams' colors. The drivers wore slaves' collars.

Malcolm had said the men who raced and fought here were either slaves, prisoners, or criminals. She wondered if the driver who'd been dragged down the track would live. She shivered. Already the chariots were pounding down the straightaway for the next lap. They skidded around the turn, bouncing across ruts left from previous laps, and rounded the turn in a cloud of glittering dust.

Three laps. Four. Five. How many laps in all? She checked the lap counters: two eggs and dolphins each remained on the crossbeams. The chariots fought one another for the lead as they swept into the turn for the sixth lap. Margo held her breath, but they all made it through the jolting one-hundred-eighty-degree turn. The sixth markers came down. Brassy trumpets sang out again. *Final lap.*

A driver in blue was battling it out with a red driver for the lead. Margo waved her red handkerchief with one hand and bit knuckles on the other. Red drivers back in the pack swung wide, blocking blue chariots from coming up to assist their team member. Two of the chariots collided. The crowd roared. Margo hid her eyes. When she dared look, she saw one broken chariot cartwheel into the wide moat with a tremendous splash. A driver in blue was being dragged wide in the turn. His body slammed into the little shrine. She screamed and hid her eyes again.

Another roar shook the stadium. She risked a peek. The surviving chariots had rounded the turning post nearest the start and were thundering toward the finish line. The red chariot shot into the lead as the driver lashed his horses. The blue chariot caught up, passed, then faltered again. The blue driver was whipping his horses mercilessly. Then the red driver swept ahead by a nose just as they flashed past the white chalk line.

The emperor's favorite had won!

Margo found herself shouting right along with the rest of the crowd. Quintus Flaminius exchanged a few coins with the man seated next to him, grinning as he deposited them in his money pouch. Margo noticed other private bets being settled, as well. Achilles' eyes glowed as he watched the driver sweep around the turning post in a wide circle and pass the emperor's platform. The driver completed the victory lap back to the finish line while the other chariots drove disconsolately off the track. The victor pulled his team to a halt. A ramp had been lowered across the moat, allowing him to ascend steps to the judging platform. Margo wondered who was handing out the prizes. She'd expected the victor to receive his reward from the emperor, but he'd stopped on the opposite side of the arena from the emperor's box. It was another man who placed a leafy crown on the driver's head, handed him a palm branch, and placed a bulging leather pouch in his hand. The crowd cheered as he descended the steps triumphantly, resumed his chariot, and drove past the emperor's box once again. Claudius saluted him to thunderous approval from the crowd.

Then he left the track. Slaves carrying baskets began climbing through the stands, tossing out handfuls of little wooden markers. Spectators dove for them, cheering if they caught one, groaning if they missed. When a handful was flung toward Margo's seat, she caught one by reflex, then wondered what it was. She couldn't read what it said. Quintus Flaminius grinned and babbled something incomprehensible. At a signal from the emperor's box, those who had caught markers descended toward the track. Margo gulped. Surely the "winners" wouldn't be sacrificed in the arena?

Those who had caught the wooden disks grinned like sweepstakes winners. Quintus snapped his fingers at Achilles. The boy bowed and took Margo's wooden disc, then hastily followed in the wake of other winners. When he and the other winners returned, Margo learned the reason that those who'd caught the disks grinned like sweepstakes winners: they *were*. Each person who had presented a "ticket" had received a prize. Achilles presented hers formally: a small leather pouch.

She opened it and shook out a blood-red gemstone carved with a racing chariot and the obelisk from the Circus' barrier wall. Margo gasped. "Ohh . . ."

Quintus Flaminius whistled softly and examined the stone. Then smiled and returned it to her. Other lucky winners nearby displayed bags of coins to their friends, or parchments that seemed important. She heard the word *terra* and concluded they'd won deeds to land parcels. Margo tucked her prize back into its leather pouch and secreted that in her money pouch as the second event began, a race where jockeys rode horses in something approaching the modern style of horse racing. They ran from the turning post near Margo's seat to the far end of the barrier where the starting stalls were located, racing past the emperor's platform in a cloud of dust.

Another chariot race began, followed by a wrestling exhibition, followed by a third chariot race. They sat through a total of ten chariot races, each alternating with other events. Most chariot races were run with four-horse teams, some with two-horse teams. Some of the races ended with the jockeys sliding off and pelting toward the finish line on foot.

Achilles broke out wine and cups, pouring for them, then handed over parcels of what looked astonishingly like fried peas. Margo tried them. Not bad. . . .

While they ate lunch, yet another chariot race began, but this time when the lightweight chariots swept down the track, Margo burst out laughing. There were no drivers. No human ones, anyway. Trained *monkeys* steered the horses around the turning posts in a ridiculous parody of the earlier races. Laughter rippled through the stands. When the leading monkey's team swept across the finish line for the final lap, slaves ran onto the track and caught the horses. Margo dissolved into helpless laughter when one of the slaves carried the victorious "charioteer" up the ramp and steps to collect his reward: a piece of fruit and a monkey-sized victory crown.

The little victor actually drove a victory lap, grinning in a simian fashion that brought roars of laughter from the crowd.

Once the final chariot had been escorted from the track, a hush fell over the vast stands. Margo wondered what was up. Slaves appeared from street-level entrances, carrying potted trees and bushes. They turned the Circus into a miniature forest, with screens of shrubbery, groves of potted trees, even tubs of flowers. When the preparations were complete, the slaves beat a hasty retreat to the other side of the podium wall. Margo noticed that all ramps across the moat had been withdrawn.

Then she heard the unmistakable grunting roar of lions. A prickle ran straight up her back. Other wild screams reached her. The crowd leaned forward. The stink of sweat and anticipation hung on the bright air. The familiar snapping sound of the opening gates cracked through the arena. Margo peered toward the starting stalls.

A dozen frantic zebras broke into a gallop, veering to avoid the trees, leaping miniature walls of shrubbery, braying and bucking as they entered the arena. Behind them came a dozen ostriches, their black and white plumage bobbing gracefully as they ran down the long course of the track, weaving between the potted trees in visible confusion. Tiny beautiful antelopes darted into the sunlight and milled about in a frightened herd near the finish line.

Down at the starting gates, slaves had closed the big doors again, resetting the bars which held them shut. Once the job was done, they scrambled up ladders which were hastily pulled up after them. Margo leaned forward, watching in morbid fascination as the racing official who'd presided over the morning's races once again lifted his white cloth as a signal. The cloth fluttered toward the ground. The gates slammed open. A defiant roar shook through the arena.

Enormous cats lunged into the sunlight. Maned lions snarled at one another and drew blood. Sleek, deadly lionesses shot past the quarrelling males, homing in on the terrified game animals that had already been released. The striking pattern of leopard skin flashed past the starting gates as half a dozen more big cats were released into the Circus. Margo tried to count. Six leopards, twenty lionesses, at least twenty more heavy male lions . . .

A scream of pain rose from the arena floor. A zebra had gone down, kicking and struggling. Lions closed in, ripping and tearing at its belly. Margo screamed and hid her eyes, More frantic cries and screeches rose on the air. Whenever she dared look, she found big cats swarming across helpless antelopes . . . leopards running down ostriches and slamming them into the sand . . . zebras torn apart while still alive . . .

She hid her eyes until it was over.

Trumpets sang out, a sound of madness in the bright April sunlight. Margo looked up. Then went cold. *Men* were entering the arena. Men with nets and trident-pointed spears, men with swords and helmets, men on foot and on horseback. Lions snarled and backed away or stood their ground over reeking lolls. The hunters advanced slowly. A few hung back near the moat, clearly terrified. Then a lion roared a challenge and charged.

It wasn't sport.

It was murder.

Of the fifty men who entered the arena, only six left it alive. They were the only living things still walking on the sand when it was over. Even the horses had been killed, pulled down by murderous cats. The crowd thundered approval of their "victory" as they limped off the sand, bleeding and stumbling. Margo sat frozen in place, shocked to her core. She'd understood at one level what a bestiary was, but to actually watch men ripped to pieces by ravenous hunting cats . . .

She could be sick. Instead she stayed in her seat and watched while slaves removed the carcasses. The sun journeyed across the sky, leaving Margo light-headed. She wished she hadn't eaten lunch. Down on the sand, another parade began. This time, the participants were gladiators. Some rode horses, some carried nets and tridents like the bestiary hunters. Some wore odd helmets with fish on top. A few rode chariots—the drivers, all but naked, were tattooed in blue over most of their bodies.

The procession wound its way between trees and shrubbery walls, circling the entire arena. Margo tried to count the number of combatants and arrived at the figure of a hundred pairs. The number horrified her. The procession ended. Trumpets blared. The gladiators saluted the emperor, who lifted his hand. Then they broke ranks and began a slow-motion exhibition across the sands, without trying to draw blood. Each gladiator demonstrated the techniques of his unique weaponry while the crowd thundered approval. Then most of them retired from the track. Ten pairs remained. Other men appeared, carrying whips and red-hot prods. Trumpets sang out again. Margo held her breath. . . .

The first pair closed. A fighter tossed his net and missed. He drew it back with a string looped around his wrist while holding off his opponent with a wicked trident. Another pair drove at one another in chariots, looping in and out between potted trees while they slashed with long swords, trying to gain advantage. The audience was shouting strange words, repeating them again and again.

Instructions, she realized suddenly. The shouts were timed to the practiced swing and thrust of the swords and tridents. A couple of men hung back, clearly terrified. Men with whips and branding irons moved in. Margo screamed when the gladiators were herded forward with furious lashes and burns across the backs of their legs.

The first gladiator went down, badly injured by a sword cut across the thigh. He lay flat, helpless under his opponent's long trident. The fallen man lifted his left arm in supplication. The crowd turned all eyes to the emperor. Claudius was looking at the fallen man, then lifted his head to the crowd. The audience broke into factions, some gesturing "thumbs up" and others "thumbs down." More of them seemed to be calling "thumbs up."

The emperor turned his attention back to the fallen gladiator, then lifted his thumb in a sharp gesture toward his breast. Margo started to relax—

The gladiator with the trident stabbed the weapon straight through the other man's throat.

NO!

Margo sat transfixed. She didn't understand. Then a whisper of memory came to her in Malcolm's voice. "Study the body language, it's different here . . ."

Somehow over time, the thumbs-up and thumbs-down gestures had become reversed.

It was symbolic of the whirling mess her life was in.

Margo found herself stumbling out of the stands, shoving past shocked spectators. She had to get away, had to get out of this madhouse of sudden death and inexplicable cruelty . . . She finally gained the street. Quintus Flaminius and Achilles had followed. Her host took her arm, asking questions she didn't understand and didn't want to answer. Margo stood panting heavily for several minutes. Her knees shook. She still felt as though she'd be ill any moment. All she wanted to do was find the Time Tours inn and hide until the gate reopened.

She didn't get the chance. Flaminius' slaves, dismissed to wait outside the Circus for their master, reappeared with the sedan chairs. Margo found herself stuffed into a seat, lifted, and carried away from the Circus before she could find the wit to argue. She slumped in the chair. *Great. Now what?*

She found herself back in her room, alone with Achilles, whose eyes were wide with concern as she sank onto her hated bed. He fussed over her until she wanted to scream at him, but that wasn't fair, so she just held silent and let him fuss. Poor lad . . . What would become of him once she left? *If* she left . . .

The situation was so maddening it was very nearly comical. Trapped in time because her host was overprotective. Margo hadn't realized how deadly serious the Romans were about rules of hospitality. *Well,* she told herself with a sigh, *looks like you'll have to engineer a jail break tonight. Over the garden wall . . .*

And hope the watchdogs didn't sound an alert.

Naturally, she fell asleep.

Quintus Flaminius' idea of dinner was a twelve-course banquet with little desserts in between and bucketsful of wine. When she woke up, the room was pitch dark. Margo blinked. Then, *Ohmigod . . . What time is it?* She groped, found her ATLS bag, dragged out her log. The chronometer's glow revealed a terrifying set of numbers. She had less than ten minutes to make the cycling of Porta Romae.

In the middle of the night, on dangerous, unfamiliar streets . . .

Margo jumped over the sleeping Achilles and shot out of the sick room as though the villa had caught fire. She hit the atrium running. The door was barred. The night watchman had dozed off. Margo flung aside the heavy wooden beam which held the door closed and heard the watchman's startled cry. She jerked open the door and pelted into the street. Panic gave her speed she hadn't thought herself capable of. She remembered the way to the Circus. And from the Circus, she could find the Time Tours wine shop where the gate would be cycling any minute. In the darkness she took several wrong turns and backtracked frantically.

A distant cry caused her to glance back. A bobbing light followed several blocks back. Margo swore under her breath and kept running. She took another wrong turn and sped back the way she'd come. The light had drawn closer: Achilles, carrying a lantern. He called out, "*Domine! Domine!*"

She didn't have *time* . . .

The boy caught up to her, gasping for breath, and followed when she homed in on the hulking silhouette of the Circus. The glances he shot her told Margo he thought his young master had completely flipped, but he was sticking by her. *Damn, damn, damn* . . . She finally found the Via Appia. Margo raced around the end of the Circus and skidded around the corner. There . . .

What time is it?

She didn't have time to check her log. She just ran for the counter and hoped for the best. Too late, she saw a familiar figure detach itself from the counter and move toward her in the darkness.

Malcolm.

Guilt and fear and relief hit her simultaneously.

As she closed the distance between them, Margo found that she had no idea what to say to him. *Hi, I really screwed up, aren't you happy you went to bed with a dolt and by the way, how do I get rid of this poor slave I seem to have acquired?* stuck somehow in her throat. So she screwed her courage to the sticking place and decided to brazen it out.

She would apologize and eat crow once they were through the gate.

Malcolm hadn't slept in days. Time Tours employees had begun steering clear of him whenever he returned to the inn. He functioned on adrenaline and hope—and the hope was waning fast. He'd never lost a customer. Never mind someone as precious as Margo. What Kit would say, what Kit would *do*. . . .

He'd already decided to remain behind when the tour left Rome. He had to find her. Or find out how she'd died. One or the other. Night closed in on their final few hours. *Nine days* . . . He'd searched from dawn until well past dark every day, asking strangers if they'd seen a young man in Palmyrene dress, searching the slave markets with sinking horror in his gut, losing hope with every additional hour that passed.

The agony of guilt was very nearly more than he could endure.

As the chronometer on his personal log ticked past eleven-thirty and crept toward midnight, Malcolm found a corner behind the deserted wine shop's front counter and waited. He had given up hope; but he would wait, anyway, until the last possible moment. Then he'd tell the Time Tours guides to return without him. The big touring company had lost tourists on occasion—it was an industry secret closely guarded with massive bribes to grieving families—but the harsh reality of a tourist's disappearance shook everyone.

The guides and even the other tourists were subdued as they made their way into the wine shop for the return trip. Malcolm huddled in his corner, refusing to meet anyone's gaze. Ten minutes until midnight. Five minutes. A ghost of white appeared in his peripheral vision. He jerked around—And swore under his breath. Just a white carthorse pulling a load of hay. The familiar ache of a gate preparing to open thrummed against the bones of his skull. The cart rumbled past. The placid carthorse tossed its head and squealed a complaint its driver echoed. The man held his ears, muttered loudly enough for Malcolm to hear, "*Absit omen* . . ." and shook out his whip. The carthorse broke into a shambling run.

Inside the wine shop, the Porta Romae had dilated open. A Time Tours guide stepped outside.

"Malcolm? Departures are through. Newcomers are arriving. You don't have any more time."

"I'm—"

A figure in white ran into view down the block. Malcolm's heart leaped into his mouth. Then he noticed the slave following behind with a lamp. Crushing disappointment blasted brief hope. Then Malcolm did a double-take. The running figure *was* wearing a Parthian-style tunic and trousers. Slender, just about the right height, same fragile, heart-shaped face . . .

He came out of his corner like a gunshot and shoved the Time Tours guide aside. *Please. . . .*

When Margo ran up to the wine counter, bedraggled as a street rat and glaring defiance, he wanted to grab her by both arms and shake her until something snapped. A bewildered boy of about thirteen skidded to a halt behind her, gasping for breath.

"Hi! Did I make it in time? Malcolm, I've got this little problem, how do I free this kid? I, uh, sort of acquired a slave . . ."

Malcolm couldn't speak. Terror had transmuted into a rage so deep he was afraid to touch her. He held her gaze for another agonizing moment, then turned on his heel and strode through the rapidly shrinking Porta Romae. He didn't even look back to see if she'd followed. Nine *days* he had burned out his guts worrying—and she'd been running around Rome *buying slaves. . . .*

His sandals slapped against the grid of the platform. Malcolm shoved aside Time Tours employees and left old friends gaping in his wake. When he hit the gym, he accomplished a lifetime first.

Malcolm Moore laid Sven Bailey flat in a sparring match.

Afterward, he took a cold shower that lasted forty solid minutes. The phone was ringing when he emerged. He jerked it out of the wall and hurled it across the room. Then, very quietly, Malcolm got drunker than he'd ever been in his life.

Chapter 16

Kit Carson was waiting in the crowd when the Porta Romae opened. Neither Malcolm nor Margo put in appearances. He started to grow seriously alarmed when the Time Tours guides who emerged wouldn't look at him. The whole contingent of tourists, guides, and baggage handlers waiting in the Commons climbed the ramp and vanished through the portal and still there was no sign of his granddaughter or the man he'd trusted with her safety. Then, just as the portal began to shrink toward closure, Malcolm shot through. One look at his face sent Kit's viscera into a tailspin.

The normally unflappable time guide burst past Kit like a damned soul pursued by gleeful demons. He didn't even glance in Kit's direction. Kit shut his eyes, convinced of the worst. Then he risked another look just as the gate shrank closed. Margo had come through. He started breathing again. But she hung back on the platform, looking defiant and sullen and scared all at the same time. She, too, watched Malcolm's stormy retreat down the Commons. Then she saw Kit standing in the crowd below.

She lifted her chin and descended the ramp.

"Want to tell me what's going on?" he asked, falling into step.

"No," she said icily. "I don't."

With that, she, too, stormed off. Kit allowed his footsteps to slow to a halt. Just what had transpired between those two? Given Margo's temper, he was afraid of the answer. But he had to know.

Kit high-signed one of the returning Time Tours guides. "What gives?"

The woman gave him a guarded look. "Uh . . . Hi, Kit. I think maybe Malcolm ought to be the one to explain." She hurried away before he could ask another question.

Kit muttered under his breath and called Malcolm's number. The answering machine picked up. He swore and headed for the Down Time, but Malcolm hadn't put in an appearance. Then Robert Li, the station's antiquarian, skidded into the bar. He announced to the room at large, "You ain't gonna believe it! Malcolm Moore just wiped up the mat with Sven Bailey. I mean put him on the ground *out cold.* What's going on? I've *never* seen an expression like that on Malcolm's face." Conversation exploded around Robert Li while Kit beat a hasty retreat. He headed straight for the gym and found Sven in his office, holding an ice pack to his head and groaning. "Whadda *you* want?" Sven muttered.

"I heard Malcolm knocked you out."

"You don't have to rub it in."

"Did he say anything?"

Sven peeled a swollen eyelid. "No. All he said was, 'Let's spar.' Next thing I know, Ann Mulhaney's bending over me and someone's yelling to call Rachel. Only thing I saw after I woke up was his back on the way out the door. What's eating him, anyway?"

"I was hoping you could tell me," Kit said grimly.

"Huh. Two weeks alone with Margo is my guess. She'd drive any man to violence."

"Great. You're some help, you know that, Sven?"

The weapons trainer just grunted and held the ice pack against his skull. Kit headed for home. Margo wasn't at the apartment. Clearly she'd been there: damp towels and dirty clothes littered the bathroom. Wet footprints crossed the carpet into the living room. But she had departed for destinations unknown well before Kit's arrival. He called Malcolm's again. In the middle of the fifth ring, the connection went dead. Kit stared at the receiver. "What the hell?" *Someone is going to give me some answers. And it had better be soon.* But when he pounded on Malcolm's door, a breakable object of unknown origin crashed against the panel and shattered noisily.

"Go away!" He sounded *drunk.* The last time Kit had known Malcolm Moore to get drunk was the night the owner of Time Ho! had fired everyone in his employ, then quietly committed suicide rather than face his creditors.

"Malcolm! It's Kit! Let me in!"

"Go the *hell* away!"

He considered breaking down the door. Instead, he leaned on the buzzer until the noise drove the younger man to distraction. Malcolm finally snatched open the door. His hair was disheveled and his eyes were bloodshot. He looked like he hadn't slept in a week. He gripped a whiskey bottle by the neck like he contemplated breaking it over Kit's head. "You *are* drunk."

"An' I'm gonna be drunker. I'm in no mood for a visit."

He slammed the door. Kit caught it before it could close all the way.

"Dammit, Malcolm, talk to me. What the hell happened down time?"

Malcolm glared at him, then dropped his gaze. All the fight leached out of him. "Ask Margo. Your granddaughter is a lunatic. An impulsive, dangerous lunatic. Worse than you, damn your eyes. And a goddamned, bloody *liar*—little bitch just turned *seventeen,* goddammit, not nineteen. Now get out and let me get soused."

Seventeen? Margo was only seventeen? Kit saw several shades of red. *I'll kill her. I swear to God, I'll teach that girl if it's the last thing I ever do not to lie to people who trust her.*

Malcolm was in the act of slamming the door when Kit caught it in one hand. "I, uh, owe you some money."

Malcolm's bitter laughter shocked Kit speechless. "Keep it. I sure as hell didn't earn it."

The door slammed shut.

Kit stared at the reverberating panel. *All right. . . .*He stalked down to the Commons on a hunt for his errant granddaughter. He found her at Goldie Morran's, exchanging her down-time currency for modern scrip. Goldie glanced up and smiled. The smile froze in place. Margo swung around and lost color.

Kit was out of patience. He backed Margo into a corner so she couldn't bolt and run. *"Just what the hell happened down time, young lady?"*

"Nothing! I did fine! It's not my fault Malcolm's an overbearing, overprotective, chauvinistic . . ."

She ranted on at length.

Kit finally figured it out.

"You left the tour?" he asked quietly, hardly able to believe his ears.

"Yes, I did! And I did fine! I'm in one piece, aren't I? I'm sick of being coddled, roped in, restricted—dammit, I proved I can handle myself this trip! I want a real scouting job!"

Kit couldn't believe it. She'd actually abandoned the tour, run off on her own. . . .No wonder Malcolm was downstairs getting drunk. Kit was tempted to put Margo straight over his knee and wallop her backside until she couldn't sit. But the fire in he wouldn't do any good.

"That's it," he said coldly. "You are clearly too reckless for your own good. I'd thought you were capable of learning something. I was wrong. Worse, you lied to me. Eighteen, hell." Margo lost color. "Pack your things. You're going home."

"*The hell I am!* You're just an over-protective, lonely old man too scared to let me try my wings! I'm ready and you're not letting me prove it!" They locked glares.

Goldie intervened quietly. "If I might suggest it, why don't you two go somewhere separately to cool off and think this over? Kit, clearly no harm was done. She's made it back just fine. Margo, why don't you come back later and we'll finish this transaction. You might think about the scare you've given everyone. Now, may I help you, sir? Yes, I can certainly exchange that for you. . . ."

Kit stalked out, leaving Margo to make her own way back to the apartment. He was so angry he couldn't think straight. Of all the bone-headed, childish, idiotic . . . He didn't care what Goldie said, Margo was clearly not ready to scout. Goldie had never set foot across a single down-time gate. She had no concept of the dangers that could threaten even an ordinary little tour, particularly when one of the pig-headed tourists abandoned her guides and struck out on her own without knowing so much as half -a dozen words of the language . . .

He stormed into the Down Time and snapped out an order for a triple. He knocked it back, then ordered another. *Gotta calm down before I face her again.* Goldie'd been right about that much, at least. He couldn't talk to her in this frame of mind. He had to recapture his composure, marshal his arguments, decide how to approach the very serious problem her rebelliousness had raised. But . . .

Whatever possessed the brainless little fool to do it? "Worse than you." Malcolm had said.

Kit winced and downed another triple. Great. That was just great. All he needed to make his life complete was a *seventeen-year-old female* carbon copy of himself bent on raising hell everywhere she turned her ambitious little gaze.

He was tempted to haul her kicking and screaming to Primary and toss her bodily through it. But that wouldn't do any good. She'd just come back. Or go to another station and try it from there. He had to find a way to reason with her, convince her to keep training, that she wasn't ready despite marginal success in surviving Rome.

The problem was, Kit had no idea how to go about it.

Everything he did or said only made matters worse.

So he delayed the inevitable and ordered another triple. Just one more for fortitude. Then he'd face her. *Lonely old man,* she'd called him. Well, that much was true. He was lonely and he was afraid of losing her. But that wasn't the reason he was holding her back. Surely he could find a way to convince her of that?

Yeah, right, just like I convinced Sarah to stick by me.

Kit tightened his hand around the shot glass.

Why was it that he always managed to find a way to flub the most important relationships in his life?

He didn't have an answer to that, either.

Margo couldn't believe it. She stood trembling in the corner of

Goldie Morran's shop and fought desperately not to cry. After everything she'd been through, after everything she'd proven . . . She'd even risked losing the gate to ask a Time Tours guide to watch over Achilles until she could properly free him the next time the gate cycled. She'd handled every adversity and responsibility chance had thrown at her, doing better than she had any right to expect, but nobody was giving her so much as a moment to *explain.* They all just assumed the worst and dismissed her as a brainless, incapable fool. Worse, Malcolm had told Kit about her lie.

She straightened her back against a weight heavier than the whole Himalayan mountain range and forced her chin up. She might have been kicked out of training, but she wasn't quitting. Somehow, Margo would prove herself. "Margo?"

She glanced around to find Goldie Morran watching her. The customers had all departed, their business transacted for the moment. Goldie smiled, a sympathetic gesture from one woman to another.

"Don't take it so hard," the older woman said. "You've clearly proven your mettle. A week down time alone, you said?"

"Yes. In Rome."

Goldie nodded. "Why don't we finish that transaction Kit interrupted? I'd like to talk to you."

Margo fumbled in her belt pouch for the coins she'd brought back to exchange. She thought about selling the Circus gemstone, but decided to send it through with a Time Tours guide the next time Porta Romae cycled. Achilles could sell it and use the money to support himself. She was proud of that plan and since ATF would only tax her for it if she tried to take it back through Primary, that was exactly what she intended to do. She might run away from her problems, but she didn't run from responsibility.

Goldie examined her coins and nodded. "Very nice. So . . . you're ready to prove yourself." It wasn't a question.

"Damn right I am," Margo muttered. "I got along fine—and I don't even speak Latin!"

Goldie's eyes widened. "That *is* an accomplishment. You should be very proud." Then she glanced at the doorway as though searching for eavesdroppers. "You want to know what I think?" The older woman's eyes were bright, merry.

"What?"

"I think you're a budding young scout in need of a place to go. And if you're interested, I think I know just the place you need."

Margo's pulse quickened. "Really?" Then she cleared her throat and attempted to assume an air of professionalism. "What did you have in mind?"

"I know of a gate that's in need of a good scout. Someone bright and ambitious. Someone who isn't afraid of a challenge. Someone who'll take a few risks to make a lot of money."

Margo's pulse slapped another few beats. "Why are you telling me?"

Goldie Morran grimaced and gestured to herself. "I'm not a scout and besides, I'm too old. And frankly, I think you've got what it takes. After all, Kit Carson did train you. You've been taught by the best and as far as I'm concerned, you've demonstrated you have what it takes. You've got fire inside you, girl. Besides," Goldie winked, "I'd like to see a woman finally crack that men's club wide open. Interested?"

Margo glared at the doorway where Kit Carson had vanished.

"You bet I'm interested. When do we start?"

"Is now soon enough? Good. First, we allay everyone's suspicions about what you're up to. . . ."

By the time Kit was ready to face Margo with something approaching calm, the "night" had advanced fairly far. Two additional gates had cycled: Edo and Primary. He'd listened to the familiar announcements regarding gate departures while brooding over his bourbon and marshalling his arguments. Significantly, none of his friends had approached his table. Kit finally left the Down Time and brushed through a crowd of new arrivals gawking at the Commons. When he arrived at his apartment Kit drew a deep breath, then unlocked the door. He expected to find her sulking on the couch. He didn't.

Margo wasn't there at all. Her things were gone.

All he found was a scrawled note.

Sorry for all the trouble. It hasn't been fun. I won't be troubling you again. Margo.

Kit crumpled the note in his hand.

Then he sank down onto the couch and cried.

Chapter 17

Margo felt free, absolutely and utterly free, for the first time in her life. Goldie Morran was a true savior. After a quick week up time learning to fly the latest ultra-light craze, she'd returned to TT-86 with a load of very specialized equipment—all paid for by Goldie. The currency expert had trusted her judgment, relied implicitly on her training and skills. That alone had been worth all the heartache of the miserable, terrifying week alone in Rome.

Margo had put hours of planning into this, deciding what to take, how to tackle the problem of overland journey and return, selecting equipment; then came the marvelous moment when she stepped through the gate into the twilight of early evening. Two hired hands trailed after her, hauling equipment.

I did it! I'm doing it! I'm really scouting!

ATLS readings widened the grin on Margo's face. "Wow!" The first stars twinkling in the darkening sky allowed her to pinpoint their location. At thirty-two degrees east longitude and twenty-six degrees south latitude, Margo was standing on the southeastern coast of Mozambique in the year A.D. 1542.

The descending African night was soft, the breeze stiff from offshore. They were very near the coast. Margo easily identified a broad stretch of water nearby from geographical records: Delagoa Bay. Around the curving bay from their position huddled a tiny settlement of ramshackle board houses and a wooden fortress, all surrounded by a wooden wall. Not a single light burned in the settlement. Margo grinned. *Like thieves in the night . . .*

She signaled her two assistants to follow, moving down the curve of the bay until they were out of sight of the primitive little town of Lourenco Marques. Then they unpacked their load and got busy. Margo took charge of the Floating Wing. It was the largest commercially available, a high-tech balloon of transparent, gas-tight Filmar shaped like a pennant flag laid flat. Margo hadn't been able to bring enough helium to inflate it, but she'd studied how to crack hydrogen from water and discovered it was dead easy. She set up the portable generator to power the equipment and got busy.

While she worked on the balloon, her two assistants worked on the gondola. She wasn't sure she approved of Goldie's choices for these two. The big Afrikaner was all right, she supposed, although he was pushing fifty-six, but she was worried about that damned Welshman. He'd tried to disembowel Margo a few weeks ago, mistaking her for Joan of Arc. Now he worked quietly under the Afrikaner's directions, which consisted mostly of hand signals punctuated by grunts and the occasional word in English. Kynan Rhys Gower had learned a few words of English, thank God, since his arrival from Orleans, but his temperament hadn't improved all that much from a month working in the garbage pits while the ribs Kit had broken healed up.

When Margo had protested the choice, Goldie explained, "We don't want anyone blabbing our plans. The Welshman's perfect. He needs money and he can't talk."

"And your Afrikaner?" The Afrikaner could, in fact, speak English, but he usually muttered to himself in his own incomprehensible Afrikaans.

Goldie grinned. "He'll look down that Dutch Afrikaner nose of his, sniff, call you English, and do his job. I know Koot van Beek. He's exactly what you'll need."

"Huh. What kind of name is Koot, anyway?" Margo had muttered, drawing laughter from her dignified partner.

Still, Koot was remarkably cooperative for a close-lipped old man who'd insisted on choosing his own rifle for the journey. He'd even insisted *she* bring a rifle.

"But I don't intend to do any hunting," she'd countered, holding up the laser-guided blowgun she'd used in training. After what she'd witnessed in the Circus Maximus, Margo wasn't sure she wanted to hunt anything for her dinner. "The darts for these are dipped in strong anesthetic. I don't want to kill anything down time unless I absolutely have to."

Koot had muttered under his breath and insisted she bring a rifle, anyway. She'd stowed it away with gear she didn't plan to use unless an emergency threatened Koot worked quietly in the starlight, assembling the PVC gridwork that would serve as the platform of their gondola. While Kynan finished tightening connections, Koot attached the ducted fans which would provide propulsion and steering capability. The triangular lifting wing began to swell against the restraining cables as it filled with buoyant hydrogen gas.

The hydrogen was one reason Margo had chosen PVC for the platform. She didn't want metal fittings anywhere on her ultra-light. Metal fittings might generate sparks. For the duration of their journey, they would be paranoid about fire prevention. She eyed the slowly filling gas bag and wished again they could have transported in enough helium to do the job, but wishing was pointless. They had what they had and Margo was darned proud of her ingenuity.

Their airship was finally ready. Kynan had covered the PVC gridwork with a "floor" of rip-stop nylon to prevent things from falling through. Koot attached cables to the hydrogen wing, then helped Kynan load on their supplies. Margo shut down the generator and packed it in the wheeled crate it had come in, then returned it to the vicinity of the gate. Next time the gate cycled, Goldie would send some down timer through to retrieve it.

Margo ran through her checklist one last time. Food. Water-purifying equipment. Picks and shovels. Her little M-l carbine and ammunition. Blowgun and anesthesia darts. Extra batteries for the laser sight. Koot's .458 Winchester bolt-action rifle. Emergency medical kit. Lightweight sleeping bags and mosquito netting. Ballast they could dump later on when the gas bag inevitably leaked some of its buoyancy. . . . Yes, they had everything.

Margo had even made certain they were all inoculated against cholera, hepatitis, typhoid, meningitis and diphtheria. They'd begun anti-malarial well before departure. And even with the extremely good water filters she'd purchased, she wasn't taking any chances on contracting bilharzias—she planned to boil all local-source water for a minimum of ten minutes before using it. The idea of becoming infected with vicious parasitic worms in her bloodstream left Margo queasy. Malcolm and Kit had trained her too well to take stupid risks.

"Are we ready?" Margo asked brightly. Koot van Beek turned from slinging his rifle across his back. He grunted in the moonlight.

"Yes, English. We're ready."

The transparent airship, a ghostly sight in the moonlight, strained against its cables. Margo grinned, then climbed onto the gondola platform and made sure everything was secure. She gestured the Welshman to a place near the front of the platform. He eyed the gas bag straining overhead with an uneasy glance, then muttered something entirely incomprehensible and took his seat. One hand strayed to the case which held his heavy longbow and quiver of arrows. Margo shrugged. They were the weapons he was most familiar with, so she hadn't begrudged him the privilege of bringing them along. How Goldie had weaseled them out of Bull Morgan was something Margo would like to have known.

"Okay, everyone, this show is about to hit the road!" Margo signaled Koot, who loosened his tether at the same moment she loosened her own cable. The airship rose silently into the starlit African night. A strong offshore wind pushed them steadily into the interior. Margo waited until they were well out of sight of the little bayside community below, then fired up the ducted fan engines.

Their noise shattered the night. Kynan covered his ears and glanced over the edge of the platform. He lost all color in the silvered moonlight. The airship dipped and plunged in the air currents like a slow-motion roller coaster. Poor Kynan squeezed shut both eyes and swallowed rapidly several times. Margo grinned and handed him a scopolamine patch, showing him how to put it on, then steered a course northward around the edge of Delagoa Bay for the mouth of the legendary Limpopo River.

⁂

Margo thrilled as the dawn came up, spreading fingers of light across the heart of Africa. Beneath their floating platform the distant Drakensberg mountains snaked away southward along the rugged Wild Coast. Directly below, the Limpopo glinted in the early light, a treacherous ribbon of water navigable only during flood stage. According to her ATLS readings, they had emerged in early December, the beginning of the summer season in this part of sub-Saharan Africa. Far to the south, clouds boiled up over the mountains. Flickers of lightning split the predawn sky as the Drakensbergs roared with another of their legendary storms.

Fortunately, Margo's route lay to the north, following the Limpopo valley in its long, arcing curve through the Drakensberg foothills. With any luck, they'd avoid the worst of the summer storms. Margo peered over the side and grinned even while pulling her jacket tighter. The crystalline chill of the high air invigorated her. The river valley below was a vast carpet of green rising steadily into the foothills. Animals moved in the early sunlight. Vast herds rippled like brown rivers. She wondered what they were. She understood being hungry; but how could anyone hunt such beautiful animals for sport?

She glanced at Koot and wrinkled her nose. *He* hunted for sport and scuttlebutt had it he'd guide down-time safaris, too, but he probably knew what those herds were. She could ask, anyway. "Koot?" The grizzled Afrikaner glanced back without speaking. "What are those?" She pointed.

"Wildebeest," he said shortly, "and Cape Buffalo. Very nasty. Most dangerous animal in Africa, the Cape Buffalo. Crocs in that river. Hippos too. Good you decided against rubber rafts."

The sarcasm was heavy enough to weight down the airship. Margo trimmed their attitude by adjusting the amount of ordinary air contained in ballonets inside the hydrogen bag. Her argument with Koot on the subject of air versus water transport had been short, violent, and conclusive. He'd won. That was all right. Flying was more exciting, anyway.

Up in the "bow," the Welshman, too, stared at the tremendous herds. Then he glanced at the hydrogen bag and shivered. Margo felt a moment's pang of pity. What must it be like for him, coming into a time and place where everything he saw smacked of "witchcraft" and left him fighting to hide his fear? She wondered if Goldie had been right to include him. He needed the work, clearly; but he was having such a difficult time adjusting, Margo would have preferred to leave him on the station and hire someone a little more familiar with modern languages, machinery, and philosophical concepts.

Then she thought about their ultimate destination and grinned. Soon she would fulfill a goal she'd set for herself the day her mother died A few weeks from now, Margo was going to walk into that prison hospital in Minnesota and show her father just how incredibly wrong he'd been about her, her dreams, everything.

Sunlight flooded the landscape and streamed through the triangular lifting wing which carried them forward into adventure, burning away all trace of bitterness. *Today is the most beautiful, perfect day of my life!* Margo consulted her compass, corrected the direction of the propulsion fans, and came about on the right heading. She thrilled at the touch of the controls. This was *her* airship, *her* expedition, *her* success come to life.

At last, something she had planned was going exactly as it should!

Finding the Seta gravel deposits Goldie had identified was so easy that Margo spent the next several days gloating over her success. They anchored the balloon, broke out digging equipment, and busied themselves excavating ore from the potholes along the Limpopo River bank.

When she encountered her first inch-wide sapphire, Margo whispered, "Oh, my God . . ." Then at the bottom of the pothole, they hit diamonds. "Oh, my *God* . . ."

Even the Welshman grinned ear-to-ear as he worked.

They removed yard after cubic yard of matrix, piling it carefully onto the gondola platform, and began hauling it upriver to the site Goldie had marked on her map. Margo had trouble finding that spot. She hovered over the Shashe River, studying the lay of the land, trying to correlate what she saw with Goldie's chart and navigational notations. She finally took an aerial snapshot with the digitizing camera that was part of her personal log, scanned in Goldie's map, and made the best correlation she could. "There," she decided.

She took the airship down and they buried the first load. They made trip after trip, digging out pits on Goldie's future landholding, seeding them with diamondiferous matrix and returning for another load. It was slow work, because the matrix was heavy. They couldn't lift much at one time. A week passed, blurred easily into two, then three. The January rains of summer hit, flooding their little camp and forcing them onto higher ground. The heat was stifling. Using filter straws which blocked out pathogens, they drank boiled water which had cooled enough to swallow, grinned like fools, and went back to work.

Margo was thrilled that her digitizing camera did double duty as a video camera. In her spare moments, she filmed vast herds of antelope, wildebeest, and zebra which stretched away across the grassy veldt. Nearer the river, where trees and scrub grew up, they saw graceful giraffes browsing in the treetops. At night the grunting cough of hunting lions sent shivers through her. Hyenas' wild cackles mingled with the cries of water birds and the bass roar of hippos in the river.

They fished to supplement their supplies. Kynan Rhys Gower and Koot van Beek dined on grilled antelope which Koot brought down. Kynan even joined the hunt, grinning as he transfixed a silver and black gemsbok with a cloth-yard shaft. He cut the long black horns for souvenirs. That night he and the Afrikaner gorged on roast gemsbok. Margo wouldn't touch anything but the fish and her own supplies. Watching them butcher their kills only reminded her of the Roman arena—and that killed her appetite and curiosity at one fell swoop.

"No, thank you," she said primly when offered a morsel.

Koot just rolled his eyes heavenward, muttered, *"English,"* and kept eating.

Elephants appeared in glorious great herds, coming down to the river to drink. Monkeys screamed and chattered in the trees and darted in to try thieving their supplies. Margo laughed and chased them away. In the hay-colored grass of the high veldt, she could even see cantankerous rhinos and long-snouted, suspicious baboons.

Those she steered clear of, having no desire to tangle with a horned tank locked on permanent bad temper or an intelligent primate that lived in structured tribal groups, ate a diet that included meat, and sported fangs as long as her fingers. But everything else was fair game, both for Margo's camera and her unbounded delight.

They'd nearly finished their work when Margo learned her first valuable lesson about scouting. She and Kynan had left the river, Kynan to hunt his dinner and Margo to stretch her legs and sightsee a little, leaving Koot to guard the camp. Margo carried the carbine slung over her shoulder, but only because Koot always pitched a fit if she didn't. Game was so plentiful Kynan never had to go far and Margo was usually thrilled by whatever they found within a few dozen yards of the campsite. Margo was creeping through tall grass with her digital camera, edging toward a herd of springbok, when it happened. She heard a snort and glanced around to see a massive Cape Buffalo. The bull stood solitary against the skyline.

Oh . . . What a gorgeous animal!

He stared at her through dark eyes, not more than seventy-five yards away. His nostrils flared. He thrust one foreleg out, stiff-legged, as though posing. She lifted the digital camera and snapped a shot. *Ooh, perfect. . . .* The bull snorted and lowered his head. The horns were enormous, sharp-tipped, beautiful.

Kynan touched her arm. She glanced around. "What?"

He high-signed her, pointing urgently toward camp. She noticed he'd notched an arrow to his longbow while backing away. "There's no danger," she told him. "He's fifty yards away." Margo clicked the camera from snapshot to video and began filming again, motion footage this time. The Cape Buffalo bull lowered his head even more and snorted again, cutting the turf with a sharp hoof.

Then he charged.

Oh, shit . . .

Margo fumbled for her laser-guided blowgun, but realized she'd left it at camp. Then she knew she was in serious danger. *That animal's as big as a car!* And he was running straight toward her, bellowing like a runaway freight train. Terror took hold. Margo fumbled awkwardly for the carbine and brought it around. The whole barrel shook, describing wild circles with the muzzle, but she managed to center the bull. She didn't know where to aim. She squeezed her eyes shut and fired. The carbine slapped her shoulder. The crack of the report sounded above the thunder of hooves.

The bull bellowed and kept coming.

WHACK!

A yard-long arrow sprouted from the bull's chest.

The buffalo bellowed furiously—and kept coming.

"Run!" Margo spun and pelted toward camp. Kynan was right behind her. The thunder of hooves bearing down told Margo they'd never make it.

"It's too far!" Margo cried. She turned and fired again, emptying the magazine into the charging buffalo.

Kynan notched another arrow and let fly. It caught the bull full in the chest. The crazed buffalo faltered only one stride then picked up speed again. Two more arrows followed, pincushioning the enraged animal. Margo fumbled for another magazine to reload the carbine. She was still fumbling with the ammunition when—KA-RUMP!

The bull went down as though pole-axed. It snorted, screamed, and staggered back to its feet. Then charged again.

KA-RUMP! The thunder of Koot's big rifle barked again.

The buffalo crumpled and slid to a stop. Margo stood where she was, shaking like a leaf. Kynan, poised between her and the maddened bull, slowly relaxed his bow. The bull had skidded to a stop less than four feet from his toes.

"You stupid English!" Koot van Beek muttered, rising from the grass behind them. "You cannot stop a Cape Buffalo with children's toys." He raised the Winchester Model 70 African Special he'd brought along. "*This* is why I brought my own rifle, English."

Margo gulped. "I—I see. Yes. I—Thank you."

Koot grunted once then jerked a thumb back toward camp. "I have fish for supper." The scathing way he said it made Margo wish she could crawl into a hole and pull it in after her. Maybe hunting *did* have its place. . . .

The Welshman slowly, carefully, replaced his arrow in the quiver at his side.

"You were very brave," Margo told him, wondering if he knew enough English to understand her.

Kynan turned to face her. Margo gulped. His whole face was pasty white. He glanced at his bow, stared for a moment at the dead Cape Buffalo, then looked past her to Koot. He said in broken English, "Koot? You show gun?"

Koot grinned. "Sure. Come to camp. I will teach you to shoot."

The look in the Welshman's eyes was one of vast relief.

Wordlessly, Margo followed the men back to camp. *Next time,* she promised, *I'll bring a* gun *powerful enough to stop anything I'm likely to encounter.* She'd made a mistake. A bad one. Fortunately, it hadn't proven fatal. This time, she'd been lucky.

Margo's second mistake was far more serious than not choosing a powerful enough rifle. Watching the falling fuel gauges—and searching the inhospitable terrain below for nonexistent landing sites—did nothing to slow the alarming rate at which they burned fuel. Far sooner than they should have, the ducted engine fans sputtered and went silent. Terror choked Margo into equally profound silence. *We're out of fuel. Dear God, we're out of fuel . . .*

Try as she might, Margo spotted nothing that looked remotely like a survivable landing site for miles in any direction. The fuel gauges read empty—and Margo knew the spare fuel canisters were just as empty as the main tanks. They started to drift rapidly off course.

It's not fair! I was so careful! I figured our exact fuel needs. I got it right for the inland flight! For all those maddening trips upriver. My calculations should've been right for the return to the coast, too. Dammit, I put in every variable I could think of to balance weight against lift—even looked up how heavy that diamond-bearing soil would be! It's just not fair!

But—as Kit and Sven had been so fond of saying—the Universe didn't give beans for "fair." It simply *was.* You got it right or paid the price. And Margo, for all her cautious calculations, had forgotten one simple, critical factor: the wind.

Year round, the wind blew off the coast of Madagascar across the

Drakensberg ranges, flowed around the foothills of the Limpopo valley and blasted inland, carrying moisture that kept the eastern half of Africa's tip from baking into desert like the Kalahari and Skeleton Coast farther west. That wind never shifted direction. In all her careful planning, Margo had forgotten to calculate the effect of bucking *headwinds* all the way back along five hundred miles of river valley while summer storms drenched them and threatened to blow their little airship off course.

It wasn't fair; it just *was.*

And now the fuel was gone.

"English!" Koot called urgently. "Fill the fuel tanks!"

Oh, God, I have to tell him . . .

"Uh . . . I can't! We're, uh, out of fuel. . . ."

The hydrogen wing bucked in the wind and dropped sickeningly, then spun lazily at the mercy of rising storm winds. From across the PVC gondola, Koot stared at her, then gave the silent ducted fans a single disgusted glare.

"English."

Margo clung to the gondola with her heart in her throat. She had no choice but to take them down. If they could *get* down. The terrain below was absolutely treacherous: broken rocks and a snaking river bordered by tangles of brush and tall trees. But if they waited much longer, the wind would push them even deeper into the interior, stranding them miles from the Limpopo with no way out but to walk.

"We're taking her down, Koot!" Margo called. "Let's go!"

He gave her a cold glare, but didn't argue. Clearly even he could see the need for getting down *now.* With all three of them fighting the steering controls and hanging on for dear life in the gusting winds, Margo managed to open valves on the lifting wing, draining out buoyant gas. The little ship descended treacherously, canting at wild angles, spinning out of control in gusting winds. Kynan tied down gear that slid and threatened to fall off, then had to grab for a cable to keep from sliding off the edge himself.

"Rope in!" Margo yelled, kicking herself for not thinking of it sooner. One of them might have been flung out. Of course, the way the ground rushed at them . . .

Koot tied himself to the gondola. Kynan and Margo did the same. She trimmed the ballonets, trying to slow their rate of descent. Then dumped ballast overboard. Their wild plunge toward the ground slowed. The flying wing sheered around, flinging Margo against the tiller, then righted itself and continued to descend.

She had no control over where they might land. She searched the ground frantically. If they landed there, they'd break up on the rocks. There and they'd crash through trees and die messily another way. The river was in flood stage, but jagged boulders stuck out of the water like teeth and massive debris including whole trees washed down the raging torrent. They couldn't land in the water. By chance, a freak wind blew them toward a bend where floods had washed out trees and brush, leaving a tiny, muddy clearing. She wasn't sure it was big enough. But if she waited, another gust would blow them past it. Margo released hydrogen with a vengeance. The gondola dropped so fast even Koot yelled.

Please . . . just a little farther . . .

Margo cut loose half their supplies and kicked the bundles overboard—they landed with a splat in the mud, The gondola slowed, settled toward the ground. Wind blew them sideways toward a snarl of broken trees. Margo yelled and yanked on the valve. Hydrogen hissed out of the balloon. The PVC gridwork thunked wetly into the mud with enough force to jolt her whole spine. *Oww . . . everything* ached.

But they were down. Down, alive, and in one piece.

Margo just shut her eyes and shook.

When she opened them again, she found Koot and Kynan staring disconsolately at their wild surroundings. Koot, at least, was busy making them fast with cables and pegs while he stared at the tangle of brush and flooded river. Margo flushed. *Some leader I turn out to be. Stranded two hundred fifty miles from the sea . . .* She wanted to cover her face and cry. But this was her expedition and it was her mistake that had put them all in jeopardy.

"Koot? What do you know about the Limpopo?"

He studied the swollen river. "It is navigable at flood stage. That I know. It will be very dangerous if we try to raft it."

Raft it? "With what?"

Koot just looked at her. "Don't you English learn to think? Our gondola will float. It is PVC plastic. All we need to do is cut up the balloon to waterproof the floor and we can raft on it."

Raft a raging river filled with rocks and whole trees and God knew what else? *Beats walking.* . . . . "Yes, you're right. That's a good idea."

He snorted. "Of course it is, English. I thought of it."

Margo flushed again, but said nothing. He might be arrogant, but he was right, as usual. Through the effort of gestures and halting explanations, they told Kynan what had to be done. They opened every release valve on the gas bag and deflated it slowly then trod on the ballonets to help deflate them as well. Kynan used his knife to carefully slice open the Filmar wing. Then they unloaded the gondola and covered the rip-stop nylon with a layer of tough, transparent Filmar. Once that was done, they lashed it securely down with the cables which had held the gas bag attached to the gondola. The engines they abandoned by sinking them in the river.

Reloading the raft was tricky as they struggled not to puncture the layer of Filmar. Once the job was done, Kynan and Koot set to work cutting poles and rough paddles from tree branches. "There will be many dangers," Koot said glumly. "Crocodiles. Hippos. Rapids. We are low on food. We may all die."

Great pep talk. "We're not dead yet!" she flashed back. "And I'm not giving up. Let's push her into the water."

Working together, they hauled the raft to the river and shoved off. Margo scrambled aboard and used her pole to help push them into deeper water. They picked up speed as the swollen current caught them and swept them downstream. She crossed her fingers, said a tiny prayer, and clutched her paddle.

Here goes nothing.

At least she wasn't hiding back home in Minnesota, waiting for life to pass her by the way it did nearly everyone else in that godforsaken little town. If she was going to die out here, she'd die trying! That, Margo supposed as she dug her paddle into the racing current, was something worthy of an epitaph.

She hoped that thought didn't turn into prophecy.

The trip back down the Limpopo was an exhausting, nerve-racking blur of incidents which haunted her at night when she didn't sleep.

"Push off!" Koot screamed. "Now! Now!"

Margo thrust her improvised paddle against a jagged rock higher than her head. The shock of wood on stone all but dislocated her shoulder. Margo went to her knees as the raft spun away from the rock. One kneecap punched through the Filmar floor. Margo dropped her paddle to rig a hasty patch across the spurting hole. Then had to grab wildly for the paddle again as another rock towered in their path. The shock of contact spread white-hot fire through her damaged shoulder. But she held onto the paddle and kept lookout for more boulders. On the other side of the gondola, Kynan hung grimly to a long pole while Koot van Beek clung to his own paddle, trying to steer a course through the flood.

Another day—Margo wasn't sure which one—storm rains lashed them. The river rose swiftly, flinging them from one muddy crest to another. Then ahead, just visible through slashing rain, a sight that brought a cry of terror: wildebeest. A whole herd was trying to cross the Limpopo, thousands—tens of thousands—of animals at a time. The river ahead was a solid carpet of swimming, drowning wildebeest.

"KOOT!"

He came to his feet, swearing. "Try to reach the bank!"

They fought the flood, cracking heavily against a submerged rock. PVC burst along one side of the raft. Then they spun off and bounded downstream again, headed slightly outward toward the far bank. Margo dug in her paddle until her back screamed for mercy—and kept paddling. *If we hit that herd, we're dead. . .* .Closer, closer, they were going to make it . . .

The bank was infested with crocodiles.

"Keep going!" Koot lunged to his feet, rifle in hand, and braced with his legs wide apart.

KA-RUMP!

The rifle barked again and again. Crocodiles died—or thrashed, wounded—on the muddy banks. Others flung themselves into the rain-lashed water or tore into wounded animals for a feast. The bank neared, spun out of Margo's view, came back around closer than before. They were going to make it. . . . They would miss. . . .

The raft grounded, flinging Margo to her chest. Koot leaped ashore, straining to hold the raft by one cable. Kynan jumped out beside him and snatched another slippery cable. Margo screamed, "Look out!"

Koot let go, whirling and bringing up his heavy rifle. He fired once at the croc lunging toward Kynan. It slithered into the roaring whitewater and vanished.

Margo scrambled onto the muddy bank, snatching at the cable Koot had dropped. The raft fought for its freedom. She dug in heels and *putted.* Rain slashed at her face, making breathing difficult. Lightning flared, but the roar of the river drowned out any thunder.

Koot yanked at another cable. The raft lifted an inch at a time. Margo worked backwards and maintained a steady pull, fearing her back would crack. The raft finally came clear of the river's maddened embrace and slid messily onto the mud. Only a dozen yards distant, crocodiles tore into other crocs brought down by Koot's rifle. Rain washed most of the blood away. Koot shot the nearest crocs then levered them into the water, creating a carcass-free perimeter around their position.

Margo panted, turning her shoulders to the driving rain to regain her breath, then found her M-l carbine. Kynan Rhys Gower tied the raft down and set about repairing visible damage as best he could. Margo shook so hard she could barely keep her grip on the rifle, but at least she was still alive to shake. Thirty yards downstream, wildebeest struggled in the water and screamed like terrified children while they died. She shut her eyes to the carnage. They'd come so close to plowing straight into that. . . .

More animals died during the next few hours than had died during the entire Ludi Megalenses. Possibly more than had died during the whole previous *year* at Rome. The death of the wildebeest herd didn't change the bloody savagery she'd witnessed in the Roman Circus, but it put life and death in much clearer perspective. Nature wasn't any nobler or gentler than human beings. It was just as deadly and just as cruel and just as savagely "unfair" to the weak. . . .

Maybe more so.

They had to wait hours past the end of the storm before the river was clear enough to risk rafting again.

That night they took turns once again standing watch.

They stayed on the river each night if no rapids threatened, trying to gain time, but dragged the raft onto the banks until dawn if the river was too rough to navigate in the dark. Tonight they'd come ashore rather than risk a treacherous stretch of white water visible just ahead in the fading twilight. That night, Margo spent a lot of time whimpering deep in her throat, glad the roar of white water drowned out the sound of her terror.

So *call me Katherine Hepburn and marry me off to Humphrey Bogart. . . .*

Margo would have settled for Malcolm Moore's strong arms in a flash. She missed him desperately, particularly at night like this when the screams of hunting leopards and dying animals drifted on the wind like clouds of enveloping mosquitoes. Every time she heard another wild scream on the night air she wanted to grab her rifle, but tonight Margo was so tired she could scarcely pick up the M-l carbine.

I'm sorry, Malcolm, she found herself thinking again and again. *I was rotten and selfish and I didn't mean it . . .*

Another drenching summer storm broke over them near midnight, jolting Margo from fitful sleep. Kynan stood watch, a ghostly figure in the flash and flare of African lightning. Koot van Beek, bedded down in his sleeping bag, stirred briefly then went back to sleep.

How could anyone sleep through this?

Lightning screamed through the clouds, slashed downward into trees and the river, dancing and splashing insanely across jagged, arc-lit boulders. Margo was too tired to flinch every time it struck, but fear jolted her with every bolt, nonetheless. *Don't let it strike us. . . .*

Then the rain struck, a solid mass of black, stinging water. Margo coughed and rolled onto her tummy, pulling the sleeping bag right over her head. Water roared louder than ever down the swollen Limpopo.

I'll hear that sound in my grave, Margo moaned. *Why 'd we have to arrive in the rainy season?* Then, because she was no longer able to hide from her own folly and its cost, *Good thing it is or we'd really be in a jam.* Rafting out two hundred fifty miles still beat *walking* it. Which they'd have had to do, lugging gear every step of the way, if this had been the dry season.

Oh, Malcolm, I really screwed up . . . She had to get back, not just to prove she could scout and survive it, but to apologize to Malcolm for the cruel thing she'd done to him. It was too late to pursue what might have been the most wonderful relationship in her life, but she could at least apologize.

When, at some later, miserable point in the night, water lapped against Margo's cheek, She thought groggily the rain must've seeped into her sleeping bag.

Then Kynan Rhys Gower appeared in a strobe-flash of lightning, drenched and white-faced. "Margo!" he cried, pointing toward the nearest edge of the raft. "River"

The raft was bobbing madly against its moorings.

Huh?

She wriggled free of her sodden sleeping bag. The river had risen swiftly—and rose visibly higher over the next few lightning flashes.

"Koot! Koot, wake up!"

He reacted sluggishly, fighting his way toward consciousness while she shook him. One good look at the rising river brought him to his feet, swearing in Afrikaans.

"Drag her higher!" Margo shouted.

"No use! Look!" He pointed inland.

Lightning revealed a tangle of impenetrable forest. At the rate the water was rising, the whole tangle would be multiple feet deep in flood waters at least five hundred yards inland from where they floated—probably within another hour.

"Can we ride this out where we are?" Margo called above the sound of river, rain, and thunder.

"Don't know. Rapids downstream looked bad!"

A terrifying *crack* nearly on top of them jolted the raft. Margo screamed. One whole end of the raft disappeared underwater. Kynan scrambled across the tilted deck, knife in hand. The raft jerked, thrashed under the tug of something monstrous. Lightning showed them why: one of their anchor trees had come down.

"Cut the cable! Cut it!" Koot van Beek screamed.

Kynan was already sawing at the taut cable where it vanished underwater. It parted strand by strand, then snapped. The raft lurched and spun sideways. Kynan went overboard with a hoarse yell. Margo lunged forward. Lightning revealed him clinging to a broken PVC pipe with one hand.

"Koot!"

The Afrikaner didn't answer. Margo wrapped both hands around Kynan's wrist. He flailed and caught her arm with his other hand. She lost him in the darkness between flashes, aware of him only through the tenuous contact of hand on wrist. Margo pulled, but her upper body strength was a pitiful match for the tug of the river.

"KOOT!"

The raft slammed around into something hard. Kynan yelled and barely hung onto her arm. Margo sobbed for breath and used toes to dig for the severed cable behind her. She found it and scooted one knee forward until the broken end was under her cheek.

"Kynan! Hold on!"

She drew a breath for courage—

—then let go with one hand and snatched the cable. Kynan yelled—

Margo flung the cable around him.

He grabbed for it as his grip on the raft broke loose.

Margo hung onto one end and Kynan clung to the other. *Please* . . . Margo sobbed under her breath. She rolled over and scooted backwards, hauling with the leverage of arms *and* legs this time. Kynan's arms appeared over the edge. Then his head and back appeared. He slithered forward, clutching at the cable, the PVC, anything he could grasp. Margo pulled until Kynan had wriggled completely onto the raft. Then she fell backwards, panting.

Grimly, Margo tied herself to a lifeline and tied one around the gasping Welshman. Koot was fighting to secure the raft to another tree, braced on one foot and one knee while he struggled with coiled cable and vicious wind and current.

"KOOT! TIE A LIFELINE!"

Before he could respond, another tree went CRACK! The raft lurched underfoot. Margo fell flat. She caught a glimpse of Koot in a strobe-flare of lightning. He was sawing frantically at the other cable with his own knife. Then they spun free. The river sucked them downstream. Margo whimpered, but forced herself to crawl forward.

"Get a lifeline on!" she shouted at him.

Koot, looking numb and shaken, fumbled for a rope.

Then lightning flared and Margo caught sight of the rapids.

"Oh, God . . . Oh, *GOD* . . ."

Margo groped blindly for a paddle, a pole, anything she could use to shove off those looming rocks. The river spat them at those rapids like a watermelon seed in a millrace. Margo found breath to scream just once. Then she was fighting for survival in the strobe-lit night. Every time lightning flared, she shoved the paddle at anything that looked dark. Usually the paddle connected sickeningly with solid stone, jarring her whole body with bruising force. The raft spun, lurched, plunged through the darkness. Spray and rain battered them. Margo couldn't hear anything but the roar of water. If anyone yelled for help, she'd never hear them.

Another shock shook them. A rock nobody'd seen. The whole raft shuddered, bounced off, rocked sideways over a lip of water, dropped sickeningly. The impact jarred her breath out, then they plunged on. She had no idea half the time if she faced upriver or down. Another jolt shook the raft. *It can't take much more of this, it'll come apart on us . . .*

The raft lurched—then either it or Margo was abruptly airborne. Margo screamed. She came down in the water. The muddy Limpopo closed over her head. Margo fought to find her lifeline. The current was savage. She couldn't move against it. She swallowed water, strangled, knew that if she hit a submerged rock, she would die—or worse—

Her face broke the surface. She was moving . . .

Kynan Rhys Gower grabbed her hair and pulled. Margo groped for his arm, his waist. She slithered forward into his lap. The raft rocked violently, spun in a new direction . . .

Then quieted.

They still raced through the darkness like a cork over Niagara Falls, but they'd made it alive through the rapids.

Margo quietly threw up in Kynan's lap, disgorging the water she'd swallowed. He pounded her back, helping her cough it out. Then he helped her sit up and made sure she'd suffered no broken bones. Margo winced a few times, but the worst she'd endured was bruises. Koot watched silently.

She finally met Kynan's gaze. "Thank you."

The Welshman pointed to himself then the river, then pointed to her and the river.

"Yes," she shivered. "We're even now. Thank you, anyway."

He spread his hands and shrugged, then busied himself checking for damage. Koot watched her without speaking.

"Are you all right?" she called over the storm.

"Yes. You?"

"I'll live. Maybe." she qualified it.

He grunted. "You're damn lucky, English. I'm going to sleep."

Without another word, he collapsed, not even bothering to crawl into his sleeping bag. Margo glanced at Kynan. He gestured for her to rest.

"My watch," he said in his careful English.

Margo just nodded, knowing she'd have found the strength to stand watch if she'd had to, but thanking God and every angel in the heavens she *didn't* have to. If another emergency threatened, Kynan would wake them. She fell asleep before her cheek even hit the sodden sleeping bag.

Five days into their wretched journey, they ran out of food—and Koot van Beek fell seriously ill. He woke with a high fever and terrible chills.

"Malaria," he chattered between clenched teeth.

"But we took anti-malarials!"

"Not . . . not a sure-fire prevention. G-get the quinine tablets."

Margo dug out the medical kit with trembling hands. She read the instructions again to be sure, then dosed him with four tablets of chloroquine and covered him with one of their sleeping bags. They had no food left to help him regain his strength. The river banks were barren of anything that could be shot and fetched back as food.

Where are all those stupid animals when we need them? I'm hungry—and Koot may be dying!

She'd have shot anything that remotely *resembled* food in a heartbeat. She'd even have cooked one of those lousy drowned carcasses, if she could've gotten close enough to one to snag it. She bit her lips and tried to cope with an overwhelming sense of failure. When they stopped for the night, pulling the raft onto the flood-ravaged bank, Margo sat in her miserable corner of the raft and held her head in her hands and started admitting the hardest truths she had ever had to face.

I am not smart. Or particularly clever. Or honest, not even with myself. Kit and Malcolm, everyone was right. I was crazy to think I was ready to scout . . .

Proving herself to her father seemed utterly pointless now. What had she expected him to do? Take her in his arms and weep on her neck? Tell her the three words she'd wanted to hear all her life? Fat chance.

Sitting there in the darkness, Margo had ample time to review every mistake she'd made, every selfish word she'd uttered, every lame-brained, dangerous risk she'd run because she hadn't learned enough. She'd nearly let a Cape Buffalo loll her because she was too busy thinking how *picturesque* it was to realize her danger. Koot had *warned* her and she'd chosen to ignore him. What was it Kit had told her? Don't put wild animals on some moral pedestal bearing no resemblance to reality?

And she'd nearly killed Malcolm in St. Giles. And in Rome, completely on her own . . . Margo had come to realize that she'd come close to being killed in Rome, too. She could've stumbled into far less scrupulous hands than Quintus Flaminius'—and his care of her could easily have soured. That lancet they'd used to bleed her could've infected her with something awful, or they might literally have bled her to death, or . . .

Margo's whole experience as a time scout was one unmitigated disaster after another, with some impatient guardian angel finally throwing hands in the air in disgust and going back to whatever heaven guardian angels come from.

All of which left her utterly alone with no supplies on a flooded river miles from help, with a dying man and a scared down-timer on her hands. The only thing that kept her going was her sense of responsibility. She hadn't left Achilles completely without resources and she wouldn't give up on Koot and Kynan, either. Somehow, she'd get them out of this mess she'd made.

Six hours later she woke Koot and dosed him with two more tablets. He complained of a raging headache and fell asleep again. Margo dug out her information on malaria and a flashlight. When she read the list of potential symptoms, Margo felt a chill of terror. The *Plasmodium falciparum* strain of malaria, which included among its symptoms severe headaches, could be quickly fatal if not treated properly. They were several hundred years as well as a hundred or so miles from the nearest medical clinic.

Kynan crouched down at her side and gestured to Koot.

"He die?"

Margo shook her head. "I don't know."

The Welshman's dark gaze flicked to the river. "Bad place."

"Yes. Very bad." She drew a ragged breath. "We have to keep going." She pantomimed paddling and pointed down the river.

Kynan nodded. His expression was as grim as Margo's fading hopes. Somewhere deep inside her, Margo found the courage to keep going. At dawn, they shoved off again. The Welshman wordlessly picked up Koot's heavy Winchester rifle and checked it as he'd been taught, then took up a guard stance in the bow. Someone had to watch for hippos while the other one steered. Margo didn't feel like arguing over which job she was best suited for. She took up position in the stern and did her best to keep them on course.

Margo was three-quarters asleep under a starry sky when their raft eddied down the last few miles of the Limpopo. Kynan Rhys

Gower shook her gently and pointed. Margo blinked and rose awkwardly. She ached everywhere, making movement difficult, and the hunger gnawing at her had left her muzzy-headed. She stared down the moonlit river for several moments before realizing why it looked so wide.

They had come within sight of the sea.

"Oh, thank God!"

Then another frightening thought hit her.

The mouth of the Limpopo was nearly a hundred miles up the coast from Delagoa Bay and the gate. A hundred miles on a raft on the open sea with no real way to steer and no food or water?

"Kynan! We have to get to the bank!"

Kynan puzzled out her meaning, then nodded and began to paddle. Margo dug her paddle into the current until her shoulders and back were on fire. They moved slowly nearer the bank—but not fast enough. The current was sweeping them inexorably out to sea. Maybe they could swim for it. . . .

Koot couldn't swim. And when she looked closely, Margo saw the gleam of crocodile eyes in the water. Terror choked her breath. *We'll drift into the Indian Ocean. My God, we could end up anywhere* . . . At the last moment, she thought to fill water cans with river water. Then they were wallowing in rolling swells. The current carried them farther from land.

"A sail," Margo muttered, "we need a sail . . ." Malcolm had taught her how to sail. But not how to build a sailboat out of a PVC and Filmar raft. "Doesn't matter. Gotta have a sail."

Margo dug for the remains of their flying wing. Not much was left. It would have to do. Margo loosened one of the broken PVC pipes and rigged a mast, using cables to tie it in place, then tied the remaining Filmar in place as a rude sail. Wind bellied it out. The raft still wallowed—but in a new direction. For a time, they made little headway. Then they left behind the influence of the Limpopo's strong current and eddied slowly down the coastline, blown slightly shoreward by the wind hitting their sail.

Kynan poured river water through their filtration equipment and used the Coleman stove to boil it. Margo was so thirsty she would cheerfully have drunk the ocean dry. He poured a cup and handed it to her. Margo sipped the hot water—

And spat involuntarily.

Salty. . . .

She stared in rising horror at the cup. She'd scooped up river water. . . . But she'd waited until they were almost in the mouth of the river to do it. The water she'd retrieved was brackish. And that water was all they had aboard.

She shut her eyes, wishing she could blot out the terrors closing in on her as easily as she did sight of the accusatory cup in her hand. Koot was dying, they were adrift at sea with no water and no food . . .

"Margo."

She opened her eyes. Kynan's brow had furrowed in the starlight. 'Water not good," she said shakily. "Salt."

He frowned and tasted it, then spat. The furrows in his brow deepened. Between them, Koot moaned. Margo checked him and bit her lips. He was extremely weak. When she tried to move him, he vomited over the side, then soiled himself with uncontrollable diarrhea. His skin burned under her hand. Margo poured sea water over him in an effort to bring down his temperature. He moaned and shivered, then subsided into delirium.

Gotta get him back to the gate. HOW?

The raft wallowed in the swells, ungainly as a beached whale. Kynan vomited over the side, too, then wiped his lips and looked embarrassed. Margo dug out another scopolamine patch and stuck it behind his ear, then dosed herself against seasickness for good measure. She wasn't sure she ought to risk dosing Koot, then decided he was so close to death she might as well chance it. If she could keep him from vomiting, maybe he'd survive? The coastline was a great deal more rugged from the ocean than it had looked from the air. Margo and Kynan took turns at the sail, steering their craft as best they could. They hardly moved in relation to the coast. At Margo's best guess, it would take them *days* to make the gate. Then, icing on a ruined cake, a line of thunderclouds rolled in from the Madagascar Straits, blotting out moon and stars. Lightning flared wildly from clouds to sea and back again. "Oh, God, no, not now . . ." The storm swept down on them. The only silver lining visible in the clouds was their increased speed as the storm drove the little raft southward. Then it began to rain. "Kynan! Fresh water!"

He'd tilted his head back, letting rain enter his mouth. "KYNAN!"

He glanced around. Margo tried to explain what she wanted, mimicking the shape of a funnel, then simply tore up part of the flooring and used the plastic to rig a funnel over one of the cans. Kynan did the same, with a bigger sheet of plastic. They filled three cans before the sea grew so rough they had to hang onto the raft to keep from being thrown off the platform. They wallowed and spun around in the swells. Rain pelted down, a wall of solid water that left them blind and drenched Margo clung to the raft, unable to let go long enough to steer.

Please, let us get out of this alive and I swear I'll do whatever Kit says, study anything Kit tells me . . . They ran before the storm, helpless in its grip for hours. Margo couldn't get to her chronometer, nestled safely in the ATLS bag looped around her torso, but given the changes in the light she guessed the storm drove them down the curving coast for more than twenty hours. She tried to remember what the curve of the coast looked like, wondered if the storm would slam them into the beach or just sweep them on southward past the Cape of Good Hope several hundred miles farther south.

Cape of Good Hope. Hah! Cape of Disasters is more like it . . .

She and Kynan drank water sparingly, giving Koot a little when he roused, but there was still no food. *Maybe I could rig something to use for a fishing line and hook? When the storm breaks . . .*

They ran aground without warning in pitch blackness.

Margo was thrown violently clear of the raft. She screamed and landed in stinging salt water. Breakers slammed her into the beach. The force of her landing knocked her breath away and left her floundering in a savage backwash. She crawled forward like a crab scuttling away from the sea, blinded by rain and deafened by the crash of thunder and maddened surf. She finally collapsed above the high water line, drenched to the skin by pounding rain.

Koot . . . Kynan . . .

Malcolm . . .

The last thing to impinge on her awareness was the knowledge that she was an utter failure.

She woke slowly, in pain. Margo heard male voices that she didn't recognize, speaking loudly and angrily somewhere above her. She stirred and moaned. *Everything* hurt. Someone slapped her, shocking her more fully awake. Margo gasped and focused on dark-haired men with light, olive-toned skin. They were dressed outlandishly in dirty clothes that reminded her of paintings of Christopher Columbus. Many of them wore slashed velvet breeches and leather armor. One wore metal chest and back plates and carried a fancy wheel-lock handgun. Margo's heart began to pound. She'd been found by sixteenth-century Portuguese from that little settlement on Delagoa Bay.

What about Kynan? And Koot? Had they survived the break up of the raft? Or had Margo alone failed to drown in the stormy surf? One of the Portuguese, the man in the metal armor, spoke roughly to her. Margo had no idea what he'd said. The man stooped over her, spoke again, then backhanded her. She tried to get away and felt a tremendous blow connect. She didn't feel anything at all for a long time after that. When Margo regained her senses, someone had stripped her naked. The traders had clustered around her, leering. They'd started to unfasten their clothes.

Margo whimpered.

When the first one shoved her knees apart, Margo squeezed shut her eyes.

Malcolm . . .

It took the bastards a long time to finish.

Chapter 18

The withered-sea landscape garden of sand and stones in the corner of Kits office had lost its ability to soothe. He slumped in his chair and shoved aside the mountain of government forms to be filled out, then stared at the raked sand and dry boulders. *Eight weeks.* It had felt more like eight years. Kit hadn't believed it possible to miss someone so keenly after such a short time—much of it spent arguing, at that. His apartment felt empty. The Down Time had lost its appeal. The Commons would have been utterly dead-flat *boring* if not for the occasional excitement of a crow-sized pterodactyl raiding lunch from shocked hands or momentarily unguarded plates.

After a while, even the giggle of watching tourists dive under lunch tables had worn off. All that was left was the intolerable weight of government paperwork and the long hours wondering where she'd gone. He'd gone up time long enough to hire an investigative agency to locate her birthplace in Minnesota and discover her real name, as well as to search other time terminals to see if she might have gone scouting at one of them. So far, the agency had drawn an absolute blank. As far as anyone could tell, Margo had dropped off the face of the earth.

Which she might have, for all practical purposes, if she'd gone scouting from another terminal.

Whatever the solution to the mystery of Margo's whereabouts, TT-86 no longer felt quite so much like home.

Kit ran a hand through his hair and sighed. "Maybe I ought to retire up time." To do that, he'd have to close his accounts, find a buyer for the Neo Edo, locate a place to live in the real world, which had changed a lot—and not for the better, so far as he could tell—during the years he'd been down time.

Kit grunted. "I'm too tired to leave and too bored to stay."

So he picked up a stack of bills and started scanning them for errors, just to avoid government forms. He was halfway through an itemized bill from the library when an entry caught his attention. He hadn't done any research on fuel-consumption and lift-capacity for Floating Wedge ultra-light airships.

"What the . . ."

He checked the access code assigned to the bill. It was Margo's. He grunted. So she had been using the library, after all. Then he noticed the date. Kit swiveled in his chair, punching up gate departures for the past two months. There was the day Porta Romae had cycled, the day his granddaughter had walked back out of his life. The library entry on the bill was dated seven days *afterward.*

"Oh, hell, she couldn't even keep her goddamned password a secret. How many other charges did this thief run up against my account?" He found several additional entries, neatly itemized by subject matter and data source as well as computer time logged onto the mainframe. Each one post-dated Margo's precipitous departure through Primary.

Kit slid the bill angrily to one side of his desk. Unless he could locate the access-code pirate, he'd be stuck for one helluva research bill. He switched computer screens, typing out a simple monitoring program to set off an alarm the next time Margo's access code was entered into the system, then e-mailed messages to Brian Hendrickson and Mike Benson, alerting them to the fact that data piracy was occurring.

Then he called Bull Morgan.

"What's up, Kit?"

"We've got a data pirate loose on the station. Someone's used Margo's access code to bill research to my account."

"I'll make a note of it. You're sure it's an account pirate?"

"Margo left a week before the first incident. Went up Primary to God alone knows where. Or when."

Bull sympathized. "I'll do some checking, put Mike Benson on it."

"I've already e-mailed him about it and Brian Hendrickson, too. Thanks, Bull."

He hung up and glared at everything in sight. Then sighed, resigned himself to a long day, and settled resolutely to work again. When the phone rang less than a quarter of an hour later, he cradled the receiver between shoulder and ear.

"Yeah, Kit here."

"Kit, it's Bull."

He sat back in his chair, faintly surprised. "Damn, I knew you were efficient, but I didn't expect you to catch the rat this fast."

Bull chuckled. "We haven't. But I did turn up something odd. I thought you'd want to know."

"Yeah?"

"Margo passed through Primary, all right. Then she came back about a week later."

He sat straight up. "*What?*"

"She came back, but hasn't logged out again. Medical hasn't out-processed her records, the ATF has no trace of her leaving a second time through Customs . . ."

"But—" He closed his mouth again. "What about other gates?"

"Mike's working on it. Hang on a sec."

Kit waited in a swivet. Then Bull came back on. "No, she didn't log out through any of the other gates, either. Not the tourist ones, anyway, and nobody's filed paperwork to scout the unknown gates off Commons."

"Bull, she has to be somewhere. La-La Land's a closed environment."

A brief silence greeted him. "Kit, there *are* unstable gates."

He shut his eyes. "No. Not even Margo's that stupid. She was scared spitless of the Nexus Gate and after Orleans . . ."

"Well, she's still here somewhere, then, avoiding you."

"For seven *weeks?* La-La Land isn't that big. Besides, Margo couldn't stay out of trouble for seven minutes, never mind seven weeks. If she were here, somebody would've seen her. She's not on the station." He thought hard. "Do me a favor, would you? See if anyone else is missing? I'll start asking around on my own, see what I can scare up. Maybe a small gate opened up somewhere we don't know about. Or maybe somebody went through one of the unexplored gates without permission." *It'd be just like that little idiot to pull a stunt like that.*

"Sure thing, Kit. I'll run some checks and let you know."

"Thanks."

Kit hung up and said several biting things to the withered-sea landscape garden, then started placing phone calls.

Kit didn't have much luck. Nobody he talked to had heard a whisper about an unknown gate. A couple of down timers who worked as Time Tours baggage handlers recalled seeing Margo return through Primary, but they had no idea where she'd gone afterward. Kit's granddaughter had managed to vanish without a trace from the heart of one of the most gossip-riddled communities in the world.

Then, when he least expected it, Malcolm Moore showed up.

The younger man had avoided Kit's company for eight full weeks. If Kit arrived someplace and Malcolm was already there, he made excuses to leave within moments. He turned down casual invitations to the Down Time for dinner and had become in general a hard-working recluse. Kit felt sorry for him. Clearly, Malcolm had taken Margo's rebellion and defection deeply to heart, blaming himself entirely. Kit had tried to apologize, to tell him it wasn't his fault, but Malcolm wasn't returning Kit's e-mail or phone calls, either.

When the buzzer on his desk lit up and Jimmy told him Malcolm was headed up, Kit actually sagged in his chair.

"Thank God . . ."

He hated to lose friends.

A hesitant knock at the door signaled Malcolm's arrival.

"Come in, it's open."

The door slid back, Japanese style. Malcolm Moore glanced into the spacious office. He looked massively uncomfortable. "Uh . . . you busy, Kit?"

Something in Malcolm's eyes told Kit he hoped the answer would be "yes."

"No. Come on in."

Malcolm sighed, then slipped off his shoes and entered. His posture told Kit he'd rather have faced the hangman.

"I, uh . . ." He faltered to a halt, staring at the floor, the walls, anywhere but at Kit.

"Malcolm, it wasn't your fault. She's a headstrong little hellion. It wasn't your fault."

A deep flush darkened the guide's cheeks. "You don't have to be nice about it, Kit. You weren't there." He shoved hands into his pockets, then paced uneasily toward the withered-sea landscape garden, leaving his back to Kit. There were holes in the toes of his socks and both heels were threadbare.

"I, uh, heard she came back. Then vanished."

"Yes," Kit said quietly. "Do you have any ideas at all?"

Malcolm halted. For just an instant his shoulders drooped. "No." Then he straightened his back again. "But I heard something odd this morning. I thought you ought to know. You know, just in case . . ."

"Park 'em. Talk."

Malcolm hesitated, then took the chair. But he still wouldn't meet Kit's eyes. "I was down in the gym working out. Ripley Sneed came in."

"Ripley? Where the hell has he been keeping himself? I haven't seen him in months."

Malcolm grimaced. "Went down an unknown gate and damn near didn't come back. Had some pretty wild stories to tell. Anyway, I mentioned you'd been asking about unknown gates anybody had explored recently. He said he'd gone through one a couple of months back, but it was completely worthless."

Kit frowned "What gate? Where?"

Malcolm rubbed the fingers of one hand. "He said it opened in the back of Phil Jones' store,"

"Phil Jones? Isn't he the nut who goes down time and rescues totem poles?"

"Yeah, that's the one. His shop gives me the creeps. Phil gives me the creeps. Anyway, Ripley said a small gate opened up in his storeroom. He went through, logged it, came back, told Phil the gate was useless."

"Why was it worthless? Where and when did it go?"

Malcolm glanced at his hands, pretending to inspect his fingernails. "He wouldn't say."

Kit tightened his hands down around the edge of his desk. "Ripley Sneed always was a goddamned bastard. How much did he want?"

Malcolm sighed unhappily and finally met Kit's gaze. "A thousand."

"*A thousand dollars?* To tell me where a worthless gate leads?" Kit swore savagely. "Where is that miserly little prick now?"

"The Down Time. He's telling everyone about his adventures in the sultan's harem."

Kit rolled his eyes. "Good God. What an idiot. Okay, Malcolm. Thanks. Maybe this'll be worth it. God knows I haven't had any other clues worth following. I'm afraid she's wandered through one of the question gates without filing proper paperwork with Bull and if she's done that . . ."

Malcolm nodded. "You may be right." He hesitated. "Margo . . . Well, she wasn't in any mood to wait any longer. Something awful happened to that lad before she came here. I'm not sure who she's trying to prove herself to, but it's riding her harder than we ever did."

Kit didn't answer. He'd spent a lot of sleepless hours doing exactly what Malcolm had been doing: blaming himself.

"That doesn't matter, does it, if she's wandered down a gate without telling anyone. She shouldn't have shadowed herself already," he said raggedly, drawing a flinch from Malcolm, "but if she's actually gone down a question gate secretly, she might as well have."

The legal consequences of stepping through an unexplored gate without filing proper forms were minuscule, a mere fine if you actually made it back alive, but the practical consequences . . .

If no one knew which gate you'd gone through, no one could even mount a rescue attempt.

❁ ❁ ❁

Kit tracked down Ripley Sneed at the Down Time Bar and Grill. Malcolm, to his surprise, followed doggedly. Kit ordered a Kirin, offered to buy one for Malcolm, then shrugged and settled into an empty chair at Ripley's table.

"Mind if we join you?"

"Sure," the scout said with a smile. "What have you been up to, Kit?"

"Oh, this and that. I hear you've been exploring unknown gates."

"Sure have," Ripley grinned. His dark hair needed washing. He smelled bad, like month-old gym socks left to soak in mare's sweat. The regulars at the Down Time had taken tables upwind of him.

Doesn't this jerk ever bathe?

"So, I hear you checked out a gate in Phil Jones' place."

Ripley took a long pull of his own beer. "Yep."

"Odd place for a gate to open up. Of course, they've opened in stranger places." Kit smiled politely.

"You're telling me. How come you're interested in gates again? Thought you'd retired?"

"Oh, just curious. I like to keep up with the business."

Ripley laughed. "You're not fooling anybody, Kit. You want to know about that gate worse than I want to get rich. It'll cost you." His eyes glinted.

"Really?" Kit leaned back and folded his hands across his belly. "You'd charge a man for information on a worthless gate? Hell, I'll just wait until it cycles again and take a look, myself."

Ripley chuckled. "Nope. You're too cautious. You've been through too damned many gates, Kit Carson. You want to step through that bad, it'll really cost you to find out whether or not you'll go 'poof!' before you hit the other side."

Kit restrained the urge to throttle him.

Malcolm leaned forward on his elbows. "You're an unpleasant louse for someone who just spent a week in some poor schmuck's harem, getting his wives pregnant while he was off fighting the Christians."

Ripley laughed, unoffended. "I can afford to be unpleasant. You can't" He belched. "Okay, Kit, I'll tell you about the gate if I see a thousand up front."

"A hundred, tops."

They fell to serious haggling. Kit finally agreed to pay Ripley five hundred. The scout dug out his log and downloaded a file, then passed the disk over. "There it is. Enjoy."

'Thanks," Kit said drily, passing back a check for five hundred.

"Better not bounce," Ripley said, tacking on a grin at the last moment.

"Watch your mouth," Malcolm growled.

"It's all right, Malcolm. Ripley can't help being abrasive any more than a monkey can help having fleas. Come on, let's see if I got my money's worth."

They left Ripley chuckling as he folded up Kit's check and stuffed it into his wallet.

The file contained very little information. Ripley had gone through the gate and logged in location and time: thirty-two degrees east longitude by twenty-six degrees south latitude, late September of 1542.

"There's a small Portuguese trading settlement about two miles north of the gate on Delagoa Bay, Mozambique. A number of native tribal groups in the region are split between Swazi and Shona dialects.

"I see some Moslem influence from contact with Islamic traders, but not much. Relations between the indigenous peoples and the Portuguese is hostile at best There is absolutely nothing of value to be found in this settlement. Delagoa Bay is merely a stopover to take on fresh water and food supplies for Portuguese ships headed to India. From what I've been able to gather, the Jesuits didn't even leave a mission here when Francis Xavier stopped in 1541. My conclusion is that this is an utterly worthless string not warranting further exploration."

The file ended.

"Well," Kit said heavily. "What do you make of that?"

"Five hundred is a lot of money to demand for that information. Something's going on here."

Kit called up a map of Mozambique and replaced the video scenes on his office wall with the chart of southern Africa. "Mozambique . . ." he mused. "That's hell and gone from anything useful. And in 1542 there wouldn't have been *any* European exploration of the interior. Nothing out there but Shona and Bantu on the high veldt and San nomads in the Kalahari."

"And the Venda-Lemba Semitic groups of the eastern Transvaal," Malcolm added. "*They* were isolated until 1898 for God's sake."

"So why would Ripley demand so much money for this information?" Kit glanced up. "I wonder what Phil Jones has been up to lately?"

"I think we ought to find out."

"Agreed. You want to tackle him or shall I?"

Malcolm managed the first smile Kit had seen out of him in weeks. "You're too conspicuous, Kit. Everybody knows you're looking for traces of Margo. I'll follow that little weasel, see what he's up to, who he's hanging out with these days."

Kit nodded. "Sounds good. I'll give Bull a call. He's trying to find out who else might be missing."

Malcolm left while Kit dialed the phone.

The station manager apologized when he came on the line. "I've been meaning to call you this morning, except that *Pteranodon sternbergi* of Sue's got sick, then we had an emergency with the water filters and . . . Oh, hell, you're not interested in my problems. Only a couple of people I can't account for, but they're interesting."

"Oh?"

"One of 'em's that Welshman you tangled with."

"Kynan? The guy from Orleans?"

"The same. He and his longbow have gone missing."

A chill chased down Kit's back. "Go on."

"Frankly, I was afraid of foul play until I noticed who else is missing. Remember that big Afrikaner who came in a few years back when South Africa went to hell?"

"Yeah, I remember him." South Africa had suffered desperate damage from earthquakes, tidal waves, even volcanic eruptions in the aftermath of *The Accident.* The government had collapsed and thousands of people had fled the ensuing riots, massacres, starvation, and rampant plagues. "Koot van something," Kit said. "Big guy about my age, if I remember right, maybe a little younger."

"Koot van Beek. Took up time guiding. Drifts from station to station, wherever there's work."

"So he's back?"

"Back and missing."

Kit gazed at the map on his video screens and tried to figure out why a freelance drifter like Koot van Beek, a displaced Welsh bowman, and Margo would have hooked up in connection with a gate that led to sixteenth-century Mozambique.

"Thanks, Bull. That's very interesting news. I'll let you know if I come up with anything solid."

Kit pulled out the itemized library bill and studied Margo's recent research. Lift capacity and fuel consumption for a helium-filled ultra-light—but with variable equations for hydrogen as an alternative lifting source. Endemic diseases of southern Africa and recommended inoculations or medical treatments where no inoculations were available. Geographical charts of Mozambique, South Africa, Zimbabwe, Botswana. Even—he grimaced—recommended medications to suppress menstrual flow.

"What the hell is that little idiot up to?"

Unless Kit were wide of the mark, Margo planned a lengthy air expedition into the heart of southern Africa, where Zimbabwe, Botswana, and South Africa met along the Limpopo River.

"But *why?*" There wasn't anything out there except crocodiles, wildebeest, and fatal diseases.

The phone rang. "Yeah?"

"Kit," Malcolm said in his ear, "this is really interesting. Phil just left Goldie Morran's. I asked around and people said he's been spending a lot of time with her. A *lot* of time."

Kit narrowed his eyes. "Goldie? Why would Phil Jones be spending time with an expert on currency, precious metals, and . . ."

It hit him. Kit widened his eyes and stared at the map. "My God . . ."

"What?" Malcolm asked sharply.

"Hang on. Hell, get back here. I have to pull a couple of files off the mainframe."

He hung up and swung around, accessing the library's mainframe in a fever of impatience. He sped through several files, correlating data against a search of known mineral sites—and hit paydirt. Kit whistled softly and sat back in his chair.

His office door crashed back. Malcolm was panting. *"What?"*

Kit swung his chair around. "Diamonds. That stupid little featherbrain has gone after a diamond source deBeers doesn't control."

"Diamonds?" Malcolm stared at the chart. "But Kit . . . the nearest diamond fields must be, what, five or six hundred miles from Delagoa Bay?"

"Five hundred miles along the Limpopo River valley," Kit said grimly, punching up the chart from the file he'd accessed, "would put you right there."

A geologic map flashed up.

"What's up there? I thought the South African diamond sites were farther south in the Kimberley region or much farther west in the Kalahari?"

Kit strode around his desk and stabbed a finger toward a spot on the Limpopo just east of the confluence with the Shashe River coming down from the Botswana-Zimbabwe border. "That, my friend, is the site of the Seta Mine. Alluvial deposits in potholes along the Limpopo, gravel matrix rich in all lands of goodies. Garnets, jade, corundum, gold, diamonds . . . That idiot grandkid of mine has vanished into the heart of Africa on a harebrained scheme to bring back diamonds. Bet you the Neo Edo on it. And I can tell you exactly who put her up to it."

Malcolm groaned and said something profoundly ugly.

Kit ran a hand through his hair. "We were in Goldie's shop when I told Margo she was through as a trainee scout. And that avaricious, conniving, greedy old . . ." He couldn't even finish the tirade. "When I get through with Goldie Morran, she's going to wish she'd never laid eyes on Margo."

Kit stormed out of his office. Malcolm Moore trailed hastily behind.

Goldie Morran's smile disintegrated the moment Kit slammed open her door.

"Why, Kit. Hello. What can I do for you?"

"You can tell me why the hell you sent my granddaughter into the high veldt after your goddamned diamonds!"

Goldie Morran actually lost color. "Kit, I don't know what you're—"

"Cut the crap!" Kit stalked over to the counter and slammed both fists down. "You're not talking to a goddamned tourist!"

Goldie adjusted the high-necked collar of her old-fashioned dress. "No, I'm aware of that, Kit. Calm down. I'm not really hiding anything."

'The hell you're not."

"Kit Carson, either control your temper or get out of my shop!"

Kit swallowed the retort on his tongue, then forcibly relaxed his fists. "Okay, Goldie. I'll be a good boy and refrain from taking your shop apart. Start talking."

She drew over a high stool and settled on it as though taking a throne. "You're aware, then, of Phil Jones' gate?"

"Yes. And where and when it leads."

"Fortunately for me, Ripley Sneed is an idiot. He didn't even think about the diamonds just lying around the interior waiting for someone to pick them up. Phil and I knew exactly where the most accessible deposits were, but we couldn't get there ourselves. Neither of us is a scout."

"You mean neither of you is crazy enough to risk your own hide. So you conned Margo into doing it for you."

Goldie's eyes flashed angrily. "Margo is an adult, Kit Carson, perfectly capable of making her own decisions. And, I might add, you've treated her very shabbily. She was only too happy to accept my offer."

"Margo is a half-trained child—a *seventeen-year-old* child." Goldie lost a little more color. "She thinks she knows enough to succeed. All she knows is enough to get herself killed. When's she due back?"

Goldie fidgeted and glanced away.

"Goldie . . ."

The severe-faced woman who always reminded Kit of a duchess he'd once known cleared her throat delicately. "Well, as to that, now . . ."

"She's overdue," Malcolm said quietly. "Isn't she?"

Goldie glanced up. "Well, yes. She is."

Kit tightened his hands on the edge of Goldie's shop counter. "*How* overdue?"

"A couple of weeks."

"A couple *of weeks?*" Kit exploded. "My God! Why the hell didn't you *tell* me?"

"Because I knew you'd blow up just like this!" Goldie snapped. "They took plenty of protective gear with them. They'll be fine! They're just a little overdue."

Kit studied her, controlling an ice-cold rage that demanded physical action. She wasn't telling them everything. For someone waiting on a shipment of first-quality South African diamonds, Goldie was remarkably untroubled about Margo's fate.

"What's your scam, Goldie?"

She widened her eyes at him. "Scam? Why, Margo was just going to dig out some of the Seta deposits and come back, that's all."

Kit leaned over the counter. "You are full of it, Goldie Morran. If Margo was supposed to bring back a shipment of diamonds, you'd have been crawling all over this station looking for someone to go after her when she was two weeks overdue. What kind of scam are you running?"

Goldie pursed her lips like someone who's tasted poison. "You are a royal pain, Kit Carson. She isn't bringing them back. Koot van Beek and I jointly invested in a little piece of property up north of Francistown, in Botswana. No one has ever found the mother lode source of the Seta alluvial deposits. So Margo's going to dig up a couple of potholes' worth of matrix and fly the ore up to our property on the Shashe River. I have a rube up time who's biting at the bait. All I have to do is confirm that Margo's seeded the land and Koot and I will 'discover' samples that match the Seta deposits. This fool will buy the land at a huge profit and we'll make a fortune. We don't even have to smuggle the diamonds past ATF this way. It's all nice and legal."

It was a nice scam. A very nice one. Neat, slick, possibly even legal, leaving out the minor problem of minerals fraud. And given the current state of government in the southern African republics, any fool crazy enough to buy the land would probably end up eating his losses.

Kit said quietly, "You had better pray real hard that nothing has happened to my grandchild, Goldie. Show me this gate."

Kit and Malcolm both scanned the gate in Phil's shop during its next scheduled opening. Malcolm double-checked his readings in rising dismay. His heart sprang straight into his throat. "Uh, Kit, are you getting the same readings I am?"

Kit nodded grimly. "It's disintegrating. Rapidly. How often does it open and how long has it existed?"

Phil Jones, a nervous little weasel of a man, cleared his throat. Totem poles loomed on every side, grotesque shapes beyond the shimmering edges of the gate. "Opens every five days, stays open about ten minutes. First saw it about ten weeks ago."

"Have you kept an exact log of its openings?"

Phil exchanged glances with Goldie. "Uh . . . should I have done that?"

Malcolm was afraid Kit might strangle the shopkeeper.

"Yes, you blithering idiot! You should have!"

The gate shrank, expanded briefly, then vanished.

"Five days," Kit muttered, noting the exact times of its appearance and departure. "I have five days to get ready."

"You're not going through?" Phil gasped. "But I thought—wouldn't it be dangerous for you to—"

One look from Kit was all it took. He gulped and shut up.

Malcolm followed Kit out of Phil's odd little shop. "Have you checked your personal log yet?"

"I have."

"And?"

"It's risky. Damned risky. There's a twenty-percent chance I'll shadow myself on stepping through. And if I stay longer than a week, if I have to wait through *two* cycles, a ninety-percent chance I'll shadow myself before getting back through. *If* the gate doesn't collapse permanently before then."

"But you're going?"

Kit's eyes were haunted. "Hell yes, I'm going. Goldie admitted Margo should've been back to the gate two weeks ago. What would you do?"

"Go with you," Malcolm said quietly.

Kit swung around. He blinked; then tightened his jaw muscles. "Malcolm, I can't ask you to risk this. You said yourself you weren't cut out for scouting."

"You're not asking and neither am I. I'm going. It's my fault Margo pulled this stunt, say what you will. I'm going."

They locked gazes for a long moment. Then a suspicious film moistened Kit's eyes.

"All right. You're going. The Portuguese aren't real cheerful about strangers in their African outposts."

"No."

"Those traders are likely to loll any European they find sneaking around their settlement."

"Yeah." Malcolm wasn't thinking about himself. He was picturing Margo in their hands.

"Jesuits," Kit said finally. "You speak Portuguese?"

"Some. I studied it for Edo, back when I was with Time Ho! My Basque is better, though."

"Good. I speak Portuguese very well. You'll be a Basque Jesuit, I'll play your superior in the Society. Let's find Connie. This is going to be one helluva rush order."

Five days.

Malcolm just prayed the gate hadn't already disintegrated so badly that it never opened again.

Chapter 19

They emerged onto a rain-lashed beach. When Kit didn't vanish like a shimmer of heat over Kalahari sands, Malcolm started breathing again. The pallor in Kit's cheeks told its own story. *Now all we have to do is try to find Margo—and beat ninety-percent odds if we don't do it in a week.*

With the entire southern tip of Africa to search, Malcolm wasn't terribly sanguine about their chances.

He finished his ATLS readings and log update a hair sooner than Kit. The retired time scout was out of practice. They hid their equipment deep in camouflaged bags beneath vestments, censers and other priestly paraphernalia. Among their personal "effects" were hand-bound copies of not only the Bible in Latin but also of the Jesuit *Spiritual Exercises* written by Ignatius Loyola, the Basque founder of the Society of Jesus. Connie Logan had outdone herself on this one.

Malcolm closed his bag and turned his attention to their surroundings. In the short minutes they'd stood on the storm-lashed shore of Delagoa Bay, their long, heavy habits were already soaked. Wind whipped sodden wool around their ankles. They had decided to approach the Portuguese first, to find out if Margo had, in fact, made it back this far or if they would have to mount an expedition into the heart of the interior to search for her.

"This storm will work in our favor!" Kit shouted above the crash of thunder. "I've been worrying about how to explain our sudden appearance. Claiming we've been shipwrecked is more credible in the middle of a storm!"

Malcolm nodded. "The Wild Coast is notorious for shipwrecks, particularly when summer storms hit the Drakensbergs. And as Jesuits, we ought to be welcomed."

They both carried bladed weapons just in case they weren't.

Lightning flares cut through the gloom of early evening, revealing the miserable little fort and ramshackle houses of Lourengo Marques huddled on the bay. A stout *kraal* wall enclosed the whole community. Kit marked the spot where the time gate had closed by piling stones into a small cairn, then he and Malcolm slogged down the rain-swept beach toward the trading settlement and prayed for the best. They passed grain fields where straggling wheat lay flat under the onslaught of the storm.

Vegetable gardens sprawled in patchwork confusion beyond an unguarded *kraal* gate. Wet chickens hid under the houses. Pens for hogs stank and leaked filth into the mud streets. Thin, forlorn cows huddled against the rain and a few sheep and goats milled uncertainly in a high-walled pen. A horse neighed once, answered by others in the distance.

"Where is everyone?" Malcolm wondered aloud. There should be a watch set, even in this storm."

Kit cupped hands over his eyes to blink them clear of streaming rain. "Probably at the fort," he decided. "The walls higher, stouter in case of emergencies. We'll try there."

When they stumbled between the houses into "town square" they halted in unison. The residents of Lourengo Marques had set up a crude pillory along one side of the square. Hanging from the stocks was a familiar, grizzled figure. Malcolm and Kit glanced swiftly around but saw no sign that anyone was watching. The whole town was shut up tight against the storm. Malcolm got to him first. Koot van Beek was dead. Had been dead for several hours, maybe as long as a day. Kit was ashen in the wild flares of lighting.

Margo . . .

They searched the body for signs of violence, but found no trace of systematic torture. Malcolm swallowed once, then followed Kit through ankle-deep mud past an idle blacksmith's forge, what was clearly a cooper's workshop, and a small gristmill. In the distance, the fort's rough wooden gates were shut.

"Lean against me," Kit muttered from cover of the gristmill.

"You're older, more likely to succumb to exhaustion. You lean against me. I know enough Portuguese to get by until you 'come around'."

Kit didn't argue. He just draped one arm across Malcolm's shoulder and let his weight sag. Malcolm hastily slid an arm around Kit's back. *All right, we're shipwrecked Jesuits who've struggled up the coast in a terrible storm . . .*

He half carried Kit across the open, muddy ground toward the gates. "Help! Hello inside, help us!" Malcolm shouted in rough Portuguese, heavily accented with Basque pronunciation. "In the name of Christ, help us!"

A suspicious sentry appeared at the top of the wall. "Who are you? Where have you come from?"

"We are Jesuits! Father Francis Xavier sent us to you from Goa. Our ship went down in this storm, south of here! This *is* Lourengo Marques, is it not? Please God let it be . . ."

The sentry's eyes had gone wide. A hasty shout relayed Malcolm's message. A moment later the gates creaked open. Then Portuguese traders swarmed outside, lifting Kit's stumbling figure to carry him while others supported Malcolm. He staggered like a man in the final stages of exhaustion and allowed his escort to take most of his weight.

The residents of Lourengo Marques stank of onions, sweat, and dirt. Their voluminous, slashed breeches needed washing. Food and wine stained leather jerkins and slashed velvet doublets. Malcolm saw at least six professional soldiers in leather armor, half of them carrying matchlock arquebus carbines rendered useless by the storm. They'd drawn wicked swords which they now resheathed, but the other half of the military detachment, carrying steel crossbows, remained alert until the gates had been closed and barred once again.

Other men had come running, dressed as rough tradesmen and humble fanners. Many carried long pikes and daggers. One burly bear of a man carried what looked like an honest-to-God wheel-lock rifle. Another man carried an enormous, full-length matchlock arquebus. None of these men wore helmets; only a few possessed leather jerkins. *Six professional soldiers and a surprisingly well-armed auxiliary of tradesmen and farmers. And those fellows over there look like sailors.* Malcolm counted five men who had probably been left behind by the last ship, to recover from illness or to be buried.

Shortly, Malcolm and Kit found themselves in a grimy, smoke-filled room which was clearly the best accommodation in the fort. Real chairs stood around a scarred wooden table covered with the remains of the evening meal. A real bed stood in the corner. A man in plate armor—at least a chest and back plate—blinked when they came in, then lowered a "high-tech" wheel lock handgun and carefully pulled back its "dog," making it somewhat safer, although still loaded and ready for use.

"Sergeant Braz, who are these men, where have they come from?"

The sergeant said importantly, "They were sent by Father Francis Xavier to us, Governor, but their ship was wrecked in this storm. I don't know any more than that."

Kit coughed violently and moaned. The soldiers carrying him asked anxiously, "May we put the Father in your bed, Governor?"

"Of course, of course. Hurry, the good Father is exhausted and ill." The governor tucked his pistol into his belt and helped lower Kit into his own bed.

Kit gasped and clutched at his benefactor's hand. "Bless you, my son," he whispered faintly. "God has preserved us in an un-Christian land." Then his eyelids fluttered closed.

Malcolm hastened to his side. He knelt and clutched Kit's hand, giving every evidence of terror. "Father Almada . . ." Malcolm turned to the anxious Portuguese. "Have you any hot broth? He is exhausted from fighting the sea and then we had to walk miles and miles up your treacherous coast. I feared God would call him away before we saw your walls."

"You sound like a Basque," one of the men dressed as an artisan said excitedly. Another had gone in search of something to feed their unexpected visitors.

"Yes, I am Father Edrigu Xabat. I had the grace to be ordained in Rome by the General of our Order, Father Loyola. Father Almada is . . ."

Kit "roused" with a faint moan. "Where . . . where are we, Edrigu?"

"God has delivered us safely to these Christian men, Inigo, praised be His name." One of the farmers handed Malcolm a cup. "Oh, bless you, my son . . ."

Malcolm held it to Kit's lips and helped him drink hot soup, then consented to eat some himself. It was terrible, no salt, no pepper, watery and thin—but it was hot. Kit struggled to sit up, then begged to know who their rescuers were.

"I am Vilibaldo de Oliveira Salazar, the military governor of Lourengo Marques," the governor introduced himself proudly, sweeping a courtly bow. He was a small man with sharp eyes and a thin face. He wore expensive velvet garments under his armor despite the grime. "This is Joao Braz, the Sergeant of my command, and these are my soldiers, Francisco, Amaro, Lorenco, Mauricio, Ricardo."

The soldiers saluted sharply.

The big man with the wheel-lock rifle shuffled forward. "Please, Father, I am Rolando Goulart, a humble blacksmith. I speak for the artisans of Lourengo Marques when I bid you welcome. This is Bastien, my assistant."

Bastien was the man who'd been so excited by Malcolm's Basque name and accent.

"And this is Vincente, our butcher and tanner, Huberto the miller, Nicolau the cooper, Xanti our baker, and Mikel his assistant . . ." *More Basques,* Malcolm realized. The farmers and husbands who tended the community's herds also proved to be Basques: Narikis, Mikolas, Peli, Kepa, Posper, and Satordi.

The other five men were stranded sailors, as Malcolm had suspected. Three were Portuguese, introducing themselves shyly as Rodrigo, Adao, and Pedro. Erroman and Zadornin were both Basques. There were no women in evidence.

"Please," Vilibaldo de Oliveira Salazar begged, "if you are strong enough, Father Almada, tell us of yourselves and your misfortunes."

Kit rose to the occasion with wonderfully fluent Portuguese, embroidering on Malcolm's original tale. He described the conditions in Goa and Father Francis Xavier's concern that the men here at this desolate outpost had no priests to confess or shrive them. He elaborated on their harrowing journey back to Africa from India, described the terrifying shipwreck which had drowned all the ship's company sparing only the two of them, spoke with tears in his eyes and a choked voice of reading last rites to the crashing waves, then of their struggle up the coast, praying that they stumbled in the direction of the outpost, not deeper into trackless wilderness . . .

Even Malcolm was impressed.

Several of the men cleared their throats and stamped their feet to hide their own emotions. Vilibaldo insisted they change out of their sodden cassocks into something warm and dry, producing good-quality, simple tunics and cloaks in which they wrapped themselves. The farmers hung their wet things to dry in one corner of the room. Vilibaldo then broke out wine and shared it around, making certain his new priests were warm and comfortable. The governor spoke of the hardships they had endured in the outpost, the troubles they had with the natives who stole Portuguese cattle or ran their own cattle through the grain fields, destroying the crops utterly, and the illnesses which had befallen them, the men they'd lost.

Finally, insisting that the soup and good company had revived him, Kit suggested that he and Malcolm hear confessions without delay. "Clearly, my son, you have been without the comforts of a priest for too long. It would be best to relieve your souls of the burden of sin you carry now, before another moment passes. I am only glad that God has sent us to minister to your needs."

The traders mumbled and looked embarrassed, then hastily rigged blankets to form two crude confessionals. Kit insisted they put on their wet cassocks again, then Malcolm took one side, Kit the other, and they began hearing confessions. They were not even through the first one when Kit emitted a roar of outrage and snatched back the curtain.

"Witches!" he cried, wild-eyed. "What say you, *witches!*"

The artisans crossed themselves. The soldiers paled.

Vilibaldo stared at the floor for a moment, then cleared his throat. "It is true, we have a prisoner who is a witch, Father. The other witch has died of some evil disease he brought upon himself."

Sergeant Joao Braz ventured, "We have closely questioned the other and—"

"You questioned this person? Are you a man of God? Do you presume to know witchcraft?"

The sergeant paled and stumbled to a halt.

"But—but Father—" one of the sailors, Rodrigo, protested. "*They were* witches! Seven weeks ago it was, I saw with my own eyes a terrifying sight, a great glowing raft of white sticks that sailed through the heavens far away to the north. Then last night terrible storms raged all night and well into the morning. You see how the witch-brewed storm has nearly destroyed even you, who are men of God? What do you think we should find on the beach, Father, but that same great white raft, broken it is true, into pieces, but there were devilish items on the sand and the man and woman wore Satan's garments and—"

Kit groped for the nearest chair and sank into it. "And the other witch? What have you learned?"

The men of Lourengo Marques glanced at one another again, clearly uneasy.

"Father, the dead witch," Governor de Oliveira Salazar said quietly, "he babbled in a possessed madness. He spoke *Dutch!*"

Malcolm and Kit exchanged glances.

"I speak a little Dutch, Father," Sergeant Braz put in. "The witch was raving about another of their company, who is not with them. We have search parties out looking for him and have told the black heathens hereabouts there is a reward for capturing this other witch and bringing him to us."

The Welshman, Malcolm realized. *Poor terrified bastard . . .*

"You must take me to the witch you have captured," Kit said severely. "I must examine the woman and see if Satan's hand is truly upon her. Has she spoken at all?"

One of the Basque farmers spat onto the floor. "No, only to scream."

Kit lost all color; Malcolm hastened to his side. "Father Almada, you are still unwell. You should be in bed."

"How can I sleep when God's work is waiting? Come, show me this witch."

What are you going to do, Kit? We can't escape through the gate for another five days. She'll tip our hand for sure.

But the desire to know what condition these men had left her in worried at him like a rat gnawing at his foot. How much worse must it be for Kit? The governor and soldiers led them through the downpour to a tiny stockade on the far side of the fort. The rest of the community trailed behind. Sergeant Braz produced an iron key. It grated rustily in the lock. The room beyond was so dim, Malcolm couldn't see a thing. Kit gestured impatiently for a lantern. The smith, Rolando Goulart, gave Kit his.

"Leave us," Kit said harshly. "Father Xabat will examine the witch with me."

"But Father Almada, she might do you an injury—"

"God is the sword of the Jesuit, my son. Do not fear for our safety. Go. We will lock her in again when we have examined her."

The soldiers shuffled uneasily, then retreated to the far end of the overhang, refusing to go farther. Kit lifted the lantern, drew a hasty breath, and stepped into the foul little room beyond.

Margo shivered in a corner of her prison, hating with a greater passion than she had ever felt in her young life. She hurt so desperately, tears formed. They tracked down her cheeks in the darkness. These brutal *animals*—no, they were *worse* than animals, that was an *insult* to animals—had raped her, beaten her, demanded things in as many languages as they spoke and hit her every time she couldn't answer. They'd finally stumbled on broken English in their efforts to find out who she was.

They had ordered her to reveal who the other man was, the one who had escaped, ordered her to explain why she and the other witches had come, demanded to know what terrible evil they planned to do Portugal. . . .

The insanity had gone on and on until Margo had been capable of nothing but screaming at them. Whereupon their pig of a leader had raped her again, then tossed her naked into this earth-packed cell and locked her in without food, water, or a blanket. They had come back only to inform her that Koot van Beek had died and that she would die next.

Margo had never known such black despair in all her life. She cried until there were simply no more tears left in her. She'd stupidly set out to prove a childish point—but the only thing she had succeeded in doing was getting Koot van Beek killed and the Welshman even more lost in time than ever. Not to mention getting herself raped and imprisoned.

Tremors shook through her at the memory. She would have killed for soap and water or a gun to shoot the bastards. *If they could even be killed.* Their sweat still stank on her skin. Every time she closed her eyes, she saw their faces, leering down at her while they held her down and hurt her. . . .

Oh, Malcolm, why did I run from you? That memory was torture, too, the sweetness and gentleness contrasted with abuse beyond anything she'd been capable of imagining. *I'm sorry, Malcolm. I'm sorry, I failed you, failed Kit, failed the men who counted on me to get them out alive. I even failed Mom—*

At least Margo's mother had died doing something to keep her child alive. All Margo had done was behave like a reckless, ungrateful brat. Locked naked in a Portuguese prison awaiting execution was a helluva time to learn one's lesson.

"I'm sorry," she whispered over and over, "I'm so sorry. . . ." She wiped her nose and sniffed, surprised she was able to conjure more tears. Life had handed her a precious friend and she'd fled, too much a baby to face what a wonderful relationship he'd offered. Now she was going to die and she would never have a chance to tell him what a thoroughgoing, cowardly *fool* she had been.

And *Kit.* He'd never know what had become of her. What she'd done to him was inexcusable. If she ever, ever had the chance . . .

But life wasn't like that. The cavalry came over the hill only in fairy-tale Westerns. And the prince on the shining charger had vanished right along with blunderbusses and sailing ships and gentlemen who tipped their top hats and smiled when a lady walked past. She'd never get to tell him how sorry she was or to beg forgiveness and the chance to go to college for several years before trying it again.

What must he have thought when he'd found her hateful little note?

"I'm sorry," she whispered again.

She didn't know what else to do.

Then, with a terrifying, rusty grate of iron turning in the lock, the door swung open. Dim light silhouetted the whole pack of slavering murderers who'd captured her. Margo bit back a terrified cry and came to a low crouch.

They would doubtless kill her. She was too weak and too badly hurt to stop them. But she could at least put up a fight. Maybe, if she were really lucky, she'd manage to send one of them to hell a few minutes ahead of her.

Kit stepped through first, lantern held aloft. Malcolm followed and hastily closed the door, then turned and found a shocking tableau. Kit had frozen in place, lantern still uplifted. Margo huddled in the corner, squinting against the lantern light. She'd come to a defensive crouch . . .

She was naked, covered with bruises. Dried blood showed dark on her thighs . . .

"Oh, my God," Kit whispered.

Malcolm whipped off his cassock to wrap around her. Her eyes widened. Then she burst into tears and hurled herself forward. Malcolm expected her to go for Kit. She flew into his arms instead, staggering him off balance. She hugged him so tightly he had to fight for breath.

"Malcolm," she was whispering raggedly. "Oh, God, Malcolm . . ."

He wrapped the cassock gently around her shoulders. She dragged his head down and kissed him so desperately all he could do was close his eyes and hold her. At length sanity returned.

"Your grandfather's here, too," he said quietly.

She turned and saw Kit. "Oh, God . . ."

Kit was staring at them, pale and silent in the lantern light. Malcolm swallowed hard and met Kit's gaze. Theeir position was painfully clear. Margo clung to him, not to Kit, had kissed him as only men and women who have become lovers kiss.

Margo forestalled the explosion by throwing herself into Kit's arms. "I'm sorry, I'm so sorry . . ."

"Shh . . ." He held her as though she might break, but his look over her shoulder boded ill things to come in Malcolm's immediate future.

Malcolm met that cold gaze steadily. He was ashamed that he hadn't told Kit sooner and he was ashamed that he'd been drunk when he'd gone to bed with Margo. But he wasn't ashamed of the way he felt about her, and it wasn't his fault he hadn't known she was only seventeen at the time. At least, that's what he'd been telling himself for weeks. So he held Kit's gaze and said quietly, "We aren't out of danger yet."

He halfway expected Margo to wail, "What do you mean?" but she didn't. She let go of Kit and carefully pulled Malcolm's cassock more tightly around herself. Then she straightened against obvious pain and said quietly, "What do we have to do?"

Her voice shook a little, but childish petulance and every trace of impatience were gone. Terrified and battered and clearly only beginning to dare hope she might live through this, Margo met his gaze and faced the possibility she could yet die. Moreover, she did it with a quiet dignity he'd first glimpsed in London, standing on a street of kosher shops and rebuilt dreams.

Malcolm swallowed hard. When Margo looked at him now, an adult met his gaze. A *real* adult, regardless of the number that represented her birth date. In that moment, he fell in love with her all over again.

"Malcolm?"

He cleared his throat. "I'd say that's up to Kit. This is his rescue, I just sort of invited myself along."

She swung her gaze around. Kit continued staring at Malcolm for another long moment, then bit out, "Yes. And now I see why." Then he met Margo's gaze. "The gate doesn't reopen for five days. *If* it reopens. The string's disintegrating fairly rapidly. I'd be very surprised if it opens more than once or twice before failing completely.

"Kynan Rhys Gower is still at large. The indigenous people in this region are being encouraged to capture and turn him in. Portuguese search parties are out hunting him. The traders are convinced you're a witch. One of them saw that damned balloon of yours seven weeks ago and now they have your 'devilish' equipment as further damning proof.

"They'll expect us," he nodded to Malcolm, "to examine you for witchcraft. Given the circumstances, there's only one verdict possible. They'll expect us to proceed quickly with the execution. We're outnumbered twenty-five to two and they're heavily armed. More so than I'd feared."

"And there's a ninety-percent chance," Malcolm added heavily, "that if we miss the next cycle of the gate, Kit will shadow himself before it reopens the next time. It's possible he'll shadow himself as it is."

Margo just covered her face with her hands. "You shouldn't have come," she whispered brokenly. "You shouldn't have risked it. I'm sorry. I'm not worth it, not even close to worth it— "

Kit lifted a hand, hesitated, then touched her hair. She glanced up, eyes brimming in the lamplight. He managed a pained smile. "Did you actually transfer those damned diamonds to Goldie's worthless piece of property?"

The ghost of a smile flickered into being. "I sure did." Then her smile crumpled. "But Koot's dead and everything's gone to ruin. It's my fault! I screwed up the amount of fuel we needed. We ran out bucking the headwinds. We had to raft out and Koot contracted *malaria* of all things trying to get downriver, and we ran out of food, then that storm broke up our raft . . ." She drew a deep breath. "I'm not making excuses. I'm to blame for all of this. You were right. I'm not cut out to be a scout."

Kit traced an ugly bruise on her cheek. "Don't tell me you're giving up so soon?"

Her chin quivered. "I—I wanted to ask for a second chance, but I—I screwed up so bad, I—"

"Promise me you'll go back up time and study. Provided we get out of this mess alive," he added with a wry smile. "You get those college degrees, okay? We'll talk about it then."

She started crying again, silently, desperately. Malcolm wanted to hold her, but left that to Kit, who pulled her close and rocked her in his arms. Malcolm's throat thickened. He'd never seen such an expression on Kit's face. Eventually she sniffed and pulled back a step. "Okay. We'll talk about that when we get there," she said, sounding exactly like her grandfather. "But first, we have to get out of here. Any suggestions?"

"None whatsoever," Kit said cheerfully. "I generally make things up as I go along. Although for the sake of verisimilitude, I would suggest you scream, very loudly and most convincingly, right about now."

Margo didn't even hesitate. She screamed, a piercing sound of agony that raised fine hairs on the back of Malcolm's neck. Then she whimpered loudly enough to be heard through the closed door. They waited for a moment, then Kit signaled to her again. She let out another gawdawful cry and started sobbing.

Kit said quietly, "I'm sorry, but Malcolm has to keep this." He took Malcolm's cassock and handed it back. Then he stepped to the door and opened it.

"Governor Salazar, whether this girl is witch or not, I have still not decided in my heart," Kit said. "But the girl has been badly brutalized." Reproach darkened his voice. "God does not approve of such violence against the weaker sex. Worse, you have left her naked and starving. We may chastise the body for the sake of the soul, but we are still Christian men. Bring the poor child a blanket, clothing, something hot to eat. Let her pray and sleep. Tomorrow we will examine her further."

He lifted his hand in a Latin benediction, then motioned to Malcolm. Margo bit her lips as he turned to leave. He said with his eyes, *Hold on, kid. Just hold on.* Then the traders brought a coarse shirt, a blanket, and a mug of soup. Kit saw to it that she was clothed and wrapped in the blanket, watched her finish the soup, then consented to lock her in again for the night.

Then—and only then—did he and Malcolm finish the "confessions" they had begun. Neither of them was in any mood for it, but the charade had to be maintained at all costs. The confessions proved astonishingly petty, yet gave great insight into the factions which split the isolated men of Lourengo Marques.

'The tradesmen." Sergeant Joao Braz complained bitterly, "act like they are in Lisbon, not this forsaken wilderness! The miller demands his twentieth part for grinding flour. What will he spend it on? And the husbands are lazy! All they do is stand around and watch their chickens scratch in the dirt while we guard their miserable lives. . . ."

The Basque baker, Xanti, ranted against the soldiers, who treated everyone in the community like peasants, putting on arrogant airs and shirking their duty. "Do they stand night watch? Ha! They *sleep* through night watch, unless a rat runs over their feet. Then they scream like women and swear that Satan himself is loose in the town. Why, that idiot Mauricio even shot at a shadow at three o'clock in the morning! Woke up the whole town. . . ."

The governor complained bitterly that the men were slovenly, undisciplined, and lazy. Nicolau the cooper's confession was one endless tirade against everyone and everything in Lourengo Marques. "The town would not even *exist* but for me! My barrels hold the water this fort was built to supply for the ships bound for India! Without me, Lourengo Marques would still be a stretch of mud held by devil-worshipping heathens!"

The blacksmith, too, had his complaints. "Three times in the past month, that idiot of a cooper has broken the handles of his drawing knives. What does he do with them, to break the handles? And the governor demands more guns, then complains at the price when I tell him what it will cost and how long it will take my assistant and myself to make even the simplest . . ."

The farmers hated the sailors with a Basque passion. "We work hard," Mikolas cried, "feeding those lazy louts. What do they do all day? They sit by the water, eat ten times what any other man would consume in a day, and sing bawdy songs while they make *rope!* Why do ships need more rope? Every time a ship comes, there are miles of rope coiled on deck, and God preserve you if you so much as step on one little pile . . ."

You know, Malcolm thought quietly while the Basque ranted, *it wouldn't take much to set these men at one another's throats.* Malcolm filed the thought away and finished hearing their bitter complaints, then doled out suitable penance for their sins, expressing shock and dismay when he learned that half the men in town didn't possess so much as a simple rosary. Malcolm might have felt guilty about deceiving these men, but for one fact: cold rage filled him every time he remembered Margo crouched naked in that filthy corner, ready to fight off her attackers.

As for Kit . . .

Malcolm glanced at the blanket separating his "confessional" from Kit's. He would deal with Kit when they came to that quarrel. No sense setting himself up for more worry than he already had. They would either get out alive or they wouldn't. Only then could he and Kit settle the matter between them.

Kit's stony silence the rest of the evening didn't bode well at all.

Kit had to plausibly stretch their "examination" of the so-called witch over five full days. He lay awake far into the night, trying to put out of his mind what these men had done to Margo. If he let himself dwell on it, he'd never be able to think straight. He knew he ought to consult Malcolm, but was too deeply angry to speak to him. *It's my fault she's pulled this stunt,* Malcolm had said.

What did you do to her in Rome, my friend? You *seduced her, hurt her, drove her away . . .*

I trusted you, Malcolm.

That hurt almost as much as what Margo had suffered.

Malcolm's breathing told him the younger man hadn't fallen asleep, either. *Good.* He hoped Malcolm Moore spent a night in hell. Kit turned over with a creak of bed ropes and presented his back to the guide.

"Get some sleep," he said roughly. "You'll need it."

Malcolm didn't answer.

At two o'clock in the morning, Kit rose and lit a lamp, then kicked

Malcolm into wakefulness. The guide stirred under dirty blankets and groaned, then struggled to his feet. His eyes showed the strain of sleeplessness. Malcolm faced him squarely, however, neither flinching nor apologizing. Kit grunted. "Time to wake these sinners up for night office. I want them half asleep and off balance for the next five days."

Malcolm only nodded. He vanished outside to search for the fort's alarm bell. Kit heard Malcolm speak with the night watch, then the bell sang out a dirge which brought men stumbling out of the houses to the fort. They clutched weapons a little wildly as they searched for danger.

"What is it?" one of them cried, darting frightened glances into the darkness. "What danger threatens, Father?"

"The danger of damnation and hell everlasting," Kit said sternly. "The Evil One has been at work among you, by your own admission. God has sent us to save your souls. All of you, put away your guns and crossbows. Kneel for Matins."

The men of Lourengo Marques exchanged dismayed glances in the dim light from Kit's lamp. Then, with a low muttering and a shuffling of feet, they knelt in the darkness. Kit began Matins in high Latin, speaking out the service in a slow, rolling way that spun out the observance as long as he could stretch it. Then, just for good measure, Malcolm repeated the whole thing. The traders yawned and dozed until Kit switched them awake with a small stick and an admonishing glare.

They finally allowed the bewildered Portuguese to get off their knees and stretch. But when the traders headed for the gate to return to their warm beds, Kit called them back. "My sons, think you that you return to bed now? Lauds must now be read before you may sleep safely in the knowledge that you are saving your souls."

When the military governor complained bitterly that his men needed to sleep, Kit held up a hand. "Until the matter of these witches is settled and I know that the souls of my new flock are safe from harm, I must ask that you abide by my decree. Kneel, then."

In the flickering lamplight, dismay showed plainly in swarthy faces. "My sons," Kit said gently, "too long have you been living ungodly lives. Have you considered that your own wickedness has brought the witches and the devil himself among you?"

Several of the men crossed themselves fearfully. No one else complained as they knelt to hear Lauds. By the time this second service had ended, dawn had begun to creep across the sky. Kit let them go, enjoining them to sleep with prayers upon their lips, then stumbled back to his own wretched bed. Malcolm glanced once at Margo's prison, then followed. They slept for exactly three hours, then roused the traders at six o'clock and conducted the Prime service. Only then did they allow the traders to eat breakfast. Kit ordered that the poor girl be fed, as well, then faced his uneasy new "flock."

"I would know what manner of devilish things these witches brought among you. Father Xabat and I will examine the evidence for what we may find of the Evil One's presence."

He and Malcolm made a great show of examining the wreckage of the raft with its PVC gridwork, the transparent Filmar and rip stop nylon, the medical kit with its shiny foil packets and brightly colored pills, and the water-purifying equipment which had washed ashore in the wreckage.

"And was this all?" Kit asked worriedly.

"No, Father." Sergeant Braz answered. "There were strange, devil-made guns which we cannot make sense of and even more frightening things."

They brought out an M-l carbine, a beautiful .458 Winchester that must have belonged to Koot van Beek, and a stained leather bag containing Margo's ATLS and personal log. Kit and Malcolm exclaimed to one another in Latin, made worried sounds, conferred at length, took apart the "devil" guns to see what might be inside, and admitted bafflement over the strange equipment.

Kit finally announced Tierce service, which ate up a good bit of time, then returned to examining the "evidence" until time for Sext. After that, he questioned each of the traders closely about everything he had seen and done and felt and thought during the past six weeks. That took them to None service, which he and Malcolm dragged out nicely.

They had just finished None when a disturbance outside the fort brought a shout from one of the traders.

"The search parties are returning! Open the gate!"

Kit and Malcolm exchanged glances, then hurried after the soldiers who ran to open the fort's high wooden gates.

Kynan Rhys Gower was a strong swimmer. But when the raft broke up, throwing him into the water, something heavy caught him a grazing blow across the temple, stunning him. He floundered in the breakers, swept away from the wreckage by a powerful southerly current. Kynan managed to keep his face above water and let the sea carry him, too dazed to struggle and wise enough to marshal his strength before trying for shore.

Lightning flares showed him the curve of Delagoa Bay and the wretched little settlement he'd first seen seven weeks previously. The current swept him past it, inexorably southward. By the time he'd recovered enough to move his arms and legs against the current, Kynan estimated he'd been swept several miles south of the settlement on the wide bay—which meant Margo and Koot were trapped north of it, on the wrong side of the bay to reach the gate.

Kynan struck out for shore, wincing slightly at pulled muscles in his shoulder, and finally groped his way onto a rocky beach. He pulled himself on hands and knees above the line of crashing breakers, then collapsed to catch his breath. Rain pelted his back. He hadn't eaten a proper meal in days, felt dizzy and weak from hunger and his struggle with the sea.

Am I going to die here? And where am I, really? he wondered bleakly. *Africa,* Margo had said, but Kynan had only the haziest idea where Africa was—somewhere far south of Wales—and he hadn't known how to interpret the glowing chart she'd shown him on her "computer." He knew the men in the bay settlement were Portuguese. Kynan shivered. No love was lost between Welshmen and Portuguese.

The other men who lived here . . . The pictures Margo had shown him were difficult to credit. *Black* men in strange garments, carrying long, wicked spears he wouldn't live wanted to face one on one, not even on his best day, which this clearly wasn't. Slowly, Kynan sat up, squinting into the rain and dark wind. Lightning flares revealed the sea, lashing furiously at the coast.

As alone as he'd felt in the time station, the isolation he felt now paled that into insignificance. He was lost a century after his own time and five centuries before TT-86 would exist, in a land where he looked nothing like the native people and where the only men born in Europe were his enemies. He had no food, no water, no weapons, and no way of reliably obtaining more. Without so much as a knife, he couldn't even make a bow to hunt game. Of course, he could probably find the gate again, if he stumbled around long enough looking for it.

Kynan grimaced. *Never thought I would long to crawl back into hell . . .*

Of course, over the past few weeks, he'd begun to doubt that TT-86 *was* hell. He'd begun to change his mind about the girl, Margo, too. She was a young fool sometimes, but she had courage to match a warrior's. He didn't understand why she had left her grandfather's protection to hunt diamonds, any more than he understood the reasons *any* " 'eighty-sixer" did anything, but he thought her grandsire would have been proud to see her on their journey down the river to the sea.

The last he'd seen of her, she'd been struggling in the sea, same as him. Kynan spat sand out of his mouth and stumbled to his feet He'd accepted her leadership of his own free will. Kynan Rhys Gower did not abandon his leaders when they were in trouble. Margo was somewhere to the north. It was up to Kynan to find her again and help her bring Koot van Beek back with them through the gate.

He started walking and kept doggedly on, pausing to rest only when his legs threatened to buckle. Each time he rested, weariness urged him to just lie where he'd fallen and sleep, but he forced himself back up. He kept going through the night and the long, steaming day which followed, moving steadily northward along the wild strand. Kynan caught the scent of the Portuguese settlement before he came within sight of the ramshackle little town.

He skirted inland past the broad bay where the Portuguese fort was, fighting exhaustion and thirst and trying to edge his way northward without raising an alarm. Kynan closed his hands, longing for some sort of weapon to defend himself, but he had none. He had only a sense of duty to drive him forward, step by aching step. Which did him no good at all when he staggered, unwitting, into an ambush.

One moment he was alone beneath a steaming forest canopy; the next, he was on the ground with Portuguese shouts in his ears and hard hands on his arms and legs. Kynan heaved and broke loose. He rolled and came to a crouch with his back against a tree trunk and swallowed hard. He faced half a dozen snarling Portuguese, all of them armed with guns or crossbows.

Honor demanded he fight. Duty demanded he try to escape and rescue his lost comrade and commander. A strong sense of practicality told him he could do neither, given his exhaustion and the unwavering weapons trained on him. One of the men grinned slowly and said something Kynan didn't understand. Then, in bad English: "Witch . . ."

Kynan's blood ran cold.

They'd found Margo or Koot van Beek or the raft—they would torture and burn him alive—

He groped behind the tree trunk, closed his hand around a chunk of stout deadwood. He'd rather be shot with gun and crossbow than burn. Then another, worse thought came to him. They would burn Margo, too, and the sick Afrikaner who had taught Kynan to shoot the semi-magical rifle. If Kynan let these men kill him now, the others would have no chance of escape at all. If he let them take him alive . . .

They had to get free only long enough to gain the gate.

Kynan caught a ragged breath.

Then quietly surrendered.

Kit and Malcolm gained the gates in time to see the search party return with a bloodied, bruised prisoner. Vines secured his wrists behind his back. The Welsh soldier was ash-pale but he stood erect, facing his doom with all the bravery in him.

One of the soldiers still inside the fort called out, "Looks like he put up a fight!"

Kynan's captors grinned "Naw. Looked like he might for a minute, but he surrendered quiet as a lamb."

Kit narrowed his eyes. They'd beaten him afterward, then, badly, from the look of it. Why had he surrendered? That didn't fit the image of the Kynan Rhys Gower who'd attacked both Kit and Margo with single-minded, near-unstoppable fury. Kynan kept his gaze stonily on the ground, clearly aware that he faced his doom.

The Portuguese were gloating.

"Put him in the stocks," the governor crowed.

"No," Kit countered, allowing weariness to color his voice. "Put him in the cell with the woman. Father Xabat and I must examine him for Satan's mark."

Kynan flinched visibly at the word "Satan." He didn't quite struggle when the Portuguese shoved him toward the stockade, but he cursed them under his breath in Welsh. One of the soldiers struck him across the mouth, splitting a barely scabbed-over lip. Kynan stumbled and glared at his captors, but made no further sound. Kit and Malcolm exchanged glances. "Brave man," Malcolm's look said. Kit just nodded, then followed. Malcolm fell into step behind him. Their heavy cassocks dragged in the mud. Sergeant Braz unlocked the cell and shoved Kynan inside, then stepped aside for Kit and Malcolm. Once again, Malcolm shut the door. Margo sat in the corner, alert and silent. She took one look at Kynan and swallowed hard, but her eyes had begun to shine with hope. Kynan swayed, clearly at the end of his strength, but he said in broken English to Margo, "I . . . I look you. Portuguese," he snarled, spitting blood onto the dirt floor, "find me. I—I come, no fight. We run gate. I help, yes?"

Margo's eyes widened. She looked past Kynan to Kit, who had difficulty finding his voice. Kynan had surrendered, knowing what the Portuguese would do to them. . . . What had happened during the past seven weeks, to change Kynan's opinion of her so thoroughly?

Kit cleared his throat. "Kynan Rhys Gower."

The Welshman jerked around. His eyes widened. His mouth worked several times before any sound came out. "*You—*"

Then faint hope began to burn in his eyes. "Have you come to help us?" he asked quietly in his native tongue.

Kit didn't answer the obvious. Instead he asked, "Did you really surrender to the Portuguese to help my grandchild escape?"

Kynan flushed and dropped his gaze. "I accepted her leadership."

Ahh . . .

"Yes, but it was still uncommonly brave, duty or not. I will not forget this. Malcolm, free his hands. Do you have any idea where and when you are?"

The Welshman paused while Malcolm untied him. "I know we are in Africa and that Africa is south of Wales," he said, rubbing his wrists. "I know those whoresons are Portuguese, a pox on them all. I think it is a hundred years after . . . after I left my home."

"Yes, the year is 1542. The Portuguese think you and Margo are witches."

Kynan lost color again. "I know. They said so when they began to kick and beat me." He winced and shrugged. "I feared for a time they would kill me without benefit of a trial."

His smile was bitter and short-lived.

Kit said quietly, "We are still in very serious danger. There is a chance I will die before the gate opens again. It's complicated and you haven't learned enough about the gates yet, but the simple truth is, a man can't exist in two times at once. I am going to come very, very close to doing that. If I stay here too long, past the time when I exist someplace else this year, I will die."

The Welshman's face went through a whole series of unguarded expressions. Then, to Kit's astonishment, he went down on one knee. "I offer fealty, then, liege lord. Command me, that I may finish your task should you perish in this rescue."

Now was neither the time nor the place to try and explain that no oath of fealty was necessary. He simply accepted the pledge of vassalage. If they lived, he'd sort it out later. Margo looked on, wide-eyed.

"Now," Kit said quietly, "what we must do is hold a mock trial for witchcraft. . . ."

❂ ❂ ❂

Malcolm ordered that the Welshman be given food and water, then treated his injuries. Kit ordained that he should be given a night's rest before the holy examination began. When they left, Malcolm felt marginally better about abandoning Margo. At least now she wasn't alone in that wretched little room.

They "examined" the Welshman in that same little room the next day, making a whole-day affair of it—and really spent the time quietly discussing their plans, coming up with alternative courses of action should something go wrong. They planned the fake trial like a Broadway production. Only this play's outcome was far more critical than any theatrical spectacular ever to hit the streets of New York City. And when they finished their plans, silent looks which passed between them said everyone was aware just how easily something could still go wrong.

The African sun was low in the summer sky when Malcolm finally stepped out of the filthy little cell and held the door for Kit. The lean time scout wouldn't look at him. Margo had clung to Malcolm before their departure, revealing her feelings so transparently a blind man would have seen how she felt. Her farewell to Kit had been far more restrained. Her demonstration had shaken Malcolm, but it hadn't done anything to heal the breach between Kit and himself. As they shut the door, Kynan moved protectively between her and the Portuguese who locked them in, bringing Malcolm's opinion of the Welshman another notch higher.

Malcolm and Kit took the traders through Vespers before consenting to sit down to the evening meal. Dark looks and angry words between several of the men convinced Malcolm to put a plan of his own into action. If Kit wanted these men off-balance, he saw a golden opportunity to set them at one another. So at dinnertime, which the entire community had begun taking together at Kit's insistence, he lifted his hands and launched into a sermon on the evils of witchcraft in his Basque-accented Portuguese.

"Know you that the Evil One has demons to sniff out all your grievous sins and tempt you to even greater evil. You must be on your guard against anything that entices you to stray from God's path. If you see your neighbor shirking his duty, be assured Satan is working within that man, leading him down the path of damnation. Be harsh with your neighbor. Correct his behavior that you might guard his soul. You must help one another to find the narrow path again. If your neighbor indulges that cardinal sin of greed, you must help him to resist the error of his ways. If you stand guard at night and see the Evil One and his minions prowling about the town, looking for ways of creating mischief, you must charge him to be gone!"

Several of the soldiers lost color. Clearly, they'd seen *something* prowling the night. Monkeys, Malcolm was willing to bet, intent on raiding the garbage middens, possibly even leopards after the livestock. Tonight's watch ought to prove interesting.

"Does your fellow man swell with insufferable pride? Teach him humility, that he might rescue his soul from damnation. Avarice, pride, *gluttony.* Watch for these deadly sins. You *must root them out!*"

He delivered a final benediction. The whole cadre of soldiers, artisans, farmers, and landlocked sailors sat speechless, eying each other with growing suspicion and fear. The governor crossed himself and began to eat—but slowly, to avoid the impression that he had fallen prey to the sin of gluttony. The other men followed his example. *Which of you,* Malcolm could practically read their thoughts, *summoned the Evil One with his wickedness?*

Later, alone, Kit eyed him coldly. "Hope to hell you know what you're doing."

"You wanted them off balance. Next couple of days ought to be interesting.

Kit just grunted and stomped off to bed. Kit's plan to keep the men unsettled and tired was certainly working on *Malcolm.* He was numb with exhaustion.

"Good night," Malcolm said quietly.

Kit's only reply was a brusque, "Hope you sleep like hell, buddy."

Malcolm held his tongue. He'd take Kit's anger and swallow it raw. *Consider it penance, Father Xabat.* Malcolm did manage to fall asleep eventually; but his dreams were violent, waking him well before midnight. He rolled over in the darkness and stared at the invisible wooden ceiling.

How could he ever patch his friendship with Kit? Malcolm owed the retired scout more favors than he could ever repay, not the least of which was the trust Kit had placed in him to guard Margo. The knowledge that she huddled in the darkness, locked into a filthy cell with nothing more than a coarse shirt and a flea-ridden blanket to cover her, when she needed medical treatment . . . He closed his fists in his own coarse blanket. Those wretched traders could have given her venereal diseases, could've gotten her pregnant—

Malcolm turned onto his side and clenched his teeth. *He* could have gotten her pregnant. He couldn't blame Kit one jot for the cold, murderous looks. Malcolm couldn't help the way he felt about Margo, but he could've restrained that wild, drunken impulse on a street in Rome. *That*, he could have prevented.

I'll make it up somehow, he promised. *Somehow.* He hadn't yet figured out how when a wild scream and gunshots shattered the silence. Another man screamed in mortal agony.

Then the alarm bell clanged wildly.

Kit rolled out of bed, one hand going for the push daggers in his ATLS bag. Then he blinked and said, "What the hell?"

"My plans coming to fruition, I think," Malcolm said drily.

Thudding footsteps ran toward their door. Then a frantic knock shook it on its hinges. Malcolm struggled to his feet and threw the door wide. "What is it?" he asked worriedly. "We heard the shots and the bell—"

"Oh, Father, come quickly, please . . ." It was Francisco, one of the soldiers. His voice shook.

Malcolm followed, with Kit hurrying in his wake. They found Zadornin, the Basque sailor, lying in the mud near the fort wall. He'd been shot through the chest. Clearly, the man was dying.

"I did see a demon, Father," the sailor gasped, "atop the wall. I screamed and the watch fired. . . ."

"It was a misshapen beast," Peli, one of the soldiers quavered. "It had the likeness of a man and it cried out with Zadornin's voice. We fired and it vanished with a screech, leaving poor Zadornin to die in its place."

The sailor was fainting from shock and blood loss. The hole in his chest was at least eighty caliber. Malcolm took his hand and spoke last rites while he died. The sailor's death shook him badly, but Malcolm steeled himself with the thought that these men had permitted Koot van Beek to die and planned to kill Margo and Kynan using the hideous methods reserved for witches. He crossed himself in time to hear a fight break out among the soldiers of the watch.

"If you hadn't been asleep, God curse you—"

"If you could shoot an arquebus as well as you shirk your duty—"

The fist fight was brutal and short. Malcolm and Kit watched wordlessly. Malcolm, at any rate, had no intention of soothing the shaken soldiers. When it was over, Amaro sported a broken nose and Lorenco spat out a couple of teeth.

"I suggest," Kit said coldly, "that you bury the man you have murdered. Do so at once. When you have finished, we will begin Matins."

The soldiers grumbled into the stubble of their beards and went in search of shovels to dig the grave.

Margo sat in her prison until nearly mid-morning, overhearing the sound of violent quarrels between her captors. Whatever Kit and Malcolm were doing, it was creating havoc. *Good!* The gunshots the previous night had jolted her out of nightmares. She had no idea what had happened, but hoped neither Malcolm nor Kit had been directly involved. Her greatest terror was that Kit would die before they could make good their escape, leaving Malcolm alone in a hostile camp of abruptly suspicious Portuguese.

The soldiers came for her shortly before mid-morning. She was clad only in a rough shirt that covered her to her thighs. Margo snatched the blanket and wrapped it around her waist as a skirt. When that hideous Sergeant Braz seized her wrists, Margo spat in his face. He backhanded her into the wall. She slid to the floor, weeping and holding her face. Dimly, she heard Kit's voice, speaking angrily in Portuguese.

Then Malcolm appeared out of the blur. She retained just enough sense not to throw her arms around him. He helped her to her feet, then escorted her outside. A table and chairs had been set up in the fort's open courtyard. The military governor—Margo shuddered at the memory—sat in the front row of seats. His soldiers stood guard, looking like they'd been in a fist fight half the night. Other men squatted on the ground or stood in uneasy clusters, watching the proceedings.

Kit seated himself behind the table and dipped a quill pen into an inkwell, writing something meticulous on thick sheets of parchment. He glanced up and gestured Malcolm to the front of the table. Malcolm led Margo to the open space between table and audience. Kit sat back and looked up at her. Margo felt a chill. If she hadn't known he was playing a part, she would have despaired.

He spoke in Portuguese. Malcolm said in English, "You are on trial for witchcraft, girl. What is your name?"

There was at least one man in that audience who understood a little English. Margo lifted her head. "Margo Smith."

"And you are English?"

"I am."

Malcolm spoke briefly to Kit in Portuguese. Kit scribbled something onto his parchment. Then he began to speak. Malcolm translated a list of charges, which began with, "You are accused of consorting with the devil to make yourself and others fly through the air by means of foul magic," and ended nearly half an hour later with, "and lastly, you are accused of summoning storms by the combing of your hair, which did cause the wreckage of a Portuguese ship and the loss of all hands but two." They even threw in summoning demons to make the sheep bleat at the wrong hour of the night.

"How do you plead to these serious charges of witchcraft?"

Margo turned her head just far enough to stare directly into the military governor's eyes. She curled her lip. "Even if I were a witch, I would not waste such powerful magic on these men. They are not worthy of it. I am innocent and they are liars, murderers, and rapists."

Malcolm translated her reply. The governor came to his feet with a roar and threatened Margo with the back of his hand. Malcolm snapped something that caused him to resume his seat.

The "trial" was the most amazing thing Margo had ever witnessed.

She was required to repeat phrases in Latin. Every syllable she stumbled over was duly noted on Kit's parchment and commented on by the sullen audience. She was stripped naked and searched. Birthmarks and a tiny mole were pointed out and recorded. She glared at Kit, who returned her gaze coldly.

Malcolm said, "Put. on your clothes, English. You offend God."

"Not as much as you do!" she snapped.

Kit glanced up reproachfully.

Then they escorted her down to the bay. Two soldiers picked her up bodily and heaved her into the water. Margo squealed in shock and landed with a heavy splash. The water was *deep.* She swam for the surface, gasped, and glared at the soldiers. The men were muttering worriedly. When Malcolm fished her out, she snapped, "What are you trying to do? Drown me?"

"Witches," Malcolm said coldly, "float. The innocent sink."

"Huh!" *Great way to get rid of a problem. Drown 'em or burn 'em.*

By the time they dragged her back to the fort, it was nearing noon. Kit asked her questions which made absolutely no sense at all. Most of them she couldn't begin to answer. Kit shook his head mournfully and wrote in his parchment. It was nearly dark when they finally escorted her back to her cell and gave her bread, soup, and wine.

If Kit hadn't made clear yesterday that he intended to find her "guilty" she would have been terrified. Margo shivered as it was. What if something went wrong? What if they began the execution and Kit simply vanished, having shadowed himself? Not only would Kit die, so would she, and most likely Kynan and Malcolm, too. The idea of burning to death left her sweating into her coarse, filthy shirt. She clenched her hands and tried to pray, then paced the little cell. Surely they would pull it off. Kit knew what he was doing.

But as Kit had admonished her time and again, even trained scouts ran into fatal trouble sometimes.

The next morning, they took Kynan away. He was gone all day, put through the same ordeals she'd been through. When the lock finally grated open and Kynan was thrust bodily inside, he was pale. In his bad English, he said, "Is not good. Portuguese scared. Mad. Not good."

"No. It isn't good. I'm . . ." She hesitated, then said it anyway. "I'm scared."

He took her hand, holding it gently. "Yes. Margo is brave. Brave have fear. Is true."

She swallowed hard. "Yes. Very true."

He managed a rueful smile. "In Orleans, Kynan fear. Fear French. Fear Margo. True."

She started to laugh and ended up crying on his shoulder. If he thought less of her for it, he didn't let it show.

During the night, more screams and gunshots rang out. Margo started awake, then muttered, "Good!" and heard an answering grunt from Kynan. No one shouted for Kit or Malcolm, though, so no one must have died this time. The next day—the day the gate was supposed to reopen—the Portuguese brought them both out to hear the "testimony" of their accusers. Not that it did Margo or Kynan any good. The testimony was all in Portuguese. But the angry, fearful looks sent their way and the sleepless hollows under most eyes told Margo that Kit and Malcolm's plans were bearing fruit.

Given the shouting match and fist fight that ensued during the afternoon, the Portuguese had begun to accuse one another of witchcraft charges. Kit ordered Margo and Kynan locked up while the soldiers broke up the vicious little fight with blows from the butts of their arquebuses. Margo wondered when Kit would make his move. They were running short on time. The gate would be opening in just a few hours—if it opened at all.

The longer they waited, the more terror stretched her nerves taut. Something had gone wrong. They'd slipped up somehow, their ruse had been discovered, or Kit had vanished, leaving Malcolm to face the whole superstitious, murderous bunch. . . .

The sun was sinking into the heart of the distant Drakensbergs when the door opened a last time. Margo's heart pounded unsteadily beneath her rib cage as she came slowly to her feet. Kynan, too, scrambled up to face the Portuguese sergeant who'd unlocked their cell. The sergeant wouldn't meet their gaze. He crossed himself and moved hastily aside. Malcolm stood behind him. He gazed coldly into the cell without speaking, then said roughly, "You have been found guilty of witchcraft, Margo Smith. You will be taken far from Lourengo Marques where you will be put to death by burning. May God pity your soul."

Margo stared at him, hardly recognizing the gentle man who had loved her in Rome. Then, recalling the part she had to play, Margo gave out a shriek and sank toward the ground. Her theatrical faint was so convincing, Kynan caught her with a cry. He held her protectively. Kit appeared behind Malcolm and said something in Welsh. Kynan didn't speak a word. He just snarled like a trapped wolf.

Oh, God, Margo thought while her heart trip hammered, *let this work!*

Soldiers herded them out of the cell. They were taken across the open courtyard while the rest of the men crossed themselves and avoided their gaze. Kynan marched stolidly between the soldiers, placing one hand protectively on Margo's waist. The gesture brought tears to her eyes.

Kit and Malcolm followed, intoning something in Latin. Both of them had slung their ATLS bags over their shoulders. It was the only hopeful sign she saw. They passed a wagon and a thin horse in harness. The remains of Margo's PVC raft and Filmar balloon and everything which had survived the wreck had been piled into it. An ominously large stack of wood and two long, thick stakes also weighed it down. Several of the Portuguese stood near it, holding pikes and lit torches. Margo let her steps falter. Then she sank to her knees, weeping. Given the fear jolting through her that something would yet go wrong, tears were remarkably easy to conjure. Kynan lifted her back to her feet and glared at their executioners.

Farther along, waiting for them to pass, were that pig of a military governor and the rest of his disgusting, unwashed swine. All of them carried weapons: black-powder firearms, cocked crossbows, swords, or murderous long pikes and daggers. Margo tried to keep her spirits from sinking, but she couldn't see how Kit planned to escape with an armed contingent that size acting as guard.

They marched completely out of the walled village and moved down the beach, heading south around the wide curve of the bay. Margo remembered the layout of the land. Kit was herding them closer to the gate. The whole parade marched down the wave-scoured beach, moving grimly, silently. Only the creak of the wagon and the crackle of the torches rose above the sound of sea and wind. Kit moved into the lead as though searching for something. Whatever it was, he clearly wasn't finding it. Margo knew the gate would open somewhere close to here, but she couldn't remember precisely where, either.

Kit finally lifted his arms and spoke in Portuguese. The wagon rolled to a halt near him. Roughly dressed men began unloading it. An enormous bear of a man hammered the terrifying stakes into the ground. Sailors piled wood high around them. Kit spoke earnestly in Latin to the skies as though she and Kynan didn't even exist. The wreckage of Margo's raft was added to the pile, alone with everything else that had survived. She checked the slant of the sun. *Any time now, surely . . .*

If the gate opened again.

Or if Kit didn't die any moment, shadowing himself.

If, if, if . . .

She noticed sweat on his face and began to tremble. Malcolm's skin had taken on a ghastly hue. He produced a coil of rope and bound one of Margo's wrists securely.

"Pretend I've tied your other wrist behind you once you're at the stake," he hissed in her ear. Then he dragged her toward the pile of wood.

Margo screamed and struggled. He caught her wrists and lifted her off the ground, doggedly climbing the stacked wood and shoving her against the stake. Margo begged for mercy, sliding to her knees and clutching his robes. He sobbed out something in Portuguese and snatched her back to her feet, then dragged her hands behind her. He jerked her wrists behind the stake. Margo screamed again. The audience hung on their every movement like hypnotized sports fans. Margo felt sick. Malcolm wound the rope around her hand without looping it around her wrist. All she had to do was let go and she'd be free. Margo slumped against the stake as though tightly bound and gave in to wretched sobs.

Kit dragged Kynan Rhys Gower to the stake. From her vantage

point, she could see that Kit repeated the same procedure with the Welshman's wrists. Kynan was white to the lips. He held his head high and intoned something in a loud voice, speaking in his own native tongue. He might have been heaping curses on the Portuguese or praying to God to let this mad scheme work.

Kit stumbled back down the piled wood and turned to face them. He lifted both hands, a crucifix clenched in one fist. He began to chant in Latin. Whatever it was, it went on and on. Sweat beaded up on his lips and dripped down his chin. Malcolm kept darting nervous glances in the direction Margo thought the gate ought to be.

Nothing was happening.

The sun sank lower, vanishing behind the distant peaks of the Drakensbergs. The crash of waves was loud in her ears. Seabirds screamed overhead. *It's not opening, oh God, it isn't going to open* . . . On the ground below the pyre, Kit sank to his knees and bowed his head. Malcolm followed suit. The rest of the company went to their knees as well. Torches crackled in the growing twilight. Still no gate opened. Kit couldn't delay this much longer. The military governor was staring at him, darting uneasy glances toward the as-yet unlit pyre. A few glimmering stars appeared in the darkening sky.

Then the bones behind Margo's ear began to vibrate.

She caught her breath on a sob—

Then let out an ear-piercing shriek.

At the first buzz of the gate, Malcolm went giddy with relief. Then Margo screamed. He started and whirled to stare at her. Even Kit jumped.

"HEAR ME!" Margo shouted. "I CALL UPON THE POWERS OF HELL!"

Malcolm staggered to his feet, holding up his crucifix. The soldier who spoke a little English began to shout that she was calling upon the Evil One himself.

Kit ran toward the pyre, snatching a torch from a dumbfounded farmer. "Minion of hell!" he cried. "Cease thy conjuring! I command thee in the name of Christ!"

Margo shouted at him to stuff it. Then she started ranting. "You will all die hideous deaths if you lay that torch to this pyre! I call on Beelzebub! I call on Satan, Lucifer, St. Nick—"

St. Nick?

From Malcolm's vantage point, Kit nearly lost it. With masterful skill, he converted sudden laughter into a cough and a cry of pain. He sank to his knees, gasping and clutching his chest as though her curses were having real effect. Semi-hysterical images flitted briefly through Malcolm's head, threatening to loose his own laughter—

But Margo was still shouting.

And the soldiers nearest her were swearing in terror, pointing their crossbows right at her. *Oh shit . . .*

Malcolm flung himself between the crossbows and the still-unlit pyre. "No! Do not interfere in God's work!"

"But Father—" one of them cried, ashen and sweating in the descending gloom.

The vibration of the gate had grown so painful several farmers and sailors had dropped their weapons. They clutched their ears, staring wildly around for the appearance of the most profoundly expected demons. Malcolm lifted his own crucifix and advanced toward the piled wood. Kit outdid himself. He twisted on the ground, then crawled to his knees, coughing and holding up his own crucifix.

In a voice faint with terror, Kit cried, "I command thee, in the name of Christ, begone Satan! God will protect us!"

"Satan will eat your entrails for lunch!" Margo screamed right back.

One of the shaking farmers let out a wail of terror—and hurled his torch straight onto the pyre. Wood shavings crackled and roared into flame. Margo screamed, then shrieked at the poor farmer, "St. Nick will have your guts for sausages!"

Kit, not to be outdone, rose tottering to his feet and lifted both arms, trembling so violently even Malcolm was halfway convinced he was about to fall down again. "Jesu Christo! Open the gates of hell itself! Send these minions of damnation to their deaths!"

Then Kit hurled his own torch like a thrown javelin—

—straight at the source of the sound that wasn't a sound.

Twenty-five yards down the beach, a crack appeared in the fabric of reality. The torch sailed straight through it. Someone behind Malcolm screamed. Someone else began chanting the Hail Mary. Another man began to sob. Half the Portuguese broke and ran for town, wailing in terror The gate dilated open, pulsing savagely in the mad rhythm of an unstable string.

"NOW!" Kit yelled.

Margo flung herself down the pile of burning wood, jumping right through the flames. Kynan Rhys Gower followed with a wild yell. Malcolm caught a blur of motion—

The huge blacksmith had aimed his weapon at Margo's back.

Malcolm lunged forward. He knocked the barrel of the smith's rifled wheel lock upward just as the piece discharged. The smith roared. Malcolm dodged away, then delivered a snap kick that flattened the arquebusier trying to fire on Margo.

Then he ran through the confused, shaken crowd. "Kit! Run!"

The time scout dove at the fire instead, snatching something out of it, then whirled, knocking aside a White-faced soldier just before his arquebus went off with a roar. A lead ball slammed into the beach less than a foot short of Margo's flying feet. The soldier snarled and charged. Kit brushed him to the ground. The man screamed. Malcolm caught the glint of push daggers in the firelight. *Nothing like Aikido and a push-dagger blade to ruin your whole day.*

Someone else leveled a crossbow at Kit's back.

Malcolm delivered a flying kick that knocked the man to the sand, then he was past and running for the gate.

"Kit!" He yelled. "It's disintegrating!"

Margo reached the gate first. It shrank savagely to a pinpoint. She sobbed out something Malcolm couldn't quite hear. Kynan skidded to a halt beside her. The gate roared open again. Kynan glanced back and shouted. Malcolm looked wildly over one shoulder. Behind them, Amaro had taken a careful bead on Margo with his crossbow. Malcolm couldn't do anything to stop him and Kit was out of position—

Kynan yelled and flung himself between Margo and the arbalester. The Welshman knocked her to the ground with a sweeping blow, shoving her out of harm's way. The slap of the steel spring was a hideous sound. Kynan screamed and collapsed like a punctured balloon. A steel shaft as thick as Malcolm's thumb slammed through Kynan's body instead of Margo's chest.

Margo sobbed once and crawled to him, trying to stanch the bleeding with her hands. Malcolm lunged the final yard to the gate. "Go!" He shoved her bodily through. She sprawled into Phil Jones' shop with a hoarse yell. Malcolm scooped up the injured Welshman in a fireman's carry. Kynan groaned and fainted. Malcolm lunged through, tripping over Margo and dropping Kynan to the concrete floor. Margo howled in pain and crawled out from under him. Malcolm came to his feet and whirled. "Kit!"

He was running for the gate.

The time scout gasped with effort and dove forward. He crashed into Malcolm just as the gate shrank with a roar like a freight train. Malcolm landed on hard concrete. Kit swore hideously and cradled one arm. A crackle of fire and thick, acrid smoke roared into Malcolm's awareness. One of the totem poles in Phil Jones' store room had caught fire from Kit's thrown torch. A crossbow bolt, covered with blood and bits of Kynan's flesh, stuck obscenely out of another.

Above them, the gate vanished as though it had never been.

Chapter 20

An instant later, the fire-control system cut in, spraying clouds of Halon into the room.

"Out!" Kit cried.

Malcolm helped carry Kynan into Phil Jones' office. Margo ran for the phone to call in a medical emergency, then ran interference, as well, driving Phil Jones bodily out of their way when he started shouting that they'd ruined his inventory, his business, and his life. When he didn't shut up, she tossed him through the doorway into his showroom. The last glimpse Malcolm had of her, she was *standing* on him.

Kit stripped off Kynan's shirt and stanched the bleeding as best he could with direct pressure. Malcolm pulled off his woolen cassock and cut thick compresses. "Here . . ."

They applied the compresses and more pressure. Kynan moaned. His eyelids fluttered, then he sought Kit's gaze. His eyes were glazed.

"My lord . . . I'm . . . dying . . ." He groped weakly for Kit's arm.

"No," Kit said roughly, "you won't die, Kynan Rhys Gower. I won't allow it."

"Aye," Kynan breathed, allowing his eyes to close again. "My life is . . . yours. . . ."

Kit had said the right thing. Maybe—just maybe—the man's superstitious faith that his liege lord could work magic would keep him alive. Long enough for station medical to arrive, anyway . . . The bleet of the medi-van's siren was the most welcome sound Malcolm had heard since the buzz of the gate in the African twilight. Rachel Eisenstein and another duty doctor raced into the office.

"Cross-bow bolt," Kit said tersely.

Rachel took over, rigging pressure bandages, stabilizing Kynan's vitals with IVs, treating for shock. "Prepare for thoracic surgery," Rachel said into her radio link with the station's hospital. "Stat! We're bringing in a bad one."

"Roger."

They lifted Kynan carefully onto a gurney and ran for the medi-van. Silence, sudden and brutal, descended on the smoky office. Kit scrubbed his brow with the heel of a bloody hand. Malcolm leaned against Phil's desk and rubbed aching ribs where Kit's lunge for safety had caught him. For a moment, neither of them spoke.

Then Kit glanced his way. "Malcolm . . ."

He looked up. A rarely seen look which everyone dreaded having pointed at *them* was leveled straight at him. Malcolm winced. *Well, you've been waiting for this.*

"All right," Kit said quietly. "Let's hear it."

"What do you want me to say, Kit? I'm sorrier than you'll ever know. Breaking a friend's trust . . . Well, I *am* British. For whatever that's worth. I've no excuses, Kit. So I won't even try to make any. But lame as it sounds, I thought she'd just turned nineteen, Kit, not *seventeen,* and . . . and dammit, that headstrong little idiot does something to me. . . ."

Kit snorted.

Malcolm adjusted himself against the hard desk, wincing slightly. "She's been hurt, Kit. Desperately. If I ever find out who did it, I think I might actually kill him. There's something fine inside her fighting to get out. I see glimpses of it all the time. First in London, again in Brighton. Then in Rome . . ." He swore softly. "We were both a little drunk. Hilaria was in full swing. She was doing so well and I was so proud of her and the next thing I knew . . ."

"Stop." Kit held up one hand. "Please."

Malcolm halted. Then, very quietly, "It isn't much, but I never meant any of this. I'm bloody sorry, Kit. I won't say I'd undo the way

I feel about her, but I'm bloody *damned* sorry for how I've handled this, the mess I've caused. If it's any consolation, I went through nine days of absolute hell, thinking I'd killed her." He groped for something else to say and ended lamely with the only thing he *could* say. "I'm sorry, Kit."

"So am I," his one-time friend sighed.

"I'll . . . I'll go to another station, I guess, get out of your way . . ."

"Malcolm."

He shut up, ready to take whatever bitter anger his friend vented.

"I ought to break your neck, you know. I'm tempted to saddle you with the Neo Edo. The punishment ought to fit the crime, after all. You *deserve* that paperwork and the government auditors and the inspections and . . ."

Malcolm winced.

"But . . ." Kit's faint smile shocked him. "At least she had enough sense to pick someone like you."

Malcolm didn't know what to say.

"It *might* have been Skeeter Jackson, after all."

Malcolm found his voice after all, surprising both of them. Kit just stared. "Where *do* you pick up language like that?"

Malcolm managed a wan smile. "Believe it or not, I overheard that one from a Praetorian guardsman the day Caligula was murdered."

"Really? Some day you *must* tell me the whole story about that day."

Malcolm let his gaze focus on something far beyond Phil Jones' sordid little office. "Maybe. I'm not sure I'll ever tell anyone the *whole* story."

Kit cleared his throat. "Know the feeling," he muttered. He scrubbed bloody hands on his ruined Jesuit cassock, then cleared his throat again and held out one hand. "I don't have enough friends to lose one. Not even for something like this."

Malcolm paused only a moment, then shook it. "I'll make it up, Kit."

The lean time scout grinned. "You sure as hell will. And if she's pregnant . . ." He let the threat dangle.

Malcolm just groaned.

The office door opened. Kit and Malcolm looked up to find Margo staring down at them. Clad in a ragged Portuguese shirt, face and hands smeared with soot and blood, eyes hardened by what she'd been through, Malcolm hardly recognized her.

"No broken bones, I see," she said quietly. "Good. Because Rome was my fault, too. In fact, Rome was *mostly* my fault." Malcolm didn't know what to say. Clearly, Kit didn't either. "I would just like to say for the record that I don't deserve either one of you. But I think I've learned my lesson—oh, hell, I've learned more lessons in the past seven weeks than I have in the last seventeen years. I screwed up *everything.* Everyone was right and I was wrong and I'm so damned sorry I nearly got us all killed, I . . . I could almost go back to Minnesota and hide. . . ."

Her voice cracked.

Oh-oh. Better try and lighten the mood a bit . . .

"You know," Malcolm said off-handedly, "there's something you really ought to know before your next scouting trip."

She blinked tears, sounding absolutely miserable. "What?"

"Mmm . . ." He glanced at Kit and winked. "There's rather a large difference between *Old* Nick and *Saint* Nick."

She stared at him, so nonplussed she forgot to keep crying. "Old Nick? Saint Nick? What are you talking about?"

Malcolm glanced at Kit. The scout's lips quirked. Then his eyes crinkled and he couldn't contain it any longer. He started to laugh. Malcolm grinned. Margo, clad in nothing but an Irish alley-cat glare and a too-loose sixteenth-century shirt, glared from one to the other as though they'd misplaced their collective wits.

"What's so funny?" she demanded.

Kit lay back and roared.

Malcolm wiped his eyes. "You called down the wrath of *Santa Claus . . .*"

Margo opened her lips over air. Then she started to chuckle. "I did?"

"Oh, Margo," Kit gasped, "you sure as hell did, honey."

Malcolm was still wiping tears. "It was priceless. I had visions of the heavens splitting open and a vengeful team of reindeer screaming down at Mach eight while the jolly old elf threw Christmas boxes like grenades. . . ."

That set Kit off again. Margo just grinned, taking the ribbing with surprisingly good humor. Then her laughter vanished.

Kit sat up hastily. "What's wrong? Oh, hell. . . . You're hurt and here we are laughing like idiots—"

"No . . . no, it's Kynan." She sank to her knees beside him. "Why did he do that? Throw himself in front of me that way?"

Kit touched a bruised cheek. "He pledged me as his liege lord. You instantly became the object of his sworn protection, his liege lady if you will. He considered it a sacred duty to die in my service, protecting you."

Margo swallowed hard. "I see. I . . ." Her face crumpled. "I'm sorry. I don't mean to snivel. Will he live?"

Kit smiled. "I'd say you earned a sniffle or two. And Rachel doesn't like losing patients. He has a very good chance, anyway." Kit dragged a scorched leather bag out of the corner. "I rescued your ATLS and log from the fire, by the way."

She opened the bag slowly, removing the ATLS, the personal log, even a folded chart.

"What's that?" Malcolm asked curiously.

"The map Goldie gave me." She thrust it at Kit. "I don't want it."

Kit took it wordlessly and tucked it into his own ATLS bag. "Speaking of Goldie . . . I think we need to hold a little chat with that avaricious old shark."

"You're telling me! She almost got us killed!"

Kit turned a reproachful glance on her.

"Well, all right, I almost got us killed. But she *knew* I was hopelessly unqualified!"

"Comes with the territory," Malcolm told her unsympathetically. "It's too bad her scam will work. She deserves to lose her shirt."

Margo sniffed. "As much trouble as I had finding that stupid spot on the river, those damned diamonds had *better* be there. I'd hate to think I put everyone through all this and got poor Mr. van Beek killed, only to find I'd screwed up and stuck them in the wrong place."

"You had trouble finding the right spot?"

Malcolm knew that tone. Kit was suddenly and profoundly interested. "What trouble, exactly?"

Margo wiped her nose. "The maps didn't match, not exactly. Here." She dug out her log and pulled up a file, then turned the screen to face him. "That's the digital snapshot I made of the river valley where we buried the stuff. I had to scan in Goldie's chart and superimpose the two. They still didn't quite match up, but I'm sure I got the right plot of ground."

Kit studied the screen intently, then started to grin.

"What?"

"Margo, I think I just might be able to pay back every scam Goldie has ever run on me. Malcolm, take a look."

Malcolm peered over Kit's shoulder. Then he, too, began to grin.

"*What?*"

"The river changed course."

"So?"

Malcolm said patiently, "Look. Here and here and here. See? It's at least a hundred yards off right here and more than fifty here . . ."

Margo frowned. Then she got it. Her eyes widened. "You mean—" She started to laugh.

Kit grinned. "Yep. Hell, it's *better* than beating her at pool." He tottered to his feet and gave Margo a hand up. "You, young lady, march straight to the infirmary. Leave Goldie to me."

Malcolm rubbed metaphoric hands in anticipation.

He could hardly wait to see this one.

Epilogue

Goldie Morran wandered into the Down Time and sank into a chair. Kit and Malcolm left their table and sat down at hers.

"What's wrong, Goldie?" Kit asked.

The gems and currency expert sniffed autocratically. "It's that stupid granddaughter of yours. She put the diamonds in the wrong place."

"Oh?" Malcolm asked innocently.

"We dug up a square fifty yards on a side around the spot on that map. Nothing. Not a trace. My up-time rube has withdrawn his offer to buy the whole parcel. I can't believe we went through all that and she didn't get the right place. God *knows* where she put them."

Kit had received his own confirmation from up-time sources that Goldie was, for once, telling God's own truth.

Malcolm put in, "Well, Margo buried them—what? Four hundred fifty years ago? Anything could have happened. A flash flood might have washed the whole mess out. Or someone could have dug the stuff up years ago and quietly sold it off. Who could tell? It was a great idea, Goldie. Too bad it didn't work."

"Yeah," she said glumly. "Too bad. *Damn* that girl. . . .

Kit consoled her by ordering Goldie's favorite. She sipped disconsolately.

"How much money did you lose?" Kit asked quietly.

"Ten thousand dollars! I paid for that whole benighted

expedition, not to mention that worthless piece of farmland! It's so riddled with tsetse flies you can't even run cattle on it!"

"I feel really terrible." Kit said earnestly. "After all, I did train Margo. Her mistake is my mistake."

Goldie sniffed again. "You always were too nice for your own good, Kit. Thanks anyway. I'm still out ten thousand."

"Tell you what. I'm determined to drive home the lessons Margo's learning from this fiasco. How about I make her pay you back?"

"Pay me back?" Goldie echoed. 'Why?"

"To teach her the value of getting her geography right."

Goldie sniffed once more, but her eyes had begun to gleam. "What did you have in mind?"

Gotcha! "Margo will be spending the next eight years or so in college. She's agreed to pay back every penny of her education out of what she earns as a scout. I'd like to tack an extra ten thousand onto the price tag. How's this? I'll buy the land. Then, every vacation Margo has, I'll go up time and make her fly, walk, and *crawl* every inch of that river valley until she learns how to do aerial mapping *right.*"

Goldie hesitated, a veteran angler playing her "fish" with seasoned skill. "I don't know, Kit. That's an awfully expensive lesson."

Kit grunted. "Not half as expensive as losing your granddaughter. Which, I might add, I damn near did."

"Not to mention my life and Kit's," Malcolm added. "And that Welshman almost died on the operating table. Koot van Beek *did* die."

Goldie hurried to change the subject. "About this proposition of yours . . . are you serious?"

"Dead serious," Kit muttered darkly. "Margo isn't setting foot across another gate until she's learned every lesson I insist she master. Getting geography right is critical. If she'd done a better job of it, Koot van Beek might still be alive."

Goldie tossed back the rest of her drink. "All right I'm willing to help teach her a lesson. Come on, I have the paperwork down at my office."

Malcolm, God bless him, maintained an absolute poker face.

Goldie couldn't sign over the deed to the Shashe River property fast enough. Kit duly transferred ten thousand from his account into hers while Malcolm witnessed the signatures. "Goldie," Kit said, kissing her hand gallantly, "you have a grandfather's undying gratitude."

"My pleasure. Young people must learn, after all." Goldie's cheeks were faintly flushed. No one loved a scam quite as much as Goldie Morran.

Unless, of course, it was Kit Carson.

Two weeks later, Malcolm Moore's e-mail queue beeped, letting him know he had a package from up time waiting at Customs. He signed for the box, which had been sealed by up-time ATF customs authorities. The return address was scrawled in Margo's hand. Malcolm spotted a second package like it for Kit.

He grinned, then made tracks for the Neo Edo.

"Kit around?"

"Yeah," Jimmy told him. "It's paperwork day again. You want me to buzz him?"

"Nah. I'll surprise him."

Jimmy grinned. "That man will do *anything* to avoid paperwork."

Malcolm laughed. "Can you blame him?"

"Hell, no."

Malcolm rapped on the office door. Kit's "Yeah, it's open" sounded vastly relieved.

Malcolm slid back the door and kicked off his shoes. He held up his mail. "Package from Margo. There's one for you, too, waiting at Customs."

Kit came around the desk like a thrown baseball. "Well, open it!"

Malcolm tore the seals and ripped open the cardboard. Inside was a metal box which he tilted carefully out. The lid slipped back to reveal a single item: a glittering diamond in the rough, nearly as big as Malcolm's thumbnail.

Kit whooped. *"She did it!"*

Malcolm held it up to the light, then whistled. She sure had. "That," Malcolm sighed, "is truly beautiful." And if she still felt the same way in a few months, maybe he'd even have it made into a ring . . .

Well, stranger things had happened to him lately. Their parting had been enough to shake both of them to the core. Who knew? Maybe she'd even broken his notorious string of bad luck?

Now *that* would be a switch.

"*I* think," Malcolm grinned, "this calls for a celebration."

Kit broke out champagne from his private stock and poured bubbly, then handed over a glass. "How about a toast?"

Malcolm waited expectantly.

Kit lifted his glass. "To the best damn time scouts in La-La Land. Partner." He slid over a signed document giving Malcolm and Margo each a third-share interest in the land Kit had bought from Goldie Morran. Malcolm just gaped.

"You earned it. We all did. Hope you don't mind paying Kynan Rhys Gower out of our joint profits?"

Malcolm's eyes misted. "Hear, hear. I'd say that's a bargain any day of the week." They touched glasses with a musical *clink.*

"Now, partner," Kit grinned, "about that story you were going to tell me . . . the one about Caligula's murder and Claudius' ascension to the Principate of Rome."

"Oh, no," Malcolm laughed. "First you have to spill the beans about what really happened when you spent the night hiding under Queen Victoria's bed."

Kit grinned. "I *never* compromise a lady. You first."

No one, Malcolm chuckled to himself, *could bamboozle and flummox his way out of the truth like a time scout.* At last, La-La Land was back to normal. Thank God. Malcolm settled back in one of Kit's chairs and started spinning the tallest tale he could concoct about that day in Rome five years previously—and two thousand years in the past—and made himself a silent promise.

If Margo could risk it, so could he. *Malcolm Moore and Margo Smith, Time Scouts . . .*

It had a nice ring to it.

Robert Asprin and Linda Evans

Chapter 1

Skeeter Jackson was a scoundrel.

A dyed-in-the-wool, thieving scoundrel.

He knew it, of course; knew it as well as anyone else in La-La Land (at least, anyone who'd been on Shangri-la Station longer than a week). Not only did he know it, he was proud of it, the way other men were proud of their batting averages, their cholesterol counts, their stock portfolios.

Skeeter was *very* careful to rub shoulders with men of the latter type, who not only boasted of *large* 'folios, but carried enormous amounts of cash in money belts declared through ATF at Primary (so they wouldn't be charged taxes for any money they'd brought with them). Skeeter rarely failed to get hold of at least *some* of that money, if not the whole money belt. Ah, the crisp, cool feel of cash in hand . . .

But he wasn't just a thief. Oh, no. Skeeter was a master *con artist* as well, and *those* skills (ruthless cunning, serpentine guile, the ability to radiate innocent enthusiasm) were among the best.

So—in honor of Yesukai the Valiant and for the very practical reason of survival—he worked hard at being the very best scoundrel he could be. Once he'd arrived (freshly scrubbed to get the New York filth off his hide and out of his soul), it hadn't taken Skeeter long to create a life uniquely his own on a time terminal unique among time terminals.

There was only *one* La-La Land. He loved it fiercely.

On this particular fine morning, Skeeter rose, stretched, and grinned. *The game's afoot, Watson!* (He'd heard that in a movie someplace and liked the sound of it.) The glow coming in beneath his door told him Residence lights were on, not in their dimmed "night" mode. That was really the only way to tell, unless you had an alarm clock with a PM indicator light; Skeeter's had burned out long ago, the last time he'd heaved it at the wall for rudely awakening him with yet another hangover to regret.

Showered and shaved with minimal time wasted, he dressed for the day—and the next two glorious weeks. After some of the things he'd worn, the costume he now donned felt almost natural. Whistling absently to himself, Skeeter—working hard as ever on his chosen vocation—contemplated his brilliant new scheme. And the one gaping hole in it.

Surprisingly, the station's excellent library hadn't been much help. To minimize information leakage, Skeeter *had* searched the computers, gleaning bits of valuable information here and there (and managing to tot up more than a week's worth of earnings against the computer-access account belonging to a scout currently out in the field). *That* little scam was actually worth the otherwise wasted effort, as the scout had once maligned Skeeter in public—wrongly, as it happened; Skeeter hadn't even been involved. Skeeter, therefore felt free to indulge his natural urge to cause the scout the greatest amount of distress possible in the shortest amount of time, all without leaving behind any proof the s.o.b. could use to prosecute.

Irritatingly elusive, the one piece of the puzzle Skeeter needed most just wasn't *in* any pilfered file. The *only* place to find what he needed was inside someone's head. Brian Hendrickson, the librarian, would know, of course. He knew—just as sharply as though he'd learned it mere moments previously—everything he'd ever seen, read, or heard (and probably more—lots more), but Brian's dislike of Skeeter was La-La Land Legend. After ruling out Brian, who was left?

Just needing one more piece of expert advice, Skeeter was running out of time to find it—and people to ask. Well, hell, folks with his chosen vocation *wouldn't* have many friends, now would they? Trust just didn't come with the territory. Having accepted that years ago, Skeeter continued to mentally rummage through the list of people he *might* be able to ask, tossed out all scouts, most guides (Agnes Fairchild was willing—mmm, was she ever!—she just didn't *know*). He hesitated—again—on Goldie Morran. She'd be motivated, all right, and she'd probably *know*, too; but he wasn't about to share potentially enormous profits by confiding his plan to *any* of the other scoundrels who made La-La Land their permanent home. To make the score himself, Goldie-the-heartless-Morran, TT-86's leading authority on rare coins and gems, was out.

What he *needed* was someone who'd *been* there, first-hand.

Other than a handful of rich visitors who'd been through the Porta Romae multiple times—most of whom Skeeter had "liberated" from the burden of their cash and were therefore to be avoided at any cost—Skeeter finally came up with a single, qualified man in the whole of TT-86: Marcus.

A startled grin passed across his face. As it happened, Marcus was probably better suited to give Skeeter advice on this particular scheme than all the so-called experts in La-La Land. *Should've just gone to Marcus in the first place and saved myself a heap of time and trouble.* But he'd been embarrassed, feeling a pang of inexplicable guilt at the thought of conning his best (and practically his only) friend into helping him. Of course, he'd also have missed racking up all those on-line hours against that asshole of a scout. . . .

By coincidence rare and somewhat miraculous, Marcus actually *liked* Skeeter. *Why*, Skeeter had not a single clue. Down-timers often came up with the strangest ideas, many of them quaintly useless, others so eccentric they passed beyond the understandable into the misty, magical realm of things like what made the gates work and what did women really want, anyway? He'd given up on both, long ago, avoiding stepping through any more gates than absolutely necessary and taking his flings where he could find them, not very discontented when he couldn't. He didn't feel proud about his ignorance; business, however, was business.

So Skeeter finished the last touches on his "business uniform" then headed for Commons to hunt down Marcus, then meet Agnes and her group for the tour.

Skeeter liked the open airy feeling of Commons. Not only did it compensate (a little) for the loss of vast, open plains of his teenage years, but more importantly, it *always* smelled to Skeeter like *money*. Vast sums of cold, hard currency changed hands here. It wasn't too much to ask of the gods, was it, that some small trickle of that vast amount fall blissfully into his deserving hands?

Theology aside (and only the many gods knew what Skeeter's was: he certainly didn't), Commons was just plain fun. Particularly at this time of year. As he strode out into the body-jammed floor, picking his way through multiple festivals and reenactments in progress, Skeeter had to shake his head and grin.

What a madhouse! There were, of course, the usual tourist gates with their waiting areas, ramps, and platforms; ticket booths for those who'd waited to arrive before deciding on a destination—fine, if you could afford the hotel bills waiting for your tour to leave; timecard-automated dispensers (hooked into the station's database and set up to match retinal scans and replace the original's temporal-travel data for those idiots who'd lost theirs); and of course, timecard readers (at the entrance and exit of every gate, to scan where and when you'd already been in a desperate effort to prevent some fool tourist from shadowing him- or herself).

There were also shops and restaurants, on multiple levels, many with entrances by balcony only; bizarre stairways to nowhere; balconies and girder-supported platforms suspended three and four stories above the floor; barricaded and fenced-off areas marking either unevenly recurring, unstable gates or stable but unexplored gates; and—the *piece de resistance*—multiple hundreds of costumed, laughing, drinking, quarreling, fighting, kissing, hugging, *gullible* tourists. With fat wallets just waiting for someone's light-fingered touch . . .

Just now Commons looked exactly like the North Pole might if Santa's elves had gone quietly mad on LSD in the process of decorating the workshop. He breathed in the smell of celebration and money and grinned up at the whole, gaudy, breathtaking length of

Commons, loving every bit of the craziness that always overtook Shangri-la Station this time of year.

"And what," a woman's voice said practically at his elbow, "are *you* grinning about, Skeeter Jackson?"

He looked up—then down—and found Ann Vinh Mulhaney, TT-86's resident projectile weapons instructor. Ann was so petite she was smaller than her teenaged son. She barely came up to Skeeter's biceps. She was, however, the second or third deadliest person on station, depending on whether Kit Carson had showed up at the range for some shooting practice most recently, or whether Ann had (since Kit's last target practice) hit the gym mats for a series of sweat-building katas and bone-pounding sparring sessions against Sven Bailey, the station's widely known Number One deadliest individual.

Skeeter felt ridiculous, towering over a woman who terrified him down to his cockles. *Uh-oh. What'd I do now?*

Oddly, Ann was smiling up at him, like that famous painting of the Mona Lisa. Like good old Mona, Ann revealed absolutely nothing in dark, knowing eyes. The strange little smile on her lips did not touch them. For a moment, he was actually cold-sweating scared of her, despite at least a foot and several inches' height advantage and a good chance at outsprinting her, even in this crowd.

Then something altered subtly and he realized the smile had just turned friendly. *What does she want? Does she want to hire me to steal something, maybe, or bring her back a special souvenir as a surprise for somebody?* Skeeter not only couldn't understand how Ann's husband could actually *live* with that deadly little viper, he honestly could find no sane reason why Ann would even talk to him.

She looked him up and down, then met his gaze. "Heard you were going through the Porta Romae."

Uh-oh. He answered very carefully, "Uh, yeah, that was sorta the plan. Me and Agnes, you know."

She just nodded, as though confirming the cinching of a wager with someone about what Skeeter Jackson was up to now.

He relaxed. Settling a wager was all right. Ann was certainly entitled to ask him questions if the answers won her a tidy sum in some bet.

But she was still smiling, friendly-like. *The Christmas season, maybe? Manifesting itself in a determined* do unto others *even if it killed her?*

She took the initiative once again. "So, what *were* you grinning about? Misadventures, schemes, and scams down-time?"

"Ann! You wound me!"

She just laughed, eyes and the twist of her mouth clearly skeptical.

"Honestly, I was just taking in all of . . . *that*."

She followed his gaze and her eyes softened. "It is, um, overwhelming, isn't it? Even crazier than *last* year's contest."

Skeeter grinned again. "At least I don't see any three-story, arm-waving Santas to catch fire this year."

She shared his laugh. "No, thank goodness! I thought Bull Morgan was going to fall into a fit of apoplexy when he saw the smoke and flames. Good thing Pest Control's good at putting out fires, too."

"Yeah. They were good, that day. You know," Skeeter said thoughtfully, "I think the holiday season is my very favorite time of year on station. All of that," he waved a hand toward the insanity surrounding them, "cheers a guy up. You know?"

Ann studied him minutely. "So, the holidays cheer you up, do they? Rachel's hands are always full this time of year with half-suicidal people who don't do holidays well. But with you, well, I think I can guess why."

"Yeah?" Skeeter asked with interest, wondering how transparent he'd become since leaving Yesukai's camp.

"Let's see . . . I'm betting—figuratively," she added hastily, "that the holiday season is usually the closest you ever come to getting *rich*. True or false?"

He had to laugh, even while wincing. "Ann, with triple the ordinary number of tourists jamming Commons, how can a guy lose? 'Course I'm happiest this time of year!" He didn't add that the pain of five missed Christmases—holidays that had nothing to do with the expensive bribes his parents piled under the tree each year—were also responsible for his determined merrymaking as he caught up on all the childhood holidays when he'd been alone.

Ann just sighed. "Skeeter, you are an irrepressible scoundrel." She caught his gaze, then, and shocked him speechless. "But you know, I think if you ever got caught and kicked off TT-86, La-La Land would be a lot less fun. You're . . . intriguing, Skeeter Jackson. Like a puzzle, where all the pieces don't quite fit right." With an odd little smile, she said, "Maybe I ought to ask Nally Mundy about it." Skeeter groaned inwardly. Not too many people knew. Skeeter's had been a fleeting, fifteen-second sound-byte's worth of fame, jammed between a triple homicide and a devastating hotel fire on the evening news, years ago. But Nally Mundy knew. Skeeter hadn't quite forgiven him for discovering that juicy little tidbit to hound him about.

Before he could lodge a protest, though, Ann said, "Well, anyway, good hunting—whatever you're up to. See you 'round in a couple of weeks."

She left before he could open his mouth.

And Ann Vinh Mulhaney wishes me good hunting, no less. La-La Land felt like it had turned upside down.

Skeeter glanced up, more than halfway expecting to see crowds of people thronging the Commons' floor, rather than the distant, girdered ceiling.

"Huh," was his only comment.

Skeeter glanced at the gate-departure board suspended from the ceiling and whistled silently. He would have to stretch his legs if he wanted to catch Marcus before he went off-shift at the Down Time Bar and Grill. But he still had several minutes' leeway until he had to catch up with Agnes for the Porta Romae Gate departure.

He picked his way cautiously through a horde of "medieval" damsels, knights in handcrafted chain-mail armor, and throngs of pages and squires, even "authentic" vendors and friars, all headed for Tournament down the newest of TT-86's active gates, the "Anachronism" as 'eighty-sixers called it after the name of the organization that used it most. It led, of all places, to North America prior to the coming of the paleo-Indian population that would eventually cross the Bering Strait and settle two empty continents. Several times a year, hordes—masses—of medieval loons flooded TT-86, every one of them just dying to step through the Anachronism to play at war, medieval style.

Skeeter shook his head. From the realities of war as he'd seen it, Skeeter couldn't find much in wholesale slaughter that *should* be turned into any kind of game. For him, it smacked a little of heresy (whatever that might be) to mock the brave dead they pretended to emulate. Clearly, they got something from it they badly needed, or they wouldn't keep doing it. Especially with the cost so high.

Not only did they have every other tourist's normal expenses, they had to get permission to take their own horses and hunting falcons along, with *stiff* penalties if any of the up-time animals got loose and started a breeding colony millennia before they should have existed. They had to haul fodder and cut-up mice for their animals; then had to find a place to *keep* said animals until Anachronism's departure date, and then, of course, they *all* had to get through the gate in time, balking horses, screeching falcons, their own provisions as well as the animals'—in short, everything required for a one-month, down-time Tournament and the honor to have fought in or attended one.

The single thing he understood about them was their detestation of nosey newsies. It was rumored that *no* newsie had ever gotten through with them. Or if they had, they hadn't survived to tell the tale. North America was a bad place, that long ago. Sabre cats, dire wolves—you name it. Meaning, of course, that Skeeter's intention of stepping through the Anachronism was right up there with his intention of walking up to Mike Benson and holding out his hands to be cuffed.

Skeeter watched with admiration as hawkers of "medieval wares" counted up their sales and tourists pushed to hand over cash for "MAGIC POTIONS!"—crystals mounted as necklaces or stand-alone little trinkets, attuned to the buyer's aura by placing it under the pillow for seven consecutive full moons; charms for wealth, health, harmony, courage, and beauty; exquisite, illuminated calligraphy with even more exquisite prices; plus relatively cheap jewelry that commanded top-rate prices because it was "handmade in the most ancient methods known to our medieval ancestors."

In Skeeter's educated estimation, they were as much con artists as Skeeter himself. They even kept back the good stuff (he knew; he'd pilfered a coveted item or two for his quarters, to liven it up a bit), keeping it hidden to sell *at* the Tournament, bringing along a supply of junk to sell to gullible tourists, to help defray expenses a little. They were con men and women, all right. They just had a different angle on the art than Skeeter did.

Ianira Cassondra—who had occasionally made Skeeter's hair stand on end, just with a simple word or two—called them fakes, charlatans, and even worse, because they had neither the training to dabble in such things, nor the proper attitude for it.

"They will inadvertently hurt people one day. Just wait. Station Management will do nothing about them *now*, but when people start falling down sick with all manner of strange illnesses, their trade *will* be banished." She'd sighed, dark eyes unhappy. "And Management will most likely outlaw *my* booth as well, as I doubt Bull Morgan is capable of telling the difference."

Skeeter had wanted to contradict her, but not only was he half scared she *was* reading the future, in the back of his own mind, Skeeter knew perfectly well that Bull Morgan wouldn't know the difference, and wouldn't care, either, just so long as the crummy tourists were protected.

Skeeter thought dark, vile thoughts about bureaus and the bureauc-rats that ran 'em, and skittered through long lines in Edo Castletown waiting for the official opening of the new Shinto Shrine that was nearly finished. He dashed past Kit Carson's world-famous hotel, past extraordinary gardens with deep streams where colored fish kept to the shadows, trying to avoid becoming a sushi lunch for some *Ichthyornis* or a *Sordes fritcheus* diving down from the ceiling.

Skeeter smiled reminiscently, recalling the moment Sue Fritchey had figured out what their crow-sized "pterosaurs" really were: "My God! They're a new species of *Sordes*! They shouldn't be living at the same time as a *sternbergi* at all. My God, but this is . . . it's revolutionary! A warm-blooded, fur-covered *Sordes*—and a *fish* eater, not an insectivore, but it's definitely a *Sordes*, there's no mistaking that!—and it survived right up until the end of the Cretaceous. All along, we've thought *Sordes* died out right at the end of the Jurassic! What a paper this is going to be!" she'd laughed, eyes shining. "Every paleontological journal uptime is going to be begging me for the right to publish it!"

For Sue Fritchey, *that* was heaven.

Grapevine or not, Skeeter *still* hadn't heard what Sue had decided about the pair of eagle-like, toothed birds that had popped through an unstable gate months ago. But whatever they were, they were going to make Sue Fritchey famous. He wished her luck.

Reaching the edge of Urbs Romae, with its lavishly decorated Saturnalia poles and cut evergreen trees, and paid actors reenacting the one day a year when Roman slaves could give orders to their masters—orders that had to be obeyed and often had the watching audience laughing so hard, both men and women had to wipe their eyes dry just to see the show, Skeeter slowed to a walk, whistling cheerfully to himself and winking at pretty girls who sometimes blushed, yet always followed his departure with their eyes.

Skeeter ducked beneath the sea of paper umbrellas that tourists and residents alike carried—protection against droppings from aforementioned wild prehistoric birds and pterosaurs—and finally hunted out the Down Time Bar and Grill where Marcus worked as a bartender.

The Down Time, tucked away in the Urbs Romae section of Commons, was a favorite haunt of 'eighty-sixers. Among other things, it was a great place to pick up gossip.

And in Skeeter's line of work, gossip usually meant profit.

So he ducked under the girders which half hid the bar's entryway (another reason 'eighty-sixers liked it: the place didn't advertise) and crossed the threshold, already savoring the anticipation of setting his newest scheme into delightful motion.

The first person to see him, however, was none other than Kenneth "Kit" Carson, retired time scout. *Uh-oh . . .* Skeeter gulped and tried on a bright grin, the one he'd learned to use as a weapon of self-defense long, long ago. He'd been avoiding Kit's company for weeks, ever since he'd tried to sweet-talk that penniless, gorgeous little redhead, Margo, into bed with him by pretending to be a scout—only to learn to his terror that she was Kit's only grandkid. Kit's *underage* only grandkid.

What Kit had casually threatened to do to him . . .

"Hi, Skeeter. How they hangin'?" Kit—long and lean and tough as a grizzled bear—grinned up at him and took a slow sip from a cold glass of Kirin.

"Uh . . . fine, Kit. Just fine . . . How's, uh . . . Margo?" He wanted to bite off his tongue and swallow it. *Idiot!*

"Oh, fine. She'll be visiting soon. School vacation."

As one very small predator in a very large pond, Skeeter knew a bigger predator's smile when he saw one. Skeeter took a vow to make himself scarce from *anyplace* Margo decided to visit. "Good, that's real good, Kit. I, uh, was just looking for Marcus."

Kit chuckled. "He's in back, I think."

Skeeter shot past Kit's table, heading for the billiard and pool tables in the back room. Very carefully, he did *not* reach up and wipe sweat from his damp brow. Kit Carson scared him. And not just because the retired time scout had survived more, even, than Skeeter had. Mostly, Skeeter Jackson had a healthy fear of the older male relatives of *any* girl he'd tried to get into bed. Most of them took an extremely dim view of his chosen vocation.

Going one on one with a man who could break major bones as casually as Skeeter could lift a wallet was not Skeeter's idea of fun.

Fortunately, Marcus was exactly where Kit had said he'd be: serving drinks in the back room. Skeeter brightened at once. Running into Kit like that—on the eve of launching his new adventure—was *not* a bad omen, he told himself. Marcus would be Skeeter's good luck charm for this venture. The old, familiar itch between his shoulderblades was never wrong. Skeeter grinned happily.

Look out, suckers. Ready or not, here I come!

Marcus had just set drinks down on a newly occupied table in the back pool room when Skeeter Jackson made a grand entrance and grinned in his direction. Marcus smiled, very nearly laughing aloud. Skeeter was dressed for business, which in this case meant a short, flamboyant tunic, more of a Greek Ionian-style chiton, really, with knobby knees showing naked below the hem and legs that were far more heavily muscled and powerful-looking than most people would have guessed from the whipcord-lean rest of him. Judging by his costume, Skeeter must be working the crowds that always gathered to watch the famous Porta Romae cycle again.

The god Janus—Roman deity of doorways and portals—had for some unknown reason decreed that the Porta Romae would cycle open yet again in less than an hour, moving the gate inexorably along to the next opening two weeks hence. Marcus hid a shiver, remembering his single trip through that portal to arrive here. He had never really believed in Rome's strange gods until his final master had dragged him, terrified and fainting, through the Porta Romae into La-La Land. Now he knew better and so never failed to give the powerful Roman gods their proper libations.

"Marcus! Just the person I'm dying to see." Skeeter's grin was infectious and genuine. Very little else about Skeeter Jackson was, which made him one of the loneliest people Marcus knew.

"Hello, Skeeter. You wish your favorite beer?" Marcus was so uncomfortable with Skeeter's lifestyle he tried hard not to mention it, in the probably vain hope he could save the young up and down-timer from the life he led. Marcus was, in fact, doubtless the only one in the whole of The Found Ones who offered the odd young man his friendship. To be raised in two times, then set adrift in a third . . .

Skeeter Jackson was greatly in need of a friend. So Marcus, busy as he was with demanding work at the bar and an equally demanding—but more fun—job as the father of two little girls, added a third Herculean task to his life: the eventual conversion of Skeeter Jackson from Scoundrel to Honest Man, deserving of the title "Found One."

Skeeter's grin widened. "Sure. I won't turn down a beer, you know that." Both men laughed. "But mostly, I wanted to talk to you. Got a minute?"

Marcus glanced out at the other tables. Most were empty. Nearly everyone was out on Commons, watching the fun as La-La Land's Roman gate prepared to open into the past. Between now and then, a whole series of antics would unfold as tourists and Time Tours guides and baggage handlers tried to get through the portal with all their baggage, money purses, and assorted children still intact, waiting impatiently while much of the previous tour exited the Porta

Romae in staggering, white-faced clumps. The rest coming back through were fine, swaggering down the ramp like aloof, supremely self-confident Roman senators.

Marcus shook off his mental astonishment that *every* tour came back like this, some pleased as kittens with a bowl of cream and others . . . Well, the drawings circulating amongst The Found Ones said it all, didn't they?

Marcus smiled at Skeeter, who waited hopefully.

"Of course. Let me get the beer for you, please."

"Get one for yourself, too. I'm buying."

Oh-oh. Marcus hid a grin. Skeeter wanted something. He was a thoroughgoing scoundrel, was Skeeter Jackson, but Marcus understood why, something most 'eighty-sixers didn't. Not even most of The Found Ones knew. Marcus hadn't even told Ianira, although with his beautiful Ianira, what she did or did not know was always a complete mystery to Marcus.

Skeeter had been so drunk that night, he probably didn't remember everything he'd said. But Marcus did. So he kept trying, hope against hope, to befriend Skeeter Jackson, asking the gods who had watched over his own life to help his friend finally figure it all out—and do something about it besides swindle, cheat, and steal his way toward the grave.

Marcus set down Skeeter's beer first, then took a chair opposite and seated himself, waiting as was appropriate for Skeeter to drink first. Skeeter had always been a free man, born into a good family, raised by another good man. Even with the eventual understanding Marcus had reached that *no one* here could call him slave, Skeeter was still Marcus' social superior in every way Marcus had ever heard of.

"Oh, I'm gonna miss that," Skeeter said after a long pull. "Now . . . You were born in Rome, right?"

"Well, no, actually, I was not."

Skeeter blinked. "You weren't?"

"No. I was born in Gallia Comata, in a very small village called Cautes." He couldn't help the pride that touched his voice. A thousand years and his little village was still there—changed a great deal, but still standing beneath the high, sharp mountains of his childhood, beautiful as ever under their mantles of snow and cloud. The same wild, rushing stream still cut through the heart of the village, just as it always had, clear and cold enough to shock a grunt from even the stoutest man.

"Cautes? Where the hell is that?"

Marcus grinned. "I once asked Brian Hendrickson, in the library, about my village. It is still there, but the name is different, just a little. Gallia Comata no longer exists at all. My village, called now Cauterets, is in the place you would know as France, but it is still famous for the sacred warm springs that cure women who cannot bear children."

Skeeter started to grin, then didn't. "You're serious."

"Yes, why would I not be? I cannot help that I was born in conquered territory and—"

"About the women, I mean?" Skeeter's expression was priceless; another scheme was taking shape visibly on his unguarded face.

Marcus laughed. "I do not know, Skeeter. I was only a child when I was taken away, so I cannot be sure, but all the villagers said it. Roman women came there from all of Gaul to bathe in the waters, so they could bear a child."

Skeeter chuckled in turn, his thoughts still visible in his eyes. "They'd have done better to sleep with their husbands—or somebody's husband, anyway—a little more often."

"Or drink less lead," Marcus added, proud of what he had learned in his few years in La-La Land. Rachel Eisenstein, the head physician in the time terminal, had told Marcus that the levels of dissolved lead in his own blood *were* dropping, which was the only reason he'd been able to father little Artemisia and Gelasia.

"Touché." Skeeter lifted his glass and drained half the brew. "Aren't you going to drink any of that beer?"

Marcus carefully poured a libation to the gods—just a few drops spilled onto the wooden floor—then tasted his own beer. He'd be scrubbing the floor later, anyway, so a little worship wouldn't anger his employers. They groused more about the free drinks Marcus sometimes gave away to those in need than they did about a little spillage.

"Okay," Skeeter took another swig, "you were born in France, but lived in Rome most of your life, right?"

"Yes. I was sold as a young boy to a slave trader coming down the Roman highway from Aqua Tarbellicae." Marcus shivered. "The first thing he did was change my name. He said mine was not pronounceable."

Skeeter blinked. "Marcus isn't your real name?"

He tried to smile. "It has been for more than eighteen years. And you probably could not pronounce my own name any more than the Romans could. I have grown accustomed to 'Marcus' and so I am content to keep it."

Skeeter was staring at him as though he couldn't believe what he was hearing. Marcus shrugged. "I have tried to explain, Skeeter. But no one here understands."

"No, I, uh, guess not." He cleared his throat, the expression in his eyes making Marcus wonder what *Skeeter* remembered. "Anyway, you were saying about Rome . . ."

"Yes. I was taken to the city of Narbo on the coast of the Mediterranean Sea, where I was put on a slave ship, sent to Rome, and kept in an iron cage until the time came for me to be auctioned on the block." Marcus gulped beer hastily to hide the tremors in his hands. Those particular memories were among the ones that woke him up nights, shaking inside a layer of cold sweat. "I lived in Rome from the time I was eight years of age."

Skeeter leaned forward. "Great. See, Agnes got me a free ticket through Porta Romae, she's guiding on the tour this trip, and it's going to be a pretty quiet two weeks. Only one day of public games, on the very last day. That's why she could get me through as a guest."

Marcus shook his head. Poor Agnes. She hadn't been in La-La Land very long. "You are shameful, Skeeter. Agnes is a nice girl."

"Sure is. I never could afford a ticket to Rome on my own. So anyway, I got this great idea, see, but I've never been there, so I thought maybe you could help me out?"

Marcus fiddled with his beer glass. "What is the idea?" He was always cautious not to commit himself to any of Skeeter's perpetually shady schemes.

"It's perfect," Skeeter enthused, eyes sparkling with glee. "I wanted to do a little betting—"

"*Betting?* On the games?" If that were all Skeeter wanted, he saw no harm in it. It was strictly illegal, of course; but Marcus didn't know of a single tourist who hadn't tried it. And it was so much less worse than what it might have been, that Marcus felt a kind of giddy relief. Maybe Agnes was a good influence on Skeeter. "Very well, what did you want to ask me?"

Skeeter's grin revealed relief and triumph. "Where do I go? To make the bets, I mean?"

Marcus chuckled. "The Circus Maximus, of course."

"Yeah, but *where?* The damned thing's a *mile long*!"

Ahh . . .

"Well . . . The best place is on the Aventine side of the Circus, near the spot where the gladiators enter the arena. They come in through the starting boxes, of course, at the square end of the Circus, closest to the Tiber River. But the public entrances closest to there are very popular betting sites, as well. There are the professional gambling stalls, of course," Marcus mused, "but I would stay away from them. Most will find an excuse to cheat a colonial blind. Of course, much of the betting takes place in the stands themselves, while the bouts are underway." He wondered what Skeeter's reaction would be to watching men butcher one another. Many tourists came back physically ill.

"That's great, Marcus! Thanks! If I win, I'll cut you in on the deal."

If Skeeter Jackson remembered that generous offer two weeks from now—and followed through on it—Marcus mused, he would have done more for Marcus than he could possibly know. Ever-present worry over finances swiftly captured Marcus' attention and swept his thoughts far away from the table where his friend was drinking his beer. Ianira, despite his protests and pride, had insisted on contributing to his "debt-free" fund a sizeable chunk of her earnings—made by giving historians whatever information she could for the "primary research source" fees. Ianira also sold genuine ancient Greek recipes for all manner of cheesecakes—though she had paid for learning to make every single variety under the whip (and more) in her first husband's house down-time.

The cheesecakes' delightful flavors and characteristics, Marcus now knew, had once been discussed in the Athenian Agora as seriously as any philosophy by the most important men in Athens. Their recipes had been lost for centuries, but Ianira, hurting still from her husband's brutality, knew them all by heart, had memorized them in a terror to survive. Now, with amusement healing old scars, she sold the recipes one by one to Arley Eisenstein, who gave her a percentage of his profits—substantial, given the cheesecakes' stunning success.

Ianira made money faster than Marcus had ever believed possible, particularly after she became the proud owner of a free-standing stall that catered to the strange and increasingly bizarre "acolytes" who sought her out as though on pilgrimage. Some of them had paid the price of the Primary Gate just to look at her, praying she would say something to them. Some even gave her money, as though she were the most revered being in the world and their money was the only offering they could give.

Ah, money. When Marcus had tried to refuse her money, out of pride and dignity, she'd caught his hand and forced him to look at her. "You are my chosen, my beloved!" Dark eyes held his, burdened with so much he wanted to erase forever. Neither money nor Marcus could erase the past: brutal marriage or, worst of all, Ianira's terrifying, heavy, close-held secret knowledge of the rituals (both public and carefully hidden private), of the many-breasted Artemis of Ephesus, where she had grown to maidenhood in the world-famous temple. At that moment, those bottomless eyes flashed with what must have been the same look that had prompted the rash Trojan prince Paris to risk everything to flee to the windy plains of Troy with the much-sought-after Helen as his mistress.

Even in memory, Marcus' head spun hopelessly under the onslaught of that look. He had, of course, melted utterly at the winning smile that followed, not to mention the touch of her hands. "I am desperately selfish of you, Marcus. I do not understand this 'honor' of yours, so stubborn to pay off an illegal debt; but if this money will help fulfill that demand inside you, then I will be sure never to allow you to deny my help." In a rare gesture of emotion, she clutched him tight as if afraid to let go. Her uptilted face revealed a sea of tears bravely held brimming on her eyelashes. Still holding him, she said in roughened voice, "Please. I know you are proud and I love you for it. But if I lose you . . ."

He had crushed her close, trying with everything in him to promise that he was hers forever, not just the way things were now, with no formal words spoken, but the correct way, the way of formally taking her as his public wife—just as soon as he could rid himself of hated debt to the man who had brought him here and set him the task of learning—and keeping secret records of—which men travelled the gates to Rome and Athens and what they brought back.

He didn't understand his one-time master's orders, any more than he understood how beautiful, highborn Ianira could love a man who had been a slave nearly all his life. So he simply kept the records, considering it a challenging puzzle to be solved, a clue to what made his former master's brain work while slowly gathering the money to pay his slave debt. He took Ianira's money, little as he wanted to, because he was desperate to get out from under such debt, to gain at least a little of the status that would put him on something approaching her own level.

Marcus' bittersweet thoughts were rudely interrupted by the unmistakable voice of Goldie Morran. Instant irritation made his skin shudder, like a horse's when big, biting flies descended to slake their thirst. Marcus sometimes wondered, looking at Goldie Morran, if she had been called Goldie for the shining, golden hair Roman women had once so coveted they'd had wigs made from the tresses of their slaves (impossible to tell now—Goldie's hair was, at present, a peculiar shade of Imperial Purple, leaving little clue as to its original color), or because she was an avaricious old gargoyle who wanted nothing in the world more than cold, hard cash—preferably in the form of gold—coinage, dust, nugget, whatever she could get her claws on.

Harpy-eyes glanced his way. "Marcus, get me a beer."

Then she sank down into one of the chairs beside Skeeter, inviting herself into their private conversation. As Marcus poured beer from the tap, seething and manfully holding it back—Goldie Morran was a regular customer—she glanced at Skeeter. "Hear you're going down time. Isn't that new, even for you?"

Marcus set the beer in front of Goldie. She took a long, slow pull while waiting for Skeeter's usual outburst.

Skeeter surprised them both.

"Yes, I'm going to Rome. I'm taking a slow two-week vacation so I can get better acquainted with Agnes Fairchild. She and I have become rather close over the last week or so and, besides, she has the right to take a guest with her on slow tours." He spread his hands. "Who am I to turn down a free trip to ancient Rome?"

"And what," Goldie glanced up coyly, the neon lights in the bar doing strange things to her sallow face and genuinely purple-silver hair, "exactly is it you intend to steal?"

Skeeter laughed easily. "I'm a scoundrel and you know it, but I'm not planning to steal anything, except perhaps Agnes' heart. I might have tried for yours, Goldie, if I thought you had one."

Goldie made an outrageous sound, glaring at him, clearly at a loss for words—perhaps a Down Time Bar and Grill first. Then, turning her back to him, Goldie gulped down the remains of her beer and slammed down a scattering of coins to pay for it. They jounced, slid, and rolled in circles; one even fell to the hardwood floor with a musical ringing sound.

Silver, a part of Marcus' mind said, having become intimately acquainted with Roman coinage and its forgeries.

Goldie, leaning over Skeeter's chair very much like a harpy sent by the gods to punish evildoers, said, "You will live to regret that, Skeeter Jackson." The chill of a glacier filled her voice. And underlying the frozen syllables, Marcus heard plainly a malice thick as unwatered Roman wine. It hung on the air between them for just an instant. Then she whirled and left, flinging over her shoulder, "Why you choose to become friends with uneducated, half-wild down-timers who can scarce bathe themselves properly is beyond me. It will be your ruin."

Then she was gone.

Marcus discovered he was shaking with rage. His dislike of Goldie Morran and her sharp tongue and prejudices had just changed in a way that frightened him. Dislike had flared like a fire in high wind, smoldering from a half-burnt lump of coal to a roaring conflagration consuming his soul—and everything foolish enough to come too close.

Marcus was proud of his recently acquired education, which included several languages, new and wonderful sciences that seemed like the magical incantations that made the world run its wandering course through the stars—rather than the stars wandering their courses around it—even mathematics explained clearly enough that he had been able to learn the new ways of counting, multiplying, dividing, learning the basics of multicolumn bookkeeping along with the new tools—all of it adding up to something no scribe or mathematician in all of Ancient Rome could do.

Perhaps a boy from Gallia Comata could be considered half-wild, but even as a chained, terrified boy of eight, he had known perfectly well how to bathe—and had amused his captors by requesting a basin each night to wash the dirt and stinking fear sweat off his skin.

He actually jumped when Skeeter spoke.

"Vicious old harpy," Skeeter said mildly, his demeanor as perfectly calm as his person was neat and eternally well groomed. "She'll do anything to throw her competition off form." He chuckled. "You know Marcus—here, sit down again—I would dearly love to see someone scam *her*."

Marcus sat down and managed to hold his sudden laughter to a mere grin, although he could not keep it from bubbling in his eyes. "That would be something to witness. It's interesting, you know, watching the two of you circle, probe defenses, finally sending darts through chinks in one another's armor."

Skeeter just stared at him.

Marcus added, "You both are strong-willed, Skeeter, and generally get exactly what you want from life. But I will tell you something important." In this one particular case, at least, Ianira was not the only "seer" in his family. The story was there, plain to witness for anyone who simply bothered to look, and knowing people as he did, the future was not difficult to predict. He finished his beer in one long swallow, aware that Skeeter's gaze had never left his face.

"Goldie," Marcus said softly, "has declared war upon you, Skeeter, whether you welcome it or no. She reminds me of the Mediterranean sharks that followed the slave ship, feeding off those who died. No . . . the sharks did only what they were made to do. *Goldie* is so far gone in the enjoyment of her evil deeds, there is no hope of salvaging anything good from her."

He returned Skeeter's unblinking gaze for several moments. Then his friend spoke, almost as coldly as Goldie had. "Meaning you think *me* worth salvaging. Is that it, *friend*?"

Marcus went ice cold all through. "You are a good man, Skeeter," he said earnestly, leaning forward to try and make his friend understand. "Your heart is as generous as your laughter. It is merely my hope that you might mend your morals to match. You are a dear friend to me. I do not enjoy seeing you suffer."

Skeeter blinked. "Suffer?" He began to laugh. "Marcus, you are truly the wonder of the ages." His grin melted a little of the icy fear in Marcus' heart. "Okay, I'll promise I'll try to be a good little tourist in Rome, all right? I still want to do that betting, but nothing more devious than that. Satisfied?"

Marcus sagged a little in his chair. "Yes, Skeeter. I am." Feeling more hopeful than he had in months, he was forced to apologize for having to abandon his friend so soon after coming to a somewhat uneasy understanding of one another's intentions in this odd friendship. "I am most sorry, my friend, but I must return to work, before the manager returns from watching the Porta Romae cycle, and I have not yet finished all the chores he set me to do. Go with the gods when you step through Porta Romae, Skeeter. Thank you for the beer. And the company."

Skeeter's grin lit up his face again. "Sure. Thank *you*. See you in a couple of weeks, then."

Marcus smiled, then busied himself cleaning vacated tables and wiping down the bar. Skeeter Jackson strolled out like a man about to own the world.

Chapter 2

Agnes Fairchild was a nice girl. Not too pretty, but sweet and generous. And great in bed. By Skeeter's standards, the shy, academic types were often the most fun: overcoming their inhibitions and showing them a thing or two about mad, wet sex was as good as getting a stunning "10" into bed. He often regretted the fact that his lovers never stayed with him long, but, hey, there were new women coming through La-La Land all the time. And after Skeeter's childhood experiences, he was *not* choosy about looks. Willingness and sincerity were what counted. A knockout in your *own* bed was great. But a bombshell in somebody else's bed was no fun at all.

So when Agnes Fairchild walked into Skeeter's life, he was more than pleased. And when she opened up the chance to do some scheming *outside* the time terminal, he showered her with every charm at his command. She even taught him enough Latin to get by in case they were separated—which he wouldn't—and did not—allow to happen—not until the day of the games. Agnes was good at her job, too. Skeeter enjoyed tagging along with her tour group almost as much as he enjoyed a passionate lover willing to share intimacy during sultry Roman nights. The ancient city come to life was like a Hollywood movie set to Skeeter—but a movie set full of real people with real money he could pry loose from real hands that wouldn't miss a few pilfered coins, because they were all dead already.

Of course, he didn't tell Agnes that. He just enjoyed her company and sights like Augustus' giant sundial and the huge Emporium of market stalls that backed the wharves and warehouses of the Porticus Aemelia—where he picked up a bit of profit with light-fingered skill—and bided his time while charming everyone from the richest billionaire in the group—whose money pouch Skeeter coveted—to the smallest, wide-eyed little girl who called him "Unk Skeeter." He even liked tickling and teasing her when she tickled and teased him. She was cute. Skeeter had discovered to his surprise that he liked kids. There'd been a time when the sight of another child—particularly boys—had made his blood run cold.

Long time ago, Skeeter. Long, long time ago. You're not everybody's bogda *any more. You're not* anybody's bogda *anymore.* And that was the best part of all. As long as he kept up the con games, the swindles, and the mastery of skills that a bitter deadly childhood had taught him, Skeeter Jackson would never again be anybody's isolated, lonely, private tribal spirit-in-the-flesh. This had been a position that, much of the time, had amounted to that of victim, unable to retaliate when teased, taunted, or hooted at in careful privacy by the other boys, because it was unseemly behavior for a *bogda* to roughhouse, no matter what the provocation. So he'd developed the knack of endurance and remained a victim because that was the only thing he *could* do, other than steal the belongings of certain tormentors and plant them in the yurts of other tormentors. He'd grown skilled at the game and enjoyed the results with bitter, malicious glee.

And all of that was something few people understood, or ever could understand, because Skeeter would sooner die than admit *any* of it to those who hadn't already figured it out for themselves.

He wondered, sometimes, if his friend Marcus carried memories as frightening as his own? After two weeks in Rome, he was convinced of it. After witnessing what went on casually on the streets, he deliberately asked Agnes to take him to see the slave markets. What he found there . . . well, if Skeeter had harbored any shred of scruple, it was erased by the sights and sounds of that place.

Anything he stole from *any* rich Roman bastard was money the wretch deserved to lose. The more, the better. For a moment, Marcus' words about him and his standing with Goldie Morran made sense.

There were levels and *levels* of depravity. Compared to these pros, Skeeter was a saint. He watched through narrowed eyes endless parades of rich, arrogant Roman men carried through the streets in fancy sedan chairs and recalled the bitter cold winds which swept endlessly across the steppes where he'd grown to teenhood.

He recalled, too, the glint of winter sunlight on sharp steel and the myriad ways of killing a man the people who'd raised him had taught their sons. And as he remembered, Skeeter watched wealthy Romans abuse helpless people and bitterly wished he could introduce the two groups for an intimate little get-together: Roman to Yakka Mongol, steel to steel.

Because that would never happen in Skeeter's sight, he elected himself the Yakka Clan's sole emissary in this city of marble and misery and money. He could hardly wait to start depriving them of *serious* amounts of gold earned on blood, not just a purse here and there just begging to be lifted by nimble fingers. His long-awaited chance finally came the morning of their last day in Rome. The entire tour group left the inn near dawn.

"Form up in your groups," Agnes called, echoed by other Time Tours guides and even a freelancer or two hired for guiding their employers safely to places not on the main tour, then safely back again. Since Skeeter was closest to Agnes, it was her voice he paid most attention to as they formed up in the silvery, pearl-hued morning. "We'll be taking seats together in the upper tier, which is reserved for slaves and foreigners. Be sure you have the proper coinage with you to purchase admission tickets and don't forget to collect a colored handkerchief to cheer on your favorite racing team. The gladiatorial games will begin after midday, once the racing is completed . . ."

Skeeter wasn't really listening. He was planning his scheme and trying to recall Marcus' instructions. He had a pouch half full of copper coins, mostly *unciae*, or one-twelfth of an *as*, the *as* being a pound of copper divided into twelve "ounces" (the first coins Romans had minted, according to Agnes). They were mixed with a few silver *denarii* and *sestercii*, plus a few gold *aurii* on top just to make it look good. Agnes had loaned him the silver and gold coins so he could—as he'd explained it—impress local merchants that he really did have money. That way, they'd be less likely to gyp him. "Agnes, I don't want them to think I'm some provincial rube not worth wasting their time on."

And like the sweet girl she was, she'd believed every word.

He wondered how long she'd be able to stomach watching what Romans did to non-Romans. Two weeks was more than enough for him, even *without* watching the games, and he'd spent five years in the yurts of the Yakka Clan.

"Skeeter?"

He glanced up and found Agnes smiling at him. "Yeah?"

"Ready?"

"Am I ever!"

Her smile was so enchanting, he kissed her, earning hoots and whistles from half the crowd. She blushed to the roots of her mouse-brown hair.

"All right, people, let's go!"

Skeeter followed eagerly as Agnes led the first group away from the inn Time Tours owned on the Aventine Hill and ushered her charges into the narrow, winding streets of an already-crowded, noisy Rome. *Games day*, Skeeter identified the electric difference from the tours' previous mornings. Skeeter hung back, letting Agnes gain distance. Tourists eager for their first—and for many of them, only—look at genuine Roman games surged ahead. Skeeter grinned, then slipped quietly away from the group and headed for the Circus Maximus by the route Marcus had given him two weeks previously.

He knew the entrance he wanted was near the starting gates of the mile-long structure. Shops selling food, wine, commemorative mugs with scenes of chariot racing molded into them, even shops selling baskets and seat cushions did brisk business despite the early hour. The morning air was clear and golden as dawn brightened the hot, Latin sky. The scents of frying peas and sausages mingled with the smell of wine, the stink of caged animals, and the sweat of several thousand men and women pushing their way toward the entrances. A few betting stalls did even brisker business, a sight that made Skeeter all but salivate.

Yesukai, your wandering bogda *has done found hisself in paradise!*

The streets were confusing, though, and so were the entrances. There were more archways into the great Circus than he'd expected. And crowds jammed each one. Which entrance, exactly, had Marcus meant? He walked all the way to the squared-off end of the Circus, down by the stinking Tiber, which flowed past the starting gates just beyond a couple of little temples he recognized from photos. The scream of caged cats and the bleating of zebras assaulted Skeeter's ears. Down here, too, were men stripped to the waist, hauling the great cages into place from barges tied up at the river. Teams of high-strung racing horses fought their handlers, while collared slaves rolled tiny, tea-cup chariots of wicker and wood into place for the first races. Men and boys who must be charioteers, given the colors of their tunics, stood around in groups, looking deadly earnest as they discussed what must have been last-minute strategy.

Well, Skeeter decided, *I'll just pick the nearest entrance to all this and hope for the best. This* ought *to be just about where Marcus meant.*

He found a likely looking spot and prepared to launch his scheme. Although Agnes had taught him some "survival phrases" he hadn't known, Skeeter had begun work several weeks previously. Through that pilfered library account, he'd learned as many Latin phrases as he could, aware he'd need them for his patter, as well as understanding the likeliest responses he'd get back from potential customers. And if he didn't understand something, Skeeter had carefully learned, "Please, I'm just a poor foreigner. Your Latin is too complicated. Would you say it more simply?" He'd even researched what kind of markers to give out to those who placed bets. No need to learn how to make payouts . . .

Since the gladiatorial fights wouldn't take place until afternoon, Skeeter had a simple plan—collect a ransom in betting money, then simply vanish while the races were on. He'd hightail it back to the inn, apologize to Agnes later this afternoon by claiming he hadn't been feeling well, then tonight when Porta Romae cycled, he'd step back into La-La Land a rich man. And an *untouchable* rich man, so long as he didn't try to step up time with any of his winnings.

Rubbing metaphorical hands, Skeeter Jackson looked over the crowd, reined in an impish grin of anticipation, took a deep breath . . . and shouted, "Bets, place your bets, gladiatorial combats only, best odds in town. . . ."

Within half an hour, Skeeter had begun to wonder if his scheme were going to pan out, after all. Most of the people who approached him declined to wager at all. Those who did were mostly poor people who wagered a copper *as*, or more likely, one of the cheaper copper coins based on a fraction of an *as. Great. Must've picked the wrong damned entrance.* He was just about to try a different arched entryway when a lean, grizzled man in his early forties, sporting a short-trimmed head of reddish-blond hair, sauntered over, trailed by a collared slave.

"Bets, eh?" the man said, eying Skeeter appraisingly. "On the combats?"

"Yes, sir," Skeeter grinned, trying to hide the sudden pounding of his pulse. Judging by the gold the man wore and the embroidery on his tunic, this guy was *rich*.

"Tell me, what odds do you place on the bout with Lupus Mortiferus?"

"To win or lose?"

A flicker of irritation ran through dark amber, lupine eyes. "To win, of course."

Skeeter didn't know a damned thing about Lupus Mortiferus or his track record. He'd simply been quoting made-up odds all morning. He smiled and said cheerfully, "Three to one."

The lean man's eyes widened. "Three to one?" Startlement gave way to sudden, intense interest. "Well, now. Those are interesting odds, indeed. You're a stranger, I think, by your accent."

Skeeter shrugged. "If I am?"

His mark grinned. "I'll place a bet with you, stranger. How about fifty *aurii*? Can your purse handle that big a bite?"

Skeeter was stunned. Fifty gold *aurii*? That was . . . that was five thousand silver *sestercii*! When he thought of the money he'd get exchanging fifty gold *aurii* at Goldie Morran's shop back in Shangri-la Station . . .

"Of course, friend! Of course. I may be a foreigner, but I am not without resources. You just surprised me." Skeeter prepared the marker.

"Stellio," the grizzled Roman addressed his slave, "fetch fifty *aurii* from my money box." The man produced a key from a pouch at his waist and handed it over.

The slave dashed into the crowd.

"I have pressing business elsewhere," the Roman said with a smile, tucking the marker into his pouch, "but I assure you my slave is trustworthy. He was a complete knave when I bought him, which is why he bears that name, but sufficient correction can cure any man's bad habits." The Roman laughed. "A slave without a tongue is much more docile. Not to mention silent. Don't you agree?"

Skeeter nodded, but felt a little sick. Once, as a boy, he'd seen a man's tongue cut out . . .

The Roman strolled off into the crowd. Clearly, Skeeter had quoted the wrong odds on Lupus whatever. But on the bright side, he wouldn't be around when this guy came to collect his hundred-fifty *aurii*. Skeeter repressed a shiver. Just as well. He wondered with a pang of genuine pity what that poor slave had done to merit having his tongue cut out.

No wonder Marcus didn't want to come back here. Ever.

Skeeter continued taking bets, filling his money pouch and giving out markers while waiting for Stellio to return. Shrill notes from Roman trumpets, sounding the beginning of the opening parade, floated on the clear morning air. A roar went up from the crowd. Skeeter took a few last bets, then spotted Stellio running toward him. The man was panting, mouth hanging open with exertion from his run. Skeeter swallowed hard. He *didn't* have a tongue.

"Nrggahh," the poor man said, shoving the pouch into Skeeter's hands.

He ran off again before Skeeter could say a word in response. Feeling a little queasy still, Skeeter opened the pouch and tipped shining gold into his hand. The slave hadn't cheated him. Fifty gold *aurii* . . . They glittered in the sunlight, striking glints like lightning against the dark Gobi sky. Skeeter grinned as he counted them back into the pouch, then tightened the drawstring and secured it to his waist. *Just wait until Goldie sees* these!

A few stragglers placed bets, mostly with copper coins ranging from full *asses* through the whole spectrum of its fractions: the *sextans*, the *quadrans* and *triens*, a *quincunx*, several *semis* coins, the cheaper *septunx*, the *bes*, and *dodrans*, one *dextans* and *deunx* each, and of course, the inevitable and popular *uncia*. He even got a couple more silver *sestercii*—then the trumpets signalling the start of the first chariot race sang out.

Time to leave.

He decided to buy a little wine to cool his throat and used some of his takings to purchase it from a nearby shop nestled under the stands, one of several hundred other little stalls, from the look of it. He noticed some shrimp set delicately on grape leaves and decided to try some. *Mmm! The Romans know how to cook a shrimp!* That finished, Skeeter noticed some cheesecakes along the back shelf. Several were molded into the shape of a woman's breast.

He asked and was told, "Almond cheesecake. Whole is all I sell."

Well, that one in the corner looked pretty small. He gestured toward it and the proprietor duly placed it in front of him, then collected the coins Skeeter produced from his "winnings." One bite and he knew that, good as this was, Ianira Cassondra's were so much superior it was like comparing caviar to potted meat. As he munched contentedly, a roar went up inside the stadium. "First race, huh?" Skeeter asked conversationally, proud of his acquired Latin.

The man looked startled. "Race? You hadn't heard? The Emperor requested a special opening to the day's games."

Paying only half attention, Skeeter said, "Really?" He was hungrier than he'd thought and this cheesecake wasn't bad. He washed down with the last of his wine.

"Yes," the shopkeeper told him, considerable surprise running through dark eyes. "A special exhibition bout by the Emperor's favorite gladiator."

"*What?*" He nearly strangled on cheesecake and wine.

"Yes. Bout to first blood in honor of Lupus Mortiferus' hundredth appearance in the arena." The man chuckled. "What a champion.

Haven't been better'n one to four odds on him since his eightieth victory. Bout ought to be finished any minute—"

Skeeter didn't wait to hear more. He didn't *have* a hundred-fifty *aurii* to pay off that idiotic bet. *Damn, damn, damn!* He shot out of the shop, leaving the half-eaten cheesecake behind. He headed down the long facade of the Circus, toward town. The Tiber ran its merry way somewhere behind him. He kept his pace at a fast walk, not wanting to draw attention to himself by running. As much money as he was carrying, someone might mistake him for a thief.

Okay, Skeeter, just stay calm. You've been in worse spots. He's not going to come collecting that money right away, even if the bout is going on right now. Just get back to the Time Tours inn and hide out until the gate cycles and you'll be just fine. You've gotten through worse. Lots worse.

Another roar broke from the high tiers of seats. Skeeter winced. Then silence fell over the great arena. Skeeter wanted to break into a run, but held himself to a brisk walk, like some businessman intent on important business.

Then, the sound of nightmare: "Hey! Hey, odds maker!"

He glanced around—and *felt* his cheeks go cold.

It was the lean, grizzled Roman who'd placed the bet, about a hundred yards behind him. Even from here, Skeeter could see the blood spattered on his clothes and arms.

Oh, man, I gotta bad feeling that IS *Lupus Mortiferus.*

Skeeter did the only logical, honorable thing he could.

He ran like hell.

"Stop! Stop, you—"

The rest of it was Latin Skeeter hadn't learned yet.

He ducked around the first corner he came to and picked up speed. The money pouches at his belt swung and bruised his thighs with every stride. The streets near the Circus were a maze of narrow alleys and crooked, twisting passageways. Skeeter dodged and ran with everything in him, convinced he could outrun the heavier Roman with ease. Given his skill at vanishing in the places he'd lived as a child, losing himself in Rome ought to be a piece of cake.

But his pursuer was faster than he looked.

Skeeter glanced back and bit back a yelp of terror. The man was still with him—and gaining. Thunderstorms rolling across the vast plains of Outer Mongolia had looked friendlier than that Roman's face. And he had a *long* knife in his hand. A *really* long one.

Skeeter skidded around another corner, crashed through a group of women who shrieked curses at him, and kept going. *Can't just go to the inn. He'd track me there and carve me up into little bits of Skeeter. Where, then?* Clearly, he hadn't studied the layout of the city adequately. Skeeter cut around another corner, dashed down a long straight-way, zipped around another corner—

And yelled, even as he tried to stop.

The street ended abruptly in a drop-off straight into the Tiber. Momentum carried him over the edge. Skeeter sucked in air, knowing the gold would weigh him down. Then he splashed feet-first into the muddy river and sank toward the bottom. Skeeter swam frantically for the surface, holding his breath and kicking with every bit of strength he had left. His face broke water. He gulped air into burning lungs.

Something hard grazed his shoulder. Skeeter yelled, went under, strangled . . . then caught at something that splashed down right in front of him. He was lifted completely out of the water. For an instant, he was face-to-face with an astonished slave rowing a large boat. The man was so shocked, he dropped the oar. Skeeter plunged like a rock back into the river. A tremendous backwash sent water into his sinuses. But he hung onto the oar and managed to drag his head above water again. He blinked river water and hair out of his eyes, coughing weakly and drawing in shuddering lungfuls of air that only set him coughing harder.

The boat above him was a shallow-draft thing that looked like a pleasure yacht of some sort. Rowers all along the side leaned over to stare at him. Several oars fouled badly, cracking into one another like gunshots. The whole yacht slewed in the water.

Great. Talk about not attracting attention.

A glance over one shoulder revealed Lupus Mortiferus on the bank, shaking his fist and cursing inaudibly. *Just get me out of this one, God, and I swear I'll never come back to Rome again. I'll stick to obnoxious tourists and government bureaucrats and other deserving UP-timers.* Skeeter clung to the oar, pulled along by the yacht's momentum for a couple of moments, allowing him to regain his breath; then an overseer stalked to the gunwales to see what was fouling the oars.

"What the—"

Skeeter lost most of the curse in translation, but the general gist seemed to be, "Get the hell off my oar!"

Skeeter was about to marshall a sob story to convince the guy to let him climb aboard when the s.o.b. snaked out a whip that caught Skeeter right across the hands. Pain blossomed like acid. He yelled and let go involuntarily—and plunged back into the river. Skeeter snorted a noseful of water before he managed to kick his way back to the surface.

Gotta get to shore . . . before I . . . wear out and drown. That gold was *heavy*. But the few minutes' rest clinging to the oar had helped. Skeeter struck out for the nearest bank, which thankfully was opposite the Circus and the wrathful Lupus Mortiferus. By the time he reached the riverbank and crawled out, sodden tunic clinging to his thighs and back, Skeeter was shaking with exhaustion. But he still had the gold. And he was still alive.

He'd just begun to celebrate those two facts with a shaky grin when a terrifying, familiar voice shouted, "There! He's there!"

Lupus Mortiferus had crossed a bridge Skeeter hadn't even noticed.

And he had friends with him.

Big, mean, ugly-looking ones.

Skeeter swore shakily under his breath and shoved himself to his feet. *Can't possibly outrun 'em.* Hell, he could scarcely stand up. Out-talk 'em? Convince 'em the whole scam had been a simple miscommunication? In English, he could probably have pulled it off. But not in Latin. The language handicap made that impossible. Wondering what Romans *did* with confidence men they caught—a roar of voices from the Circus gave him a clue—Skeeter looked wildly around for some way out of this.

What he saw was a group of horse handlers loading racing teams onto a barge for the trip across to the Circus. The horses were between him and the group of enraged gladiators. Skeeter didn't have many skills, but as a result of living in a yurt of the Yakka Clan, one thing he *had* learned to do was *ride*. If it had four legs and hooves, Skeeter could ride it.

So he ran straight *toward* the men hunting him and caught a glimpse of shocked amazement on Lupus Mortiferus' face. Then he said to a surprised animal handler, "Excuse me, but I need that," and snatched the bridle of the nearest racehorse still on shore. He was on the animal's back in a flash. The startled horse reared and screamed, but Skeeter had stayed with horses more ornery than this. He slammed heels into the animal's flanks and brought its head and forelegs down with a savage jerk on the reins. The horse got the message: *This ain't no novice rider on my back.*

Skeeter hauled the horse's head around and kicked the animal into a fast gallop. The racing handlers yelled and cursed him, but he put distance between himself and *all* his pursuers in nothing short of miraculous time. This horse could *run*.

Skeeter laughed in sheer delight and leaned low over the animal's neck. The whipping mane caught his face with a wiry sting. The muscles bunching under his thighs rippled in perfect rhythm. He missed the iron Mongol stirrups, shaped like the tips of Dutch wooden shoes, to which he'd grown accustomed, but he hadn't lost his sense of balance—and he'd learned to ride bareback, just to prove to Yesukai that he could, and hopefully to be permitted the chance at learning to ride proper ponies with proper saddles. Pedestrians scattered out of his way with curses and screams. He laughed again at the horse's astonishing speed. "Must've liberated me a champion!"

It was several years overdue, but Skeeter had finally completed his manhood ritual. *Wow! Finally! My first real horse-thieving raid!* Too bad no Yakka clansmen were around to witness it and celebrate the occasion. The Yakka khan had not permitted Skeeter to go along on such raids, fearing his funny little *bogda* might be injured, which would bring bad luck. Skeeter grinned. *Never thought I'd get a chance to do this. Not bad for a kid who fell through an unstable gate and ended up in a place nobody thought he'd survive!*

He hated to give up the horse.

But riding a stolen race horse through Rome while its handlers and several really pissed off gladiators were chasing him was not a smart move. And neither his mama nor—particularly—his foster mama had raised a fool. In fact, Yesukai's stolen bride had not only accepted her marriage, but had begun to rule her husband's yurt like a queen born to the task—and, alone among strangers, she had adopted the funny little *bogda* who was in much the same predicament, teaching him a great deal and smiling on him with great favor.

So, having learned caution from *both* his adoptive parents, Skeeter pulled the animal to a walk, cooling him out, then halted as soon as he dared and patted the beast on the neck. Dried sweat clung to his hand.

"You did good by me, fella. Thanks. I owe you. Too bad I can't make it up to you."

The horse blew softly into his face and nudged his chest, friendly-like. "Yeah," Skeeter said with a smile, stroking the velvety-soft nose, "me, too. But I gotta run and you've gotta race."

He tied the reins to the nearest public fountain, so the horse could at least get a drink of water, then set out to find himself a good, deep hidey-hole until the Porta Romae cycled sometime near midnight. The jingling of gold in the pouch at his waist sounded like victory.

Skeeter grinned.

Not a bad day's work.

Not bad at all.

Chapter 3

Lupus Mortiferus didn't like losing.

In his line of work, defeat meant death. And like most gladiators, losing a wager was an almost omen-like foreshadowing of trouble to come. The Wolf of Death, as the school had named him, was going to find that miserable street vermin and shake his money loose, or see him die in the arena for thievery.

All he had to do was find him.

He and his friends stood muttering in a group as the cheat escaped on Sun Runner, one of the greatest champions ever to run in the Circus. The handler was beside himself with fury. Already several other handlers had mounted to give chase, but the thief had a good lead on a fast horse. Lupus Mortiferus didn't hold out much hope that *anyone* would catch the rat.

"So," Quintus nudged him with an elbow, "you were gonna make a hundred-fifty *aurii*, just like that, huh?"

"Guess the Wolf isn't as smart as he thought," another friend laughed. "Getting a little long in the tooth and a little short on savvy?"

Lupus just ground his teeth and held silent. He'd *needed* that money to start a new life. Having just purchased his own freedom last year, he'd barely begun to save enough to leave the arena for good. Then, in one glorious moment, some country rube offers the chance to get there three times faster . . . and he turns out to be a sneak thief.

"You go on back," Lupus growled. "My big matches aren't for hours, yet. Think I'll follow those racing handlers, see what I can find. The Wolf does not give up *this* easily."

He took another round of ribbing—he had, after all, walked right into the rat's smiling arms—then stalked in the direction that the racing handlers had gone. *I will find that little puke and I will by Hercules break every bone in his cheating body to pieces and after that I'll break the pieces into pieces—*

He met the riders coming back, leading Sun Runner by the bridle. Sweat had dried on him, but he'd been properly cooled out or the handlers wouldn't have been smiling in such enormous relief.

"Found him tied to a public fountain," one of them explained when asked. "Three blocks farther on."

Lupus nodded and stalked on. He found the fountain, but no trace of the thief. So he started bribing shopkeepers for information. He hit paydirt on the third bribe.

"Yeah, he strolled off that way, whistling like he owned the Emperor's palace."

"Thanks." Lupus flipped him a second silver *sestertius* and headed that way. The streets here weren't quite as twisted and winding as they were across the river. Lupus spotted him within five minutes. Every impulse in him said, "Now!"

But he held back.

If he followed the little snake back to his lair, he might recover more than just the money he'd lost. Who knew how much this rat had swindled since coming to Rome? The thief led him a merry chase. Evidently, he was intent on touring the whole blasted city. He paused now and again to buy wine and sausages with money he'd swindled from other victims, then bought a few trinkets a woman might enjoy wearing.

By the time the little rat recrossed the Tiber and stopped to stare at the great temple complex atop the Capitoline hill, Lupus was out of time. Either he had to shake the rat down *now* and get back his money or he'd miss the fighting matches for which he was scheduled today. He was actually advancing, hand on the hilt of his gladius, when a third alternative occurred to him.

He had noticed a couple of wide-eyed beggar brats staring at him and paused to consider what use he might make of them.

"Are you really Lupus Mortiferus?" the bolder of the two asked, eyes round with wonder and a glint approaching fear.

"I am."

Wide eyes went rounder.

Lupus smiled coldly. "Want to earn some money?"

Mouths dropped open. "*How?*"

"See that man?" he pointed out the thief. "Follow him. Find out where he lives and tell me and I'll give you enough silver to buy slaves of your own."

The boys gasped. "We'll follow him! But how can we let you know where he's gone?"

Lupus sighed. Starvation left a man stupid and these boys looked like they hadn't eaten properly in years. "One of you stay wherever he's gone," Lupus said patiently. "The other of you, come find me. I'll be at the starting boxes, waiting."

He gave each boy a couple of copper *asses* as incentive, showing them the silver in his purse as greater incentive, then headed grimly back toward the Circus. He had some fights to win. Given his mood, Lupus Mortiferus pitied his opponents today. The crowd ought to be *very* pleased with his performance. And afterward . . .

Afterward, a certain foreign thief would learn the bite of Roman revenge.

Agnes Fairchild's voice rose on a half-scream of hurt rage. "You *used* me, Skeeter Jackson! How . . . how *dare* you—"

"Agnes—"

"Don't touch me! My God, to think I gave you a ticket, money, *slept* with you! I hate you! All you wanted was a chance to sneak away and make a bunch of illegal bets!"

"Now, Agnes—"

"I could lose my job!" Tears in her eyes sparkled in the lamp light, but they were angry tears more than fear. "I can't believe you would do this to me." She hugged both arms around herself and refused to look him in the eye.

"Look, kid, you're a nice girl. I happen to like you a lot. But business is business. Good God, Agnes, you take a bunch of bloodthirsty perverts to the arena to watch men butcher each other, you ferry around zipper jockeys so they can rape prostitutes in downtime brothels, and you don't bat an eyelash, but let a man make a little wager—"

"Get out of my sight! I wish I'd never laid eyes on you, Skeeter Jackson! If I thought I could get away with it, I'd . . . I'd maroon you here! That'd be rich, leave you stuck in Rome with all the people whose money you swindled!"

Skeeter gave up. He'd broken up with his share of women, although he rarely understood why, exactly, but he'd never had one react this violently. Well, there was the exception of Margo. She'd said a few choice things to him, after she'd found out he wasn't a time scout after all. And he hadn't even managed to get her into bed!

All of which was useless to pursue. He would miss Agnes' company, particularly in the sack, but the amount of gold in the pouches at his belt was more than incentive to dismiss her serious overreaction. It'd only been one little day's wagering, for God's sake. Yesukai would've been singing his praises to the entire clan around the cookpots.

Oh, well. Easy come, easy go. So much for this scheme. Guess I'll have to come up with something else that doesn't involve a down-time gate. Of course, with his winnings today, he could take all the time he wanted, deciding his next intrigue. He left Agnes sitting in her private room at the Time Tours inn and rejoined the festivities in the dining room, aware that she was crying as he shut the door, aware of a pang of guilt down inside himself, but also aware that she'd brought most of her anguish on herself.

Sheesh. One little bet.

You'd have thought he'd stolen her heart or something. *Women. Can't figure 'em, any way you look at it.* When he got back to TT-86, he was going to march straight into the Down Time Bar and Grill and get roaring drunk. Hell, he'd buy drinks for everybody there and get well and truly Mongolian *drunk* with friends. After the fit she'd pitched, he deserved a little celebration.

Maybe he'd even find someone willing to console him in the privacy of his apartment afterwards. Some sweet, soft-skinned tourist willing to assuage the sense of loss and loneliness he couldn't quite dismiss as he entered the raucous main room of the Time Tours inn. Yeah, that was the ticket. Wine and women. Age-old cure for what ailed the heart.

Skeeter put on his best smile and wondered how many pockets he might have the chance to pick before the Porta Romae Gate cycled a few hours hence.

The thief had taken up lodgings at an inn situated pleasantly on the Aventine. It bustled with customers. Lupus paid both boys and watched them scamper off, then stepped into the crowded room. A few people gave him odd looks, but he was served with good food and better wine than he'd expected. The man he sought was in a far corner, all smiles and triumph, talking to a plain-looking slave girl who smiled at him the way a well-bedded woman smiles at a man who's tumbled her frequently. Lupus hid his own smile as they left for more private surroundings, then heard the beginnings of an argument through their closed door. It ended with the thief storming back into the main room, thunderclouds in his eyes, whereupon he struck up a lively discussion with the nearest girl.

All does not go well, then, between master and concubine. He chuckled, finished his meal, and left the inn to wait for darkness. All he needed to do was wait until the guests bedded down for the night and the thief was his.

He *could* have called for the city watch to arrest the man, but his reputation was already damaged. So far, only his closest friends knew of his foolish loss. Let the city watch discover it, and his name would become a laughingstock from the Janiculum to the Campus Martius. This was a score he intended to settle personally. To his great chagrin, however, a banquet or great party of some kind was being celebrated inside, with loud laughter and singing in some barbaric tongue he couldn't place. It went on until the night grew very late.

"Will these colonial clods never bed down and sleep?"

Carts and heavily laden wagons rumbled past in the darkness, casting lantern light on weary-faced drivers and dark, rutted paving stones. Another hour passed, then another, and still the party roared on. Hugging his impatience to his breast like a well-honed dagger, Lupus waited.

What happened next surprised him beyond all belief.

Every single one of the revellers left the inn in a packed group, led by lantern light and collared slaves through the wagon-jammed, dangerous streets. The man Lupus sought was there amongst them, grinning like a trained monkey. Lupus followed, one hand on the pommel of his sword. He trailed the group to a wine shop on the Via Appia. Judging from the positions of the stars, it must be nearly midnight, yet nearly forty people entered the dark, silent wineshop. Some were giggling, some reeling, while some looked like they might be ill at any moment.

Lupus' prey entered without so much as a backward glance over his shoulder. An open door at the rear of the shop spilled lantern light into the now-empty shop front with its counters, stone benches, and tight-lidded amphorae of wine. Beyond was clearly a small warehouse where the shopkeeper stored his stock. Lupus slipped across the street and cautiously entered the public area just as someone closed the warehouse door. Darkness smothered him in an instant. He swore under his breath and waited for his night vision to return. He listened at the edge of the door, but could hear nothing.

Then a strange buzzing began to vibrate the bones of his skull. There was no real *sound*, but he clapped hands over both ears, trying to shut out the unpleasant sensation. *What manner of wine shop* is *this?* Sweat started out on his brow. He wasn't afraid, exactly—

The warehouse door opened again, unexpectedly.

Lupus hurled himself into the shadows behind the counter.

Some fifty people emerged from the warehouse room—*but none of them were the ones who'd gone inside moments before.* The last person through closed the door to the warehouse, leaving Lupus hidden in shadows while lanterns swung in the night and giggles and whispers in that same foreign tongue reached his ears. Lupus stared at the departing group, while the bones of his skull ached. Gradually the sound that wasn't a sound faded away. The men and women who'd just left the warehouse disappeared around a street corner.

Lupus emerged slowly from behind the humble limestone countertop, glancing from the closed warehouse door to the street corner and back. Then he tried the door. It wasn't locked. Someone had left a lamp burning; the shop owner must mean to return shortly, else he'd have blown out the lamp. Lupus searched the room thoroughly, if somewhat hastily, but found absolutely no trace of the forty-odd people who had entered this room moments earlier. Nor could he find a doorway or hidden trap in the floor. The room was absolutely empty, save for racks of dusty amphorae. The nearest of those, shaken gently, proved to be full.

Standing in the center of the deserted room, Lupus Mortiferus felt an unaccustomed trickle of fear run up his spine. His quarry had vanished, apparently into thin air, taking Lupus' hard-won money with him. Lupus swore softly, then returned the amphora to its place in the rack, turned on his heel, and strode out again. He *would* discover the secret of that wine shop. The people who came and went from it had to come through *somehow*, as they were not spirits from the underworld, but flesh-and-blood men and women. And since Lupus—superstitious though he might be—did not believe in outright magic, he would find that way through. All he had to do was follow the next group more closely.

And once through . . .

Lupus Mortiferus, the Wolf of Death of Rome's great Circus, smiled cruelly in the starlight. "Soon," he promised the thief. "Soon, your belly will meet my blade. I think you will find little enough stomach for my revenge—but my steel will find more than enough of your stomach."

Laughing darkly at his own joke, Lupus Mortiferus strode away into the night.

Gate days always packed in the customers at the Down Time Bar & Grill. With the Porta Romae cycling, Marcus had all he could handle keeping up with drink tabs and calling sandwich orders to Molly. The clink of glassware and the smell of alcohol permeated the dim-lit interior as thickly as the roar of voices, some of them bragging about what they'd done/seen/heard down time and others drowning whatever it was that had shaken them to the core and yet others denying that anything at all was bothering them.

All in all, it was a pretty normal gate day. Marcus delivered a tray full of drinks to a table where Kit Carson and Malcolm Moore were sharing tall tales with Rachel Eisenstein. The time terminal's physician wasn't taken in by either man, but she was clearly having a good time pretending to believe the world's most famous time scout and La-La Land's most experienced freelance time guide. Marcus smiled, warmed more by their welcoming smiles than their more-than-generous tips, then moved on to the back room, shimmying skillfully between pool players intent on their games, to a corner where Goldie Morran was deeply involved in a high-stakes poker match with Brian Hendrickson.

Marcus knew that look in Goldie's eyes. He held in a shiver. She must be losing—heavily. Brian Hendrickson's face gave away nothing, but the pile of money on his side of the table was a good bit larger than the pile on Goldie's. Several interested onlookers watched silently. Goldie (who somehow reminded Marcus unpleasantly of a certain haughty patrician lady a former master had visited on carefully arranged assignations), glanced from her hand to meet Brian's steady regard. Her lip curled slightly, sure of him. "Call."

Hendrickson showed his cards.

Goldie Morran swore in a manner Marcus still found shocking. More money travelled to the librarian's side of the table.

"Your drinks," Marcus said quietly, placing them carefully to one side of cards, money, and outthrust elbows.

Out in the main room, a familiar voice sang out, "Hey, Marcus! Where are you?"

Skeeter Jackson was back in town. He hid a pleased grin.

Marcus quietly collected empty glasses from the poker table, noted the lack of a tip from Goldie and the modest tip from the librarian, then hurried out and found his friend beaming at the entire roomful of patrons.

"Drinks," he announced elaborately, "are on the house. A round for everyone on me!"

Marcus gaped. "Skeeter? That is . . . that will be very expensive!" His friend never had that kind of money. And the Down Time was *crowded* tonight.

"Yep! I scored big for a change. Really big!" His grin all but lit up the dark room. Then he produced a wallet *full* of money. "For the drinks!"

"You won the bets?"

Skeeter laughed. "Did I ever! Serve 'em up, Marcus." He winked and handed Marcus a heavy pouch, whispering, "Thanks. That's for your help." Then he sauntered over to a table, where he found himself the center of much attention, most of it from tourists. The pouch Skeeter had given him was very heavy. Marcus began to tremble. When he opened the drawstrings, the number—and *color*—of the coins inside made his head swim. There must be . . . He couldn't see properly to count the money. But if it wasn't enough to pay off his debt, it was close. Very, very close. His vision wavered.

Skeeter had remembered.

Marcus knew that in this world of up-timers and 'eighty-sixers, grown men did not weep, as Roman men did with such free abandon. So he blinked desperately, but his throat was so thick he couldn't have spoken to save his own life. Skeeter had *remembered.* And actually followed through on the promise. *I won't forget,* Marcus made a silent vow. *I won't forget this, my true friend.*

He stuffed the money into a front jeans pocket, deep enough to keep it safe from pick pockets, then blinked fiercely again. He wished desperately he could leave the Down Time and share his news with Ianira *now*, but he had several hours left on his shift and she would be in the middle of a session with an up-time graduate student, one of many who consulted—and paid—her as a singular, primary source. She had told him once that some up-time schools did not allow students to use such recordings or notes, considering them faulty, if not downright fraudulent, sources. Anger had sparked like flint against pyrite in her eyes, that anyone would dare to question her honesty, her integrity.

But a lot of other schools *did* accept such research as valid. Marcus discovered a deep, abiding joy that Ianira would no longer have to reduce herself to selling off little pieces of her life just to save money for Marcus' debt. He could tell her later of his good fortune, of their good friend and ally. Already he anticipated the joy in her dark eyes.

Perhaps I can even support another child. A son, if the gods smile on us. Thus preoccupied with dreams, Marcus started taking the drink orders Skeeter's generosity had prompted. Skeeter plopped down enough cash to buy the drinks he'd promised and then some.

Goldie Morran and Brian Hendrickson emerged from the back just then, evidently because Goldie had run out of either money or patience. Their admiring entourage followed like schooling fish.

"What's this about drinks being on Skeeter?" Goldie demanded.

Skeeter rose lazily from the seat he'd taken and gave her a mock bow. "You heard me right. And you know I've got the money." He winked at *her* this time.

Ahh . . . Goldie had done the money changing for Skeeter's winnings. Goldie's expression deepened into lines of bitterness. "You call a couple of thousand *money*? Good God, Skeeter, I just dropped that much in one poker game. When are you ever going to graduate from the penny-ante stuff?"

Skeeter froze, eyes going first wide then savagely narrow. He was the focal point of the entire room, tourists and 'eighty-sixers alike. A flush crept up his face, either of embarrassment or anger—with Skeeter, it was never easy to tell.

"Penny-ante?" he repeated, with a dangerous glint in his eyes. "Yes, I suppose from your point of view, that's what I am, Goldie. Just Skeeter's penny-ante bullshit, same as always. Now, if I had your juicy situation, maybe I'd hit it big a little more often, too. You're no better than I am, Goldie, under all that fancy crap you hand your customers."

A sewing needle dropped to the wooden floor would have sounded like an alarm klaxon in the silence that followed.

"And just what do you mean by that?" Goldie was breathing just a touch too hard, nostrils pinched one moment, flaring the next, lips ash white.

"Oh, come off it, Goldie. You can't con *me*, we're too much alike, you and I. Everyone in La-La Land knows you scam any customer you can." Several tourists in the room started visibly and stared at Goldie with dawning suspicion. Skeeter shrugged. "If I had a fancy shop and the chance to snatch rare coins at a fraction of their worth, or had the kind of bankroll you've conned over the years, hell, I could drop a few thousand in a poker game, too, and not miss it.

"Like I said, you're no better than I am. You scam, I scam, and everybody here calls us backstabbing cheats. If you didn't use all that fancy crap in your head about coins and gems, you couldn't scam half of what I do in a week. Frankly, coins and gems is *all* you know. Hell, I could probably top you two or three to one, if you had to make a living the way I do."

Goldie's cheeks went slowly purple, nearly matching her hair.

"Are you issuing a challenge to *me*?"

Skeeter's jaw muscles clenched. Something in his eyes, a glint of steel harsh as the Mongolian desert skies, caused Marcus to shiver. Then Skeeter grinned, slowly, without a trace of mirth in those steely eyes.

"Yeah. I think I am. A challenge. That's a good idea. What about it, Goldie? Shall we give it a week? Anything you make using knowledge of rare coins, gems, antiques and the like doesn't count. At the end of the week, the person with the most cash takes the whole pot. How about it? Do we have a bet?"

The reek of tension and sweat filled the crowded room as every eye swivelled to Goldie Morran, the dowager con artist of La-La Land. She merely curled a lip. "That hardly seems like a stake worth bothering myself over, considering how little you manage to rake in during an average week." Her eyes narrowed and a smile came to thin lips. Marcus shivered. *Walk carefully, my friend, she means to have blood.* "I don't make fools' bets."

Skeeter took a dangerous step forward, eyes flashing angrily in the dim light. "All right, how about we up the stakes a little, then? We'll make it a *real* bet. Let the wager run for *three* weeks—hell, let's make it one month, even. That'll take us right through the holidays. At the end, loser leaves TT-86, bag and baggage, and never comes back."

Goldie's eyes widened for just a moment, causing Marcus to bite his lips to hold back his protest—never mind a dire warning to take care. Then she actually laughed. "Leave TT-86? Are you mad?"

"Are you chicken?"

For an instant, Marcus thought she might actually strike him.

"*Done!*" She spat out the word like a snake spitting venom. Then she whirled on poor Brian Hendrickson, a man who wouldn't have cheated a stray flea. He was watching the whole affair round-eyed. Goldie stabbed a long-nailed finger at him. "You. I want you to officiate. This is a for-goddamn-real bet. I win and we're rid of that two-bit little rat for good."

Skeeter's cheeks darkened. But that was the only sign of emotion. He smiled. "I win and we're finally rid of the Duchess of Dross."

Goldie whirled on him, lips open to snap back something scathing, but Brian Hendrickson stepped between them.

"All right, we have a wager challenged and accepted." The librarian glanced from one to the other. "You two have no idea how much I would give to get out of this, not to get stuck in the middle, but with a wager this serious, somebody's got to keep you two as honest as possible."

He sighed, then reluctantly admitted, "I guess I'm the man to do it, since I know as much about rare coins and gems as you do, Goldie. All right, every day each of you reports to me. I hold all winnings and track all losses. I judge whether a winning counts. Goldie, you are forbidden to use your expertise to scam tourists. You'll have to find some other way to cheat your way to victory."

Brian's eyes revealed clearly how little pleasure he was taking in this, but he went doggedly on. "Money earned legally doesn't count. And one more thing. If either of you gets *caught*, you automatically lose. Understood?"

Goldie sniffed autocratically. "Understood."

Skeeter glared at her for a moment, naked desire for revenge burning in his eyes. Marcus remembered what Skeeter had said, that night he'd been so drunk he'd started confiding secrets Marcus had never dreamed existed. He'd known already that his friend carried with him a monstrous capacity for cold, calculating vengeance. That icy-cold desire now left Marcus terrified for Skeeter's safety. He wanted to shout, "You don't need to prove yourself!" but it was far too late, now. The money in his jeans pocket felt heavier than ever, nearly as heavy as his heart.

His friend would spend the next few weeks doing exactly the kinds of things Marcus was trying to make him *stop* doing, or he would risk having to leave the station forever. Marcus didn't want to lose a friend, any more than the Downtimer Council would want to lose a "Lost One" located and identified by one of their members. Marcus prayed to any Roman *or* Gaulish gods and goddesses that might be listening that Skeeter would win this bet, not Goldie.

She could afford to start over somewhere else.

Skeeter Jackson couldn't.

In that moment, Marcus felt a loathing of Goldie Morran he couldn't begin to put into words. He turned away, busying himself behind the bar, as Brian Hendrickson finished laying down the rules. He didn't notice when Goldie left. But when he glanced around the room and failed to find her, the relief that flooded through him left him weak-kneed. Conversation roared to a crescendo and he was so busy serving drinks, he didn't see Skeeter leaving either. He swallowed hard, sorry for the lost opportunity to speak with his friend, but he still had work to do.

So, very quietly, Marcus served drinks, collected bar tabs, and stuffed tips into his jeans, all the while worrying about the fate of his one good friend in all the world—or time.

Chapter 4

Lupus Mortiferus had not survived a hundred combats in the Roman arena by giving up easily. He waited from the Kalends of the month until a single day remained before the Ides, either he or his slave following the strangers who had emerged from that wine shop on the Via Appia in the middle of the night. Lupus watched men, women, quarrelsome children, and puckish teens gawk at marble temples, enter brothels with erect-phallus signs poking out of the sides of dingy brick buildings, or file excitedly into the circus to watch the racing and the combats.

For all that time, nearly half the lunar month, Lupus bided his time and whetted the edge on his gladius as sharp as he whetted his desire for revenge. He endured stoically the jokes and jibes that still continued. A few of the jokesters took their jests to the grave, blood and entrails spilling on the sands of the arena while the crowd roared like a thousand summer thunderstorms in his cars.

And then, the waiting was done.

They left in the middle of the night, as before, slaves showing the way with lanterns. Following them was ridiculously easy. Lupus ordered his slave home and slipped from one shadowed shopfront to another, booted feet soundless on the stone paving of the sidewalk. Several of the young men had clearly drunk too much; they reeled, clutching at slaves or at one another, and tried to keep up. As the group approached the wine shop on the Via Appia, Lupus quietly insinuated himself into the group, hanging near the back.

A slave near the front called out something in a barbarous tongue. The group entered the wineshop by twos and threes. Lupus noted uneasily that the slaves assigned to guard the group were carefully taking count of those who passed into the shop's warehouse. Just when he feared discovery, one of the young men near him began to void the contents of his alcohol-saturated stomach. Lupus hid a grin. *Perfect!* Slaves converged on the boy, holding his head and trying to urge him forward. The sight and smell of the boy's vomit triggered a chain reaction amongst the drunken youths. Another boy spewed as he stumbled into the warehouse. Lupus took his arm solicitously, earning a smile of gratitude from a harried woman wearing a slave's collar.

Elated, Lupus dragged the sick youngster into a corner and let him throw up the wine and sweetmeats he'd obviously gorged on during the day. Yet another boy in the group began to throw up. Women in stylish gowns moved away, holding their breath. Frowns of disgust wrinkled painted lips and manicured brows. A little girl said very distinctly, "Yuck." Lupus wasn't certain just exactly what the word meant, but the look on her face was clear enough. Even the older men were giving the sick boys a wide berth. Lupus was pressed into the corner with the sick youngsters, ignored by everyone except the boy who clung to his arm and groaned.

Then the air began to groan.

It wasn't an audible sound, but it was *exactly* like the painful buzzing in his skull the last time he'd been close to this warehouse. Lupus swallowed a few times and tried to find the source of the noise that wasn't exactly a noise. A hush fell over the crowd, punctuated messily by the sounds of wretchedly ill boys and a few murmured words of encouragement from their slaves. Lupus glanced at a blank stretch of wall, wondering yet again why everyone had crowded into this particular warehouse—

The wall began to shimmer. Colors scintillated wildly through the entire rainbow. Lupus gasped aloud, then controlled his involuntary reaction. A quick glance showed him that no one had noticed the sweat that had started on his brow. That was a relief, but it still took all his courage to continue looking at the pulsing spot on the wall.

Captivated by the sight, he couldn't look away, not even when a dark hole appeared in the scintillating, circular rainbows, his hindbrain whispering to *run*! The hole widened rapidly until it had swallowed half the warehouse wall. Lupus fought back once more the instinct to run, then swallowed instead and whispered softly, "Great war god Mars, lend me a bit of your confidence, please."

People started stepping into it.

They flew away so fast, it was as though they'd been catapulted by a great war machine. Someone took the other arm of the boy Lupus was "helping" and pulled him toward the gaping hole in the wall. Lupus wanted to stand rock-still, terrified of that black maw that swallowed people whole down its gullet. Then, thinking of vengeance and his carefully sharpened gladius, he drew a deep breath for courage and moved forward in the midst of the half-dozen boys who were manfully struggling to overcome their illness. Lupus hesitated on the brink, sweating and terrified—

Then squeezed shut both eyes and stepped forward.

He was falling . . .

Mithras! Mars! Save me—

He went to his knees against something rough and metallic. Lupus opened his eyes and found himself kneeling on a metal gridwork. The boy who had gone through with him was vomiting again. Men hauling baggage stumbled past them, struggling to get around. Lupus hauled the kid to his feet and dragged him in the direction the others had taken, down a broad, gridwork ramp. Chaos reigned at the bottom, where several other of the boys were still holding up the line, vomiting piteously all over a young woman in the most outlandish clothing Lupus had ever seen. Everyone in line was trying to slide some sort of flat, stiff vellum chip into a box-like device, but the boys were making a mess of the entire procedure. The young woman said something that sounded exasperated and disgusted and glanced the other way.

Lupus, who had no flat, stiff vellum chip to insert into the device, slipped quietly past and fled for the nearest concealment: a curtain of hanging vines and flowering shrubs that screened a private portico. Panting slightly and cursing the fear-borne adrenalin that poured through his veins the way it did just before a fight, Lupus Mortiferus took his first look at the place where the thief who'd stolen his money had taken refuge.

He swallowed once, very hard.

Where am I? Olympus?

He couldn't quite accept that explanation, despite the terrifying magic of a hole through a wall that sometimes existed and sometimes didn't. Atlantis, perhaps? No, that had been destroyed when the gods were young, if it had ever existed at all. Where, then? Rome *was* civilization in this world, although traders spoke of the wonders of the far, far east, from whence expensive silk came.

Lupus didn't know the name of the cities where silk was spun into cloth, but he didn't think this was one of them. It wasn't a proper "city" at all. There was no open sky, no ground, no distant horizon or wind to rustle through treetops and evaporate sweat from his skin. The place was more like an enormous . . . room. One large enough to hold the towering Egyptian obelisk on the spine of the Circus Maximus—with room to spare between its golden tip and the distant ceiling. The room was large enough that he could have laid out a half-length chariot race course down its length, had there not been shops, ornamental fountains and ponds, decorative seats, and odd pillars with glowing spheres at the top scattered throughout its length, along with a riot of colorful Saturnalia and other, unfathomable, decorations from floor to ceiling. The delighted shrieking of young children brought home just how lost he was: a mere child of five clearly knew more about this place than he did.

Staircases of metal *everywhere* climbed up to nothing, or to platforms which served no sane purpose Lupus could divine. Signs he could not read scattered strange letters colorfully across the walls. A few areas were fenced off, leaving them inaccessible despite the seeming innocuous blankness of the walls behind them. The image of the wine shop's wall opening up into a hole through nothingness was so powerfully and recently embedded in his soul, Lupus shuddered, wondering what lay behind those innocent-seeming stretches of wall. People dressed as Romans mingled with others in costumes so barbaric and foreign, Lupus could only stare.

Where am I?

And where, in all this confusion of shops, staircases, and people, was the thief he sought? For one terrible moment, he shut his eyes and fought the urge to charge straight up the ramp and back through the hole in the wall. He managed to bring shuddering breaths under control only with difficulty, but he did control himself. He was the Death Wolf of the Circus Maximus, after all, not a milk-fed brat to fear the first strangeness life hurled his way. Lupus forced his eyes open again.

The hole in the wall had closed.

He was trapped here, for evil or good.

For just a second, terror overrode all other concerns. Then, slowly, Lupus gripped the pommel of his gladius. The gods he worshipped had answered his hourly prayers in their own mysterious fashion. He was trapped, yes.

But so was the thief.

All Lupus had to do was find a way to pass himself off as a member of this sunless, closed-in world long enough to track the man down, then he would wait for the next inexplicable opening of the wall and fight his way back home, if necessary.

The corners of his lips twisted into a mirthless smile.

The thief would rue the hour he had cheated Lupus Mortiferus, the champion Death Wolf of Rome. That decision holding hard-fought fear at bay, Lupus clutched the pommel of his sword and set out on his hunt.

Wherever populations of illegal refugees spring up without legal status inside an existing, "native" population, certain networks are formed almost as automatically as baby whales swim straight for the surface to gulp that first, essential breath of air. Almost by unconscious accord, mutual-aid systems will emerge to help illegal aliens survive, perhaps in time even thrive, in a world they do not understand, much less control.

In the time terminals that had grown around those areas where gates formed in close-enough profusion to warrant building a station, this unwritten rule held as true as it did in the squalid streets of Los

Angeles or New York, in the streets of every major coastal city, in fact, where refugees of The Flood which had followed The Accident crowded together for safety, almost without hope of finding any, each and every pitiful one of them without papers to prove their identity or country of origin. Those up-time refugees struggled to survive under even worse conditions, sometimes, than refugees trapped forever on the time terminals. It didn't bear mentioning the living conditions of the tidal waves of refugees fleeing endless, senseless wars raging throughout the Middle East and the Balkans. Whole armies of them fled illegally across national borders, fleeing genocide at the hands of enemies, many of them dying in the attempt.

Men and women, children and strays, those who wandered into the terminals through open gates and found themselves trapped without up-time legal rights, without social standing, protected by the thinnest of "station policies"—because the up-time governments couldn't decide what to *do* about them—set up social systems of their own in courageous attempts to cope. A few went hopelessly mad and wandered back through open gates, usually unstable ones, never to be seen again. But most, desperate to survive, banded together in sometimes loosely, sometimes tightly knit confederations. Often speaking only the common language of gestures, they shared news and resources as best they could, sometimes even going so far as to hide from official notice any newcomers who might be exploited or injured by regulations and officialdom's sometimes harsh notice.

On TT-86, management under Bull Morgan made such extreme efforts necessary only rarely, but all down-timers shared a common bond few up-timers could really understand. It was the experience of being lost together. Like the Christian sects of Rome which had once met in the catacombs beneath the city or the cells of Colonial American patriots hiding out from British armies and meeting in any root cellar or thicket they could find, La-La Land's down-timer Council met underground. Literally underground, beneath the station proper, in the bowels of the terminal where machinery (which filled the air with chaos and noise) kept the lights running, the sewage flowing, and the heated or chilled air pumping; down where massive steel-and-concrete support beams plunged into native, Himalayan rock, the refugees created their culture of survival.

Amidst the noise and whine of machines they barely understood, they met in the cramped caverns of La-La Land's physical plant to bolster one another's courage, pass along news of critical importance to their standing, and share fear, grief, loss, and triumph with one another. A few had taken it upon themselves to hold special classes in up-time languages, while those most able to understand the world in which they were trapped did their best to explain it to those least able.

Up-timers knew about it, but most didn't pay much attention to the "underground society's" activities. On TT-86, management cared enough to provide an official psychologist on the payroll, whose sole duty was to help them adjust, but "Buddy" didn't really understand what it meant—emotionally, in the depth of one's belly—to be torn away from one's home time and become trapped in a place like the bustling time terminal that La-La Land had become over the years.

So down-timers turned to their own unofficial leaders in times of need or crisis. One of those unofficial leaders was Ianira Cassondra. Sitting and waiting for Marcus to return home to her, she spent a quiet moment bemused with the thought that her own history was, in many ways, more unlikely than the odd world in which she now led others through an unlikely existence. Ianira, born in Ephesus, the holy city of the Great Artemis Herself, had learned the secrets of rituals no man would ever understand from priestesses who followed the old, old ways. Ianira, secluded from the world as only a priestess of Artemis could be, was then, at sixteen, ripped from that world and sold into virtual slavery through the marriage bed—tearing her away from beloved Ephesus to the high citadel of Athens, across the Aegean Sea. Ianira, abandoned by her kinsmen, was left in the shadow of the dusty Agora where Athenian men met under blazing clear light to stroll amidst vendors of figs, olive oil, and straw baskets while they discussed and invented political systems that would change the world for the next twenty-six hundred years. Secluded from all that she knew, Ianira had tried to learn the mysteries of the patron goddess of her new home, only to be kept a virtual prisoner in her new husband's gyneceum.

Ianira the "Enchantress," who had once danced beneath the moon in Artemis' sacred glade, bow in hand, hair loose and wild, had prayed to her mother's ancient goddesses to deliver her—and, finally, *They* had heard. One night, Ianira had fled the gyneceum and its imprisoning "respectability," driven by grief and terror into the night-dark streets of Athens.

Half bent on seeking asylum in Athene's great temple at the crowning height of the city—and half intent on throwing herself from the Acropolis rather than endure another night in her husband's home—Ianira had run on bare feet, lungs sobbing for air, her body weak and shaking still from the birthing chair in which she had so recently been confined.

And there, in those silent, dusty streets where men changed history and women were held in bondage, her prayers to Athene, to Hera, to Demeter and her daughter Proserpina, Queen of the Underworld, to Artemis and Aphrodite and even to Circe the Enchantress of Old, were finally answered. Pursued by an enraged husband, she ran as fast as she could force her flagging body, knowing all too well what fate awaited her if her husband caught her. Ianira's bare toes raised puffs of dust in the empty, moonlit Agora, where the columns of the gleaming white Hephestion rose on a hillock to one side and the painted Stoa where philosophers met to discourse with their disciples rose ghostlike before her in the haunted night.

Still bent on trying to reach the shining Parthenon above her, Ianira darted into an alleyway leading up toward the Acropolis and heard a beggar man seated on the ground call out sharply, "Hey! Don't go through there!"

A glance back showed her the figure of her husband, gaining ground. Terror sent her, sobbing, up toward Athene's great temple. She literally ran into the solid wall of a small cobbler's shop hugging the cliff face, staggered back—

—and saw it happen.

Inside the open doorway of the cobbler's shop, the dark air had torn asunder before her disbelieving eyes. Her gown fluttered like moth's wings as she faltered to a halt, staring at the pinpoint of light and movement through it. Dimly, she was aware of people crowding around her, her husband's curses at the back of the crowd. She hesitated only a moment. At the embittered, battered age of seventeen, Ianira Cassondra lifted her hands in thanks to whichever goddess had listened—and shoved past startled men and women who tried to stop her. She stepped straight into the wavering hole in reality, not caring what she found on the other side, half expecting to see the grand halls of Olympus itself, with shining Artemis waiting to avenge her defiled priestess.

She found, instead, La-La Land and a new life. Free of many of her old terrors, she learned to trust and love again, at least one man who had learned caution from harsher masters than she had yet found. And even more precious, something she had not thought possible, she had found the miracle of a young man with brown hair and a laughing heart and dark, haunted eyes who could make her forget the brutality and terror of a man's touch. He would not marry her yet. Not because she had left a living husband, but because—in his *own* mind—he was not honorably free of debt. Ianira had never met this man who owned Marcus' debt, but sometimes when she went into deep trance, she could *almost* see his face, amidst the most unlikely surroundings she had ever witnessed.

Whoever and wherever he was, waiting for Marcus to finish his days' labors, Ianira hated the hidden man with such a passion as Medea had known when she'd snatched up the dagger to slay her own sons, rather than let a replacement queen raise them like slaves. When—if—he returned, Ianira mused, she herself would find no barriers to taking up her own dagger and punishing the man who had treated her beloved so callously. It would not be the first time she'd offered the pieces of a sacrificial human male to ancient Artemis, she who was called by the Spartans Artamis the Butcher. She had thought herself long past the need for such bloody work; but when her family was threatened, Ianira Cassondra knew herself capable of *anything*. Quite a change from that time in her life when the thought of sleeping with a one-time slave would have been revolting to her—but the contrast between a year of "honorable" marriage and Marcus' tender concern for a stranger lost in a world the gods themselves would have found bewildering, had worked a magic Ianira could recognize. Sharing Marcus' bed, his fears and dreams, Ianira gave him children to ease the pain in his heart—and her own.

To her surprise, Ianira found she not only enjoyed the humble, mundane chores she had never before been forced to do, but also she enjoyed the surprising status and acclaim her abilities and personality had earned her. Odd to be so suddenly sought after—not only by other lonely down-timer men, but by tourists, up-timer students, even professors of antiquities. In this strange land, Ianira had discovered she could make many things, beautiful things: gowns, baubles and ornaments, herbal mixes to help those in suffering. After a few of these items had sold, demand was suddenly so great, she'd asked Connie Logan if she would please teach her to use one of the new machines for sewing, to make her gowns faster.

Connie had grinned. "Sure. Just let my computer copy down any embroidery or dress patterns you use and you've got a deal!"

Connie was a shrewd businesswoman. So was she, Ianira remembered with a smile. "The embroidery? No. The dress patterns? Yes, and welcome."

Connie shook her head and sighed. "You're robbing me blind, Ianira, but I like you. And if that Ionian chiton you're wearing is any example of what you can do . . . you've got a deal."

So Ianira used Connie Logan's workshop to create the chitons she was stockpiling toward a future business of her own. She'd spent her entire pregnancy with Gelasia sewing, making up little bags to hold dried herbs, learning to make the simple but beautiful kinds of jewelry she recalled so clearly from her home—and her now-dead husband's. And finally it paid off, when she got the permit from Bull Morgan to open a booth, which Marcus made for her in his free time. They painted it prettily and set up for business.

Which was good, if not as phenomenal as she'd once or twice hoped. But good, still, more than enough to pay for itself and leave extra for family expenses, including Marcus' debt-free fund. Theirs was an odd marriage—Ianira categorically refused to acknowledge the year of rape and abuse in Athens as a legitimate marriage, as she had *not* consented—but the odd marriage was filled with everything she could have wanted. Love, security, children, happiness with the kindest man she'd ever known . . . sometimes her very happiness frightened her, should the gods become jealous and strike them all down.

Marcus reeled in from work the night the Porta Romae cycled, far gone in wine he rarely took in such quantities, and shook his head at the supper she'd kept warm for him. Ianira put it away efficiently in the miraculous refrigerator machine, then noticed silent tears sliding down his cheeks.

"Marcus!" she gasped, rushing to him. "What is it, love?"

He shook his head and steered her into the bedroom, not even bothering to undress either of them, then held her close, nose buried in her hair, and trembled until he could finally speak.

"It—it is Skeeter, Ianira. Skeeter Jackson. Do you remember me laughing when he left for Romae, promising to give me a share of his bet winnings?"

"Yes, love, of course, but—"

He shifted a little, pressed something heavy inside a leather pouch into her hand. "He kept his promise," Marcus whispered.

Ianira held the heavy money pouch and just listened, holding him, while he wept for the kindness of an *up*-timer friend who had given him the means at long last to discharge his heavy debt and finally marry her.

"Why?" she whispered, not understanding the impulse which had driven a man universally regarded as a scoundrel to such generosity.

Marcus looked at her through eyes still flooded with tears. "He knows, I think, a little of what we have known. If he could only find what we have found. . . ." Marcus sighed, then kissed his wife. "Let me tell you." Ianira listened, and as Marcus' tale proceeded, vowed to store in her heart the story of Skeeter Jackson, who had, in his boyhood, stumbled through an open gate into an alien land.

"He was drunk that night," Marcus whispered to her in the darkness, so as not to waken their young daughters in the crib beside their shared bed. "Drunk and so lonely he started to talk, thinking I might understand. What he told me . . . Some of it I still do not understand completely, but I will try to tell it to you in his own words. He said it began as a game, because of his father . . ."

The game, Skeeter had recalled through a haze of alcohol and pain, had begun in deadly earnest. "It was my father's fault, or maybe my mother's. But you know, even when you're only eight, you can figure the score, figure it 'bout as accurately as any bookie making odds in New York. Dad, he bought the whole Pee-Wee League basketball team matching uniforms. Made sure our games got local TV coverage. Did the same for my Junior League baseball team. Spent a lot of money on us, he did. And you know what, Marcus? He never came to a game. Not one. Not a single, stinking, stupid game. Hell, it wasn't hard at all to figure the score. Dad didn't give a damn about *me*. Just cared 'bout how much prestige he could buy. How many customers his publicity would bring in, God *damn* him. He wassa good businessman, too. So rich it hurt your teeth just thinkin' about it."

Marcus, only vaguely comprehending much of what Skeeter said, knew that the young man was hurting nonetheless, worse than any resident he'd ever listened to on a late, slow night at the Down Time Bar and Grill. Skeeter stared into his whiskey glass. "Fill 'er up again, would you, Marcus? That's good." He drained half the glass in a gulp. "Yeah, that's good . . . So, it's like this, I started stealing things. You know, things at the mall. Little stuff at first, not because I was poor, but because I wanted something I got by myself. I guess I just got too goddamn sick of having Dad throw some expensive toy at me like a bone to some flea-bitten dog that had wandered in, just to keep it quiet."

He blinked slowly and gulped the rest of the whiskey, then just reached for the bottle and poured again. His eyes were a little unfocussed as he spoke, his voice a little less steady. "In fac', I was at th' mall the day *it* happened. After The Accident, you know, that caused the time strings, ever'body knew a gate could open up anywhere, but, hell, they usually cluster together, you know, like the TV said all my life, in one little area small enough to build a time station around 'em and let the big new time tour companies operate through 'em. But, my friend," he tipped more whiskey into his glass, "sometimes gates just open up, no warning, no nothing, in the middle of some place ain't no gate ever been seen before."

He drank, his hand a little unsteady, and entirely without his volition, the story came pouring out. He'd been careless, that time, they'd caught him shoplifting the big Swiss Army Knife. But he was little and blubbered convincingly and was slippery enough to dodge away the minute their guard was down. He'd considered, for a few moments after the guard grabbed him, *letting* the scandal hit the papers and television news programs, just to get even with his father. But Skeeter didn't want the game to end that way. He wanted to perfect it—*then* present his dad with a scandal big enough to wreck his life as thoroughly as he'd wrecked Skeeter's, game after missed baseball and basketball and football game, lonely night after lonely night.

So away he dodged, into the crowded mall, with the angry guard hot on his heels and Skeeter whipping around startled shoppers, dodging into department stores and out again through different exits on upper levels, and skidding through the food court while the guard giving chase radioed for backup.

It was all great fun—until the hole opened up in the air right in front of him. The only warning he had was an odd buzzing in the bones of his head. Then the air shimmered through a whole dazzling array of colors and Skeeter plunged through with a wild yell, face flushed, hair standing on end, T-shirt glued to his back with sweat and his sneakers skidding on nothing.

He landed on stony ground, with a sky big as an ocean howling all around him. A man dressed in furs, face greased against a bitter wind, stared down at him. The man's expression wavered somewhere between shock, terror, and triumph, all three shining at once in his dark eyes. Skeeter, winded by the chase and badly dazed by the plunge through nothingness, just stood there panting up at him for endless moments, eye locked to eye. When the man drew a sword, Skeeter knew he had two choices: run or fight. He was used to running. Skeeter usually found it easier to run than to confront an enemy directly, particularly when running allowed him to lay neat traps in his wake.

But he was out of breath, suddenly and shockingly frozen by the bitter wind, and confronted with something a few thieving raids at the mall had not prepared him to deal with: a man ready to actually *kill* him.

So he attacked first.

One eight-year-old boy with a stolen Swiss Army Knife was no match for Yesukai the Valiant, but he did some slight damage before the grown man put him on the ground, sword at his throat.

"Aw, hell, go on and kill me, then," Skeeter snarled. "Couldn't be worse'n being ignored."

To his very great shock, Yesukai—Skeeter learned later just exactly who and what he was—snatched him up by his shirt, slapped his face, and threw him across the front of a high-pommelled Yakka saddle, then galloped down a precipitous mountainside that left Skeeter convinced they were all going to die: Skeeter, the horse, *and* the madman holding the reins. Instead, they joined a group of mounted men waiting below.

"The gods have sent a *bogda*," Yesukai said (as Skeeter later learned, once he could understand Yesukai's language. He had heard the story recounted many times over the cook fires of Yesukai's yurt.) He thumped Skeeter's back with a heavy hand, knocking the breath from him. "He attacked brave as any Yakka Mongol warrior, drawing the blood of courage." The man who'd slung him over his saddle bared an arm where Skeeter had cut him slightly. "It is a sign from the spirits of the upper air, who have sent us the beginnings of a man to follow us on earth."

A few younger warriors smiled at the ancient Mongol religious tenet; grizzled old veterans merely watched Skeeter through slatted eyes, faces so perfectly still they might have been carved of wood.

Then Yesukai the Valiant jerked his horse's fretting head around to the north. "We ride, as I have commanded."

Without another word of explanation, Skeeter found himself bundled onto another man's saddle, thrust into a fur jacket too big for him, a felt hat with ear flaps tied under his chin—also too big for him—and carried across the wildest, most desolate plain he had ever seen. The ride went on for hours. He fell asleep in pain, woke in pain to be offered raw meat softened by being stored between the saddle and the horse's sweating skin (he managed to choke it down, half starved as he was), then continued for hours more until a group of black-felt tents he later learned to call *yurts* rose from the horizon like bumps of mold growing up from the flat, bleak ground.

They galloped into the middle of what even Skeeter could tell was some kind of formal processional, scattering women and children as they smashed into the festive parade. Screams rose from every side. Yesukai leaned down from his saddle and snatched a terror-stricken young girl from her own pony, threw her across his pommel and shouted something. The men of the camp were running toward them, bows drawn. Arrows whizzed from Yesukai's mounted warriors. Men went down, screaming and clutching at throats, chests, perforated bellies. Deep in shock, Skeeter rode the long way back to the tall mountain where he'd fallen through the hole in the air, wondering every galloping step of the way what was to become of him, never mind the poor girl, who had finally quit screaming and struggling and had settled into murderous glares belied by occasional whimpers of terror.

It was only much later that Skeeter learned of Yesukai's instructions to his warriors. "If the *bogda* brings us success, I command that he be raised in our tents as a gift from the gods, to become Yakka as best he can or die as any man would of cold, starvation, or battle. If he brings the raid bad luck and I fail to steal my bride from that flat-faced fool she is to marry, then he is no true *bogda*. We will leave his cut-up body for the vultures."

There was no compassion in Yesukai for any living thing outside his immediate clan. He couldn't afford it. No Mongol could. Keeping the Yakka Clan's grazing lands, herds, and yurts safe from the raids of neighbors was a full-time job which left no room in his heart for anything but cold practicality.

Skeeter had come to live in terror of him—and to love him in a way he could never explain. Skeeter was used to having to fend for himself, so learning to fight for scraps of food like the other boys after the adults had finished eating from the communal stew pot wasn't as great a shock as it might have been. But Skeeter's father would never have troubled himself to say things like, "A Yakka Mongol does not steal from a Yakka Mongol. I rule forty-thousand yurts. We are a small tribe, weak in the sight of our neighbors, so we do not steal from the tents of our own. But the best in life, *bogda*, is to steal from one's enemy's and make what was his your own—and to leave his yurts burning in the night while his women scream. Never forget that, *bogda*. The property of the clan is sacred. The property of the enemy is honorable gain to be taken in battle."

Boys, Skeeter learned, stole from one another anyway, sometimes starting blood feuds that Yesukai either ended cruelly or—on occasion—allowed to end in their own fashion, if he thought the wiser course would be to drive home a harsh lesson. Hardship Skeeter could endure. Fights with boys twice his age (although often half his size), nursing broken bones that healed slowly through the bitter, dust-filled storms every winter, learning to ride like the other boys his age, first on the backs of sheep they were set to guard, then later on yaks and even horses, *these* Skeeter could endure. He even learned to pay back those boys who stole from him, stealing whatever his enemies treasured most and planting the items adroitly amongst the belongings of his victim's most bitter enemies.

If Yesukai guessed at his little *bogda*'s game, he never spoke of it and Skeeter was never reprimanded. He desperately missed nearly everything about the up-time home he'd lost. He missed television, radio, portable CD players, roller blades, skate boards, bicycles, video games—home versions *and* arcade games—movies, popcorn, chocolate, colas, ice cream, and pepperoni pizza.

But he did not miss his parents.

To be accepted into the Yakka Clan, with its banner of nine white yak tails, as though he actually were *important* to someone, was enough, more than enough, to make up for a father who had abdicated all pretense of caring about his family. Not even the mother who—after her son had been missing for five years only God knew where, more than likely dead, the son who had been rescued by a time scout who'd given his life rescuing Skeeter—had welcomed him home with a cursory peck on the cheek, obligatory for the multiple media cameras. She had then, in her chilly, methodical way, calmly set about making lists of the school classes he'd need to make up, the medical appointments he'd need, and the new wardrobe that would have to be obtained, all without once saying, "Honey, I missed you," or even, "How did you ever survive your adventure?" never mind, "Skeeter, I love you with all my heart and I'm so glad you're home I could cry."

Skeeter's mother was too busy making lists and making certain he was antiseptically clean again to notice his long, still silences. His *father's* sole response was a long stare of appraisal and a quiet, "Wonder what we can make of this, hmm? TV talk shows? Hollywood? At least a made-for-TV movie, I should think. Ought to pay handsomely, boy."

And so, after two weeks of bitterly hating both of them and wishing them gutted on the end of Yesukai's sword, when Skeeter's father—in the midst of signing all the contracts he'd mentioned that first day—decided to send him to some University school to have his brain picked on the subject of twelfth-century Mongolian life and the early years of Temujin, first-born son of Yesukai—merely for the *fee* it would bring, Skeeter had done exactly what Yesukai had taught him to do.

He had quietly left home in the middle of the night and made his way to New York by way of a stolen car to continue his real education: raiding the enemy. The man and woman who'd given him life had become members of that enemy. He was proud—deeply proud—of the fact that he'd managed to electronically empty his parents' substantial bank account before leaving.

Yesukai the Yakka Mongol Khan, father of the one-day Genghis Khan, had begun Skeeter's formal training. New York street toughs furthered it. His return to La-La Land, a time terminal he recalled as a half-finished shell of concrete with few shops and only one active gate open for business, run by a company called *Time Ho!* was the journeyman's equivalent of completing his unique education.

So, when Skeeter said, "My father made me everything I am today," he was telling the bald-faced, unvarnished truth. The trouble was, he was never sure which father he meant. He possessed no such uncertainty about which man's values he'd chosen to emulate. Skeeter

Jackson was a twenty-first-century, middle-class, miserable delinquent who had discovered happiness and purpose in the heart and soul of the Yakka Mongol.

And so he smiled when he worked his schemes against the enemy—and that smile was, as others had sometimes speculated, absolutely genuine, perhaps the only "genuine" thing about him. 'Eighty-sixers had become the closest thing Skeeter now had to a family, a tribe to which he belonged, only on the fringes, true; but he never forgot Yesukai's lesson. The property of Clan was sacrosanct. And there *was* no greater pleasure than burning the enemy's yurts in the night—or, metaphorically, scamming the last, living cent out of any tourist or government bureaucrat who richly and most royally deserved it.

If others called him scoundrel because of it . . .

So be it.

Yesukai the Valiant would have applauded, given him a string of ponies for his success, and maybe even a good bow—all things that Skeeter had coveted. La-La Land was the only place where a latter-day Mongol *bogda* could practice his art without serious threat of jail. It was also the only place on earth where—if life grew too unendurable or the scholars caught up with him—he could step back through the Mongolian Gate, find young Temujin, and join up again.

"Y'know," Skeeter slurred, downing yet another glass of whiskey, "nights when m' luck's down and I got no one, sometimes I swear I'm gonna do just that. Walk through, next time th' Monglian—Mongolian—Gate opens. Haven't done it yet, Marcus. So far," he rapped his knuckles against the wet surface of the wooden bar, "m' luck always takes a turn for the better, jus' in time. But my Khan, he always said luck alone don't carry a man through life. Tha's why I work so damn hard. It's pride, don' you see, not jus' survival. Gotta live up t' Yesukai's standards. And genr'ally—" he hiccuped and almost dropped his glass, "—genr'ally it's fun, 'cause a' bureaucrats anna' damn arrogant tourists are a bunch a' idiots. Incomp'tent, careless idiots, don' even know wha's around 'em." He laughed a short, bitter laugh. "Let'm stay blind 'n deaf 'n stupid. Keeps the money coming, don't it?"

He met Marcus' gaze with one that was almost steady, despite the appalling amount of whiskey he'd consumed.

"If no one else unnerstan's, so be it. 'S not their life t' live. 'S mine." He thumped his chest, staining a Greek chiton of exquisite cut and embroidery when the remaining whiskey in his glass sloshed across the garment and puddled in his lap. "Mine, y'unnerstand. My life. And I ain't disappointed, Marcus. Not by much, I ain't."

When Skeeter began to cry as though his heart were breaking, Marcus had very gently taken the whiskey glass from his hand and guided him home, making sure he was safely in bed in his own apartment that night. Whether or not Skeeter recalled anything he'd said, Marcus had no idea. But Marcus remembered every word—even those he didn't quite understand.

When Marcus shared the precious story of Skeeter Jackson with Ianira, she held her beloved close in the darkness and made sacred promises to her goddesses. They had given her this precious man, this Marcus who cherished not only Ianira herself, but also their beautiful, sloe-eyed daughters. They had given Ianira a man who actually *loved* little Artemisia and tiny little Gelasia, loved their cooing laugher and loved dandling them by turns on his knee and even soothing their tears, rather than ordering either beautiful child left on the street to die of exposure and starvation simply because she was *female.*

There in the sacred privacy of their shared bed, Ianira vowed to her goddesses that she would do whatever lay in her power to guard the interests of the man who had given her beloved the means to discharge his debt of honor. When Marcus joined with her in the darkness, skin pressed to trembling skin, she prayed that his seed would plant a son in her womb, a son who would be born into a world where his father was finally a free man in his own soul. She called blessings on the name of Skeeter Jackson and swore a vow that *others* in the down-timer community would soon know the truth about the smiling, strange young man who made such a point to steal from the tourists yet never touched anything belonging to residents—and always treated down-timers with more courtesy than any 'eighty-sixer on the station, with the possible exceptions of Kit Carson and Malcolm Moore.

Ianira understood now many things that had been mysterious to her. All those cash donations, with no one taking responsibility for them . . . Down-timers had a champion they had not dreamed existed. Marcus, not understanding why she wept in the darkness, kissed her tears and assured her in ragged words that he would prove himself worthy of the love she gave so freely. She held him fiercely and stilled his mouth with her own, vowing he had proven his worthiness a thousand times over already. His response brought tears to *her* eyes.

In the aftermath of their love, she held him while he slept and made plans that Marcus would neither understand nor approve. She didn't care. They owed a debt which was beyond profound; Ianira would repay it as best she could. And the only way she could think to do that was to further the fortunes of the man who had given Marcus the means to purchase back his sacred honor.

Ianira kissed Marcus' damp hair while he slept and made silent, almost savage, decisions.

Chapter 5

Wagers in La-La Land were big news. Essentially a closed environment for full-time residents, gossip and betting took the place of live television and radio programs, except for a couple of new on-terminal news programs run more like "gossip hour" than a real news broadcast. The Shangri-la Radio and Television Broadcasting system, an experimental outfit, to say the least, ran taped movies and canned music when down-and-out newsies weren't conducting official gossip sessions.

And like all other newsies, who were snoops at heart, if someone bet on something, everyone in La-La Land would eventually hear about it, the process just speeded up a little now thanks to S.L.R.T.B.'s inquisitive, intrusive staff. Even minor bets, like how long it would take a new batch of tourists to react to pterodactyl splatters on their luggage, became juicy tidbits to pass along over a beer, across the dinner table, or over the new cable system.

When two of Shangri-la Station's most notorious hustlers made a wager like the one Goldie Morran and Skeeter Jackson had made, not only did it spread like wildfire through the whole station, it captured the top news slot of the hour for twenty-four hours running and made banner headlines in the *Shangri-la Gazette*: POCKETS—PICK 'EM OR PACK 'EM! The banner headline was followed immediately, of course, by intimate details, including the full set of rules laid down by librarian Brian Hendrickson.

Skeeter read that article with a sense of gloom he couldn't shake. Everyone who *lived* on TT-86 knew he never went after residents, but now the *tourists* would be warned, too, drat it. He crumpled up the newspaper and glared across Commons, wondering how much Goldie had scammed so far. Goldie had no such principles where cheating and theft were concerned, which meant residents were watching their wallets and possessions with extra care. It hurt Skeeter that many now included *him* in that distrust, but that was part of the game.

He glanced up at the nearest chronometer board to see which gate departures were scheduled and pursed his lips. Hmm . . . The Britannia Gate to London tomorrow, Conquistadores this afternoon, medieval Japan through Edo Castletown's Nippon Gate in three days, and the Wild West gate to Denver in four, on a clockwork routine of exactly one week. He didn't like the idea of going after tourists headed for the ancient capital of the Japanese shogunate. Some were just gullible businessmen, but lots of them were gangland thugs—and all too often the businessmen travelled under the protection of the gangs.

Skeeter had no desire to end up minus a few fingers or other parts of his anatomy. If he were desperate enough, he'd risk it, but the other gates were better bets. For now, anyway. The nearest gate opening would be the South American Conquistadores Gate. That would present plenty of opportunity for quick cash. He could set up more elaborate schemes for the later gates, given the time to work them out. And, of course, he kept one eye eternally peeled for Mike Benson or his security men. He did *not* want to get caught and Benson would have security crawling around all the gates, now that word of the wager was out.

Skeeter cursed reporters everywhere and went to his room to get into costume. If he had to dodge security, he'd better do something to disguise himself. Otherwise, he'd be looking for a new home next time Primary cycled. The fear that he would be forced to do just that put the extra finishing touches on his disguise.

When Skeeter finally finished, he grinned into the mirror. His own birth mother—God curse her—wouldn't have recognized him. He rubbed his hands in anticipation—then swore aloud when the telephone rang. Who could possibly be calling, other than Security or some damnable snoop of a reporter who'd somehow dug up the truth about Skeeter from some dusty newspaper morgue?

He snatched the phone from the hook, considering leaving it to dangle down the wall, then muttered, "Yeah?"

"Mr. Jackson?" a hesitant voice asked. "Skeeter Jackson?"

"Who wants to know?" he growled.

"Oh, ah, Dr. Mundy. Nally Mundy."

Skeeter bit his tongue to keep from cursing aloud.

That goddamned historical scholar who interviewed down-timer after down-timer had been here so long he was practically considered a legitimate 'eighty-sixer. Well, Skeeter wasn't a legitimate down-timer and he wasn't about to talk to Nally Mundy or any *other* historical scholars about *anything*, much less his years in Mongolia. In some ways, scholars were *worse* than newsies for nosing around in a guy's private life.

Mundy must've seen the news broadcasts or read the *Gazette*, which had reminded him to make The Monthly Call. Sometimes Skeeter genuinely hated Nally Mundy for having come across that years-old scrap of newspaper clipping. Some thoughtless fool must've put it into a computer database somewhere, one that had survived The Accident, and Mundy—thorough old coot that he was—had run across it on a search for anything that survived relating to Temujin.

He actually groaned aloud while leaning his brow against the cold wall. The sound prompted a hesitant, "Have I called at an inconvenient time?"

Skeeter nearly laughed aloud, imagining all too clearly what the good historian must be thinking. Skeeter's reputation with women being what it was.

"No," he heard his voice say, while the rest of him screamed, *Yes, you idiot! Tell him you're screwing some tourist through the bed so you can get out of here and steal anything you can get from all those Conquistadores! They're even stupider than you are!* But he couldn't very well *say* that. Fortunately, Dr. Mundy rescued him from saying anything at all.

"Ah, well, good, then." The good doctor—like all 'eighty-sixers—knew better than to ask Skeeter anything about his current affairs (business or otherwise), but some men were stone-hard persistent about Skeeter's *past* affairs. "Yes, then, well, to business." Skeeter reined in considerable impatience. He'd heard all this before from the fussy little man. "I'm starting a new series of interviews, you see, with generous compensation, of course, and there is so much you could reveal about Temujin's early years, the father and mother who molded him into what he eventually became. Please say you'll come, Skeeter."

Skeeter actually hesitated a moment. Generous compensation, huh? The old fiddler in other people's lives must've received a beaut of a grant from somewhere. And Skeeter *did* need money badly, for the bet. But Brian Hendrickson would *never* allow money earned from an interview with Nally Mundy to count toward his bet.

"Sorry, Doc. Answer's still no. Don't want my name and photo scattered all over the goddamned world. I've made a few enemies, you know, over the years. Professional hazard. I'd be pretty goddamned stupid if I let you put my name and photo all over your next little research paper. Hell, it wouldn't be stupid, it'd be *suicidal.* Forget it, Doc."

A nasal sigh gusted through the receiver. "Very well, then. You do have my number?" (Skeeter had thrown it into the trash a *long* time ago.) "Good." Mundy took his silence for assent, a trick Yesukai had taught him: when to speak and when to hold silent as a lizard on the sun-warmed rocks. "If you change your mind Skeeter, whatever the reason, whatever the hour, *please* call me. We know so very little, really about Temujin, his early childhood, his relatives—anything that could shed light on the boy who grew up to be Genghis Khan."

Skeeter did realize enough to know that sending researchers down the gate would be tantamount to murder. The scout who'd brought him back had died in the attempt. Either Temujin's band of hunted brothers and followers would kill them, or Temujin's enemies would. He really *was* the only source. And since Yesukai had taught him the knack of remaining silent, he did so. The Dreaded Call would come every month of every year, anyway, regardless of what Skeeter did. Maybe one of these days he'd even be desperate enough to accept Mundy's terms. But not yet. Not by a long shot.

"Well, then, that's it, I suppose. I always hate letting you go, young man. One of these days I'm going to read in the *Gazette* that you've ended up dead through one of your endless schemes and that would be a great loss to scholarship. A very great loss, indeed. Do, please call, then, Skeeter. You know I'll be waiting."

Skeeter ignored the nearly overt sexual overtone to that last remark and thought, *Yeah, you'll be waiting in a pine box before I tell you a single syllable about Yesukai and his wife and their son . . .* The moon would turn blue, hell would freeze over, and Skeeter would settle down to a nice, *honest* way to make a living before he talked to Nally Mundy.

Yakka Mongols did not betray their own.

He snorted, checked his disguise in the mirror, smoothed out the smudge on his forehead where he'd leaned against the wall, then put Nally Mundy and his grandiose dreams of a Pulitzer or Nobel Prize—or whatever the hell he'd win for Skeeter's interview—all firmly out of mind. He was actually whistling a jaunty little war tune when he locked his door and headed for the Conquistadores Gate with its truncated pyramid, colorful wall paintings, fabulous Spanish restaurants, "peasant" dancers whirling to holiday music played on guitar and castanet, their full skirts and rich, black hair flying on a wind of their own making—and, of course, dozens of piñatas in wild colors and shapes, hanging just out of reach, due to be smashed open at the appointed hour by as many kids as wanted to join in the fun.

Skeeter was whistling to himself again as he pilfered the equipment he'd need, then headed off to the Conquistadores Gate to see what profits might be drummed up.

Goldie Morran tapped slim, age-spotted fingers against the glass top of her counter and narrowed her eyes. Publish their bet, would they? She'd find a way to get even with that idiotic reporter, make no mistake about that. And the editor, too—another score to settle. Goldie smiled, an expression that signalled to those who knew her well that someone's back was about to be stabbed with something akin to a steel icicle.

Goldie did not like to be crossed.

That ridiculous little worm, Skeeter Jackson, wasn't the only upstart on this time terminal who would pay for crossing her. The *nerve* of him, challenging *her* to such a bet. Her smile chilled even further. She'd already made arrangements for his eviction and up-time deportation, through a little side deal she'd made with Montgomery Wilkes. "I'll rid you of that little rat," she'd purred over a glass of his favorite wine.

Montgomery, nostrils pinched as though speaking to her were akin to smelling a skunk dead on the road for five days, said, "I know the kind of games you play, Goldie Morran. One day I'll catch you at them and send *you* packing." He smiled—and Goldie was smart enough to know that the head ATF agent on TT-86 had the power and the authority to do just that, if he caught her. Light glinted in his cold, cold eyes, always shocking with their contrast to his bright red hair. His smile altered subtly. "But for now, I'm more interested in Skeeter Jackson. He's a pest. Technically, he never enters my jurisdiction, so long as he doesn't try to take anything up time, but he's bad for business. And that's bad for tax collection."

He leaned back in his chair, black uniform creaking where the creases bent, and held her gaze with a glacial smile.

Goldie, maintaining a smile that hurt her face, nodded solemnly. "Yes. I understand your job very well, Montgomery." Better than he understood it himself, the autocratic . . . "Believe me, I know just how bad for business the Skeeters of this world are. So . . . it's in our mutual interest to be rid of him. I win a harmless little wager, you say goodbye to a thorn in your side forever."

"If you win."

Goldie laughed. "*If*? Come, now, Monty. I was in this business before that boy was *born*. He doesn't have a chance and he's the only one in Shangri-la Station who doesn't know it. Draw up the papers. Date 'em. Then toss him through Primary and good riddance."

Montgomery Wilkes actually chuckled, a laugh Goldie got on tape—thereby providing the necessary proof she needed to win that little private wager on the side with Robert Li about the outcome of her conversation with the head ATF agent. Montgomery Wilkes had then drained his glass, nodded as pleasantly as she'd ever seen him nod, and taken his leave, plowing through a crowd of tourists like a wooly rhinoceros charging through a scattered herd of impala.

Back in her shop, Goldie once again tapped her fingertips against the cool glass of her counter, then swept away the latest copy of the *Shangri-la Gazette* in one disgusted movement. The newspaper fluttered into the trash can at the end of the counter, settling like dead butterflies. *Skeeter win? Ha! That little amateur is about to eat his boast, raw.* The shop door opened, admitting half a dozen customers due to depart in a few hours through the South American Conquistadores Gate. They needed to exchange currency. Goldie smiled and set to work.

Marcus' shift ended shortly after the cycling of the Porta Romae, which left him rubbing shoulders with crowds of men and women dressed as wealthy Romans. Although he knew them to be impostors, he could not overcome the ingrained need, beaten into him over years, to scurry deferentially out of their way, to the extreme of hugging the wall with his back flat against the concrete when necessary to avoid offending any single one of them. Most were decent enough and a few even smiled at him—mostly women or young girls, or swaggering little boys full of themselves and willing to share their excitement with any passerby.

Several young men, however, had been seriously ill—a common enough occurrence for returning tourists. Down-timers like himself, hired as cleaning staff for the time terminal, were busy mopping up the mess. Marcus nodded to one he knew passingly well, a Welshman from Britannia who had pledged some sort of lifelong oath to Kit Carson—a time scout Marcus held in awe, almost more because of the kindness he showed Marcus than because he had once survived the Roman arena.

When Marcus nodded to Kynan Rhys Gower, he received a return grimace and half-hearted smile. "Stupid boys," Kynan Rhys

Gower said carefully in the English everyone here used—or tried to. "They drink much, yes? Make stink and mess."

Marcus nodded in Roman fashion, tipping his head back slightly. "Yes. Many tourists come back sick from Rome. Especially boys who think they are men."

Kynan's sun-lined face twisted expressively as he rolled his eyes toward the ceiling. "Yes. And Kynan Rhys Gower washes it."

Marcus clapped his shoulder. "I have done worse work, my friend."

The stranded Welshman—who had no hope at all of ever returning home, having stumbled into La-La Land through an unstable gate that had not opened again—met his gaze squarely. "Yes. Worse work. In Rome?"

Marcus didn't bother to hold in the shiver that caught his back. He couldn't have, had he tried. "Yes, in Rome." He was just about to speak again when a man dressed in an expensive tunic, wearing a gladius belted to his waist, stepped out from behind a vined portico and shot a tentative glance both ways before heading past them. Marcus blinked. He knew that face. Didn't he? He stared at the man's retreating back. Surely he was wrong. The face in his memory, the face *that* man wore, didn't belong to a tourist—it was someone he'd seen in Rome long ago, before his latest master had brought him to Time Terminal Eighty-Six then vanished uptime on his ever-mysterious business.

"Marcus?" Kynan asked quietly. "Something is wrong?"

"I—I'm not sure. I—" He shook his head. "No. It could not be. It is only a man who looked like someone I once saw. But that is impossible. All tourists look alike, anyway," he added with a feeble attempt at a grin.

Kynan laughed dourly. "Aye. Ugly and rude. I finish, yes? Then maybe you come to my room, we eat together?"

Marcus smiled. "I would like that. Yes. Call me on the telephone."

Kynan just groaned. Marcus laughed. Kynan Rhys Gower still called the telephone "Satan's trumpet"—but he'd learned to use it and was beginning to enjoy its convenience. Marcus had no idea who "Satan" was supposed to be. He cared very little for the religious beliefs of others in La-La Land, figuring it was a man's own business what gods he worshipped.

Whoever this "Satan" was, Kynan feared him mightily. Marcus admired the courage it took the Welshman to use the telephone. He was hoping time would cement the tentative friendship growing between them. Marcus had many who called him "friend" but very few he could truly call on *as* friend when trouble struck.

"I will call," Kynan agreed, "when I wash this. And myself." His grimace was all too expressive. Kynan's disgust of tourists ran far deeper than Marcus', who found most of their baffling antics amusing more than maddening.

"Good." Marcus gave him a cheery smile, then headed in the direction of his own rooms in Residential to shower and change clothing and see what he might contribute to the joint meal out of the family's meager supplies—riches, compared to what Kynan Rhys Gower would have at *his* place, though. He wondered if Ianira might have left one of her famous cheesecakes in the refrigerator. He grinned, recalling the sign Arley Eisenstein had posted in the Delight's menu-holder the last time Ianira had sold him a recipe: "A Bite of History . . . A Taste of Heaven." If she'd left any of their last one, he could raid a slice or two to contribute. Marcus' grin deepened as he recalled Ianira's astonishment over the *serious* discussions even important politicians and philosophers of Athens had held routinely on the merits of this or that type of cheesecake. He hadn't known the delicacy was so ancient.

Arley had paid her enough money that she'd been able to open that little stall he'd made for her in the Little Agora section of Commons, near the Philosophers' Gate, which was owned by the up-time government. Even Time Tours, the biggest company in the business, had to pay to send its tour groups through Philosophers' Gate. Tickets to ancient Athens were *expensive*. Several touring companies had even approached Ianira about guiding, for a fabulous salary and benefits. She'd turned them down in language they'd found shocking—but which Marcus understood in his bones.

He would not have set foot through the Porta Romae again for anything less than rescuing his family.

He was strolling toward her booth, to ask if she might like to join him at Kynan's place for dinner, when he spotted the man with the gladius again. Whoever the fellow was, he ducked furtively through a door which led to the storage rooms of Connie Logan's Clothes and Stuff shop.

Finding that peculiar, Marcus paused. Was the man on Connie's payroll? He knew the eccentric young outfitter constantly hired agents to travel down time researching costumes, fabrics, utensils, and other assorted items used in daily life on the other side of La-La Land's many gates, but Marcus didn't know this man.

And there was still that odd tingle of near-recognition chilling his spine. It couldn't be . . . could it? He decided to wait, settling down beside a shallow pond stocked with colorful fish, and watched the door. Brian Hendrickson strolled by, deep in conversation with a guide. They were speaking Latin. From the sound of it, Brian was in the middle of a language lesson, stressing the finer points of conversational Latin to the relatively new guide. Across the way, Connie's storeroom door opened again. The man Marcus was following stepped out into the open. A woman nearby started to giggle. Even Marcus gaped. Cowboy chaps over jeans, topped by a Victorian gentleman's evening jacket, finished off by a properly wrapped but ludicrous toga and stovepipe hat . . .

For an instant, his gaze locked with the other man's.

A dark flush stained weathered cheeks. The man Marcus was positive he'd seen before ducked back into Connie's warehouse. The giggling tourist caught a friend's attention and hurried over to tell her what she'd just seen. The door opened again moments later; this time, his quarry emerged wearing only the jeans and chaps and a western-style shirt. Marcus noted that he still wore the gladius, however, hidden carefully beneath the leather chaps. That worried him. *Should I report this?*

Concealed weapons were against station rules. Openly carried weapons were fine. But only when stepping through a gate was one permitted to conceal one's personal weapons. Those were the rules and Marcus was careful to live by them. But he also knew it wasn't always a good idea to mix one's affairs with those of a stranger. Well, he could always report the fellow anonymously to Mike Benson or one of his security men through a message on one of the library computers.

Or he could simply ignore the whole thing and go take that shower. He had just about decided on the latter course of action when the stranger turned to glance back at him. Something in the movement, the set of the mouth and the dark light in those eyes, clicked in Marcus' memory. Shock washed through him like icy water. He gripped his seat until his hands ached. It wasn't possible . . . yet he was *certain.* As certain as he had ever been about anything in his life. Sweat started under his shirt and dripped down his armpits.

Rome's Death Wolf, Lupus Mortiferus, had come to Shangri-la.

What purpose could the Circus' deadliest gladiator possibly have in coming here? Marcus the former slave didn't know—but he intended to find out. He owed the men and women who'd befriended him here that much. Heart in his throat, blood pounding in his ears, Marcus waited until the Wolf of Death turned his attention elsewhere, then cautiously eased from his seat and began to follow.

Skeeter Jackson, in heavy disguise, wheeled his cart toward a tourist near the Conquistadores' Gate. The man was in the middle of a nasty harangue directed at a harried tour guide. Her face was flushed with anger, but her job prevented her from venting it. Skeeter stepped in with a smile.

"Sir, baggage check for leave-behind luggage?"

The man turned to note the other tagged suitcases on Skeeter's cart, each tag with the owner's name and hotel scrawled across it, with the tear-off stub missing. The tour guide's eyes met Skeeter's and widened in recognition. For a second, he thought he'd been blown for good. Then her eyes flashed briefly with unholy joy. She winked and fled, leaving Skeeter's quarry to his just deserts.

"Why, yes, that would be convenient. That idiotic guide—"

It was the same old story. Stupid tourist doesn't read the rules, then takes out his mad on the guides. Skeeter smiled as charmingly as he could—which was *very*—and tagged the man's expensive leather bags, tearing off numbered receipts which he handed over. "Thank you, sir. All you need to do to reclaim your luggage on return is present those claim stubs to your hotel. Have a good trip, sir."

The man actually tipped him. Skeeter hid a grin, then maneuvered his now-full cart toward the edge of the growing crowd. And there, just as he was passing a woman whose cases were also on his cart, it happened. He came eye to eye with Goldie Morran.

"Is that the man?" Goldie asked the tourist whose cases Skeeter had "checked."

"Yes!"

Goldie smiled directly into Skeeter's eyes. That was when he noticed security ringing the area.

"All's fair in love and bets, Skeeter, darling." Goldie's eyes glinted far back in their depths with murderous amusement.

It was either ditch hard-won gains or lose the bet—and his home. Skeeter did neither. Goldie's own mouth had uttered his one chance for salvation.

"Mike!" he yelled. "Hey, Mike Benson! Over here!"

Goldie's eyes went round and her pinched mouth fell slack.

Benson lost no time approaching. "As I live and breathe . . ."

Before he could finish, Skeeter said indignantly, "Here I am saving these poor folks from Goldie's clutches, making sure she doesn't make a grab for their luggage, and *she* has the nerve to accuse *me*—well, Mr. Benson, I want you to take a good look at these tags, here. I was on my way to all these hotels to turn over these cases, when Goldie, here, furious I'd got in her way, started making nasty accusations."

Every tourist within earshot was goggle-eyed, listening to nothing else.

Mike's forehead creased with vertical *and* horizontal lines. "And you just expect me to swallow that pack of—"

"Not only do I insist you believe it, I *demand* an escort to every one of these hotels so I can make sure every bag is locked safely away. Don't trust Goldie, Mr. Benson. She might have me waylaid by some of those paid thugs of hers."

Mike Benson stared from one to the other, then started—

astonishingly—to laugh. "Look at the pair of you. Priceless! Okay, Skeeter my boy, let's go put these cases in the hotels' lock-up rooms. I'll go along just to be *certain* nobody waylays you on the trip."

Skeeter seethed inwardly, having hoped Mike would let him just trundle his cart away for some time to rifle the contents of watches, cameras, jewelry, etc. Instead, he smiled and said, "Sure thing."

"Just a minute!" Goldie snapped. "If you're so altruistic, why the disguise?"

Skeeter smiled into her eyes, noting the fury in them. "Why, Goldie, so your agents wouldn't recognize me and drop a sap across the back of my head to get these." He waved expansively at the suitcases. "There's gotta be a fortune in up-time jewelry in 'em, and who better than you to break up the pieces and fence the stones?"

Without waiting for a smarter and potentially deadlier protest from Goldie, Skeeter shoved his cart forward through the gaping crowd and sang out, "Coming, Mr. Benson? Gotta lot of work waiting, getting these good peoples' cases back safe."

Benson did as he'd promised, following Skeeter to each and every hotel on Skeeter's list. He verified each case as it was put into storage, then checked his list against Skeeter's supposed-to-be-fake manifest of names, hotels, up-time addresses, the works, not to mention the claim-ticket numbers. He grunted when the work was finally done. "Huh. Kept you clean this time, at least."

"But—Mr. Benson, you wound me. Honest."

"Don't 'Mr. Benson' me, punk. I was a damned fine cop before you were even born, so give it a rest. You came close, buddy, but you slithered out of it. Just be sure I'll be watching you double-close from now on."

"Well, sure. Hey, thanks for the escort!"

Benson just gave him a dour look. Skeeter lost no time vanishing into the thick holiday crowds, heading for the hotel from which he had "borrowed" the cart and claim tickets. He didn't want to leave any loose strings if Benson should question the hotel manager or bellhops. Not that Benson could prove anything. He just didn't want to go through what Benson benignly referred to as his "lean-on-'em-a-little-and-they'll-sing" speech.

Although as the head of ATF's presence on TT-86, meaning that technically, Montgomery Wilkes was the highest-ranking officer of the law on the station, Monty's actual jurisdiction was limited to the Customs area near Primary (much to Monty's everlasting, abiding rage, since he guessed how often he got hoodwinked outside that jurisdiction).

In all else, Benson reigned supreme. And if he wanted to keep Skeeter locked up for a month on bread and water, just for questioning, there was nothing in the station's charter that prevented him from doing just that. It was one of the reasons Skeeter was always so careful—and it was also the impulse behind his effort to try a little scamming down time, away from Benson's watchful eye.

Of course, that'd nearly gone sour, *would have* if not for that gorgeous racehorse. The Lupus Mortiferus incident had prompted Skeeter to give up any further thoughts of down-time scamming until he knew a *whole* lot more about the culture he was planning to rip off. He understood far better, now, why guides and scouts spent all their free time—most of it, anyway—studying.

That Skeeter's target would be Rome again was a foregone conclusion, despite his somewhat desperate, drowning promise. He intended to hit rich Romans often and hard, because the arrogant bastards *deserved* it so much. But not just yet. He needed a lot of hours in the library and its soundproof language booths. And before he could do so much as that, he needed to win a little bet, first. Goldie had already proven ruthless enough to *arrange* for him to get caught.

Goldie'd get what she had coming, of *that* Skeeter was certain.

He could hardly wait to wave bye-bye as she hauled as much as she could afford to pay taxes on when she was forced up time and use the rest of her assets to make bail. Skeeter chuckled. If things *really* went his way, he might even have enough at the end of the bet to buy out what Goldie couldn't take with her, including that breeding pair of Carolina parakeets some visitor had brought back from Colonial Williamsburg. Extinct birds, and she had a breeding pair of 'em. Could get more any time she wanted, too, by pulling the right strings—the ones attached to her down-time agents. Skeeter made a little wager with himself that Sue Fritchey didn't even know they were on station.

Well, if it came down to those birds (rumor had it Goldie was actually attached to them, emotionally) or Skeeter's continued life on TT-86, he'd know exactly what to do. Call up Sue Fritchey and make her famous all over again. Undoing Goldie in the process.

The klaxon and announcement came over the Commons' big speakers, warning of the impending cycling of the Conquistadores' Gate. Skeeter grinned, wondering what had happened to Goldie after he'd left. Hopefully, at least a *third* of what she deserved, interfering like that in one of his scams. At least now he'd been warned about the way she intended to play this out, which *might* give him the edge he needed to win. Disconsolately, thinking of the *thousands* of bucks' worth of easily sold items in those lost suitcases, Skeeter headed for the library to have Brian value his "tips" into the official betting ledger.

Skeeter hunted him out behind the front desk, where the librarian was busy updating the computer's research index, actually deleting the lurid red "stamp" across the face of an entry page that read: all known copies destroyed in aftermath of the accident. librarian will update this listing should this status change.

Brian didn't get a chance to remove very many of those stamps from the system.

"Hey, Brian. What turned up somewhere?"

Hendrickson swung around to face him. "Oh, it's you." His accent was wildly at odds with his appearance, which was that of an ex-military, scholarly gentleman. His dark face curved into a genuine smile. Despite the words, he kept smiling. "Somebody found a copy of Pliny the Younger's collection of histories hidden in their grandparents' attic. Asked the nearest university were they interested or should they just toss it out? The university *paid* 'em for it—a hundred-thousand, I believe it was—and had an armored car with armed guards pick it up for safe transportation. *After* they sealed it in a nitrogen atmosphere.

"Anyway, the university scanned the whole bloody thing and started selling copies on CD to every time terminal library, every other university or public library that wanted one. Library of Congress asked for *five*."

Skeeter, who had no idea who Pliny the Younger was, managed to pull off a sufficiently impressed whistle of appreciation. "Weren't taking any chances, were they?"

"No. It's the last known copy in the world. A translation, as it happens, which is too bad, but still a copy, nonetheless. To scholars and scouts, it's absolutely priceless."

"Huh. I know you're not supposed to try and steal artwork from down time unless you can prove it would've been destroyed anyway. Same goes for books and such, huh?"

"Oh, absolutely." Brian's eyes twinkled. "And Skeeter—don't even *think* of trying it. Stolen antiquities are out of both Mike's *and* Monty's jurisdiction. *That's* a federal matter and the bully boys up time don't look too kindly on somebody breaking—at least, getting *caught* breaking—the First Law of Time Travel."

"So that's why Robert Li's our official representative of—" he had to stop a moment to recall the actual *name*, not just the acronym "—the *International Federation of Art Temporally Stolen*? So he can copy the stuff for everybody's use, then send an I.F.A.R.T.S. agent down time to put it back where it came from?"

"Precisely. There's an enormous uptime market for such things." Brian looked at him. "And if you decide to join ranks with the breakers and smashers raping our past of its treasures, I'll testify at your trial and urge the death penalty."

Brian Hendrickson's intensity scared him a little. Skeeter held both hands up, palms toward the librarian. "Hey, I was just curious. I've got a lot of catching up to do myself, you know, since I never really finished grade school—never mind high school."

Homesick longing struck him silent before he could go any further.

Brian looked at him in an odd fashion for a moment, then—in a much gentler voice—asked, "Skeeter? Just why *did* you come here?"

"Huh? Oh." He dug into his pocket, pulled out the coins and bills he'd received as tips on the almost-successful suitcase pilfering he'd attempted, and explained what had gone down.

Brian glanced at the money, repeated Skeeter's story *word for word* (not scary—*terrifying*) then shook his head.

"What do you mean, the tips don't count?"

Brian Hendrickson, his dark face set now with lines of distaste, all trace of his earlier joy wiped away by deep unhappiness, said coolly, "You earned those tips for fair labor. If you'd succeed in stealing the luggage, the contents would've counted, but the tips still *wouldn't* have. So I can't count them now, even though they're all you managed to hang onto."

"But—but the damned tourists are *warned* they're supposed to check leave-behind luggage at the hotels, not with 'curbside' guys like me. The tips *are* stealing, same as the luggage would be."

Brian just shook his head. "Sorry, Skeeter. A tip is, by definition, something earned as part of a service accorded someone else. The cases are safely locked away, the tips are income—pure and simple—so your twenty-oh-seventy-five doesn't count."

Skeeter stuffed the bills and coins back into his pockets and stalked out of the library.

Who'd ever heard of such a thing, not counting scammed tips?

Chapter 6

"Please have your timecards ready so the scanner can update them as you approach the gate . . ."

Goldie had, fortunately, managed to escape the angered, hot-blooded Spaniards who were the most frequent customers through the Conquistadores' Gate. One lady about ten years Goldie's junior shoved through the crowd to follow.

"Wait! Wait, please, I wanted to thank you!"

Goldie stopped and turned, allowing a puzzled smile to drift into place. "Thank me? Whatever for?"

"For . . . for saving my luggage." The woman was still out of breath slightly. "You see, my husband and I were going down time to research some of our ancestors. We'd planned to attend the hotel's Christmas ball as a kind of celebration after we got back and, I know I'm silly, but I packed away my gown and great-grandmother's diamond tiara, necklace, and a few other matching pieces *in* that suitcase. You've saved me so much grief! I never *did* believe the ridiculous story that young man told the security chief and neither did Rodrigo. Please, let me say thank you."

She was holding out a slightly used bill with a one and an undetermined number of zeroes after it.

"I couldn't possibly," Goldie protested weakly, having deciphered the number of zeroes. *A thousand dollars?*

"Oh, please, Rodrigo and I have more money than we know

how to spend, but those jewels are absolutely irreplaceable. Please. Take it."

Goldie faked reluctance beautifully, allowing the other woman to push it into her slack hand. She closed careful fingers around the bill, and while she maintained an outward mask of surprise and lingering reluctance, inwardly she was gloating. *A thousand bucks! A thousand! Wait until Skeeter hears about this! Maybe he'll choke on envy and we'll be rid of him even sooner!*

Goldie thanked her generosity, pocketed the bill, reassured her that she hadn't missed the gate departure yet, then watched her disappear into the crowd milling around the waiting area. Then, exulting in her good fortune, Goldie headed toward the library, grinning fit to crack her skull. *Strike one, you little fool. Two more and you're out for the count!* Nobody loved a wager more than Goldie Morran—and nobody else in La-La Land came remotely *close* to Goldie's orgasmic pleasure at cheating to win. It was *not* how the game was played that counted with Goldie. It was about how much she could rook out of the opposition's wallet, down-time coinage, or bank account.

Just a few more days and Skeeter Jackson would be gone.

For good.

She passed Kit Carson, who was sitting at a cafe table sharing a beer with his pal the freelance guide, Malcolm Moore. She grinned and waved, leaving them to stare after her.

Let 'em wonder.

After what Skeeter had tried to do to Kit's grandkid, those two would surely be more appreciative than most when Goldie's plans came to full fruition. Goldie very carefully did *not* think about what *she* had very nearly done to Kit's granddaughter. Even Kit had eventually admitted the whole disaster had been entirely Margo's doing, accepting the challenge to go after those diamonds through an unstable gate.

Too bad about losing that scheme, though. Goldie sighed. Win some, lose some. At least Margo was up time at school, toiling to repay her grandfather the money Kit had paid Goldie for that worthless hunk of African swampland. Goldie patted her pocket and regained her smile, then headed for the library so Brian Hendrickson could record her "take" in his official bet ledger. He might even laugh when she recounted her tale of that cretinous woman giving her a *reward*. La-La Land's librarian had so far found very little humor in Goldie and Skeeter's bet. This ought to change his tune.

Goldie didn't exactly *need* to stay in Brian's good graces to continue her own profitable business, but burning bridges unnecessarily was just plain-and-simple foolishness. There were certainly times when Brian's encyclopedic memory had proven useful to her. And there would doubtless be other times in the future she'd want to call on his knowledge. So, scheming and dreaming to her heart's content, Goldie Morran smiled at startled scouts on their way into or out of the vast library and found Brian Hendrickson on his usual throne.

The expression in his eyes was anything but welcoming.

"Hello, Goldie. What are you doing here?"

She laughed easily. "What do you think, silly?"

Brian just grimaced and turned back toward the master computer file he was updating.

"Here." She set out the thousand-dollar bill that idiotic but *wonderful* woman had given her. "Put this on my ledger, would you, dearie?"

He eyed the money. "And how, exactly, did you come by it?"

She told him.

Then stormed out of the library, money stuffed back into her pockets. How *dare* he not count it?

"Reward for good deeds doesn't count, my eye! That overstuffed, self-important—"

Goldie *seethed* all the way back to her shop.

Once there, among her shining things, Goldie comforted herself with the knowledge that Skeeter's "tips" hadn't been counted, either. Then she got to work. Part of her mind was busy figuring out how to scam the next batch of tourists unfortunate enough to enter her shop, while another part was preoccupied with how to foil Skeeter's next attempt. That—plus a swig from a bottle she kept in reserve under her counter and fifteen minutes' solitude with her beloved, deeply affectionate Carolina parakeets—got her through a long, dead-flat afternoon. Not a single tourist entered to exchange up-time money for down-timecredit or down-time coinage for up-time credit.

By the time Goldie closed her shop for the day, she was ready to do murder. And Skeeter Jackson's grinning face floated in the center of every lethal fantasy she could dredge up. She was going to win this bet, if it was the last thing she ever did.

And Skeeter would pay in spades for daring to challenge *her*!

Goldie entered the Down Time Bar and Grill, ordered her favorite drink from Molly, the down-time whore who'd stumbled through the Britannia Gate into TT-86, and settled in the billiards room to wait for some drunken tourist who *thought* he knew how to play the game to wander in and become her next victim.

Lupus Mortiferus was afraid—almost as afraid as he'd been his first time on the glittering sands of the Circus. He struggled not to show it. Nothing about this insane world made sense. The languages bombarding his ears were very nearly painful, they were so incomprehensible. Every now and again he would hear a word that sounded almost familiar, making the wrenching dislocation even worse. Some of the lettering on the walls reminded him of words he knew, but he couldn't quite make out their sense. And everywhere he turned were mysteries—terrifying mysteries—that beeped, glowed, hummed, screeched, and twittered in alien metals and colors and energies he would have called lightning or the ominous glow of the evil-omened lights in the northern night skies, had they not been imprisoned by some god's hand in pear-shaped bulbs, long tubes and spiralling ones, plus all manner of twisted shapes and disturbing colors of glass.

And the sounds . . .

Voices that erupted from mid-air, coming from nowhere that he could see, blaring messages he couldn't begin to understand.

Have I fallen into a playground of gods?

Then, unbelievably, he caught a snatch of Latin. Real, honest Latin.

" . . . no, that isn't at all what I meant, what you have to do is . . ."

With a relief that left him almost in tears, Lupus found the speakers: a dark man who was certainly of African origin, Carthaginian, perhaps, or Nubian—although his skin was too light for Nubia—a shorter, nondescript man in shades of brown at whom no one in Rome would have given a second glance.

Lupus followed them eagerly, desperate for someone he could actually communicate with in this mad place. He followed them to a room—a vast, echoing chamber of a room—filled with shelves of squarish objects made from thin vellum and rows of . . . what? Boxes men and women sat before and *talked* to—and the boxes talked back, their glowing faces flashing up pictures or streams of alien words.

Lupus held in a shiver of terror and wondered how to approach the dark man who clearly knew Latin better than the brownish one. He was about to approach when two *other* men entered and collared the dark-skinned man first. Lupus melted into the shadows behind a bank of tall shelves and hugged his impatience to his breast, biding his time until the dark man who could speak Lupus' tongue would be alone and approachable.

"So," Kit Carson asked, relaxing back into his chair, "what do you have planned for Margo's visit?"

Malcolm Moore flushed slightly. The light in Kit's eyes told him exactly what Kit expected them to do. Fortunately, Kit approved—provided Malcolm's intentions were honorable and he took reasonable precautions against pregnancy.

"Well," Malcolm said, running a fingertip through the condensate on the tabletop, "I was thinking of a little visit to Denver. I've checked my log entries—there shouldn't be any risk of Shadowing myself. I wasn't in London during the week the Denver party will be down time."

Kit nodded. "I think that's a good idea. Margo should like it, too—and it'll complement her American History studies very nicely."

Malcolm grinned. "Sure you won't come along?"

Kit just grimaced. "I *was* in London that week. That whole month, in fact. You two lovebirds go along and have a good, careful time." Kit sighed. "It's strange. I didn't think it would happen, but . . . her letters are changing, Malcolm. Their tone, the intelligence behind her observations and comments."

Malcolm glanced up, noting the furrow on Kit's brow. "So you did notice? Figured you wouldn't miss it. She's growing up, Kit." That brought a flinch to his friend's eyes. He'd just barely begun to know her when she'd vanished: once, almost for good; the second time off to college. Trying to help his friend get used to the idea, Malcolm said, "Hell, Kit, she *grew up* in that filthy little Portuguese gaol. But now she's growing in ways it's hard to put into words."

Kit nodded. "Yeah."

Malcolm punched Kit's shoulder. "Don't take it so hard, Grandpa. Her mind's coming alive. I can hardly wait to see what direction her thoughts take her next."

Kit laughed sourly. "Just so long as it isn't toward a South African diamond field." Then Kit blinked and stared past Malcolm's shoulder. "Speak of the devil . . ."

Goldie Morran passed, smiling so sweetly at them Malcolm wondered who'd just died.

"What can *she* be up to?"

Kit laughed sourly. "Given that wager between her and Skeeter, God knows. Want to play tag the nanny goat and follow along?"

Malcolm grinned. "If that sour old goat has ever had kids, I'll eat this table. Goat I'll allow. Nanny? Not even in the British sense, Kit." His grin deepened, however. "Sure sounds like fun, though. Quick, before we lose her!"

Kit's eyes glinted as they scurried for the door, dropping more than enough money on the front counter to pay for consumables plus tip. Each of them knew the consequences should Goldie ever discover the double scam they'd pulled on her with Margo's help—not that she could really *do* anything, not legally, anyway. Their up-time diamond strike was one of La-La Land's best-kept secrets. And *that* was a monumental achievement in its own right.

Malcolm and Kit quickly determined that Goldie Morran's goal was the library. They took up places at computer terminals near the counter, ostensibly doing research, but more than close enough to overhear Goldie's screech when her "take" was disallowed.

She stalked out of the library in a towering rage.

Kit stepped over to Brian's counter. Malcolm abandoned his computer, too, and leaned on his elbows beside Kit.

"So what's new?" Kit asked casually.

His long-time friend gave him an evil stare, then shrugged. In his wonderful, outlandish accent, he muttered, "Oh, why not. You're not involved, after all." Brian Hendrickson grimaced expressively, the skin around his eyes tightening down so much Malcolm grew alarmed. Then, curtly: "They have begun a war of attrition. A *serious* one. Goldie just spoiled one of Skeeter's schemes in a way that could have been fatal—for Skeeter, anyway. I suppose spoiling each other's schemes is better than letting them rip off unsuspecting tourists, but this . . . I didn't think their idiotic wager would turn this deadly. I suppose I should've seen it coming from the very start."

He wiped his brow with a handkerchief plucked from a pocket, then neatly folded and replaced it with such style, Malcolm found himself seriously envious of the librarian's unconscious panache. Malcolm clearly needed to do a covert study of Brian's movements and work until he'd copied them motion-perfect. On London tours, those elegant movements would serve him well. Particularly with the hopeful plans he'd been developing in the back of his mind. Then Brian sighed mournfully. "I still can't believe I allowed myself to be drawn into this."

Malcolm, who was about to comment that Brian had voluntarily put himself exactly where he was, abruptly spotted a man in Western getup watching them ferally from the shadows across the room. He blinked. *Not a scout, not a freelance guide, not even a Time Tours, guide.* Malcolm made it his business to keep close watch on the competition—particularly since Time Tours, was indirectly responsible for the death of his previous employer and close friend.

The mystery-man's face arrested his attention for a moment. *But I've seen that face before, I* know *I have. But where?* Maybe a tourist Malcolm had approached at some point, looking for a job? God alone knew, he'd begged work from thousands of transient tourists over the past several years, before he and Kit and Margo had become repugnantly wealthy. (They didn't flaunt it—didn't need to—but it certainly was a great deal of fun, just *looking* at his bank account's balance, which had hovered near negative numbers for so long.)

Maybe one of the tourists had remembered him and was looking for a good guide?

No . . . whoever he was, his attention was focused directly on Brian. For some reason he couldn't explain, that very fact sent a chill racing up Malcolm's spine. He wondered if he should speak, then thought better of it. If Brian Hendrickson had a profitable side deal going with someone, it was none of his business. But he did use it as an excuse to leave, now they'd discovered what they'd wanted.

Malcolm nudged Kit with an elbow. "I think there's someone waiting to talk to Brian. Why don't we grab a bite of lunch. I'll fill you in on my plans for Margo's visit."

Brian's expression cheered immensely. "Miss Margo is returning? Capital! Have her come by and say hello, would you?"

Kit laughed. "Count on it. Malcolm's taking her to Denver. Even *with* her studies at school, she'll have time-scout-type research to do before they step through the Wild West Gate."

Brian chuckled. "It's a date, then."

Malcolm cast a last, uneasy glance at the man in cowboy getup standing in the shadows, then shrugged the whole thing off. He had better things to look forward to: like Margo's kisses. He grinned in anticipation. The ring he'd had made from the sample diamond she'd sent was ready and waiting. All she had to do was say yes. Counting the hours and minutes until Primary cycled and brought her back into his life again, Malcolm strolled out of the library with his hopefully future grandfather-in-law and suggested the Epicurean Delight for lunch.

"We haven't been in a while. And I understand Ianira Cassondra's been selling Arley some ancient Greek cheesecake recipes—long lost delicacies and confections."

Kit nodded. "The Greeks were so fond of cheesecake. We have written complaints from a Greek, a married man who asked for cheesecake for his dinner and was, um, to put it delicately, irate when he didn't get it. Weren't there supposed to be dozens of different flavors?

Malcolm nodded. "Yeah. And from what I've heard, just one slice of whatever type of cheesecake he's made for the day is enough to make a California billionaire pay a thousand or more just to get the whole thing!"

Kit laughed, an easy, relaxed sound that reassured his friend. "Sounds great," Kit agreed—vehemently. "I've been hearing those same rumors and *I*, my friend, am a cheesecake-a-holic. Let's test it out, eh?"

Malcolm chuckled and thumped his friend's wiry, granite-hard gut and said, "At least you work it off somewhere."

Kit grimaced. "Sven Bailey is a fiend from Hell. He even *looks* like one."

"So I'd noticed. And so Margo complained—bitterly—those first few lessons with him. And then, would you believe it, our little imp started to *love* having Sven kick her around the mat like a sack of squashed potatoes."

"Ah, yes; but she learned, didn't she? C'mon Malcolm, let's eat! Skimpy lunch and all the cheesecake we can hold!"

They set out, laughing like kids. The "cowboy" they'd left lurking behind in the library was so far from his thoughts, it was almost as though the man had never existed.

Ianira Cassondra was attempting to sell an amber-and-silver bracelet and necklace set to a genuine tourist through the howling idiocy of her self-proclaimed acolytes. Did up-timers have nothing better to *do* with their lives than hound and harass her, day and night, month after tedious, temper-provoking month? The Little Agora was seething with gossiping 'eighty-sixers when Chenzira Umi, a grey-haired, stately Egyptian merchant who'd fallen in a drunken accident through the Philosophers' Gate not too many months after Ianira had stumbled through, elbowed and shoved his way to the side of her little booth.

In Greek, which he spoke only well enough to dicker—*nobody* else on station (except the Seven) spoke his ancient Egyptian (although Ianira knew well enough that Chenzira earned much of his meager living by teaching his long-dead language's proper pronunciation, including some odd inflections, to uptime scholars), Chenzira reported. "Goldie badly done. She broke attempt by Skeeter."

"*What?*"

Ianira paled so disastrously that the tourist dickering over the jewelry actually noticed—and frowned in genuine concern.

"My dear," he said in the drawling tones of an American Texan, "what in thunderation's wrong? You're whiter'n the underbelly of a rattler what's just shed his skin. Here, honey, sit down."

"Thank you, no, please, I am fine." She fought off shock and worry and mastered both, *plus* her voice. "I apologize profoundly for causing you distress. Did you want the bracelet and necklace for your wife?"

He glanced from Ianira to the jewelry, the calmly waiting Chenzira, bringer of bad tidings (noticeable in *any* language), then up at the surrounding vultures. He scowled impartially, evidently not liking his face and voice recorded without his permission any more than she did.

"How long these nosy bastards—uh—vultures been after you, honey?"

"Too long," Ianira said, half under her breath.

His pop-up grin startled her. "Hell, yeah, I'll take 'em, and throw in some of those funny-lookin' scarves there. Marty, my wife, she's nuts about stuff like that—yeah, those, right there—and what's this little doo-hicky here for? *Love* charm? Well, hell, gal, gimme a dozen of *those*!"

His friendly grin—despite Ianira's inner turmoil—was infectious. She rang up the bill, bagged everything into velvet bags that she'd sewn herself nd handed him one large easy-to-carry parcel with a secure drawstring, and the itemized bill she'd written out in a somewhat shaky hand.

He handed back double the price listed, gave her a jaunty wink and said, "It'll be fine, honey, don't you fret, now, hear?" vanished into the crowd before she could protest or give back the extra money. She stood trembling for a moment, the sounds and bright sights of Commons washing over her like a dim, color-puddled dream, while she stared at the money that she and the father of her children so desperately needed, while on all sides, six to seven deep, her maddening acolytes Minicammed, voice-recorded, and jotted notes on every single second of that interchange. She wanted to scream at them all, but knew from experience that any action other than business as usual would bring twice as many watchers who'd stay another week hoping a revelation would be near.

Chenzira leaned closer, his disgusted tone of voice helping to bring her whirling mind back on track. "If I your beauty and charms had, Ianira, I, too, such deals make would. You demon are—under soft skin!" Gentle, deep laughter took any possible accusation from Chenzira's words. Along with the other down-timers in The Found Ones community—not to mention being elected to The Council of Seven almost from his first few weeks here—Chenzira was a born haggler, as many an unfortunate down-timer had discovered to his or her woe.

And since Chenzira Umi was as shrewd a man as Ianira had ever met, she, too, merely smiled. "And had I your canny wits," she countered calmly, "I would not be a huckster of this junk."

Chenzira smiled, but, in that mysterious Egyptian way of his, said nothing. Ianira received the impression—a strong one—he still deferred to her as Head of the Seven. Then he leaned close again and said very quietly in his own language, which *all* of The Seven now had to learn, "You must convene the Council. The Seven must decide what is best and summon a general Council immediately afterwards to vote on it. This atrocity, this interference *must stop*."

"Yes," she agreed, already somewhat proficient in Chenzira's native language. A smile tugged at her lips as she imagined the idiotic, eavesdropping throng trying to translate *this* conversation!

She asked—also in Egyptian—"Could you watch my shop a little?"

He nodded.

Ianira bolted from the booth, outrunning her merciless followers by a few staggering strides to a nearby hotel lobby. "Private in-house phone?" she gasped, damning the fact that women's clothing from her own time was *not* designed for an all-out, freedom-winning dash.

The desk clerk, who knew Ianira's reputation—and pitied her for the never-ending madness of her enthralled seekers—stepped back and all but shoved her into the hotel office, muttering, "Lock the door and I'll hold 'em at bay."

She gave him a startled glance of thanks, then banged shut the door and snapped the lock. It was cool and quiet inside the hotel office. She lifted the receiver and dialed a trustworthy in-house line. One phone call, she knew, would lead to others. Many others.

Having set things in motion, she returned to her stand, pushing her way through angry Seekers, all of whom were taller than she was, and forced on a bright smile for a couple of genuine customers who'd stopped to "window shop."

"Thank you, Chenzira Umi," she said formally. "You have been of great help."

Chenzira's unexpected grin (as the Seekers took up their disgruntled positions, furious they'd missed even those few, short moments of The Great One's words) startled Ianira.

"What?" she asked.

Chenzira nodded at the man and woman peering at her stock. "Your previous customer knows them. They lost no time seeking out this 'find of the year' if I remember the words. I am not yet so good at English."

"Thank you, Chenzira Umi," she breathed as she turned toward her customers with a bright smile.

Chenzira Umi was long gone, faded into the crowd as nondescript as any other bald tourist, before Ianira noticed the new price markers. Her eyes widened ever so slightly. In her absence, he had doubled the price on *everything* she carried. And the customers were buying: jewelry, Greek-style clothing for both men and women (in a matching pattern she'd lovingly sewn), scarves, and charms of all sorts.

Even all the copies she had a little, hand-done booklet that Dr. Mundy had helped her write, print, and bind, which they'd titled, *There I Lived: Athens in Its Golden Age and Ephesus, 5th Century* B.C. *Trading Center and Home to The Great Temple of Artemis, Seventh Wonder of the Ancient World*. The booklet was nothing, of course, compared to the scholarly work he was building from the sessions she spent with him, but it was a decently scripted, informal "chatty" little booklet full of odd little facts and anecdotes, some previously unknown until Ianira's arrival. It was a popular item, even outside the sales to maddening Seekers.

One of her long-term plans as First of the Seven was to assist other down-timers in writing similar booklets, which she would then sell and pass along the money to the authors, taking no commission, for this would be The Found Ones' business, not her own.

By the time La-La Land's first-shift "business day" was over, that single phone call made from the cool, quiet hotel office—she must remember to reward that wonderful, understanding clerk with some little trinket of thanks—had borne its intended fruit. Ianira made her way to the madhouse of La-La Land's School and Day-Care Center where her daughters played with the other children. She picked them up, then took back-station staircases down into the bowels of Time Terminal Eighty-Six for a secret meeting of The Found Ones.

Since this was an informal meeting, no ceremonial garb was needed nor were her daughters a nuisance to anyone. Others of the Seven who had arrived ahead of her were already discussing the news. The day after Skeeter Jackson's gift to Marcus, Ianira had passed word of his true standing to other women in the down-timer community and they, in turn, had passed it to their men. Word had traveled through the entire community before bedtime. For the first time since their arrival, the down-timers of La-La Land knew that, alone of the up-timers, they had found someone who *understood.*

Many who had looked on him with disgust as a simple thief had immediately begun to cheer on his exploits. *Anything* to punish the up-timers who used them for grunt labor, without a single thought for their welfare, was worth a cheer or ten. Astoundingly, in a few short days, Skeeter had rapidly taken on the status—thanks to Ianira's judicious' meddling—of their champion and hero for causing up-timers to suffer monetary losses and public humiliations.

Also thanks to Ianira, it became unwritten law that Skeeter's past was a private secret to be kept from all up-timers on the station. Parents warned children—and those children held their tongues.

Word of the wager between Skeeter and Goldie Morran, at first simply an affair between up-timers, had abruptly taken on new significance. Fear like the shock-waves of an earthquake travelled through their community. If Skeeter Jackson lost his bet, they would lose their spirit-champion. So when Ianira placed that phone call and word spread that Goldie Morran had deliberately spoiled one of Skeeter's attempts, and that a general session would follow a meeting of the Seven, narrow-eyed men and women gathered in the depths of Shangri-la Station to discuss what should be done about it, while wide-eyed children listened in silence to the anger in their elders' voices.

"We could slide a knife between her ribs," one grey-haired man muttered.

"Poison would be better," a younger man countered. "She would suffer longer."

"No, we don't need to kill her," Ianira said over the babble of voices as she joined the other Six on the low dais. Silence fell as abruptly as night fog rolled over the wharves of Ephesus. The Seven had previously decided the only course they *could* safely take. Now it was up to the Seven to convince the others.

She held her daughters close, partly from protective love she could scarcely give coherent tongue to, and partly because she was—as a former high-ranking Priestess of Artemis—aware of the symbolism their stance of togetherness roused. Those who stood nearest to her saw not only a mother and her children, but looked at her little girls and understood in their viscera that the children's father owed more than anyone on this station to Skeeter Jackson.

Which was precisely what she *wanted* them to think.

Had she been born up time rather than down, she'd have been running the government inside two years.

Although most of the gathered Found Ones came from times and places where women were expected to remain silent on pain of beating, even men who had grown to grey-beard stature had learned to respect Ianira—and in this matter, she had the right of a mother whose children were threatened. That right was so universal, even those men who had found the adjustment to TT-86 and—in particular—the status of women in TT-86, held their tongues and listened in respectful silence.

She looked from face to silent face and nodded slowly, understanding their message without the need for words. "We don't need to kill her," Ianira repeated. "All we need to do is ensure she loses her bet."

The smiles that lit multiple eyes—dark eyes and light ones, black and grey and brown and blue ones, and the occasional clear amber or green ones—all were smiling, cold as Siberian ice.

"Yes," someone on the edge of the crowd murmured, "the gems dealer must lose that bet. Which would be the better strategy, Council? Help Skeeter with his work? Or plot to destroy the money-changer's schemes?"

Ianira laughed, tossing thick, black hair across one pale shoulder. "Destroy the money-changer's schemes, of course. Skeeter can hold his own when it comes to stealing from the up-timers who kick and rob so many of us. All we have to do is make sure the money changer steals less. *Much* less. It ought to be fun, don't you think?"

Laughter rippled through a group which moments before had been grim enough to contemplate violent murder, consequences be damned—just the thing the Seven had feared. Agreements were made to watch the money-changer's every move. Assignments were given to those best suited to the task of foiling Goldie Morran's schemes—or, if necessary—stealing her winnings before she could "log" them with Brian, as the rules of the wager demanded.

Ianira kissed her daughters' hair and smiled softly.

Goldie Morran would rue the day she had dared interfere with Marcus' patron and champion. Rue it as bitter as wormwood and never once guess why she failed in her every effort. Ianira pledged silent sacrifices to her patron goddess Artemis of moon-pale hunting dogs and silver arrows notched through eternity to her moon-wrought bow, as well as pledges to her adopted goddess, Pallas Athena of spear and shield, Athenian war helmet and above all *Justice*, should they secure victory for Skeeter Jackson.

She left the meeting with her own assignment and returned home to put supper into Artemisia and Gelasia, then put both girls into their little beds. She worked on Council business, while waiting with great anticipation for Marcus to finish his shift at the Down Time Bar and Grill.

She hummed an *old* tune as she worked, one her grandmother had taught her as a child, all the while quietly hugging to herself the secret of the astonishing money she'd made at the booth today—thanks to wise, old, mercenary Chenzira's meddling with her prices. In the all-but-silent backdrop of their apartment, the dinner she'd prepared for her love bubbled and simmered its way toward perfection in the endlessly miraculous oven.

Goldie was cashing out money for tourists returning up time from a tour when she spotted them: three small, innocent-looking coins that were worth several thousand dollars each, they were so rare. Avarice warred with caution. She wasn't supposed to make use of her knowledge to obtain them. She couldn't buy them at a fraction of their value and claim the collector's price or Brian would disallow them completely. So she smiled in her cold heart and simply short-changed the tourists. Stealing the coins should certainly count. She waited until the batch of tourists had gone before putting up her "Out to Tea" sign and locking up the shop.

She could hardly wait to gloat to Skeeter about the day's success. Goldie headed for the library at full tilt, a battleship plowing through seas of disgruntled tourists, and cornered Brian behind his counter.

"Brian! Just take a look at these! Stole 'em fair and square!"

Brian examined the coins with care. "Very nice. Mmm . . . Yes, very nice, indeed. Let's see, now." He glanced up, a frosty look in his dark eyes. "Valuing these is really quite simple. This one, that'll give you a bet credit of twenty-five cents, this one's face value is what, thirty-five cents? Hmm . . . The silver content of this one's a little thin. I'd say about a buck thirty for the three."

Goldie stared, mouth agape and not caring who saw it. She honestly couldn't find her voice for whole seconds. When she finally *did* find it, heads turned the length of the library.

"*What?* Brian Hendrickson, you know perfectly well what those three—"

"Yes," the librarian said repressively, interrupting her before the tirade could build momentum. "Their *collector's* value is probably in excess of five thousand dollars. But I can't give you that kind of credit for them and you know it. Rules of the bet. You stole a couple of coins. Face value—or metals value, whichever is higher. That's it. Feel free to sell them for what they're really worth, but you won't get credit for that on the bet."

He pulled out a little ledger book and made an entry. Goldie couldn't believe it. A dollar and thirty stinking cents. Then she caught sight of Skeeter's last entry in a column next to hers: zero.

That was something. Not much, but something.

Goldie stormed out of the library, determined to eat Skeeter Jackson's liver for breakfast. Chuckles behind her only rubbed salt in a raw wound. She'd pay Brian back, too, she would. Just wait and see if she didn't. A buck-thirty. Of all the humiliating, backstabbing—

A feathered *Ichthyornis* screamed past on a power-dive into a nearby fishpond. The splash drenched Goldie from waist to knees. She screeched at the toothed bird and cursed it in language that caused mouths in a fifty-foot radius to drop. Then, catching herself, Goldie compressed her lips, glared at the people staring at her, and sniffed autocratically.

Skeeter might be behind, but a dollar and thirty cents wasn't a lead, it was an insult. She'd show that upstart little pipsqueak what an amateur he really was or her name was not Goldie Morran. She smiled tightly. The expression hurt the skin of her face and started a nearby toddler whimpering against its mother's skirts.

Goldie Morran had not yet *begun* to scam.

Skeeter, having successfully picked several pockets in a crowded cafe, returned to the library to hand over his take for Brian to hold, per the rules of the bet. When he caught sight of Goldie's last entry, he laughed out loud.

"A buck-thirty?" His laughter deepened, the primal joy of a half-wild Mongol who has pulled one over on the enemy.

Brian shrugged. "You're taking the news more cheerfully that she did."

"I'll bet!"

Brian said repressively, "You already have, Jackson. Now beat it. I have *real* work to do."

Skeeter laughed again, refusing to be insulted, and let his imagination linger on what Goldie's face must have looked like as she received the unpalatable news. Bet her face had gone nearly as purple as her hair! He strolled out of the library, hands in pockets and whistling cheerfully. The Commons certainly was a pretty place this time of year . . .

A heavy hand grabbed his shoulder, spinning him roughly around. His back connected with a concrete wall, driving the breath momentarily from his lungs. Skeeter blinked and focused on the face of a man he'd last seen standing on the banks of the Tiber, cursing him for all he was worth.

Oh, shit—

Lupus Mortiferus.

In modern clothes and a towering rage. "Your entrails aren't really worth a hundred-fifty gold *aurii*—but they'll do!"

"Uh . . ." Skeeter said, trying to buy time before the gladiator choked and/or stabbed the life out of him. *How the hell did he get onto the station?* Not that it mattered. He was *here*—and one look into those dark, murderous eyes told Skeeter he was about to die.

Or worse.

So Skeeter did the only thing that might possibly save him. He dropped to the floor like a limp rag doll. His opponent paused just an instant too long. Skeeter rolled, kicked Lupus Mortiferus' feet out from under him, scrambled up, and *ran*. A bull's bellow of fury followed him. One quick glance showed the enraged gladiator in close pursuit. *No river to jump into this time. No horse to steal, either. How the* hell *did he get into TT-86?*

He wove and dodged through the dense holiday crowds, ducked past a cluster of blinking, six-foot-five decorations, and shouldered someone aside when they blocked his way. An autocratic screech and a splash were followed by Goldie Morran's voice cursing him in language almost as colorful as Yesukai at his best. He took a brief second to wish he'd had the time to enjoy the sight of Goldie dripping wet from purple hair to spike-heeled toes—but that gladiator was right on his heels. He rounded the fish pond and pounded through Edo Castletown. In his wake, men dressed like samurai shouted obscenities at his pursuer, who shoved several of them bodily to the floor in his charge.

Ooh, Yakuza, Skeeter thought with a wince as he glanced back to see tattooed men swearing at the gladiator's back. Too bad they hadn't managed to lay hands on him.

He pounded out of Edo Castletown into Frontier Town, with its Wild West Gate, bars, saloons, and show-girl halls. Frontier Town's saloons offered a confusing maze of darkened rooms where bar girls served whiskey, poker games lasted until all hours, and rinky-tink piano players hammed it up on artificially battered upright pianos. Skeeter ducked into the nearest, sliding *under* a series of tables in the dim-lit bar, scattering card players and whiskey glasses as men jumped back in startled surprise. Then whole tables crashed to the floor behind him. The gladiator had waded in, snarling something in Latin. A fist fight broke out somewhere to his rear. Skeeter didn't care. He dove across the bar, catching a glimpse of the barkeeper's shocked expression in the mirror, then hauled butt back for the door while Lupus Mortiferus battled his way through a mob of really pissed-off "cowboys"—including at least one wrathful time scout who knew martial arts.

Having bought himself a couple minutes' lead, Skeeter blasted through the saloon doors into the bright Commons again and pelted back through Edo Castletown, where the first Shinto observances had begun at the new shrine. A deep bell tone shimmered through the air as the first worshipper pulled the bell-rope to sound the gong that would catch the attention of the resident, sacred *kami*. A glance over his shoulder revealed the irate gladiator battling his way past a dozen *really* irate Yakuza thugs. Lupus Mortiferus had knocked them down on their first dash through Castletown, causing them to lose serious face in public. They were out for vengeance. He grinned, leaped the low fence marking off the new shrine, gaining traction in the expanse of white gravel, ducked *under* the shrine, and vaulted the fence on the other side while outraged Japanese curses poured after him in waves. One swift glance showed Lupus Mortiferus in even greater trouble as the worshippers vented righteous ire upon the gladiator.

Sorry about that, really, Skeeter told the certain-to-be-offended *kami. I'll, uh, come ask your pardon later. Honest.*

Skeeter cut hard into a side corridor leading toward the maze of corridors that made up Residential. A bellow in the distance told him the chase, although badly slowed for Lupus Mortiferus, was still on.

Skeeter pelted up a staircase and rounded a wicked bend at a full run, grabbing a heavy rope garland and swinging around the *outside* of the girder that supported a balcony platform above, using it like Tarzan's vines to whip around at maximum speed. Below him, gasps of shock and fear arose from the packed Commons floor. *Great. All I need's an audience.* Three changes of corridors, two more staircases, and another turn brought Skeeter out onto a wide balcony of shops and restaurants overlooking Commons.

Far back, but rounding the corner after him, Lupus Mortiferus was still coming. *Cripes, doesn't anything stop that guy?* Skeeter tipped over clothing racks, cafe tables, and fully lighted Christmas trees. He kept running, providing any and all barriers he could that the gladiator would have to jump or pick up first, then skidded down a gridwork staircase, mostly sliding down the banister. A flock of roosting pterosaurs screeched and took wing in protest. They swooped and dove, knocking wreathes, plastic candy canes, and all sorts of other decorations off girders and balconies—which created panic amongst the tourists gaping in his wake.

Skeeter heard curses—but they were farther and farther behind. He hit the next balcony level still running flat out, slammed a seven-foot plastic Santa to the balcony floor behind him, and spotted an open elevator. Skeeter grinned and dove into it. He punched "5" and the doors closed. The elevator shot upward, carrying him to the upper floor of a hotel's graceful balcony. Skeeter stepped out onto lush carpet, rather than bare gridwork, hearing the very distant sounds of pursuit below, then slipped into the hotel's hallway, covered with a different color carpet, but just as luxurious as the balcony's. Skeeter jogged easily down the line of gilt-numbered doors and found an interior elevator which took him to the basement.

Under the hotel were weapons ranges and a gym. Skeeter ducked through the gym, found another elevator tucked back in the men's shower area, which had been placed there for the convenience of residents who wanted to head straight up after a workout. He rode it up to the third level of Residential.

When he finally stepped out into a silent corridor, there was no sign of the gladiator. Skeeter leaned against the wall and drew several deep breaths, then slowly relaxed. He couldn't help grinning. What a chase! Then reality settled over him like a blast of Mongolian snow. With Lupus Mortiferus on the station, Skeeter was in real trouble. What to do about it? Skeeter narrowed his eyes. He could always go to Bull Morgan and report the down-timer, but that would mean having to confess his down-time scam to the Station Manager. And that would get him into serious legal trouble with Management—with a probable eviction from TT-86 as the result. He wouldn't need to lose the wager to lose his home.

If the gladiator were reported—and questioned—the result would be the same. The damned gladiator would be given refuge, but Skeeter would be kicked up time to fend for himself in a world he had grown to hate. And if that gladiator caught up with him, he was a dead man.

"Great," Skeeter muttered to the listening walls. "Not only do I gotta win this bet, now I gotta stay alive while doing it."

He straightened his shoulders and lifted his chin. The boy who'd survived life in Yesukai's camp wasn't a quitter. He was no professional fighter—certainly no match for someone like Lupus Mortiferus—but he knew a few tricks. He wasn't happy, but he'd cope.

He always had, no matter what life handed him.

Tired, hungry, and thirsty, Skeeter headed for his little apartment, hoping Lupus Mortiferus didn't know that any computer in La-La Land listed his address as bold as a Mongolian sky, on an entry screen Skeeter couldn't hack into and purge—not without drawing serious attention to himself from Mike Benson's sharp-eyed gang. He thumbed open his door and retreated into his private refuge to fret over the problem, knowing as he opened the fridge for a beer and turned on the shower that wishing would *not* make this particular problem vanish.

He took a long pull from his beer and made the wish anyway.

From his viewpoint, Skeeter figured the gods owed him a break or two. For once, maybe they'd listen?

Lupus Mortiferus stood panting in the middle of an empty corridor, hand on the pommel of his gladius, eyes narrowed in a rage that filled his veins until his ears roared with it. *Where* had that little bastard slipped away to? So close . . . and the rat had vanished into thin air.

Again.

"I will find you, *odds maker*," Lupus swore under his breath. "And when I do . . ."

Meanwhile, he had to find someone to communicate with. That dark-skinned man had answers Lupus needed. It took him nearly an hour of confused wandering through the mad place before he found it again, but find it he did. And the man was still there, perched comfortably behind a wooden counter. Girding on courage as though it were armor, Lupus strode up to the counter and greeted him in Latin.

The man glanced up, surprise showing in deep brown eyes. "Hello. Guide? Or scout? Don't think I've seen you before. Just in from another station? Brian Hendrickson, Station Librarian."

The man stuck out a hand.

Lupus stared at it, wondering what in the world the man was babbling about. The words were Latin, but their meaning . . . He might as well have been speaking some obscure desert tongue like Palmyrene or the incomprehensible babble of a Scythian horseman.

"Well," the man was saying, staring at him with rising curiosity, "the computers are at your full access, of course. In that getup, I'd thought you were headed down the Wild West Gate. Planning on a freelance trip to Rome? It's a lucrative gate, certainly, and thanks to Kit's leaning a little on Bax, Time Tours is giving freelancers a freer hand with the customers. You shouldn't have any problem at all making a good living if you decide to stay."

The man made no sense at all. With a rising sense of panic he couldn't control, Lupus tried to marshall a single question, but found his tongue glued to the roof of a mouth gone dry with fear. *The gods make sport of me for fun. . . .*

Whatever the man said next, it wasn't in Latin. His brow furrowed in open puzzlement. That was more than Lupus could take. He couldn't afford to be found out as an imposter in this place of divine madness. He bolted for the door. *Mithras, help me,* he prayed in growing misery. *I don't know where to go or what to do.* Lupus didn't quite run down the bewildering confusion of staircases, ramps, shops, ponds, and imitation streets that made up the main room of this world, but he moved fast enough to put distance between himself and the man who was most certainly coming to the conclusion that Lupus did *not* belong here.

He was halfway down the long, long stretch of room when he realized he was being followed. The man was younger than he, brown-haired and slender enough that Lupus could easily break him in half with bare hands. Lupus knew a jolt of fear that stabbed from heart to groin, anyway. The gods who ran this mad playground had found him out.

Then anger, pure and simple, scalded him to his bones.

I have been swindled, cheated, and dragged out of my very world. I will not *submit meekly to this!*

He took a side corridor that led into a quiet, private part of this world and hid in a shadowed niche. Sure enough, the young man following him took the same turn. Lupus gripped his sword and slid it sweetly out of its scabbard. *Someone* would give him answers or pay the consequences of their refusal.

He waited patiently for the quarry to come close enough to strike.

One moment, Marcus was completely alone in the Residential corridor, having lost sight of his quarry. The next, he was crushed painfully against the wall, sword at his throat. He gasped. Lupus Mortiferus . . .

Shock detonated in the other man's eyes. Marcus realized he'd gasped the man's name aloud when the gladiator demanded, "You know who I am?"

"I—" Marcus thought he might well faint from terror. How many men had the Wolf of Death killed during his bloody career? The thought of leaving Ianira and little Artemisia and Gelasia alone, trying to survive without him, drove him nearly to gibber. "I know—I know you, yes. I saw you, once. Many years ago. Before a fight. At—at one of the gladiator feasts—"

The sword blade stayed pressed against his throat. "Where am I? What place is this? And why have the masters of it sent you trailing my steps?"

Marcus blinked in surprise. "Nobody sent me. I saw you earlier and thought I recognized you. I—I just wanted to ask what you were doing here. You shouldn't be here at all. Please, I beg of you, Lupus Mortiferus, don't kill me. I have children, a family—"

The blade remained at his throat, but the pressure eased up just a bit. "Kill you?" the gladiator snorted. "The only man in this mad place who speaks Latin that makes sense? Do you think the Wolf of Death a complete fool?"

Marcus began to hope he might survive. "How *did* you come here? The Roman gate is very well guarded—" His eyes widened. "Those boys who got sick, when the gate cycled. You must have come through during the confusion."

Lupus Mortiferus narrowed dark eyes. "Gates? Talk sense. And answer my question! *Where am I?*"

Marcus knew he'd once been a slave, but it had been years since anyone had used that tone with him. "The last time I saw you," he dared flare back, "you were still a slave. Where is your collar? Or have you run from the school?"

Lupus' dark eyes widened. For an instant, Marcus saw his own death reflected there. Then—shocking him beyond all reason—the Wolf of Death lowered his sword. "I bought my freedom," he said quietly. "Then the money I earned with this sword, the money I was saving to start a new life, was stolen by a black-hearted street-rat of a foreigner. I followed him here." The threat returned to his eyes. "Now tell me, *where is 'here'?*"

Marcus blinked several times, struggling with emotions that ran the gamut from pity to terror and back again. "If you will put away the gladius, I will tell you. In fact, if you put away the gladius, I will take you to my own rooms and try to help you as best I can. What I have to say will not be easy for you to understand. I know you are a proud man, Lupus Mortiferus—you have a right to be—but you will need help to survive here." Some glint in Lupus' dark eyes told Marcus he'd hit a raw nerve. "I have a woman and daughters to support, but I will do my best to help. From what I remember, you didn't begin your life in Rome either. In that, we have something in common. You have asked for answers. I offer them and more. Will you come with me?"

The gladiator paused for several heart-shattering moments, then sheathed his sword under the ridiculous cowboy chaps. The gladius snicked softly into place under the concealing leather. "I will come. I think," he said softly, "the gods have left me no choice."

The admission shocked Marcus speechless.

But he recalled all too vividly his own first days in La-La Land, with their wrenching, sick dislocation and the terror every sight and sound brought. This man had been badly wronged by someone from TT-86. Marcus would do what he could to make amends.

The Wolf of Death followed silently behind as Marcus led the way toward his small apartment. He wondered with a sinking terror in his gut what Lupus Mortiferus would do when he saw Ianira's delicate beauty. He was strong enough—and ruthless enough—to take her while Marcus watched helplessly from the floor, bloodied and dazed, perhaps even bound and gagged. Surely Lupus would adhere to guest/host laws? But Lupus was neither Roman nor predictable. Marcus had no idea what he would or wouldn't do.

But he had given his word and Lupus Mortiferus had been wronged.

And the laws here, he recalled with effort, were not those of Rome. If Lupus Mortiferus tried to hurt his beloved, he *could* call for help—or send her and his daughters to live with others who could and would protect them.

Afraid and torn between honor and multiple duties, Marcus led the gladiator to his little home deep in the recesses of Residential.

Ianira had just taken a cooling cheesecake out of the oven, placing it on a rack on the counter beside simmering pots and sizzling pans filled with their dinner, when the apartment door opened. She glanced up, a smile on her lips . . . and let the smile die, unborn, at the look in Marcus' eyes. His face was ash pale. He held the door for a stranger dressed for the Denver Wild West Gate. Eyes downcast, Marcus' posture screamed his feelings of fear and inferiority. The stranger's dark gaze darted about the room, paused briefly on her, then returned to a scrutiny of the room as though expecting it to contain lethal traps.

With her eyes alone, Ianira sought Marcus' gaze and begged the question: *Is this the man? Your former master?* She realized she'd begun to tremble only after the slight movement of Marcus' head indicated, *No, this is not the one.*

The relief that flooded her whole being was short-lived. If this were not Marcus' mysterious up-time master, who, then, that he inspired such terror and deference in her beloved? When Marcus spoke, he spoke in Latin and kept his voice soft—the voice of a slave addressing a social superior from his own world.

"Please, you are welcome to my home. This is Ianira, the mother of my children. A high-born woman of Ephesus," he added with just a touch of defiant pride in his eyes and voice. The dark-eyed stranger gave Ianira a long, clear-eyed stare which left her trembling again—from anger, this time. She knew the look of a man hungry for a woman's body. That look was a ravening fire in this man's eyes when he stared at her.

"Ianira, Lupus Mortiferus has stumbled through the Porta Romae in pursuit of a man who stole his money. He needs shelter and our help."

Ianira relaxed marginally, but remained alert for trouble. Why was Marcus so visibly shaken, so subservient, if all he offered was asylum to a fellow down-timer in need? By rights, he should be playing the role of social superior, not struggling to hide obvious terror.

Taking the plunge, Ianira recalled her duties as hostess in Marcus' home. "You are welcome as our guest," she said in her careful Latin. Marcus spoke Greek better than she spoke Latin. Their common household tongue was English. Living as they did, it was a survival ritual they practiced as much for the sake of their children as for the practice speaking the dominant language of the time terminal. Most of the languages Ianira heard spoken on the station—particularly Japanese—were utterly beyond her. But English she learned from necessity and Latin she learned from love. She could even understand a little of Marcus' native Gaulish, although he rarely used it except to swear at or by gods neither Athens nor Ephesus had ever known.

Marcus gazed worriedly at the man who continued to stare at Ianira as though the jeans and T-shirt she wore didn't exist. The look sent chills down her back and made her long to close her hands around a weapon to defend herself.

"Ianira," Marcus added with a touch more courage in his eyes, "is highly placed on the Council of Down-timers in this world. She owns her own business and is well respected even by those from up time, who control the fate of all down-timers who stumble into the station. She is important in this world." The warning in his voice was unmistakable—and it had effect. Lupus Mortiferus' look changed from that of a man who is considering taking what he desires by force to that of speculative curiosity.

Marcus ended the introductions by saying quietly, "Ianira, Lupus Mortiferus is the most famous gladiator to fight in the Circus Maximus at Rome. He has won the Emperor's favor many times and has killed his way to victory in more than a hundred fights by now, I should guess. He will need our help adjusting to La-La Land and to find the thief he seeks. It is his desire to find that thief, recover his stolen money, and return home."

That was against the law. They both knew it.

But a man like Lupus Mortiferus, who had survived combat in the arena, wasn't likely to abide by any such rule. Clearly, Marcus wanted only to help him regain his money as quickly as possible so the man *would* leave again. Ianira found herself agreeing with that silent desire which burned so brightly in Marcus' frightened eyes. She did not want Lupus Mortiferus to stay on TT-86. The shorter his visit, the greater her peace of mind. But until he left, he was an invited guest in the home of the father of her children.

She gestured gracefully, playing the role she had learned so well under the lash in her husband's home. "Please, come in. Sit down. The evening meal is nearly ready. It is very simple fare, but nourishing, and there is Greek cheesecake for afterward."

Lupus Mortiferus' eyes came back to hers. "Greek? I thought you were from Ephesus?"

"I was born in Ephesus, yes, but came to live in Athens for a year before stumbling through the Philosophers' Gate, as it is called here. You came here by way of the Porta Romae."

Lupus treated them to a mirthless laugh. "Gate of Rome. How incredible. So you really did live in Athens? The cheesecake is genuine?"

She held back a proud, haughty smile by main force of will. Romans felt a humble respect for anything Greek, believing—as well they ought!—that Greek culture *was* culture.

"I have heard much of Greek cheesecakes from wealthy patrons."

Ianira forced a light laugh. "Indeed, my recipes are genuine. I knew them by heart—and I *was* born about six hundred years before you were."

Shock detonated in the man's dark eyes.

Ianira laughed again, knowing she played a deadly game, but knowing also that she could more easily risk it than a man. "Welcome, Lupus Mortiferus, to La-La Land, where men and women from many different places and times come together under one roof. You have much to learn. Please. Sit down and rest. I will bring refreshments for you and serve the dinner. Then we will talk of things you must know in order to survive here."

The piercing look he gave her was difficult to interpret, but he took a seat on their plain brown couch. The vinyl squeaked as the leather of his chaps rubbed it. Ianira noticed the sword half-concealed beneath them, but said nothing. Guest laws notwithstanding, Lupus Mortiferus was a man lost in a world he could not possibly comprehend—one that Ianira herself, after three years, took mostly on faith, translating "technology" into "magic" for anything she didn't understand.

For what it was worth, she knew there were *up* timers who did the same when confronted by the power of the gates through time.

As for the weapon, keeping it would reassure him, more than any words of welcome they could offer. Ianira served fresh fruit juice to the men, deciding against the wine she'd previously planned for their dinner—she had no intention of serving alcohol to a potentially explosive guest—then returned to the kitchen. Marcus would normally have joined her to help, but the presence of their guest held him against his will in the room that served double duty as living and dining area.

Artemisia, strapped into her toddler's high chair beside the device that kept foods and drinks wonderfully chilled, even frozen, cooed and giggled at her mother's reappearance. Ianira stooped to kiss her child's hair, then filled a bottle with apple juice and gave it to the little girl. While Gelasia slept peacefully in the crib in their one bedroom, Artemisia sucked on the rubber nipple contentedly, gurgling occasionally as her wide, dark eyes followed her mother's movements around the kitchen.

Low male voices, intense and frightening, crept like ghosts into the warm kitchen. Irrationally, Ianira wanted to stand with the gun Ann Vinh Mulhaney had taught her to shoot, between her children and their new guest. She *knew* her reaction was irrational and overprotective, but the Goddess' warnings of impending danger were not to be lightly ignored.

Why hast thou sent this man, Lady? she asked silently, addressing her frightened prayer to the great patroness of Athens itself, wise and fierce guardian of all that was civilization. *I fear this guest, Lady. His glance causes me to tremble with terror. What warning is this and how should I listen for Thy answer? Is* he *the danger? Or merely the messenger? The portent of a greater danger to follow?*

In the closed environment of La-La Land, there were no sacred owls to give her omens by the timing of their cries or the direction of their flight. But there was in-house television. And there were birds—strange, savage, toothed birds so ancient that Athene herself must have been young when their kind flew the darkling skies of Earth. Artemisia, her attention caught by the moving colors of the television screen, dropped her bottle of juice against the highchair's tray with a bang. A chubby finger pointed.

"Mama! Fish-bird! Fish-bird!"

Ianira looked—and felt all blood drain from her face. She had to clutch the countertop to keep from sliding to the floor. An *Ichthyornis* had struck a brown fish and was devouring it while it struggled. Blood flowed in all-too-lifelike color. Ianira lunged across the narrow kitchen, driven by terror, and snapped off the machine with shaking hands. The screen went dark and silent. Fear for Marcus rose like sour bile in her throat.

No, she pled silently, *keep this death away from our threshold, Lady. He has done nothing to merit it. Please . . .*

Ianira's hands were still trembling when she carried the dishes out to their small dining table and offered the food she had prepared for their evening meal. It took all her courage to smile at their guest, who tore into the food like a ravening wolf. Lupus Mortiferus . . . Wolf of Death . . . Ianira did not yet know precisely *how* danger would come to Marcus through this man, but she was as certain of it as she was certain that her shaky breaths were barely holding terror at bay.

Ianira Cassondra had lost one family already.

She would do murder, if necessary, to keep from losing another.

Chapter 7

The Britannia Gate was rich with possibility.

Skeeter chose a likely looking mark dressed in expensive, Victorian-style garments and followed him discreetly until the "gentleman" entered a public restroom. Skeeter entered behind him, took care of business, then—while they both washed their hands at the automatic sinks—he dared break the cardinal rule of silence in the men's washroom.

"Travelling to London, too?" he asked, buttoning the fly of his own Victorian-era togs.

The man shot him a startled glance. "Er, yes."

Skeeter smiled. "Take some friendly advice. That place is *crawling* with pickpockets. Worse than you'll ever read in Dickens." That, at least, was God's own truth. "Don't carry all your money in some predictable place, like a pocket wallet. Some nine-year-old kid'll snatch it and be gone before you even know it's missing."

"I—yes, we were warned about pickpockets," the man stammered, "but I wasn't quite sure what I should *do* about it. Someone suggested maybe I should ask an outfitter, you know, for a moneybelt or something—"

"I'll show you a trick I learned the hard way." Skeeter winked. "Wrap your money in a handkerchief and tuck it inside your shirt, so it sits inside the waistband of your trousers."

The mark looked doubtful.

"Here, let me show you what I mean." He pulled out a standard white handkerchief stuffed with his own money and demonstrated. "Here, I have a spare hanky. You try it."

The man looked doubtful for a moment longer, then relaxed. "Thank you. I will." He pulled a *huge* bankroll out of an expensive leather wallet and tucked the money into the center of the hanky, tying it clumsily.

"I'm afraid I'm not very good at this."

"Here, let me help."

Skeeter tied the corners expertly and tucked it into place, showing the mark exactly how the handkerchief was supposed to fit. Then he retrieved it and said, "Try it again" as he tucked his own money-filled hanky back into his own waistband.

The mark—having no idea that Skeeter had deftly switched handkerchiefs on him—tucked Skeeter's much smaller "bankroll" into his slacks. "Yes, that works wonderfully! Thank you, young man. Here, let me give you a tip or something . . ."

"No, I wouldn't dream of it," Skeeter reassured him. "Hope you have a good visit in London. Some really spectacular sights. Can hardly wait to get back, myself."

He grinned at the other man, then strolled out of the washroom gloating over his success. With any luck, the tourist wouldn't discover the switch until he was *through* the Britannia Gate. Time Tours would bail him out for the duration of the tour—although they'd charge him double price as refund for their trouble—and he'd learn a valuable lesson he clearly needed about hanging onto what was his.

Meanwhile, this haul ought to put Skeeter several hundred dollars ahead of Goldie. He headed directly for the library to have his winnings logged, whistling cheerfully. A group of half-grown boys in Frontier Town—*aw, nuts, looks like the up-time abandonees just cut class again*—dashed out of a restaurant directly in his path, yelling and whooping in an excess of energy. Crashes and yells inevitably followed their retreat. Skeeter snorted. Bunch of mannerless hooligans, smashing up anything they could lay hands on just for jollies.

Time Tours, and the smaller touring outfits tried every trick they could to keep parents from taking kids down time. After that kid in Rome had gotten himself killed and Time Tours had ended up settling for a huge sum of money (despite the fact it was entirely the fault of the stupid kid and his too-bored-to-be-bothered parents), the outward ripple was as simple as it was inevitable: *no* touring outfit wanted *any* kid running wild down time.

So the new policy to cope was simple: parents either signed a waiver and paid an enormous extra fee for kids' down-time tickets, or they "abandoned" the kids on the station. Theoretically, Harriet Banks, the station's school teacher, was assigned to watch them. In practice, Harriet had to watch—and teach—Residents' kids, keep tourists' kids from leaving, and make certain that none of the toddlers or infants in the Day Care Center were injured, sick, or just plain obnoxious with the other kids. Skeeter thought Bull should've done something ages ago or one of these days he was going to find himself with a full school and day care center and *no one* to mind the store.

Bored, usually spoiled, tourists' kids got out of hand constantly, running wild through the station like feral dogs through a butcher's shop. Skeeter found himself caught up in their midst while they darted in mad circles, shouting, "Bang, I got you!" and, "No, you didn't, you louse, you missed me clean!"

Several caromed off his shins in their antics.

"Hey! Watch the toes!"

"Sorry, mister!"

They darted away, still shouting and playing their idiotic game. Those boys were too old to be playing cowboys and indians. They were at that uncertain age when their games should've been more like "who can look up the prettiest girl's skirt first?" He muttered under his breath—then halted mid-mutter.

The next words out of him were so foul, an *Ichthyornis* took offense, shook out its oil-free, sodden feathers, and flopped over to another bush to finish drying its wings.

There was no mistake. Skeeter felt nothing but emptiness inside the waistband of his pants. Disbelieving, he actually jerked his shirt out of his slacks and stared. The handkerchief was gone. So was his own wallet, from his back pocket.

Those murderous, conniving little—

The boys had run in the general direction of Goldie Morran's shop.

That she'd stoop to bribing *tourists*—tourists' *kids*—to roll him, right there in public . . . The humiliation was unendurable. Bet or no bet, Goldie was gonna pay for this one. Skeeter stormed toward her shop in a towering rage, not even certain what he meant to do. A dark-haired girl stepped into his path, barring his way. Skeeter tried unsuccessfully to step around, felt his mind go strangely grey and distant, then blinked and found himself staring into Ianira Cassondra's bottomless eyes. The exotically beautiful girl who lived with Marcus took hold of his arm, her grip urgent.

Skeeter saw the self-styled acolytes who followed her *everywhere* closing in through the holiday crowds.

"There is no time to explain properly, Skeeter. Just let it go," she murmured softly. "Goldie Morran is not the only one on this station with supporters. She will not win her bet. This I swear by all I hold sacred."

She was gone so fast, he wasn't certain for several moments that she'd actually been there. He stared after her, wondering what in the world she had meant, and confirmed that his senses hadn't lied, because there went her entire retinue of acolytes clutching cameras, notepads, vidcams, and sound recorders in eager hands, trailing after her like boy dogs after a svelte little bitch in heat. Skeeter really didn't know what to think. Sure, he'd given Marcus that money, which meant he and Ianira must be grateful to him, and he'd been donating money to The Found Ones for months and months, but even if they were serious, what could Marcus and Ianira do against Goldie Morran? The Duchess of Dross had powerful allies and agents *everywhere*.

Still, Ianira's impassioned words disturbed him. They could get themselves thrown off the station, interfering with an up-timer's business which Skeeter profoundly did *not* want to happen: the only place they *could* be sent would be an up-time prison. Without their kids. Skeeter gulped. Things were getting too far out of hand, much too fast, all because that purple-haired *harpy* couldn't content herself with putting into motion her *own* scams.

No, she had to do everything possible to destroy *Skeeter's.*

Another part of him, the scared-kid part hidden down inside, and desperate to stay on TT-86 at any cost, actually prayed Ianira *had* cooked up some scheme that would cause all sorts of hell for Goldie Morran—just one that wouldn't put Marcus and his little family in danger. Whatever she'd meant, she'd diverted Skeeter's dangerous rage long enough to cool into sensibility. If he'd actually gone into Goldie's shop, there was no telling what he might have done.

Standing for murder charges would *certainly* get him kicked off the station.

Rubbing his chin speculatively, Skeeter decided to kiss goodbye the lost bankroll and wallet. He could always get the station ID cards replaced, even the Residents-Only ATM cards, allowing access to on-station bank accounts. Not that his had much in it, currently. Most of his winnings from Rome were already gone. He grimaced, realizing he'd have to eat his pride to go into Bull Morgan's office and admit a vividly edited version of what had happened so he could get replacement cards. As for the lost bankroll he'd stolen, he'd just try again somewhere else, with some other scheme or maybe just some other restroom and mark. He didn't have much choice. Even if he *did* face Goldie down, he couldn't prove anything. And she'd make him a laughingstock for falling prey to one of his own tricks. Ianira was a smart girl. Skeeter owed her more than he'd realized.

He sighed philosophically and changed course, heading for Bull Morgan's office before trying the Prince Albert Pub to see what action he might pick up there. If he didn't score something big soon, he was a lost man. As he took the lift to the Station Manager's capacious office on the second floor, Skeeter realized Ianira's comments had shocked him in another way: he *did* have people rooting for him, friends among the down-timers he hadn't realized would back him so staunchly.

Very well, he would try harder. For their sake as well as his. It was comforting to know he wasn't entirely alone.

Kynan Rhys Gower had no love for Skeeter Jackson.

It was said by those who knew that Skeeter had attempted to

seduce the grandchild of Kynan's liege lord, Kit Carson, by passing himself off as something he was not. Kynan had not been a resident of Time Terminal Eighty-Six when Skeeter Jackson had lied about being a time scout. But during the period when Kynan was struggling hardest to adjust to his new life, he had very nearly been killed protecting the lady Margo. Therefore, any man who would stoop so low as to besmirch her honor was—and had to be—a sworn enemy.

However, life in this place he had been forced to call home was never as simple and straightforward as it had been in his own time. He began to realize the depth of that truth when Ianira, a Greek beauty some called the Enchantress, but who seemed to Kynan a very devoted wife and mother, called for a Down-Timers' Council meeting in the bowels of the time terminal. There, she revealed word of the latest development in the bet between the scoundrel and Goldie Morran—and what he heard made Kynan Rhys Gower's blood sing.

Goldie Morran was stealing from the scoundrel. But Ianira wasn't pleased. Instead, she was asking their help. Ianira Cassondra was actually asking them either to steal back from Goldie, or to ruin as many of her schemes as possible, to pay a debt she and Marcus—unbelievably—owed the scoundrel, along with all other Found Ones. He'd missed the last meeting due to his work schedule and hadn't had a chance to catch up on Council business since. Everything he heard amazed him.

A thief had actually given money to a down-timer, to the whole community of down-timers, keeping his word. Kynan despised the philandering scoundrel. But the chance to act against Goldie Morran, with the Found Ones' full Council blessings . . .

Kynan Rhys Gower, too, had a score to settle, one it would give him great pleasure to set right. The scars on his back and chest were mute testament to what Goldie Morran's greed and persuasive, silver tongue had wrought—mute testament to the near loss of his life in the fetid, steaming heat of an African twilight, with witch hunters hard on his heels and a crossbow bolt aimed dead at the lady Margo's breast.

Goldie Morran had lied to him about the conditions under which he was to work for her, had lied to him about the extensive, potentially fatal dangers, then had arrogantly refused to pay him because their "adventure" had failed. It was his liege lord, Kit Carson, who had risked death in more ways than even Kynan could understand, Kit Carson who had rescued Kynan from the clutches of the Portuguese witch hunters, Kit Carson who had made certain that the wounds Kynan had sustained were mended by the great magic available to healers here. And it was Kit Carson who had paid him solid coin for his part in the work Goldie Morran had hired him to do. And paid him, moreover, twice the amount Goldie had named.

Kit Carson was Kynan's liege lord, Goldie Morran a proven enemy. Kynan might not love Skeeter Jackson, but if helping that scoundrel's cause brought disgrace and banishment for Goldie Morran, well, there were worse ways a man could spend his time and effort. He needn't actually help Skeeter *make* money, all he needed to do was prevent Goldie from earning any. The stranded Welshman chuckled to himself and began laying careful plans.

Goldie was sipping wine at an "outdoor" cafe table in Victoria Station, listening to the tourists preparing for departure down the Britannia Gate. One of them, seated nearby, was a florid-faced man who kept wiping his brow with a handkerchief and patting his coat pocket.

"I tell you, Sally has been after me so long I finally agreed to bring her on this tour, but I had no idea it would all be so *expensive*! The ticket into Shangri-la, the ticket through the Britannia Gate, the hotel bills here and down time, the *costumes*. Good God, do you know how much money I just dropped in that Clothes and Stuff place? I tell you, I'm down to my last five thousand and Sally will pitch a fit beyond belief if I don't buy her expensive presents in London, and then there's the ATF tax to pay on whatever we bring back. . . ."

His companion, looking bored, just nodded. "Yes, it's expensive. If you can't afford it, don't go."

The disgruntled man with the florid face huffed. "That's easy for you to say. You don't live with my wife."

The other man at the table glanced at a pocket watch. "I'm due on the weapons ranges. See you later, Sam."

He paid his bill and departed, leaving the florid Sam to mop his brow all by himself. Goldie smiled and moved in. She picked up her wine glass and approached his table.

"Mind if I join you?"

He glanced up, surprise widening his eyes, then belatedly mumbled, "Sure, sure, sit down."

Goldie took her seat with the dignity of a dowager empress settling into the ancestral throne. "I'm sorry, but I couldn't help overhearing your conversation. I hope you don't think it forward of me, but there are ways to cut the cost of a time tour. Considerably. You can even turn a tidy profit on occasion. If," she smiled, "you're . . . mmm . . . willing to bend the rules a little? Nothing genuinely illegal, mind you, just a tad . . . exciting. I've tried it dozens of times, myself, or I wouldn't recommend it."

She sipped her wine and waited, smiling politely.

Her mark blinked a few times, taking in Goldie's expensive Victorian-era tea-gown and glittering jewelry. He blinked a few times more, swallowed loudly enough to be heard two tables away, then went for it. "What ways?"

Goldie leaned forward slightly, just touching Sam's hand with well-manicured fingertips. Diamonds winked from one ring, sapphires from another. "Well, as you know, we up-timers are legally forbidden to bet on sporting events down time—boxing, horse races, that sort of thing—because we might be able to find out the results in advance. ATF considers that an unfair advantage."

She allowed a tinge of aristocratic disdain to creep into her voice and glanced derisively in the direction of Primary, with its Bureau of Access Time Functions tax collectors, luggage-searching busybodies, and officious bureaucrats.

Sam grunted once. "So I've been told. Our guide said we'll be watched to keep us from doing any betting while we're in London. Interfering, high-handed . . ."

Goldie let him rant at length, then brought the conversation around toward her intended direction again. "Yes, I know all that, dearie." She patted his hand. "As I said, I've done this dozens of times. It's very simple, really. You find out the winners of whatever race you want to bet on, then give that information and your money to one of the down-timers hanging around the station. Many of them pick up odd jobs at the last minute for Time Tours as baggage handlers, so it's really a very simple matter to arrange. The down-timer places your bet and collects your winnings. You give him a small cut, and *voila*! You've helped defray expenses, at the very least. And best of all, you split the earnings *down time*, so you can either convert it to up-time money the ATF can't touch or buy a few trinkets to bring home as souvenirs."

Goldie lifted her wineglass, tilting it so that the endless light in Commons glittered on the jewels adorning her fingers. *Come on, Sammie boy. Go for it. Not that any down-timer'll come near your lovely bankroll.* She smiled politely and sipped wine as though the outcome of his decision meant nothing whatsoever to her. *Hook him, then tell him the idiot down-timer wandered through a gate and Shadowed himself, went "Poof!" money and all. Complain to management if you like, but of course, it's your word against mine and there's that matter of admitting an attempt to place an illegal bet. . . .*

Sam wiped his brow one last time with a wilted handkerchief, then said decisively, "I'll do it! I will. Tell me how."

Goldie set her wineglass down. "As it happens, I've already made arrangements with a gentleman to place a bet for *me* this trip. He can place a bet for you, as well, on the same race. The wagering stands at ten-to-one. I'm placing ten grand on it. This time next week, I'll have a cool hundred thousand more in my retirement fund."

Sam, his face flushed now with excitement rather than nerves, reached for his coat pocket and pulled out a fat wallet. Goldie salivated and swallowed while toying idly with her wineglass to keep her fingers from trembling in anticipation of all that lovely money.

"How much . . ." Sam was muttering. "How much to risk? Oh, hell, here. Have him bet it all."

The man handed her British pound notes which added up to five thousand dollars, American. Goldie smiled again, her predatory heart singing. Then a shadow fell across the table. They both glanced up. Goldie widened her eyes in astonishment.

"Kynan Rhys Gower!"

"I come, lady, as I promise. The bet, lady. Do I hear right? I make bet for this man, too?"

Goldie blinked once, owl-like, aware that her lips had fallen into a round O of surprise. Then she forcibly recovered her composure. "Why, yes, that's right, Kynan. I just didn't realize you'd come early to collect my stake."

"I prompt, lady. Place bet good. All bets." He winked.

Then he plucked the money from nerveless fingers before she could part lips to protest. Kynan bowed and kissed her hand gallantly, then bowed to Sam, who was beaming, clearly impressed by the charade. Goldie didn't know what to do.

But if Kynan Rhys Gower thought she'd let him out of her sight, he was a greater fool than she thought.

The Welshman bowed again and started to leave.

"If you'll excuse me," Goldie said hastily, "Kynan and I have business of our own to finish."

"But—"

"Don't worry, we'll be on the tour together. I'll catch up to you at the Britannia Gate, Sam."

Goldie fled after the Welshman, who had already vanished around a corner of Victoria Station's cobbled, twisted "streets" of shop fronts, cafes, and pubs. She spotted him ahead and picked up speed.

"Kynan!"

The Welshman ducked into a pub and vanished in a wooden-floored room with air so thick from cigar smoke and alcohol fumes, it was as though a marshland miasma rose from dozens of beer mugs, brandy snifters, whisky glasses, and stinking black stogies. Goldie stood glaring from the threshold until her eyesight adjusted, but there was no sign of Kynan Rhys Gower.

"Has anybody seen Kynan Rhys Gower?" she demanded of the crowded room at large.

"Headed toward the loo, love," someone sang out.

Grim-faced, Goldie stormed into the men's room, not caring a fiddle for the shocked men who grabbed at open flies and cursed her in scalding terms when she started searching stalls.

Kynan was *not* in the loo.

She emerged, color rising high in her cheeks from sheer ire.

Then someone came past, saying, " . . . won't believe it! Biggest domestic screaming fight I've ever seen! Yelling cat and dog, they are, her waving a fist full of money at him, and the poor schmuck trying to explain it was for her he'd got himself swindled. . . ."

Goldie cursed once aloud, explosively, earning curious stares from several 'eighty-sixers hanging on this gossip.

"Something wrong, Goldie?" Rachel Eisenstein asked, her brow furrowing slightly.

"Not a thing!"

Rachel shrugged and turned back to the storyteller. "Think it'll require stitches before they're done?"

Goldie stormed away from the terminal's head physician and the rest of the gossipers yammering about *her* money.

That . . . that honor-bound, incompetent, down-time *rat*!

He'd given the blasted money back to Sam's *wife*!

She beat a dignified, hasty retreat toward her money-changing shop, seething inside as she tried to come up with some other scheme that would net her a big gain over that mongrel cur, Skeeter Jackson.

Goldie slammed shut the shop door so hard, the bell jangled wildly against the glass. She stalked behind her counter and indulged in at least five minutes of unrestrained, sulky *cursing* where nothing but her glittering coins and jewels could hear.

Then, drawing several savage breaths, she added Kynan Rhys Gower to the list of names she owed serious paybacks. And then—caution overcoming wrath—she carefully struck his name off her list again. For reasons personally painful to recall, Kynan Rhys Gower was under Kit Carson's personal—and far-reaching—protection. After what Goldie Morran had suffered as a result of Kit's wrath, she did *not* want to find herself on the losing end of another deal with Kenneth "Kit" Carson, world-famous time scout and land-shark businessman.

Goldie muttered under her breath. "Damn meddling scouts, guides, *and* down-timers, one and all." She turned her savage anger toward a more productive target: Skeeter Jackson. She had to know what he was up to. After that blitzkrieg attack by those boys she'd hired, he'd gone virtually underground. Goldie tapped long, manicured nails against the glass countertop, noticed the rings she'd borrowed from her inventory. She replaced them in the glass case with a snort of disgust, then reached thoughtfully for the telephone. She might not have won this battle, but the war was far from over.

All communities, no matter their size, have rituals by which they measure the passage of time and gauge the meaning of life. These rituals serve purposes beyond seemingly superficial appearances; they provide necessary cohesion and order within the primate group to which humanity belongs, they sustain continuity in the endless chaos of life, they ensure proper passage from one phase of life into the next as the individual grows from childhood into adulthood responsibility and from there into old age, all within the context of the social group to which that individual belongs. This need for ritual is so profound, it is locked within the genetic code, transmitted over the generations from the vast distance of time when Lucy and her predecessors roamed the steaming plains of Africa, learning to use tools and language in a hostile, alien world—a world whose harsh beauty struck awe into the soul, a world where the terror of instant death could not be fully comprehended.

And so humans learned to survive via the evolution of rituals, changing not so much their physical bodies as their cultural, social patterns of behavior. In a world without rituals, humans will create their own, as in the gangs of lawless children who had before and still did, after The Accident, terrorized the streets of major cities.

The more chaotic the world, the greater the need for ritual.

La-La Land was an utter morass of conflicting cultures, religious beliefs, and behavior patterns. Its very nickname reflected the insane nature of the small community of shopkeepers, professionals, law enforcers, medical personnel, scholars, con artists, time tour company employees, stranded down-timers, freelance time guides, and the most insane of all the residents, the time scouts who explored new gates, risking their lives with each new journey alone into the unknown past.

In order to keep the peace, Station Management and

representatives of the up-time government both had laid down sets of rituals—codified into law—by which residents and tourists alike were required to abide. Others sprung up naturally, as such things will any time human beings come together into more or less permanent groupings of more than one. (And, in fact, even hermits have their own rituals, whether or not they care to admit it.)

In La-La Land, there were two rituals of paramount importance to every resident: Bureau of Access Time Function's incessant attempts to enforce the cardinal rule of time touring, "Thou Shalt Not Profiteer from Temporal Travel," and the residents' unceasing attempts to thumb their collective noses at said cardinal rule.

The high priests of the two opposing factions were Bull Morgan, Station Manager, whose sole purpose in life was to maintain an orderly, profitable station where a body could do pretty much as he or she pleased, so long as the peace was kept—and the other was Montgomery Wilkes, head ATF agent, a man dedicated to enforcing the cardinal rule of time touring at all cost.

Inevitably, when Bull and Montgomery locked horns, sparks flew. This, in turn, had given rise to a third universal ritual in La-La Land. Known affectionately as Bull Watching, it involved the placement of bets both large and small on the outcome of any given encounter between the two men. In its classic form, Bull Watching provided hours of entertainment to those men and women who had chosen to live in a place where light blazed from the ceiling of Commons twenty-four hours a day, but where the only real sunlight came from the occasional trickle through an open gate.

In this sunless, brightly lit world, it was inevitable that Montgomery Wilkes would grow ever more bitter as residents flouted his authority at every possible moment and made bets that infuriated him about every word he did or did not utter. When Goldie Morran came to him with her plan to rid the station of Skeeter Jackson, he saw a golden opportunity to rid it of Goldie Morran, as well—a woman he knew in his bones broke the cardinal rule of time touring with every gate that opened, but was slick enough not to get caught.

In taking that wager with Skeeter—and then coming to him—she had sealed her own doom.

Montgomery Wilkes intended to deport *both* of the scoundrels before this business was done. That decision made, he indulged in a little ritual of his own. He called it "inspecting the troops." The ATF agents assigned to TT-86 called it words impossible to repeat in polite company.

Dressed in black uniforms that crackled when they walked, their hair cut to regulation length (Montgomery had been known to use a ruler to measure hair length to the last millimeter), every ATF agent in the ready room snapped to attention when he stalked in, six feet, one hundred eighty pounds of muscle, close-cropped red hair, crackling green eyes, and set lips that underscored the lines of discontent in his face.

As he faced his agents, eyes alight with a martial glow that struck terror into their collective hearts, he said, "The time has come for you to start living up to those uniforms you wear. This station has hemmed us in, crowded us into a corner, prevented us from doing much more than searching luggage and levying taxes on the few items that actually get transported uptime. Meanwhile, we sit by and watch while out and out crooks scam fortunes under our very noses."

Shoe leather creaked in the silence as he paced the front of the room. He turned to glare at the nearest agents. "*Enough!*"

With brisk movements, he switched on a slide projector and clicked controls. Goldie Morran's pinched countenance filled a ten-foot wall.

"This is Goldie Morran. Gems and rare coin dealer, money changer, currency expert, and con artist." Slides clicked in the silence. "This is smiling Skeeter Jackson. I don't think I have to tell you what kind of rapscallion this two-bit thief is." He cleared his throat deliberately, pinning the nearest agent with a baleful green stare. "I also know that every one of you has heard by now about their little bet."

Not a single agent in the room dared crack a smile; not with the boss pacing three feet away. A few began to sweat profusely into their stiff black uniforms, wondering if their side bets on the outcome of "the wager" had been discovered.

"Ladies and gentlemen," he folded his hands behind his back and stood in the center of the projected image of Skeeter Jackson, so that the colors from the slide wavered across his uniform and face like stained glass taken from a madhouse, "we are going to let these two have enough rope to hang themselves. I have had a *bellyful* of watching these 'eighty-sixers hoodwink their way through life, as though the sacred laws which we have been hired to uphold didn't even exist. We may not be able to deport them all and close down this station, but by God, we can catch these two! And I intend to do just that. By the end of the week, I want Goldie Morran and Skeeter Jackson in custody for fraud, theft, and anything else we can think up and make stick. I want them deported up time to jail where they belong, or I'll have the reasons why a crack troop of ATF agents is incompetent to catch two small-time crooks in a closed environment. Is that understood?"

Nobody said a word. Hardly anybody breathed. Many kissed pensions goodbye. Without exception, they cursed the fate that had landed them in this career, on this station, under this boss.

"Very good. Consider yourselves warriors in a timeless battle of good against evil. I want undercover teams combing this station, looking for anyone who might testify against either of those two. I want other undercover teams to set up sting operations. If we can't catch them in a fair scam, we'll by God entrap them in one of our own making. And if I hear of *anyone* betting on the outcome of this wager, I'll have pensions, so help me! Now move it! We have work to do!"

Agents in black fled the room to receive assignments from their captains and lieutenants and sergeants. Montgomery Wilkes remained behind in the empty ready room and gazed cold-eyed at the projected visage of smiling Skeeter Jackson. "I'll get you," he said softly to the colored light on the blank, ten-foot wall. "I will by God get you. And it's about time Bull Morgan understood just who the law around here really is."

He stalked out onto Commons on course for the Station Manager's office.

Chapter 8

Like most time terminals, TT-86 attracted gifted scholars from around the world, many of them the very best at what they did. Robert Li was no exception. As an antiquarian, he was sought out by private collectors and museums alike as a consultant and had been instrumental in identifying numerous quality forgeries.

There was good reason for this: no one excelled like Robert Li at *producing* forgeries of the genuine article. His work was—usually—strictly legal. Tourists and museum reps often brought items up time to his studio to be reproduced in exquisite detail; these replicas were then exported to museums around the world as legal replicas bearing the Li trademark. Occasionally, however, like most other 'eighty-sixers, Robert Li would get a bellyful of ATF's high-handed tactics.

He had an exceptionally strong—if unique—sense of right and wrong. The closer Montgomery Wilkes' people watched his operation, the more ire he swallowed until, inevitably, it broke out in such indignant expressions as assisting thieves smuggle out their wares! (Of course, only *after* he'd charged them a substantial amount of cash to reproduce the item.)

Even so, far more frequent were the times when scouts had returned "stolen" items to their original times when he felt an item *shouldn't* go missing—although, again, he usually reproduced it, first. And occasionally, an item crossed his counter that was so breathtaking, so unique that he simply couldn't resist. He could wax rhapsodic about Ming porcelain, but Greek bronzes threw him into utter fits. Unknown to ATF—or anyone else, for that matter—Robert Li kept a private safe the size of his bedroom, where he stored his most precious belongings. His collection of ancient bronzes rivalled that of the Louvre and surpassed that of up-time collectors with far more money than he had.

Some things, one simply did not sell.

Greek bronzes were one; friends were another.

Goldie Morran was, at heart, a cheating scoundrel who would've sold her own teeth if they'd been worth enough, but she was also a friend and one of the few people in the world whose knowledge of rare coins and gems approached his own. Goldie had done him a favor or two over the years, obtaining items here and there that his heart had coveted, and he harbored a secret admiration for her skills.

Unlike Kit Carson, he never tried to best her at billiards or pool, knowing his own limitations as fully as his strengths. Normally, Goldie would've respected his lack of desire to wager against her. He was equally aware, however, that with Goldie's livelihood on the line, she would consider nothing sacred. So when she entered his studio, Robert Li buttoned his pockets, locked the cases and cabinets he could reach, and put on his best smile.

"Why, Goldie, what a surprise to see you."

She nodded and placed a carbuncle with ornate carving across its upper surface on a velvet pad left lying on the countertop.

"What do you think of it?"

He eyed her speculatively, then picked up the gem and a jeweler's loupe. "Mmm . . . very nice. The depiction of the statuary on the spine of the Circus Maximus is excellent and I've never seen a better representation of the turning posts. Who forged it for you?"

Goldie sniffed, eyes flashing irritation and disappointment. "Bastard. How'd you know?"

He just gave her a sorrowful look from under his brows.

Goldie sniffed again. "All right, but would it fool most people? Even a discerning collector?"

"Oh, without a doubt. Unless," he smiled, "they hired someone like me to authenticate it."

"Double what I said before. Triple it. How much?"

Robert laughed quietly. "To keep quiet? Or provide authentication papers?"

"Both, you conniving—"

"Goldie." The reproach in his voice was that of a lover wounded by his lady's mistrust.

"Robert, you owe me a few. I'm desperate."

"ATF's watching me like a hawk. Word's out: Monty's planning to nail you *and* Skeeter, send you both packing to an up-time jail."

Goldie could swear more creatively than anyone Robert Li knew—and he knew *all* the time scouts operating out of TT-86.

Robert knew better than to pat her hand, but sympathy seemed called for. "Well, I suppose you could always poison Wilkes, but I think it would be easier to steer clear of anyone you don't know for the next few days. This place is *crawling* with undercover agents."

Goldie's eyes, sharper than ever, flashed dangerously. "Bull know about that? If ATF's undercover, they're way outside their jurisdiction and Montgomery Wilkes for damn sure knows it."

Before Robert could answer, Kit Carson entered the shop, sauntering over with a gait calculated to appear lazy, but which covered ground with astonishing speed. "Hi. Heard the news?"

"*Which* news?" Goldie demanded, exasperation coloring her voice.

Kit chuckled and winked at Robert. "Reliable eyewitnesses said the shouting could be heard *through* the soundproofing."

"Bull and Monty?" Robert asked eagerly. "Ten says Monty stepped over the line just a tad too far this time."

"No bet," Kit laughed. "You'll never guess what Bull's done now."

Goldie, carefully covering the carved carbuncle with her hand, asked, "Bull 'fishpond him'?"—referring to the time Margo had taken offense at being mauled by a multibillionaire with a thing for nubile redheads. Margo had thrown him into the fishpond.

Kit laughed heartily. Robert Li was sure Goldie had *intended*, with careful calculation, to remind Kit of that particular incident. And such a ruckus the dripping-wet old goat had raised, too, threatening to sue everything and everyone he could.

Fortunately, Bull Morgan had pointed out that said goat would have to file suit in the jurisdiction where the assault had taken place, then explained that no lawyers *at all* were permitted to hang their shingles anywhere inside TT-86. Better that way for *everyone.*

Of course, the way Margo looked and moved . . .

A man could hardly be blamed for trying. Malcolm Moore was one lucky son if she said yes.

Kit leaned forward conspiratorially. "Good guess, but nope, you're *way* off the mark."

Kit's little audience leaned forward, unaware they did so. Kit grinned. "Bull Morgan had Mike Benson place dear old Monty *under arrest.* Threw him into the brig with seventeen boozers, half a dozen brawlers, and three flea-bitten thieves clumsy enough to get caught."

"*WHAT?*" The demand came out in stereo, Goldie's screech hitting soprano.

Kit's grin lit his thin, mustachioed face like an evil jack-o-lantern. "Yep. Seems like during their, er, meeting over jurisdiction up in Bull's office, Monty's sense of outrage and diligence to the letter of the law prompted him to, um, an assault."

Robert Li gasped. "Monty *hit Bull*? And he's still alive?"

"Oh, no," Kit laughed, eyes twinkling. "Much better than that. Monty *assaulted* Bull's prize porcelain of the Everlasting Elvis. You know the one, sat on his desk like some serene Buddha for years after he, er, borrowed it from that cathouse in New Orleans."

Goldie's eyes went as round as the carbuncle she'd tried to hide from Kit's sharp-eyed gaze. "He broke Bull's *Elvis*?"

"They're still digging pieces out of the wall. And ceiling. And carpet."

"Oh, dear God," Robert said hoarsely, covering his eyes. "You know what this means?"

"Oh, do I ever. Open season on ATF agents *and* station security alike. The fights—and they're getting dirty, fast—have already started. Just thought I'd warn you. Things are likely to get hot around here for a while. Oh, one last thing."

He winked at Robert. "That carbuncle you're trying to hide,

Goldie? Forget selling it to that sweet young thing who asked if you could find her one. She's the newest narc on Monty's payroll."

Goldie's mouth dropped open. Robert grinned. Kit rarely had the pleasure of catching her so completely off-guard. Goldie very primly closed her mouth. Then, with as much dignity as she could muster, she said, "I am not even going to ask. Good day, gentlemen."

She took her carbuncle and left.

Robert glanced curiously at Kit. "This girl you're talking about. Is she really Monty's?"

Kit chuckled. "Hell if I know. But she walks and talks like ATF, for all the lace and perfume and goo-goo eyes she's been making at Skeeter Jackson. He hides every time she comes near. And I've *never* known that boy's instincts about undercover cops to fail."

"She sounds guilty to me," Robert chuckled. "Poor Skeeter. Poor Goldie. What terrible, tangled webs."

Kit grinned. "Yeah, well, hey, they wove 'em all by themselves, didn't they? I just don't like the idea of ATF throwing its weight around where it's got no real jurisdiction. They mind their checkpoints, we mind our business. Problems like Goldie and Skeeter, we handle internally."

Robert Li laughed aloud, recalling just how Kit had "handled" his own family "problem" with Skeeter. The youngster was still gun-shy whenever Kit was around.

"When's Margo due in?" he couldn't resist asking.

Kit's world-famous grin flickered into existence. "Next time Primary cycles. Malcolm's taking her to Denver."

"So I heard."

"Is nothing secret around here?"

Robert Li chuckled. "In La-La Land? Get real. Whoops, here comes a customer."

Kit wandered out past a young woman who wandered in. Kit paused in the doorway, giving Robert the high sign that *this* girl was trouble, then left whistling jauntily. Robert Li watched the tourist narrowly as she paused to look at antique furniture brought up time from London, then glanced appreciatively at a cabinet filled with jade jaguar gods.

"Is there anything in particular I can help you with?" Robert asked politely.

"Hi. I was wondering if you could help me out? I'm interested in buying something for my dad's birthday and he's crazy about Roman antiquities. And he's a sports nut, too. So when this gems dealer showed me a gorgeous stone with a carving of the Circus Maximus on it . . ." She batted eyelashes a half-inch long and let the sentence trail off. She *was* all lace and perfume and goo-goo eyes. And her voice would've liquefied thousand-year-old honey. But Kit was right: this kid walked like a trained agent and despite the melt-in-your-mouth patter, her voice held a burr that told Robert, *Monty's riding 'em hard, all right. This kid's out for blood.* Robert Li folded his hands into the sleeves of the Chinese-style Mandarin robe he affected while in his studio and waited for her to continue. Having a Chinese maternal grandfather gave him certain physical attributes that came through despite his mother's Scandinavian heritage; it also gave him an excuse to go inscrutable on demand. The tactic, so effective with other customers, even threw *her* off-stride. She floundered visibly for a moment, then recovered.

"I was hoping you could give me an appraisal, you know, so I'd be sure I was paying a fair price for it."

"I am an antiquities dealer," Robert said humbly, "with some small knowledge of furniture and a slight interest in South American jades, but I do not presume to claim expertise in valuing gemstones."

"There's an IFARTS sign in your window," she challenged, as perfectly well aware as he what was required to become an IFARTS official representative.

"Dear lady, I fear my consultation fee would be a complete waste of your money."

"Consultation fee?"

"A trifling charge for my time and services. It is not against IFARTS rules and one *does* have to make a living." He smiled politely. "I fear a thousand dollars to tell you 'I don't know' would be a great strain on the budget of someone as sensible as I perceive you to be. Surely you could go to one of the gems dealers on the station for such an appraisal?"

Her eyes narrowed in dawning suspicion. "Everyone recommended you."

"I would, of course, be happy to do my best, but there is also my reputation to consider. Think what damage I would do if I valued such a thing wrongly. You would be cheated, the current owner of the gem would be cheated and possibly greatly offended, and no one would trust my judgment again. I know my limits, dear lady, and my reputation will not stand such a strain as you ask."

She compressed her lips. He could all but see the thoughts seething behind her eyes: *You're in on it, you bastard. You're all in on it and I'll never prove a thing on her. . . .*

"Thank you," she said curtly. All trace of sweetness and goo-goo eyes had vanished. "I hope you have a pleasant day."

The hell you do, girlie. Robert smiled anyway. "And a pleasant day to you. And your father. May his day of birth be blessed with the freedom in life he so earnestly desires."

Robert thought for a moment she would actually break cover and scream at him that Montgomery Wilkes wouldn't be in jail long, by God!—but she didn't. She just marched out of his studio as though she were on parade ground. *She's young,* Robert sighed, *and that idiot Wilkes is ruining her already. What a tight-fisted, anal-retentive fool.* Then Robert reminded himself that the ATF—no matter how attractively packaged—was the enemy and busied himself placing a few phone calls. There were friends who deserved fair warning before that little number came to call.

Clearly, she was out for Goldie's blood.

Robert Li sold many things, for many prices. But he had never sold a friend. Not even a snake of a friend like Goldie Morran. Just because she'd sell *him* out at a moment's notice didn't mean *he* needed to reciprocate her lack of morals, never mind plain bad manners. And that was something ATF agents just didn't seem to comprehend. Not the ones trained by Montgomery Wilkes, anyway. Sometimes Robert wondered what drove the man so. Whatever it was, it boded ill for many an 'eighty-sixer before this business with The Wager was finished.

He dialed a number from memory.

A voice on the other end of the phone said, "Hello?"

"There's a sweet young thing on Monty Wilkes' staff making the rounds, trying to sting Goldie, and maybe you in the process. She just left here and she's goddamned good. All honey and goo-goo eyes until she realizes she can't have what she wants. Can't miss her. Just thought you ought to know."

"Huh. Thanks. I'll start passing around word, myself. You wanna take A to M or N to Z?"

"I'll finish in the group where I started. A to M."

"N to Z it is. Thanks for the tip-off."

The line went dead.

Robert grinned. Then punched another set of numbers.

"Your attention, please. Gate One is due to open in five minutes. All departures, be advised that if you have not cleared Station Medical, you will not be permitted to pass Primary. Please have your baggage ready for customs inspection by agents of the Bureau of Access Time Functions, who will assess your taxes due on downtime acquisitions . . ."

Malcolm Moore leaned over to Kit and said, "I wouldn't want to be in that line today. Those agents look bloody angry."

Kit chuckled. "You'd think with their boss in jail, they'd be more relaxed, not edgier than ever. Of course, after the fights some of 'em have been in . . ."

Half the male agents in sight sported blackened eyes and bruised knuckles. A few of the women bore scratches down their cheeks. Mike Benson had been forced to discipline half his own staff—then, he'd had to order the ATF agents into temporary quarters in one of the hotels nearest Primary, just to separate them from Station Security until the worst blew over.

"I rather expect most of them wish Skeeter Jackson and Goldie Morran had never been born, never mind made that idiotic wager," Malcolm noted wryly.

Kit glanced up at the chronometer board again.

Malcolm laughed. "The clock won't move any faster just because you keep staring at the numbers."

Kit actually flushed, then rubbed the back of his neck. "Yeah, well, I guess I've missed the brat."

Malcolm cleared his throat. "Well, since you mention it, I am rather anxious to see her again."

Kit gave him an appraising glance. "Yes. She might say no, you realize."

"I know." The quiet anguish in his voice betrayed him. He couldn't shake the fear that his notorious luck might still be holding steadily on "bad."

"She might say no to what?" a voice boomed behind them.

Malcolm winced. He and Kit turned to find Sven Bailey, hands on hips, watching them like a bemused bulldog.

"What in bloody hell are you doing here?" Malcolm muttered.

Sven grinned, a sight that made most men's blood run cold. "Waiting for my pupil, of course. Gotta see if she remembers anything I taught her."

Kit chuckled. "If she doesn't, we'll *both* wipe up the mat with her."

"Oh, goodie." Sven Bailey, widely acclaimed the most deadly man on TT-86, rubbed thick-fingered hands gleefully. "I can hardly wait. I never get to have that much fun with the tourists."

Malcolm rubbed one finger along his nose. "That's because the tourists would sue."

The terminal's martial arts and bladed-weapons instructor grunted. "No lawyers allowed in La-La Land and you know it."

A new voice said, "Good thing for you, too, isn't it, Sven?"

They glanced around to find Ann Vinh Mulhaney grinning up at him. Very nearly the only person on TT-86 who dared laugh *at* Sven Bailey, the petite shooting instructor's eyes sparkled with delight. Their matched heights produced a comical appearance: squat fireplug, stolid beside a sleek bird of prey.

"What is this," Malcolm muttered, "a welcoming committee?"

"Well, she *is* my student," Ann pointed out. "I'd like to say hello and see if she remembers anything." Her eyes flashed with unspoken humor, whether at Malcolm's discomfiture or in remembrance of Margo's early lessons, Malcolm wasn't sure.

Sven just snorted. When Ann glanced curiously at her

counterpart, Kit chuckled. "That was Sven's excuse, too. You two are complete fakes. Why you should even like that brat after what she put us all through is beyond me."

"*Like* her?" Sven protested. He managed to look hurt—an astonishing feat, considering that his eternal expression was that of a rabid bulldog about to charge. "Ha! Like her. That's good, Kit. I just want another look at that Musashi sword guard of yours. You know, the one you said I could peek at if I trained her."

"And I," Ann said sweetly, pulling off the wheedling tone far more effectively than Sven, "covet another week in the honeymoon suite at the Neo Edo." She batted her eyelashes prettily.

Kit just groaned. Malcolm grinned. "You're as bad as they are, Kit, if you expect me to buy that theatrical groan any more than I buy their excuses."

Kit just crossed his arms and compressed his lips in a pained expression, as though he'd crunched down on a poisoned seed pod and didn't know whether to spit or curse. "*Friends.*" Disgust dripped like ice from his voice.

"Kit," Ann laughed, touching his shoulder in a friendly fashion, "you are the biggest fake of any 'eighty-sixer walking this terminal. It's why we love you."

Kit just snorted rudely. "You sound like Connie Logan. Do all the women on this station get together and compare notes?

Ann winked. "Of course. You're famous. Half the tourists who come here are dying for a glimpse of *the* Kit Carson."

Kit shuddered. His loathing of tourists was La-La Land legend. "I would remind you, I'm not the only famous 'Kit Carson' by a long shot."

Sven nodded sagely. "But you're both scouts, eh?"

Kit grinned unexpectedly. "Actually, I'm not named for Kit Carson, Western scout, at all."

All three of them stared. Malcolm scraped his jaw off the floor before the others. "You're not?"

Kit's eyes twinkled wickedly. "Nope. I used to build balsa airplanes and launch 'em when I was a kid, then shoot 'em down with a slingshot off the side of some cliff. Dahlonega, Georgia," he added drily, "might not have much left but a checkered history, but cliffs we had in plenty. So when I started hitting every little balsa plane I'd made with a nice, fat rock, he took to calling me 'Kit' for his favorite WWII Ace Pilot, L. K. 'Kit' Carson. Came darn near to matching Chuck Yeager's record."

"A fighter pilot," Sven said, eyes round with lingering astonishment. "Well, hell, Kit, I guess that's not too bad a thing, being named after a flying ace. Ever have a chance to do any real flying?"

Kit's expression went distant. Malcolm knew the look. "Yeah," he said very softly.

Before anyone could pry, the station announcer interrupted.

"Your attention, please. Gate One is due to open in one minute . . ."

The four watched in companionable silence as the circus of a Primary departure wound up to a crescendo of baggage searches, purple faces, outraged protests, and the exchange of shocking sums of money collected by agents in no mood to put up with anyone's lip on this particular departure. By the time the gate began to cycle, causing the bones behind Malcolm's ears to buzz, tempers were ragged on both sides of the tables.

"Good thing the gate's about to open or we'd have a fight or two, I think," Malcolm muttered to no one in particular.

"Yep," Sven said with characteristic loquacity.

The sound that was not a sound, heralding the opening of a major gate, intensified. Beyond the imposing array of barriers, armed guards, ramps, fences, metal detectors, X-ray equipment, and dual medical stations stood a broad ramp which rose fifteen feet into the air, then simply ended. Light near the top dopplered through the entire visible spectrum. Then Shangri-la Station's main gate—and sole link with the rest of the uptime world—dilated open.

Up-timers streamed into the station, hauling baggage down that long ramp toward the Medical station barring the way. One by one, station medical personnel scanned and logged medical records. Malcolm waited in a cold sweat for the one slight figure in all that crowd he'd waited months to see—and dreaded meeting again. Then, before he was ready for it, she was there, hair back to its natural flaming red, all trace of brown dye banished until she was ready to take up time scouting as a professional.

Margo . . .

Malcolm's belly did a rapid drawing in. How could he have forgotten what that little slip of a girl could do to a man's body chemistry, just by walking down an ordinary ramp? Margo was dressed—to Malcolm's astonishment—in a chaste little floral-print dress that came nearly to her ankles. The swing of its long skirt and the way it clung to skin he vividly recalled the taste and touch of did bad things to Malcolm's breath control. Her hair was longer, too, and—if possible—sexier than ever as it curled around her ears. *Oh, God, what if she says no? Please, Margo, don't walk down that ramp and tell me you've met some boy at school. . . .*

She caught sight of him and her face lit up like Christmas on Picadilly. She shifted a heavy duffle bag to wave and blow a kiss right at him. His belly did another rapid drawing in that made breathing impossible. He waved back. His knees actually felt weak.

"Buck up, man," Kit muttered in his ear. "You're white as a sheet."

The ring in his pocket all but burned him through the cloth. He'd thought to give it to her here, but with all these well-intentioned onlookers . . . Then, again before he was ready, she'd cleared station medical and dropped the duffle bag to run straight into his arms.

Margo Smith had not forgotten how to kiss.

By the time they disentangled, spontaneous applause had broken out even amongst tourists Malcolm had never laid eyes on. Margo flushed, grinned, then flung her arms around Kit.

"I missed you!"

"Humph!" Kit said, crushing her close despite the attempt at pretense. "The way you greeted Malcolm, I thought you'd forgotten your grandfather existed!"

Margo shocked them all by bursting into tears. "Forget you?" She hugged him more tightly than ever. "Don't you count on it!"

Malcolm cleared his throat while Kit shut his eyes and just held her. After the losses Kit had suffered, Margo's impromptu demonstration meant more than she could possibly know. And after the terrible fights they'd had, it was good to see that look on Kit's face.

Eventually she dried her eyes and sniffed sheepishly. "Sorry. I really did miss you. Sven! And Ann! You came to see me!"

Ann hugged her former pupil tightly. "Welcome home, Margo."

Sven Bailey, true to his nature, demonstrated his affection by launching a snap kick right at her midriff. Margo wasn't there when it should have connected. Despite the hampering cloth of her long dress, she danced aside and managed to land a stinging punch before grabbing Sven and hugging him tightly. He made a single sound of outrage, turned as red as Margo's hair, and extricated himself with slightly less than excessive force.

"Huh. Good to see you remembered some of what I drilled into you, girl."

Margo grinned. "Just a little. Care to spar later? I've been practicing."

Sven Bailey's eyes lit up like an evil gnome's. "You're on!"

Then, shocking everyone, he picked up Margo's luggage and set out with it, calling over one shoulder, "Neo Edo? Kit's apartment? Or Malcolm's place?"

Margo flushed bright pink, glanced guiltily at Kit, bit one lip, and said, "Uh, Malcolm's?"

Kit's face fell until Margo hugged him again and whispered, "Just for tonight, okay? I mean, well, you know."

Kit turned brighter red than Sven had.

Ann laughed aloud. "That's twenty you owe me, Kit."

Kit just produced the money and said repressively, "You had *better* be safe about it, Margo."

Margo put out a pink tongue. "I promised *that* before I went off to school. And I don't break my promises." At his look, she added, "Not anymore. I *learned* that lesson! But I want dinner with you at the Delight, so you'd better not have any dates lined up for tonight!"

Kit relaxed into smiles again. "Arley's already reserved our table."

"Good! College food sucks!"

"Watch your mouth," Kit said mildly.

"Well, it does." But she smiled as she said it.

Her gaze caught sight of the brave decorations strangling

Commons and her mouth and eyes turned into little Os of wonder. "Oh, Malcolm, look! When did *that* happen?"

Kit laughed. "Another new 'eighty-sixer tradition you haven't been introduced to yet. Winter Holiday Decorations Contest. The vendors around each gate try to outdo one another. *Last* year, a three-story, arm-waving plastic Santa caught fire."

"Oooh, bet the stink of that took a while to clear."

Malcolm chuckled. "Yes. *Whichever* way you choose to interpret that."

Margo sighed. The gaudy spectacle was clearly, in her eyes, utterly enchanting. Then she shook herself and glanced at Kit. "Oh, uh, by the way? I've decided going back up time to that school you got me into is a complete waste of time. Brian's got a much better library and, well, it's just *awful*!"

Before Kit could erupt into a violent temper, Margo held out one hand. "Just think about it. We'll, uh, talk more later. Okay?"

Kit hrumphed and said, "All right, my girl, but you're gonna have to talk pretty fast and damn convincingly to change my mind."

Margo laughed, a grown-up burble more than a child-like giggle. "Oh, I will. Don't you fret about that."

When she grabbed Malcolm's hand, Malcolm felt like the air around his brain was fizzing and sparkling. He wondered if Margo could actually feel how hard his heart was thumping through the contact of her fingers against his.

"Any interesting prospects in that group?" Ann, who'd taken in the entire by-play with wide, fascinated eyes, asked. She nodded toward the other up-timers as they headed down the brightly lit, gloriously garish Commons.

"Hmm . . . actually, yeah. There's this group of paleontologists headed down time through the Wild West Gate. Couple of Ph.D.s, three grad students. They're all set—they think," she chuckled, "to study the Bone Wars."

"Bone Wars?" Ann echoed, sounding astonished.

Margo glanced up at Kit, looking smug as a cat that's sneaked a choice morsel off someone's plate. "Yeah, the Bone Wars. There were these two paleontologists, see, Cope and Marsh, who got into a war with one another collecting fossils from the American West. It was kind of an undeclared wager to see who could name the most new specimens and mount them in museums back east. Heck of a wager, too, let me add. Their agents would actually sneak into one another's camps and smash up specimens, shoot at one another, real exciting stuff. But they brought out a king's ransom in dinosaur bones, between them, because of the competition. Named tons of new species and genera and stuff. So, anyway, these guys—well, one of the grad students is a woman—they want to study it first-hand. Said they've already got their own weapons, rifles and pistols, but they were all cased up for the trip through Primary. I made 'em promise to show me their rifles and stuff before they left and made 'em swear to God and all the angels they'd see you for lessons first. I think one of 'em would rather touch a live rattlesnake than the guns he brought along."

Ann grinned. "Good girl!"

Margo chuckled. "It was easy. The four of 'em who were guys were drooling all over themselves for an excuse to talk to me." She rolled her eyes. "*Men.*"

The stab of white-hot jealousy that shot through him stunned Malcolm. Margo glanced up quickly. She must have felt his hand twitch, because she said, "You all right, Malcolm?"

"Fine," he lied. *Just what do these so-called paleontologists look like?* He studied the incoming up-timers, but there were so many, he wasn't sure which group they might belong to.

Margo squeezed his hand. "Hey. Malcolm. They were boring."

The way her eyes sparkled when she smiled made his insides go hot and cold. "Really?" *There, that had come out reasonably steady. Buck up, man, as Kit says. She hasn't said no yet.*

Margo flounced as only Margo could. Malcolm followed the movement with a tortured gaze. She added, "Hah! Their fossils would've been more interesting! I just wanted a peek at their rifles."

Kit laughed. "Malcolm, I'd say you just won *your* standing bet, eh?"

Margo colored delicately. "I wouldn't say that. The time limit on *that* bet ran out ages ago."

Malcolm sighed. "Well, there are other ways of getting your life's story, I suppose."

"Hmm. We'll just have to see how creative you are, Mr. Moore." But she squeezed his fingers.

"At least," Kit said, eying them askance, "you seem to be picking up your American History nicely. Maybe Malcolm's idea wasn't such a bad one, after all."

"Malcolm's idea," Malcolm growled, "was supposed to be Malcolm's surprise."

Margo just looked up at him, wide-eyed. "You planned a surprise for me?"

Heat rose into his face. "Yeah. And Grandpa's doing his damndest to spoil it."

"Got a bet on?" Margo asked suspiciously.

"Not me," Malcolm sighed. "But I wouldn't be surprised if Kit does."

"Kit and everyone else in La-La Land," Ann laughed. "Mind if you have company for dinner, or is this a family affair?"

Margo blushed. "Uh, would you mind if we had lunch tomorrow, instead?"

"Not at all." Ann had to reach up slightly to ruffle Margo's hair. "Imp. It's good to have you home."

She strolled off with a backward wave.

Kit rubbed the back of his neck. "I, uh, have some things I have to take care of . . ."

"So soon?" Margo wailed.

He glanced at Malcolm. "I think Malcolm wants you to himself for a while. Grandpa can wait. But not long," he added with a fierceness in his voice that his playful smile could not quite disguise.

She hugged him tightly. "Promise."

Kit kissed the top of her head, then gently disentangled himself. "Dress up pretty for dinner, okay?"

"I will."

He ruffled her hair much the way Ann had, then left Malcolm alone with her. Malcolm swallowed hard, finding his throat suddenly dry. "Did you, uh, want to catch a bite to eat first?"

Margo's green eyes smoldered. "I'm starving. But not for food. C'mon, Malcolm. It's me. Margo."

He ventured a tentative smile. "That therapy of yours seems to have helped."

She grinned. "Yeah, the rape counsellor I've been seeing is good. She's helped unkink me a whole lot. But I like being in your arms better." Without warning, those smoldering eyes filled with tears and she threw her arms around him. "God, I've missed you! My head *aches* with everything that horrid school stuffs into it! I want you to hold me and tell me I'll get through this."

"Hey, what happened to my little fire-eater?"

Wetness soaked through his shirt. "She got lonely."

Had any up-time boys comforted her during that loneliness? Malcolm hoped not. "My place is this way," he murmured, wrapping an arm around her. "We, uh, have a lot to talk about."

"Yeah?" She brightened and sniffed back tears. "Like what?"

"Oh, lots of stuff." They caught an elevator for Malcolm's floor. "Goldie and Skeeter are in the middle of a *wager*, for one. Whichever of them scams the most in a month—and Goldie can't use her knowledge of rare coins and gems—gets to stay in La-La Land. The other one has to leave."

Margo's eyes widened. "You're kidding? That's a serious wager!" Then she grinned, evilly. "Any way we can help Skeeter?"

"I thought you hated him!"

Margo laughed, green eyes wicked as any imp newly arrived from Hell's own furnace. "I do. But Goldie deserves worse than what we gave her. *Lots* worse." The steel in her voice reminded Malcolm of his favorite poet:

But when hunter meets with husband,
each confirms the other's tale:
The female of the species
is more deadly than the male. . . .

"Huh. Remind me never to get on your wrong side, young lady." The memory of those terrible days in Rome, searching for her, were almost more than he could bear. Margo's squeeze on his hand said a great deal more than her eyes, and *they* spoke of a pain and longing that hurt Malcolm like a physical blow. His faltering hopes began to regain their feet.

Sven Bailey had left Margo's luggage in the "lock-me-tight" mail bin outside each Resident's apartment. Malcolm unlocked the bin, rescuing Margo's cases, then opened his door and ushered her inside.

"You've redecorated! Wow! You actually have *furniture*!"

Malcolm shrugged. "A little money never hurts."

Margo laughed. "Don't be upset with me, Malcolm. I know it's my fault I nearly got us killed, but see. Something good *did* come of it." She swept a grand gesture at the room, nearly knocking over a lamp. "Whoops! Sorry."

That was his Margo, all right. But would she be *his* Margo?

"I, uh, had a little something, I, uh, that is . . ."

"Malcolm," she took both his hands in her own, "what *is* it? It's *me*. The addle-brained brat you had to rescue off a Portuguese witch-burning pyre. You're actually shaking! What's wrong?"

He stared into those bottomless green eyes, filled now with worry and even the beginnings of fear. When she reached up and brushed her lips across his, he felt something inside his soul melt. If she said no . . .

"It's okay, Malcolm. Whatever it is. Just tell me."

No more stalling, he thought grimly. Then he fumbled in a pocket for the little velvet box. "I, uh, went up time for a little vacation, had this made for you."

She opened the box curiously, then went absolutely white.

"Malcolm?" Her voice wavered. So did those luminous green eyes.

"Will you?" he whispered.

An agony of indecision passed across her heart-shaped face, causing Malcolm's heart to cease beating.

"Malcolm, you know my heart—my whole *soul's* set on scouting," she whispered. "You—you wouldn't object?"

He cleared his throat. "Only unless you objected to my coming along."

Her eyes widened. "But—"

"I thought it was high time I got over being a coward."

Margo was suddenly in his arms, crying and kissing him at the same time. "*Don't ever say that! Do you hear me, Malcolm Moore? Never, ever say that!*"

Then she handed back the ring and held out her hand. Her fingers were trembling. It took Malcolm three tries to fumble the ring onto the engagement finger. A golden band to circle the heart line and hold it fast to his heart . . . Margo closed her fingers around the shank of the heavy ring and gazed silently at it for long moments. A diamond she'd nearly died locating in Southern Africa glittered in soft lamplight. "Yes," she whispered. "Oh, yes, Malcolm. I will."

Then, before Malcolm could do more than start breathing again, a look of stricken dismay widened her eyes. "Oh, Lordy, what's Kit going to say?"

Malcolm managed a wan chuckle. "Grandpa approves."

An Irish alley-cat glare he knew so well transformed her adorable, heart-shaped face as the eyebrows dove together and green eyes smoldered. "He does, does he? Am I the only one on this station who didn't know I was getting married?"

Malcolm rubbed his nose in embarrassment. "Well, uh, you know La-La Land."

"Do I ever." But the look in her eyes softened. "Margo Moore. I like the sound of that."

The sound of his name linked with hers did strange things to Malcolm's blood chemistry. The light in the room dimmed. "So . . . How's Denver sound for the honeymoon? I've got tickets. . . ."

Margo's kisses were enough to drive a sane man over the brink. When they came up for air, Margo breathed against his lips, "Sounds perfect. Now stop stalling, Malcolm Moore, and take me to bed!"

He carried her there, long dress trailing, without another word spoken. He was afraid the brutal violations she had suffered at the hands of those damnable Portuguese traders would somehow raise a barrier between them that neither could overcome. But the softness and passion he remembered so well from Rome redoubled in the silence of his bedroom, sending Malcolm nearly out of his mind with the need to touch and cuddle and bring joy where she had suffered so much pain. After their loving came to a shuddering, reluctant end, Margo cried again, nearly as hard as she had that terrible day in

Rome. But this time instead of running, she clung to him and let him comfort her with silly, nonsensical words meant to reassure. Evidently they did, because she fell asleep cradled against the hollow of his shoulder, tear trails streaking her cheeks and his bare skin. Malcolm kissed her hair and marvelled, wondering if she would ever trust enough to share her mind as she had come to trust sharing her body.

The ring glittering softly on her left hand gave him hope. It was a start, anyway. Just as this joining had been. Malcolm lay awake, languorous and wondering, for hours, just holding her while she slept. When she finally woke, their second coming together was even sweeter than the first. And this time, as she drifted off once more against his chest, the words he had longed to hear came like a sigh in the darkness.

"I love you, Malcolm Moore. Hold me . . ."

And so he did.

Chapter 9

"His name is Chuck," the voice on the other end of the phone said. "Chuck Farley."

Skeeter had no idea who the caller was, but it had his undivided attention. "Yes? What about him?"

"He came through Primary alone. Without a tour group. He's wearing a money belt he didn't declare through ATF. Right now, he's asking around at the hotels for the best time periods to visit."

The line went dead before Skeeter could ask who the caller was, why they'd called him, or how they'd obtained this juicy tidbit of information. Was Goldie setting him up? Or the ATF? Or was this legit? He hadn't forgotten Ianira's strange intensity on the subject of who was going to win this bet.

Maybe he possessed more allies than he'd realized.

Skeeter decided to hunt up Mr. Farley and see for himself what this lone up-timer might be up to. And if that money belt were for real . . . then Skeeter might just win his wager in one fell swoop. All it would take was a little finesse on his part. The question was, which scheme to use in the initial approach? Rubbing his hands in anticipation, Skeeter set out to do a little snooping of his own.

Scouting the territory in advance, Yesukai had taught him, was key to any victory. He'd find out what Chuck Farley was up to and use that to craft his plans to deprive the gentleman of that well-filled, undeclared money belt. Skeeter grinned and headed toward Commons with a jaunty whistle.

❖ ❖ ❖

"Undeclared? You're sure?" Goldie's voice came out sharp, excited.

"Positive. I saw it under his shirt when he went to the can. And it's *fat*. Could be thousands tucked into that thing."

Golden dreams floated before Goldie's eyes, like sugar plums and gallant Nutcracker princes, along with visions of Skeeter in handcuffs, hauled kicking and protesting through Primary by Montgomery Wilkes while she waved bye-bye like a sweet little grandmother.

"What's his name and where is he now?"

The voice on the other end chuckled. "Calls himself Chuck Farley. He's hotel hopping, asking questions. Like what gates are the best to visit. Doesn't seem to have any particular destination in mind. Thought that was a might odd, so I started asking around. Time Tours says he doesn't have a ticket through any of their gates and none of the little companies have him booked through the state-owned gates, either."

"Well, well. Thank you very much, indeed."

Goldie hung up the phone thoughtfully. Either they had a speculator on their hands, intent on making an illegal fortune, or they'd stumbled across a rich fool looking for a thrill. No telling, until she had the chance to chit-chat him personally. Whichever the case, she intended for that money belt and its delightfully undeclared contents to end up in *her* possession. Idiot. Chuck Farley had no idea that he'd just stepped into Goldie Morran's parlor. And like the nice, gentle spider she was, she set about weaving her silken web of deceit to pull in this fat little fly all for herself.

Skeeter stood in the shadows of a fake marble column across from the Epicurean Delight, watching a slim, nondescript fellow with dark hair and unremarkable eyes read the posted menu. Chuck Farley wasn't much to look at, but the trained eye revealed the unmistakable presence of that money belt the anonymous tipster had telephoned about. Skeeter was about to step out into the open to join him in perusing the menu when Kit Carson, Malcolm Moore, and—of all people—Margo Smith showed up, chatting animatedly. Skeeter swore under his breath and kept to the shadows. Margo sported an enormous diamond on her left ring finger. *Huh. What she sees in that guide is beyond me.* Malcolm Moore was even more nondescript than Chuck Farley, with a notorious string of bad luck dogging him, to boot.

Of course, he'd been a little more prosperous lately. Some scheme he and Kit had going—and the fact that Skeeter couldn't get the real dope on it was driving him crazy. Nonetheless, he kept a tight rein on his curiosity—Skeeter was more curious than the average 'eighty-sixer, but he steered far clear of *anything* connected with Kit Carson. Yesukai had taught him well—Skeeter knew when he was outgunned. The clever warrior chose his prey with care. Glory was one thing; stupidity quite another. Five years in Yesukai's yurt had more than taught Skeeter the difference.

The group paused outside the Delight, exchanging polite words with Farley as they glanced over the menu. *Come on, go inside, already, before he decides to take a seat.*

Farley nodded courteously in return and joined the long line of up-time patrons waiting for a table. Unless one were a Resident, tables at the Delight were difficult to come by. Reservations were booked weeks in advance and long waits were the norm. But Residents always found a spot at one of the "reserved" tables Arley Eisenstein held for 'eighty-sixers. Skeeter's mouth watered. The scents wafting out of the world-famous restaurant tantalized the senses, but Skeeter didn't have the kind of money to foot the bill for a meal at the Delight, not even when he *wasn't* saving every scrap of cash he owned to win a wager like this one.

Of course, he *had* conned his way in a time or two, getting some trusting uptimer with more money than sense to buy him a gourmet meal. But that didn't happen often, and the fact that Skeeter was ravenously hungry only made matters worse. Voices from waiting patrons floated across the Commons, making it impossible to hear what Kit Carson and his party were saying. Skeeter hugged his impatience to himself. If they would just go in, he could wander over and find a reason to strike up a conversation with Chuck Farley.

A down-timer Skeeter recognized as the Welsh bowman who'd come through that unstable gate from the Battle of Orleans a few months back pushed a wheeled dustbin past, then paused and exclaimed aloud. Margo hugged him, laughing and asking questions Skeeter couldn't quite hear. When she showed off the ring on her hand, the Welshman made deep, deferential bows to both Kit and Malcolm.

Kynan Rhys Gower was one of the very few downtimers Skeeter didn't feel comfortable around. For one thing, the man had pledged some sort of medieval oath of fealty to Kit, which made his business very much Kit's business—and therefore very much *not* Skeeter's. For another, the Welshman looked murderous every time he glanced in Skeeter's direction. Skeeter had no idea what he'd done to antagonize the man, having never recalled even speaking directly with him, but then, the Welshman's temper *had* manifested itself in decidedly odd ways since his arrival. He was unpredictable, at the least. At times, he'd bordered on certifiable—like the time he'd attacked Kit with nothing but a croquet mallet, bent on murder.

Skeeter crossed both arms over his chest and slumped against the column. *Great. An impromptu welcome home party right in front of my rich little mark. Talk about luck* . . . Maybe Malcolm Moore's was contagious? Skeeter certainly hadn't had much luck bringing any of his schemes to fruition since challenging Goldie to this stupid bet. *What was I thinking, anyway? Everyone knows it's impossible to beat Goldie at anything. If anyone's certifiable, it's me.* Still, the challenge she'd thrown down had stung his pride. He hadn't really had a choice and he knew it. Probably she'd known, too, blast her for the backstabbing harpy she was. At least Brian Hendrickson's records proved Goldie's lead a small one. A couple of good scams and he'd be ahead. Well ahead.

Skeeter leaned around the column to see where his "mark" was—and heard a solid *thunk* next to his ear. Startled, he turned his head. A knife haft quivered in the air, the metal blade still singing where it had buried itself in the plastic sheathing of the fake column. Skeeter widened his eyes. If he hadn't leaned around just when he had . . .

He jerked around, looking through the crowd—

Oh, God.

Lupus Mortiferus.

The gladiator charged.

Skeeter bolted, yanking the knife out of the column as he went, so he wouldn't be completely weaponless if the enraged Roman actually *did* catch up with him this time. Diners waiting patiently in line stared as he dashed past, knife in hand, with a gladiator in cowboy chaps in hot pursuit. A sting made itself felt along the side of Skeeter's neck. He swore and swiped at it, then gulped. Blood on his fingertips told him just how close he'd come. A swift glance down showed a thin line of drying blood on the edge of the knife he'd snatched.

Holy . . . if that was poisoned . . . then he'd be in *big* trouble, and soon. His legs went shaky for a couple of strides, then he dodged up a staircase and pounded down a balcony crowded with shoppers. Weaving in and out between them, Skeeter made it to an elevator. The door opened with a soft ding. He dove inside and punched the button for top floor. The elevator doors slid closed just as the enraged gladiator stormed past an outraged knot of shoppers.

The car surged smoothly upward. Skeeter collapsed against the wall, pressing a hand to his neck. *Damn, damn, damn!* He needed to go to the Infirmary and have Rachel Eisenstein look at this. But pride—and fear—sent him plunging into the heart of Residential, instead. If he reported the injury to Rachel, he'd have to explain how he'd managed to sustain a long slice across the side of his neck. And that would lead to unpleasant confessions about profiteering from time travel . . .

Nope, a trip to the infirmary was out.

And that blasted down-timer might have learned enough about La-La Land by now to anticipate him going to the clinic, anyway. Skeeter cursed under his breath and headed for home. By the time he made it to his apartment, Skeeter was trembling with shock and blood loss despite the hand he kept tightly pressed to the wound. Blood seeped between his fingers to drip down his shirt. He was tempted to call Bull Morgan and report the attack, consequences be damned. That gladiator *scared* him. Winning the wager with Goldie was one thing; dying for it was quite another. Hand shaking, he locked the door and stumbled into the bathroom, swearing softly at the ashen cast of his face when he switched on the light.

He dabbed gingerly at the long, shallow slice, hissing between his teeth. "Sorry, Yesukai, but that *stings*." Antiseptic, antibiotic cream, and bandages made him look like the victim of a wide-jawed vampire. "Turtleneck sweaters for a while," Skeeter muttered. "Just great. I really, genuinely hope that goddamned knife wasn't poisoned."

If it had been, he'd know soon enough.

He still wavered between calling Bull Morgan and keeping silent as he switched off the bathroom light and stumbled into his living room. He switched on the in-house TV news channel and flopped into his favorite chair, exhausted and scared and still trembling slightly. He needed food and sleep and painkillers. Food and sleep could be had without leaving the apartment. Painkillers . . . well, aspirin thinned the blood, which was no good. He'd have to settle for something like ibuprofen, if he had any.

The evening newscast's theme music swelled through the darkened little apartment. La-La Land's news program was, like the *Shangri-la Gazette*, more a gossip forum than a real news show. Most of the so-called journalists who drifted into and out of the anchor job were muckrakers who couldn't get work up time for one good reason or another. They tended to shift from time terminal to time terminal in the hope that some juicy tidbit worthy of a real network job would relaunch their uptime careers. They also complained perennially about the lack of budget, equipment, and studio room. Skeeter shrugged—and winced. After his return up time as a child, he'd grown utterly disgusted with them; they had camped out on the lawn waiting for a chance at a photo session and maybe even an exclusive with the kid who'd lived with Genghis Khan's father and the toddler who would become Genghis Khan, himself.

Journalists had been a large factor in his decision to simply leave during the night and head for New York City.

In the Big Apple, rotten to its scheming, seamy core, stories like his could easily be buried under the sensationalism of exposé after exposé on corrupt politicians, waving crime, and the spreading violence and sin that made the City *the* place for one little half-wild adopted Mongol to practice hard-won skills. Skeeter sighed. Those had been rough years, rougher in many ways than living in Yesukai's camp. But he'd survived them. The thought of going back . . .

I could always walk through the Mongolian Gate again, he told himself. *Temujin's out there somewhere fighting for his life against Hargoutai and his clan right about now. Temujin would take me in, might even remember the boy who used to do tricks to amuse him at night while the men were busy eating and telling stories and drinking themselves so sick they'd have to go outside and vomit. Living with Temujin'd certainly be better than going back to New York.* Just about anything would be better than going back to New York. He wasn't sure he'd live long, if he went back, and Skeeter Jackson had become terribly fond of creature comforts, but there were fates worse than dying young in battle.

Speaking of which . . . should he call Bull Morgan or not?

The news program he'd been waiting for had come on, flashing the familiar, sickly sweet face of "Judy, Judy Janes!" onto the screen. She smiled at the camera, looking (as always) every eyelash-batting bit as idiotic as she *sounded*. But her opening statement caught Skeeter's attention *fast*.

"A disturbance this evening on the Commons just outside the Epicurean Delight has left 'eighty-sixers mystified and Security baffled. An eyewitness to the event, well-known station resident Goldie Morran, was willing to share her impressions with our viewing audience."

The camera treated Skeeter to a close-up of The Enemy.

Skeeter swore creatively. In Mongolian.

"Well, I couldn't be sure, everything happened so fast, but it looked to me like Skeeter Jackson bolted from behind that column over there and ran from a man I've never laid eyes on."

"Are you positive about that identification, Ms. Morran?"

Skeeter's official station identification photo appeared briefly on screen, grinning at the audience. The caption read "Unemployed Confidence Artist." Skeeter saw red—several seething shades of it.

The camera cut back to the Commons and Goldie's moment of triumph. Her eyes glittered like evil jewels. "Well, no, I couldn't swear to it, but as you know, Skeeter and I have made a rather substantial wager, so I've been at some pains to keep track of his movements.

I'm afraid I wouldn't do Station Security much good as a prosecution witness, but it certainly did *look* like him. Of course," she laughed lightly, "we get so many scoundrels through, and so many of them look alike . . ."

The rest of the report was nothing more than innuendo and slander, none of it provable and every word of it calculated to wreck any chance he had at conning a single tourist watching that broadcast out of so much as a wooden nickel. Skeeter closed his fists in the semidarkness of his apartment. Report his injury? Hell would freeze first. He'd win this wager and kick that purple-haired harpy from here to—

Skeeter punched savagely at the channel changer. His apartment flooded with soothing music and slowly-shifting vistas taped both down time as well as up time. He'd deal with that pissed-off gladiator as best he could, on his own. *Nothing* was going to sour this wager. Not even Lupus Mortiferus and his fifty goddamned golden *aurii*.

He grabbed the knife and closed his hand around the hilt. Skeeter Jackson wasn't a trained fighter—he hadn't been old enough when "rescued" by an astonished time scout—but he knew a trick or two. Lupus Mortiferus might just be in for as big a surprise as Goldie Morran. He flipped the knife angrily across the room, so that it landed point-first in the soft wallboard. *Nice throwing blade*. Bastard. That knife was *not* an ancient design. Either he'd stolen it . . . or someone was helping him.

Skeeter meant to find out which. And, if someone were helping him, *who*? The sooner he found out, the better. Neutralizing that gladiator had become imperative.

Unlike most Mongols, who learned early to place a very low value indeed on human life, Skeeter Jackson valued his most highly. He did not plan to die at the hands of a disgruntled down-timer who went around cutting out the tongues of the poor wretches he owned and gutting people for sport and coin.

Stranded as he was between the two worlds that had molded him, Skeeter Jackson listened to music in his darkened apartment, endured the thumping pain in his neck, and wrestled with the decision over whether or not to kill the gladiator outright by some devious method, or scheme some way to send him back where he belonged—permanently.

It was a measure of how deeply those two worlds tugged at him that he had not resolved the question by the time he nodded off to sleep in the early hours of the morning.

Malcolm joined Margo as she emerged from the shower, aglow in a healthy, sexy way that made his insides turn to gelatin. He managed to find his voice and keep it steady. "You always did look great in skin, Margo."

Margo just beamed and winked, then adjusted her towel invitingly to dry her back.

Malcolm groaned and seized the towel, but managed to dry her back as gently as he might a frightened fawn. "Been doing your homework, then?" He couldn't believe how husky his voice sounded.

Margo started to laugh. "You bet! Every free moment I get outside of classes. You wouldn't believe the nickname some of my friends have given me."

"Oh?" Malcolm asked, raising one brow to hide the knot of fear that some of those friends might be young and masculine enough to capture her attention.

"Yes. Mad Margo. That's what they call me. I don't go to parties or overnighters or field trips—unless they're related to something important I'm studying—and I positively *never* go out on a date."

"Sure about that?" Malcolm half teased.

Green eyes that a man could get lost in turned upward and met his, quite suddenly serious and dark. "Never." She squeezed his hand. "Do you honestly think all those little boys who swill beer and brag about their conquests could possibly interest me? After what we've been through, Malcolm? It'd take an act of God—maybe more—to pry us apart."

Malcolm dropped the towel and kissed her tenderly. It didn't stay tender long. When they finally broke apart, panting and on fire, Malcolm managed, "Well. I see."

Margo's eyes laughed again, the green sparkle back where it belonged. "Just wanted to convince you, is all."

Malcolm ran the tip of his tongue over swollen lips, then grinned. "Good!" But when he bent for another go-round, Margo laughingly danced away, causing his mind and gut actual pain.

"Oh, no. I'm squeaky clean. I'd like to stay that way for at least another hour, Mr. Moore!" Then she darted into the bedroom they shared and emerged less than two minutes later, clad in very chic black jeans, a sweater that would've made an old man's eyes pop, and dark, soft boots. Malcolm realized with a jolt that her clothing had Paris stamped all over it. She didn't flaunt herself in trendy, gaudy colors but stuck by well-made items that would be in style forever. "All right," she said, fluffing her hair as it dried—hair that looked like a Parisian salon had styled it—"you mentioned something about lunch?"

"Mmmm. Yes. I did, at that. Very well, Margo, gentleman I shall be—for now!"

He wriggled his brows wickedly. Margo laughed, secure of him. They left the apartment and found the corridor to the nearest elevator shaft. They moved easily, hands locked. The air between them sizzled with unseen but palpable heat. When they stepped into the elevator, Margo said huskily, "Your place or mine? After lunch?"

Malcolm couldn't hold back the jolt of need that went though him, but he retained enough presence of mind to recall that Margo, while nominally on vacation, needed to spend some educational time *outside* Malcolm's bed. Or couch. Or dining room floor. Or . . .

He sighed. "Neither just yet. There's someone I think you ought to meet."

Green, expressive eyes went suddenly suspicious. "Who?"

Malcolm chuckled and tickled her chin. "Margo Smith, are you turning jealous on me? Anyway, you'll like her. Just trust me on this one. She lived here already, but hadn't set up her shop yet when you first came to La-La Land. But she's well worth meeting. Trust me."

"Okay, I'm game. So after lunch, show me!"

For a moment Margo sounded *exactly* as she had just a few short months ago. Nice to know not *everything* had grown up quite yet. He didn't *ever* want that part of her to change. "I'll show you, all right," he chuckled. "But *before* lunch. I insist."

Margo pouted while Malcolm punched the button for Commons. The elevator whirred obediently upward. Malcolm steered her into the Little Agora District, vastly different from the genuine Agora's golden era. For one thing, there were no tethered or caged animals waiting to be purchased and ridden or eaten. For another, neither Socrates nor his pupils were anywhere to be seen. Instead, there was one particular booth positively jammed with customers. Other booth vendors looked at the crowded one with expressions that ran the gamut from rage to deep sorrow. Malcolm drew Margo straight toward the jam-packed booth.

Of course.

"Are you sure whoever this is won't mind interrupting her sales? She's got a ton of business there."

Malcolm grinned. "She'll thank *us*. Trust me."

He shoved and elbowed his way through the crowd with shocking rudeness, until Margo found herself staring at the most exotically beautiful woman she had ever seen. Her eyes, black as velvet, were far older than the early twenties she seemed to be. Even as Margo stared, wondering what it was that was so compelling about her, the woman broke into an exquisite, somehow ancient smile. "Malcolm! Welcome!"

Margo felt herself shrink in stature and confidence. While she'd been off at college, alone, Malcolm had been free to . . .

"Ianira, this is Margo. She is Kit Carson's granddaughter and the woman I plan to marry."

Another dazzling smile appeared, this time directed disconcertingly toward Margo. "I am honored to meet you, Margo," she said softly. "Malcolm is a twice-lucky man." The dark eyes seemed to pierce her very soul. "And he will take away the pain in your heart, as well, I think," she said in an even softer voice. "He will make you forget your childhood and bring you much happiness." Margo stared, unable to figure out how she could *know*, unless someone of the few who *did* know had gossiped. Which in La-La Land would be entirely in character, except the only people who *knew* were her father, her grandfather, and Malcolm Moore.

When she glanced around for Malcolm, she realized with a jolt that every "customer" at the booth was busy either writing furiously, holding out a tape recorder, or fiddling with the focus on a handheld vidcam. Sudden fury swept her; she made a grab at and barely hung onto her temper at the intrusion into her privacy. Margo took a deep breath, then deliberately turned back to Ianira. Margo found a smile far back in those dark eyes, a smile which understood her anger and the reasons for it. "Thank you," she said slowly, still rather confused, because she was *certain* neither Kit Carson nor Malcolm Moore would have told *anyone*. And she was utterly certain her *father* had never set the first toe on TT-86's floor. Ianira's return smile this time was every bit as enigmatic as the Mona Lisa's, yet reminded her of graceful white statuary recovered from lost millennia to stand, naked or artfully draped, in vast, marble museums.

Malcolm said quietly, "Ianira Cassondra came to TT-86 a few years ago. Through the Philosophers' Gate."

"You're a down-timer, then? I hadn't guessed," Margo added, as Ianira nodded slightly. "Your English is fabulous."

A brief smile like sunlight on cloud tops passed over Ianira's face. "You are too kind."

Nervous, Margo focused her attention on the actual booth and its contents. Exquisitely embroidered cotton and linen gowns similar to the one Ianira wore were neatly folded up amidst dress pins, hair decorations, lovely scarves, tiny bottles of God only knew what, piles of various kinds of stones and crystals—with a select few hanging on cords to catch the light—charms of some kind which looked extremely ancient, carved carefully from stone, wood, or precious gems, even little sewn velvet bags closed by drawstrings, with tiny cards on them which read, "Happiness," "Wealth," "Love," "Health," "Children" in fake "Greek-looking" letters. There were even incense sticks, expensive little burners for them, and peeking out here and there, CDs with titles like *Aphrodite's Secret: The Sacred Music of Olympus.*

And, topping it all off, extraordinary jewelry of an extremely ancient design, all of which looked real, and from the prices could've been.

"You have quite a booth," Margo said, hearing the hesitation in her own voice.

Ianira laughed softly, a sound like trickling, dancing water. "Yes, it is a bit . . . different."

Malcolm, ignoring the crowd around them with their scribbling pens, tape recorders, and vidcams, said, "Margo, you remember young Marcus, don't you?"

"The bartender from the Down Time? Yes, very well." She could feel the heat in her cheeks as she recalled that first, humiliating meeting with Kit. The blush was innocent, as it happened, but Ianira might wonder. "Why?"

Malcolm smiled and nodded toward Ianira. "They're married. Have two beautiful little girls."

"Oh, how marvelous!" Margo cried, completely forgetting her earlier doubts. "Congratulations to you! Marcus is so . . . so gentle. Always so anxious to put a person at ease and treat them like royalty. You must be very happy."

Something in those fathomless dark eyes softened. "Yes," she whispered. "But it is not wise to speak of one's good fortune. The gods may be listening."

While Margo pondered that statement, Malcolm asked, "Have you had lunch, Ianira? Margo and I were just on our way. My treat, and don't give me any lame excuses. Arley Eisenstein's made enough money over the cheesecake recipes you've already given him, you might as well share the taste, if not the wealth."

Unexpectedly, Ianira laughed. "Very well, Malcolm. I will join you and your lady for lunch."

She lowered prettily painted plywood sides and locked the booth up tight with bolts shot home from the *inside*, then finished off with a padlock. They smiled when Ianira finally joined them. Ianira held a curious, largish package in brown paper tied up with string, which reminded Margo of a favorite musical with nuns and Nazis and narrow escapes.

"Special delivery after lunch?" Malcolm asked.

Ianira just smiled. "Something like, yes."

Margo, oblivious to that exchange, found herself envying the way Ianira walked and the way that dress moved with every step she took. She tried, with some fair success, to copy Ianira's way of moving, but something was missing. Margo vowed silently to buy one of those gowns—whatever it cost—and try out the effect on staid, British Malcolm Moore, who melted in her arms and kissed her skin with trembling lips as it was, every time they made love.

Unhappily, the entire mass of curious scribblers, tapers, and vidcammers followed close on their heels all the way down the Commons.

"Who *are* those people?" Margo whispered, knowing that whisper would be picked up and recorded anyway.

Ianira's lip curled as though she'd just stepped in excrement. "They are self-appointed acolytes."

"*Acolytes?*"

"Yes. You see, I was a high-ranking priestess in the Temple of the Holy Artemis at Ephesus before my father sold me in marriage. I was only part of the price to close a substantial business transaction with a merchant of ivory and amber. The man he gave me to was . . . not kind."

Margo thought of those horrid Portuguese in South Africa—and her father—and shivered. "Yes. I understand."

Ianira glanced sharply at her, then relaxed. "Yes. You do. I am sorry for it, Margo."

Margo shrugged. "What's past is past."

The statement rewarded her with another brilliant smile. "Exactly. Here, it is easier to forget unhappiness." Then she laughed aloud. "The day the ancient ones"—she pointed to the rafters, where fish-eating, crow-sized pterodactyls and a small flock of toothed birds sat—"came through the big unstable gate, I hid under the nearest booth and prayed *someone* would rescue me. When I dared peek out, I found the huge one covered in nets and the small ones flying about like vengeful harpies!"

Both Margo and Malcolm laughed softly.

Malcolm rubbed the back of his neck, while his cheeks flushed delightfully pink. "You should've seen *me*, that day, trying to hold that monster down and getting buffeted around like a leaf in a tornado. I finally just fell off and landed about ten feet away!"

They were still laughing when they reached the Urbs Romae

section of the time terminal. Malcolm steered them into the Epicurean Delight's warm, crowded interior, toward one of the tables eternally reserved for 'eighty-sixers. Frustrated acolytes seethed outside, unable to get in without the requisite reservations or status as 'eighty-sixers. Tourists, most of whom had made reservations months in advance, stared at them with disconcerting intensity. Margo heard a woman nearby whisper, "My God! They're 'eighty-sixers! *Real* 'eighty-sixers! I wonder who?"

Her lunch companion gasped. "Could he be Kit Carson? Oh, I'm just dying to catch a glimpse of Kit Carson!"

"No, no, didn't you see the newsies? That's Malcolm Moore, the mysteriously wealthy time guide, and that's Margo Smith, Kit Carson's granddaughter. I remember it because it was a granddaughter he didn't even know existed. Made headline news on every network for an entire half an hour! I taped the stations I wasn't watching, just to compare versions. I can't *think* how you missed it. And that other woman seated with 'em? Just you take a guess as to who *she* is?"

"I—I'm afraid I don't recognize her—"

"You know all those churches of the Holy Artemis that've been springing up all over the place? Well, that's Ianira Cassondra, the *Living Goddess*, an enchantress who knows the *ancient* ways. Lives here, now, to escape persecution."

The other woman's eyes had widened so far, just about all that remained of her face was eyes. "*Really?*" It came out a kind of repressed squeal. "Oh, oh, where's my camera—?"

She fumbled a small, sleek camera and pointed it toward them.

Margo flushed red. Ianira looked merely annoyed. Malcolm just grinned, first at Margo, then at the ladies who'd been whispering so loudly; then he rose from his chair and bowed at the waist, tipping an imaginary tophat. The flash momentarily blinded Margo, catching Malcolm mid-hat-tip. Both women went white, beet-red, and hungry-eyed all in the space of two seconds. Then they beamed what they thought were seductive—or at least winning—smiles back at him.

"Hey," Margo said, wrapping her fingers around his, "you're took. An' don't you go 'round forgettin' it, now, or I'll hafta take a skillet to you!"

He chuckled. "Just part of the show, dear. Never know when it'll get you a rich customer. Besides, you're not allowed to hit me until *after* we're married." He lifted one brow, then. "And just *when* did you start learning Wild West lingo?"

"Oh, a while back, I reckon."

He wrapped gentle fingers around her wrist and scowled his blackest, enraged scowl. "You two-timin' me, woman, with some no 'count cow-punchin' range rat?"

"Oh, God, that's depressing. And I thought I was actually making progress with it." She batted his hand away from her wrist. "You're terrible. Love you anyway." Then, "I didn't notice tourists doing that sort of thing last time."

"Oh, they were. You just didn't notice because you were too busy turning that alley-cat glare on everything and everyone who stood in your way—even those poor, abused books you used to read and fling across Kit's apartment whenever you got frustrated. Or attempting to toss Sven on his backside, if it killed you."

Margo went beet-red again. "Didn't know Kit'd told you about the books," she mumbled, noticeably not apologetic about trying to mop up the gym with the instructor who'd given her multiple bruises every single night.

His eyes softened. "Hey, Margo. It's okay. We all got out in time and you're doing wonderfully well, now that you're into your studies so deeply."

Margo just nodded, afraid to try her voice.

Ianira, who had taken in the entire exchange silently, began to chuckle. "You will do well, the pair of you." Two heads whipped around guiltily. Ianira laughed aloud. "Oh, yes. Fire of Youth and Caution of Experience—with streaks of child-like play and frightened love in you both. Yes," she smiled, "you will do well together." Before either of them could speak, Ianira stretched slightly. "Oh, what a relief to get away from those hounds." She pointed silently with her glance toward the window where her acolytes stood with despairing expressions, then said something low in ancient Greek, something that sounded holy and apologetic.

When she'd finished, and Margo was *sure* she'd finished, she asked curiously, "Don't they drive you crazy? Do they follow you around like that all the time?"

"Very nearly, and yes." Expressive eyes went suddenly tired. "It does get a bit wearing at times. Still, a few of them are actually teachable. I am told, for I will never be allowed up time, that I have sparked an entire revival of Artemis worship. You heard those women. Simply by being here and occasionally speaking directly to a few of them," again, she nodded very slightly to the window, "I have accidentally begun something that even I do not know where the ending will lie."

"Yeah, you have. Believe me, have you ever. There are no less than *three* Artemis temples just on campus, because response was so high they had to build another and then a third one to hold all the students attending the ceremonies. How many are in town, I don't think anyone knows."

Ianira pondered that in silence—and judging by her eyes—sorrow.

"Hey, Ianira, don't feel so terrible. I mean everything we do or don't do, say or don't say has an impact on something or someone else. And none of us know even half, never mind *most* of the endings. I mean, look at the Church of Elvis The Everlasting."

"El-vis?" Ianira asked uncertainly. "I do not know this god."

Margo giggled. A genuinely delighted, little-girl giggle. "Yeah. Elvis Presley, singing star. Here's an aging rock 'n' roll legend found dead on the *toilet*, for God's sake, with a whole bunch of chemicals in his blood. That was back in 1976. Wasn't too long before folks started writing songs about him, or claiming they'd seen The Everlasting Elvis at some grocery store or in their living rooms, or maybe hitchhiking some interstate and a trucker lets him in, talks to him for a while, then he'd say something like, 'Gotta go, now friend. Good talkin' to you. See you at Graceland some day.' Then he just vanishes."

Ianira was laughing so hard, there were tears in her eyes. "Please, Margo, what is a 'rock 'n' roll' singer? Why was this El-vis so popular?"

Surprising them both speechless, Malcolm shoved back his chair, ran impromptu fingers through his hair so it looked more or less appropriate, then in an astonishingly good imitation of Elvis' voice, sang a stirring, blood-pounding rendition of "Heartbreak Hotel" complete with world-famous hip thrusts. He grabbed up the vase from their table and sang into the pink carnation as though it were a microphone and crooned the chorus to applause, whistles, and feminine shrieks. Then with a single movement, he whipped the dripping carnation and tossed it—straight at Margo. She let out a sound somewhere between scream and fainting ecstasy while the transformed Malcolm bowed to the thunderous applause all through the Delight. He bowed to every corner in turn, saying, "I wanna thank you for comin' and sharin' my show. I love you all, baby. Gotta go, now. My 'nanner sandwich is waitin'."

He sat down to another thunderous round of applause, shrieks for "MORE!" and an entire hailstorm of carnations. All three ducked, finding themselves covered in no time with dripping wet flowers.

"See," Malcolm grinned, coming up for air—with a red carnation stuck sideways in his hair—"no sequined suit, no fancy guitar—in fact, no guitar at all, and I'm not nearly as good an imitator as lots of guys are. But you saw the response from the people in here." They were still brushing off carnations. Malcolm signalled for a waiter. "They went completely nuts. *That's* the definition of the ultimate rock 'n' roll star: being so good at what they do, their audiences go crazy. Happened with the Beatles, too; but they called Elvis 'The King of Rock' *long* before he died and got himself apotheosized."

Margo took up the rest of the explanation as best she could. "Pretty soon, there was a single 'Church of Elvis the Everlasting.' The main temple was—is—his estate at Graceland, Elvis' mansion in Memphis, Tennessee. Trouble was, while lots of folks made the pilgrimage, lots more couldn't afford it. So before you know what's happening, there are *thousands* of Churches of Elvis the Everlasting, all over the country. And all of 'em mail their cash tithes overnight express to the High Temple at Graceland."

Margo grinned. "Man, you should *see* that place! There was a documentary on it one Friday night a few weeks back, and since I didn't have much to do, I watched it." She rolled her eyes. "A *real* king would be jealous. There's an altarpiece, must be twenty-four feet of black velvet, with another piece coming down the pulpit to the floor. Believers who can sew are still working on it. The Everlasting Elvis on the pulpit is finished—gold and silver threads, diamonds, rubies, emeralds, you name it, they used it to decorate that drop of cloth.

"And no cheap, synthetic velvet, either, but the real stuff that would cost me, let's see, at *least* seven weeks of saving up every bit of my allowance, just to buy a piece of real velvet as big as the altar piece, never mind the twenty-four-foot runner. *That* is supposed to illustrate the entire *life* of the Everlasting Elvis."

Margo giggled. "I can't help wondering if they're going to show him ascending as the Elvis Everlasting, rising into grace from that toilet seat he died on? Oh, that whole *place* is crazy. The whole *fad* is crazy. Worshipping a dead rock 'n' roll singer? Puh-leeze."

Ianira was still wiping tears of hilarity from the corners of her eyes. "Your whole up-time world, I think, is just as crazy as worshipping a dead man. You have a gift, Margo, for telling a story." Ianira's smile was brilliant. "You could go into training, fire-haired one. So few see so clearly at your age."

Margo flounced in place. "Humph. It ain't the age, it's the mileage," she muttered, paying tribute to one of her favorite last-century classics.

"You see what I mean?" Ianira said softly. "You just did it again. You *should* get training before you go scouting on your own. You may well have need of it someday."

Margo couldn't say anything. Once again, Malcolm came to her rescue. He passed menus around and said lightly, "Ianira, who has accumulated quite a bit of 'mileage' for *her* age, has become something of a celebrity up time, as you mentioned with all those temples on your campus. Right after The Accident, there was a group of kooks, I forget what they called themselves—"

Margo supplied the answer: "The Endtime Saviors."

"Yes," Malcolm said, and pantomimed a "thank you" and a kiss, "these Endtime Saviors decided right after The Accident that the End was upon us. They kept looking for a sign. A prophet who would usher in the next age of mankind. Or should I say 'womankind'? Unfortunately, they've decided Ianira *is* that sign. She's regarded as a prophetess, the Voice of the Goddess on Earth."

Margo rubbed the tip of her nose. "Well, if she can say to everyone what she said about me and my poor, checkered past, I can understand why."

"No," Ianira laughed softly. "It is just that you and I resonate so closely. Our experiences, different as they are, have enough similarity to feel the resonance and understand clearly its source."

Margo shook her head. "I dunno. I guess if that's how you do it . . ."

Ianira smiled slightly. "It is part of my training in the Mysteries of Artemis, you see, in the great Temple at Ephesus, where I was born. Oh, how I miss Ephesus!" Her exotic eyes misted for just a moment and it came to Margo with a jolt just how terribly homesick most downtimers must be, torn away from everything they knew and loved, never allowed to go home, wandering at best from menial job to menial job, maybe even switching stations in the hopes of improving their situation—

Margo thereby swore a sacred oath to treat *all* down-timers, not just Kynan Rhys Gower, a great deal more courteously.

Ianira was still speaking. "After marriage, when my *husband* carried me across the Aegean Sea to Athens, pride of Greece, I vowed to study as best I could the Mysteries of the majestic Athene who guarded his city. Not even *he* could deny me that, not with my stature from Ephesus. So I learned—and learned to hate my life outside the Temple, inside *his* gyneceum."

Margo, round-eyed, could only reply, "Oh. I—I'm sorry."

Malcolm chuckled. "Hits most people that way. Ianira's name means the Enchantress, you know. She's what you might call an international, temporal treasure, locked away safe and sound inside TT-86's concrete walls."

Ianira flushed and made a small sound of disagreement.

"Say what you will," Malcolm said mildly, "an international, temporal treasure is exactly what you are. Dr. Mundy—a professor of history who interviews the down-timers," he added for Margo's benefit, "—says it constantly. Best information he's found in all his life, he says, and he's getting it all in glorious detail from *you*, Ianira. Besides," he winked, "being an international, temporal treasure does pays the bills, doesn't it?"

Ianira laughed aloud. "You are impossible, Malcolm Moore, but yes. It does, handsomely. It was a good idea Marcus had, to put up such a booth when crassly miseducated, up-timer fools began to seek me out. We're almost out of debt to the Infirmary, now."

"That's great, Ianira. I've very happy for you. I know how close it was with your little girl."

Ianira gave him a sad, sweet smile. "Thank you. It was in the hands of the gods—and Rachel Eisenstein, may the Lady bless her eternally—but she is now healthy enough to return to the Station Babysitting Service and School. I would dearly *love* to get my hands on the tourist who brought that fever back to the Station with him! Malcolm, after lunch, perhaps you would care to join me? I always go there after lunch to check on my babies. And I have an idea which may help relieve a bit of the strain on poor Harriet Banks. She tries so hard and it is just not fair."

Malcolm just said, "Yeah. I know. I'll be happy to come along. Got a few ideas of my own, I do. We'll compare notes after lunch. Margo?"

She shook her head, eyes apologizing to Ianira as best she could. "I have to get in some weapons practice before we go to Denver. I'm a little rusty and even if I weren't, I'd still practice because my scores just weren't all that good before my, uh, adventure. So I thought I'd try out a couple of period rifles, a few handguns, see how I do with them."

"You are wise," Ianira smiled that archaic, mysterious smile. "A woman who thinks herself without limits is a dangerous fool—and I have seen so very many of them." The acolytes were still outside, filming and scribbling notes. Ianira glanced their way with the merest flick of her gaze, but managed to convey utter contempt for the lot of them. Margo blinked, having no earthly idea how she'd just done that, but wanting to learn the secret of it for herself.

Ianira reached out and covered Margo's shocked hand. "You have begun to understand that you have limits, Margo, even as all humanity has limits. What I find even more astonishing—and delightful—for a girl your age, you have already discovered what many of them," she nodded toward the window, "will never discover." Then once more, the offer came, causing even Malcolm to stare.

"It would be my great joy to train you, Margo, for there is such a fire in your soul as I have not seen since my childhood, when my own dear instructor, the sister of my mother, was chosen as High Priestess. Light would dance from her hair, her fingertips, there was so much fire inside her. She did many great things and was everywhere honored as a great and shrewd leader during times when leadership was desperately needed.

"You look nothing like her, Margo, yet you could *be* her. And, youthful as you are, you have already taken the first steps on your own journey to wisdom." Then, letting go Margo's hand, which tingled as though live electricity had poured through it, Ianira fished under the table and slid the brown-paper packet over toward Margo. When Margo gave her a puzzled look, Ianira said softly, "Your Malcolm is a man with a beautiful soul. He is dear to us, to the Council of Seven, to the whole community of down-timers, The Found Ones. Consider the contents of the package a wedding gift from all of us, so that you might please Malcolm even more than you do now, and so that Malcolm will not just love you, but worship you, for that is what you both need and deserve. Nothing less will do. I can only hope this offering of silly trinkets will help."

"Uhm," Margo cleared her throat. "Do I open it now? Or save it for the wedding night?"

Ianira laughed. "That is your decision. But the way Malcolm is staring from you to that package and back, with such speculation in his eyes, I would suggest you open it now."

Margo glanced over and saw the intense hunger in Malcolm's face, which turned bright red when he realized he'd been caught. Hastily he cleared his throat and said, "I was only curious, after all."

Both women laughed. Margo dipped into an across-the-shoulder purse no bigger than a diskette box and pulled out a small but useful

Swiss Army Knife. She made quick work of the string, then turned the carefully tucked package onto its back, took a deep breath, and opened it.

Inside lay the most exquisite gown from Ianira's rack and jewelry nestled in its fold: not the cheap stuff, but the stuff that had the look and feel of genuine antiquity.

"Oh!—My God! Oh, my *God*! Ianira, you shouldn't have—I can't possibly accept—"

Ianira stopped her attempted refusal by leaning forward and placing soft fingertips across Margo's lips. "Just accept. As a friend."

Margo's eyes filled. "Why are you doing this? I just met you—"

"Oh, no, child. We have known each other through many lifetimes. Wear it and please each other, that you also may be together for many lifetimes."

Margo didn't hear much through the next few seconds. She kept staring at the lines of sparkling embroidery, the heavy silver necklace, bracelets, earrings, with all the stones in them prepared in the ancient way: simple, round-topped cabochons, even the diamonds. It was beyond beautiful. Margo could find no words to say how beautiful it was.

Ianira and Malcolm were speaking, forcibly yanking Margo out of uncustomarily deep thoughts. "—firearms practice schedule on her own, same with the martial arts. And she studies, my God, the girl studies!"

Ianira laughed softly. "Would you have her any other way?"

Malcolm said without hesitation, "No."

Ianira glanced over to Margo. "I will ask the Lady's blessing on your practice."

"Hear, hear," Malcolm agreed. "After lunch, you go play with guns. I'll come down later and see how you're doing, get in a little practice, myself. Then we'll get clean, eat in, and try on that," he nudged the half-opened package, "before bedtime. *Well* before bedtime."

Margo smiled her best, heart-stopping smile. One elderly gentleman—well, he was hardly a gentleman—at finding himself the focus of that smile, had literally collapsed on the street, leaving strangers to hunt his pockets for the nitroglycerin and to call the ambulance. After that experience, Margo was careful just how far she turned on that particular smile—and then realized with a jolt that she and Ianira weren't so different, after all. It startled her into meeting the other woman's gaze.

Ianira knew. Somehow, she knew exactly what Margo had just discovered. Moreover, she approved, eyes twinkling merrily. Margo swallowed hard as the silent invitation passed over Malcolm's bent head. *Someday*, Margo attempted to convey with eyes and tiny gestures. *Someday I will seek you out for training. I have the funniest feeling I'm* supposed *to study with you, that I* am *going to need to learn what you teach me.*

Ianira merely nodded and smiled again, a mysterious little smile full of knowledge and agreement. Margo smiled back her acceptance.

Malcolm the Ever-Vigilant (missing the exchange entirely) glanced up from his menu and smiled at them both. "Well, then, what shall we order for lunch?"

Chapter 10

One look at the firing line and Margo's gut muscles tightened in dismay.

Please, anyone *but that bunch!*

Maybe they were just finishing up their session?

Margo's nostrils pinched tight, causing her upper lip to curl in a completely unconscious expression of disgust. The group of five intent paleontologists she'd met at the up-time station in New York, where Shangri-la's Primary opened, were just beginning to unpack a luggage cart, laying out their sundry gun cases for a private lesson.

Aw, rats. Some of Ann's lessons took *hours* to complete.

She didn't dislike the paleontologists, exactly. Well, not the woman, anyway. But three of the four men had spent their entire time in Primary's up-time waiting lounge all but drooling while they stared directly at her. Or, rather, at her chest. It was a reaction she was more than accustomed to, but she still didn't like it.

Chalk up another change, Margo. You don't like being stared at anymore.

Already, the group had noticed her and the renewed stares made her feel like a sleazy 42nd Street hooker. Margo began to consider—seriously—buying some of the uglier but more fully concealing peasant clothing in Connie Logan's Clothes and Stuff.

Paleontologists, hah!

The only truly interesting thing Margo had discovered about

them was where and when, exactly, they were heading. Cope and Marsh had fought over a *huge* chunk of territory. She shook her head slightly.

The damned fools were deliberately walking right into the middle of the fight, hoping to rescue one of the new-species fossil skeletons that one side or the other had smashed up into tiny, useless fragments, so that it had been lost to science forever. The girl, one of three graduate students selected for this trip, had explained; at least, she'd mentioned something about a diary one of their professors had stumbled on in a used bookstore, written by one of the actual field agents charged with bringing back as many intact new specimens as possible.

Using that diary as a guide, they'd plotted out this madcap adventure and actually expected not only to find and rescue one or more of the smashed skeletons, but to get the bones back through the Wild West Gate and up time to the museum affiliated with their university.

Margo was glad they'd had enough sense to take her advice and get some good instruction on how to use whatever they'd brought along, but that did *not* mean she wanted to practice with them.

Come on, Margo, bear up! Maybe if I take that farthest lane? If it's not reserved already, it ought to do. The lanes were sometimes reserved in advance for a scout who was planning to push an unexplored gate and wanted to learn to use a nice, little hide-out gun. It was a practice Kit disapproved of—and a habit he had very carefully made certain she *never* picked up—but scouts were independent agents, so to speak, so each made his own decisions on what to take down time. Kit had warned her there were a few really marginal scouts who routinely broke what he considered to be *the* sacred rules of scouting.

Carrying a gun down time into an unknown time and place, where any gun might be an anachronism, wasn't stupid. It was suicidal.

She didn't spot anyone else on the range, though, which bolstered her hopes. The paleontologists were talking excitedly while dumping gun cases onto Ann's benches. *Lots* of gun cases. Margo winced at the way they just casually bounced the stuff around, allowing them to slide to the floor, banging them together, using the muzzle end of a thin leather case to shove a larger, much heavier case farther down the bench to make room for the rifle with its now possibly ruined front sight. They'd be learning about sighting in and zeroing rifles, or Margo didn't know Ann Vinh Mulhaney.

When Ann noticed that only one of her five students was opening the gun cases for inspection, while four of the group had their attention directed elsewhere, she glanced around. Then smiled so brightly Margo's eyes misted a little.

"Oh, it's you," Ann laughed. "I thought maybe Marilyn Monroe's ghost had jiggled in or something."

That statement caused several reddened faces and sudden diligence with as-yet-unloaded gear. Margo's face had gone terribly hot. Marilyn Monroe, the twentieth-century sex goddess? *That*, Margo would never be, but she enjoyed the compliment just the same. Ann nodded her over. Margo would have *loved* a long heart to heart with Ann—but now was not the time.

Oh, well, she thought as she headed resolutely toward them, *at least I'll finally get to see what firearms these "learned" idiots brought along.* Making the best of it, Margo covered the intervening space with a cheery, "Hi, Ann! Hope things have been fantastic."

Ann laughed and gave her a swift, hard hug, then stepped back. She had to look up a fair ways to find Margo's eyes—and Margo was not even remotely tall. Ann was just *tiny*.

"Yes, they have been. Utterly and completely fantastic. I'm going to have another kid in about seven months." She patted her belly gently. "So no wrestling," she chuckled. "Anyway, that's Sven's forte, not mine." Her eyes crinkled in a fond smile as she studied Margo. "Just look at you, girl. You're still growing! I thought so, earlier, but the way Malcolm was mauling you, it was hard to tell."

Margo's cheeks flushed again, hotter than before. The ring on her finger tugged downward, it was so heavy. She knew Ann had noticed it the moment she'd walked into the range.

"Good!" Ann decided, hands planted on hips in her usual stance. "You look better with some meat on those bones and some color in your cheeks, you scrawny little Irish alley-cat. One thing's for sure, that baleful green glare hasn't changed. Not a bit."

Margo grinned. "How're the wagers going?"

Ann blinked. "Wagers?"

"About how soon I'll be in your condition."

"Oh, *that* wager." Ann's eyes crinkled again. "Hot and heavy betting, both for and against. Everyone knows how determined you are about your profession, but everyone also knows that Malcolm Moore is a very, um, how to put it—intense individual when it comes to getting what he wants."

They grinned at one another. Then Margo noticed the paleontologists, who stood listening in silence, several of them round-eyed with shock. *Aw, rats. Here I am doing just what I said I* wouldn't *do.*

Ann, perhaps guessing some of what was happening inside her head, just touched the back of Margo's hand with her fingertips, bringing her back to the reality outside Margo's thoughts. Margo blinked. Ann asked gently, "Have you come to brush up with a lesson? If you did, you'll have to wait a while. Or do you just want to brush up with a stack of targets and whatever you care to shoot?"

Margo nodded. "Thought I'd try a Winchester model 73 first. Malcolm's taking us to Denver, so I thought I might as well tackle period rifles. I'll try a model 76 Centennial later."

"Just those two?"

Margo let go a genuine, healthy laugh. "And who taught me to carry only the right weapon for the job? This is just this *morning's* practice session. Tomorrow morning I have a date with handguns of every imaginable design and manufacture, just so long as they were invented *before* 1885; then Sven gets a crack at me before lunch."

Anne's eyes brightened. "Oooh, can I come watch? I don't have a class scheduled . . ."

Margo just rolled her eyes. "I can't stop you. Besides, I might need help crawling out of the gym."

Ann laughed heartily. "Okay, imp. It's a deal." Ann's eyes sparkled with anticipation. "You're head's on straight, kid, even if you *were* stuck in an up-time college for six months. A college I'm *certain* does *not* have a shooting range."

"Are you kidding?" It came out sour as early Minnesota apples, still green and hard as walnuts on the tree. "A *shooting* range? No way real." That new bit of up-time slang hadn't filtered down to La-La Land yet, given the startlement in Ann's eyes.

"They just outlawed metallic emery boards, for God's sake."

Ann shook her head, eyes dark with sorrow. "It's been lousy up time for a *long* time. Why do you think we moved our family to Shangri-la Station?" She shivered at some memory she was unwilling to share, then sighed. "Well, you might as well get started. Use lane four, if you don't mind. I'm going to start the class on basic safety before we move to pistol and rifle types. You know where the keys are, right?"

Five sets of jaws dropped—again.

Margo grinned back. "Yep. I even"—she dropped a wicked wink—"know where you hide the pole guns and laser-guided dart guns, never mind the *really* cool stuff. Hey, is that Browning Automatic Rifle working again? I really liked shooting it before it malfunctioned." She considered pride versus humility in front of this bunch of geeks, and decided on humility—hoping it would be a lesson to *them*. "And I'm still utterly mortified that I, uh, caused it to malfunction last time I used it, then couldn't figure out how to machine a new part. Is it fixed yet? I did send the money to repair it." She batted pretty lashes and sounded wistful as a half-drowned kitten.

Ann just laughed. "Oh, you're impossible as ever, imp. Weepy one second, hellbound for leather the next. Go on and get whatever you need and let me get back to *paying* customers." Her smile took any possible sting out of the words. But she had not answered Margo's question about the B.A.R. *Rats!*

Before she left, Margo glanced at the rifles and pistols that had been quietly laid out on the benches while they spoke. *Uh-oh. Thought so. Smart—but stupid. Typical academicians. You'd think they'd eventually change.*

Margo found the keys right off, then unlocked a largish room built inside the range itself. Made entirely of steel four inches thick in every dimension, with a heavy door whose hingepins were on the *inside*, it contained firearms of literally every time period from their invention in the 1300s onward. Door still open, she half heard Ann say lightly to her new students, "Why did I . . . Margo . . . keys? Oh, that's only because . . . time scout. Still in . . . already very good at her job. Her first scouting adventure . . . very dangerous . . . unstable gate. But she got everybody out but one . . . malaria."

Margo squirmed—*all* 'eighty-sixers knew who'd pulled her bacon out of the fire (literally) on that trip; but she was still young and vain enough to wish she could've seen the expressions on those stuffy academic faces as it registered: a *woman* time scout. She grinned—then suddenly sucked in air as a horrifying thought sent her belly plummeting groundward.

Oh, damn! She figured she had about three months before those five idiots out there blabbed to every up-time newsie in the business that a *woman* time scout by the name of Margo Smith was working out of TT-86. She'd be *swarmed* over by reporters, particularly the tabloid kind. And they were nearly *impossible* to shake off once they got interested in you.

Now she'd *never* get any studying done. She abruptly understood her grandfather's uncompromising, lifelong hatred of news reporters. *Well, Margo, my girl, just make the best of it and maybe you'll build up a reputation big enough to satisfy even* your ego.

She grinned at herself, having learned quite a few things about Margo Smith this day she'd never even guessed existed, and plucked a beautiful Winchester Model 73 .44-40 from the rifle rack, automatically checking to be certain it wasn't loaded. She laid it carefully aside, muzzle pointed away from the open door. She found ammo for a Model 76 Centennial in .45-75 Winchester, remembering vaguely that Ann carried a couple of the rifles in stock. She discovered a beauty of a lever-action Winchester Model 76 Centennial—clearly *original*—which was very similar to the 73, but beefier and in a more powerful caliber. It, too, was safely unloaded. The Centennial was for *serious* shooting. She'd have to remember to ask Ann to reserve them for the Denver trip.

The size of the 76 caused Margo to remember Koot van Beek's

rifle and that great, horrid Cape Buffalo. That was a barely scabbed-over memory, too. She hastily snagged the Centennial, along with a modern cleaning kit with brushes for both rifles. Never, ever again would Margo travel down a gate without the right weapons close at hand.

Putting aside the memory, Margo carted all the items to an empty shooting bench on lane four. Ann glanced up and nodded approvingly, her goggles in one hand, her earmuffs slid down around her neck, in "lecture mode."

"Let me know when you're ready to go 'hot,' Margo," she called down the line.

Margo nodded and curiously studied the beginning of the lesson as she prepared to practice. It looked from here like the paleontologists were giving Ann a *very* difficult time.

One of them—Margo's electronic earmuffs picked up conversations from an astonishing distance—demanded in a voice that would have frozen lava, "We are *not* renting and wearing this crap! Why would we possibly need eye and hearing protection? This is *supposed*"—the word dripped venom—"to be a trial run for our fieldwork. We'll have none of this junk down time! Will we?"

Margo continued shamelessly eavesdropping—how else did one survive in a cruel world, particularly when one was studying to become a real scout whose *job* was to overhear and remember just such conversations? Ann was clearly working hard not to shout obscenities in Vietnamese *and* Gaelic at her recalcitrant pupils.

As Margo's first, lamentable lessons had shown, while Ann could instruct willing students to a high degree of skill, she couldn't instill intelligence. Result? Some customers refused to listen, went down time improperly armed and/or trained, and usually came back needing a hospital—or staying down time in a long pine box.

Time Tours, of course, liked to keep that kind of publicity to a strict minimum, but the company executives—looking for ever more gate profit—did nothing about *requiring* weapons or self-defense training before allowing a tourist to go down time. Lessons with the terminal's pro's were strictly on a voluntary basis.

Maybe she ought to suggest required classes to Bull Morgan. She snorted. He'd no doubt tell her it was a tourist's business to get training, not his, and if they were stupid enough to go down time without it, they deserved whatever they got. Besides, Bull Morgan would *never* pass such a rule, because La-La Land was a place where folks fought, ignored, and thumbed noses at rules, rather than making new ones.

At any rate, it looked like Ann could use some help corralling this bunch of jerks into *listening* instead of tossing their academic credentials around like spiked morning stars. She sighed and left everything on her chosen bench, muzzles pointed down range, then plunged in.

"Hi, guys!" Margo called, friendly-like, baiting her hook with a honeyed voice. Margo smiled sweetly, a dire warning to every person who knew her well—Ann actually winced—then she swept off shooting glasses and protective earmuffs and shook out vibrant hair.

"See these?" She held out the earmuffs, determined to give this her best effort. "These are hearing protectors. On a firing range, you wear them. Period. You can lose most of your hearing mighty fast unless you put hearing protection on *before* somebody starts target practice."

"How would you know?"

One man she couldn't quite see shot the question in her general direction.

She shrugged. "Because I lost part of my hearing in this ear on a deadly little street in Whitechapel one bitter cold morning in 1888."

Silence reigned.

She didn't add that Malcolm had done the shooting. But the hearing loss, slight as it was, was genuine. She added, "I lost more when an unstable gate opened up and I fell through it right into the Battle of Orleans. Joan of Arc and some really pissed off English knights and archers and some even *angrier* French nobles were taking a beating and hating it. Orleans was a really *intense* battle. Damn near got myself killed—twice—before I was back safe in the station's infirmary.

"Then some more of my hearing went bye-bye in South Africa, running from sixteenth-century Portuguese traders. I got caught in the middle of a firefight. Some friends of mine who'd figured out I was in trouble had come to help and I got caught between them and a whole, unwashed *mass* of murderous traders who were *really* riled up. They'd already decided to burn my assistant and me at the stake."

Margo managed to hold back the near-instinctive shudders such memories brought—and in suppressing them, understood her grandfather more than she'd ever believed possible. It was little wonder he'd turned her down so rudely in the Down Time Bar and Grill that first day.

"Believe me, black powder guns are *loud*. You *do* want to be able to hear when you get down time?" Margo questioned sweetly.

"As for these," she wiggled the clear, wrap-around shooting glasses between two fingers, "even a novice should be able to figure out what they're for. I do take it that nobody *wants* to go blind?"

Nobody answered, despite an angry stirring near the back of the group. Margo shrugged. "They're your eyes and ears. You got replacements lined up for 'em, go right ahead without the safety equipment. But then," she smiled sweetly again, "I'm wagering you're just the teeniest bit brighter than that. By the time you've earned a master's, never mind a Ph.D, you've supposedly learned what's irrelevant and beneath notice from what's not only correct, but essential. Right?"

Behind the paleontologists, Ann had covered her lips with both hands to hold in laughter. Tears appeared in her eyes when five heads nodded like marionettes in sync.

"Thanks, Margo, for taking your time to help out. I'm sure these folks will save their ears from the noise you're about to generate!" Ann added pointedly. The group sheepishly picked up its safety equipment and began donning it.

Margo retrieved her Winchester Model 73—the most popular rifle in the Old West—from her own shooting bench. She loaded the Model 73 and called out, "Ann, I'm going hot!" She then lined up her first shot.

BOOM!

To her right, all five paleontologists jumped, despite the dampening qualities of their hearing gear.

BOOM! *A little high and right*, she muttered to herself, correcting her aiming point rather than adjusting the sights, using a method called "Kentucky windage," where you simply moved the sight picture to the other side of the target the same distance you missed or until you simply "felt right." The third BOOM! put the bullet exactly where she wanted it: inside the ten ring. She finished the magazine, pleased that the only shots outside the nine ring were those two initial placement shots. *Didn't throw a single round!* And that, despite months without even picking up a gun. She continued with her practice, nonetheless.

After a while, Margo smiled at her latest target and put the rifle down. She was tempted to return to the group, if only to see what sort of firearms they had, but was reluctant to disturb Ann's class any more than she already had. As if divining her interest, Ann looked up and waved Margo over.

Upon her arrival, Ann motioned almost imperceptibly for Margo to hold her own inspection. Margo realized this inspection—and everything that went with it—was, in fact, a lesson Ann was using to judge *her* improvements, her judgment. She took a good, long look at the neatly arranged firearms. She confirmed at a glance what she'd suspected earlier.

"Mmmm . . . they do have some nice Winchester Model 94s here, don't they, Ann? It really is too bad." She glanced over toward the paleontologists. "You're gonna have to ditch 'em, every last one. Anachronistic as he-heck. For one thing, the whole feed system on a 94's different from the Model 73 and 76."

A deep, angry voice behind the knot of grad students demanded, "What does that have to do with anything? Standing right here they look just alike!"

Hooo, boy. Ivy League and pissed. Not good.

She shook her head. "Sorry, but no, they don't look alike."

"Not at all," Ann chimed in, startling Margo at first until she saw the tiniest bit of a dip from Ann's left eyelid. She felt better immediately.

"Now," Ann was saying, "where you're going, some folks are going to see those Model 94s up-close enough to notice."

"Can't be avoided," Margo added, enjoying the see-saw rhythm as they took turns. *Maybe if I'm desperate for something to do on weekends, I could try my hand at teaching. I've got pretty good credentials, after all.*

Modest, Margo was not. And finally she could revel in it to her heart's content, the way cats simply fold their bodies into pretzel-twists around *anything* loaded with catnip.

"Young woman," one of the men began, voice surprisingly deep for the acceptably trendy cadaver he called a body, "are you questioning *my* judgment? *I*," he went on, arrogant as a New York cabbie, "either suggested or chose each and every one of these firearms myself." He cleared an Ichabod Crane throat delicately, feigning (and not very well) humility. "NCAA Rifle Team four years running. Harvard."

Harvard? Aw, nuts! I'm losing my touch. She'd have bet for sure he was a Yalie.

She caught and held his gaze squarely, long enough to let him know she wasn't impressed, then replied politely, "Well, sir, I'm sure you were wonderful with a perfectly balanced match rifle—Anscheutz Model 54? Thought so," she added as he nodded stiffly.

Someone behind the tall professor said, "Wow! A real classic!" to which someone else whispered, "And a college rifle team! Do you have any idea how scarce those are now?"

Margo hid a smile as the man's face went red—though humiliating him would be so easy and so fun, the point was to get the folks to learn. Before the man could turn and chastise the speakers, Margo said forcefully, "An Anscheutz Model 54's a great match rifle—but choosing a gun to bet your *life* on is a little bit different.

"No," she revised, "a *whole lot* different."

The professor, his pride clearly damaged, opened his mouth to reply. In the pause, Ann stepped in, a savvy businesswoman smoothing ruffled feathers.

"You'll have to forgive Margo's abrupt manner, Dr. Reginald-Harding. I do assure you, all time scouts are usually a bit . . . direct."

The professor's scowl lightened. Ann Vinh Mulhaney gave him her most winning smile, a sure sign that she personally detested him, all the while coveting as much of his grant money as she could shake loose. "But scouts *do* know what they're talking about—if they didn't, they wouldn't survive long. And this one," she nodded toward Margo, "has had the best possible training available. I taught her firearms and other projectile weapons, Sven Bailey taught her martial arts and bladed weapons. 'Kit' Carson set up her whole training schedule and did a good bit of the teaching. Then, of course, the best freelance time guide in the business taught her what the rest of us didn't. Like how to really survive down time in the East End of London, 1888."

Sounding as if he were sucking lemons, the professor said, "Well then, would you please explain why our firearms are either anachronistic or unsuitable?"

Ooh, bet it hurt your platinum tongue to say that.

"All right." She could be civil if he could, although it cost her considerable effort. But she *was* learning. It was a skill that would doubtless stand her in *very* good stead as a scout. It was also, she realized abruptly, a skill her grandfather had perfected long ago to stay alive and had retained as a life-long habit, just to protect himself from crowds of awestruck up-timers gawking and asking him stupid questions. He'd shouted and fumed at her because he *knew* what she had yet to learn for herself: controlling pride and anger were utterly critical for a scout, something she hadn't realized before.

Good grief! These idiots were actually *teaching* her something!

"All right. First, open the actions—Ann will assist you, if necessary—and check to be sure your rifle is unloaded."

They went through the drill, she and Ann moving back and forth along the line, correcting here, demonstrating there. Clearly, La-La Land's expert firearms instructor was having the time of her life, taking Margo's orders—for this, too, was a test of everything Margo had learned from her. *Good thing I kept studying at college with those books Kit sent.*

Margo nodded. "Okay, work the action and look down into the top of the loading mechanism while you do it."

They obeyed, opening and closing the actions slowly.

"Notice anything?"

One of the younger men spoke up first. "The loading ramp flips up, like a toggle. And there is not so much room in the loading ramp and chamber as with many rifles."

"Very good."

The young man started, looking up in brief astonishment; then grinned belatedly. "Thanks."

"Okay, class," Ann took her turn in an astonishingly commanding voice, "anybody guess why the Model 94's feed system is constructed that way?" It was clear that only the younger man had much knowledge about guns in general. He glanced at all the others, finding only blank faces, before clearing his throat. "It would be a fairly smooth way to bring a cartridge into the chamber. Not so many moving parts, I think."

Ann nodded. "Very good." She glanced at Margo, silently saying, "Over to you."

Margo drew a deep breath for courage and plunged in feet first, her limited experiences gripped in both hands like daggers.

"Yes, you've noticed something very important about the Winchester 94. The 94's feed system *does* flip like a toggle, or to use an easier analogy, it tips like a teeter-totter every time you shoot, to bring a new cartridge up into the chamber. Okay, everybody lay down their rifles and gather 'round me."

In a moment, she was loosely surrounded by the group. "Now look," she picked up the Model 73 and proceeded to tip it up so everyone could watch, "at the difference here." She worked the lever slowly, so they could *see* the difference. "On a Model 73 or 76, the feed system just moves straight up and down. Like an elevator. That's important to all of you for your down-time research. Anybody care to guess why?"

Several chewed their lips. The young woman spoke up. "Because somebody'd notice the difference while we're getting our gear together in Denver?"

"Too right. No Old Westerner's going to miss *that* difference. They pay attention to guns. All guns. For one thing, guns keep 'em alive, and I haven't met a man yet who didn't just *love* tinkering with the toys—or tools—of his choice."

Both male grad students went red at the unintended double

entendre. She ignored them as she ignored most *boys*. "Now, go get your Model 94s and keep the muzzles pointed toward the ceiling."

Eventually, they all returned to her side, Model 94s held carefully, muzzles rigidly pointed toward the ceiling.

"Okay. Look at the outside of each rifle. This side plate on my Model 73, for instance, doesn't exist at all on your Model 94s. Again, every Old Westerner who notices that *your* rifles don't have a side plate—and believe me, someone, maybe *several* someones, will notice! So the second they spot that little detail, they'll know it's something they've never seen before. And they'll get mighty curious about it. Curiosity about your group or your gear is the very *last* thing you want."

She smiled coldly and drove home the point like hammering in a wooden stake.

"Any Old Westerner seeing these 94s is going to wonder just what in heck they are and where in heck you got 'em. I think the only other Model 94s in existence in 1885 were in a workshop in Ogden, Utah, where the Browning brothers were just finishing up inventing it. Winchester bought up the rights like a fish snapping up a fly, because the improvements the Browning brothers had made over the Model 73 and the Model 76 were so good.

"But the Model 94 didn't come out for a while, because Winchester had to buy manufacturing rights from the Brownings, and they had to play with the design a little until it was as good as *they* could make it, then Winchester had to tool up their factory to accommodate the changes the 94 would require, that sort of thing—all the normal delays between prototype and commercial release."

Before she could say anything else—or any of the paleontologists could draw upon their courage to ask a question—the weapons-range door opened, admitting a cool draft, Malcolm, and closely following him, Kit Carson.

Chapter 11

Gasps went up from those who'd seen photographs. Malcolm just grinned, ignoring the sound, which set her heart beating so fast that cute young grad students might have never existed. Malcolm had a breathtaking smile that turned her insides—and occasionally her very bones—to melted marshmallow.

"So *there* you are!" Malcolm exclaimed, relief on his long, craggy, sun-and-wind-scoured face. "I thought maybe you'd come down here to spar with Sven. We looked. He's miffed."

Margo said smugly, "I'm saving up for that. If he throws me twice, I'll fast for a whole day."

Kit grinned. "I'll make sure you honor that one, my girl."

She put her tongue out, then kissed Malcolm, just thoroughly enough to set him on fire, but not quite thoroughly enough to push him over the edge and *carry* her out of here. She finally broke the kiss, smiling up into his eyes with a promise of more to come later, then all but crushed Kit's ribcage. It startled him, but he didn't let go before she did. He did lower his head to kiss her hair several times, as though he couldn't believe this was happening.

When she looked up into his eyes, she saw joy and tremendous pain there. "I'll make it up," she whispered, "all of it. I'll even tell you my whole life's story. I should have a long time ago, but I was scared. After class, okay?"

Kit just closed his eyes.

"I'll—yes, please." Then he opened his eyes again, cleared his throat. "I believe you have a class to teach?"

She sighed, then commented wryly, "Yeah. Like everything else I do, it appears to be part of my training."

Kit and Malcolm nodded approvingly, Kit adding, "A fine lesson for you to learn—and all on your own, too." Margo wrinkled her nose at him, then turned back to the class of goggle-eyed scientists.

Margo took Malcolm's arm, wrapping it possessively around her waist so he all but surrounded her. Determined to do this right if her tongue shattered from all the gilding one was supposed to learn to master gracefully, she said, "This gentleman with his arm around me is Dr. Moore, Freelance Temporal Guide, sought out by members of the very oldest names and fortunes in the world, men and women who bear European titles of nobility, Americans of the greatest industrial and computer families in the nation, prestigious members of the press and the glittering stars of New Hollywood.

"They seek Dr. Moore for assistance with private tours away from the main Time Tours itineraries so they won't have to endure the endless chatter of the riff-raff who take the same tours. Dr. Moore is also a successful gemstone speculator," Malcolm squeezed warningly, "a doctor of philosophy in both anthropology and classics, and, to my greatest happiness, my fiance."

A few faint groans reached them, bringing laughter to Malcolm's eyes when she glanced up.

Kit, however, was staring at her oddly.

"And this renowned hero," she said, slipping loose of Malcolm's grip just long enough to take her grandfather's calloused hand, "is the most famous recluse on Earth. You are deeply privileged to meet one of *the* original time scouts who pushed the major gates the first time they began popping open and closed on a regular, stable schedule. Knowing the danger that he might shadow himself, he continued pushing gates until the odds were simply too great, then settled down as owner of one of the world's most prestigious hotels, the New Edo, right here in TT-86, where he pushed most of the tourist gates that Shangri-la Station possesses. It is, indeed, my intense pleasure to introduce the legendary time scout of Shangri-la

Station, Kit Carson." She deliberately left out the fact that he was her grandfather.

Round eyes stared back at Kit, with *all* the grad students looking as though they might faint in the presence of a living god.

Kit, moving very close to her, muttered, "Where the hell did you learn to speak all that flowery bullshit?"

Margo, eyes flashing, answered in an equally soft whisper, "At that moronic college you sent me to. Make me take *etiquette,* will you!"

Etiquette was another class she'd been forced to take, in place of the math class she'd needed—badly. Margo had desperately wanted to master her log and ATLS—Absolute Time Locator System—with greater skill, and that meant plowing through mathematics. So, when she could not argue, wheedle, or tempt her way into the class she really needed, above all others, she'd left the registrar's office in a storming rage—and made other plans, which included buying all the requisite books for the class she'd been denied and studying them until slow comprehension dawned for each and every formula or proof the books contained.

With her greater understanding, she performed the same ritual each night: she'd finish supper and rush from the cafeteria back to her room, where she studied until it was nice and dark. If the night sky was clear—as it often was in winter—she'd grab her ATLS and log and jog down to the courtyard which four dormitories completely enclosed. Margo then shot one star fix after another, recording her findings by whispering into her computer log.

She would then return to her room, ignoring the odd looks from other students who'd seen her in the courtyard, talking to herself and pointing a little box at the sky over and over, and the lustful looks of those who didn't care how crazy she was, just so long as they could get their hands on what was beneath her designer jeans that fit her derriere like they'd been sewn on. Margo, completely aware of both types of stare, ignored each equally, regained her room and checked her calculations very carefully, for each star fix she'd shot.

She still wanted that class, but she was getting much better at the mathematic formulae needed to calculate exactly where you were by shooting a star fix. And she *had* learned her accursed "etty-ket." Got a stinking A+ for it. *Some use modern etiquette and oratory is going to be down time through an unknown gate.*

Then she realized there was something wrong with her grandfather's expression. Kit's eyes actually blazed with anger and his sandy eyebrows dove until his entire forehead was a mass of wrinkles—a few of which she, herself, had regretfully put there.

"We'll talk about this later, in private," he muttered. "I want to know everything there is to know about that place. *Everything.*"

At least he's not mad at me, Margo thought cheerfully. Nobody, not even Margo, wanted to be on the downside of Kit Carson's temper. She'd been there all too often to want to find herself there again.

"And Margo," Kit added, without a trace of a smile, "do Grandpa a favor, huh? Cut the etiquette crap and sound like yourself, or I'll drag you over to the gym and slam the living daylights out of you until you start sounding like my grandkid again."

Margo, a little angry, a little relieved, a whole lot aware of how much he loved her—and the only way he knew to express it most of the time—met his gaze with a wicked twinkle in her eyes and a dangerous smile on her lips. "Tsk-tsk, child-beating? Shame on you." Her smile deepened. "As for slamming the living daylights out of me, you could try."

Kit's black scowl was part of the way she always remembered him. Before he could speak, she whispered, "Oh, don't worry, I hate that stuff, too. I'll be good."

Kit relaxed visibly, then grinned, and ruffled her hair affectionately. "Okay, fire-eater. Go show 'em your stuff. *After* you finish introductions." As Margo did not know the names of any of the scientists, she turned to Ann for help. Surely Ann would know the names of her clients.

As the introductions progressed, Margo found that Kit could still surprise her. She told herself she shouldn't have been so startled when Kit greeted each politely—in whatever language they might happen to speak besides English: Yiddish with Dr. Rubenstein; honest-to-God Ukrainian with Vasylko, whose eyes widened until just about all you could see was a vast double pool of blue under a shock of ice-blond hair. Vasylko stammered out his reply in Ukrainian, saying something that caused Kit to smile. A greeting in Arabic brought a flush to Katy's cheeks. Clearly, she remembered enough Arabic to understand what Kit had just said.

Then he turned to assess the other Ph.D. paleontologist. "I've admired your work, Dr. Reginald-Harding. I saw the American Museum of Natural History after The Accident. What you've done to raise money to restore the building, never mind repair and remount the fossil skeletons and other priceless displays approaches the miraculous. It's a pleasure to meet you at last."

Both men shook hands, Dr. Reginald-Harding just a little bit awestruck, if Margo were judging accurately his body language and the stunned look in his eyes. Kit, evidently noticing the same thing, gave out his world-famous smile.

Then Kit turned his attention to the remaining graduate student. Adair MacKinnon just stared at him, whole face slack and increasingly red when Kit addressed him in Gaelic.

"No?" Kit sighed. "Ah, well, your education isn't complete, then, anyway, is it? You'll have plenty of time to learn it before earning your Ph.D."

Adair flushed, even more and stammered, "Always . . . always meant to learn it, 'cause I've got to, you know, before I become The MacKinnon. Sometimes . . . never mind."

Kit nodded his understanding of what Adair had left unspoken.

Introductions completed, Dr. Rubenstein stepped forward immediately, shaking Kit's hand, then Malcolm's. "Gentlemen, it's an honor, believe me. You, sir, are known *everywhere*," this to Kit, "and you, Dr. Moore are a lucky man. Damned lucky. You both trained this young lady? She's a bit blunt," he said with a smile, rubbing his chin, "but she knows what she's talking about. Very, very well. And her, mmm, 'forceful' suggestions have all been to the point and excellently stated." This time, Samuel Rubenstein smiled at her. "I can see, now, where your excellent education comes from."

Perversely, she was peeved. *Not good enough on my own, but the minute Kit Carson strolls in, I'm a sensation. Buddy, you ain't seen nuthin' yet.* Outwardly, she said a bit breezily, "Oh, well, there certainly is that, and believe me, their tutoring is *profoundly* educational"—she could *feel* the snort Kit held in—"but there's a lot of bookwork, too. A *whole* lot. So much, you *never* stop learning. Do you, Grandpa?"

It was the first time she'd ever called him that. He stiffened momentarily, speechless, while he stared down at her.

"That's right," he managed. "Even though I'm retired, I'm still learning, just in case. I've recently tackled an ancient Chinese dialect and Croatian stripped of all Serbian influences, vocabulary, and so on, to add to my other languages, and I've been reading and taking notes from a complete history of the Croatian people, both of which I'll have to transfer to memory sufficiently for instant recall if I ever decide to risk going down that new gate at TT-16. Not a tourist gate, not at all; but the research potential is said to be fabulous." His eyes actually glittered with intense interest.

The paleontologists were clearly impressed.

Kit just ruffled his granddaughter's hair, saying everything he wanted to say with that touch and the look in his eyes.

Margo cleared her throat, wishing desperately for once that they were alone and someplace private where they could just *talk*. She *needed* to tell him what had really happened to her mother, Kit's lost daughter—whom he hadn't known existed until Margo told him about her, at least the little she'd been *able* to tell him: her name and that she was dead. Margo cringed at the memory of that talk by the fishpond on Commons. She'd been so inexperienced, so uneasy, so afraid of him, she literally *hadn't* been able to tell him what his eyes had begged to know.

This time, she wouldn't be such a coward. And she'd hold him while he cried over her mother's brutal murder, robbing him of a child he'd never met.

Whoops, getting too maudlin, Margo. You have a job to do and you can't do it snuffling goddamned tears, of all things.

So she said to her somewhat abashed students, "Oh, by the way, all of you should stop by Connie Logan's Clothes and Stuff, not just for period-appropriate clothing—she's got the best and you can rent it for much less than buying it—but also be sure to buy a good Old

West dictionary, so you won't sound quite so green. Old Western speech is nearly unintelligible to anybody else from *anywhere* else. To Old Westerners, anybody who *can't* speak it is a greenhorn. Learn the language you'll need to know."

She'd picked up a little at school, but she'd have to study it like mad before she and Malcolm went to Denver.

"But," Adair MacKinnon asked, swallowing hard and sweating, "isn't it just a dialect of English?"

"No," Malcolm said quietly. "Unless you can tell me the *exact* Old West meanings and pronunciations—without having to think about them—of churn-twister, cienaga, a Jerusalem undertaker, the word 'jewelry' or the phrase 'jewelry chest,' then you'd better hit the library and find yourself a good Old West-English/English-Old West dictionary and start memorizing it. You're going to *need* it for three months in rough country, away from the more 'civilized' vicinity around Denver."

Adair stuck to his guns. "I can understand the need to speak like a native, but why so adamant about it? So-called dudes from the East wouldn't have spoken it, after all. And just exactly what do 'Jerusalem undertaker' or a perfectly normal word like 'jewelry' really *mean*?"

"Yes," Malcolm replied, "dudes don't speak Old West when they arrive. They're lost in an alien culture, trying to survive and blend in gradually with what they find. In short, they're intrusive greenhorns, and greenhorns are considered fair game."

"Very fair game," Kit added solemnly. "The range wars weren't quite as bad as depicted in the movies, although they were bad enough, and Dodge City had a lower per capita murder rate than, say, New York or Washington, D.C. during, oh, the mid 1990s. But attacks on dudes by a single, experienced man, or a gang of them, were very common. Even swindlers could make a killing, saying one thing that meant another altogether, which the dude would find out too late, once his money or land or horse or whatever he'd risked was long out of his possession. And having made a legal contract, there was absolutely nothing the poor sop could *do* about it. Except maybe hire himself a gun-hand—if he had enough money left—to hunt down the rat and kill him."

Margo took Kit's hand again, more carefully this time, realizing she was squeezing it so tightly, his fingernails were turning purple. "Grandpa pushed the Wild West Gate," she put in, eyes aglow as she gazed up at Kit.

He harrumphed and muttered, "Lots of time scouts pushed lots of gates. Nothing heroic in walking through the Wild West Gate, of that I may assure you. There were other gates that were *much* harder to step through."

A subtle reminder of Margo's disastrous mission into Southern Africa. She flushed, but held tight to his hand.

Dr. Rubenstein nodded. "The Roman Gate, I expect, was an extremely difficult one."

Kit laughed. "Oh, it was easy to get *in*. Getting *out* again proved a rather interesting test of wit and skill."

And that was how he dismissed one of the most dangerous, nearly lethal adventures he'd ever encountered. His involuntary fight in the Circus Maximus was legend the world over.

"Well," Margo muttered, "I, uh, guess I'd better get on with my own practice and let you take over the class, Ann."

The diminutive firearms instructor nodded gracious thanks for helping break the class the way a horse-breaker might soften up and civilize a particularly unruly horse.

Kit said very softly, "We'll wait on the benches until you're finished."

She nodded, holding in another sigh. *Another bleeding test . . .*

But this time she put up no arguments, no protests, no childish tantrums. She simply put on her safety gear, called out, "Line's going hot!" so everyone else donned safety gear—including Kit and Malcolm—and got busy finishing the other two boxes of .44-40s, scoring well in toward the center of the black despite her nervousness; then she switched to the heavier Centennial and did herself proud with three boxes of almost perfect nines and tens. She did throw a couple of rounds here and there from sweating palms and aching arms and eyes that burned and wouldn't focus properly, but even though she was out of practice, her scores were good and she knew it.

"Well?" she asked as she handed over the targets.

The two most important people in her life put their heads together, poring over the targets, marking each shot outside the nine ring. Finally they looked up again.

"Well, frankly," Kit began, "you could use some more practice and work on your upper arm strength, but pretty damned good for a first try after several dry months."

Margo let go her tense fear and abruptly felt like she was floating on fizzy bubbles that tickled her all the way to the ceiling.

"Hey," Malcolm called, "come down out of the clouds, will you?"

She sighed inwardly and allowed the wonderful fizzing bubbles to waft her gently toward the floor. She blinked and found herself staring into Malcolm's eyes. "Yeah?" she asked softly.

He didn't say a word. He just kissed her until those dratted, wonderful fizzing bubbles came back. When she came up for breath, she was actually dizzy.

"Wow! Where'd you learn to do *that*?"

Malcolm touched her cheek. "From a certain red-headed imp I know. She's very, um, motivational."

Margo blushed to her toes. Malcolm only smiled.

"Shall I, um, put everything away so we can get the heck out of here?"

"Y-e-s," Kit drawled, devilment in his eyes, "I think that would be appropriate. We'll stuff down some dinner, then if it's possible, I think I'd like to pry you away from Malcolm for a while, so it's just you and me, okay?"

"Yeah," was all she could manage.

They helped her clean the rifles, just to speed up the process, then she put away all her gear and locked up the gun room, returning the keys carefully where they belonged. That done, Margo Smith hooked arms through both Malcolm's and Kit's. They left the range aware of the still-awestruck gazes that followed them.

Once outside, beyond the soundproof glass, they all started laughing like complete idiots. But it was a healing laughter, as well, washing away awkwardness and lonely pain and leaving only the new closeness and the utterly reaffirmed love Margo felt for both of these men. It was a love she felt she didn't deserve, but was by God going to *try* to deserve.

"Last one to the elevator's a goose's egg!" Margo called, sprinting off like a gazelle.

Not at all surprisingly, Kit arrived just behind her, his hand covering hers just as she punched the elevator button. Malcolm wheezed up a moment later.

"Out of shape," Kit chided.

"Hah! Blame that on your insatiable granddaughter."

Kit just laughed and winked at Margo, who flushed red as a beet. But she was still laughing. The elevator carried them and their hilarity upward in efficient silence, until the doors opened again and their laughter spilled out onto Commons. They headed for the Epicurean Delight and a dinner that would certainly be a momentous occasion.

At least, it would if Kenneth "Kit" Carson had anything to say about it!

Chapter 12

Marcus was on duty in the Down Time Bar and Grill when *he* strolled in, casual and cool as a general surveying newly levied troops on the Campus Martius. A glass slipped from nerveless fingers and shattered on the floor behind the bar. *He* glanced Marcus' way, noted him briefly with a flick of disinterested gaze, then took a seat near the back as though Marcus didn't exist.

Fear and anger both ripped through him, piercing as the shockwaves of an unstable gate. The years he'd spent on TT-86 had changed him more than he'd realized, had eased the harshness of certain memories with the fair treatment he'd received here, where men like Kit Carson and Skeeter Jackson saw him as a man, not a possession. He'd come to realize over the years that he was free, that no one had the right to call him slave, but in that single, blinding instant when his one-time master's eyes had slid dismissively away from his, the memory of his slavery had crashed down around him like a cage of steel bars.

Marcus stood rooted to the floor, unable to believe he had actually forgotten that terrifying, familiar, casual dismissal of his very humanity. What it felt like in his soul to be reminded—

"Hey, Marcus, clean up that mess!" called the manager, frowning at him.

Hands shaking uncontrollably, Marcus knelt and swept up broken shards of the bar glass. When the job was done and the pieces dumped into the trash bin, Marcus washed and dried hands that refused to hold steady. He drew a deep breath for courage. He didn't want to cross that short distance of space, but knew it had to be done. He still owed a terrible sum of money to this man whose name he'd never actually known, merely calling him *Domus*, same as any other slave would address a master. He recalled all too clearly the cold humor in the man's eyes when he'd first laid eyes on Marcus in that stinking slave pen.

He left the relative safety of the space behind the bar and approached the dim table near the back. *His* glance flicked up again, studied Marcus with brutal appraisal, a herdsman judging the health of prize stock. Marcus' insides flinched.

"Your order?" he whispered, all voice control gone.

His one-time master had not changed much during the intervening years. A little leaner, a little greyer. But the eyes were the same, dark and glittering and triumphant.

"Beer. Whiskey chaser."

Marcus brought the drinks as ordered, trying desperately to still the jittering of glassware on his small, round tray. Quick eyes noted the dance and smiled.

"Very good," he purred. "That will be all."

Marcus bowed and departed. He felt the dark touch of the man's gaze on him through the next hour, watching him work as he served drinks, collected bar tabs and tips, made up sandwiches and snacks for the ebb and flow of customers, and prayed to all the gods to get him through this ordeal. *Why has he come?* pounded behind his eyelids. *Why has he not spoken to me again? I have the gold to repay the debt of my purchase price. I have it . . .*

And above all other questions, again and again, *Why does he not* speak? *He just sits and watches.* The man finally finished his beer and left money on the table, departing without a backward glance. Marcus had to brace himself against the bar to keep his feet.

"Marcus?"

He jumped so badly he nearly went to the floor. The manager braced him with a hasty arm.

"You feeling okay? You look sick."

I am sick! Marcus wanted to cry out. "I—do not feel well, I am sorry . . ."

"Hey, you got plenty of sick time coming. Go on home and take some aspirin, get some rest. I'll call Molly—she could use some overtime pay. If you don't feel better by tomorrow, call Medical."

Marcus nodded, numb to his bones. "Thank you." Very carefully, he wiped his hands on a bar towel. He hung it up with great deliberation, then crept out of the Down Time Bar and Grill into the brilliance of Commons. His former master was nowhere to be seen. What was he to do? The man had said nothing, left no instructions to meet him, made no arrangements to turn over the notes Marcus had so carefully compiled over the years. He didn't know what to do. He didn't even know the man's name, to check the hotel registries. Perhaps he meant to save the meeting for the privacy of Marcus' little apartment?

To return to the apartment, he would have to pass Ianira's booth in Little Agora. What could he tell her, when he knew nothing, himself? Marcus half hoped he could slip past her without being seen, but Ianira spotted him straight away. Her lovely eyes widened. The next instant she'd left a customer and a whole retinue of devotees gaping after her. She flew to his side like an arrow into his heart.

"What is it? You're ill . . ." She laid a hand against his cheek.

Marcus, aware that his former master might be anywhere, watching and assessing and planning, felt himself unbearably torn between the desire to crush Ianira to him and draw comfort from her strength versus the even fiercer desire to protect her and their children.

"*He* came into the Down Time today," Marcus said a little unsteadily. "The—my old master." Ianira's luminous dark eyes widened; her lips, exactly the shape of Artemis' divine silver bow fully drawn to strike, parted in shock. Before she could speak, Marcus added, "Can you—can we afford it if you close up the booth?"

Worry furrowed Ianira's brow. "Why?"

Marcus had to draw an unsteady breath before he could speak. "I want you to take Artemisia and Gelasia and go someplace safe until I know what he wants. He said *nothing*, Ianira, just came in, watched me for an hour, and left without a word. I was once his slave, Ianira! He still thinks . . . will act as though . . . if I cannot protect you and our children, what kind of man *can* I be?"

The look in her eyes wounded him. He forced himself to continue. "And no down-timer has real rights in this world. I am afraid for you. He could so easily do terrible harm, make trouble with the up-timers whose laws bind us, maybe even try to take you for his own—by force!"

His hand on hers trembled. He would die to protect her and their children. He was just afraid his one-time owner would move on Ianira before Marcus could take proper precautions.

Ianira's glance darted around the brightly lit Commons as though searching for their unseen enemy. Tourists, oblivious of their terror, sauntered past, laughing and chatting about upcoming adventures down time. Her retinue of idiotic followers had left the booth and half surrounded them. Ianira, glancing at that follow-her-come-what-may crowd, compressed soft, sensuous lips until nothing remained but a hard, white line.

"You are right to fear," she whispered, her voice so low even Marcus had a hard time catching the words. "I feel that someone watches, someone besides these people," she waved a negligent hand toward her awestruck devotees, "but I cannot find him. There are so many minds in this place, it confuses the senses. But he *is* here, I know it." Marcus knew she had innate gifts he could barely understand, plus training in ancient ways and rites no man could ever comprehend. Her glance into his eyes was frightened. "I will stay with friends in The Found Ones until we know. You are wise, beloved. Take great care." Then the look in her eyes shifted, hardened. "I *loathe* him," she whispered fiercely. "For putting that look in your eyes I hate him as much as I hate my pig of a husband!"

Her lips crushed his, all too fleetingly, then she whirled and left him. The "costume" she wore—no different from the ordinary chitons she'd worn on the other side of the Philosophers' Gate—swirled in a flutter of soft draperies and folds. Astonishingly, down-timers from all parts of Commons, summoned only the gods knew how, appeared from nowhere and surrounded her, most forming an impenetrable barricade to keep her acolytes from following. Others formed a guard—and unless Marcus were greatly mistaken, theirs was an *armed* guard—to protect the Speaker of the Seven and her offspring. He knew they would be taking a swift, back-corridor route to the station's School and Day Care Center to pick up the girls. Then she vanished around a corner in Residential and was gone.

Marcus stayed where he was, making sure she was not followed. A few of the acolytes tried to, but that living wall managed to discourage them—forcefully for one or two insistent, insolent vidcam operators—then they, too, were gone around the same corner.

With The Found Ones, Ianira and their children ought to be safe from the monster who'd brought him here, who had then left him up time with nothing but instructions that made no sense. That master had then blithely joined the line to depart TT-86, leaving Marcus—who was deep in shock from *everything* he heard and saw—to fend for himself. He recalled nearly every detail of that nightmare of a day. No one here had seemed to speak his native tongue.

Instead, he'd heard smatters of barbaric tongues, so many and spoken so fast he felt dizzy. He'd recognized none of them. Haphazard stairs that went nowhere had eventually led him into the arms of the "gods" who ruled this place. Eventually, he'd met the man named Buddy and after that, a group of men and women in more or less his same position, who took him in and helped him adjust through the worst of the transition.

Marcus was startled from his painful memories by a down-timer named Kynan Rhys Gower. Marcus knew this man to be a close friend of Kit Carson's. He was casually closing up Ianira's booth, setting items on the counter inside and locking the sides down, and fending off Ianira's followers with a helpless gesture and a convoluted sentence in Welsh that only the gods could probably decipher. He escaped the crowd, which settled itself around the booth as though they meant to wait forever. Kynan pushed his wheeled waste bin past Marcus' chosen place of vigil.

"Your woman and children are safe, friend," the Welshman murmured, pausing to pick up some bit of trash near Marcus' feet. He deposited the waste in his bin and moved on. Marcus closed his eyes, thanking all the gods for that miracle. Then, straightening his shoulders and drawing in a deep breath, Marcus headed resolutely for their apartment. His old master would doubtless seek him there and reveal his orders. What he would do when Marcus repaid him the price of his purchase and asked him to please take the records Marcus had compiled and never return . . .

A *Roman's* reaction, Marcus could have judged without giving the matter a second thought. But Marcus' one-time master was not Roman. He was an up-timer with unknown motives, unknown ways of thinking. He had set Marcus a very specific—if mystifying—task. Would he be willing to give up a source of information placed so well to gather the details he clearly wanted very badly? What would he do? What would he say? Marcus could always appeal to Bull Morgan for help—if it came to such desperate straits. The Station Manager would protect him, if no one else would. The thought of his one-time master facing down Bull Morgan and a squad of Station Security helped soothe the tremors ripping through his insides.

But he was still deeply afraid.

"Mr. Farley?"

The man who'd emerged from the Down Time Bar and Grill glanced around, surprise evident in his dark eyes. "Yes?"

Skeeter Jackson gave him a brilliant smile and a fake business card. "Skeeter Jackson, freelance time guide. I heard you were looking for a down-time adventure, checking out the gates we have here at Shangri-la Station."

Farley glanced at his card, then studied him. "I'm gathering information," he allowed cautiously.

Skeeter, maintaining that smile at all cost, wondered if Chuck Farley had witnessed Skeeter's panic-stricken flight from that double-damned gladiator—or the newscast which had followed. "If you wouldn't mind a friendly piece of advice . . ."

Farley nodded for him to continue.

"Time Tours offers some nice packages, but frankly, they'll gouge you for every extra service they can conjure up. The small outfits that rent the government-owned gates are a better deal, although the gates don't lead to quite as interesting time periods. Your best bet is to hire a freelancer. Then, if you decide on a non-Time Tours gate, all you do is pay the government's gate fee plus your guide's fee, plus down-time lodging, meals, that kind of thing. Much cheaper than a package tour. Of course, it depends on what you want, doesn't it?"

Farley's eyes were cool and unpleasantly alert. "Yes."

"If you do settle on a Time Tours package, you might still consider a private guide." Drawing on the patter he'd heard Malcolm Moore use so frequently, he added, "There are some extraordinary experiences the package deals simply skip over, because they can't herd that many people around and not be noticed. Hiring a freelancer to go along with you lets you break away from the main tour group whenever you want. You could," he dredged up an example he'd researched on the computers, "go down towards Ostia, for instance, and look at the big Claudian harbor under construction. Magnificent sight, that harbor, but it isn't on the package tour."

He smiled again, winningly.

Farley merely pocketed his card. "Thanks for the advice. I'll consider it."

Without another word, he simply turned and walked off.

Skeeter stood rooted, silly grin still pasted on his face. His insides seethed. *Goddamnit, I'm losing my touch! Just when I need it most, too. What's with people this month?*

He *had* to get access to that guy's money belt.

Skeeter headed for the library and started checking hotel registries on one of the computer terminals. Farley had to be staying *somewhere*. He started with the less expensive hostelries and worked his way up to the luxury hotels before he found the entry he sought: Farley, Chuck. Room 3027 Neo Edo. Skeeter just groaned and leaned his brow against the cool monitor screen. The Neo Edo. It figured. Kit Carson's hotel.

Well, he hadn't run out of disguises yet.

If he could get into the hotel without being recognized, he could get into Farley's room. And if he could get into the man's room, he could steal anything in it. If he were lucky, he'd catch the guy during a shower and simply make off quietly with the money belt around his *own* waist. He still couldn't quite believe the guy had turned him down as a freelance guide.

Swearing softly under his breath, Skeeter headed home to try out one of his disguises on the employees of the Neo Edo Hotel.

Goldie Morran found Chuck Farley seated at a table in Wild Bill's, a saloon-style bar in Frontier Town. He was reading the latest copy of the *Shangri-la Gazette* with apparent interest.

"Mind if a lady joins you?" she purred.

He glanced up, blinked, then set the paper aside. "Suit yourself."

The measuring look he gave her and the coolness of his greeting didn't bode well, but he did signal for a waitress. The rinky-tink jingle of the upright piano at the back of the room, its player costumed with gartered shirtsleeves and a battered beaver hat, rose above the sound of laughter, conversation, and the clink of glasses. The waitress, a saucy down-timer who—if rumor were correct—had earned more gold flirting with miners than the miners themselves had earned over an average year's digging, winked at Goldie, one hustler to another, friendly-like. Goldie smiled.

"What'll it be?" She rested hands on well-curved hips, while her breasts all but spilled out of her tight-laced costume. If Chuck Farley was affected by the sight, it didn't show in any way Goldie could see. Maybe he preferred men? Goldie didn't care who he slept with, or why, so long as she obtained possession of his money.

"A drink for the lady. I presume," he added sardonically, "that she's buying, since I didn't invite her."

Goldie managed to keep smiling, although she'd vastly have preferred slapping him. "Whiskey, Rebecca. Thank you. And yes," she added smoothly, "I am buying. I did not come here to steal a drink or two off an unwary tourist."

Some hint of mirth stirred far back in his eyes. "Very well, what *did* you come here for?"

As Rebecca threaded her way back through the crowded bar to fill Goldie's order, Goldie leaned back in her chair. "I am given to understand you're looking for something besides the usual tours."

Farley's smile was thin. "News certainly moves around fast in this place."

Goldie laughed. "That is too true. Which is why I wanted to talk to you before someone disreputable tried to swindle you." She handed over her card. "I have a shop on Commons. Money-changing, rare coinage, gems, that sort of thing. My expertise is considerable."

Farley's thin smile came again, although it didn't touch his dark, watchful eyes. "I've heard of you, yes. Your reputation precedes you."

How he meant that, Goldie wasn't quite sure. Nor was she at all sure she liked the way he continued to watch her, like a waiting lizard.

"Not knowing what you had in mind, of course," she said, accepting the whiskey glass Rebecca brought and pointedly dropping money onto the table to pay for it, "I thought we might chat for a few minutes. Since you didn't seem interested in any specific tours, I thought perhaps you'd come to Shangri-la with something else in mind."

His eyes narrowed slightly. "Such as?"

"Oh, there are all sorts of reasons people come here," Goldie laughed. "Some people come just to eat at the Epicurean Delight. Then there's that Greek prophetess all those wacky up-time bimbos follow around like she was Christ on Earth." She smiled at the memory of Ianira's hordes. Goldie had made more than a little profit from them.

"But I didn't come here to talk about oracles and the fools who believe them. Occasionally we're visited by the shrewd individual who understands the investment potentials a place like Shangri-la has to offer."

The corners of Farley's lips twitched. "Really? What sort of investments?"

Goldie sipped her whiskey. Farley was cool, all right. Too cool by half. "Well, there are any number of lucrative ventures a man with wit and capital could turn to his advantage. There are, for instance, the shops that supply the tourists, restaurants—even the small ones turn a fabulous profit. Captive audience, you know." She laughed lightly. Chuck Farley allowed a small smile to touch his lips. "Then there are businesses like mine. Capital invested in rare coins obtained by down-time agents could increase nine, ten times the initial investment."

Again, that small, sardonic smile. "I thought the first law of time travel was, 'There will be no profiteering from time.' The ATF has copies of it posted everywhere, you know."

Somehow, Goldie received the impression from the mirth far back in those dark eyes that Chuck Farley didn't give a damn about the first law of time travel.

"True," she smiled. "But money exchanged from down-time purchases which is then invested right here in Shangri-La isn't covered by that law. You're only in violation if you try to take your profit up time.

"So, the possibilities for shrewd investment are limitless for a man with capital and imagination." She sipped at her whiskey again, still watching him over the rim of the glass. "Best of all, the money you invest in, say, a business here on Shangri-la is taxed only at the rate it would be up time. Frankly, you can make a killing without ever breaking a single law."

She smiled politely while he leaned back in his chair and studied her face. The corners of his lips moved slightly. "You interest me, Goldie Morran. I like your style. Gutsy, polished, sincere. I'll be in touch later, perhaps."

He tossed some coins onto the table to pay for his own drink, gathered up his copy of the *Gazette*, and left her sitting there, seething. She knocked back the remaining whiskey and followed him out, but he'd vanished into the mob milling around Commons. People gawking at the stores, the ramps, the chronometers, the gates, the waiting areas, the prehistoric beasts picked up from that absurd, unstable gate into the age of the dinosaurs—that was all she could see every direction she turned. She compressed her lips, furious that he'd turned her down and then simply vanished.

Just what the devil was Farley after, anyway?

Disgruntled in the extreme, Goldie set out for her shop. She'd gone only a few strides when she noticed Skeeter Jackson deep in conversation with a tourist. Drat the man! She was seriously of a mind to march over and tell that luckless tourist what a cheating fake he was, to spoil whatever profit he expected to pick up. Why she had ever agreed to this idiotic bet—

Goldie blinked. Someone was stalking Skeeter. A reddish-haired man in Western-style clothing that somehow didn't match the way he moved . . . Her eyes widened as recognition hit home: the down-timer who'd chased Skeeter before. Then she noticed the truly wicked blade he was silently drawing from beneath a set of leather chaps. Goldie drew in her breath sharply.

For an instant, spite and malice held her silent. Spite, malice, and greed. If Skeeter were dead, all bets were off and she could stay in La-La Land with no one to fault her. The man crept closer. Goldie's stomach churned at the look of hatred in the stranger's eyes, etched into his attentive, absorbed face. Skeeter was Goldie's rival and a scoundrel and probably deserved what he was about to get more than anyone she knew. But in that instant, she realized she didn't want to watch him die.

Not particularly because she cared what happened to Skeeter, but murder was messy. And bad—very bad—for business. And for a fleeting instant, she also realized victory by default over a dead man would be about as sweet as vinegar on her tongue. So she found herself moving across Commons faster than she'd moved in years.

Skeeter and his target were deeply engrossed in conversation near the waiting area for the Wild West Gate. The man creeping up on him sidestepped around an ornamental horse trough filled with colorful fish and tensed, ready for the final lunge. Goldie glanced around, wondering if she could find a weapon, or someone from Security, even something to use as a diversion.

Overhead, ten leathery, crow-sized pterodactyls perched in the girders, eying the fish in the horse trough. Skeeter talked on, oblivious to the closeness of impending death. *Ah-ha!* Goldie darted over to a vending cart which sold hats, T-shirts, and other trinkets, and said, "Sorry, gotta borrow this," to the startled cart owner.

She snatched up a toy bow and arrow set and nocked the arrow, pulled back expertly, then let fly. The arrow whizzed true to its mark: the rubber tip smacked right into the flock of startled pterodactyls.

The whole lot of them took wing with ear-bending screeches and dove straight down. Goldie ducked under the cart. Skeeter jerked his gaze up and around—and saw the man with the long knife. His eyes widened.

Then he took off faster than Goldie had *ever* seen him run.

The man with the knife swore in what had to be Latin and bolted after him. Angry pterodactyls swarmed in his way, screaming like maddened crows mobbing a jaybird. Leathery wings buffeted the man's face. Claws raked his hair. He yelled something furious and tried to cut at them with his long knife. Skeeter's tourist, a pretty redhead, screamed and took refuge behind the horse trough. Other tourists scattered while those at a safer distance started to point.

Someone shouted for Security. Someone else yelled for Pest Control. The man fighting off the pterodactyls abruptly realized he was attracting attention to himself. He swore again and took off in the opposite direction Skeeter had taken—none too soon, as Security arrived hard on his heels.

"What's going on?"

The shaken tourist Skeeter had been trying to swindle crawled out from behind the trough. "A man with a huge knife! He tried to attack the guy I was talking to—then those things—" she pointed at the pterodactyls still flitting angrily above their heads "—started diving everywhere and—and I don't know where he went. I just hid behind this."

Security officers took the man's description from the shaken tourist while Goldie slipped quietly away in the confusion. The vendor she'd borrowed the bow and arrow from just gaped after her. Goldie returned cautiously to her shop, making sure no one from Security had followed, then locked the door and sat down to do some very serious thinking. Skeeter Jackson had picked up a lethal enemy somewhere. Or somewhen. He *had* changed an enormous sum of money after that last trip of his through the Porta Romae. Goldie would've bet the very gold in her teeth that Skeeter's attacker had been swindled down time and had somehow come through the gate looking for revenge.

She shivered slightly behind her glass cases filled with coins, gems, and other precious items brought up time by various gullible tourists. Wager or not, she was glad she'd acted. But there was one thing she intended to find out, or her name was not Goldie Morran, and that was the identity of the man who'd come so close to killing Skeeter.

Yes, finding out who he was and why he was after that wretched little con artist might just come in very handy. She might not want to see Skeeter murdered, but she had no qualms at all about seeing him arrested. Tapping her fingers thoughtfully against the cool glass countertop, Goldie wondered who to contact about the mystery man's identity. She had all sorts of agents spotted about the station, willing to do a little spying for her as well as the odd down-time courier job. Goldie sniffed autocratically and picked up the phone.

Time was running, but she *would* find out.

There were, after all, only so many places in La-La Land a man could hide. Someone would know. And once *she* knew, the man chasing him would know. And when *he* knew, Skeeter Jackson's days on Shangri-la would be over for good. She started calling her paid agents all over the station.

Chapter 13

Marcus made his way home and entered the cramped apartment. It was echoingly empty. Ianira had packed in haste, leaving most of her own things in favor of taking the children's necessities. He touched one of her Greek gowns, breathing in its scent, almost smiled at the sight of prosaic jeans hung neatly on hangers in her half of their closet. He crushed the heavy fabric beneath his hands.

Marcus had known this day would eventually come.

He just hadn't known it would tear his vitals so mercilessly.

Marcus swore savagely in a language no other man, woman, or child on TT-86 ever used—with the rare exception of his beloved Ianira, to whom he had taught a little of it—then found the aspirin in the medicine cabinet. He downed five tablets to relieve the fierce throbbing in his head and wished bitterly he could afford strong alcoholic beverages like Kit's special bourbon, brought to TT-86 from some secret, down-time escapade. But he didn't have the money for such luxuries.

He didn't have money for *anything.*

Marcus swore again, hating himself for the tremors he couldn't quite suppress. He'd come to believe in himself as a free man. But the man who had purchased and brought him here would—sooner or later—demand an accounting. Marcus brought out the notes he had laboriously compiled over years of bartending and listening to the talk of men and women far gone in their boasting. He brought out the money he had so carefully stockpiled in the little metal box at the top of the bedroom closet. He changed out of his working clothes into a clean pair of blue jeans and a respectable shirt, one Ianira had surprised him with from a shop in Frontier Town on his last birthday. He smoothed down the fringe with unsteady fingers and swallowed down a throat gone dry. His face in the mirror was ashen despite the stubble of beard along his chin.

If he tried shaving now, he'd cut himself to ribbons.

Able to think of nothing else to do to prepare himself, he sank into a chair facing the door to wait. When the telephone shrilled, Marcus actually knocked the chair over. He disentangled himself, and made it to the phone before the answering machine switched on.

"Hello?"

"Marcus," that familiar voice said—notably in English, not Latin. "We have business to discuss. Come to the Neo Edo, Room 3027. Bring your records."

The line clicked in his ear.

Marcus swallowed once in the silence. He still didn't even know the man's name. He swallowed again, against unreasoning fear. Nothing could really happen to him. And it was Kit's hotel he'd be going to, not some out-of-the-way corner of the terminal. Kit Carson was a friend. A powerful friend. Marcus clung to that thought.

Then he gathered up moneybox, records, and courage and headed resolutely toward Kit Carson's world-famous hotel.

Getting into the Neo Edo was simple.

There were *lots* of ways into the luxury hotel besides the main lobby. Probably more, in fact, than Kit Carson knew existed, unless the previous owner, the legendary Homako Tani, had left blueprints behind when he'd deeded the enormous hotel to his long-ago time-scouting partner. The Neo Edo's architect, working under Tani's direct supervision, had put in more melodramatic secret passageways, hidden entrances, and blind rooms built into the rocky foundations of the Himalayas themselves than even the gods of the mountaintops knew.

Skeeter had tried to pick locks on those doors more than once, slipping in through one of at least fifteen secret entrances he'd discovered thus far (and he hadn't even attempted the top three floors of the five-storey hotel yet, for fear of opening a hinged panel and emerging straight into Kit Carson's palatial office on the fifth floor. A gilt-and-wood dragon-shaped balcony, whose "scales" were Imperial Chrysanthemums, snaked completely around the open, atrium-style upper floor, which boasted bedrooms larger than Skeeter's biological parents' entire home floorplan.

Rumor had it (and Skeeter's sources were pretty reliable) that Kit had learned he owned the Neo Edo when a bunch of lawyers he didn't know had been allowed into La-La Land just long enough to hand-deliver a copy of Homako Tani's will, a brief letter, and the deed to the hotel.

Lawyers, however, were barred from conducting *any* official legal business (never mind set up a law firm!) in La-La Land by edict of none other than Bull Morgan. The squat, fire-plug of a Station Manager, who chewed cigars the way eight-year-olds chewed bubble gum, had put into place iron-clad rules he bent only when the "official lawyering" dealt with wills and inheritances.

In its way, so long as you obeyed the rules (or didn't get caught breaking them), La-La Land was a sanctuary beyond compare. Skeeter grinned. No one—probably not even Kit—knew whether or not the Neo Edo's builder was really dead. Rumors (and here, even Skeeter's sources were of wildly mixed opinions) ran the gamut from Homako Tani dying at the hand of Japan's greatest warrior-artist-poet-swordsmith ever to live, Miyamoto Musashi, to Tani walking up into the ceiling of the world and ending his last years as Dalai Lama in Tibet (not so far, actually, from the geographical, if not temporal, site of TT-86).

The world-famous temple at the roof of the world had finally been refurbished after tidal waves, earthquakes, famine, disease, and war with their hated northern neighbors had caused the great, sprawling bastion of communist socialism to crumble and finally leave Tibet to its prayer wheels, its solitary temples, its bamboo-munching pandas, and its mountains, where new snow falling on the great Himalayan peaks blew harshly.

Whatever the true story, Skeeter simply strolled into the lobby in his disguise, passed the huge mural of *Sunrise over Edo Castle*, which was supposed to be a copy of one that the same Musashi (who *might* have killed Homako Tani, for *any* possible reason, given Musashi's temper) had painted. Skeeter reached the elevator and pinged the little lighted circle.

Moments later, he was on the third floor, stealing toward Charles Farley's expensive room on a carpet as thick and fine as any the kings of Persia might have ordered woven for their winter pavilions. The subtle pattern of black and white reminded him of snow leopards, or those elusive creatures of the Mongolian steppes, the silent white tiger glimpsed through blasts of snow and wind. Skeeter shivered, recalling his terror when ordered by Yesukai to join a winter hunt in the sacred mountains of the Yakka Clan's homeland. He still didn't know whether it had been skill or luck that his arrow had brought down the snow leopard before the huge cat could claw him to death, but he would take to his grave the scream of his pony, knocked from under him and mortally wounded before he knew anything was near.

Skeeter shook off those memories with some irritation and concentrated on the matter at hand: breaking into Room 3027. First, he listened, ear bent to the door with a stethoscope to hear what might be taking place beyond the closed door. He caught the sound of the shower and a man's voice singing Gilbert and Sullivan off key. Skeeter smiled, carefully slipped the lock while disabling the alarm with a little tool he'd invented all on his own, and entered the darkened hotel room.

Farley sang on, as Skeeter began a methodical hunt of the well-appointed bedroom. He rifled through the discarded clothing on the bed, searched every drawer, under the mattresses, in the closet, under every piece of furniture, and even managed to open the room safe, only to find it empty.

Where? Skeeter fumed.

He eased the bathroom door open and risked a peek inside.

Steam hit his face, along with an unpleasant bellow about mausers and javelins, but there was no sign of a moneybelt draped over the toilet, sink, or towel rack. Had he worn the damned thing *into* the shower?

The song—and the spray of water—came to an abrupt end. Farley's shower was over. Skeeter cursed under his breath and ran for the hall. He slipped outside, locked Farley's hotel room door behind him, and leaned against it, breathing heavily as his heart raced.

"What are you doing here?" a familiar voice demanded.

Skeeter yelped and came at least three inches clear of the floor. Belatedly he recognized Marcus. "Oh, it's only you," he gasped, sagging again into the door for support. "For a second, I thought Goldie'd set Security on me again."

Marcus was frowning intensely. "You were attempting to steal from the room."

Skeeter planted hands on hips and studied his friend. "I do have a wager to win," he said quietly, "or had you forgotten that? If I lose, I get tossed off station."

"Yes, you and your stupid bet! Why must you cheat and steal from everyone, Skeeter Jackson?"

Marcus' anger surprised him. "I don't. I never steal from 'eighty-sixers. They're family. And I never steal from family."

Marcus' cheeks had flushed in the soft lighting of the hall. His breathing went fast and shallow. "Family! When will you learn, Skeeter? You are not a Mongol! You are an up-timer American, not some unwashed, stinking hordesman!"

Shock detonated through him. How had Marcus known about that?

"'A Mongol doesn't steal from his own kind,'" Marcus ranted on, evidently quoting some conversation Skeeter didn't remember at all. "Pretty morals for a pretty thief, yes? That is all you are. A thief. I am sick of hearing how the tourists deserve it. They aren't your enemies! They are only people trying to enjoy life, then you come and smash it up by thieving and lying and—" His eyes suddenly widened, then went savagely narrow. "The money you gave to me. The bet you made in Rome. You did not win it honestly."

Skeeter wet his lips, trying to get in a word edgewise.

"He came to me for *help*, damn you, because you'd stolen the money for his new life! Curse you to your Mongolian hell, Skeeter Jackson!"

Without another word, Marcus turned and strode toward the distant elevators, passing them and opting for the staircase, instead. The door banged against the wall in an excess of rage. Skeeter stood rooted to the snowy carpet, swallowing. Why did he feel like bursting into tears for the first time since his eighth birthday? Marcus was only a down-timer, after all.

Yeah, a voice inside him whispered. *A down-timer you called friend and were drunk—or stupid—enough to confide the truth to.* Skeeter could lie to any number of tourists, but he couldn't lie to that voice. He had just watched his only real friendship shatter and die. When the door to Room 3027 opened and Farley stuck his head into the corridor, Skeeter barely noticed.

"Hey, you. Have you seen a guy named Marcus, about your size, brown hair?"

Skeeter stared Farley in the eyes and snarled out yet another lie. "No. Never heard of him."

Then he headed for the elevators and the nearest joint that served alcohol. He wanted to feel numb. And he didn't care how much money it took. He closed his eyes as the elevator whirred silently toward the Neo Edo's lobby.

How he was going to regain the friendship he'd managed to shatter into pieces, Skeeter Jackson had no idea, but he had to try. What was the point of staying on at TT-86 if he couldn't enjoy himself? And with the memory of Marcus' cold, angry eyes and that wintery voice sinking into his bones, he knew he would never enjoy another moment in La-La Land unless he could somehow restore good faith with Marcus.

He stumbled out of the elevator, completely alone in a lobby crowded with tourists, and realized that being the object of Marcus' anger was infinitely worse than all those long-ago baseball games where he'd played his heart out, alone, while a father too busy to bother stayed home and stole money from customers who didn't need the expensive junk he sold tthem.

The comparison hurt.

Skeeter found that nearest bar, ignoring tattooed Yakuza and wide-eyed Japanese businessmen, and got roaring, nastily drunk. Had his luck gone sour? Was all this a punishment for screwing over—and thus guaranteeing the loss of—his only friend? He sat there amongst the curious Japanese businessmen and thugs who stared at the gaijin in "their" bar, and wondered bitterly who he hated worse: His father? Marcus, for pointing out how much Skeeter had turned out like him? Or himself, for everything he'd done to end up just like the man he'd grown up despising?

He found no answers in the Japanese whiskey or the steaming hot *sake*, which he consumed in such enormous amounts even the Japanese businessmen were impressed, eventually crowding around to compliment and encourage him. A girl dressed as a geisha—hell, she might have *been* one, since time terminals could afford to pay the outrageous salaries their careers demanded—refilled his cup again and again, attempting vainly to flirt and draw him out with conversation and silly games that the others played with enthusiasm. Skeeter ignored all of it, utterly. All he wanted was the numbing effect of the booze.

So he let them talk, the words washing over him like the cutting winds of the wide, empty Gobi. There might not be any answers in the whiskey, but alcohol made the emptiness a little easier to bear.

Three sheets to the wind (a sailing term, Skeeter had discovered years earlier when his father had taken them on a short cruise so everyone of any importance would see his new sloop), Skeeter was just about to give into to drunken stupor when the phone rang. He snagged the receiver, tripping and knocking over a chair on the way. "Yeah?"

"Mr. Jackson? Chuck Farley, here."

Surprise rooted him to the carpet. "Yes?" he asked cautiously.

"I've been thinking about your offer the other day. About time guiding. You had a good point. If you're not engaged, I'd like to hire you."

Skeeter recovered from his surprise gracefully. "Of course. What gate did you have in mind?"

"Denver."

"Denver. Hmm . . ." He pretended to consult a nonexistent guiding calendar while pulling himself together. "The best time for Denver's just a tad over two weeks from now, after the Porta Romae makes a complete tour cycle. Yes, I'm free for that Denver trip."

"Wonderful! Meet me in half an hour in Frontier Town. We'll discuss details. There's a little bar called Happy Jack's . . ."

"Yes, I know it. Half an hour? No problem. I'll be there."

"Good."

The line clicked dead. Happy Jack's was a wild place, where anything could happen. Especially to one particular fat money-belt. Skeeter grinned as he emerged from his apartment.

Profit, here I come!

Happy Jack's bore an enormous wooden sign over the entrance, of dancing, dueling cowboys shooting at one another's feet. A large glass window was painted in bright Frontier Town colors, as well, proclaiming the bar's name in red, blue, and garish gold. Skeeter pushed open the Hollywood-style saloon doors and entered the raucous establishment, where a piano player was already busy pounding out tunes popular in Denver—the lyrics of which would've given the NAACP a collective fit of apoplexy. Many of those popular old tunes, heard and bellowed in dance halls and saloons from New York to San Francisco during the 1880s, were *not* flattering to the darker races.

There was a running war between up-time delegations and Frontier Town bar owners over the playing of those songs, but no resolution was in sight. So the pianists played on, accustoming patrons to what they'd actually hear down time—shocking, crude, racist, and all. Skeeter figured it beat having some up-time type throw a fit in the *real* down-time Denver, where more modern attitudes publicly and forcefully expressed would get a tourist into hot water fast.

Skeeter shook his head. Some folks just didn't get it. Human beings weren't nice, given half a chance not to be. If crusaders with legitimate gripes wanted to fix things, getting into legal wrangles with station bar owners wasn't the way to do it. Couldn't change the past, no matter what you did, and the barkeepers were just doing their part to acclimatize customers, after all. Crusaders needed to stay up time and pour their resources into causes that might actually do some good: like raising the level of education for up-timers of *all* colors and breeds of human being. Same went for those enviro-nuts who wanted to go down time and save the environment. Besides, it was plain wrong to murder a bunch of down-time commercial hunters and loggers for doing what their time thought perfectly normal.

For a half-wild, adopted Yakka Mongol, Skeeter just couldn't figure out what was so horrible about taking a good, long, clear-eyed look at one's past and facing whatever one found in it. Making up the past to fit whatever idea some politically correct group wanted to pass off as reality this week seemed a lot more dangerous to him than facing brutal facts, but then, he *was* just a half-wild, adopted Yakka Mongol in his innermost heart. What did he know from social theory and up-time politics?

Chuck Farley was there ahead of him, sitting at a table near the front and sipping whiskey. Skeeter smiled his best and slid into a chair. Above the roar of piano and human voices, he said, "Evenin' pardner."

Chuck smiled slowly. "Evenin'. Have a drink with me?"

"Don't mind if I do."

Farley signalled the waiter. A moment later, Skeeter was sipping some fine whiskey. *Ahh* . . . "Now. You wanted to plan a trip to Denver?"

Farley nodded. "What I really need is an experienced time guide to set up my trip and show me the ropes before I go through the gate."

"Well sir, then I'm your man. But my fee is high."

Farley reached into a coat pocket and extracted a bulging envelope. "Half of this is yours before we leave, half when we get back."

"You realize, sir, that tickets to the Denver Gate go quickly; we'll need to purchase them right away." Skeeter half hoped that Farley would hand over the money right then.

Instead, Farley put the envelope back and said, with the air of a man relieved not to have to bother with petty details, "I'll leave it to you, who knows the ropes, to make arrangements, then."

Skeeter grinned philosophically. "Sure thing. Where and when shall we meet next?" If this envelope was only a fraction of what Farley carried in that undeclared moneybelt, Skeeter would soon be a rich man.

Farley named a spot off Commons in a quiet corridor near the Epicurean Delight. "We'll meet there in, say, an hour?" Farley added.

"I'll be there." Skeeter smiled.

"I'll be lookin' for you, pardner." Farley lifted his glass. "To adventure."

Skeeter clinked glasses and drained his whiskey. "To adventure. See you in an hour." *Perfect*, he gloated. *Just where I want him. Goldie's gone for good.*

He strolled out of the saloon and headed straight to the nearest money machine. He regretted having to front the ticket money himself, but he figured he needed to bait his hook with high-class worms to catch a rich fish. He then made his way to the Wild West Gate Time Tours ticket booth. "Hi, I'd like two spots on the Denver trip two weeks from now."

"Sure, plenty of tickets left." The woman behind the glass—who knew Skeeter as well as any long-time 'eighty-sixer—frowned and said, "But let's see the cash, Jackson."

He grinned, producing it with a flourish. The woman groaned. "Poor sucker. I pity him—or her. All right, here are your tickets."

She stamped generic tickets for the correct departure date and handed them over. "Don't forget to tell your rube he'll need his time card with him," she added sarcastically.

Clearly, she didn't expect Skeeter's supposed victim to make it anywhere near the Wild West Gate. Skeeter cheerfully blew her a kiss, then headed for the assignation with Farley behind the Delight. He whistled as he walked, tickets in his pockets, along with a little remaining cash of his own to buy supper with. He chuckled midwhistle. After he got possession of that money-belt, the little bit of his own money he carried would be insignificant by comparison.

Dinner at the Delight would be a welcome change from frozen

soy patties with "seared-in" so-called grill patterns to look like beef. After the diet he'd grown accustomed to as a boy, they made him want to gag, but they kept body and soul together and just now, with the wager on, he couldn't afford luxuries like real beef in his freezer.

The corridor behind the Delight was long and deserted at the moment. Bins and chutes leading to composting rooms and incinerators in the bowels of the station lined the walls. Skeeter propped his back and the sole of one foot against the wall, whistling still, and waited. A sound off to his left distracted him. He glanced down that way—

Pain exploded through the back of his skull. He went down, knowing he was hurt, and felt his face connect with a the hard floor. Then a cloth soaked in foul-smelling liquid covered his nose and mouth. He struggled briefly, cursing his stupidity and carelessness, but slid inexorably into a black fog even as hands searched his pockets.

Then the darkness closed over him and left him inert against the floor.

When he regained his senses, slowly, with a taste like the Gobi on his tongue and a sandstorm pounding the insides of his head, Skeeter groaned softly, then wished he hadn't. *Drugged* . . . He struggled to sit up and nearly retched, but made it to a sitting position propped more or less against the wall. Fumbling hands searched, but the tickets and all of his money were missing. Had Farley rolled him? Or some opportunist amateur new to the station? Or—just as likely—one of Goldie's agents?

He cursed under his breath, winced, and gingerly touched his throbbing head. He couldn't exactly report this mugging to Bull Morgan, now could he? "Hi, I was about to scam this up-timer when somebody jumped me with a sap and a chloroformed rag. . . ."

No, he wouldn't be talking to the Station Manager or anyone else about this one. Skeeter managed to gain his feet, then slid dizzily back to the floor and spent several miserable minutes bringing up the contents of his stomach. He was still coughing and wishing for a glass of water to rinse his mouth when hasty footsteps ran lightly his way.

"Skeeter?" a female voice said anxiously.

He looked up, wondering who she was. He didn't remember seeing her before.

"Skeeter, you are ill! Oh, Ianira will be so upset! Here, let me help you."

Her accent pegged her as a down-timer, probably Greek. Legs so wobbly he could barely stand unaided, he let her guide him through the back corridors to his own apartment, where she levered him expertly into the shower, stripped him down, and sluiced lukewarm water over his shivering body to clean up the mess. He leaned against the tiles, groaning, and pressed gingerly at the swelling on the back of his head.

Whoever she was, she reappeared with a towel and helped him out of the shower, dried him expertly, and got him into a comfortable robe, then assisted him across the short stretch of floor to his bed. He couldn't have made the walk unaided. She disappeared again, returning with a glass of liquid.

"Here. Sip this. It will settle your stomach and ease the pain in your head."

He sipped. It didn't taste as bad as he'd expected. Skeeter finished the glassful, then groaned softly and leaned back into the pillows. She pulled the covers up over him, switched off the lights, and settled into a nearby chair to watch over him.

"Hey," Skeeter mumbled, "thanks."

"Sleep," she urged. "You have been hurt. Sleep will heal."

Unable to argue with either her logic or the heaviness stealing across him, Skeeter closed his eyes and slept.

Marcus found Lupus Mortiferus in Urbs Romae, skulking near the entrance to the Epicurean Delight. The gladiator's eyes widened when Marcus charged right toward his place of concealment. He thrust his hand into the box of money he'd so carefully saved up and yanked out a fistful of coins from a bag that matched the amount Skeeter had given him.

"Here. This is yours."

Lupus took the wad of heavy pouch without comment, just

staring at him. He glanced down at the money, then back at Marcus. "What has happened?"

Marcus laughed, a bitter sound that widened Lupus' eyes. "I have discovered an ugly truth, friend. I am a very great fool. The man who stole from you gave me that money. I thought he had won it fairly, betting at the Circus. Why I thought that, when he has never done an honest day's work in his life . . ."

Lupus caught him by the shirt. "*Who is he? Where is he?*"

For just an instant, Marcus almost answered. Then he jerked loose. "Where?" The laughter was even more bitter than before. "I don't know. And I don't care. Probably out trying to steal from someone else gullible enough to call him friend. As to who he is . . . I have given you hospitality. My woman and my children are in hiding and now I do not have enough money to repay the debt of my purchase price to the man who brought me here. And thief and scoundrel though he may be, I have called him friend. You mean to kill him. You will have to discover him yourself, Wolf."

Goldie's network of contacts paid off. Specifically, a brilliant, impudent down-timer aged about fifteen, known to everyone in La-La Land simply as "Julius" had been the one to hit paydirt. Goldie sat down on a bench in Victoria Station, where the Britannia Gate would be cycling soon. According to Julius, all she had to do was *wait*. People strolled past three and four times as they explored the brilliantly decorated Holiday La-La Land—and Victoria Station had pulled out the stops in the annual competition, hoping to regain respect again after that enormous raptor of some sort had crashed through and fallen five stories, only to land with smashing force on cobblestones, wrought-iron benches, even smashing over a dainty street lamp with etched glass in its multiple panes. She hoped they took the prize money with a thousand points between them and their nearest competitor.

Goldie shook off too many memories and watched intently the tourists taking in the exuberant display, complete with a Victorian kid-sized railroad that began at Victoria Station and quickly picked up steam to circle the entire, lavishly decorated Commons. Many parents had vidcams with them to record junior or their darling little miss, eyes aglow and their laughter sparkling like Christmas bells.

Goldie snorted under her breath. Truth was, she hated children as much as she hated that tinkle-winkle noise of thinly silver-plated brass bells.

Goldie shrugged. She couldn't help being cynical. She'd seen it all before, year in and year out, as relatively poor up-timers with their big families took advantage of the special "one-cycle-pass" tickets to step through Primary and absorb as much of the holiday spirit as possible in the Wonderland of La-La Land before the Primary cycled again. But she'd put up a few requisite lights and bows around her shop and counted it time wasted. And speaking of time wasted . . .

Where was Skeeter's nemesis?

Ordering herself to remain patient and seem the very picture of innocence, she sat regally on her bench in Victoria Station, watching the crowds surge past, many pausing to take pictures of overhead decorations. Goldie noted they were tattered a bit in places by the prehistoric birds and pterosaurs that tended to roost in the girders.

One camera-bedecked geek got more than he had bargained for. An offering from one of the leather-winged screechers above splattered hideously across camera lens and body, the photographer's face, the eye not on the eyepiece, both cheeks, mouth and chin, never mind the mess running down into his hair. Laughter, most of it sympathetic, with the delighted, devilish kind coming from the kids in their mothers' tow, broke out across Victoria Station.

Goldie, chuckling along with everyone else, almost missed him. A pair of cow-chaps caught her attention. Her field of visual acuity narrowed as she looked this man over. Someone staying in the Wild West section, out to see the rest of the station's gilt offerings. Oddly enough, he wasn't laughing with the rest. Then he turned and Goldie looked straight into his face. *Ahh* . . . yes, that was him, all right. The dark scowl, the shock of short-cut reddish hair, the play of muscles as he moved, all confirmed the identity of the man with the knife. Just where he was sleeping was not immediately obvious; he looked tired, like a man who hasn't eaten enough in the past few days, and somehow frustrated. She didn't know his name—yet—but this very much the worse-for-wear gladiator was going to solve *all* of Goldie's problems and rid Time Terminal 86 of that weasel Skeeter Jackson forever.

With a wave of her hand, Goldie signalled. Two *very* large, very muscular down-timers in her employ casually moved in, then grasped the astonished gladiator's arms—pinning them behind him (probably a career record for sudden, brutal defeat)—then steered him over to Goldie. A moment later, a young lad slid across the cobblestones on in-line skates, sending showers of sparks as he moved on the sides of his wheels rather than the bottoms. He did an impressive sliding stop on the bench rail, earning admiring looks from uptime kids on a tighter leash.

Born showman, Goldie thought. It was a very good thing that he'd ended up adopted by that down-timer couple Goldie'd run into. The pair had been running from taxes they couldn't pay and, in their terrified flight from slavers, accidentally ran straight through the Porta Romae into La-La Land. They'd had coins she'd been able to "help" them with.

"That him?" he asked.

"Yes," Goldie said, ginger-honey in her voice. "Would you please tell him that all I want is to talk to him about what he wants most. Tell him if he will make a promise not to run, I will deliver his enemy into his hands."

Young Julius spoke, his Latin pure and flawless, in a quiet, dignified manner that would have pleased even Claudius himself. (Goldie suspected Imperial blood in him, because he hadn't been left on the city's heap of dung to be taken into adoption or—far more often—slavery, but had been exposed, instead, outside the gates of the Imperial palace, with a little placard around his neck that read, "So all shall know, this is Julius, son of a concubine who has died in childbirth. It is fit that her issue die also.") Goldie watched the gladiator's face as Julius translated her offer. His expression changed drastically in the space of five seconds. First, incredulity, closely followed by suspicious disbelief, then his glance darted this way and that, searching for nonexistent station security squads, from that to puzzlement, and finally very cautious acceptance of the truly odd situation in which fate had placed him.

"Please, Julius, ask our guest to sit beside me."

Julius didn't particularly get along well with the plebeian parents who'd raised him—he found them clinging and mindless—but he thanked all the gods for having landed them here. He absorbed more in one *day* in La-La Land than he'd ever learned from his adoptive parents. They didn't *want* to adjust. (Jupiter forgive them if they attempted something new and radical, like flipping on a lightswitch rather than filling the apartment with smoke from candles and lanterns scattered here and there, too dim to see much of anything except shadows dancing on the wall.)

Goldie Morran drew him out of deep thought. "Julius, would you be so kind as to explain to this man the location of the enemy he seeks?"

Julius grinned. Then turned to the big man beside him and started speaking rapidly in Latin.

Chapter 14

Marcus turned on his heel and stalked away, leaving the gladiator to gape after him. He was aware that Lupus tried to follow, so he dodged through Victoria Station, only half aware when Julius' Lost and Found Gang hijacked Lupus Mortiferus for Goldie Morran, of all people. By the time he returned to the Neo Edo, Skeeter had abandoned his attempt at theft and had long since gone. Marcus took the stairs, pounding angrily so the noise echoed up and down the stairwell, and emerged on the third floor, his meticulously kept records and depleted moneybox tucked under one arm.

"Curse him!" Marcus spat to the empty corridor.

He pounded on the door to Room 3027 with a closed fist and wondered what he would say to the man whose debt he could not now pay. The door opened with alacrity. Marcus swallowed hard and faced down the man who'd bought him out of a filthy, stinking slave pen and brought him, fainting with terror, to La-La Land.

"Marcus," the man said with a tiny smile. "Come in."

He didn't want to go into that room.

But he stepped across the threshold, fingers white around the metal moneybox, and waited. The click of the door closing reached him, then a tinkle of ice against glass came in the silence. Liquid splashed. Marcus recognized the label. His one-time master had a taste for expensive liquor. He did not, Marcus noted, offer a second glass to him. Cold and angry, Marcus waited while the man sipped and studied him.

"You've changed." The Latin rolled off his tongue as neatly as it had that day in Rome.

"That is your doing," Marcus replied in English.

One brow rose toward a greying hairline. "Oh?"

Marcus shrugged in that Gallic gesture which had survived the centuries. "You brought me here. I have listened and learned. I know the laws which forbid slavery and the laws which forbid you to bring men like me into this world."

Dark eyes narrowed.

"I owe you money," Marcus went on doggedly, "for repayment of the coin you spent for my purchase. But your slave I am not. This is La-La Land. Not Rome."

He dropped the record books on the bed. "There are the notes you sought. Men who travelled with the zipper jockeys to the brothels of Greece and Rome. Men who returned with the art you seek. Men who did business with Robert Li when they returned and men who did not."

He thrust out the moneybox. "Here is most of what I owe you. In another few seven-days, I will have earned the rest. If you would tell me your name," he allowed sarcasm to creep into his voice, "I will have it sent to you up time."

His former master stood very still for a very long time, just watching him. Then, slowly, he accepted the moneybox and set it aside, unopened. "We'll discuss this later, Marcus. As for my name," a brief smile touched mobile lips without reaching dark, watchful eyes, "it's Chuck. Chuck Farley. At least," he chuckled hollowly, "it is today. Tomorrow . . ." He shrugged. "Let's see those records of yours, shall we?"

He held out a hand for them.

Marcus, torn between the desire to stand his ground and the hope that his one-time master understood and would be reasonable about the arrangements for the rest of the money, hesitated. Then slowly picked up the record books and handed them over.

"Ahh . . ." Chuck Farley settled into a chair and flipped on a light, sipping whiskey and poring over Marcus' notations, making occasional comments that meant nothing to Marcus. "Very interesting. Hmm, now I wonder—of course." And he laughed, darkly. Marcus fought a shiver. Farley read through each book before glancing up again. "You've done very well, Marcus. I am impressed by your eye for detail and the thoroughness of your notes." He gestured with the glass toward the ledger books. Ice cubes tinkled like bones against the glass. "Now, as for the other matter, let's just see how much you have left to pay off, shall we?"

He opened the moneybox at last and counted out everything Marcus owned—and almost every bit of what Ianira had earned. They'd kept back just enough to buy food for the children.

Farley whistled softly. "You managed to save all this while keeping a roof over your head on the terminal? I'm impressed again." His glance was full of smiles this time. Marcus repressed a shiver. "Here." He shoved the metal box aside and found another glass, poured whiskey for them both, this time. "We'll celebrate, shall we? Your emancipation. Yes, we'll drink to your emancipation. You should be able to earn the balance in no time."

Marcus accepted the glass automatically. In truth, he felt a little numb, unsure what to think or believe.

"In fact, you could discharge the rest of that debt in one little job, tonight."

Whiskey untouched, Marcus just waited.

Farley smiled. "Drink. This is a celebration."

He drank. The whiskey burned his throat. He managed—just barely—not to cough. Whiskey, of any kind, was not something his palate was accustomed to, despite the amount of it he dispensed to others in the course of a week.

Chuck Farley—or whoever he really was—was speaking. He tried to pay full attention, despite the heat and disconcerting dizziness spreading rapidly through him.

"Now. I'm heading through the Porta Romae tonight to do some art collecting. I have quite a bit of baggage with me and I don't want to leave it behind. Things always manage to get stolen from luggage left in the care of a hotel." His smile sent a shiver down Marcus' overheated back. "Hmm . . . I'll tell you what we'll do. Act as my porter tonight, help me get all that baggage to the inn, and we'll call the debt even. I know down-timers work as porters all the time. I'd save myself a good bit of money, if you agree, and you'd be out of debt." His eyes twinkled, but darkly, like black diamonds.

Farley was smiling, now, while the whiskey sank into Marcus' veins. Farley refilled his glass. "Drink up, Marcus! We're celebrating, remember?"

He drank, feeling the burning heat sink into his belly and spread like dizzy fire through his whole body. His head whirled. Return to Rome? The very thought terrified him so badly his hand, unsteady around the glass, sloshed expensive liquor onto even more expensive carpet. He drank just to empty the full glass and spare Kit Carson's cleaning bill.

Actually *return* to Rome? But it would be a quick, simple way to discharge the remainder of his debt.

Carry a few bags through the Porta Romae, then return free of debt to the woman he loved and the children they had made together. It sounded so simple. Farley was smiling and chatting easily, now, refilling his glass, urging him to sit down, drawing him out about the men in his dry, factual notes. Marcus found himself talking about them, about the sexual art they had smuggled through for rich, up-time collectors greedy for rare, explicitly sexual items in pottery, stone, and ivory. Frankly, Marcus didn't understand the fuss. He'd grown up with so much of it around him, it was like walking past Connie Logan's and seeing the familiar figure in wildly mismatched clothes she was trying on for fit.

With Farley drawing him out, he talked and drank and through a haze of whiskey, heard himself agree to the bargain over his debt. Porter for a trip to Roma for complete freedom of debt. His honor was satisfied. But he couldn't help wondering if he'd made a bargain with the gods of the underworld themselves.

"Good! Very good." Farley glanced at his watch. "Just another hour, or so, and the gate will be cycling. We'd better get into costume, eh? I'll expect you back here in, say, fifteen minutes?"

Marcus found himself nodding dumbly, then stumbled into the hall and made his unsteady way down and down still farther to his empty apartment. He still had the tunic and sandals of his first days on the station, tucked away in a box at the back of the closet. They felt alien against his skin. He left the fringed shirt Ianira had given him sprawled across the bed, along with a note in an unsteady hand, leaving word of where he was going and why, then—garbed as a Roman of the poorest, most abused classes—returned resolutely to the Neo Edo.

In an hour, he would be free of all debt and obligation to the man calling himself Chuck Farley. He knocked on the door to Room 3027 and quietly collected the man's bags, following silently to the brightly lit Commons and the crowded waiting area surrounding the great Porta Romae.

"Wait here," Farley told him. "I have some money to exchange."

Marcus just nodded, standing guard over the bags as told. He wondered where Ianira was, wished he could tell her everything was turning out fine, after all, then noticed that Farley'd disappeared in the direction of Goldie Morran's shop. He considered warning the man against her, then shrugged. Farley clearly knew what he was doing. Exhausted, head still befuddled from the whiskey he'd swallowed, Marcus simply waited for Farley's return and the end of the coming ordeal.

Chuck Farley wasn't his real name, but it was admirably suited to his line of work—and sense of humor. Chuck was close enough.

He hid a smile, looking forward to the little scene about to unfold. Passing through the Urbs Romae section of the terminal, he paused to change clothing in a men's room, slipping into a custom-made harness arrangement under up-time clothes and stuffing his Roman disguise of tunic and toga into a shoulder satchel, then sought out the shop of that appalling, purple-haired gargoyle of a money-changer. He entered as quietly as an owl on the hunt for a particularly delectable mouse.

The gargoyle glanced up from another customer. Goldie beamed at him. Chuck smiled politely back and waited, laughing inside already.

Ah, what joy it was, setting up someone who thought themselves a pro. . . . She finished hastily with the other customer, all but shoving him out the door in her greed.

"Mr. Farley, what a lovely surprise! Have you reconsidered?"

Chuck allowed himself a small smile. "Not precisely." He reached into the satchel holding his Roman garments and extracted from a side pocket the bait. "I wanted to discuss this with you." He rubbed the back of his neck as though self-conscious. "I was told you were the expert on such things." With well-practiced deference, he handed over a faded newspaper clipping.

Eyes glancing curiously from his face to the bit of paper, Goldie Morran scanned what he'd handed her. Avarice gleamed for a lovely instant. *Hook, line, and sinker.*

"Well, that is most interesting," Goldie Morran said with a slight clearing of her throat. "This is legitimate?"

"I assure you, it is. I'm something of an amateur historian and I was tracing some of my family's history. I came across this in my uptime researches into the Gold Rush in Colorado. Imagine my surprise." It came out droll enough to cause Goldie to laugh. He smiled and gestured to the newspaper clipping. "There I am, preserved for posterity, standing over the gold mine I discovered, while some primitive cameraman takes my photograph for the folks back home." He chuckled. "So, you see, I have this opportunity—destiny?—and all I require to fulfill it is a grubstake to purchase the blasted bit of ground."

"Ahh . . ." Goldie smiled and beckoned him to a comfortable seat on the customer side of her counter. "You'll be wanting to exchange uptime currency for American currency of the proper type for the Wild West Gate, then?"

"Exactly. I'll need a lot of money down time to buy the camping gear, mining equipment, horses, and so on, to develop the mine quickly and make me seem legitimate. And you understand I don't want to exchange such a large sum of money officially—the ATF is suspicious, you know."

Goldie chuckled unexpectedly. "No wonder you weren't interested in any of my suggested investments. You had your own nicely arranged. Very clever, Mr. Farley." She wagged a talon at him. "How much did you have in mind to exchange?"

"A hundred thousand."

Goldie Morran's eyes widened.

"I did bring the cash," he added with a small smile.

"All right. A hundred thousand. I'll see what I have. There will, of course, be a small transaction fee included in the exchange rate."

"Oh yes, I quite understand," Farley reassured her.

She walked down the counter and opened up a locked drawer. She returned with a large wad of oversized bank notes and a handful of gold and silver coins.

He then dutifully unbuckled the moneybelt under his up-time clothing and counted out a hundred thousand dollars in bills. Goldie's eyes gleamed. She swiftly counted the money he handed to her, and pushed the unwieldy pile of down-timer money to him.

The exchange completed, Goldie smiled. "You realize sir, that you'll also need a good quantity of gold nuggets to take into the assayer's office as proof of your strike, in order to stake a proper claim."

Chuck looked taken aback. "I hadn't realized that. But I was told I'd need at least this much money to buy the new gear in 1885 because of the high prices during the gold rush. And this is all I have."

Goldie nodded, reminding Chuck of a cathedral downspout he'd once seen, come to full and hideous life. "Well, maybe I can help you. As it happens, I have a good bit of my own assets in the form of gold. I'll give you the gold you need to substantiate your claim if you cut me in for a percentage of your strike. Say about fifty percent?"

Farley looked eager, then less so when she named the percentage. "Well, that seems a bit steep. How about twenty percent? After all, I did find it."

"Yes, but without my gold, you'll have to spend a lot of back-breaking, sweaty work just to rush into town to make your claim before the gate closes. Then you'll have to get back to your mine, wasting time that could be devoted to getting more gold out of the ground."

"True enough. Hmm, how about fifty percent and you agree to exchange my share of the gold dust I bring back without charging your usual fee?"

"Done, sir."

She dove into back room and after a short time came back with a rolling cart on which were piled small sacks with odd lumps sticking through the cloth. She pulled out a set of scales and calibrated weights from a shelf underneath the counter, and sat down.

"Now, mostly what I have is dust, but there are a few nuggets," she said with a smile. "This should be enough to convince the assayer about your strike." She set up the scales carefully, filling one side with brass weights designated in troy ounces. She opened a sack and tipped gold into the other pan until the scale read level. "At the current rates of exchange, that's a hundred dollars."

She was lying—it was actually more like thirty-five. Chuck said diffidently, "Er, isn't that a bit light?"

"Oops, sorry, these are the ones I reserve for the zipper jockeys. Let me get the real ones." She opened a drawer behind her, and pulled out another set of counterweights, and continued measuring out hundredweights until she'd finished with the pile. It was a big pile.

"You probably think it's odd that I happen to keep this much gold around. But I went through the big crash after The Accident, and I don't trust banks, not anymore."

Chuck rubbed the side of his nose and murmured sympathetically. "My dear lady, you are a life saver. A fortune saver," he added with a small laugh. "But I still have one problem." He gestured to the bags of dust and nuggets laid out across the top of the counter. "I can't very well go walking through the Wild West Gate with that in plain sight. I've got to look like someone who's been in the field for months, accumulating it. Do you have a period-style leather satchel, perhaps, that I could carry everything in?"

Goldie smiled in what she probably considered her most winsome manner. "I have just the thing. A set of saddlebags brought up time by one of my agents—for you, no charge. I'll just go and get them."

She vanished into the back of her shop yet again.

Chuck was tempted to steal back his bills, just lying there on the counter, but he didn't want to risk being arrested when he came back. His fake ID was good, but why take unnecessary chances? Besides, getting caught by his boss for his little extracurricular activities on TT-86 would be bad for his health. Permanently.

He and Goldie concluded their business with a handshake, and Farley headed for the nearest public restroom to ditch his clothes, settle the heavy bags of gold into his carrying harness, and don his toga for the Roman gate. He rejoined Marcus, who waited quietly with his luggage. He smiled at the younger man, then headed up the ramp with the other tourists.

By the time Goldie discovered the scam and reported it, he'd be long gone. Chuck laughed aloud, softly, drawing a curious look from the slave he'd purchased all those years ago. Yes, he'd have given a great deal to see the look on her face under all that purple hair. *Amateurs.* Still chuckling, he slid his time card with its fake identification into the reader, had his departure time and date duly logged, and gestured to Marcus. The young man hoisted the baggage and followed silently through the gaping portal in the concrete wall of Time Terminal Eighty-Six.

Unable to leave his apartment because he felt so ill, Skeeter—in looking for ways to make some illegal profit during his convalescence—hit quite suddenly on the answer. Something Marcus had once said brought new inspiration when Skeeter needed it most. He was still hung over and hurting, a particularly nasty throb where Farley had struck the back of his skull. Or whoever it had been. He was also, however, running out of time. So he quietly bought up a supply of small glass bottles, corks, and paper labels from various outfitters, ordering them over the computer and asking to have them delivered immediately to his apartment. When everything arrived, Skeeter got busy, diligently gluing handwritten labels onto each filled, corked bottle of tapwater, tinged just slightly with a drop of ink. The longer he counted the potential profits to be had in the patent medicine business, the more cheerful he grew, despite headache and hangover from too much alcohol combined with too much chloroform. Each label exclaimed in gorgeous, "antique" script (Skeeter could, among other odd skills, forge just about any signature he'd ever seen): miracle water—direct from down-time importer! famous springs of cauterets! own a bottle of mystic history from gallia comata, A.D. 47! a thousand passionate nights GUARANTEED with ancient world's most sought-after love potion!

He hadn't spent much and the uptime tourist crowd was just as gullible as any nineteenth-century Iowa farmer. The descendants of twentieth-century new-ager crystal mystics, in particular, ought to be "medicine show" pushovers. As Ianira Cassondra's little booth on Commons had proved, they'd buy anything even moderately wacky—particularly if he hinted that the stuff had not only been bottled in Gallia Comata, but that the water from the famous spring actually bubbled up from the sacred rivers of lost Atlantis. He pasted another label, wondering how much he could get per bottle? Ten? Twenty? Fifty? Shucks, some fools might go as high as a hundred.

Gingerly humming a little ditty Yesukai the Valiant's aged mother had taught him, the tune war-like and lighthearted, Skeeter was as happy as any exiled Yakka tribesman in a *lot* of pain could be. He had several bottles left to label when someone buzzed his doorbell frantically. Curious, he peered through the peephole.

"Huh?" Skeeter opened to the door to find Ianira Cassondra outside his apartment, literally wringing her hands in the folds of a pretty, Ionic-style chiton. "Ianira! What are you doing here?"

He ushered her in, shocked by the tears sparkling on pale cheeks and ashen lips. The door clicked softly behind him, the latch catching, but he was so distracted he didn't bother with the deadbolt. Ianira had clutched at his arm.

"Please, you must help him!"

"Who? Ianira, what's happened?"

"Skeeter, he's going with that terrible man, and I don't trust him, and it's your fault he's going at all—"

"Whoa, slow down. Now. Who's going where?"

"Marcus! To Rome!" The words were torn from her.

Skeeter blinked. "Rome? Marcus is going to Rome? That's crazy. Marcus would never go back to Rome."

Her nails dug painfully into his arm. "His cursed *master* came back! You know his pride, his determination to pay that man his purchase cost, to be free of the debt!"

Skeeter nodded, wondering what on earth had happened. "He should've had plenty, I'd think. I mean, I know the new baby was expensive, and all, and what with little Artemisia getting so sick from the fever that idiot tourist brought back they had to quarantine her, but there's that bet money I gave him—"

"That's just it!" she cried. Her nails drew blood. "He found out how you got it and gave it back!"

"He . . . *gave it back?*" Skeeter's voice hit a squeak. "You mean . . . he just *gave it back?*" Then: "Oh, shit, that means he knows how to find that maniac that's been—"

"Yes, yes," Ianira said impatiently, "Lupus had been staying with us, because he needed help and we didn't know it was *you* who had stolen the money he needed to start a new life away from the blood and the killing!" Harsh accusation rasped along Skeeter's nerves. After that fight with Marcus, this new accusation felt like Ianira had just dumped a whole shaker of salt into an open wound.

"Okay, I really screwed up with that gladiator. I've known that a while, Ianira, and I'm sorrier than you know. But, *what does that have to do with Marcus going to Rome?*"

Ianira gave out a strangled sound like a sob. "How can you be so *blind*? That man came back, the one who bought him. Marcus didn't have quite enough money to pay him back. Not after all the medical bills. So Marcus agreed to carry his luggage to Rome to finish paying off the debt."

Skeeter relaxed. "Is that all? He'll be back, then, in a couple of weeks, free and clear."

"*No, he won't!*" Petite little Ianira, snarling like an enraged wolverine, backed Skeeter into a corner. He'd seen that look in a woman's eyes before—more than once and usually when Yesukai's new bride had vented her temper on some hapless victim in her imprisoning bridal yurt.

"Can't you see it, idiot?" Ianira demanded, raising the fine hairs on his neck and arms. "He's made Marcus keep records of certain people who come and go. The man who calls himself Farley, a name which does not match the soul-darkness in his eyes, *steals* things, down time. Expensive things. Artwork. Some of it sexual and very rare! Once they're in Rome, Marcus will be just another expendable bit of profit to be auctioned off! That horrible Farley man has tricked him. I can *feel* it—and I was trained in such arts nearly three thousand years before you were born!"

A touch of coldness settled in Skeeter's belly. *Chuck Farley was Marcus' old master?* That put a whole, new—and utterly terrifying—wrinkle on the situation. After his own experience with Chuck Farley, Ianira had to be right. Hell, Ianira was never *wrong*. The lump on the back of his head still ached, making rational thought nearly impossible. Torn by helplessness, he asked quietly, "What do you want me to do? I can't afford the price of a ticket to Rome."

Dark eyes flashed rage. "You mean you can't and still save enough to win your horrible wager!"

Skeeter groaned. That damnable wager, again. "Ianira, the man kidnapping Marcus robbed *me* of almost everything I had left. And Brian Hendrickson is holding every red cent of what I've accumulated for that stupid wager."

"So steal it back! Before it's too late! There are still a few minutes before the Porta Romae opens! Marcus is in line, Skeeter, looking confused and scared, just standing there guarding that miserable man's luggage." Her nails dug even deeper into his arm. Skeeter winced. "I've got The Found Ones out there, but we don't have the money between us, and he won't listen to them if he can't pay off that debt. Please, Skeeter, he is your friend. *Help him!*

"I—" He stopped. He didn't have many resources at the moment and if he were going to stop Marcus from stepping through the Porta Romae, he'd have to come up with some fast cash to pay off Farley before the gate opened. "Oh, hell!"

He switched on his computer and searched out the listing he needed, then picked up the telephone and dialed. The elderly Nally Mundy answered a bit testily.

"Yes, yes, hello?"

"Dr. Mundy? It's Skeeter Jackson. I—I know you're going to think this is a scam, because of that damned wager I made with Goldie, but a friend of mine, Marcus, the bartender from Rome, he's in trouble and I need money to keep him from doing something stupid. *Dangerous* and stupid. If—if you still want to do that interview with me about Yesukai and the Khan's boyhood," he swallowed hard, "I'll do it. I swear. And Ianira Cassondra's here to witness it."

A long silence at the other end ticked away precious seconds. "Put her on the phone, Skeeter."

Ianira took the instrument and spoke rapidly to the elderly historian—in Archaic Greek. Then she handed the telephone back to Skeeter.

"Very well, young rascal. I should probably be committed to an asylum for such folly, but I'll authorize the transfer. You can pick up the money from a cash machine in five minutes. If you cheat me on this one, Skeeter Jackson, I swear to you I will make *certain* you get tossed off this station into the highest security uptime prison I can land you in!"

Skeeter winced. He'd pledged his word—and besides, the elderly and utterly harmless Dr. Nally Mundy was an 'eighty-sixer. "Thank you, Dr. Mundy. You don't know what this means."

If he could just get to the Porta Romae departure line with that money in time . . .

The door imploded.

Skeeter swung around, shocked, even as Ianira gasped with fright. Lupus Mortiferus stood in the shattered remains of his door, face flushed with murderous anger.

"Now," he growled in Latin, "*now* we will settle accounts!"

Chapter 15

The unnatural quiet, broken at regular intervals by a high, beeping sound, convinced Goldie she was neither in her shop nor her apartment. Confused, disoriented, she turned her head and found an IV bottle hanging near her head and a heart monitor beeping softly beside her. The slight movement tugged at monitor leads placed at seeming random about her torso. Then Rachel Eisenstein came into her frame of view and smiled.

"You're awake. How do you feel?"

"I—I'm not sure. What am I doing in the infirmary?"

"You don't remember?"

Goldie frowned, but nothing came back to explain this.

"You collapsed in the library. Brian thought you were dead, started hollering for help." Rachel smiled. "I was afraid you'd had a heart seizure or a stroke, but it seems you simply fainted for some reason."

Fainted? Why in the world would she have—

Memory returned, shocking and brutal. Farley had conned her. There was no such mine—the article had been a fake.

Rachel uttered a little cry and fumbled for something, then injected it into Goldie's IV lead. The room stopped spinning as drowsiness tucked itself around her awareness like a woolly blanket, but memory remained, harsh and inescapable.

Rachel had found a chair. "Goldie?"

She managed to look up.

"Goldie, what is it? What happened?"

She started to laugh, high-pitched and semi-hysterical. Laughter gave way to hiccupping sobs as the reality of her loss sank in. Nearly her entire life's savings, gone. All of it, except for a few coins and the odd gem or three. And, thank God, her precious parakeets, which were safe at her apartment. She'd have to raise cash to live on by selling what little was left—except for her beautiful birds, which she'd sell only after she'd sold everything else she possessed—including her soul. She found herself blurting it all out between sobs, mortified yet strangely comforted when Rachel eased her up and put both arms around her, letting her cry it out. By the time she'd told it all, Goldie realized that whatever Rachel had slipped into that IV line was more potent than she'd realized. Drained of tears and energy, the drug took hold with triumphant strength. The last thing she was aware of was Rachel's hand on hers, comforting. Then she was asleep, face still wet with tears she hadn't shed in many, many years.

Skeeter barely had time to think, *Aw, nuts . . .* before the enraged gladiator dove at him. Skeeter lunged across the bed, scattering labelled and corked bottles as he went. He ducked as the gladiator threw something. The mirror above his dresser shattered. Skeeter scooped up a couple of water bottles and hurled them back in the gladiator's general direction. He heard a meaty smack and a roar of pain and anger, but didn't wait to see what damage he'd done. He scrambled for the door, shoving Ianira aside as gently as he could. She shrieked behind him and he heard a loud curse in Latin, then he was around the corner and running hard.

Damn!

Lupus Mortiferus' voice roared out behind him. The chase was still on. A swift glance over one shoulder revealed the gladiator, shirt dark and wet with ink-stained water, face contorted with murderous fury, gaining ground. Skeeter put on a burst of speed and skidded around a corner into the corridor leading toward Commons. He caught his stride and shot into the midst of a packed crowd gathered to watch gate departures. He slithered between tourists and 'eighty-sixers who'd gathered to watch the usual antics of a gate departure unfold.

Cries of dismay and anger in his wake told Skeeter that Lupus was still back there, dogged as a cursed snow leopard after its favorite prey. Skeeter vaulted over a cafe table in Victoria Station, startling screams from the diners and scattering glassware and lunches in several directions. A bull's roar and more screams accompanied the crash of the whole table. Skeeter raced and dodged through Victoria Station, whipping around iron lamp posts, jumping park benches whether they were occupied or not, flinging himself past gaping tourists and residents while his mind raced in several directions at the same time.

He had to save Marcus. To do that, he had to get that money and stop Farley from taking Marcus through the gate. To get the money, he'd have to stop running. That meant Lupus the Murderous back there would chop him into minced Skeeter. He skidded into Urbs Romae, splashed straight through a shallow goldfish pond—scattering a flock of *Ichthyornises* with a flapping of wings and shrill, toothy screams of protest—and risked a glance back.

Lupus was still coming, inexorable as a Mongolian sandstorm.

Skeeter passed a cash machine without time to stop. *Shit! Now what?* Maybe he could sprint around the waiting area, double back somehow, grab the money, and snatch Marcus? Even as the thought formed, the klaxon for a gate departure sounded.

"Your attention, please—"

Skeeter ignored the loudspeakers and concentrated on the crowd waiting to step down time to Rome. Maybe if he just burst up to the pair of them and offered an IOU? *Yeah, right. Cash deal or nothing, buddy. Your credit's no good.* It was a bitter pill to swallow. The line had already started to move up the long ramp as returning tourists exited the gate. Skeeter caught sight of Marcus, but was too winded to call out. He and Farley were near the front of the line, almost to the portal already.

With no time to stop for cash, no breath to call out anything—much less the deal he'd made with Dr. Mundy—Skeeter did the only thing he *could* do. He jumped the roped-off waiting area's steel fence, caught a ramp girder, swung himself up and around, and landed on his feet next to a Time Tours guide so shocked she actually screamed. More screams behind him told Skeeter that Lupus, curse him, was still back there. He put on a burst of speed, clattering up the steel meshwork ramp, trying to catch up to Marcus before he could step through the portal.

"*Marcus! Wait!*"

His heart plummeted to his toenails.

Just ahead of him, Farley and Marcus vanished into the distortion of the open gate. Skeeter would've sworn in a court of law that Farley had bodily dragged Marcus through after hearing Skeeter's desperate shout.

Skeeter had two choices. He could jump off this platform and elude Lupus yet again, leading him on another merry chase through the station, or he could crash the gate and find a way to get Marcus back through. Time Tours, was going to fine him something dreadful—

Skeeter drew a deep breath and threw himself bodily through the portal. He landed in the familiar wine shop, momentum hurtling him past shocked tourists. Skeeter crashed into a rack of stacked amphorae and knocked the whole thing over. Wine, like foaming seawater against rocks, spread out in rushing waves across the entire floor. Tourists screamed and tried to dive out of the way. He couldn't see Farley anywhere in the confusion.

"Marcus!"

No familiar voice answered. He grabbed the nearest guide he spotted and gasped out, "Farley! Where'd Farley go with Marcus?"

The man shook his head. "They just left, in the first group. For the inn."

Skeeter laughed semi-hysterically. "If Farley ends up at the inn, I'll eat your shoes."

He was just about to dodge into the street when a heavy hand closed on his shoulder. Someone spun him around with brutal force. Screams of panic rose all around. Lupus Mortiferus' visage loomed enormous in Skeeter's vision. He had just enough time to think, "*Oh, shit—*" before a massive fist and darkness crashed down.

* * *

Sights and smells overwhelmed Marcus from both past and present the moment the door to the wine shop's warehouse opened onto the street. A tremble hit his knees. Farley glanced around.

"Stop dawdling," he said irritably in Latin.

Marcus clutched the man's luggage with sweating hands and followed the rest of the group toward the Time Tours inn on the far side of the Aventine Hill from the great Circus. They headed down the Via Appia toward the hulking edifice of stone bleachers, rising in tiers to the arches high overhead. When the rest of the group turned left to skirt the Aventine, Farley surprised him by heading the other way, toward the Capitoline Hill.

"Mr. Farley—"

"Be quiet and follow me!" Farley snapped.

Marcus glanced once at the tour group disappearing into the crowd. Then, hesitantly, he followed Farley. He'd given his word. And he needed to clear this debt. But the longer they walked, passing the Capitoline Hill and moving through the great Forum, where the rostrum towered with its glittering trophies of war, the battering rams of ships taken in battle, the greater grew Marcus' sense of wrongness.

"Mr. Farley, where are you going?" he asked in English as they left behind the Forum.

"To a place I've arranged," Farley answered carelessly.

"What place?"

Farley glanced over his shoulder. "You ask too many questions," he said, eyes narrowed.

Marcus stopped dead in the street, setting down the man's bags. "I believe I'm entitled."

Farley's mouth twitched at one corner. "You? Entitled?" He seemed to think this outrageously funny. "Hand me that bag. That one."

Marcus stooped without thinking, handing it over automatically. Farley opened it—

And the next thing Marcus knew, his face had slammed into a brick wall and Farley's fist into his left kidney. He gasped in agony and felt his knees begin to go. Farley held him up with a fist twisted through his tunic. The next moment, Marcus' hands were manacled in iron chains.

"Now listen, boy," Farley hissed in his ear, "you're not in La-La Land any longer. This is *Rome.* And I am your master. I paid good, goddamned gold for you and I intend to do with you as *I* see fit. Is that clear?"

Marcus tried to struggle, knowing even as he did that any fight was hopeless. Farley put him on the ground with another punch to his kidney. He groaned and lay still at the man's feet.

"Get up."

Marcus fought to catch his breath.

"I said get up, slave!"

Marcus glared up at him through a mane of fallen hair across his eyes. "Bastard!"

"Get up, slave, or I'll have you branded as a runaway."

Marcus blanched. The letter *F* burnt into his cheek . . . He struggled and lurched, but finally made it to his feet. Curious onlookers shrugged and returned to their business. Farley fastened a long rope to Marcus' chains, then signalled to a couple of idle fellows at a wine stall, their sedan chair leaning against the wall.

"You, there! Is your chair for hire?"

"It is, noble sir," the broader of the two said eagerly, setting aside a chipped earthenware mug of wine. "You have merely to tell us your destination."

In a daze of disbelief and growing terror, Marcus watched Chuck Farley climb into the sedan chair and accept his luggage, which he balanced on his lap. The porters struggled and grunted to get him airborne and settled onto their shoulders. "Come here, slave!" Farley snapped. "I don't want you getting tangled up in traffic and causing me to fall!"

Marcus stumbled behind the sedan chair, wrists weighted by the heavy cuffs. Chains clanked with a sound of buried nightmare. He remembered being chained . . . chained and worse. *Ianira!* he cried silently. *What have I done, beloved?* If opportunity had presented itself, he would cheerfully have plunged a dagger through Chuck Farley's black heart. But he knew opportunity would *not* present itself.

The porters carried Farley to an imposing villa, where one of them pounded on the door. A slave chained to the interior wall of the entryway opened the door and bowed low, asking their business.

"Tell your master the man he was told to expect has arrived," Farley said, his Latin flawless. "With the goods, as promised."

The slave bowed and passed word to someone deeper in the house. A moment later, the porters had set down their burden, sweating and gasping for breath as though they'd just carried five men, rather than one. Farley paid them and sent them away with a wave of his hand. Then he turned to Marcus, an unpleasant smile lighting his eyes.

"This way, if you please, young Marcus. You are about to meet your new owner."

He wanted to run. Everything in him shouted the need. But in broad daylight, with hundreds of Romans to take up the cry "Runaway!" trying to bolt now was tantamount to suicide. He swallowed down a dry throat. Farley jerked him off balance with the rope, dragging him forward into the villa. He said in an ugly whisper, "You'll have to work a few years to pay off this debt, boy."

Marcus felt sick—sick and trapped. He knew in his soul that no man had the right to own him, but that was in a world two thousand years away. Here, now, to gain his freedom and satisfy the law and his sense of honor, he would have to obtain his purchase price, somehow. Or compromise the values he'd come to believe in so highly and simply run.

It was even money at the moment which he would choose.

Then he was stumbling into the presence of a wealthy, wealthy man. Marcus actually went down, catching himself on hands and knees. *Gods* . . . He had seen this man many times, at public functions, on the Rostrum, in the law courts. Farley was selling him to . . .

"Farlus, welcome! Come in, come in."

"Your hospitality is gracious, Lucius Honorius Galba. Congratulations, by the way, on your election to *curule aedileship*."

Tremors set in, chattering his teeth. Lucius Honorius Galba had been elected *curule aedile*? As powerful as his hated first master had been, Galba was a thousand times more so. Escape this man? Impossible. Galba glanced down at him.

"This?" the man said, disdain dripping from his voice. "This cowering fool is the valuable scribe you offered for my collection?"

Farley jerked on the rope. "Get up, slave." He said to Galba, "He didn't wish to be sold from my household. And he doubtless knows your illustrious reputation very well." The smile Farley gave Marcus was cool as a lizard's. "I assure you, he knows his job well. I purchased him some years back when the estate of one of the *plebeian aediles* was being disposed of due to the man's death. As to the terror, his desire to make a good impression has left him shaking like a virgin."

Galba chuckled. "Come, boy, there's nothing to fear. I'm a fair man. Get up. I have need of a new scribe and your master, here, has offered a fine trade, a very fine trade. Come, let's see a demonstration of your skills."

Marcus, hands trembling as Farley unlocked the chains, wet his lips, then took the stylus and wax tablet handed him.

"Now," Galba said with a slight smile, "let's see if you can take this down properly."

The stylus jittered against the soft wax, but he did his best to take the dictation, which ranged from a partial letter to a business partner to household accounts to cargoes and trade sums earned at interest. Galba nodded approvingly over the result.

"Not bad," he allowed, "for a man trembling in terror. Not bad at all. In what capacity did you serve your *plebeian aedile*, boy?"

Marcus' voice shook as badly as the rest of him. "I kept records . . . of the races, at the Circus, the inventories of the wild beasts for the bestiary hunts, and the records of gladiators who won victories and those who did not. . . ."

Memory closed in, harsh and immediate despite the time elapsed since those days. He heard Galba say, "I do believe you've brought me a boy who'll settle in nicely. Very well. The bargain is agreed upon."

They retired to a small room off the atrium and its splashing fountain. Chuck Farley and his new master bent over papers, signing their names and exchanging coins for Marcus' life. A moment later, his new owner had called for the steward of his house.

"See to it the new boy is made comfortable, but confined. I want to be certain he doesn't run at the first opportunity. Now, about the pieces you wanted in trade . . ."

Dismissed entirely from the man's awareness, Marcus stumbled dazedly between a burly steward and another thickset man who guided him toward the back of the house. The room they put him in was small and windowless, lit with a lamp dangling from the ceiling. A shout from the steward brought a collared slave girl running with a tray of food and drink. Marcus had to hold back a semi-hysterical laugh. If they thought he could possibly eat now without being sick . . .

They left him and the untouched meal alone in his cell, locking the door from the outside. Marcus sank onto the only piece of furniture, a bed, and closed his hands into the thin mattress until his fingers ached. The blur of the alcohol Farley had plied him with was beginning to wear off, leaving him colder with every passing moment. Light from the oil lamp gleamed against the sweat on his arms. He felt like screaming, cursing, battering down the door with the bed. . . . Instead, with as much calm as he could dredge up from the depths of his soul, Marcus forced himself to eat and drink what he'd been given.

He would need to keep up his strength.

Marcus was aware that it would be ridiculously easy, in a few weeks' time, to simply slip away and run for the Time Tours wine shop on the Via Appia. Everything in him screamed to do just that. Everything except his honor.

And that honor—the only bit of his parents, his family, his whole village and the proud tribe of the Taurusates, kinsmen to the great Aquitani themselves, left to him—demanded he repay the debt of coin his new "master" had paid for him. Somehow, someday, he would find his way back through the Porta Romae and hold Ianira in his arms again. It would take years of work to repay his purchase price and he had no guarantee that beautiful Ianira would wait. Perhaps he could send a message, somehow, with a Time Tours employee? How, he didn't have the faintest idea. But he would. And he *would* get back to her, somehow. Or die trying.

Kit Carson was on his way to a business luncheon he'd rather have avoided—he *hated* the monthly business meeting of TT-86 hoteliers—which was scheduled to take place at the Neo Edo's expensive *and* excellent restaurant this month. 'Eighty-sixers and tourists alike appreciated Kit's kitchen. But these stupid monthly meetings, where everyone talked, no one *did* anything, and Kit invariably sat through, silently fuming . . . he'd accomplish *nothing* except the loss in revenue to the Neo Edo from a group of men and women more interested in the delicacies of his kitchen than they were in Guild business.

Thank God the meetings rotated from one hotel to another, so Kit didn't suffer too often. He was nearly to the doorway of the *Kaiko no Kemushi*, the Silkworm Caterpillar—any form of bug, particularly *caterpillars*, elicited greater disgust from Japanese than even cockroaches did for Americans, so most of his Japanese customers found the restaurant's name hysterically funny—when *it* happened: The miracle he'd been hoping would rescue him from this interminable luncheon.

His skull began to buzz in the old, familiar way, but he was constitutionally certain that no gate was due to open today. He grinned suddenly, transforming in a blink from serious businessman to imp of mischief ready for some fun.

"Unstable gate!" he crowed, racing into Commons, even as warning klaxons blared. What would it be this time? Another peek into the late Mesozoic? No, the buzzing of his skull bones wasn't intense enough for a gate that big. The eerie, nonsound told him that this would be a smallish gate, open for who knew how long? Would it cycle several times, then vanish, or set up a steady, long-term pattern? *Where?* Kit wondered, having seen everything from giant pterodactyls to murderous Welsh bowmen stumble through unstable gates.

Kit arrived a few instants earlier than Pest Control, with their innocuous grey uniforms and staunch faces, discontinuity detectors sweeping the whole area. They also carried rifles, shotguns, and capture nets to be ready for *whatever* roared through. Mike Benson and several of his security men raced up next, followed by a puffing Bull Morgan. Mike looked terrible—eyes bloodshot, bags under them so dark a purple they looked nearly black, jawline unshaven.

Bull looked sharply at his Chief of Security as well, then snapped out, "Any ideas?"

Pest Control's chief, Sue Fritchey, always had a quiet, almost demure air about her—and it often fooled people. Sue was twice as strong and at least four times as smart as she generally looked. Kit chuckled silently. There she stood, looking exactly like a carbon copy of all the other Pest Control agents. You'd never guess to look at her that she held doctorates in biological/ecological sciences, nematological/entomological sciences, had large- and small-animal veterinary and zoo degrees, and a paleontological science Ph.D. to boot: in both flora *and* fauna. With a master's in virology thrown in for good measure.

Sue Fritchey was *very* good at her job.

A shimmering in the air opened ten feet above Time Tours' Porta Romae gate platform—and about four feet to one side of it. The air shimmered through a whole doppler range of colors and indescribable motion, then the dark, ever-shifting edges of an unstable gate slid open. Little yellow-brown things fell through it, all the way to the concrete floor below, where they smacked with a bone-cracking sound. A flood followed them, a tidal wave. Kit widened his eyes when he realized what it was. He laughed aloud. "Lemmings!"

Pest Control tried desperately to stem the flow *at* the gate, using nets to capture and toss back as many as possible while leaning dangerously far over the rail of Porta Romae's gate platform. For every batch of five or six they caught and hurled back, twelve or fifteen more got through, falling messily to their deaths on the now enormous pile of silent, brown-furred bodies. Tourists, aghast at the slaughter, were demanding that Pest Control *do* something, it was cruel, inhuman—

Kit interrupted a group of five women dressed in the latest Paris haute couture, all of them badgering Sue while she tried to direct one group at the gate, tried to get another squad into position from a different angle, and put a third squad to work shovelling the bodies into large bags.

"'Scuse me, ladies," he smiled engagingly, "I couldn't help overhearing you."

They turned as one, then lost breath and color in the same moment as they recognized him. Kit hid a grin. Sometimes world-famous reputations weren't such a curse, after all.

"Mr.—Mr. Carson?"

He bowed. "As I said, I couldn't help but overhear your conversation." He drew them adroitly away from Sue Fritchey a few steps at a time and was rewarded with Sue's preoccupied smile. "Are you ladies by any chance acquainted with the behavior patterns of the ordinary lemming?"

They shook their heads in time, well-practiced marionettes.

"Ah . . . let me help you understand. Lemmings are rodents. Some live on the Arctic tundra, where predators generally keep their populations in check. But they also live in cold, alpine climates like you'd find in, say, the northern tip of Norway. Without sufficient predators our sweet little rodents breed out of control, until they've destroyed their environment, not to mention their food supply." Five sets of eyes went round. "When that happens—and it does to many a herd of lemmings, I assure you—then something in their genes or maybe in their brain structure kicks in and causes them to leave their environment, sometimes by the thousands. You see, that unknown signal is a warning that their population has become too large for the land to sustain it. It's as unstable as that gate up there."

He pointed, and waited for five sets of shocked eyes to return to him. "So they leave. Now, the herds that live in very rocky country, with lots of cliffs, have the perfect suicide mechanism built right into their habitat. Some of those cliffs drop into deep, jagged valleys. Some shadow a deep, narrow bay. One full of water," he added, not sure that their collective IQs were above those of a *live* lemming. "And you know what those cute little buggers do? They run straight for those cliffs, almost as though they knew, *wanted*, to throw themselves and their pups over the edge. Those," he pointed to the avalanche of small rodents still falling through the gate, "have jumped off a cliff somewhere. They'd be dead already, even if the gate hadn't opened ten feet over the station floor. You can't change history—or the deep genetics of certain species. Fool about with their genetic structure, get rid of the signal—if you could—that triggers the suicidal migrations, and pretty soon you'd be hip deep in starving lemmings. And there wouldn't be anything green left for thousands of square miles."

Round eyes stared at him from pale, pinched faces. He tipped an imaginary hat and left, humming a delighted tune under his breath. He gave out a short, humorless bark of laughter, wondering what those five would say when they went back up time?

He then joined the crew sweeping bodies into containers supplied by shopkeepers and other willing 'eighty-sixers. Kit found himself scooping warm, still little bodies into an ornate brass wastebasket that could only have come from the *Epicurean Delight.* Kit grinned, then got to business filling it. He sighed. It *was* a shame; lemmings were so darned . . . cute. But their biology and behaviors were as they were, which meant that on this particular day and time in La-La Land, Kit Carson was shovelling up hundreds of dead rodents, same as everybody else on volunteer duty. Really, anything was better than attending pointless meetings!

Of all people, Goldie Morran appeared in the crowd, sniffing disdainfully but eyeing all those lemmings with speculation. What in God's name was she up to *now*? Hadn't she been in the infirmary recently? Didn't take *her* long to recover. *I sometimes think Goldie's too mean to die.* She turned on a stilt heel and sought out Sue Fritchey, who listened intently for a moment, then nodded impatiently and shook Goldie's hand. The look on Goldie's face as she tried to figure out where to wipe her hand, covered now with blood and lemming hair, was priceless. Then, when she leaned over an intent newsie's vidcammer and cleaned her hand thoroughly while asking him sweet-voiced questions to distract him from the motions she was making against his back, it was almost too much to bear.

In fact, when one film crew caught it on camera, Kit did laugh—but softly enough Goldie couldn't possibly hear him.

Whatever she'd wanted, she'd clearly gotten, as she left with a contented smile on her face. Kit worked his way toward Sue.

"What'd Goldie want?"

"Hmm? Oh, hi, Kit. She wanted the skins. Said she'd pay a down-timer to skin 'em and tan the skins for her, then maybe the big *sternbergi* might take a fancy to lemming meat. God, I hope so. Have you got any idea what it's going to *smell* like, all through the station, if we have to incinerate these little beasts?"

Kit shuddered. "Yeah. I got a real good idea."

She glanced sharply at him. "Oh, damn, I'm sorry, Kit. I was distracted . . . forgot all about that witch's burning you were forced to watch. . . ."

He forced a shrug. "Thanks. I appreciate the apology, but that's one of 'em I sometimes still wake up screaming over. And it's the *smell* that lingers with you, like a spirit as malicious as the goddamned Inquisitors who ordered the burnings in the first place." He cleared his throat and pointed his gaze into the far distance. "Sue, one of those so-called witches was a little girl, curly red-blond hair, couldn't have been above two years old, screaming for her mommy—who was burning on the stake right next to her."

Sue had squeezed shut her eyes. "I will never, ever again complain about my job, Kit Carson."

Kit thumped her on the shoulder. "Go ahead and complain away. Makes me feel good to hear other people's problems. Not my own."

Sue swallowed hard, then managed a shaky smile. "Okay, Kit, one helluva big job complaint, comin' at you. *Why the hell are you just standing there in that bloody three-piece suit? Pick up a goddamned shovel and start shovelin'!*"

Kit laughed, hugged her, then swung his own shovel like a baton, whistling as he returned to work.

At last Pest Control hummers with attached sidecars for hauling whatever needed hauling, pulled up. The cleanup crew dumped their loads into the hoppers. Kit did the same, then turned back for more.

Fortunately, the unstable gate closed before the entire herd of several thousand fell into TT-86, but a final lemming, halfway through as the gate closed shut, was sucked back with an almost startled look in its button-black eyes, the inexorable shutting of the gate sending the animal back into its own time—and a probable fall with its fellows off whatever cliff they'd found. Judging from the size of the piled little bodies, at least a quarter of that herd had ended up on the floor. It took hours of back-breaking work to get them all into hoppers, never mind cleaning bloodstains from the floor. The newsies from up time covered the whole event, not only for the on-station television network but for the hope of a potential scoop by getting the video through Primary first.

They tried, without success, to interview him where he knelt hip deep at one edge of the miniature mountain, blood all over his expensive three-piece suit and previously immaculate white silk shirt. Despite his absolute, categorical refusals—"I'm busy, can't you see? Talk to someone else."—they hovered around him like hornets, vidcams whirring with the sound of hornets' wings.

Ignoring the newsies as best he could, he continued shoveling bodies into the Pest Control hoppers. While most of the lemmings had landed on concrete, several hundred had splattered against expensive, exquisite mosaics funded by the Urbs Romae merchants and built by a down-timer artisan who had designed and placed mosaics in his native time. Now the beautiful, tiled pictures of grapevines, gods and goddesses, even the portraits of Imperial family members done with astonishing accuracy from memory, had not only to be cleaned, but cleaned with painstaking care to get the blood out of the grout between colored tiles no larger than Kit's pinkie fingernail.

A voice he'd know anywhere growled, "Goddamn mess."

He glanced up into Bull Morgan's face. "Yes, it is."

"Those tiles under there cracked?"

Kit used his hated necktie to scrub away enough blood and intestines to see. "'Fraid so. Some cracked, some shattered to bits. Damn."

Bull echoed him. Then he shouted, "Sue!"

Sue Fritchey slewed around, then began walking toward him. When she arrived, covered in even more blood than Kit, Bull said, "Show her, Kit."

He pointed out the damage done to the mosaic. Sue groaned. Already news was spreading to the Urbs Romae shopkeepers, hoteliers, and restaurateurs, mostly thanks to newsies who rushed at them to "get their reactions on record." Bull narrowed his eyes. "Sue, when the worst of this mess is gone, get your people to digitally map each damaged mosaic. Station Manager's office will foot the bill for any repairs. Spread the news to 'em and fast, before they start mobbing your people." Sue hurried off to spread the word and instruct her crews to spread it farther—the faster, the better.

Bull grinned abruptly, looking very much like a fire-plug riveted to living human arms, legs, and head. Kit, his shoulders aching almost worse than his knees, took in Bull's grin and muttered, "Want to share the joke? I could use a laugh. Goddamned newsies crawling across me like flies . . ." He shivered.

Bull's laugh only deepened as he thumped the taller, slighter man's back. "Never heard of Kit Carson giving in to a newsie."

"And you won't, either," Kit muttered, "unless they doctor the tapes, in which case I can sue. And lose my fortune, my reputation, and my case, all in one fell swoop."

"Yeah," Bull said through narrowed eyes as he watched them pestering anyone they could for a story. "Can't win a case against a newsie, that's for goddamned sure. Gotta think up a reason to toss 'em all up Primary and keep any more from coming in."

Kit's full, blazing grin was seen so rarely, even the stolid Bull Morgan blinked. "And what, exactly, are you thinking, Kenneth Carson?"

"Oh, nothing too mischievous. I was just thinking you might want to plant a little bug in someone's ear, you know, just a hint about courageous newsies coming to the rescue in a Station Crisis. Get their flunkies to film 'em scooping up busted-open lemmings. Ought to be good for, what, fifteen points on the Nielsons just for the gore content alone?"

Bull Morgan slowly pulled a cigar from one pocket and lit it, sucking until it created clouds of obnoxious blue-grey smoke. His eyes crinkled. "Yeah," he said around the cigar, starting to smile. "Yeah, that's a good, solid idea you got there, Kit. Keep 'em out of our crews' hair, away from the shopowners, 'til they've had their fill and leave to shower someplace where the water's endless and hot enough to wash away the blood, the stink, and their own puke."

Kit chuckled. "You, Bull Morgan, are a wicked judge of human character."

"Hell, Kit, thought you'd figured it out by now: *all* human character is wicked. Just varies in degree is all."

Leaving Kit to ponder that odd, un-Bull-like bit of philosophy, Bull Morgan waded through the slop and bent to murmur into the ear of the nearest newsie. She looked startled, then delighted. Soon, every newsie in the place was down on hands and knees, scooping up dead rodents alongside the Pest Control crews and 'eighty-sixers who'd seen, done, and been through *everything*. Or at least enough to know that a mountain of dead lemmings wasn't exactly a dire crisis, just a massive pain in the butt.

True to Bull's prediction—Kit was glad he hadn't wagered—the newsies didn't last long. They retreated to their hotel rooms with their vidcams and flunkies and were not seen again until much later that evening, when La-La Land's very own in-house TV network ran various tapes and commentaries. Kit didn't bother to watch the broadcast. If it contained anything truly terrible, friends of his would let him know—and probably hand him a recorded copy or six.

Once the dead lemmings had all been carted away, and the blood scrubbed away with toothbrushes and ammonia, Pest Control filmed every cracked or shattered tile in every single mosaic affected. Bull's generous offer settled several upset merchants. Sly cuss, their Station Manager. He had to be, or he'd watch La-La Land's artificial world crumble apart like dry cake left outside too long in brittle, harsh sunlight, slowly turning to dust.

Yeah, Bull Morgan was just the right man for the job, a man who found the law useful in how far it could occasionally be bent to save a friend. He chuckled aloud, drawing startled stares from the Pest Control crews still filming damaged mosaics. He didn't care. This would make a great story, full of places for artistic embellishment—and Kit Carson knew he could spin a *very* good yarn. He laughed again, anticipating the reactions of his granddaughter and his closest friend, soon-to-be his grandson-in-law.

He grinned like a fool and didn't care about *that*, either. For the first time in years, Kit Carson realized he was genuinely happy. The last of the hummer-trains groaned into motion, then Kit glanced down at himself. His three-piece suit—from the same designer who'd fashioned clothes for that idiotic quintet of rich, empty-headed women—was soaked in blood and thick with yellow-brown fur. And the *smell* was even worse. No wonder Bull had smiled. He sighed. *Maybe* the suit and silk shirt could be salvaged.

Kit returned to the Neo Edo, managed to sneak past the still-in-progress hoteliers' meeting, and took the elevator to his office. He didn't feel like going home and he *did* feel like putting on the kimono left in the office for the sole purpose of comfort during work. There was a shower, too, hidden away behind a screen that had once been the pride of some ancient Edo nobleman's house.

He stripped, showered, towelled off, then found the kimono. *Ahh . . . much better.* He left the suit on the shower floor, unwilling to touch it; this kimono had cost him a small fortune. More, actually, than the suit. He telephoned the front desk for a runner and soon heard the breathless knock of one of his employees.

"C'mon in, it's not locked!"

"Sir?" the wide-eyed runner gasped, trying to appear that he was *not* staring, awestruck, at Kit's office.

Kit chuckled and said, "Come on in. Stare all you like. It *is* a bit different for an office."

The boy, a down-timer who Kit had rescued and employed, stepped into the office.

The boy's gaze drank in Kit's eclectic office, with its wall of television screens, some of which played tapes of views up time and some of which showed views of various parts of the Neo Edo and Commons. The sand-and-stone garden, with its artificial skylight, drew his attention so powerfully, he actually bumped right into Kit, who had paused at the edge of the screen hiding his bathroom.

The boy reddened clear down into the neckline of his green-and-gold Neo Edo tunic. "Oh, sir, please forgive me—"

Before the apology could turn into an avalanche as thick as those lemmings, Kit smiled and said, "It *is* rather impressive, isn't it? I remember the first time I saw it, after Homako Tani vanished and left this white elephant on my hands. I think I dropped my teeth clear onto the floor."

A hesitant smile passed over the boy's face, revealing as clearly as though his face were made of mountain-stream water, rather than flesh and blood, how unsure he was that he might be taking liberties.

"Through here," Kit smiled, "I, er, rather made a mess of that suit scooping up dead lemmings."

The boy brightened. "I heard about that, sir. Were there really millions and millions of 'em?"

Kit laughed. "No, but sometimes it *seemed* like it. There were probably at least two or three thousand, though."

The boy had gone round-eyed with wonder. "That many? That's a big number, isn't it, sir?"

Kit reminded himself to be sure this youngster was included in orientation and education sessions he held at the Neo Edo for down-timer employees and their families. Many had profited enough from the lessons to leave the Neo Edo and drudgery work behind forever, finding or even making better jobs for themselves. Kit prided himself that none of *his* down-timer employees—current or former—had walked through a gate and shadowed him- or herself, vanishing forever the moment they crossed to the other side.

The boy took the ruined suit and promised he'd take it to the best drycleaner in the station—there were only two—then bowed and ran for the elevator.

Kit chuckled, then sighed and decided he might as well tackle the four stacks of triple-damned government paperwork *every* shop owner on TT-86 was required to file weekly. Sometimes, he pondered as he sat down and began on the first tedious document, Kit wondered if Bull Morgan was seen so rarely because he had locked himself into his office to cope with *his* mountains of paperwork.

Chapter 16

The pain in Skeeter's head registered first. The next sensation to impinge on his awareness was his nakedness. Except for a cloth at his loins, he'd been stripped clean as a Mongolian sky. He blinked and stirred. That's when he discovered the chains. Skeeter moaned softly, head throbbing savagely, then blinked and focused once again on his wrists. Iron manacles and a short length of chain bound them together. A circlet of iron around his throat caught his Adam's apple when he swallowed nausea and fear. Further exploration revealed chains and manacles around his ankles, hobbling him and locking him to an iron ring in a stone wall.

He was alone in a dim, tiny stone cell, iron bars forming a sort of door-cum-fourth wall. Beyond, he could hear distant voices: shouts, cries of pain, screams of terror, pleas for mercy. He managed to sit up. The unmistakable snarl of caged cats—big cats—somewhere nearby brought a shiver to his naked back. He'd seen snow leopards and Mongolian tigers during Yesukai's famous hunt drives. He didn't care to go one-on-one with *anything* feline that even remotely approached *that* size. The claws and teeth would be far too sharp and his death would be far too slow . . .

Despite the iron ring around his throat, Skeeter gagged and voided the contents of his belly onto the cold stone floor.

Footsteps approached his cell with a clatter of hobnailed boots. Skeeter looked up, still feeling sick and dull of mind, and gradually focused on two men grinning in at him. One of them he'd never seen in his life. The other was Lupus Mortiferus. The fear and nausea in his belly turned to sour ice.

"Hello, odds-maker," Lupus smiled. "Feeling comfortable?"

Skeeter didn't bother to answer.

"This," Lupus gestured to the other man, a thick-set individual with arms big around as Skeeter's thighs, "is your *lanista.*" *My trainer?* "Thieves are condemned men, you know, but you will have a chance." Lupus' eyes twinkled as though this were hilariously funny. "If you survive, you will remain the property of the Emperor and fight for his glory." At least, that's what Skeeter thought he'd said. His Latin wasn't very good. "You and I," Lupus laughed, "will meet again, thief."

That's what I'm afraid of, he groaned silently.

Lupus strode off, a wicked chuckle echoing off stone walls.

The other man smiled coldly and unlocked the door.

Skeeter wanted to fight, to break free and run—

But not only was he chained and hobbled, the *lanista* who unlocked his chains from the wall dragged him around as though he were a mere babe to be dandled in one hand. Skeeter held back a groan of pain and allowed the man to drag him through a confusing maze of corridors. Then, past a set of heavy, iron-bound doors, bright sunlight blinded him. He blinked, overwhelmed by harsh light, the odd clack of what sounded like two-by-fours smashing together, and the screams of wounded men. He balked instinctively and received a terrible buffet to the side of his aching head.

Reeling, Skeeter found himself dragged forward into the middle of a practice session on a sandy floor. High iron fences and armed soldiers surrounded the area. Gladiators in armor, wielding wooden swords, practiced what looked like set-piece moves, as carefully choreographed as a ballet, while "trainers" called out moves to them. Other men were engaged in calisthenics, jumping low hurdles, wrestling, practicing hand springs and tucked rolls, hacking at straw men or thick wooden posts. Still others sighted along javelins and hurled their weapons at—

Skeeter stumbled as a mortal scream tore the air.

A slave tied to a post at the far edge of the practice ground sagged, a javelin embedded in his bowels. A nearby soldier grunted, stalked over, and yanked the weapon out again, then slit the suffering man's throat with a neat slice from a dagger. Skeeter had seen such casual cruelty before, many times, in Yesukai's camp—but that had been a long time ago. He'd grown more civilized than he'd thought during the intervening years.

Skeeter's *lanista* dragged him past and thrust him into the group doing calisthenics. He was unchained and forcibly prodded into movement with the tip of a long spear. Sweating, head spinning uselessly, Skeeter did what he was forced to do, vaulting low hurdles awkwardly and going through the motions of the calisthenics. Then he was handed a dull-edged wooden sword and a shield and found himself facing his trainer. He swallowed again, dizzy and terrified.

"Shield up!" the man shouted—and lunged with a short wooden sword.

Skeeter's reaction time, dulled by pain and shock, was slow. The wooden sword caught him in the gut, doubling him over with a retching pain. His trainer waited until he'd caught his breath, then dragged him up again and shouted, "Shield up!"

This time, Skeeter managed to drag his arm up to catch the blow across the wooden shield. The smack and force of the blow drove him to his knees.

"Thrust!"

Over the next two miserable, wretched weeks, his trainer beat the drills into him, until he could at least follow the instructions. He learned the various methods of fighting, tried to use the various types of weapons that different classes of gladiators used. His *lanista* spent a great deal of time grumbling, while Lupus Mortiferus stalked the training arena like a god and laughed at him, besting every opponent sent against him with lazy ease.

Disheartened and bruised, Skeeter slept in chains, too exhausted to move once allowed to collapse on his hard bed. He ate the gruel he was given as fast as he could shovel it in. It tasted faintly of beer; barley gone a little too far toward fermentation, perhaps? Occasionally Lupus Mortiferus would visit his cell, grinning and taunting him from beyond the iron bars of his cage. Skeeter returned his gaze steadily and coldly, while his insides quaked with deeper terror than he had ever known, deeper even than his terror at falling through the unstable gate into Yesukai the Valiant's life.

Each night as he drifted into bruised sleep, Skeeter dredged up from memory everything Yesukai had ever taught him, every trick and dirty move he'd ever learned on the plains of Mongolia. Then it occured to him that perhaps he was reviewing the wrong memories. And he thought of his time on the broken, filthy streets of depraved New York, where a boy, even a grown man, could find himself fatally trapped before he knew anything had gone wrong. Certain areas of New York were said to be as deadly as the ancient Roman gladiatorial combats. Looked like he was about to find out.

At the moment, Skeeter would take the concrete-and-glass canyons of New York, even the washed-out ruins of New Orleans, over *this*. He just prayed he had time to come up with some sort of escape plan before Lupus Mortiferus killed him in the arena. Given the diligence of the guards, he didn't hold out much hope.

"QUIET!"

Brian Hendrickson had sufficient command presence to be heard—and obeyed—when he wanted. The babble in the library sliced off like a dagger cut. He glared at Goldie Morran, whose nostrils flared unpleasantly as she breathed hard. Ianira Cassondra, clutching her pretty little children close, glared at Goldie, hatred and possibly even murder in her dark, ancient eyes. This had to be defused, and fast.

"Goldie," he said, speaking as gently as possible, considering her recent release from the infirmary—and the reasons for it, "I know as well as you do the terms of the bet. The most cash at the end of a month. But this evidence about Skeeter's disappearance complicates matters. Considerably."

He glanced at Ianira. "You will swear by all you hold sacred," he asked her gently—in archaic Greek—"that Skeeter Jackson was trying to rescue Marcus when he crashed the Porta Romae?"

"I swear it," she hissed out, with another murderous glance at Goldie.

"Do you have any way to prove that?"

"Dr. Mundy! I spoke with him on the telephone! He arranged for Skeeter to pick up money to pay that man Farley. He will speak the truth for me! And my 'acolytes' were following me. Someone must have taped it!"

"All right." He glanced across the growing crowd, many of them the loons who followed Ianira wherever she went. "Any of you catch on vid Skeeter Jackson crashing the Porta Romae?"

One timid, mousy little man near the back cleared his throat five times, casting awestruck, terrified glances at Ianira, then managed, "I—I did—"

Brian nodded. "Cue it up, would you, while I place a call?"

The loon began fiddling with his camera as Brian picked up the telephone behind the library counter, placidly ignoring the crowd which grew by fives and tens as word of the argument over the wager's terms spread through La-La Land. The telephone was answered testily by Nally Mundy.

"I'm in the middle of a session, here, so if you'd please call back—"

"Dr. Mundy, Brian Hendrickson here."

"Oh. Yes, Brian? What is it?"

"Ianira Cassondra tells me you offered Skeeter Jackson money to help Marcus the bartender pay off a debt."

A long silence at the other end of the line caused Brian to sigh. Skeeter had ripped off the old man, after all, and vanished down time—

"Yes, I did. But he never picked up the money. Odd, you know. Heard about that ruckus at the gate. I'd say Ianira's telling the truth. If Skeeter'd had time, he'd have picked up that money and something tells me young Marcus would still be with us. Don't trust that dratted Jackson much, blast him, but he didn't take the money. If I could just get one decent session taped with that boy, the mysteries about Temujin that we could solve—"

"Yes, I know," Brian hastened to interrupt. "You've been very helpful, Dr. Mundy. I know you're busy, so I'll let you get back to your session."

The historian hurrumphed into the phone, which then clicked dead. Brian cradled the receiver. "Well. Have you cued up that camera?"

The little man pushed his way through the crowd and handed over the camera, then knelt and kissed the hem of Ianira's gown. "May my humble camera bring you comfort and victory, Lady."

Brian watched the whole thing unfold, from Lupus Mortiferus kicking down Skeeter's door to Skeeter's desperate lunge up onto the ramp, the hoarse cry he'd uttered for Marcus to wait, the man with Marcus bodily snatching him through—and, finally, Skeeter vanishing through the gate after them. He clicked off the camera thoughtfully, wondering what in the world had possessed Skeeter to such altruistic rashness. Then he roused himself slightly and handed the camera to Ianira, who returned it to the man at her feet. He uttered a tiny cry and pressed lips to her hand, then snatched the camera and scuttled more than a yard away before rising to his feet again, face alight as though he really had touched the hand of Deity.

Odd bunch of folks, Ianira's followers.

Brian cleared his throat. "It seems Ianira is telling the truth. Nally Mundy *and* that videotape prove it, beyond any question in *my* mind." When he glanced up, he wasn't surprised to find a crowd of nearly a hundred 'eighty-sixers pressed as close to the reference desk as they could get, with more peering in through the door.

"Well. As I said, this unexpected gesture of altruism by Skeeter changes everything. I'm afraid, Goldie, I can't declare you winner by default on the grounds that Skeeter will be gone for at least two weeks down time. Your wager stipulated a month, true, but that doesn't mean the month has to run straight through, uninterrupted. I declare this wager on hold until Skeeter returns. If he returns."

Ianira blanched and blinked back sudden tears. She clutched her children more closely to her breast. Alerted by their mother's sudden fear, communicated in that mysterious way between mothers and their offspring, the two little girls began to whimper.

Goldie sniffed. "*If* he returns, indeed. That maniac who's been chasing him has probably carved out his entrails by now. And it would serve him right!"

A tiny sound broke from Ianira's throat.

Brian caught Goldie's eye. "In the interim, you are hereby barred from scamming, scheming, or accumulating *any* stolen funds toward this bet. I wouldn't dream of interfering with legitimate business, particularly considering your recent loss, but in the interest of fairness, I would suggest placing an impartial witness with you at all times until Skeeter's return."

Goldie let out a sound like an enraged parrot and turned purple. "*A guard!* You'd set a guard on me? Damn you, Brian—"

"Oh, shut up, Goldie," he said tiredly. "You agreed to this idiotic wager and dragged me into refereeing it. Now live by my decisions or default in favor of Skeeter."

She opened and closed her mouth several times, although no sound emerged, then she compressed white lips. "Very well!"

"That's decided, then. Now. Goldie, I have it on good authority you've been selling lemming-fur cloaks down near the Viking Gate."

"And if I have?" Her chin came up several notches.

"Calling them blond mink, I think it was?"

"It seemed appropriate." Her eyes were dark and watchful as a vulture's.

"Yes. Well, that constitutes a scam. All proceeds you've earned up to now and haven't logged in yet, you will hand over in the next fifteen minutes. Oh, and bring along the cloaks. You can sell 'em to your heart's content—*after* this wager is officially over."

"Curse you," Goldie hissed. "And what am I supposed to *live* on?"

"You got into this, Goldie. You're going to have to get yourself out of it. That's it, then, folks. Now, if you all would kindly get the hell out of my library so I can get on with my work?"

Chuckles in the crowd drifted to him, then people began ambling out the door. Brian saw money exchanging hands as multiple, impromptu bets on the outcome of his decision were settled. Brian sighed. What a mess. Then, before the fellow could leave, Brian high-signed Kynan Rhys Gower, who hovered near the edge of the crowd.

"Kynan," he said gently in the man's native Welsh, "I know your integrity is beyond question and I am also aware," he allowed himself a small smile, "that Goldie Morran cannot possibly bribe you. Would you agree to stay with her during the next two weeks, watching to be sure she does not cheat, until the Porta Romae cycles again?"

Kynan's wind-tanned cheeks crinkled into a broad, twinkle-eyed grin. "It would be my honor, should my liege lord give his permission."

Somewhere in the dispersing crowd, Kit Carson's famous laugh rang out. "Not only my permission, Kynan, I'll make up all lost wages from your sweeping job."

Goldie just glowered.

Ianira smiled grimly. "Thank you, *kyrie* Hendrickson. We down-timers have few friends. It is good to know there are honest people here who will champion our cause." She gave Kynan Rhys Gower a swift smile of thanks, then vanished into the dispersing crowd.

Kynan grinned at Goldie, eyes alight with savage mirth.

She said something profoundly unladylike and stalked out of the library. Kynan followed at his ease, winking at Brian on the way out. Brian suppressed a grin of smug satisfaction. With Kynan on the job, Goldie'd stay honest for the next two weeks. She wouldn't have a choice. And if Brian were any judge of solidarity in the down-timer underground community, more than Kynan's pair of eyes would be watching that purple-haired harpy through the days to come.

He allowed himself a soft, wicked chuckle, then waved off the rest of the crowd and got back to work.

After seeing Hendrickson, Ianira went to the top.

Bull Morgan saw himself as a fair man. Tough—God alone knew he had to be, to do this job—but fair. So when Ianira Cassondra walked into his office with her two daughters, he knew he was in serious trouble. There was only one thing she could possibly want from him. He wasn't wrong.

"Mr. Morgan," Ianira said in her beautiful, oddly accented English, which was neither quite Greek nor quite Turkish, but something far more ancient, "I appeal to you for help. Please. The father of my daughters has been taken away. The man who took him has broken the law before, by bringing him here, and now he breaks it again by taking him away. Please, is there nothing you can do to help me find the father of my children?"

Tears trembled on thick, black lashes.

Bull Morgan swore silently and steeled himself. "Ianira, there is nothing I would like more than to find Marcus. Please believe that. But I can't." The tears spilled over, even as her mouth tightened into a thin line of anger. "Let me try to explain. First of all, Marcus went down time with him willingly. Second, you and Marcus are down-timers. The up-time government can't make up its mind what to do about people like you, so it's a confused mess as to what I can and can't do. Besides, this Farley bastard was smooth. There really isn't anything I can pin on him."

"So you will do nothing to find Marcus!"

"I *can't*," he said quietly. "I have a very small security staff. We're not authorized to go down time to rescue people who are *from* down time."

"But you have told us we cannot go back, even if we wanted to, to live downtime in the places of our births! How can you permit Marcus to return permanently to Rome, when your own law says he cannot?"

Bull groaned inwardly. "That's station policy, yes. I'm doing my best to interpret the law. Down-timers can work as porters through the gates, so long as they return. But, Ianira, there just isn't any way I can *enforce* that." Even as he said it, he knew it would have terrible repercussions in the down-timer underground community he knew existed on his station. "If I could," he said as gently as possible, "the next time the gate cycles I'd send in a division of Marines to find him. But the reality is, I can't even send down one security man. Our budget is so tight, I can't afford to lose the man-hours of even one security guard for two entire weeks—with no guarantee he or she could even *find* Marcus."

More tears spilled over, silently. But her head remained high and her eyes flashed dangerous defiance. "So I am just supposed to sit and wait to see if I must put on widow's weeds and weep the death of my children's father aloud?"

Bull shook his head slowly. "The only thing I can do is talk to some of the guides, some of the scouts. They like Marcus. If I can persuade some of them to go down time to Rome, I can get the necessary paperwork approved quickly. It's the best I can do—and I can't promise that another man will do as I ask."

To Bull's surprise, Ianira nodded slowly. "No one can ever speak for the behavior of another. Only for one's self can you speak, and even then, do we not lie to ourselves far more often than we lie to others?"

"You'd make a damn fine psychological therapist, Ianira. You should talk to Rachel Eisenstein about training with her."

Ianira's laugh was brittle as shale. "I am a Priestess of Artemis, trained at the great Temple of Ephesus where my mother's sister was High Priestess. I do *not* need more *training*!"

Without another word, Ianira Cassondra gathered up her beautiful little girls, both of whom looked scared, and swept out of his office like a primal force, siphoning away every erg of his willpower to continue going through the motions of his job.

It was a long, long time before Bull Morgan answered his phone or moved a single sheet of paper on his desk from the "to do" to the "done" stack.

If he'd been able, he'd have gone down time himself. But he'd told her nothing except the naked, brutal truth. Manager of the time terminal he might be, but there was absolutely nothing he could do to help her, except call a few guides and scouts who were currently in and ask them for a favor they wouldn't be too wild about granting.

Bull sighed mightily, dislodging several sheets of paper from the "to do" stack, which landed on the floor beside his massive desk. He ignored them completely and reached for the telephone. If he were going to make those calls, he'd better start making them, before Ianira did something stupidly desperate.

As the phone rang on the other end of the line, Ianira Cassondra's ancient, bottomless eyes haunted him like a whiff of perfume diffused through his entire awareness, inescapable and unutterably damning.

"Yeah?" a surly voice on the other end of the line said.

Bull sighed again, dislodging more papers, and said, "Bull Morgan here. I've got a favor to ask . . ."

⁂

Malcolm nudged his fiancee. "Margo, that young woman over there. By the exit ramp?"

They were waiting, along with half of Shangri-la station for the cycling of the Porta Romae. After Skeeter and Marcus had both disappeared down time, Malcolm had canceled their reservations for the Wild West Gate, to wait and see if a rescue would need to be mounted.

"Yes," Margo stood on tiptoe to see over taller heads. "Isn't that the woman you introduced me to at the Delight? The Enchantress?"

"Yes. Ianira Cassondra. She'll be waiting to see."

He didn't have to tell Margo *what*—or rather *who*—Ianira was waiting to see. News of Marcus' disappearance down time with a con man so slick he'd fooled even Goldie Morran was still the talk of the station—particularly since Skeeter Jackson had crashed the gate going after the young bartender.

"I think perhaps," Malcolm murmured, "we ought to get a little closer. Just in case."

Margo glanced up, swallowed once, then just nodded. She'd grown up a very great deal in the past few months. Her hand closed tightly around his, tacit admission that she understood just how close she'd come to losing him forever.

Several down-timers were standing close to Ianira but gave way with surprise when Malcolm edged through, his hand still tightly gripping Margo's.

"Hello, Ianira," he said quietly.

She flashed a stricken look into his eyes. "Hello, Malcolm. And Margo. It is good of you to wait with me."

He tried to smile reassuringly. "What else are friends for?"

Just then the klaxon sounded, drowning out further conversation as the Gate departure was announced from blaring loudspeakers the length of Commons. The message repeated in three other languages. The line of tourists stirred expectantly, while porters gathered up baggage, fathers snagged unruly sons they'd paid a ransom in extra fare to take downtime, and mothers gripped daughters' hands tightly, admonishing them to be quiet and behave. Elegantly gowned women whose appearance and carriage would have screamed *money* in any society sipped at the last of their wine and tossed paper cups into trash cans in the fenced-off waiting area.

Always the same, Malcolm mused, *the rich ones who've been before, the families who've scraped and saved for the family vacation of a lifetime, the millionaires out for a sightseeing jaunt, the zipper jockeys ready to go brothel hopping.* Always the same, yet always different, with new wrinkles and near-disasters each time.

Then the gate dilated slowly, causing a painful sensation in the bones of his skull as the sound that was not a sound resonated harshly at subsonic level through the station. Gate Six rumbled open, then disgorged the inevitable staggering, pallid tourists, exhausted guides, chattering women comparing their shopping sprees in the bazaars and markets of Rome, and the teenaged kids who'd drunk too much and were that peculiar shade unique to a boy about to puke.

But there was no Marcus. And no Skeeter. Ianira scanned the departing tourists frantically, but they simply weren't there. She did hiss at one point. "Him!" she said viciously. "That's him!"

"You're sure?" Malcolm asked quietly.

The man Ianira pointed toward looked nothing like the man who'd gone down time as Chuck Farley. Lightly bearded, beard and hair a different color from Farley's, even his eyes were a different shade. Contact lenses, no doubt. Malcolm wondered just how many pairs he owned, as well as how many bottles of hair dye and glue-on beards to match?

"I swear it by Artemis! That is the man who took Marcus to Rome with him. Now I know why his face has always remained hidden to me: he changes his face every few weeks!"

That was good enough for Malcolm. Several of the down-timers near Ianira began to mutter, most of the mutters having to do with violent, slow deaths in the bowels of the terminal.

"No," he said aloud, cutting across bloodthirsty plans. "Let me take care of him. I understand how creatures like *him* think."

"Yeah, leave it to *us*," Margo said darkly, watching the man who'd once been Charles Farley slide a time card through the reader and step off the ramp. She wondered just how many time cards, under how many names, the snake owned. "We'll take care of him, all right." Her eyes flashed that Irish-alleycat glare that did such deadly things to Malcolm's insides.

Malcolm drew a quick, steadying breath. "Everyone spread out, discreetly mind, and follow him. When we've established where he's staying, we'll watch him, day and night. Ianira, you can identify him better than the rest of us, even through the disguises. How long can you hold up, watching?"

Her eyes met his. "As long as it takes."

He didn't pretend to know the ways of her ancient training. She *might* be able to stay awake for days, for all he knew. The fakirs of the Far East could do some amazing things. And if Farley's next destination were somewhere beyond the Philosophers' Gate? Malcolm was a good guide through Athens, but Ianira had spent the bulk of her young life in the fabled city of Ephesus, across the Aegean Sea on the once-beautiful coast that the Balkan Wars had pounded into rubble over the decades. He wasn't even sure if the archeological ruins still existed.

Ephesus . . .

Malcolm really would have to get away on a little vacation of his own, to satisfy his scholarly itch. Purchase a ticket to Athens, arrange down-time transportation on a sailing vessel, and then . . . Ephesus, in all her ancient tragedy and glory. See the city of Artemis, whose magnificent temple, finally pulled down by Christian zealots. Its magnificent porphyry pillars had been transported away to be built into the Haghia Sophia.

He shook himself slightly, to find a faintly puzzled line between Ianira's dark brows. "You point him out and we'll take our vengeance, never you fear that, Ianira. I am *not* fond of people who sell my friends into slavery."

She nodded and strode away purposefully in the wake of Charles Farley.

Malcolm found Margo looking up at him with a glow in her eyes akin to hero-worship. He quite suddenly felt eleven feet tall and more than capable of taking on the dragon, St. George, *and* his horse. "Let's go," he said a bit gruffly.

Margo, clearly as moved by what they'd just witnessed as Malcolm, simply nodded.

As it turned out, following Farley was easier than either of them had expected. He took a modest room in the Time Tripper, then went downstairs to breakfast in the hotel restaurant. This new version of Farley was far quieter than the last. Once he returned to his room, he didn't leave it again, ordering tickets (Margo batted eyelashes and smiled at the Time Tours clerks until she got his new alias and destination) over the phone, eating only through room service—delivered by a down-timer—doing only God knew what up there by himself until the Wild West Gate departure was announced.

Malcolm and Margo repurchased tickets through Malcolm's computer, then scrambled into their "Wild West" duds well in advance of departure. Although the tour was full, Bull Morgan had pulled some strings at Time Tours to let Malcolm and Margo be added to the group. A few hours later, dandied up for what was to have been a celebratory vacation for their engagement, Margo and Malcolm found themselves appointed as the posse, stepping through the Wild West portal, along with the group of pre-dust-coated paleontologists carrying their assorted arsenal (they'd delayed departure to get in more practice with their firearms, one of them had explained diffidently to Margo) in correct period holsters . . . and Chuck Farley, still with blond hair and beard.

Once through the portal, the trick was not to be spotted following him. Denver of 1885 spread out in all its nouveau riche splendor against the backdrop of snow-capped Rockies. The better streets were bricked; many were dirt. Chuck hired a horse at the livery stable, hired a second as pack animal, and tied his baggage to it, trotting away with a clatter, not even bothering to glance back.

Cocksure bastard, Malcolm thought darkly as he paid for hacks for himself and Margo. Spreading out her riding skirt gracefully across the leathers, she gathered up the reins, gave a curt nod, and sent her mount down the street at a brisk trot, riding sidesaddle as though she'd been born in one. Malcolm followed, his heart soaring at the sight of her—and positively burning with fierce, primitive joy when he caught sight of Chuck Farley and his pack animal ahead.

He caught up with Margo. "Not too fast, dearest. We must *not* let the blighter catch on to us."

She nodded. "Quite right. Forgive me." She flashed him a brilliant smile. "In my zeal, I forgot myself."

He wanted to crush her against him and kiss those laughing lips—

But there was work waiting to be done.

What *sort* of work would depend entirely upon Mr. Farley's activities over the next few days.

Chapter 17

The day he returned to the great Circus was the most terrifying day of Skeeter Jackson's life. He came in a cage, like one of the big cats trapped so close to his iron box on the long barge. Their snarls of rage beat through him, making him wonder how long it had been since they'd been fed anything except prods from sharpened stakes and taunts from their keepers. Skeeter knew very much how they must feel.

Some of the gladiators on shore walked around freely, some of them still under armed guard, not yet dressed for combat or given the weapons with which they would slaughter one another. Those not under guard were free men who'd taken up the insane game of life or death and glory; those guarded were valuable slave-gladiators who'd earned grand reputations and were proud of their skills—not condemned criminals awaiting a mockery of a fair chance at survival.

The previous night, though he wasn't sure where they'd actually been, he and the other prisoner-gladiators had been paraded into some kind of public banquet hall and feted, given anything they cared to eat—or could hold down. More than a few men said goodbye to family members, clearly expecting never to see them again. Skeeter didn't have even that. All he had were Yesukai's lessons to get him through a last meal under the eyes of jeering, laughing, *betting* Romans.

Now, with the sun high in the sky, and the races at the Circus, which took place in the mornings, just about to end, it was time for the next part of the show. Skeeter's barge halted and the cages were hauled one by one onto shore near the back of the great Circus itself, where the starting gates of the races were. Inside, the crowd was cheering so loudly it startled the raging cats—leopards, lions, sleek cheetahs—into even greater frenzy. Caged antelopes bleated their terror and hurled themselves against narrowly spaced iron bars, unable to escape.

Some of the other prisoners near Skeeter's cage, also doomed to the arena, were crying for mercy to such men as passed, none of whom listened. Skeeter wanted to do a little crying of his own, but he didn't see the good it would do. Yesukai the Valiant had taught him endurance, tenacity. He called on those lessons now with everything in him and managed—just barely—to remain silent. But he could not stop the shakes quite so easily.

Far down the line, some slave with a stack of wax tablets was busy making his way past each cage, noting down contents or checking off his list, something like that. *Inventory clerk*, Skeeter thought with a sudden, near-uncontrollable desire to laugh insanely. Those infuriatingly thorough, meticulous Romans. Keeping their records right down to the last doomed prisoner and bleating antelope.

But when the slave got close enough that Skeeter could hear his voice asking questions of each caged gladiator, such as his name and fighting style, Skeeter gave a sudden start and grabbed the bars, straining to see. *He knew that voice!* He knew . . . but didn't quite believe it until he came face to face with Marcus through the bars of his filthy cage.

Marcus went deathly white in a single instant.

"Marcus, I—"

"Skeeter, what—"

They began, and halted again, simultaneously.

Marcus went to one knee, to be on the same level as Skeeter. His eyes were dark with emotion. "Skeeter!" He swallowed hard, consulted his tablets as though confirming the nightmare, then slowly met Skeeter's eyes. "They have paired you with the Death Wolf." His voice broke a little as he said it.

"Yeah. I know." Skeeter managed a sickly version of his old smile.

"Nothing like justice, huh? I'm just—I never meant for this"—he gestured to Marcus' collar—"to happen. Never, *ever*. You . . ." He couldn't finish it. Couldn't say, "You were the only friend I ever had." The enormity of his loss was just now opening inside his mind.

"I am sorry," Marcus whispered. "My master . . . I will be on the balustrade above the stalls, watching the fighting. I . . ." He swallowed hard, tapped the wax tablets he carried. "I have to record who wins."

Skeeter tried, and failed, a bright smile. "Yeah. Well. Maybe I'll surprise everyone, huh? At least you can run away, get to the gate next time it opens."

Marcus was shaking his head, 'eighty-sixer fashion rather than Roman. "No. I have an enormous debt to repay. I know, here," he touched his breast, "that no man has the right to hold me slave. But I must repay the money, Skeeter. The honor of the Taurusates is all I have left, now."

There were tears in his eyes as he said it.

"Taurusates? That your real name?"

Marcus started to laugh, ended up crying. "No," he choked out. "My tribe's name. We . . . we were both betrayed, you know. The money-changer, Goldie? With the hair of purple? The one against you in the great wager." His voice came out bitter, brittle as the hot sun beating down on them both. The stink of terrified men and the reeking musk of enraged lions engulfed their awareness.

Skeeter narrowed his eyes, trying to drive present reality out of existence at least for the moment. Sweet memories of Time Terminal Eighty-Six were almost too much. "Yeah, Goldie Morran," he managed. "What about her?"

"She told . . . she told Lupus about you. How to find you. This I *heard* her do, right before I returned to the Neo Edo to give Farley what I owed him. As much as I could of it, anyway."

Skeeter winced, writhing inside as he recalled the tears and bitter accusation in Ianira's voice. "So she told him, did she? Too bad I won't get a chance to throttle that old witch by the throat."

Marcus shrugged, very Gallic. "She will not be doing so very well, either. Farley stole a great deal of gold from her, just before we left. He laughed as he told me of it, *after* my sale. I . . . I asked him how he had brought so much gold through Primary. He said he took it from Goldie."

Despite the genuine calamity to Goldie Morran, Skeeter found himself laughing a little too shrilly, even as tears formed in his eyes, tears of helplessness, rage, terror. "So he got her, too, eh?" Marcus' dark eyes widened. "Christ. Both of us. What a couple of suckers we were. So goddamned sure—"

He glanced through the bars at Marcus. "I don't suppose you'd believe me, anyway, if I told you I was trying to stop you from going through the Porta Romae?" Marcus' eyes widened even further. "That's when Lupus crashed the Gate behind me and cracked me across the head."

Marcus' tightly pressed lips came adrift. "But—*why?*"

"I'd . . . I'd arranged to borrow some money, see, to do some sessions with Dr. Mundy, and to pay Farley the rest of what you owed him."

The look in Marcus' eyes told Skeeter he should've taken pity and kept his mouth shut. Skeeter cleared his throat roughly. "You'd better get on with your job," he said, "before your master gets pissed off and thinks you're loafing."

Marcus swallowed. "I had thought, until the moment I saw you in that cage, that I hated you, Skeeter. But now . . ." He trailed off helplessly. "May the gods fight on your side."

He made a hasty mark on his wax tablet and hurried on to the next cage, and the one beyond it, until he was out of sight and hearing. Skeeter slumped against the bars, feeling the throb of hurt inside him turn slowly to bitter rage. Goldie Morran, curse her, had sent him to this. Skeeter deserved to be punished, that much he could at least admit, but to just sell him out, knowing he'd be murdered, in order to win that accursed wager . . .

Skeeter owed Marcus, owed him his freedom, his family, a debt *he* needed to absolve himself of before he met the gods of the high Mongolian mountains, where the bite of ice in the sharp winds could kill a man in minutes. "If I get out of this alive," he vowed, "I'll get you back to Ianira and your kids. Somehow. And when I do . . ." He thought blackly of Goldie Morran. "When I do, I'll wring that scrawny old buzzard's jewelled *neck*!"

Rage sustained him through the exhibition before the start of the real games. Paired off with Lupus, whose laughing eyes and grinning mouth told of supreme confidence, Skeeter went through the motions he'd been beaten into learning, doing the whole, maddening drill in slow motion to the cheering encouragement of the crowd. Lupus' shield, Skeeter noted as he studied his adversary's every move, every potential weakness, was decorated with an odd, painted motif: a coiled serpent inside a circle of feathers painted a lurid shade of green, like First Officer Spock had bled all over them. Realizing that he was thinking about a television show some fifty years old, Skeeter gave a short bark of laughter that caused shock to detonate in Lupus' eyes for just a second.

Good! Skeeter thought savagely. *Keep the bastard off balance, maybe you'll live through this yet.*

Some of the men near him were literally gibbering with terror. Skeeter *should* have been shaking, too, with fear of what Lupus was about to do to him. But all Skeeter felt was a cold, dark rage at what Goldie had done. A Yakka Mongol knew only too well that death would come sooner or later, pleasantly or in agony, which was why he lived life to the fullest every day he still breathed; but what Goldie had done, had deliberately set in motion—

That could not be forgiven. He prayed to gods he thought he'd forgotten the names of, sky gods and mountain spirits and the demons which drove the great, black storms of sand across the valleys and open plains, and waited to match weapons for real with Lupus Mortiferus.

Lupus just might have a surprise or two in store.

While even in 1885 Denver was a fair-sized city, with many stately buildings in brick and stone, most of the streets were dirt. Puffs of dust from their horses' hooves rose behind them as Malcolm set out with Margo on Chuck Farley's trail. Fortunately, that same dust made trailing him very easy. He left town completely, heading out to a spot that would one day become, if Malcolm were correct, a public park in the twenty-first century. He and Margo slowed their horses, which blew quietly as they slipped into the cover of a grove of trees, and watched Chuck dismount. He was whistling cheerfully. The sound carried on the slight breeze, straight toward them. The backdrop of the snowclad Rockies was breathtaking and the air was so clean, it smelt of bright sunshine and clear wind.

Malcolm glanced at Margo and smiled. Clearly she was entranced by the setting, the chase, the whole deadly game they played. Although she rode sidesaddle, a Winchester lever-action Model 76 Centennial rode in a saddle scabbard, and her skirts concealed a beauty of a revolver, one of the Colt .41 Double Actions. *This* time, Malcolm had no qualms at all about her ability to use—with deadly accuracy—any weapon she was forced to bring to bear. Out in the clearing, Chuck had begun to dig with a heavy spade unloaded from his pack horse. If he caught sight of them, they might well have to fight it out. But Malcolm, glancing at his own firearms, hoped it didn't come to that.

At least Margo had set those idiotic paleontologists straight. *They* were now properly armed with rifles and pistols that would arouse no one's curiosity. Malcolm hid a grin. What a way to begin their first adventure together as Smith and Moore, time guides, soon to be Moore and Moore, time *scouts.* He edged his horse just far enough toward hers to catch her hand and squeeze it. She glanced up, startled, then grinned and squeezed back. Malcolm quietly unstrapped the leather satchel holding his computerized log and ATLS, opened the flap, and slipped out a digitizing video camera attached to the log. He turned it on and was gratified when Margo copied his action efficiently, setting up her own digitizing camera and training it on Chuck, still busy digging. The images both cameras captured would feed directly into their individual logs—and could be used as legal evidence, along with the sworn affidavits, in most any uptime court of law.

Chuck's hole was getting larger by the minute. What was he burying, a crate the size of a steamer trunk? Malcolm narrowed his eyes. From the looks of the luggage tied to that pack horse's back, he'd need a *big* hole.

Chuck finally laid the heavy spade aside and straightened his back, grumbling audibly. Whatever he was burying, he was going to a great deal of personal trouble about it. Antiquities smuggler was Malcolm's private bet with himself. It was the only reasonable explanation he could devise for a man who went down time with a vast sum of money, and returned with a great deal of clearly precious luggage.

What, Malcolm mused, had he brought back? Manuscripts? The way Chuck grunted when he unstrapped one case quashed that idea. That box was *heavy*. Chuck set it on the ground beside his deep hole, then unpacked several other cases. Then he sat down and opened them one by one. Apparently he had been too careful to examine them while in TT-86.

"Mother fucking—" Chuck's curse was loud and startling. He was glaring into the first box, which he'd angled enough that Malcolm and both cameras could see its interior—and complete lack of contents. "Goddamned gold must've been used for something else later in history. Shit! After the trouble I went through to get those pieces . . ." He muttered something under his breath, then tossed the case aside. "Just like what happened with those goddamned jewels of Isabella's. How was I supposed to know those rocks would end up in her collection, never mind Chris Columbus' greedy Italian hands? Damn. Wonder if *any* of it managed to come through the goddamned Porta Romae intact?"

Malcolm held back a chuckle at the look of glee on Margo's face. She was absolutely intent on her work, recording Chuck's every move, every savage curse, every case he opened. Another foul expletive cut through the air. "—gold inlay vanished!" He held up a piece that Malcolm at first couldn't identify. Then the shape took on abrupt, crystal-clear meaning. It was an ivory dildo, complete with testes, which were evidently missing a detailed inlay of some sort. Malcolm zoomed in on the piece and thought, *Yes, I do believe there was supposed to be golden "hair" on that thing, and inlay for the veins along the shaft. Good Lord, what's he done, robbed or bribed every brothel in Rome?*

A quick glance at Margo showed him flaming cheeks and even a pinkened throat, but she was still recording as steadily as any pro. *Good girl!* Chuck laid the dildo back in is velvet-lined case and examined the rest of the contents. All of them were sexual in nature, although not all of them were actual sex toys. Each new case brought to light exquisite statuary in marble, ivory, bronze, even—Chuck gloated through the digitizing camera lens—a few surviving golden pieces. A delicate little silver statue of Aphrodite in flagrante delicto with one of her lovers came to light, followed by a marble statue of Hermes with a *very* erect—and removable—phallus.

Very carefully, Chuck recovered his treasures in their lined cases, dragged out a small, battered notebook and made a few notations in it, then bagged each case in waterproof plastic which he heat-sealed with a handy little battery-operated gadget. He then gently laid them in the deep hole he'd dug, clearly planning to return up time and reclaim his treasures without having to pay ATF taxes on them. It was a nice little scam. Those pieces would bring a fortune on the black market—even if they hadn't been commissioned by some up-time collector. Chuck filled in his hole again and tamped the dirt down, then carefully replaced the sod he'd cut out and tamped it down, too, pouring water from two entire canteens over it to ensure that it wouldn't die and turn brown, which if it did, would stick out like a neon sign saying, "Somebody buried something here!"

Chuck then pulled out an ATLS, surprising Malcolm considerably, and shot geographic coordinates using lines of magnetism, the position of certain mountain peaks in relation to his treasure trove, and so forth. He'd have gotten a better reading at night, when he could shoot a complete scan, with star-fixes to be completely sure of his location, but Malcolm decided he'd get an accurate enough reading to find his little treasure with minimum difficulty once he'd returned uptime.

Having taken his ATLS reading, Chuck stowed the instrument generally used only by trained time scouts in its leather bag on the pack horse—which now had a *much* lighter burden—and started whistling again. He mounted his saddle horse, glanced back at the watered sod, and said quite distinctly, "Not a bad haul. Not bad at all. Boss is going to be pissed as hell about the lost pieces, but that's the risk you take in this business." He chuckled. "Ah, well. I should've known better than to buy that whole lot from one source. Rotten little Egyptian. Too bad I won't be able to zip back down to Rome and settle the score." With that, he clucked to his horses and set off at a brisk trot toward town.

Malcolm waited until he'd been out of sight for a full fifteen minutes, then signalled Margo to wait. She thinned her lips, clearly seething at the restriction, but this time she stayed put with no arguments. She was learning. Good. Malcolm walked his horse around the clearing several times, but Chuck showed no sign of returning. He filmed a closeup of the tamped-down, wet sod, then signalled Margo to join him. She did, grinning like the evil little imp she was.

"Okay," she said, fairly bursting with excitement, "what do we do? We've got him dead to rights—but how do we *catch* him?"

Malcolm chuckled. "We notify the up-time authorities the moment Primary opens to stake out this spot. He'll show up to dig up his booty one nice quiet night and they'll nail him. Meanwhile . . ." He turned off his camera, stowed his log, and said, "Keep filming, would you, Margo? I'm going to leave a nasty little surprise for our dear friend Chuck Farley, or whatever his real name might be. Let's see, now . . ." He sorted through his saddlebags until he found a short-handled camp spade he'd planned to use on a jaunt he'd wanted to take Margo on out into the countryside.

Instead of camping, they had something much more enjoyable lying ahead of them. Malcolm chuckled, carefully laid Chuck's wet sod aside, then began to dig. He uncovered every single plastic-wrapped case, then filled in the hole with rocks while Margo recorded the whole thing. "What I intend to do," he said, puffing for breath as he heaved the final rock into place, "is return these antiquities to the . . . proper authorities. There." He tamped dirt down around the rocks until the entire hole had been filled, then settled the sod back in place, watering it from his own canteen.

Then he glanced into Margo's digitizing camera. "I am Malcolm Moore, freelance time guide, working out of Time Terminal Eighty-Six. I hereby do solemnly swear that a man known to me as Charles 'Chuck' Farley acquired the antiquities in these bags, which we recorded him commenting upon as he buried them; that said Chuck Farley should be apprehended by up-time authorities for antiquities fraud; for violation of the prime law of time travel; for tax evasion on objects of immense artistic and historical/archaeological value; and potentially for kidnapping, as two residents of TT-86 are missing as a result of his actions.

"I also hereby solemnly swear that as soon as the Wild West Gate reopens, I will turn over each and every antiquity recorded here to the proper, designated representative of IFARTS on TT-86 for cataloging, copying, and return to its point of origin. I freely agree to serve as a witness at any deposition or trial should the man calling himself Charles Farley be apprehended."

He signalled to Margo to hand him her camera. She passed it over and he settled her face in the viewfinder. Her normally vivacious countenance was unusually stern as she repeated approximately the same statement Malcolm had just made, adding only—but significantly: " . . . and should be charged for murder or manslaughter, should one Skeeter Jackson be determined to have died in an attempt to stop Chuck Farley's intended plans, an attempt witnessed by several hundred individuals in Time Terminal Eighty-Six and recorded by one of the tourists. This can also be corroborated by Time Tours, Inc., as Mr. Jackson 'crashed' the gate in a desperate bid to stop the kidnapping of a TT-86 resident. Should Mr. Jackson's remains be discovered down time, I strongly urge whatever court may hear this testimony to charge the man known to us as Charles Farley with murder, manslaughter, or whatever charge the prosecution may deem appropriate under the circumstances. Chuck Farley is an evil, ruthless man who will stop at nothing to gain what he wants and if caught should be denied bail and punished accordingly."

Malcolm was nodding silently, pleased that she'd thought of those finishing touches. Jackson was no friend, but his action at the Porta Romae two weeks previously had elevated him in Malcolm's estimation by several notches of respect. Malcolm just hoped that whatever was happening down time in Rome, Skeeter and Marcus would make it back to La-La Land safely.

Malcolm thought of Ianira and those two beautiful little girls and silently told himself that going after Farley in person and calling him out to a duel here and now in Denver would not only be suicidal, it would put Margo in desperate danger, as well. Nevertheless, his hands itched to line up Farley's bearded face in the sights of the Colt single-action army revolver strapped to his waist and squeeze off as many shots as it held.

Malcolm did *not* like losing friends. If Marcus and Skeeter didn't return by the next cycling of the Porta Romae, Malcolm would be ready to go through the other direction and hunt for them. Rome was a big city, but Malcolm had his sources and so did Time Tours. Losing two 'eighty-sixers—even if one were a downtimer and the other a gate-crashing con man and thief—would definitely *not* be good for their public image or their business. Malcolm would personally make them see that, if necessary.

Malcolm smiled grimly. Oh, yes, there would eventually be a reckoning with Mr. Chuck Farley, if Malcolm had to go up time and hunt him down, himself. He just hoped Skeeter Jackson and Marcus were still alive and able to testify when that reckoning finally came.

Chapter 18

The Roman sun beat down fierce as any Mongolian desert sky, and the sand underfoot was hot enough that Skeeter could feel it through the thin leather soles of his shoes—sandals that were mostly straps. Heat radiated off the arena sands, boiled off the embossed plaques of the great bronze turning posts, blinded the eye with reflections from tier after tier of stone and wooden seats and marble temples built right into the stadium itself. Sound roared down, assaulting his ears until his head ached, with the heart-freezing beat of a hundred thousand voices screaming in one solid mass nearly a mile long on each side.

Skeeter swallowed, briefly closed his eyes, and thought, *If Ianira's right, then I could use a little help here, Artemis. And Athene, Ianira says you even beat the God of War in battle once. I sure could use some assistance.* He even prayed to the Mongolian sky and thunder gods, as well as the singular Trinity of the Methodist church to which his mother had dragged him as a small boy. When it came to prayer, Skeeter wasn't too particular at just this moment Who answered, so long as they helped him get out of this fight alive. He wondered how many other prayers were winging their way heavenward with his.

He counted the pairs: twenty men, fighting in ten pairs, all at the same time. Two pairs of *essedarii* would be fighting from chariots drawn by a couple of horses each. A pair of *laqueatores* would fight one another with throwing slings—he'd seen what they could do during practice and was glad he wasn't fighting one of *them*. Two pairs of *myrmillones* in their weird, Gaulish helmets with the fish soldered on top would slash and stab it out with swords. Two *retiarii* were paired off against their traditional pursuers, the heavily shielded *secutores* with their massive, visored helmets, shields, and short swords. A duo of mounted *andabates* brought a dull, burning anger to Skeeter's gut. Mounted, he could've held his own for at least a little while, by running his horse in circles around the gladiator until Lupus fell down from exhaustion, if nothing else. But he didn't have a horse. The last two pairs were armed the same way he and Lupus were: the underdogs with nets and tridents, like the *retiarii*, with lassos as backup weapons, while they faced seasoned champions who fought nearly naked—but with a wicked sword in each hand.

As a group, they marched stolidly out across the burning arena sands to the Imperial Box, while the slam and *whap* of the starting-gate boxes being closed up reached his ears. A deep water moat at least ten feet across an iron fence tall and solid enough to keep an elephant from breaking through it, separated the fighters from the crowd. A few massive dents which even blacksmiths hadn't quite been able to unkink caused Skeeter to wonder if injured elephants *had* tried an escape through that fence.

The only hiding place anywhere out here was up on the spine, a collection of long, rectangular pedestals between the racing turns, on which stood statues of various deities, winged Victories that Skeeter hoped were smiling on *him* today, and an enormous Egyptian obelisk right in the center.

Skeeter's *lanista* prodded him. The gladiators were bowing to the Emperor. They shouted as one, "We who are about to die . . ."

Skeeter stumbled over the words, more because his Latin just wasn't very good than from a shaking voice. Besides, he didn't feel like saluting the Roman Emperor. Claudius was sitting up there like a deformed god, gazing coldly down on them like they were insects about to provide some trifling amusement. As a displaced Mongolian *bogda*, that made Skeeter mad. *For five years, I was a god, too, dammit. I was lonely as hell, but I'm just as good as you are, Imperator Claudius.*

Anger was far better than fear. He fed it, cunningly, as a fox fed his craftiness to catch unsuspecting the prey that thought itself safe.

The champion of a hundred or more victories, Rome's wildly popular Death Wolf, bowed low and received the adulation of tens of thousands of voices: "Lupus! Lupus! Lupus!"

Skeeter glanced at his trainer who held a whip in one hand and a red-hot branding iron in the other, tools of encouragement . . . if necessary. He laughed aloud, visibly disconcerting the man, then turned his back. He wouldn't need *that* sort of encouragement. A swift glance at Rome's Death Wolf showed a grinning, overconfident champion already counting his victory. Skeeter knew he should've been scared to his bones, but the knowledge that Marcus was standing somewhere to his left, watching helplessly because both of them had been betrayed, burned away fear as effectively as the Mongolian desert sun.

The Emperor raised his hand, then dropped it. A monstrous roar beat at him—then he was dancing aside, away from Lupus' flashing double swords. He narrowed his eyes against the glare, wishing for a pair of sunglasses, a suit of chainmail made from titanium links, and an MP-5 submachinegun with about fifty spare magazines of ammo, and began the fight for his life.

The roar of the crowd faded from his awareness. Skeeter's whole concentration narrowed to Lupus Mortiferus and his flashing swords and grinning face. He danced this way and that, feinting and falling back, getting the champion's rhythms down, then made his first net cast. Lupus lunged aside barely in time. The crowd's roar penetrated his concentration even as he danced backward, away from those deadly blades and reeled in the net by the attached string. He held the heavy trident out to block thrusts or slashes and allowed his mind to race ahead with ideas.

The great spine of the Circus wasn't solid. It had gaps in it, wide enough for a man to duck into—or through. Skeeter ducked. Lupus swore hideously, his bulk too large to follow. He ran around the long distance of the spine to catch him on the other side. Skeeter simply ran back the other way. The crowd's roar turned to howls of laughter. Lupus' face, when Skeeter glimpsed it, was almost the color of pickled beets. The gladiator, veins in neck and throat standing out in clear relief, charged back down the long wall of the spine.

Gee, maybe he'll have a stroke and I'll win by default.

No such luck, though. Lupus scrambled through sideways this time, grunting and cursing at him as he scraped belly and back on rough stone. Skeeter dodged out into the open, where he most profoundly did not want to be, but avoided a deadly sword thrust aimed at his side. Shouts and cries from the stands indicated that someone had gone down. Skeeter's peripheral vision showed him one of the netmen down, left arm upraised in supplication. The crowd was roaring, thumbs turned up. The Emperor copied their motion, jerking his thumb upward from gut to throat.

The *secutore* who'd hacked his opponent's leg out from under him plunged the sword through his fallen opponent's chest. The crowd roared its approval. Skeeter ran, Lupus chasing him, and dodged around behind one of the racing chariots, drawing curses from its driver as well as from Lupus. Skeeter caught the harness of one of the horses and hung on, letting the horse save his strength while Lupus fought to get past the encumbering chariot. Down where the dead gladiator lay, a man raced out from the starting stalls and smote the poor bastard a skull-cracking blow from an enormous hammer, then dragged the body away.

Okay. Thumbs up means you're a gonner and if the guy you're fighting doesn't do it properly, they'll finish you off. Good things to know, Skeeter, my boy.

He let go of the chariot horse's harness and darted between a pair of circling horsemen, ducking *under* one horse's belly. The startled animal screamed and reared, blocking Lupus' way. The crowd roared its approval with cheers and laughter. Sweat dripped into his eyes, along with a pall of dust—stirred up from the speeding, circling chariots and horsemen—forcing him to blink tears from his eyes. *Not near as bad as a rip-snorting Gobi sandstorm, though*, Skeeter decided. He was quite abruptly very glad Yesukai the Valiant had made him go on that hunt so many years previously.

If I can take a snow leopard with a bow, I can take this bastard.

Maybe.

If I'm really damned careful.

When Lupus closed, Skeeter dove for the ground, rolling under the stabbing swords, and came up with a fistful of sand and a net, both of which he flung at the cursing gladiator. Lupus snarled, swiping at his eyes with the backs of his hands while fighting blindly to free one entangled leg. Skeeter hauled—hard. Lupus went down—harder. The crowd surged to its collective feet, screaming its bloodlust. Lupus hacked at the net, managing to free himself before Skeeter could close with the lethal trident.

Shit! Goddamnit, I don't really want to kill this cretin, but what am I supposed to do? Ask him to dance? Skeeter skipped back out of range while Lupus fought to clear sand from his eyes. Skeeter unwound the lasso from his waist. He formed a hasty loop and swung it easily. A lasso, he knew how to use. Skeeter grinned, a taut, fang-bearing grin. During his brutal training he'd deliberately fumbled the lasso exercises, same as he'd tossed the net with awkward casts. They'd thought it a monstrously funny joke, sending him out with the weapons he'd done poorest with.

Bless you, Yesukai, wherever you are, for teaching me a sneaky trick or two.

The crowd roared again, three times in rapid succession as gladiators fell to their opponents and died. The next one was spared and limped bravely from the sands while Skeeter ducked and dodged and felt his own strength ebbing under the cruel sun and Lupus' inexorable stalk.

Gotta do something spectacular, Skeeter, or it's shish-ka-bob a lá Skeeter as the main course.

A charioteer went down, dragged behind his spooked horses. The crowd screamed its decision and the other charioteer pursued, stabbing his opponent to death on the run before collecting his prize and leaving the arena under armed escort.

Okay, so even if you win, a bunch of soldiers are waiting to haul your butt back to barracks. Another good thing to know.

A slice of fire along his ribs sent the breath rushing out of him in a hiss. He brought up the trident, cursing his momentary lapse of attention, and managed to entangle the bloody sword in the prongs. He gave a heave and a twist and the sword snapped off halfway down. Lupus snarled and lunged forward while the crowd went mad, on its feet and screaming. The cut along his ribs burned like a thousand ant bites. If it'd been a slashing blow instead of a stabbing one, he'd be on his back in the sand, bleeding to death from the deep wound.

Skeeter stumbled away, too tired to dance lightly on his feet any longer. Lupus grinned and closed in for the kill. Skeeter, unable to think of anything else, began to sing, his voice hoarse with pain and fatigue. Lupus' eyes widened. Skeeter sang on, a wild, hair-raising Yakka Mongolian war song, while the crowd nearest them fell silent, as disbelieving as Lupus. Skeeter pressed the slight advantage and whirled the lasso expertly. It settled over Lupus' body and slid down to the knees. Skeeter jerked. Lupus went down with a startled yell.

Skeeter couldn't understand individual words in the immense wall of sound that beat down across him, but he gathered the general gist of it was, "Skewer his belly with the trident, you fool!"

Skeeter didn't. Lupus hadn't asked for quarter, but Skeeter wasn't about to take the man's life unless ordered to do so. And maybe not even then. What happened to a gladiator who refused the express orders of crowd and Emperor? *That maniac with the hammer probably crushes your skull or something.* While Skeeter was thinking such happy thoughts, Lupus hacked at the rope binding his legs. It gave way with a snap, leaving Skeeter with half the length of the original lasso. He took to his heels, fashioning another knot and threading it as he ran—

—and then it happened.

The answer to all those prayers he'd sent heavenward.

A mounted *andabate*, mortally wounded by his opponent, toppled to the sand. While the crowd was cheering and the victor was collecting his prize and the hammer-happy executioner was making damned sure the poor sap was dead, the loose horse ran within lassoing distance. Skeeter flipped the rope expertly and tightened it down. The poor horse reared once, half heartedly, more confused than ornery. Skeeter ran toward it, leaping into the saddle with old skill he'd never quite forgotten. There were no stirrups, as there had been on Mongolian ponies, but the saddle was a good one and the horse, after one snort, settled down and responded to the hastily gathered reins.

Skeeter whirled the animal's head around and caught a glimpse of Lupus gaping up at him. Skeeter laughed aloud, started his war song again, and charged, trident lowered like a medieval jousting lance. Lupus hurled himself out of the way, barely missing the horse's thundering hooves. The crowd went maniacal. Even the Emperor had straightened in his chair, leaning forward intently.

Wonder if this is a foul or just something they didn't expect?

Skeeter worked Lupus in circles, harried him with the tip of the long trident, tripping him up and letting him rise again, just to let his opponent—and the crowd—know he was toying with a doomed victim. Skeeter's blood sang in his veins. *This* was living! Driving your opponent back against the wall, looking him in the eye and seeing nothing but shock and dawning terror. . . .

Lupus tried to bring up the single remaining blade he carried, but Skeeter caught it in the prongs of the trident and ripped it out of his grasp. A collective gasp went up from the crowd. Unarmed, Lupus snarled up at him, then grabbed the trident. For a few seconds, no more—although it seemed like minutes—they played tug-of-war, Skeeter skillfully backing and turning his mount with legs and reins. Lupus was forced to follow, putting all his weight into the effort of wresting the trident loose.

Skeeter glanced along the barrier wall of the long spine—and felt his heart leap with wicked joy. A long, long hunting spear from an earlier fight had tumbled to the sand at the foot of some enormous, golden goddess in a chariot drawn by lions. Skeeter grinned—and let go of the trident. Lupus staggered backwards and fell, wounding himself inadvertently as he went down, the weight of the trident's barbs cutting one arm and drawing blood on his bare chest.

Under a solid wall of noise from a hundred thousand human throats, Skeeter kicked his mount into a startled gallop and leaned forward and down, his head mere inches from the wall of the spine. A miscalculation at this speed would be death—then he closed his hand around the hunting spear, clutching it solidly in one hand. He whirled his mount around, bringing the long shaft up and around even as he regained his seat in the saddle. Then he charged, spear held like a medieval lance.

Lupus parried awkwardly with the trident, a weapon he was clearly not accustomed to using. Skeeter raced past at full speed, passed the turning post at the far end of the straightaway, then whirled and sent his horse leaping *over* a tiny shrine on a circular pedestal set right down on the track. Another gasp went up from the crowd. *If that was sacrilege, sorry about that, whoever you're dedicated to.*

Whoever it was, they didn't seem to mind.

The crowd started chanting what sounded at first like "mercy," then resolved into a single word: "Murcia! Murcia! Murcia!"

Skeeter had no idea who or what Murcia was. The only thing of immediate concern to him was the stumbling figure of Lupus Mortiferus ahead, trying to bring the trident around, its tines aimed low this time, to catch his horse. Skeeter windmilled the spear in his grasp, letting it slide butt-first until he gripped it near the lethal tip. At the last second, he jerked his mount's head, sweeping past just out of range of the trident. The solid butt-end of the spear clanged against Lupus' head with such force that it lifted the gladiator off the sands, bent in his helmet, and hurled him at least four feet across the arena floor.

Skeeter whirled his mount for another charge, but there was no need. Lupus didn't stir on the sands. He was—thank all gods—still breathing, but he was clearly down, and out for the count. The crowd had gone absolutely mad, waving colored handkerchiefs, screaming words he couldn't begin to translate, throwing flowers, even coins, through the high fence and across the wide gap of water. Skeeter drew another wild burst of enthusiasm when he dipped from one side to another, scooping up anything that gleamed silver or gold in the sands.

He ended in front of the Emperor, sitting his mount easily, breathing quickly and lightly against the fire in his side where Lupus' sword had grazed him. The Emperor met his gaze for long moments. Skeeter, who had met without flinching the gaze of the man who'd sired Genghis Khan, stared right back at Claudius, neither of them speaking. The Emperor glanced at the crowd, at the fallen champion, then back to the crowd. Then, with a swift gesture, he drove his thumb down, sparing a brave man's life with a single movement.

Skeeter would've sagged with relief and exhaustion had he not faced a yet worse challenge: escaping the Circus alive. He had absolutely no intention of being hauled back to that training camp in chains. The Emperor was beckoning him forward. Skeeter moved his horse closer. A slave ran from the Emperor's box and hurled a laurel crown and a heavy sack down to him. Skeeter caught them, felt the bulge of coins inside, knew the prize was a really *big* one and felt the skin of his face stretching into a savage grin as he donned his honest-to-God victory crown.

All he had to do now was figure out a way to: One, escape the soldiers who were even now galloping toward him from the starting stalls—which had already been shut behind them; Two, figure a way over that high iron fence; Three, somehow rescue Marcus from his so-called master; and Four, hide out until the Porta Romae cycled again.

After what he'd just been through, his impudent mind whispered, *Piece of cake.* The rest of him, aware how close it had been, resumed intense prayers to Anyone who'd listen. Even the mysterious Murcia, with his or her little shrine down in the track itself, next to a scraggly little tree growing from the hard-packed sand.

He caught a thrown handkerchief, which landed on the sands nearly at his horse's hooves, with the tip of his spear and brought it up, snapping bravely in the wind of his horse's canter as he rode *toward* the soldiers, carrying that handkerchief like the pennon of victory it was. He tucked the coins he'd scooped from the sand into the quilted, chain-studded sleeve that protected his net arm, shoved the money pouch's leather thong into his waistband, and sent his horse flying past the soldiers in a sweeping victory lap of the Circus. The crowd was on its feet, hurling money at him which he scooped up as best he could on the gallop, aiming for golden gleams in the sand. And as he rode, Skeeter looked for a way—any way—out of this pit of sand and death. He rounded the far turn, mounted soldiers riding easily behind him, and headed down the long sweep of the straightaway toward the starting stalls, with their wooden doors, metal grills set above into marble, and above that, the open balustrade where officials stood, having doubtless watched with delight the show he'd put on saving his skin.

He measured the height critically, glanced at the long spear in his hand, studied the looming marble wall he and his horse thundered toward—and made the only decision he could. He'd mounted horses that way dozens of times, learning to do what the older boys and warriors could do, earning their grudging respect as he mastered skill after skill. He'd never scaled a fifteen-foot wall off the back of a horse, but with the horse's momentum and the long axis of the spear . . .

It was his only hope. He headed his mount for the starting gates at a rushing gallop, aiming between the tall, semi-human stones that stood on round stone bases between each starting stall. When he was certain the horse wasn't going to shy on him, he stood *up* in the saddle, drawing a gasp and thunderous roar from the crowd. Skeeter narrowed his eyes, timing it, timing it—and planted the butt of the spear solidly on the pavement in front of the starting stalls. Momentum from the galloping horse and the long arm of the spear helped as he leaped and swung his body up, higher and higher as he twisted like an Olympic pole vaulter, up past the heads of the statues, up past the grillwork on the stalls, up and up past the marble facade of the balustrade . . .

Then he was over the top, rolling like a cat across an incredibly hard stone floor. His laurel crown, loose around his head, fluttered back down to the arena sands. Shocked officials simply stood rooted, staring open-mouthed at him as he continued the roll and came to his feet, weaponless but free of the suddenly astonished soldiers in the arena below. Then his eyes met the stunned gaze of his one-time friend.

Marcus, standing behind a richly dressed man who was gaping at Skeeter, ignored everything, even his "master," to stare, jaw slack, even *hands* slack as he completely failed to write down the winner of this particular bout. Obviously, he still couldn't believe it. What had Marcus told him? Honor was all he had left of his tribe? Skeeter's throat closed. The money in the pouch still tucked through his belt seemed to burn him, saying, *I will win your wager. Cut your losses and run, fool!*

Instead, he hurled the heavy prize pouch at Marcus' master. It thumped off his chest and fell to the marble floor with a solid chink of gold. "I'm buying and you're selling," Skeeter snarled in bad Latin. Then, in English, "All debts paid in full, pal. Now *run like hell!*"

Without bothering to see if Marcus followed, Skeeter did just that, bursting down the stairs to the street level before the soldiers down there could recover their wits enough to ride him down. Every stride hurt him, hurt his ribs, hurt with the knowledge that he'd lost his wager for sure—

"This way!" Marcus' voice yelled behind him.

A hand grabbed his iron collar and forcibly jerked him into a narrow alleyway that wound down around the Aventine Hill away from the Circus. The roar from the great arena was deafening, even at this distance.

"We've got to get you out of that gladiator's getup or we're lost!" Marcus yelled practically in his ear.

Skeeter just nodded. The next man they came to, Skeeter simply tackled and stripped, top to toe. The fellow protested loudly until Marcus, showing a ruthlessness Skeeter had never witnessed, simply kicked him in the head until he passed out.

"Hurry!" Marcus urged, scanning the street for any sign of pursuit.

Skeeter wriggled out of his protective sleeve, forming a bag of it with knots at both ends to hold his coins, then skinned into tunic and perniciously awkward toga while Marcus dragged the unconscious man into an alleyway. "Hey, Marcus, know where we might find a blacksmith's shop?"

Marcus laughed, a little shrilly. "Follow me."

Skeeter grinned. "Lead the way."

The blacksmith was close, tucked between a potter's stand and a bakery. Before the blacksmith knew what was up, Skeeter had grabbed a dagger, a sword and belt, and cutting tools, then he and Marcus were off and running again, dodging into twisting alleyways until Marcus pulled him into a rutted little snaking pathway between tall wooden tenements.

"Here! Give me the cutting tools! Bend your head!"

Skeeter did as he was told, even as he strapped the swordbelt on and hid the sleeve full of money in the awkward folds of his badly draped toga. The lock on his collar snapped.

Skeeter grabbed the tools. "You next."

"But—I can't pass for a citizen!"

"Then pass for a freedman!"

"But I have no freedman's cap or—"

"Shut up and turn around! We'll *get* one! Or would you rather get caught by whoever's been sent after us?"

"The Praetorian Guard?" Marcus shuddered and bent his head. Skeeter went to work on the lock holding his friend's collar in place. The lock gave with a screech, then broke. Marcus jerked the collar loose with a low snarl.

"I have been keeping track of the days. The Porta Romae cycled last night."

Skeeter swore. "Then we hide out for two weeks and make our getaway next cycle. Broad daylight'll work to our benefit, anyway. More chances for a diversion to get *you* back through."

Marcus paused, dark eyes blazing with unspoken emotion.

"Don't mention it. All in the package deal. One combat, two escapes. C'mon, let's make tracks before those guards figure out which alleyway we dodged down."

They waylaid a hapless freedman by simply racing past him and snatching off his peaked cap. They rounded two corners and Marcus jammed it onto his own head.

"Hope he doesn't have head lice," Marcus grumbled.

Skeeter laughed aloud. "Rachel Eisenstein will disinfect you nicely, if he does. And I don't think Ianira would give a damn even if Rachel *didn't* disinfect you. Okay, one more block, down that little alley, then we slow down to a nice leisurely walk, a citizen and his freedman out for a stroll. . . ."

About ten minutes later, mounted Praetorian guardsmen tore past them, searching the crowds for a fleeing gladiator and his collared companion. Marcus waited until they were out of sight to sigh in heartfelt relief. Skeeter grinned. "See? Told you it'd be a piece of cake." He didn't mention that his knees were a little weak and his insides shook like gelatin in a blender.

Marcus glared at him. "You did not say any such thing, Skeeter Jackson!"

His grin widened. "No. But I thought it, to give myself the nerve to try pole-vaulting out. And look at us, now; we're alive and we're free. Let's keep it that way, if it's all right by you."

Dark emotion bubbled up in Marcus' eyes again. "It is very much all right by me."

"Good. I think I see an inn up ahead. Know anything about it?"

Marcus peered through the crowd. "No. But this is a good part of town. It should be safe enough and serve food worth eating."

"Sounds good to me." He chuckled. "Nothing like that proverbial purloined letter."

"The *what*?"

"A story I read once. Sherlock Holmes. Best place to hide something is right out in the open, where nobody expects to find it."

Marcus laughed, not from mirth but from sheer amazement. "Skeeter Jackson, you astonish me more and more the longer I know you."

Skeeter rubbed the side of his nose, feeling heat creep into his face. "Yeah, well, I've had an interesting sorta life. I'd about ten times rather have a great wife and a couple of kids, right about now. Hell, I'd settle for a friend." Marcus cast a glance in his direction, but didn't speak. Skeeter felt the silence like a punch to his gut. He dragged in a deep breath, even *that* hurting, and muttered, "Okay, here we go. Your Latin's better than mine and something tells me rich guys don't do the dickering."

Marcus smiled. "You learn quickly. Keep closed your mouth and no one will be the wiser."

Skeeter grinned, then dutifully closed his mouth, shook loose some coins, and handed several of the silver ones over. "That be enough?"

"I'd say so. Now hush and let me play the hero this time."

They stepped into the cool quiet of the inn and met the bright smile of the proprietor. Marcus launched into Latin too rapid to follow, but it got results. They were taken to a private room and shortly were feasting on chilled wine, roasted duckling, and a pot of boiled beef and cabbage. Skeeter ate until he couldn't hold another bite.

"Gawd, that was heavenly."

Marcus wiped his mouth and nodded. "*Much* better than wheat gruel." He paused, then added awkwardly, "If—if you will take that tunic off, Skeeter, I will wash and bandage your injuries."

Skeeter didn't argue. His wounds stung and burned every time he moved in his stolen garments of wool. Marcus tore up some of the bedding and laved the long slice with clean water, then wound strips of cotton around Skeeter's torso. "There. That should keep the blood from seeping out and giving you away." He cautiously dabbed at the stains on the side of the tunic, which the long toga had hidden. Most of them came out with the application of cold water. Marcus finished that chore and hung up the tunic to dry, then cleared his throat. "If you will give me the sword, I will stand guard. You are exhausted, Skeeter. Sleep. Anyone looking for you will have to kill me."

Skeeter held his gaze for a moment and realized Marcus meant it. He didn't know what to say. Maybe . . . just maybe . . . all those prayers he'd uttered back at the start of the fighting had given him back not only his life, but a chance at winning back the friendship he'd so thoughtlessly shattered?

Because he couldn't have spoken to save his half-wild soul, Skeeter sank back on the denuded mattress without a single word and was asleep before Marcus had finished setting aside the dishes from their meal. His final thought was, *If I do have a second chance, don't let me screw it up. Please.*

Then all was silence and peaceful sleep while Marcus stood guard over him, placing his life between Skeeter and the door.

Goldie Morran spent an unhappy two weeks waiting with the rest of TT-86 for word of Skeeter Jackson. As she'd discovered already, she didn't want Skeeter dead. Kicked off the station had seemed like a grand idea, but now . . . all she could do was wonder what he was up to downtime. Rescuing Marcus? She snorted. Goldie really couldn't credit that, Dr. Mundy and vidcam evidence notwithstanding. A person could *always* interpret a bit of evidence ten different ways from Sunday. Besides, Skeeter was too much like Goldie to spend his time rescuing a worthless slave when he could be scamming so much gold down time, she'd never catch up. Of course, Brian might disallow it, on the grounds that the wager was on hold. Or—she shuddered delicately behind her cold, glasstop counters—that dratted librarian might just decide that since Skeeter would have had no way of *knowing* the wager was on hold, his earnings *would* count.

Curse the boy!

She was theoretically ahead, with more than half the bet's term left to run. If Skeeter returned.

What if Skeeter *never* returned? Some people thought Goldie was a heartless sociopath. She wasn't—although she put out considerable effort to seem that way. So if Skeeter Jackson, never mind that nice kid who tended bar at the Down Time never came back, she'd have their fates on her conscience.

And backstabbing cheat that she knew herself to be, that was something she knew she couldn't live with. *Please*, she whispered silently, *bring them back. I miss that obnoxious little bastard.* She was discovering she actually missed watching that boy con tourists out of cash, cameras, wristwatches, wallets, and anything else he could lift to turn a buck. She even missed the arguments over whiskey and beer at the Down Time while tourists who wandered in watched, goggle-eyed. . . . *I miss them. Bring them back, please. Whatever I felt before, I never meant for this to happen.*

Goldie didn't realize she was crying until the tears dripped with a soft splash onto her glass counter. When she sniffed and looked around to find a handkerchief, she found a young Asian woman she'd never laid eyes on standing in front of her counter. The girl offered a clean, beautifully embroidered handkerchief.

"Here, Miss Morran, you are hurting. You have much to be sorry for, but we understand."

Without another word, she slipped out of Goldie's shop, moving with the unobtrusive grace of a girl trained in one of the finest geisha houses in Japan. Goldie stared at the embroidered handkerchief, stared at the doorway, then very slowly dried her face and blew her nose. It wasn't easy, facing the fact that if those two boys didn't return, it would be largely her fault.

"All I ask," Goldie muttered, blowing her nose miserably again, "is a chance to tell that miserable, thieving, no-good cheat that I'm sorry—to his face."

A tiny whisper at the back of her mind warned her to be wary of what one asked the gods for, lest they grant it.

Just where was Skeeter Jackson? And what the living hell *was he doing down there in ancient Rome? Playing hero? Or playing the cad?* She hoped she'd have the chance to find out which.

Goldie sniffed one last time and wadded up the exquisite handkerchief until her hand hurt.

"Come back, damn you!"

Only the chill of her glass cases, filled with cold, rare coins, cool, smooth miniature sculptures in precious stones, and the frozen glitter of a few scattered jewels on shivering velvet heard.

Chapter 19

For the remainder of their stay in Denver, the man calling himself Chuck Farley spent his time visiting one cathouse after another. Margo wrinkled her nose as they watched quietly in the darkness while he entered yet another establishment of ill repute.

"I hope he catches something really nasty!"

"He might, at that," Malcolm muttered. "He's doubtless been inoculated, because smallpox is still rampant in these parts, but he might catch a social disease and be put into quarantine. Dr. Eisenstein could either heal it or recommend permanent quarantine. Up time, too; Rachel Eisenstein takes her job very seriously, she does. She wants to ensure diseases like that don't get passed on to anyone in the real world." A bitter chuckle issued near her ear. "He would certainly deserve it. But it's more likely he's gathering additional inventory."

"To make up for the pieces that didn't come through the gate with him?"

"Exactly."

Margo flounced as only Margo could do while standing perfectly still. Her dress rustled like wind through aspens at her movement. "He's disgusting," she muttered under her breath. "And he doesn't look or act rich enough to keep those for himself. Wonder who his uptime buyer is?"

Malcolm stared at her with considerable surprise. He hadn't

expected her to pick up on that part of it so fast. But there *were* up-time billionaires who paid agents to loot the past for their collections. A tiny number of the agents moving down time then up time again had been caught, their stolen antiquities confiscated and turned over to IFARTS for evaluation and return down time. Disgusting was far too mild a word for the kind of man who'd pay others to take the risks, do the legwork—the dirty, often lethal work. The payoff from the actual client would, of course, be only a fraction of what the antiquities were worth, but enough to keep them busily moving back and forth time and again, to steal even more artwork.

Malcolm glanced at Margo and realized, she'd like to do murder when Farley exited the house. And with the gun concealed in her fur muff, she probably could have drilled him through whichever eye she chose. As though following his thoughts, she glared at the cathouse Farley had entered. He half expected a Margo-style explosion or an outright attack murderous with pent-up emotion, but all she said was, "Creeps."

The deep silence of the late Denver night was shattered abruptly by the rumbling, squeaking, and groaning Conestoga wagons—a long line of them—which began forming up nose-to-tail on a long, dirt road that led southeastward out of town. "Malcolm," she whispered, "is that what I think it is? A real, honest-to-goodness wagon train?"

With the ease of long practice, Malcolm shifted into his Denver persona.

"Yeah, I s'pect so, ma'am. Lots of prairie schooners in that train."

Malcolm's uncanny ability to mimic local languages, even dialects, always amazed Margo. It was his way of reminding Margo that she, too, would have to master the knack.

"But I thought all the wagon trains were a thing of the past? I mean, I read somewhere that the whole continent had been settled by 1885 or so."

Malcolm shook his head. "Nope. With book learnin' you has to go deep to ferret out truth. Lemme 'splain somethin', ma'am. This here city o' Denver weren't nothin' more'n paper plans, laid out nice and neat, back in '59. Then along comes the Pike's Peak rush—over what?"

Margo's brow furrowed delightfully. Then her whole face lit with an incandescent glow. "Gold! The '59 Gold Rush."

Malcolm chuckled. "Very good. 'Cept nobody could find any. Miners called it the biggest humbug in all history, they did, and left in disgust. But the experienced men, now, the ones who'd sluiced and dug out the big Georgia and California motherlodes, they stayed on. Saw the same signs, they did, same as the signs they'd noticed before. So they stayed on and come late '59 and into '60, made the really big strikes. Caused another rush, o'course," he chuckled.

"Yes, but what's that got to do with that?" She pointed toward the wagons.

"W-e-e-l-l-l, that's another story, now, ain't it? There's still odd bits and pieces o' land rattling around this big country, pieces that're still unclaimed for homesteadin'." He lowered his voice to a nearly inaudible murmur. He whispered into her ear, "In fact, four times as many acres were homesteaded after 1890 than before it, but you'd never guess it from period attitudes about land. It borders on sacredness." Then at a slightly higher volume and a more discreet distance, he said, "Take careful note 'o what those wagons is carryin'. And what they ain't."

Another lesson, even during the very serious duty of watching for slug-like Farley? Malcolm Moore was always so sure of himself, yet so gentle compared to the men in her old life. She studied each wagon in turn, trying to ignore weird shadows thrown against the canvas tops as those departing checked over their equipment. She saw the usual rifles and pistols, bandoliers and boxes of ammunition to hunt game for the table, dozens of tools whose use Margo could only guess at, and a few rough-hewn bits of furniture.

"No women's things," Margo said abruptly. "No trunks for clothing or quilts, no butter churns, no barrels of padded china from back East. And no children. Those men aren't married. No farming equipment, either, and no livestock except the oxen and horses pulling those wagons. Not even a single laying hen—and you can hear them clucking a fair distance away. And believe me, they cluck *loud* when they're upset. Do *you* hear any chickens?"

Malcolm shook his head solemnly.

"No, me neither."

"Very nice, indeed," Malcolm purred. "You've a good eye—and ear—for detail. Now just keep up with the bookwork and you'll make one damned fine time scout."

Margo's fierce blush was, thank God, hidden by the dark night.

"Those," Malcolm continued very quietly, "are hardened frontiersmen, always on the move. They follow the remnants of the buffalo herds for their hides, which are commanding good prices again, now that there are so few buffalo left. They follow hints and whispers of gold found on this creek or that. Or they work for hire as ranch hands, even drovers, although that profession is just about as extinct as the poor buffalo. Now that bunch," he turned Margo's head toward the front wagon in the caravan, "is bound for the Indian Territory, or my name isn't Malcolm Moore."

"Indian Territory?" Margo echoed.

"Later renamed several things, but Oklahoma was generally mixed in there somewhere. Right now men are streaming in by the hundreds to support David Payne, a cutthroat frontiersman leading a band of even more violent frontiersman in a war against the Indians given that land, even against the Federal Government."

"Your accent's slipping,"

"Right you are, ma'am, and thank you it is for the reminder."

"So," Margo concentrated, her brow deeply furrowed as she thought it through, "these men are going to stir up Indian tribes by taking part of their land illegally?"

"Yep. Worse trouble'n anybody thought they'd stir up. But the whole country's clamorin' to kick out the 'savages' and open up Oklahoma for 'decent' folk to settle."

Margo shivered, watching these men pack away their clothes, excess weapons, and whatever they considered valuable enough to take along. The rest, they abandoned along the road, in bundles and boxes, for anyone to salvage. "The more I learn about history, the more savage I find it was. These men are going out to murder as many Indians as they can get into their goddamned sights, aren't they?"

"My dear lady, you shock me! Such language!"

It was a gentle reprimand, with a steel-hard warning behind it.

Ladies of quality did *not* curse like sailors in 1885, not even on the Frontier. Of course, barmaids and whores could be expected to say anything and everything . . . but Margo did most emphatically not wish to be associated with them.

Not Minnesota prudishness this time—she'd lost a lot of that on a beach in Southeastern Africa—but a cold, calculated decision in the direction of survival. Time scouts, as her grandfather Kit Carson put it, had to be bloody careful anywhere down time. Especially if scouting an unknown gate. Shaking inside her frontier, multi-button, impossible-to-fasten boots (until Malcolm, shaking with silent laughter, handed her a button hook and explained its use), Margo recalled her formidable but lonely grandfather, a man who'd stepped through a gate to rescue her, not knowing if he'd survive the trip to the other side; then glared at the men in those murder-wagons, at the ones standing outside in little knots, smoking some kind of foul-smelling cigars, their boasts of killing no-account Indians like it was some insane game where they tallied score by the number of people they butchered.

Not that she thought the Indians shoved into that Oklahoma Reservation to be the peaceful, nature revering, squeaky clean role-models the TV ads and movies made them out to be. She'd read with a clinical, removed-from-the-dreadful-scenes detachment as her only defense against descriptions of massacres perpetrated by desperate and enraged young warriors, young men with their blood up, refusing to give up either tribal or manly pride. *Pride!* How much trouble that one little word had caused the world . . . That was new—these insights and connections she'd begun making about all kinds of subjects, to the everlasting astonishment of her professors and the steady rise of her GPA.

She slitted her eyes slightly against the sting of wind-borne cigar smoke, thinking it all through as carefully and thoroughly as possible—as Kit and Malcolm had jointly taught her to do. No, the Native American tribes hadn't been peaceful nature lovers at all, even before the coming of Europeans; before that momentous date, they'd made war on one another in just as savage a fashion as they later made war against the pale invaders of their continent. But what the

American government had later done to these people was hideous, unforgivable.

Margo liked getting her facts straight, more and more so the longer she was in college, delving through books she had once abhorred, so she could *understand* the real message behind admittedly biased writing on Native American Indians—contemporary accounts by trappers, traders, settlers, mountain men—as well as modern scholarly research-hero-worship crap about people who—according to several archaeological site analyses written by the archaeologists themselves—tossed their meal scraps right out of the tepee's front door for weeks, maybe even months on end (at least, that was true of some of the plains tribes, well before the arrival of the European); people who thought nothing of making their immediate surroundings a latrine/cesspit and thought their women attractive in hair dressed in bear grease applied six months previously. Margo shuddered delicately.

Ultimately, what she had found were two differing stories of two very different peoples, each savage in their own way. Who was to say which was worse? Warriors taking scalps as trophies of victory or men who calmly plotted the obliteration of entire tribes. She finally managed to choke out, "Will they give a damn about shooting women and children, too?" And this time, notably, she received no scolding for her anachronistic manners.

After a look of pain passed through Malcolm's expressive eyes, he said very quietly, "W-e-e-l-l-l, not really. Least, not everywhere. But yeah, ma'am, it happens, here 'n there, all across the whole land. They say the first known record of biological warfare was takin' a load of blankets from a smallpox victim still aboard ship and delib'retly handin' 'em over to a tribe of six-foot Indians down in Florida, men who could put a long, heavy arrow through a man's leg, his horse, and mebbe catch his other leg on the way out again."

Margo nodded silently, letting him know she'd read about that already. "Now, these men," he nodded toward the wagoneers, "they're a tough bunch o' claim-jumping cutthroats with one aim in mind. They'll settle down in parts of the Oklahoma Reservation that don't no one tribe actually own, massacre a bunch from one tribe, just so's another would go on the warpath. Not just for revenge for a fellow tribe. Hell, the poor bastards just figure they're next, anyway, and who wants to be shot in bed, like a fat, lazy cow waitin to be milked?

"It's been gettin' so bad, Fed'ral troopers have done come in to stop it all and toss the Boomers, as they style themselves, out o' Indian land. But shucks, there's always ten, twelve men waiting to replace every corpse or kickin', cursing Boomer tossed out or arrested. That's decent farmland, compared to what was left everywhere else at a cheap price. What them men wanted was decent, *cheap* land to homestead. And the only place left to get it was in Indian land, see? Hell, ma'am, and 'scuse the language, but some o' them Boomers mean to have as much as they can beg, borrow, or steal by murderin' whoever's already there that ain't got a white hide. It's a dirty, rotten land-grab of a business, played like some damned child's game, only a long-sight bloodier."

"And there's nothing we can do to stop it?"

A sigh gusted past her ear. "Nope. Not a goddamned, helpless thing. History cain't be changed. One of the first rules of time travel, and you should know 'em all by heart now."

Margo's sigh echoed Malcolm's. "Rule One: Thou shalt not profit from history nor willfully bring any biological specimens—including down-timer human beings—into a time terminal. Rule Two: Do not attempt to change history—you can't, but you *can* get killed trying it." She halted the rendition of "The Rules" to glare at the wagons. "Too bad. I'm a pretty good shot, these days."

Malcolm, who'd witnessed her performance in the "Lesson for a Few Rattled Paleontologists," silently agreed. "Quite a good one, in fact, at least with modern cartridge guns and most of the black-powder stuff. But we're not here to stop Indian wars. We're here to track Chuck Farley's movements and discover what disguise he'll wear back up time to the station. Believe me, if it would do any good, Margo, I'd shoot every one of those mother's sons and leave 'em to bleed into the dirt.

"But," and he placed warm hands on her shoulders, which tingled at the contact through thin cotton calico, "that wouldn't stop the massacres of hundred of millions of innocents since the beginning of human existence, now, would it?" Margo shook her head, trying to hide the grief in her eyes, none too successfully given the look on Malcolm's face. "We can't, Margo. We simply cannot change it. Something *will always go wrong*, leaving you in the delicate position of run like hell or be painfully shot/stabbed/sliced/burned/scalped/or done in through other, even more gruesome methods. Can you really imagine me just popping in to visit the Pope and saying, 'Hey, I'm an angel of death. God's really pissed over your little crusade against the heretics in France. Ever hear of a thing called Black Death? It's the prize your butchers have earned for themselves.' Or maybe I could wait a few years, let Temujin grow up a good bit, then show up at his yurt one fine evening and change his mind about slaughtering half the population of Asia and Europe." He snorted. "Rotten as he is, if you ever get the chance, ask Skeeter Jackson sometime about that."

Margo blinked, surprised. "Skeeter? He spent time with Temujin?" Then, as no answer was forthcoming, she swallowed a little too hard. "I know nothing important can be changed. It's just so . . . hard." She thought about a certain, terrible fight with this man who wanted to spend the rest of his life with her, thought about a dingy London street that bordered the true, deadly slums where her ignorance had nearly gotten them both killed, and fought a lump in her throat.

"Malcolm?" Her voice was whispery and unsteady as she reached for his hand in the darkness. The security of his strong hand wrapping around hers gave her courage again.

"Yes?" he asked, quite seriously.

"Why is it that whenever I go down time with you, thinking it'll be a special treat, I end up seeing so much misery?"

Malcolm didn't speak for quite a while. Then he said, "It's just like that bloody wretched day in London, isn't it?"

Margo nodded. "Yes. But only worse, because some of these people have no hope. That's what's going to give me nightmares."

Malcolm squeezed her hand gently. "It's a rare scout who doesn't suffer damned *terrifying* nightmares." Margo, recalling those her grandfather had suffered, simply murmured agreement. "And," he said more gently than before, "it's a very rare man *or* woman who sees past the glitter and romance to the scalded hands of Chinese coolies washing clothing for others.

"It takes . . . I don't know . . . *heart*, something truly alive inside, to possess the wit and courage to grieve for victims of the world's great migrations, to see the scars of rejection in their eyes and hearts. A Chinese, an Indian, a Brit, all of them see the world through vastly different eyes. Do they see the same things? Mere facets of the whole? Or something else entirely? Classic case of the blind men and the elephant." He sighed. "I don't have the answers to that, Margo. But finding them out . . . together . . . is as good a lifetime's work as any I can think of."

Margo squeezed his hand, glad of the deep shadows. She didn't want him to discover the tears on her face. She swallowed hard to avoid snuffling the mess in her nose and sinuses.

"How *do* they manage to make this—" she gestured around them "—so confounding *dull* in school when it's so absorbingly human, so marvelously, tragically interwoven, it makes me ache and want to cheer at the same time?"

Malcolm's only answer was a long, desperate kiss that somehow conveyed the fear that he would lose her to someone else, someone who outshone him, had more money than he did, or an estate and noble lineage longer than many a champion horse's, to a man who was younger and more attractive than he was, or had ever hoped to be. In answer, she crushed herself against him, returning the kiss with such fervor, holding him so tightly that for a moment she thought he meant to join with her right then and there. But being British in his soul, a tumble in the weeds along a dirty Denver roadside was *not* seemly—and it was *her* reputation he so carefully guarded.

"Oh, Malcolm," she sighed against his lips, "my beloved, my silly, insecure Malcolm. Do you honestly think any other man could take the place of a certain person I know who sold eel pies and green glop along the streets of Whitechapel, saving my idiotic life in the process? I almost got us both killed because I hadn't studied enough, hadn't learned my shooting lessons properly, not to mention my sense of when to strike and when to just give 'em what they want. I nearly got us both killed!" She crushed him close. "Don't *ever* let me go, Malcolm! Whatever my role down time as a scout turns out to be, even if it's a skinny boy—"

"Hey, you're not skinny!"

Appreciative hands ran across curves until Margo flushed in the darkness. "It's all these wretched underthings and bustles and gewgaws that make me look fat. Playing the role of a young boy is *much* more comfortable. No bustles, no corset stays, no drawers, no layers of camisoles and underskirts and no final dress which I have to be literally wedged and *cinched* into just to avoid being called a loose woman—and pursued as such."

"Mmm . . . sounds like romantic illusion number twenty-seven hitting the ground and shattering into zillions of pieces."

"That's not funny!"

"I didn't mean it to be. It's just that being a guide is tough enough. Tackling the job of scout . . . that's scary, Margo. I almost panic when I think about watching you leave me, maybe never to return and I'll never know why or how you vanished from my life—"

"Then come with me."

Malcolm stiffened at her side, then covered her entire face in kisses, paying sweet attention to wet eyelashes and tender, trembling lips. "I've prayed you would ask me that. Yes, I'll go, when and wherever it is. I'll go."

During the clench and flurry of kisses and hasty promises on both sides, Margo's eyes widened. "Malcolm! It's Farley! Looks like you were right. New inventory."

Malcolm said something truly creative *and* extremely filthy, giving the lie to those brave words earlier about their mission being to follow Farley everywhere. He swore once more beneath his breath, then turned slightly in her arms as Farley left the brothel with a heavy leather satchel which bulged in odd places.

"You don't suppose he'll try to add it to the hole he's already dug and discover our tampering?"

Malcolm chuckled. "Nope. If we'd attempted to change history, something would have stopped us from carting off that prize of erotic loot. He'll make a second treasure hole, all right, near the first. We'll mark its position, then leave it for the up-time authorities as incriminating evidence in his arrest."

Margo grinned. "Malcolm Moore, have I ever said, 'I love you'? Your evil genius is beyond compare."

"Huh," Malcolm muttered, "just a few tricks and pointers I picked up from your grandfather."

She nuzzled his arm. "I like that. Hey, if we're going to follow that lout, we'd better get moving!"

They mounted up, Malcolm giving her a leg up, not because she needed it, but because it was what just about any man in this time period would have done. Cautiously they followed the lone rider into the darkness while shadows raced across a three-quarter moon, bringing with it the taste of ice and waist-deep snow in the high mountains above Denver on a chilly night sometime late in 1885.

It was a good night to be alive. If they hadn't been stalking a criminal to his hoard, Margo would have burst into exuberant song. Instead, she held rigidly quiet, as did the remarkable man at her side, both of them intent on the figure ahead, bathed in the faltering light of a cloud-cocooned moon.

Neither the Praetorian Guard nor the city's watch patrol found them. Skeeter's and Marcus' disguises were good—and no Roman would think to look for an escaped gladiator in the fine tunic and toga of a citizen, with his freedman accompanying him. But, just as a precaution, they changed inns often, paying for each night's lodging and meals with the dwindling amount of money Skeeter had picked up from the arena sands.

Late one night, the only time they risked speaking English, Marcus asked in a troubled voice, "Skeeter?"

"Mmm?"

"When you gave over your winnings to pay the debt I owed," his voice faltered a little, "all you had left was the coins you plucked from the sands. I have nothing. Do we have enough money to survive until the gate opens again?"

"Fair question," Skeeter answered. "I've been worrying about that a little, myself."

"May I make a suggestion?"

"Hey, it's me. Skeeter. You're not a slave, Marcus. If you wanna talk, I'll listen. If I'm bored, I'll probably fall asleep. Hell, I might, anyway. I'm bushed and my back and arm muscles are screaming bloody murder."

Marcus was silent for a moment. "That leap you made. I've never seen a thing like that, ever."

Skeeter snorted. "Obviously you've never seen a tape of the Summer Olympic Games. It was just a pole vault, after all. A little higher than most pole vaulters are used to, maybe, but then I had the added advantage of my horse's height. So enough. Wipe that worshipful look off your face and tell me what's on your mind."

"I—at the Neo Edo—what I said—"

Very quietly, Skeeter muttered, "I deserved every word, too. So don't go feeling bad about that, Marcus. God, I was stupid and selfish to fool you, to force you into a position where you had to decide between honor and your family." For a moment, neither man spoke. Then Skeeter continued, "Your village, the one in France, the men there must've taken honor very seriously if an eight-year-old boy who grew into a man as a Roman slave still puts honor ahead of everything."

Marcus took a long time answering. "I was wrong about that, Skeeter. Since the moment Farley tricked me back here and sold me to the arena master, I have discovered that such honor is cold and empty compared with protecting those of your own blood. I have hurt Ianira terribly, and my children . . ."

It took a moment to realize that Marcus was crying. "Hey. Hey, listen to me, Marcus. We all make mistakes. Even me."

That brought a watery snort of near-laughter.

"Point is, when you fall flat on your backside or put a new dent in your nose from smashing it into the ground, you learn something. From whatever stupid thing you've done wrong this time, file away the lesson learned as a warning against the same mistake, then just keep on going. I'd never have survived in Yesukai's camp if I hadn't been able to learn from the multi-bejillion mistakes I made there. You know, it's funny. I came to feel like that murderous old Yakka

Mongol was more of a father to me than my real one. Did I ever tell you he made me Temujin's uncle? Believe me, that's a helluva responsibility and honor in Mongol society: uncle to the Khan's first-born son. And you know, he was a decent little kid, toddling about the yurt, curling up to sleep against his mother, maybe begging "Uncle *Bogda*" to play with him. When I think what he went through as a teenager, what all that did to him, made him into, I sometimes just want to sit down and bawl, 'cause I can't change it."

Marcus' silence puzzled Skeeter. Then, "There is much hurt inside you, Skeeter, a very great much. One day you must let it out or you will never heal yourself."

"Hey, I thought Ianira was the mind-reading wizard of the family?"

Marcus' laugh was thin but genuine this time. "Amongst my people—my family—there were certain . . . talents that passed from generation to generation."

"Oh, God, please don't say you're psychic."

"No," Marcus said, the smile in his voice clear even to Skeeter. "But . . . you have never asked me about my family."

"Thought that was a bit too private, friend."

An indrawn hiss of breath was followed by Marcus' shaking voice. "You can still call me friend? After what I have done to you, can I still be your friend?"

"I dunno. Can you? I got no problem with it."

Dark silence passed. "Yes," Marcus said quietly. "Perhaps I am mad to say it, knowing what you are, but after what you sacrificed to wrench me out of slavery . . . I seldom know what to think about you any longer, Skeeter. You steal from good, ordinary people to make your living, yet you give part of your stolen money to The Found Ones to help us stay active—"

"How'd you find that out?" Skeeter demanded, voice breathless.

Marcus laughed quietly. "You are so certain of your privacy, Skeeter. The Found Ones have many ways to find out things we desperately need to know. In one such search, it became clear to us where some of the money was coming from."

"Oh." Then, "Well, I hope my goddamned ill-gotten gains

helped." He turned on the hard bed and groaned as aching muscles sharply called attention to themselves from his shoulders to his thighs and from his biceps down to his wrists.

A stirring of the darkness gave him scant warning. Then, when hands touched his naked shoulder in the darkness, panic hit. "Marcus, what are you doing?" The other man was kneading his sore shoulders as though they were bread dough.

"I am doing what I was trained to do from boyhood. To give my master soothing back- or shoulder- or foot-and-leg rubs when he requested them. Just lie still, Skeeter. I'll work through your tunic cloth, since you do not have the mindset—that is the right word?—of a Roman. Your privacy is a dark shroud you pull about yourself. That is your choice; every man needs his privacy intact."

A certain darkness in Marcus' voice connected quite abruptly with other things he'd said on occasion, leaving the truth about Marcus' boyhood lit by a scathing spotlight. He knew; but he found he had to confirm it to *believe* it. "Marcus?"

"Yes, Skeeter? What is wrong? I have hurt your shoulder?"

"No. No, that's fine. Feels like maybe I'll be able to move it tomorrow after all."

"It would be better with liniment, but we have no coin to buy it."

"Marcus, would you please shut up? I have something really important to ask. You don't have to answer; but I have to ask it. Your old master, the one before that bastard Farley dragged you through the Porta Romae . . . when you gave him rubdowns like this, did he request—order—other things as well?"

The sudden stillness of the hands on his shoulder and the utter silence, broken only by rattling breaths, gave Skeeter all the answer he needed.

Surprisingly enough, Marcus answered anyway, in a whisper torn from a proud man's soul, leaving it filled with nothing but pain and fear. "Yes. Yes, he did, Skeeter. He was . . . not the first."

Skeeter blurted out, "He wasn't? Then who the hell *did* rape you first?"

Marcus' stilled hands on his shoulder flinched badly. "A man. I never knew his name. It was on the slave ship. He was the first."

It hit Skeeter harder than most, for he'd seen prisoners of the Mongols buggered before being split open from throat to genitals and left to bleed out. "My *God*, Marcus! How can you even bear to touch another person? To father children, to give my aching muscles the rubbing they need. I mean, the rubbing they want?"

He said simply, "Because for whatever foolish reason, I have come to trust you again, Skeeter. My life is literally in your hands. If we are caught, they will take *you* back to the gladiatorial school. You have become famous in the Circus, so you are valuable. I am only a scribe. I've grown too old for the other, thank all gods and goddesses, but even as a scribe, I am worth little compared to you. If we are caught, our faces will be branded with the *F* of a fugitive. That's all that will happen to me, if I'm lucky. My so-called master could well cripple me to keep me from running again, or turn me over to the state for execution, or sell me to the bestiary masters, to be torn apart by ravening wild animals." He drew a deep breath. "So, I stay with you, Skeeter, as my only hope of survival until the gate opens. And . . . I wish to ease your pain because you *are* my friend, and you acquired that pain saving *me* from the arena master's ownership. *I* knew that was wrong, but not another man in Rome would have questioned it, never mind defended me."

"Hey, I wasn't just helping you. As I recall, I had some pretty selfish reasons to get the hell out of that arena, too, you know."

"Yes, but . . ." He gave up with a sigh, and said instead, "What I said at the Neo Edo, Skeeter . . . I had no right to say it. Any of it. The truth of what happened between you and Lupus Mortiferus I will never know, for I was not present, and I know now the kind of professional killer he is. So . . . who am I to judge?"

"Huh." Skeeter remained silent a moment. "Well, just to set the record straight," he couldn't keep a bitter hoarseness from creeping into his voice as, for once, he told the gods' own truth about what he had done, "I swindled and pickpocketed every bit of the money I brought back from that profitable little trip. Right down to the little copper *asses* and their fractions."

Marcus was silent a long time, kneading muscles along Skeeter's back until they felt like pudding.

"There are many ways of growing up, Skeeter, and I have no right to judge when I, of all people, know your truth—the way *you* were brought up. Your childhood, Skeeter, was far worse than mine."

"*Huh?* How the hell do you figure that—?"

Marcus wasn't listening. He gave out a little, wan laugh just this side of anguish. "Believe me, Skeeter, when I say mine was hell. But yours was far worse. I was every kind of fool for judging you so cruelly."

"The hell you were." Silence fell between them, both of them stilled to the point that the sound of an unknown voice outside their hideaway would have drawn indrawn, ragged screams from them both. Skeeter finally broke the silence with a sigh. "No judging, huh? Is that how your Found Ones operate their business?"

"First," Marcus dug into a muscle under Skeeter's shoulder blade with enough force to wring a yelp of pain from him, "we are not a 'business.' We are a survival necessity for those of us ripped from time and left stranded at TT-86. We serve as what Buddy would call a 'support group.' And we have to accommodate the religious and political beliefs of many, many differing times and nations and kinds of men and women. It is not easy to be a leader of that group."

"And you are?"

"*Me?*" Honest shock filled his voice. "Great Gods, no! I am neither talented nor patient enough for such demands." A brief pause. "I *did* say that the right way, did I not? It is 'either/or' and 'neither/nor' is it not?"

Skeeter knew far better than to chuckle. Marcus was a man with little but battered pride left and Skeeter didn't want to make more mistakes than he felt he already had. "Yes," he said quietly, "you got it right, Marcus. But if you're not a leader, who is? You've adapted better than almost anyone else, you're smart and driven to improve yourself—"

"Skeeter! Please . . . it is some other man you must be speaking of, not I." He drew a deep breath and let it out. "It is Ianira who leads us, with a few others who take responsibility for certain tasks. Things like making sure no down-timer goes hungry." He chuckled, then, clearly over his embarrassment. "Do you have any idea how long it took to convince Kynan Rhys Gower that we were not devil-worshippers damned for all time? Yet now he comes to our meetings and speaks up with ideas that are good."

"Humph. I didn't know you were that organized, or even if you *were* organized, but I figured you needed help. I gamble away most of my money, anyway, you know, a habit I picked up in Yesukai's yurt, so I just take some out first and send it to you, so I can tell myself I'd done *something* decent as judged by *this* world."

His voice caught slightly on the word. Surprising himself immensely, he found himself saying, "Do you have any idea how *my* two worlds tug at me? Some days . . . some days they come near to ripping me apart. In my most secret heart, I still yearn for the honor of riding on raids as a Yakka warrior. But I *lived* in the squalor and deadly dangers under which they live, Marcus—lived in it for five years. It is a perilous life, usually brutally short; yet I still want it. And another part of me is pulled the other way, into the now in which I was born. The now where I hated my father so much for not caring, that I became an accomplished thief and swindler by the age of eight. In that same heart, I know Yesukai would have been proud of me, these past years. But here I am tolerated only because I don't steal from 'eighty-sixers. They don't seem *ever* to understand they're the only family I have left." It was Skeeter's turn to suffer hot, stinging eyes. "What you said, about my lying to myself? Maybe you were right. I just don't know, any more."

Marcus said nothing, just moved magical hands down his spine, kneading burning muscles as he went. "Those were harsh words, I know," Marcus finally said, "and I am sorry I said them the way I did. But I worry about you, Skeeter. If you are caught often enough, Bull Morgan will have you sent up time for trial and I would lose a friend . . . and not merely a dear friend, but also a Lost One."

Skeeter, puzzled, stopped feeling sorry for himself long enough to ask, "Lost one? That's silly, when you know my apartment number, my phone number—"

"No, Skeeter, you do not understand. A Lost One is a down-timer in need of help, but from fear or terror of being discovered, disguises himself or hides until starvation drives him to action. Until we find them, we cannot help. They are lost to us, to the whole universe, until they make themselves known. And even then, it may take weeks, months, sometimes years before such a one trusts us enough to become a Found One.

"You remember, Skeeter, the Welshman I spoke of, Kynan Rhys Gower? He was such a one. *Weeks* it took to convince him we were not after his soul. Fortunately, one of us was a Christian—an early Christian, true, who had come through the Porta Romae—but he managed to convince Kynan that it would be safe—no, that it would be God's will—to join us." Marcus sighed. "It always brings great pain to know there is a Lost One amongst us and be unable to reach him, through word or action."

Vast astonishment like light pouring into his soul, drove away the vestiges of lingering self-pity. "Are you talking about *me*, Marcus?"

The answer was very soft in the darkness. "Who else?"

It was too much to take in that fast, all at once. Retreat was literally the only course he could take in that moment. "Huh. Well, thanks for the backrub, anyway. I don't think I could move now if I had to. Felt good, Marcus. I'm glad you're my friend again. It gets awful lonely when a man loses his only friend."

And with that statement, he drifted to sleep.

Marcus sat up in his own bedding for a long time, gazing blindly in the direction of Skeeter's sleeping breaths. *At least he is willing to become a friend again.* Marcus was struck with such pain he could scarcely breathe. The words " . . . only friend" kept battering at him. He didn't know quite how, but if they did manage to get back through the Porta Romae, Marcus would do everything in his power to give Skeeter more than one friend in the world. He swallowed hard, recalling the terms of the wager with Goldie Morran. They might step through to find Goldie declared the winner in the face of Skeeter's long absence. To go through what Skeeter had gone through already and then be thrown off the station, bag and baggage . . . it was simply not to be borne. Should that happen, Marcus and the other downtimers would make *very* certain that Goldie lost her entire business and was driven, bankrupted, back up time to the world

Marcus would never know first-hand. Somehow, the Council of Found Ones (a very great many of whom were capable of very long-lived blood wars, indeed) would find a way.

Marcus smiled bitterly in the darkness. Very few up-timers took *any* down-timer seriously. Tourists considered them unmannered savages with just brains enough to carry luggage through the time gates. Up-timers didn't even seem to mind that more than a few had vanished through shadowing themselves because no one had thought to warn them of the danger. Time Tours. took great measures to protect their customers, but no measures at all to protect the men who hauled baggage for them.

Such up-timers were in for a rude shock, very soon, if Marcus had anything to say about it.

If he and Skeeter got back safely through the gate.

If . . .

Well, he told himself prosaically, *there is not a thing you can do stuck in this inn, waiting for the Porta Romae to cycle. Better get some sleep while you can. Tomorrow may find us in the hands of the slave-catchers, or worse, the Praetorian Guard.* He shivered involuntarily, having heard the tales of what happened to runaways caught by the elite Praetorians. Marcus settled down in his hard bedding—far superior, of course, to the slave cots he'd grown reaccustomed to, but a miserable bed, indeed, compared to the wonderful one in his apartment on TT-86, where Ianira waited with no word of his fate.

Marcus drifted into sleep planning his reunion with his family and plotting either Skeeter's salvation or Goldie's ruin.

One or the other would come to pass as surely as the sun rose and set on a blazing hot Roman day or a crisp and lovely one in Gaul.

One or the other . . .

Marcus finally slept.

When the Wild West Gate dilated open at the back of a Time Tours livery stable, Malcolm and Margo stumbled under the weight of their luggage. Both had managed to get digitized video of Farley burying his Denver haul on their scouting logs. Farley had, as predicted, chosen a site just a few yards away from the original site they'd already dug up and camouflaged. They shot more video with their scout logs when Farley emerged from his hotel sporting blond hair going grey at the temples, a different nose, and an enormous moustache which matched the color of his hair. He carried with him almost no baggage at all.

If they hadn't been tailing him for a week, neither would have known him. This guy was *good.* Too good. A whole lot of up-time money had to be paying for a professional of this caliber. Farley stepped through the Wild West Gate ahead of them, a new man (doubtless with new ID forged to perfection in New York, right down to the retinal scans and med records). Fortunately for Malcolm and Margo, he did not suspect a thing was amiss, even though Malcolm staggered under the weight of the fortune in antiquities they had so carefully unearthed. Margo was having an even worse time. She stumbled and staggered like a teenager who'd drunk one too many beers. Margo was stone cold sober, but even her luggage was enormously heavy, despite the fact that Malcolm had packed the heaviest items in his own bags.

Mike Benson, Chief of Station Security, was nearby, scrutinizing returning tourists when they emerged, clearly watching for any signs of illegal activities. Someone must've tipped him off. Goldie? Couldn't have been Skeeter—he'd been gone nearly a month, now. When Benson caught sight of them, his eyes widened, then narrowed again into angry slits.

"Mike!" Malcolm hissed, aware that Farley was still near enough to hear. "Need your help! *Official* help."

Benson, whose biggest excitement came when an unstable gate broke open inside the station, or when kids left behind with the station's babysitter got loose and went on a rampage, clearly recognized An Important Event about to unfold. His expression moved through vast, sudden relief to deep curiosity and a cold anger that built in his eyes. He motioned curtly for Kit Carson, who'd come to see his granddaughter and almost grandson-in-law return. Kit was looking puzzled, as well, and murmured in Mike's ear. The relief on *Kit's* face was actually comical. Both men waited until they'd descended the ramp all the way, passing their timecards through the automatic reader at the bottom of the ramp, to be updated in a Time Tours effort to keep its customers from shadowing themselves.

"What is it?" Benson asked quietly.

"See that guy up there, greying blond hair, protruding nose, huge moustache?"

Benson squinted through the crowd. "Yeah, I've got him. What's so special about him?"

Kit put in quietly, "If I'm not mistaken we've just seen Chuck Farley in a new face."

Benson glanced sharply at Kit, eyes a bit wide, then nodded abruptly. "Yeah, I expect you're right."

Kit laughed quietly, puzzled eyes still studying their massively heavy luggage. "Mike, you should know by now, I am *always* right." He let that sink in, then forestalled any outburst by adding, "Unless I'm wrong, of course. That's actually happened, oh, eight or nine times, and most of them"—he tickled Margo's chin "were over this little fire-eater."

Margo blushed to the roots of her hair.

Malcolm broke through their levity with a low-voiced, "Mike, I really think you should have someone tail him until Primary cycles, but not so close that he bolts the second he's gone through."

Mike nodded. "My men are very, very good. Most of 'em got dumped on the street after The Accident when the DEA was torn down and its employees let go. They're good, Malcolm."

He nodded his trusting acquiescence. "I've got this plan, you see, Mike, to catch a member of that gang of notorious 'antiquities acquisition specialists.' A really slick one. We'd appreciate your escort to the IFARTS office. We'll tell you the entire story there."

Kit put in wistfully, "I know this is police business, but could I come, too? After all, my only relative *is* involved."

Mike Benson snorted. "Kit Carson, you could wheedle your way into Buckingham Palace."

Kit laughed. "I already have, Mike. *Long* story." His eyes twinkled.

"Oh, you're impossible. Suit yourself. Hell, you probably know almost as much about antiquities as Robert Li does."

With that, Benson plucked off his belt the in-station radio unit all TT-86 security wore and efficiently set up the undercover tail.

"There. Now lets go find Li, shall we?"

They started toward Robert Li's antiquities shop, which also served as the IFARTS office in La-La Land. Every station had an IFARTS facility, staffed by at least one thoroughly trained expert, and sometimes more than one for the really *big* stations with twenty or thirty active gates. Since carbon dating was now useless, experts had to be relied upon to judge fake from genuine, to assign an approximate date as well as detailed descriptions, photos, the whole bit. Mike noticed Margo's red-faced struggle with her baggage only a few feet closer to their goal. Evidently, so did Kit, because before Mike could call for a baggage cart, Kit took the heaviest bag, earning a dazzling smile from his granddaughter.

Mike sighed, jealous of Malcolm Moore because he'd found her first—and because Kit had asked him to help train her. Given the looks that passed between the two lovebirds, each was as smitten with the other just as surely as Goliath had been smitten by little David. He shook his head over mixed metaphors and quietly herded them toward the IFARTS office.

They were approximately a third of the way there when Kit changed the suitcase to his other hand—again. "Thundering—" Kit cut off the oath midsentence, shaking out his cramped hand. "What the living hell is *in* this thing? Solid gold?"

Margo grinned up at him. "Yep. Mostly. Our Mr. Farley had expensive if disgusting taste in collectibles."

Mike gave her a long, measuring look, but all she did was wink at him. *Damn* that lucky bastard, Moore. That one smile had seriously interfered with the transfer of oxygen-laden blood from his brain to a spot somewhat considerably lower. Grumbling, he grabbed one of Malcolm's bags to hide it, and actually staggered under the weight.

"Warned you," Malcolm laughed. "You're not gonna believe what that rat buried. And we even left the other motherlode intact, so up-time authorities can nail him digging it back up."

"That's . . . great . . . can we just . . . get a move on, please?"

In minutes, he was as red-faced as they were. Margo laughed, Kit chuckled, and Malcolm gave him that irritating smirk-smile that was uniquely his own. From necessity, they stopped chatting and sped up. Thank God. He wasn't as young as he'd once been and the strain was telling in his heart-rate, painful spasms in arms, shoulders, and bone-deep pain down his back from an old gunshot wound sustained while still working as a cop. *This had better be worth it, Moore, or you're going to find yourself in deep, deep trouble whenever I'm around.*

But when they opened the cases and spread the contents (except dirty clothes) across Robert Li's counter, Li gave out a strangled sound like a cat in orgasm; Kit Carson's eyes widened until his whole face was little more than luminous, shocked eyes; and Mike Benson forgave Malcolm with a low whistle. He glanced from one glittering figurine to the next, open-mouthed, unable to believe *he* had a chance to catch an international thief of this magnitude.

Malcolm explained their whole story, recording it on his guide/scout's log, then sighed and added, "He was really angry that some of the pieces had vanished, obviously because the gold on them or in them was destined for something important. He made quite a haul in Denver's cathouses, too, and buried that a few yards from the hole he'd dug for these." He gestured carelessly at what amounted to an entire room's worth of display cases in some museum that didn't mind putting erotic devices of antiquity on display.

"Well," Robert Li rubbed his hands in anticipation, "shall we begin?"

It took several hours, with Kit occasionally arguing over a date for some weird little piece made of gold or wood where gold inlay hadn't survived stepping through the Porta Romae. Malcolm drew up a stool and watched quietly. Margo leaned against the counter, chin resting on elbows, drinking in every word, every date assigned. She was charming, leaning there like that, still in her Denver getup, so absorbed in the cataloging he doubted she would hear her own name if he said it.

One by one the pieces were examined, determined genuine, and carefully packed away. Occasionally a piece wrung groans and exclamations from Robert Li—and a few times, even from Kit.

"My God, Kit, look at this! It's a solid gold herm, you won't believe the detailing! Look, there, at the back end. The face and attributes of Hermes himself, and look at the expression on his face!"

Kit took what looked like a slightly larger-than-lifesize phallus, turned it carefully in reverent hands, and held it up to the light. The beautiful art on what should have been the flat "base" was muttered over in tones of ecstasy. "I've read of pieces like this," Kit said with a low moan in his voice, "but to *hold* one . . ."

"Know what you mean," Robert said softly.

"The detailing is incredible. Lost wax?"

"Possibly. Or mold and the mold lines rubbed out."

Kit held it up to the bright light again. "No, I don't think so. That would leave marks and I don't see anything like that."

"Lost wax would leave similar marks," Robert mused. "How the hell did they do it?"

Surprisingly, Margo spoke up. "Well, maybe it's a real man's, uh, you know, dipped in gold after it had been severed."

All three men stared at her. Then Robert Li managed a strangled-sounding reply. "That's, uh, not a bad guess, Margo," he started, breaking off to cough and get his voice back under control, "particularly considering the detailed veins, ridges, and foreskin, but a phallus dipped in gold wouldn't be nearly as heavy as this. It's solid metal."

"A copy of the original palladium of Athens, perhaps?" Malcolm offered quietly. "I doubt Farley could wrest away the real one. After the Romans stole it, it was used in annual secret rituals which only the Pontifex Maximus was allowed to attend. But a copy, perhaps, carved from an ingot?"

"Carved from an ingot?" Robert echoed. Then, sudden realization hit. "Yes, that must be how it was done. Carve it from a solid piece, polish out any tool marks left over . . . my God, it must have taken a master artisan months to craft this!"

Kit was nodding agreement. He said, grinning slightly, "Sometimes we forget your doctorates, Malcolm."

He bowed slightly in acknowledgement of the compliment. Then said a bit smugly, "Apology accepted. And coming from *you*, Kit, any apology on professional matters is an honor to hold forever."

Kit flushed. "Huh. Ever since you got engaged, you've gone soft-headed and sentimental."

Malcolm just grinned, neither defending himself nor admitting guilt.

"Oh, you're impossible." Kit ignored him in favor of Robert Li. "Bob, do you have that phallus logged in?"

"Yes. And the next piece is . . ." He simply stopped talking. His gaze was rivetted to an exquisite little jade figurine.

Margo gasped. "Why, that's Kali-Ma, dancing on her dying consort, Shiva! But—they're deities of India. However did that little statue end up in Rome? And without breaking any of those delicate little pieces off?" The hands, the feet, the nearly translucent crown, were so fragile light poured through them as though the solid stone had gone transparent.

Kit said slowly, "There were some unsuccessful forays into India. An officer might have plundered it, wrapped it carefully, carried it on his person. Then again, by the time of Claudius there were some trade routes open to the East. Or a slave artisan might have carved it from memory. We'll probably never know."

With reverent hands, Robert Li lifted the little multi-armed, multi-legged dancer. "Flawless," he whispered. "Absolutely flawless." A low moan of pleasure escaped him as he turned it around and around in his hands, absorbing details with his dark, quick eyes, caressing it with trembling fingertips. "But why would a man who collected those," he gestured toward the small hoard of sexual implements, representations, and brothel art, "want *this*?"

Margo cleared her throat. "Well, the dance of Kali-Ma and Shiva *is* sexual in nature. Very much so. They dance the dance of life, meant to regenerate the entire universe each year. Shiva *has* to die, so his blood will fertilize Kali-Ma, impregnating her so she can give birth to his reincarnated self, plus all the grain crops, the fruits of the earth, the birds and game animals, the deadly snakes that could kill a man within three dizzy steps . . ." She trailed off, suddenly uncertain under the stares of all three men, each of whom was qualified at least five times more than she was.

Kit spoke first. "Margo, I see you *have* been hitting the books hard." He shook his head. He leaned across the corner of the cabinet and ruffled her hair playfully. "You done good, kid. *Real* good."

Margo's delighted grin brightened the room.

Robert Li smiled, too, then entered the Kali-Ma/Shiva statue into his computer, carefully wrapped it up, and—with a sigh—moved to the next piece.

Chapter 20

Dawn of Gate Day left Marcus and Skeeter in a tense sweat. They intended to remain in hiding until nearly ten-thirty that morning, since this was to be a daylight opening. No games, though, which meant Lupus Mortiferus—a man very much smarter than he looked—would be there in the crowds on the Via Appia.

"We'll *have* to watch out for him. He's got his life back," Skeeter groaned, "but I made a fool of him in sight of practically all Rome. Not to mention the Imperator, Claudius. He's going to want blood, and the more he gets, the more his reputation will be soothed. *If* that happens, blend in with the tourists, offer to carry baggage, anything—just get through that gate!"

"Without you?" Marcus asked in a low voice. "Without the man who has brought me safely this far? No, Skeeter, I cannot in good conscience leave you behind to die."

"You ever *see* Lupus play with his victims?"

Marcus' shudder was his answer.

"You break in, try to stop him from killing me, he'll tear you apart like kindling."

"So we must avoid his notice. Go through carefully, perhaps in disguise?"

Skeeter considered that. "Not a bad idea. With a quick expedition, I could acquire just the right costume for you. At the market," he added, seeing the stricken look on Marcus' face. "Now . . . I'm going to be a little trickier, since I don't have any of my makeup kit with me."

"Well, we could always ask the innkeeper to send for a barber. With a close shave and a few changes in costume, you could pass for an Egyptian merchant."

"Close shave, hmm. Just how close are we talking about?"

Marcus' face burned. "Well, Skeeter, you would need to, um, buy an Egyptian robe and neck collar—no Egyptian would be seen in public without one—and then, um . . ."

"Yes?" Skeeter, having guessed the reason for the barber and the stalling tactics. He just wanted it confirmed, so no misunderstandings loused up their chances.

Resignation darkening his eyes, Marcus met Skeeter's gaze. "You would need to shave your head bald."

"Bald," Skeeter echoed aloud, his guess confirmed, while to himself he thought, *Poor Marcus. He thinks I'll be shocked. He never saw me in Mongolia, thank all the gods of the air.* "Very well, I'll go and fetch what we need and when I come back, you can ask the innkeeper to send in a barber."

Marcus hesitated. "Can we afford this?"

Skeeter snorted. "We can't afford *not* to. Besides, I thought you knew. Several gold *aurii* were amongst the coins I scooped out of the sand on my victory lap. Quite a few silver *denarii* and *sestercii*, too. We can't afford to waste it, but these purchases are *necessary*."

Marcus nodded. Skeeter rose to his feet and squeezed Marcus' shoulder. "Lock the door, Marcus. If it won't lock, push a couple of chests in front of it, and pray Lupus doesn't trace us here. When I come back, if I say, 'The weather's going to change,' you'll know I'm being held hostage to catch the other runaway. Get out through that little back window, if you can."

Marcus glanced at it, nodded. He could probably squeeze through. He was no longer as thin as he'd been as a slave, but the time spent in the arena master's household had taken a few pounds off his frame. He could still taste the gruel that had been his only meal for so much of his life. "And if you are alone?"

"I won't say the code words." With that, Skeeter departed, leaving

Marcus to move furniture around with deep, scraping sounds and more than a few grunts.

Skeeter was genuinely in his element at the marketplace, an enormously long colonnaded building which sat right behind the wharves and warehouses along the river's edge, busy with the cargoes from ships that had sailed from gods-only-knew what part of the empire, only to unload at Ostia's deep-water harbor and send their goods upriver on heavy, shallow-water barges. It was just like a mall. He recalled it fondly from the trip here with the unfortunate Agnes. The roofed-over portico ensured a wild babble of voices rising to a roar in the market itself, crowded with slaves running errands for their masters, merchants looking over goods with resale—and profit—in mind, and everywhere the haggling, shouting, ear-bending roar of voices engaged in bargaining with merchants for a better price.

Skeeter ignored the cacophony. He'd lived in New York City, after all, mostly on the streets for several years; by comparison, the market seemed almost quiet: no sirens screaming in the distance, no semi–trailer truck horns blaring at smaller cars to get out of the way, not even the screech and roar of taxicabs dodging through the perpetual traffic with the nimble, reckless grace of a gazelle with a leopard snarling hungrily at its heels.

Intent on his errand, the displayed goods he shouldered his way past did nothing to attract him. A glance here and there showed fine cloth, imported wines, bulging sacks of wheat for making bread (the staple of a poor man's diet), delicately hand-blown glass vases, baskets, cups, even glass amphorae which rested in wrought-iron tripod stands.

Skeeter dragged his attention back to concentrating on his job. He figured Lupus was going to be skulking around the Via Appia wineshop, so he should be perfectly safe here in his disguise as a toga-wrapped citizen, but he wanted to take no chances whatsoever. It took some time to find what he wanted, not only for his own disguise, but one for Marcus, too. He hoped Marcus didn't mind losing *his* hair, as well. Frustrated, he skillfully lifted a couple of heavy-money purses from distracted Roman men and continued shoving his way through the throng of eager shoppers snapping up the goods that every conquered province was required to send to the capitol. Skeeter looked wistfully at some of the more primitive pieces, reminded of the time spent in a yurt and wanting them, just to remember. But he wasn't here for souvenirs.

He finally found what he wanted: a whole booth devoted to Egyptian wares, all of it dreadfully expensive. *Good thing I lifted those extra money pouches and dumped them into mine.* He bargained with the shopkeeper in his slowly improving Latin, fighting to bring down the prices. He succeeded on two exquisite linen robes, the pleats sewn down and neatly pressed where they weren't sewn. The shopkeeper moaned, "You have robbed me, Roman," and put on a mournful face that neither of them believed for a single second.

Skeeter said, "Wrap them."

The shopkeeper bowed and did as told.

"What else may I offer to interest your Eminence? Collars? Rings? Ear-bobs?"

Skeeter, who did not have pierced ears—and even if he had, the hole in his earlobes wouldn't be nearly large enough to wear those earrings—declined the latter with an air of distaste, then perused the collars and rings.

"How much?" he pointed to two collars and several rings.

"Ah, a man of perfect, exquisite taste. For you, only ten thousand *sestercii.*"

"Who is the robber now?" Skeeter demanded, carefully choosing his words from his limited Latin vocabulary.

The bargaining began in earnest, delighting Skeeter, who had spent five years watching—and occasionally taking part in—haggling over the price of a pony, a bauble for Yesukai's wife, a strong, new bow. He talked the shopkeeper down by seven thousand, quite an accomplishment. Glowing inside with pride, Skeeter maintained a polite smile for the shopkeeper, instructing him again with the simple words, "Wrap them."

The shopkeeper, who seemed nearly in tears—conjured by who-knew-what method—wrapped the new items, put them with the parcels containing the robes, and added a small basket for nothing, so Skeeter could carry his purchases. *Should've haggled even lower,* Skeeter realized, glaring at that innocent basket. Despite the mournful face, Skeeter caught the satisfied gleam in the back of the trader's eyes. Skeeter gestured and his purchases were carefully piled into the basket. Skeeter hefted it, moving and watching carefully lest some pickpocket steal one of his parcels, then left the shopping district.

He returned cautiously to the cramped upper room of the inn where they'd taken refuge, taking great care to ensure he was not followed, then finally knocked on the door. "Marcus, it's me. Shopping's done."

Inside, Marcus waited for the code phrase. When it was not forthcoming, Skeeter heard the scrape of heavy furniture. Then the door opened, barely wide enough for Skeeter to peel himself and his purchases through the slit. He shoved the door closed again and said with a relieved smile. "Did it. Not a tail, not a hint of pursuit."

Marcus was shoving the furniture back into place. "While you were gone, I slipped downstairs and told the innkeeper that my patron was in need of a haircut and shave and could he please send a barber up. The man should be here momentarily."

"If that's the case," Skeeter mused thoughtfully, "this room has got to look normal." He started shoving furniture away from the door, returning each piece to its correct place. Marcus, eyes dark with fear, did the same. Not five minutes later, a knock on the door startled Marcus to his feet.

"Easy. It'll be the barber."

Marcus swallowed, nodded, and went to the door like a man on his way to the executioner. It *was* the barber. Marcus actually had to lean against the doorjamb to keep his knees from shaking.

"I was told to come," the barber said uncertainly.

"Yes," Marcus said in a good, steady voice, "my patron wishes a haircut." He gestured toward Skeeter, seated regally in one of the better chairs.

"Patron, eh?" the barber asked, glancing from Marcus' peaked, freedman's cap to Skeeter. "Looks like you didn't take that cap too seriously, if you ask me."

Marcus' face burned at the insinuation, but then the barber was moving toward Skeeter. Marcus managed to shut the door.

"Better if we had sunlight," the barber complained.

"Lamplight will do," Skeeter said shortly. "Marcus, explain what I want."

"My patron wishes you to shave his head."

The barber's eyes widened. "Shave it? All of it?"

Skeeter nodded solemnly. "And Marcus' hair must come off, as well."

Behind the barber, Marcus' eyes widened and he put involuntary hands to his longish brown hair.

"But—*why?*" the barber stammered.

"Vermin picked up accidentally."

Marcus, picking up on the cue, added, "I believe we have found most of them and their filthy egg sacs, but to be safe, the patron wants you to shave our heads."

The barber nodded, then, in perfect understanding. "Let me get my things."

In a very short time, neither of them recognized themselves in the polished bronze mirror the barber held up. Nearly bald, the barber having carefully scraped away most of the stubble left over, Skeeter nodded and paid the man. The barber bowed, murmured, "I thank you for the business," then left the room.

"Unless I miss my guess," Skeeter said quietly, while unconsciously running one hand across his bare pate, "we have about half an hour to reach the gate. Here." He tossed a couple of parcels to Marcus, who caught them with a numb, clumsy motion.

Skeeter ripped open his own, glanced up, and said impatiently, "Come on. We haven't much time."

Marcus opened the packages slowly, then gasped. "Skeeter! This . . . this must have cost you thousands. How could you pay for such things?" He shucked out of his rough tunic and freedman's cap and slipped on the exquisite robe.

"Lifted a couple of heavy purses. And don't give me that look. Our goddamned lives are at stake."

Marcus only shook his head, regretfully. He slipped on the collar

and glittering rings, set with precious gems. Skeeter was already dressed in similar getup when he finished.

"Ready?" Skeeter asked with a grin for the way they looked.

Marcus managed a snort of laughter. "No. But I will come with you, anyway. I want to be rid of Rome forever."

Skeeter nodded and opened the door.

Stepping through it was harder, this time, with his head bare and vulnerable, and wearing enough jewelry to look like a New York drag queen. Marcus closed the door softly behind them, then caught up at the bottom of the staircase. "Let's go," he said roughly.

Skeeter nodded sharply, and led the way to the Via Appia, eyes alert for any sign of Lupus Mortiferus in shadowed streets no bigger than alleyways, in the dark interiors of wine shops, in the crowd pushing its way past the vast facade of the great Circus. He repressed a shiver, and found the Time Tours wine shop. Men, women, and a fair number of children converged slowly on the shop. Street urchins, their faces filthy, their hollow eyes screaming their hunger, lined both sides of the great road, begging for a few small copper coins from Romans and rich Greeks and Egyptians and others Skeeter didn't recognize. A rich litter carried by sweating slaves approached from the side away from the Circus.

Skeeter narrowed his eyes; then smiled, a chilled, savage smile that caused Marcus, standing courageously straight and alert at his side, to shiver.

"What is it?" Marcus asked in Latin.

Skeeter shook his head, the movement feeling strange without hair to shift about around his ears. "We wait. It is almost time."

The street urchins continued begging in pitiful tones. Some had lost limbs, or were—or pretended to be—crippled, to increase the sense of pity in those who might give them coins. Skeeter averted his face, judging the timing of the approaching litter. Just as it neared the wine shop, the familiar sound-that-was-not-a-sound began buzzing inside his bald skull.

Now!

Skeeter tossed an entire handful of glittering, gold coins into the center of the street. Begging children scrambled for them, creating a

mass of limbs that was impassable. The slaves bearing the litter were caught dead in the center of the miniature storm. The litter swayed dangerously. One slave lost his footing and the litter crashed to the street, accompanied by a high, feminine scream.

"*Move!*" Skeeter snarled. He dodged around the confusion, Marcus at his heels, and dove into the Time Tours wine shop. He cold-cocked the guard at the sound-proofed door, then yanked it open and ran inside, a juggernaut that no one in the room could stop. He was aware of Marcus at his heels. New arrivals were already pushing their way into the shop, creating confusion, but Skeeter plowed right through them, as well. Cries of protest rose behind him, some of them from Time Tours guides, then he glanced around, making sure of Marcus, grabbed him by the arm just to be extra sure, and dove headfirst through the gate. The sensation of falling was genuine: the moment his body hurtled through the portal, he fell flat on the steel grid and rolled violently into the solid railing with leftover momentum.

Marcus slammed into him in much the same manner.

Sirens were already sounding. Skeeter didn't care.

"We did it!"

Then he gulped. He'd have an *awful* fine to pay, crashing the monumentally expensive Porta Romae *twice*, plus Marcus' fine, which Skeeter had already decided was his own responsibility to pay for having let him down so badly earlier.

"C'mon," Skeeter said more quietly. "Might as well go down and confess to Mike Benson and take our punishment, 'fore they come and slap us in handcuffs."

Marcus' eyes showed fear for just a moment—fear, Skeeter realized, that was focused on *him*, not for his own sake—then he nodded and pushed himself painfully up while Skeeter grabbed for the railing and hauled himself to his own feet. In the crowd below, Mike Benson stood out like an angry beacon. Security men were converging on all the ramps. Skeeter sighed, then started down the one closest to Benson. Marcus followed silently.

The return of Marcus and Skeeter was a nine-day wonder, even

for TT-86, which always had *something* exotically strange to gossip about. But their return, together—that was something unheard of in the Station's annals. An up-timer crashing a gate, going missing for a whole month, then crashing the gate again *with* the missing down-timer? It was a thing to twist and turn and talk and argue over endlessly, late into the Station's night and on into the early morning hours, the passage of time hardly noticed under the eternal glow of Commons' lights. Everyone wondered—and laid bets on—how long Marcus and Skeeter would be quarantined in one of Mike Benson's unpleasant cells.

Many another wager was laid on how soon Benson would kick Skeeter's backside through Primary into the waiting arms of prison guards.

The 'eighty-sixers waited, laid their bets, and talked the subject to death with one theory after another to explain the inexplicable *why*.

And just outside Benson's office door, a gathering of silent down-timers, including Ianira Cassondra and her beautiful little daughters, sat blocking the door, waiting for news or sitting in protest, nobody was quite certain. Many an 'eighty-sixer had been shocked that the down-timers, previously regarded as nonentities, had managed to organize themselves enough to hold a silent but well-orchestrated "sit-in" vigil that Gandhi himself would've been proud to claim.

More than a few bets were wagered on that, alone.

Inside Benson's interrogation room, an exhausted, pain-riddled Skeeter Jackson went through the whole story again, aching from the cut in his side, bruises sustained in the arena and their flight from the Circus, even from rough scrapes and tiny, stinging nicks along his scalp. Bronze razors were not particularly kind to the skin. Skeeter was so tired, he wasn't even certain how many times Benson had forced him to repeat his story. A *bunch*, anyway. Hours and hours of it. His body cried out for sleep: healing, heavenly sleep. How long he'd been here, he didn't know, but Skeeter's bleary vision spotted the strain in *Benson's* bloodshot eyes, on his sagging cheek muscles. He, too, was clearly fighting sleep.

Marcus, defiant to the last, had submitted under protest to the drugged-interrogation method Benson felt necessary to get at the truth. Skeeter, as an up-timer, was safe from such tactics, but Marcus *had* no such protection, no rights to keep the needles out of his arms. He, too, repeated his story again and again, including his re-enslavement, his discovery of Skeeter amongst the caged men and beasts he was inventorying, then the rest of it, which matched Skeeter's so closely, that despite the grueling hours of interrogation, Skeeter *knew* Benson had found not a single discrepancy. When his final, drug-induced, mumbled story ended, Marcus collapsed, boneless and silent, across the table, perhaps into a coma or a foetal withdrawal to escape this unexpected torture instead of the joyful celebration of homecoming they'd both longed for.

Skeeter managed through a slurred, furred tongue, to get out the question, "What now? Hot boiling goddamned oil?" He would cheerfully have killed Benson if he'd been able to move. But he knew if he tried to stand up, he'd crash to the floor.

"Lookit him." Skeeter more or less nodded toward Marcus, who still lay collapsed across the interrogation table, oblivious to everything—including Skeeter's continued suffering.

"Gonna kill us both, Benson, to get the goddamned truth out of us? You'd like killing me, wouldn't you? *Wouldn't you, Benson?*"

An odd flicker ran through Mike Benson's exhausted eyes.

"Before *this,*" he, too, gestured awkwardly toward Marcus' inert figure, "I . . . I just dunno. You're a thieving rat. Put a lot of rats like you in jail, while I still wore a City badge. Nothin' but scum of the earth, those bastards." He sat and looked unblinkingly at Skeeter. "But this . . ." He gestured toward Marcus. "This changes the whole thing, doesn't it?"

"Does it?" Skeeter asked, exhaustion causing his voice to quiver. "Aren't I still just a thieving rat, Benson? Can't have it both goddamned ways. Either I'm a worthless scoundrel or I finally managed to do something decent—something *you're* ripping to fucking *shreds.*"

Mike Benson scrubbed his face and eyes with both hands. "Not thinkin' straight," he muttered, to which Skeeter added a silent, snarled, *Amen, you stinking pig.* Benson said through his hands,

"Yeah. It does make a difference, Jackson. To me, anyway. Can't figure why you did it, what was in it for you, but your story's consistent and airtight with his." He nodded toward Marcus.

Benson sat back in his chair, letting both hands fall to his lap. "All right, Skeeter. You can go now. Your pal, too. I'll, uh, speak to Time Tours about the fines for crashing the gate, seeing as how it really was a mission of mercy."

Skeeter just looked at him. Benson's face flushed. He refused to meet Skeeter's eyes. "Can't promise anything, you realize; it's *their* gate and Granville Baxter . . . well, Bax is under tremendous pressure during the holiday season and Time Tours has laid down some new rules he's going to have to enforce, despite the fact they're just not enforceable." He sighed, evidently gathering from Skeeter's closed, set expression that Skeeter didn't give a damn *what* Bax's management problems were.

"Anyway, Skeeter, I can be pretty persuasive. And so can Bull—and I expect he will be *very* persuasive when I make my report." Again, Skeeter simply blinked and looked at him. *Does he honestly think this bullshit makes up for the last God-knows-how-many hours?*

"Huh," was all he could find to say. Short, derisive, and abrasive.

Benson had the good grace to flush. He looked away and muttered, "Need help getting home?"

Skeeter desperately wanted to grab Benson's shirt collar and shout, "No, you stinking bully!" Pride alone demanded it. But his strength was shot and he knew it. And there was poor Marcus to consider. "Yeah," he finally muttered. "Yeah, I could use some help." He continued without a hint of a smile anywhere in him. "Don't think I could walk across this room on my own, thanks to your hospitality."

Benson flushed again, darker this time. He dropped his eyes to his own hands, knotted on his side of the tabletop.

"Marcus is gonna need help, too." Skeeter jerked a thumb at his friend then dropped his arm abruptly, shaking all over. "I could cheerfully murder you, Benson, over what you did to him. He sure as hell didn't deserve needles and drugs and hours of questioning."

Benson was staring at him oddly, as though he wasn't quite sure what he was seeing, then he finally nodded. "All right, Jackson. Some of my men will drive you. If," he added dully, "we can get a hummer in through that bunch of protesters out there."

Skeeter drew a blank. "Protesters?"

Benson said slowly, "Down-timers, all of 'em, organized in a sit-in protest. They're blocking the goddamned door twelve deep."

Skeeter didn't know what to think until Benson added, "His, uh, wife and kids are out there, center stage. If looks could kill, I'd be a stone statue right now."

A hollow emptiness in Skeeter's belly froze his breath into ice. *A welcome home for Marcus. But not for me. Never for the stinkin' rat of a thief.* He tried to shrug it off, knowing what they must think of him after betraying their faith, as it were, by causing Marcus to step through that portal with Chuck Farley. Skeeter wondered absently, thoughts drifting, what had become of that rat. *Prob'ly never know.*

Mike Benson prodded the still-unconscious Marcus' shoulder with astonishing gentleness, considering what he'd just put the young bartender through. Slowly, Marcus swam toward the surface, moving small bits of himself one at a time. He finally opened his eyes. The sight of Benson stooping over him brought a terrible flinch, both in body and eyes.

"It's all right, Marcus," Benson said quietly—and in pretty damned good Latin. "I believe your story. Both your stories. You can go home, now. I have a hummer and driver on the way to take you there. But I'd better warn you, just so the shock won't kill you, there's a bunch of down-timers outside, blocking the door, waiting for news, I guess, and what else, I can't guess. Your family's in the crowd, right near the door.

Marcus sat up straighter. "Ianira?" he choked out. "My daughters?"

Benson nodded. Marcus surged to his feet, swayed badly, shrugged off Benson's hand, which the Chief Security Officer had held out in an offering to help, then finally steadied. "I will go to my family, now. Thank you for my freedom," he said, irony heavy in his voice. Skeeter and Benson both knew who was genuinely responsible for that.

He made it to the door, then vanished into the corridor, back stiff, knees a bit unsteady.

Well, hell. If he can, I can. A straight back was agony to maintain, a fact Skeeter hid from Benson with a light, "Thanks for *my* freedom, too." Benson looked uncomfortable. Then it was over and he finally managed to stand completely straight. The pain in his body was bearable. Maybe. Benson said nothing as Skeeter limped his way out, teary-eyed from a stab of knife-hot, pinched nerves down his sciatic channel. The pain stabbed all the way to his left foot. But he made it to the door, too, moving woodenly. By the time he gained the outer door, he was gasping, *gulping* for breath. His vision kept going dark, fading back in again to show him the way out, then straying dizzily back into darkness.

When he opened the door, he glimpsed Ianira and Marcus clutched together, their daughters holding tight to Marcus' unsteady legs. Neither of them even noticed him. Skeeter felt abruptly empty, defeated. All he had left were a few of the coins he'd scraped from the arena sands. Benson hadn't searched either of them, it being clear through the semi-transparent Egyptian linen that neither of them carried anything. So it wasn't really Benson's fault, because he didn't know about Skeeter's injuries, but when he stumbled in a drugged haze against one of the down-timers fading back into whatever they called home or job, the jostle was too much. Overbalanced, Skeeter tried to compensate, but exhausted, bruised, fire stinging along his ribcage, and a pain like torn muscles down his side from that pole vault, rendered him abruptly helpless. Not a single, abused muscle in his back and legs obeyed his commands.

He went down hard. As complete darkness settled over him, he realized the down-timers would simply leave him here, after what he'd done to Marcus, involving him in that gods-cursed scam of Farley's. Promising himself to hunt down Farley and kill him, Skeeter's face connected with a cold, rock-hard cement floor. The settling darkness became complete in that instant and he knew nothing more.

Skeeter woke slowly, with bits of his body making themselves known by varying degrees of screaming pain. The headache alone thundered through his skull like a Gobi lightning storm. He lay very still, trying to breathe around the pain, hoping it would lessen just a bit if he remained perfectly frozen in place.

It didn't work.

Gradually, Skeeter realized he was not lying face-first on the Commons' concrete floor. *Someone*—probably Benson's gang—had moved him. He thought bitterly, *Probably didn't want the tourists to see a passed-out con man apparently drunk out of his mind on Commons floor. Bad for business.*

For a moment, he wondered if Benson had put him in one of the private detention cells of La-La Land's little jail. Then, startling him beyond all measure, came the incongruity of a child's voice. *Mike Benson does not lock up children. Not one that young.* He moved his head slightly on the pillow to hear better and gasped at the pain in his neck and the sensation of a hairless skull sliding across the pillowcase. He dealt with those startling facts each in turn, finally recalling the reasons.

The child's voice spoke again. He couldn't understand the kid's words; but they flowed like music. A female voice answered in the same liquid language. Skeeter blinked. He knew that voice. Deep, throaty, as beautiful as its owner. *What am I doing in Ianira Cassondra's apartment?*

Not that he minded, so long as Marcus didn't—

Where's Marcus?

He strained to hear, but didn't catch a single syllable of Marcus' voice. Then he strained to remember, but Mike Benson's interrogation blended into one, long stream of ruthless, sleepless, pain-filled questions. He vaguely remembered being told he could go, vaguely recalled collapsing outside Benson's office . . . but he did *not* remember what had become of Marcus.

Somehow, that was intolerable. He tried to swing his legs over the edge of the bed, shove covers aside, and get up. He really tried. Instead, he got about halfway between horizontal and vertical, blacked out, and fell back with a faint cry of pain, which exploded through the whole of him like an electric shock prod wired to his insides and left set on full charge—one whose existence he'd completely forgotten. The next thing of which he was clearly aware was a soft touch on his brow, a hot towel that brought ecstasy when it soothed the throbbing behind his eyes, and a murmuring voice he'd last heard raised in desperation, begging help from *him.*

"Skeeter?" Her voice came like rich, deep bell tones. "Don't worry, Skeeter, you're safe now. Marcus has gone to fetch Dr. Eisenstein for you."

Skeeter was really glad the wet towel on his brow leaked water down his face, because quite suddenly his eyes filled and spilled over, completely out of his control. No one but Yesukai had *ever* treated him so kindly. As though she had divined the source of his greatest pain—and maybe she had, at that; everyone called her the Enchantress—she touched his face in various places, featherlight, drying tears on his cheeks, pressing against places he'd never realized would feel so . . . so warm, so comforting.

"It is all right to weep out the pain, Skeeter. A man can go only so long alone, untouched, unloved. You miss your fierce Khan, I know that, but you cannot go back, Skeeter." Her words tore something inside him, something he'd realized but not acknowledged for a long, long time. "From here," she murmured, still touching his face gently, "the road unwinds in only one of two directions for you, Skeeter Jackson. Either you will remain on the road you have been traveling all your life and your loneliness will destroy you, or you may choose the other road, into the light. It is a choice neither I nor Marcus can make for you. Only you can decide such a profound question. But we will be travelling beside you, trying to help and support as best we can, whatever road you choose."

He fought a thickening in his throat.

"Oh, Skeeter, Cherished One, you risked everything, even life's blood in the test of the gods' arena, to save Marcus."

Then, when the deep emotions her words evoked wrenched him impossibly in too many directions, she massaged his temples and crooned a song, or perhaps an ancient incantation, while he turned his head as far away from her as he could and cried as he hadn't since the age of eight. The words she'd whispered kept reverberating through his whole being: *Cherished One. . . .*

Then Marcus' worried voice rang out and a moment later, Rachel Eisenstein bent over him, ignoring his tears or taking them as a reaction to pain. She turned him with clinical, gentle expertise, examining the damage front and back, the scars of the lash across ribs and spine, the muscles strained and knotted from shoulder to shank from that tremendous vault from his horse's back, the slash across his side.

He was eased back down and covered warmly. "Skeeter? Can you hear me? It's Rachel."

Rather than nodding, he managed to croak past the tightness in his throat. "Yeah." It was a sound of defeat and even he knew it. He hoped Ianira and Marcus understood. He was simply too exhausted, in too much pain to struggle any longer.

"Skeeter, I need to take you to the infirmary. Nothing that won't mend, but there's more of it than I like to see in one patient. Do you understand, Skeeter?"

Again, the thick-throated, "Yeah."

He closed his eyes, praying Ianira would understand his need to escape for just a little while the intense, soul-cracking emotions she'd roused with so few words. That portion of himself needed healing, too. Maybe he'd go see Dr. Mundy, after all, tell him everything, get all the secrets and the pain and the memories of good times and terrifying ones out of his system.

Someone removed the cooling towel from his brow, then Ianira's voice came low and velvety: "Remember, we will always be here, ready to help."

Then the metallic clanging of a gurney came to his ears and he was lifted and slid with professional gentleness by two orderlies. He only bit his lip once during the entire process. Then the gurney was moving and he thought he heard the sound of a woman weeping, but he wasn't sure of much in this state.

They slid him neatly into the miniature ambulance used on station and moved away with lights flashing, evidently taking back ways down, since their speed didn't slow for the throng of holiday party-goers jamming the station just now. In the cramped quarters of the little ambulance, Rachel Eisenstein deftly lashed his gurney to tie-downs on the ambulance wall. Then, before he knew it, she'd threaded an IV into his arm. "Dehydration," she explained, "plus a mild painkiller. You need it."

That's for goddamned sure. But he had no voice left to say it.

Then, almost conversationally, she added, "Spoke to Mike Benson earlier today." Skeeter pricked up his attention. "Let him have it between the eyes, I did." She chuckled. "Should've seen the expression on his face. By the time I was done, I do believe he understood clearly that when injured people fall through a gate—regardless of who they are—they are to be brought directly to *me*, not abused for nearly a whole day in a sham investigation."

She touched his brow. "You can mop up the floor with him as soon as you're back on your feet with all your muscles working properly again."

Skeeter tried to smile, grateful she understood. "Promise?" he croaked hoarsely.

"Promise."

He might spend time behind bars, but by all the gods, he had a score to settle with Mr. Michael Benson.

"Easy, now. We're nearly there. Just hang on, Skeeter. Soon you'll be asleep again, mending faster than you realize." When he furrowed his brow, worried about money, she correctly guessed the cause. "Don't worry about the bill, Skeeter. Someone's already agreed to pay it."

"Who?" he croaked through his still-tight voice.

Rachel chuckled and tickled his nose. "Kit Carson."

Skeeter's eyes widened. "*Kit?* But . . . but *why*?"

Rachel laughed warmly this time. "Who ever understands why Kit does *any* of the things he does? He's an original. Like you."

Then the back doors opened and his gurney was untied, slid backwards, and the wheels lowered. Skeeter closed his eyes against the dizziness of the moving ceiling overhead and pondered Rachel's revelation. Why would Kit Carson, of all people, agree to pay for Skeeter's medical bills? He couldn't understand it. Still didn't when they injected something incredibly potent into his IV's heplock. The room swam in dizzy circles for just a second or two, then darkness closed around him.

Chapter 21

When Skeeter, aware of a new inner strength, cold-cocked and then mopped up the floor with Mike Benson, the big cop didn't even press charges. "Rotten bastard," Skeeter growled. "Bad enough you tortured *me* for hours—I might actually have deserved it, given my reputation—" another punch sent Benson reeling into the wall, whereupon he slid comically to the floor like a wrung out cartoon, "—but no, you had to do the same thing to *Marcus*, who's never done a goddamned thing wrong in his life. This one's for Marcus." And he slammed the flat of his hand against Benson's nose, with just enough force to break it, but not enough to drive a sliver of bone fatally back into the brain. Blood poured in streams. His eyes lost all focus. He was still sitting there, unable to move so much as one arm, as Skeeter stormed through the astonished crowd of onlookers.

He'd found the Security Chief near Primary, which was due to cycle soon. Montgomery Wilkes, with his red hair, black uniform, and steel-cold eyes, routinely prowled the whole area. When Wilkes deliberately put himself in Skeeter's way, growling out, "You are under arrest, you filthy little rat," a collective gasp went up.

Skeeter said dangerously, "No way, Herr Hitler. *Way* outside your jurisdiction."

"Nothing's outside my jurisdiction. And people like you are a danger to peace in our time. And I'm the one who's going to take you off the streets." When Wilkes actually grabbed Skeeter by the arm, he slammed his other fist into Monty's solar plexus. Monty doubled over with a gasp of shock, letting go of Skeeter's arm to hold his middle. Skeeter, coldly enraged, took advantage of Wilkes' doubled-up condition and added a nice chop to the back of his neck. Skeeter then kicked him to the floor. That felt good. Wilkes had been begging it for years. He said loudly enough for Wilkes to hear, "Look, I haven't broken any of your laws. And you just assaulted me. Just remember, I'm hell and gone outside *your* jurisdiction, Nazi. Or do you really want to spend another couple of weeks in Mike Benson's lockup?"

Wilkes, too winded to reply, glared coldly up at him, eyes promising retaliation.

Skeeter gave out a harsh bark of laughter that startled Wilkes into widening his eyes. "Forget it, Monty. You do and I'll press charges so serious, you'll end rotting in a cell forever. *I* grew up as a living god in the yurt of Genghis Khan. I could kill you in so many different ways, not even *your* lurid imagination could come up with all of 'em. So take some advice. Go hassle taxes out of honest tourists who can't or won't fight back."

He spat, the wad of saliva landing right next to Monty's chin. The head ATF agent didn't bat so much as an eyelash. "Face it, Wilkes. You're no better than I am. You've just got a badge to hide behind when you swindle people and pocket the stuff you skim off the top, before it's ever recorded where government accountants might find it. So cut the Mr.-Upholding-Law-and-Order-Good-Guy crap. I ain't buyin' it and I ain't scared of you or any of your underhanded tricks. Got that, Monty?"

Monty looked cold and pale on the floor. He nodded stiffly, his face nearly cracking with the movement. Skeeter had him dead to rights and they both knew it.

"Good. You leave me the hell alone and I'll leave *you* the hell alone."

God, that felt good.

When he stalked away, anger palpably radiating from him, *everyone* got out of his way. Even ATF agents. It reminded Skeeter of that Charlton Heston movie, where the sea had peeled back for the Israelites to flee Pharaoh's wrath.

So far, so good. Two thrashings down, one yelling match to come. Next stop: Kit Carson's office.

He shoved impatiently past the Neo Edo's front desk, grabbed an elevator, pressed the unmarked button, and rose swiftly upward into Kit's private domain. When he stormed into the office, not bothering to remove his shoes, Kit's brows knotted above a deeply disapproving frown. Skeeter didn't care. He knew Kit would put him down in about two seconds if he started anything physical, so he gritted his teeth, leaned his palms on the enormous desk, and said, "All, right, Carson. Let's hear it. *Why?*"

Kit hadn't moved. The stillness scared Skeeter, despite his momentum and the fire in his blood.

"Sit down, Skeeter." It was not an invitation. It was an order and a fairly forceful one at that.

Skeeter sat.

Kit finally moved, leaning back slightly in his chair and observing Skeeter closely for several silent moments. His clothes were disarranged slightly from the knock-down, drag-out with Benson and his knuckles were a scraped-up mess from bringing Monty the Monster down a peg or two. Kit finally pointed to the wall-sized rank of monitors to Skeeter's right. He turned cautiously, wondering why Kit wanted him to look at them, then understood in a single flash of understanding. One of the screens showed live feed directly from a security camera at Primary. He saw Mike Benson staggering to his feet, still bleeding, with the help of two of his men. The sway in his knees warmed Skeeter's heart. Yesukai would have approved: honor avenged.

"That, Skeeter, was quite a performance." Kit's voice came out dry as a Mongolian sandstorm.

"I wasn't performing," Skeeter growled. "And you haven't answered me yet." He ignored the monitors and glared at Kit, whose abrupt bark of laughter startled him so deeply he almost forgot why he'd come up here. "Do you have any idea," Kit said, actually wiping tears, "how long I've wanted *someone* to put that overbearing ass on the floor so hard his brains rattled? Of course, this *is* going to start another round of battle between ATF and Station Management. Oh, don't look so scared, boy. I just got off the phone with Bull Morgan, who was laughing so hard he just about couldn't talk." That world-famous grin came and went. "No need to worry about charges being pressed or getting thrown off station. Both of those idiots got what they richly deserved."

Word travelled fast in La-La Land. Skeeter sighed. "Okay. So everybody's cheering my fight of honor. Big deal. But you *still* haven't answered my question."

Kit studied him some more. Then rose and walked barefooted except for black tabi socks to a sumptuous bar. He chose an ancient-looking bottle, handled it with the greatest reverence, and found two shot glasses. He poured carefully, not wasting a drop, then put the bottle cautiously back into the depths of the bar. Skeeter realized he was being granted some special privilege and didn't know why.

Kit returned and set a shot glass in front of him then resumed his chair. His brown eyes were steady as they met Skeeter's. "Marcus is a friend," he said softly. "I *couldn't* go after him, which damn near broke my heart. I've watched that boy grow from a terrified slave into a strong and self-confident young man. I've offered him jobs dozens of times, but he always shakes his head and says he prefers friendship over charity."

Kit paused a moment, shot glass steady in his hand. "You and I haven't had much love for one another over the years, Skeeter. The way you make your living, what you tried to do to my granddaughter . . ." He shook his head. "Believe me, I understand all too well the fear behind your eyes, Skeeter Jackson. But four weeks ago you did something so out of character, it shook me up. Badly. You tried to save Marcus from that bastard Farley, or whatever his real name is. Word is, you suffered some pretty rough treatment down time before both of you escaped."

Skeeter felt heat in his cheeks. He shrugged. "Gladiator school wasn't so bad, if you didn't piss off the slave master enough for him to rake your hide with the whip. And I beat Lupus, hands down, in the Circus. No big deal."

Kit said quietly, "Yes, very big deal. Remember, I've fought for my life in that arena, too." Skeeter *had* forgotten in his anger. "So far as I can tell, that fight was an important first in your life. First time you put somebody else's life ahead of your own."

Skeeter felt uncomfortable again.

Kit lifted his glass. Clumsily, Skeeter took hold of his.

"To honor," Kit said quietly.

Skeeter's throat closed. An 'eighty-sixer had finally understood. He gulped the bourbon, astonished by the smooth flavor of it. Where, he wondered, had Kit acquired it? And why share it with Skeeter?

Kit set his shot glass upside-down on the desk; Skeeter did the same.

"I offered to pay the hospital bill," Kit finally said, "because you acquired those injuries in a desperate fight to get Marcus back where he belonged—with his wife and children. And I *know* exactly how much money you don't have."

"There's the wager money Brian's holding—hey, what *about* that wager? Do you know anything?"

A smile came and went. "Goldie screamed and kicked for a whole week when Brian put the wager on hold until you returned. It's still on hold until you officially visit Brian in the library."

Skeeter thought that one out. The wager seemed almost irrelevant, now. But he could use the money Brian was holding. He *did* rather enjoy the mental image of Goldie purple-faced enraged. Then he sighed and startled himself by admitting, "Wish I'd never made that goddamned wager."

Kit nodded slowly. "Good. That's one of the reasons for the bourbon." He chuckled. "It's illegal, you know. Brought a few bottles back with me from a scouting trip."

Skeeter couldn't believe it. Not only was *the* Kit Carson speaking to him man-to-man, but he'd shared a chink in his squeaky clean honor, shared it knowing it made him vulnerable.

He rose slowly to leave. "Thanks, Kit. More than you know. And thanks for the 'vodka,' too. It was bracing and I needed that." It was the only way Skeeter knew to tell Kit he would keep his mouth shut about the wonderful, illegal bourbon.

Kit's lips twitched and a wicked gleam touched his eyes, but he said only, "Any time. I think Brian's waiting for you."

Skeeter nodded, headed for the door, then turned and said, "Sorry about the shoes. Won't happen again." Provided, that was, if Skeeter were ever invited back to Kit's sanctuary, which he deemed improbable at best. He closed the door, stood in the corridor for a moment, a little unsure just *what* he felt, then he sighed, found the elevator, and left the Neo Edo, heading toward the library. The few coins left from his victory lap jangled in his pocket. If the wager was still on, he was still in very hot water. Any tiny bit of coin he could scrape up would help.

When he entered the library, Brian Hendrickson looked up and said in his impossible accent, "Ah, heard you were up and about again. Glad to see rumor true, for once. I've been waiting, you know, for a month."

Skeeter, his mind and blood cooled by the time spent in Kit's office, pulled the coins out of his pocket and set them on the counter.

"Mmm . . . very, very nice. And a gold *aurii* amongst the lot." Brian looked up. "However did you come into possession of these?"

Skeeter wanted to tell him they'd come from the purses he'd stolen; but that wasn't the truth. He'd spent every last copper *uncia* of that money getting Marcus and him through the gate. All that remained were a few coins from the arena sands. So he said, very quietly, "I snatched them from the sand when the crowd at the Circus Maximus started throwing coins to me on my victory lap. I'd, uh, beaten the favorite champion in Rome, and, uh, things got pretty wild for a few minutes."

Curiously, "Did you kill him?"

"No," Skeeter bit out. "But I beat the hell out of him and Claudius spared him."

Brian Hendrickson gazed at nothing for a moment. "That," he said, "would have been something to witness. Claudius spared very few." Then he shook himself slightly and a mournful look appeared on his face. "I'm afraid these *cannot* count toward your wager, Skeeter. You earned them honestly."

He'd half expected that answer, anyway, so he just nodded and scooped up the coins.

"Going to exchange them somewhere?"

"No." They represented a pivotal moment in his life, when—for just a few minutes—the crowd really had treated him as the god Yesukai the Valiant had once called him. He stuffed the coins back into his pocket. *Some god.* All the years he'd spent fooling himself into thinking that what he did was correct was simply time wasted from his life, on delusions and fantasies that kept him from seeing what he was and where he was inevitably headed with genuine clarity. Thank God for Marcus. Without him, Skeeter might never have woken up.

"Thanks, Brian."

He stalked out of the library, unsure what to do next, or where to go. Surprisingly, he ended up at Dr. Mundy's door. A few minutes later, relaxed in a deep, easy-on-the-back chair with the whir of a tape recorder in the background, Skeeter started spilling all of it out, every single thing he could recall about Yesukai, Temujin, and the yurt he'd lived in as *bogda* and then as uncle of the Khan's firstborn son. Then, under Dr. Mundy's gentle persuasion, he let out the rest of it, as well. When he'd finished, he knew the hurt and fear weren't gone, but much of it now inhabited that whirring strand of metallic recording tape rather than Skeeter's belly and nightmares.

He refused the usual payment, startling Mundy into stutters, then left quietly and closed the door on that part of his life forever.

Margo and Malcolm got word from Primary just about the time Skeeter Jackson was punching Mike Benson into the ground. A sealed letter with official letterhead and stamps arrived for them.

"Open it!" Margo demanded.

"Patience," Malcolm laughed.

"You know I haven't got any!"

"Ah, yet another lesson to explore."

The Irish alley-cat glare, at least, had not changed since she'd begun college. Malcolm carefully slit the envelope with his pocketknife, replaced the little folder in his pocket, then slid out a crisp, official reply.

"Re: William Hunter, a.k.a. Charles Farley. Above was apprehended while digging up an illegal hoard of down time artwork from Denver. Your recordings were most helpful in getting his cooperation and should serve very nicely at trial. I know you're wondering, and ordinarily I wouldn't commit words to paper before a trial, but you are, after all, on TT-86, many, many years in 'our' past. He was, indeed an agent, collecting unusual pieces of art from the past and returning with them to his employer." Malcolm's eyes bugged when he saw that employer's world-famous name.

"We'll have a separate trial for him, of course. Seems he and another rich gentleman, on whom we have not a shred of evidence beyond Mr. Hunter's statements, had several years ago engaged in a little wager as to which of them could smuggle up time for their private collections the most, ah, aforementioned artwork. We've already seized one collection and will be turning it over to an IFARTS office as soon as the trials are completed. No one expects either trial to be long. I thought you should know, as you went far beyond the extra mile—and citizens, not law enforcement, at that—to bring this temporal criminal to justice. Good luck to you and thank you most sincerely for your incalculable help in cracking this illegal wager wide open."

The signature block caused even Margo's eyes to pop. "Wow! The actual Justice Minister, not one of his flunkies!"

Malcolm chortled and folded up the slip of paper, sliding it back into the envelope. "I'd like to have seen old Chuckie's face when they caught him with the goods. He'll get life for the illegal trafficking alone and probably a death sentence for the people he killed along the way." He sighed slightly. "I always did fancy happy endings," he mused, smiling down at Margo.

She leaned up and kissed him, not caring who was watching, then breathed against his mouth, "Let's go make a few copies, eh? Give one to what's left of Benson's carcass, another to Bull Morgan, maybe even one to that horrid Montgomery Wilkes. Tax evasion is, after all, in *his* jurisdiction."

Malcolm laughed hard enough to draw stares, then brushed a kiss across her lips. "Sounds good to me, fire-eater."

"Huh. Fire-eater. You just wait until I get you alone, you prudish, staid old Brit, you."

They set out toward Bull Morgan's aerie of an office, grinning like a couple of cheshire cats.

Wandering aimlessly, Skeeter finally ended up inside the Down Time Bar and Grill, where—of all people—Marcus was on duty at the bar. He flushed and nearly walked out again, but Marcus was pouring his favorite brew and saying, "Skeeter, have a beer with me, eh?"

He halted, then turned. "No money, Marcus."

"So what?" Marcus said a shade too seriously. He came around the end of the bar, handed Skeeter a foaming mug, then sat down with his own. They drank in silence for a few minutes, popping peanuts in between sips and longer pulls at the beer.

"Been wanting to thank you," Marcus said quietly.

"Huh. Been wanting to do the same."

Another long silence reigned, filled with peanuts and beer.

"Just returning the favor," Marcus said at last. "Isn't nearly enough, but it's a start."

"Now look here, Marcus, I'm not going to put up with any more of your honor is sacred bullshi—"

Goldie Morran appeared at the entrance.

Marcus winked once at Skeeter and resumed his place behind the bar. Goldie walked over and, to Skeeter's dismay, took a chair at his table. "Marcus, good to see you back," she said, with every evidence of sincerity. He just nodded his thanks. "Would you get me a tall bourbon with a touch of soda, please?"

Back in his bartender role, Marcus made the drink to Goldie's specifications, then delivered it on a tray with another beer for Skeeter.

"Well," Goldie said. "You have been through it, haven't you? I didn't expect you to survive."

Skeeter narrowed his eyes. "Not survive?" he asked, his tone low and dangerous. "Five years in the yurt of Genghis Khan's father, and you didn't think I'd survive?"

Goldie's eyes widened innocently; then, for some reason, the mask shattered and fell away, leaving her old, tired, and oddly vulnerable. She snatched at her drink the way Skeeter had snatched at that hunting spear in the stinking sands of the Circus.

He wondered which of them would say it first.

Before either of them could summon up the nerve, Mike Benson—both eyes blacked, limping a little—entered the bar a bit gingerly and sat down very carefully at their table. He looked from one to the other, then said, "Got a copy of a communique from the Minister of Justice today." Skeeter's belly hollowed. "I, uh, just wanted to ask for the record if either of you had run into a professional antiquities thief by the name of William Hunter during these last few weeks? He's one of the best in the world. Steals ancient pornography for an up-time collector as part of a wager with another collector. Oh, by the way, one of his aliases was Farley. Chuck Farley."

Skeeter and Goldie exchanged glances. Neither of them spoke.

"Well, do let me know if either of you've seen the bastard. They'll be needing witnesses for the trial next month."

With that, Benson left them.

Goldie glanced at her drink, then at Skeeter. "Professional, huh? Guess we were a couple of damned amateurs, compared to that."

"Yeah." Skeeter pulled at his beer while Goldie gulped numbing bourbon. "Funny, isn't it? We were trying to win our stupid little wager and he cleaned us both out to win his boss' wager. Feel a little like a heel, you know?"

Very quietly, Goldie said, "Yes, I know." She stared into her drink for several seconds, then met his gaze, her eyes troubled and dark. "I, uh, I thought I really needed to apologize. I told that gladiator where to find you."

Skeeter snorted. "Thanks, Goldie. But I already knew."

Goldie's eyes widened.

"Marcus told me, right before I went into the arena to fight Lupus Mortiferus."

Goldie paled. "I never meant things to go so far."

"Me, neither," Skeeter muttered. "You should feel what *I* feel every time I move my back and shoulders. Got a bottle of pain pills this big." He measured the length and diameter of the prescription bottle. "Not to mention the antibiotics, the muscle relaxants, and whatever it is Rachel shoots into my butt every few hours. Feel like a goddamned pincushion. One that's been run over by all *twelve* racing chariots in a match."

Goldie cleared her throat. "I don't suppose . . ." She stopped, visibly searching for the right words and the courage to say them. "That stupid wager of ours—" She gulped a little bourbon for bravery. "I think we ought to call it off, seeing as how it's done nothing but hurt a lot of people." Her eyes flickered to Marcus, then back. "Some of them *good* people."

Skeeter just nodded. "Terms accepted, Goldie."

They shook hands on it, with Marcus a silent witness.

"Suppose we ought to go tell Brian," Skeeter muttered.

"Yes. Let's do that, shall we, before I run out of bourbon courage."

Skeeter slid his chair back and took Goldie's chair, assisting her up. She shot a startled glance into his face, then fumbled for money.

"Goldie," Marcus called from the bar, "forget it. You're money's no good for that one."

She stared at the young former slave for a long time. Then turned abruptly and headed for the door.

"Thanks, Marcus," Skeeter said.

"Any time, friend."

Skeeter followed Goldie out into Urbs Romae where workmen were busy patching broken mosaics. They stepped past as carefully as possible, then headed for the library.

Word travelled far faster than they did. Telephones, word of mouth, however it happened, the alchemy proved itself once again, because by the time they reached Brian Hendrickson's desk, an enormous crowd of 'eighty-sixers and newsies holding their vidcams aloft and trying to shove closer, all but filled the library. Goldie faltered. Skeeter muttered, "Hey, it's only 'eighty-sixers and some lousy newsies. Isn't like you're facing a champion gladiator or anything."

The color came back into her face, two bright, hot spots of it on her cheekbones. She strode into the crowd, muttering imperiously, "Get out of the way, clod. Move over, idiot."

Skeeter grinned to himself and followed her through the path she plowed. When he caught sight of Kit Carson, Kit's grin and wink shook him badly enough he stumbled a couple of steps. But he was glad Kit was there, on his side for once.

Then, too soon, they both faced Brian Hendrickson. Voice flat, Goldie said, "We're calling off the bet, Brian."

A complete hush fell as every eye and vidcam lens focused on Skeeter. He shrugged. "Yeah. Stupid wager in the first place. We're calling it quits."

A wave of sound rolled over them as minor wagers were paid off, vidcam reporters talked into their microphones, and *everyone* pondered the reason. Skeeter didn't care. He signed the paper Brian shoved at him, watched while Goldie signed it, too, then collected his earnings, stuffed them into every pocket he possessed, borrowed an envelope from Brian to hold the arena coins, then moved woodenly through the crowd, holding mute as questions were hurled in his direction. *Let Goldie cope with it*, he thought emptily. *I don't want any part of it.*

A fair percentage of the crowd followed him up to Commons and down its length, whispering wagers as to what he'd do next. He ignored the mob, including at least two persistent newsies, and stalked through Castletown, Frontier Town, and into Urbs Romae.

The only warning he received was the flash of light on a sharp metal blade. Then Lupus Mortiferus—*how the hell did he slip though the gate again?*—charged, sword and dagger in classic killing position. Skeeter did the only thing he *could* do, while unarmed. He turned, shot through the startled crowd, and *ran*. The coins and bills in his pockets slowed him down, but not by much. Lupus remained behind him, running flat out, but the gladiator wasn't gaining. At least, not yet. A quick over-the-shoulder glance showed Lupus and, incongruously, two newsies in hot pursuit, vidcams capturing every bit of the lethal race.

Skeeter cursed them, catskinned over a railing—and howled at the pain which made itself abruptly known all over again—then charged up a ramp, shouting at tourists to get out of the way. Startled women lunged for children or shop doorways as Skeeter pelted past. His shirt pockets were lighter by a fair percentage, having dumped money to the floor while in the middle of that catskinning move. *Damn.* He kept running, aware from the screams that Lupus was still back there. *Doesn't this guy ever give up?* Then he had to admit, *C'mon Skeeter, you robbed him then humiliated him in front of the Imperator himself, never mind all his fans. Either you outrun him, or he's gonna chop you into deli-sized slices of Skeeter. And you'd deserve it.*

With Lupus and both panting newsies in pursuit, Skeeter whipped around a corner, grabbed an overhead girder, and swung himself up and around, then dropped to the catwalk the moment Lupus and the confused newsies rounded the corner. He sped back the way he'd come, hearing a roar of rage far behind. The next roar was much closer. Skeeter knew he was getting winded, and cramps the length of his body slowed him even further. He dropped to the Commons floor and headed for Residential, hoping to lose the man in the maze of corridors and elevators. Maybe, if he were lucky, he could grab an elevator for the gym and find a weapon. Preferably one of those fully automatic machineguns Ann kept in her little office, with a full belt of ammo in it.

Lupus charged down the corridor, shouting obscenities at him in Latin and gaining ground. Winded, aching from wrenched muscles that hadn't quite healed yet from his battle in the arena, Skeeter didn't notice it at first. Then, as he fell against an elevator door and frantically pressed the button, a shimmer dopplered wildly and a gate opened up between him and the enraged gladiator. The gate's edges pulsed raggedly in the typical configuration of a very unstable gate. It grew, shrank to a pinhole, then engulfed the entire hallway. Through the intense vibration of his skullbones, Skeeter thought he heard a startled yell. He peered hard at the pulsing, black opening, wondering if anyone had ever studied the *back* side of a gate, or could see what was on the other side.

Before he could make out any details, the gate shuddered closed. Skeeter slid to the floor, panting, when he realized there was no sign of Lupus, just two gaping newsies. One of the stammered, "D-did you see what I think I saw?"

"I think I did. Our vidcams should've caught it."

They exchanged glances, ignored Skeeter completely, and dashed down the corridor the other way. Wearily, Skeeter found a stubby pencil in one pocket, and pushed himself to trembling legs, marking out the gate's position and size as best he could, dragging the pencil down walls and across the floor, with arrows pointing toward the ceiling, since he couldn't reach it.

Unstable gates were nothing to mess with. Whenever possible, their location and duration were logged. He'd call Bull Morgan as soon as he got home. Exhausted, he dug for keys that the slave master must've taken away from him at least a month ago, then remembered that Lupus had shattered his door a long time ago. He hadn't needed a key since his return. Eventually, he might even have enough money to have the door fixed. He stumbled in the direction of his apartment and found it exactly as he'd left it earlier in the day. The bottles of water he'd planned to sell as a con he'd already shoved angrily into the wastebasket. Skeeter hunted a little desperately for the pill bottle he'd described to Goldie. He shook out two tablets, reconsidered, and shook a third into his palm.

He swallowed them dry, then tumbled into bed. By some odd chance, he'd left his small television on this morning. The television, even his apartment still looked and felt alien. He was about to shut it off by remote when a newsflash came on, showing Skeeter running from Lupus, with a breathless commentary on the long-standing feud. Skeeter grunted and reached again for the remote. Then froze, hand in midair.

"This, as you can see, is a blowup of what our vidcam lenses picked up through the unstable gate. Rumor is, it has already started a heated debate among on-station scholars." Skeeter stared at the screen as Lupus, larger than life, plunged into the gate with a startled yell, then stumbled on a stone step. One of a huge number of stone steps, leading to the crest of a flat-topped pyramid. Lupus, grasping sword and knife, was staring down at an enormous crowd of feather-clad Indians. They were prostrate on the ground.

"Clearly," the voiceover said as Lupus just swayed there, stupefied, "this will begin an intense scholarly debate over the legendary origins of the god-like Viracocha, who came to Central America wearing a pale skin, taught the people a great deal of knowledge they didn't possess, then vanished across the ocean to the west, vowing to return. Speculation about the classic legend should fuel debate for years to come. Whatever the truth, this tape represents a scholarly as well as journalistic victory in the search for knowledge of our past."

Skeeter finished the motion he'd started with the remote and turned off the television with a deep sigh. He was almost sorry Lupus had suffered such a fate. He knew in his bones the shock of dissonance caused by plunging accidentally through an unstable gate, with no way home again. But in his inner soul, he was even gladder that he was still alive. *Still selfish, aren't we, Skeeter?* He realized sadly he probably always would be. But the painkillers had already begun to hit his system, so that he couldn't quite raise enough anxiety to worry about it now. Within moments, he drowsed into blissful oblivion.

"Marcus?"

Her voice came drowsily in the darkness. He'd been lying quietly, wrapped up in the miracle of holding her again and wondering if the gods would bless them with a son this time.

"Yes, beloved?"

Ianira's tiny movement told her how the endearment, new to his lips, had startled and pleased her. "Oh, Marcus," she breathed huskily into his ear, "what would I have done if—"

He placed gentle fingertips across her lips. "Let us not tempt the Fates, beloved. It did not happen. Let us not speak of it again."

Her arms tightened around his ribcage and for a moment she buried her face in his shoulder. A marvel of sensation, of need . . . but she wanted to discuss something, so he willed it back, ran his fingers through her silken black hair and murmured, "You had something to say?"

She turned just enough to kiss his wrist, then sighed and said, "Yes. That telephone call you were so angry about earlier?"

Marcus felt the chuckle build deep inside. "Not angry, love. Impatient."

His reward was another brush of her lips across his. Then she settled back into his arms, wrapped around him as warmly and contentedly as any cat. He'd had a kitten, as a child, tamed from the wild as the only survivor of its litter. Perhaps they should ask permission to get a kitten for their children? It would be a delightful surprise—

"Marcus, you haven't heard a word I've said!"

"I'm sorry, beloved. I was just thinking of asking the Station Manager for permission to get a kitten. For the girls."

It was Ianira's turn to chuckle. "Always my romantic dreamer. I would never have you be otherwise."

"What were you saying, beloved?" Strange, how the endearment he'd never been able to say before *now* came so easily to his lips.

"The phone call. It was Council business. They were taking votes over the phone, to move as quickly as possible."

Marcus turned his head slightly. "What could possibly be so urgent?"

She said very softly, "Skeeter."

Ahh . . .

"He is no longer Lost. He must therefore be given the chance to become Found."

Marcus nodded. "And your answer?"

"Yes, of course. Who do you think started the round of calls in the first place?"

Marcus laughed, softly enough not to waken their sleeping children, then turned until Ianira was beneath him, both arms still wrapped around him. This time, he could not hold back the love in him. Ianira cried out softly, moaned his name and sought his mouth. Marcus moved slowly, dreamily, thinking of kittens and sons and the miracle of this moment in whatever time Fate gave them together.

Epilogue

Skeeter was dreaming again. He'd dreamed often, these last few weeks, all of them terrible and strange, so at first he felt no great alarm, only a frisson of fear and a great deal of resignation as to what horrors his unconscious mind would put him through this time.

The dream began with dark figures, faces masked in black, bodies sheathed in black, hair covered with black, sinister figures which touched and lifted him, began to wind strips of black around his feet and lower legs so tightly he couldn't move even his toes. Then he realized he wasn't sleeping anymore. He began to fight—was subdued thoroughly and expertly. Sweat started along his back and chest and face as the black strips rose higher, covering thighs, hips, lower belly, like some monstrous black mummy casing. But they wouldn't get his arms. He had to have his arms free, to struggle, to plant a fist in *someone's* face before his strength ran out.

He fought savagely. He thought he heard a faint curse from one of the figures holding him and fought even harder. But his other fights, never mind that final run from Lupus, had taken nearly everything left in him. Eventually, his strength began to wane. And then, before he could react, an unknown person grabbed his shaved head and bent it back until the pain was so deep all he could do was blink tears down an open mouth and fight for air through the strain on his windpipe.

When they let him go, black wrappings swathed arms, chest, and neck. He could not move.

Coming slightly out of shock, Skeeter thought to use the other major skill he possessed: language. "Hey," Skeeter began, "look, whoever you are—not that I care, really, that's your business—but what're you doing? With me, I mean? Kidnapping's illegal on TT-86." At least, he thought it was. He hadn't ever gotten around to actually *reading* the rulebook they'd given him at Primary. "Look, have a heart. You can see I'm helpless, here. What could it possibly hurt to just *tell* me?"

Then, he became terrified as a new set of wrappings, covered his head and brow, wound around his eyes in one gauze-thin layer after another, Skeeter fought a whimper that had been building since childhood. "Please," he said while his mouth, at least, was still free, "what harm have I done to you? Just tell me, please, and I'll make it up to you, I swear it—"

His eyesight disappeared completely, both eyes covered in layer after layer of thin black cloth until there *was* no light. He struggled again, far too late. He could not move *anything* beneath the wrappings more than a quarter inch. Genuinely terrified now, a one-time Mongol battling claustrophobia, his breath came in ragged gasps. They left his nose clear—small comfort—then forcibly closed his jaw over a thick gag and tightly wrapped his mouth closed until the loudest sound he could utter was a faint, muffled, "Mmmmf," which even *he* had difficulty hearing. Getting enough air through his nose to fuel the mindless terror ripping through him proved futile. As he was lifted and carried toward his shattered apartment door, Skeeter blacked out.

He came to in ragged bits and pieces, aware of movement, of jostling as those carrying him grew tired and rearranged his weight in their grasp. He saw no light whatsoever and could catch no scent that might tell him where he was. He drifted out of consciousness again, then faded back into it, pondering this time *who* had him? ATF? Benson's men, intent on wresting whatever "unofficial" confessions they could beat and starve out of him? Or maybe Goldie Morran's henchmen, hired to do only the gods knew what—kill him, cripple him, send him uptime as luggage through Primary . . . Despite her capitulation on the bet, Goldie must still hate him with all her greedy, cold little heart. Or perhaps it was simply a tourist with a taste for revenge, who'd hired enough men to do this, maybe dump him down the garbage incinerator. . . .

A chill shook him inside the wrappings. Burned alive, like so many captives over the centuries. He'd heard the crazy stories about Kit's grandkid and that crazy Welsh bowman, both of whom had nearly been burned alive. His skin crawled already, anticipating the suffocating heat and the flames searing him while he writhed inside his black bindings and screamed himself to death.

He finally was set down on a cold, hard surface, unable to move. Someone unfastened the wrappings from his eyes, allowing him sight. At first, he thought he must've gone blind during that semi-conscious trip, for whatever room he'd been brought to was black-dark. Then he noticed specks of light as his eyes adjusted. Candles. Candles? He blinked a few times, clearing his eyes of dried tears and grit, and noticed shimmering golden draperies which formed a quiet, snug little room filled with candles—hundreds of 'em—and with warmth beyond any possible heat those candles could've given off and . . . he felt a fool for saying it even to himself . . . welcome.

Some welcome, Skeeter, wrapped up tight so you can't move, in black mummy bandages.

He noticed a dais, then, low and right in front of him. It was wide enough to hold seven people comfortably. Currently six stood on it, with a gap in the center for someone unknown. The six were men of various builds and heights, robed in black, faces masked in black, but unmistakably male. *The ones who brought me here, then.* A shuffling of many feet and the sound of dozens of lungs in the utter silence told Skeeter that a crowd had gathered to witness . . . what?

He shivered inside his imprisoning layers of cloth and looked up. He'd never gone lower in the terminal than the basement where the gym and weapons ranges were, having a Mongol's fear of tightly closed-in places. This must be the level beneath the basement, nothing but steam pipes, sewage drains, electrical conduits, and computer cables strung everywhere, festooning the girdered ceiling like the web of a very large and completely insane spider.

Skeeter shuddered again.

He didn't much like spiders.

Being caught in one's web was even worse.

At just that moment, the golden draperies stirred behind the dais, admitting darkness in the guise of a slim figure also robed and masked in black. *Looks like it's showtime.* Skeeter swallowed hard around the thick wad of cloth in his mouth. The gag forced every sound he tried to make shrivel and die in a parched throat. He gazed up at the seven robed figures, aware of dozens of figures still crowding into the already claustrophobic little space.

It's a court, Skeeter realized with a tremor. *It's a court and they're the judges and prob'ly the jury, too.* Probability that he'd be sentenced without defense was decidedly high—but for what crime? And what would that sentence be? Skeeter had come through so much over the past few days, he couldn't credit the evidence of his eyes: robed, silent judges, a rack of what looked like knives and instruments of torture just visible at the edge of his restricted gaze, a neat, terrifying coil of rope, just the right diameter and heft for hanging a man.

Skeeter, claustrophobic twice over, struggled in vain while the back of his brain whispered that any one of those ducts, pipes, and concrete supports overhead would make a great platform for a hangman's rope. And even if he hadn't been gagged, who would've heard him screaming, anyway, down in the bowels of the terminal where concrete met native Himalayan rock and merged with it?

Well, Skeeter'd survived a bloodbath, giving the spectators their money's worth; he'd won the damned laurel crown and the money prize fair and square. He'd even managed to rescue Marcus, alive and uninjured, except for the desperation in his dark eyes that spoke eloquently of how much his one-time friend wanted simply to go home and forget everything that had happened.

Skeeter hadn't expected elaborate thanks from the former slave and he certainly couldn't blame Marcus for wanting to forget those few weeks when circumstance and his stubborn, Gallic pride had forced him to pick up the burden of slavery again. True to his expectations, Marcus had not offered an elaborate, embarrassing

demonstration of gratitude. A couple of beers; but no elaborate show of gratitude. Yes, Skeeter had predicted that and it had come true.

A little bitterly, Skeeter wished he possessed a quarter of his former friend's character.

But in of all his long musings over Marcus' eventual reaction Skeeter had not predicted *this*. Not in his wildest, most terrify nightmares.

Before he was ready, a deep, male voice began speak language so archaic Skeeter didn't understand a single syll the robed judge had made his statement and retire another stepped forward. At least *he* spoke English

"I will speak the words of our most learned Umi, a scribe of pharaohnic Egypt, in English common language now, necessary for sur own thoughts for your consideration."

Skeeter didn't recognize either o inverted spins like a dying aircraft

"Chenzira Umi speaks agai than a common thief and cut off to end his career of thiev might expect of a worshi even our very Lord, w of Chenzira Umi."

Beneath his bindings wer what gave him? H but th ar

in a sc I'd say ha for the childr

Skeeter close

One by one, th

violent retribution. One for mercy, because he'd never stolen from *them*, whoever the hell *they* were, although Skeeter was beginning to form a pretty good guess. Then, surprisingly, another vote for mercy for the sake of the children Skeeter had saved over the years with his large donations. Skeeter narrowed his eyes. *How's he know I've been donating, never mind why?* Dimly, Marcus' voice came back to him, explaining how The Found Ones had known about his gifts of money for a long time. Based on that alone, Skeeter knew he ought to know the man, but the voice was completely strange to him. Maybe they wore voice synthesizers under those masks? The sixth vote was also, onishingly, for mercy, leaving the vote at a tie.

Then the seventh, small-statured person stepped forward.

keeter knew her voice in an instant. He stared, aghast that she be a part of such a bloodthirsty organization, but there she ier voice as clear as ancient temple bells.

a Cassondra's voice, issuing from the black mask, said, "The the Council of Seven stands at three against, three for. ote either way . . . well, either decision's outcome would be uld it not? I will not, *cannot* break a tie in this vote. As Council, I may vote to create a tie, for some things must very cautiously. But I may not cast the deciding vote. given reasons for our vote, I will speak as a special will poll the Committee members again, lest any r minds, hearing others' testimony."

e what's his name, that ancient Greek guy the s had forced to drink poison. Ianira herself had ne time over dessert in the apartment she and Skeeter was the guest of honor. *So fare the* r thought bitterly, *when seven wolves and a* ch. *Perfect democracy: everybody got to vote.*

wd would even bother *asking* this lunch aphorically speaking?

o soft she might have been whisperi ll projected Skeeter was certa hear her perfectly, began

Must've picked up that little trick in that big temple of hers. He waited for the betrayal to come.

It didn't. Instead, disbelieving, Skeeter listened while she wove a thread that became the yarn of a great tale of evil and danger, with Skeeter caught at the center of it, Skeeter who had, indeed, donated large sums of his earnings to them, donations which had saved many a child's life—and many an adult's, as well.

Then, as he was beginning to squirm with embarrassment, she launched hypnotically into the tale of Skeeter's run for life—Marcus' life—all the way from the back of Residential to the Porta Romae gate, already open with tourists filing through, while he dodged a man determined to kill him. How Skeeter had at last been forced to crash the Porta Romae to try and save his friend from the evil clutches of the man who'd planned all along to kidnap and sell Marcus back into slavery.

A craning, strained glance backwards showed Skeeter a roomful of people leaning forward, intent on her every word.

Damn, I'll bet she was impressive in that temple. In her flowing robes and flowing hair and that voice . . . Many a man would've thought she was whatever equivalent to angel he knew.

Ianira's magic voice then softened in horror at the fate of each man: one sold to the master of the games and ordered to keep track of inventory—men and beasts. Beside that, she wove the story of the other man, kidnapped and sold to be a gladiator, hardly able to communicate with his captors, beaten and tortured into learning the art of butchering others to stay alive, when his own presence in Rome spoke eloquently of the fact that he could be no killer, that he had come here because he had promised to save Marcus, whatever it took. In trying to keep that promise, he had lost his freedom and was slated to die in the arena on the end of a grand champion's sword.

By this time, there were murmurs in the back rows, murmurs that sounded angry. Skeeter didn't dare hope that note of anger was for *him* and the foul treatment he'd received.

"And then," Ianira Cassondra cried out, raising both arms in a graceful, possibly symbolic motion, "our Skeeter defeated th[illegible] champion *and refused to kill his opponent!* The Caesar—" s[illegible] pronounced it Kai-sar "—gave him both laurel crown and purse as rightfully his. Aware that only more slavery awaited him, victory and prize notwithstanding; aware also that he had not yet freed his friend, who stood with his evil master on the great balustrade above the starting boxes for the races, Skeeter did what only a man with the smiles of the gods at his back could possibly have done."

She deliberately stretched out the tense silence. Then, all but whispering, as if in holy awe herself, "He galloped his horse for the starting-gate wall. Leapt to his *feet* on the galloping horse's back—" a number of people, men from the sound of it, gasped in shock— "then dug the butt of his spear into the blood-drenched sand and spun himself up and over the balustrade. While every guard on the balustrade gawked just to *see* him there, instead of fifteen feet down in the arena, Skeeter tossed the heavy purse that was his well-earned prize to Marcus' new master as payment for his friend's freedom."

Somewhere behind them, a ragged cheer broke out. Skeeter began to pray with the tiniest smidgen of hope that he might yet live through this.

"And then?" Ianira's voice demanded of her audience. "Then our resourceful Skeeter arranged for them to impersonate more highly placed persons than they were, to throw off the slave trackers after them. They hid. They changed disguises and hiding places, again and again. And when gate time came for the Porta Romae, Skeeter caused a great diversion so that he and Marcus could win through to the time gate and come safely home.

"Now," and her voice turned abruptly hard as diamond and angry as a rattlesnake stirred up in the rocks, "I ask you, members of The Found Ones, what was his reward for this? A monstrous fine from that evil group calling itself Time Tours whose employees use us badly and care not a bit for our health, our dependents left behind should we die, our very lives squandered like spare change without anyone ever warning us of the dangers! They actually had the gall to *fine him*! *Both directions!* And what followed that? Imprisonment by Station Security—during which he was starved, beaten, humiliated!

"I ask!" she cried, sweeping off her mask, shaking out her hair, revealing her face, alight now with startling holiness—it was the only way Skeeter could find to describe the light that seemed to flow outward from her—"I ask you, each of you, is this any *fair* way to treat a man who has risked his very life, not once, but many times, for *one of us*?"

The roar echoed in the confined space like a Mongolian thunderstorm trapped in the confines of a canyon deep in the high, sharp mountains.

Very, very slowly, Ianira allowed her head to fall forward as though infinitely wearied by the gruesome story of treachery, courage, and betrayal she'd just been forced to reveal. When her head rose again, the mask was back in place. *Symbolic, then,* Skeeter realized. But of what?

Voice carefully neutral again, Ianira said, "He has the qualifications. All of you know already the story of this man's childhood, lost in a time not his own. He has faced all that we have faced—and worse. Yet he has survived, prospered, remained generous in his heart to those in greater need than he. I now ask for a new and final poll of the Seven. Do we Punish? Or Accept?"

One by one the answers came to Skeeter's sweating ears.

In thick-accented English came the single word, "Punish," from the ever-condemning voice of the Egyptian.

A pause ensued. The man who had previously translated the Egyptian's longer speech said very quietly, "Accept."

The next man refused to be swayed, which, if Skeeter were reading the body language under the robe correctly, deeply irritated Ianira Cassondra.

Down the line it went, skipping over Ianira: "Punish." "Accept." "Accept." "Accept."

Skeeter wasn't certain he'd heard—or counted—correctly. *Was that really four versus two? Now what?*

Ianira stepped forward, the final member of the Seven to cast her vote. Skeeter waited to hear her confirm what he thought he'd just heard. "The vote stands at four to accept, two to punish. As there is no chance for a tie, I may cast my vote freely." She looked down at Skeeter, lying helpless on the concrete floor at her feet. "I cannot deny that Skeeter Jackson is a scoundrel, a thief, and a man who charms people out of their money and belongings, to his own benefit.

"Yet I must also repeat that he has saved the lives of many in this very room through donations he thought anonymous. And then, on nothing more than a promise, this *scoundrel* and thief risked his life to save a down-timer, a member of The Found Ones. I admit difficulty in putting aside personal feelings, for Marcus is the father of my children, but this is a thing in which I was trained at the Temple of Artemis at Ephesus: to look beyond personal feelings to the heart of the truth.

"And that is why, peering as we have into this man's heart, his soul, judging him by his actions—*all* his actions—I *must* vote to Accept."

Another thunderous roar went up while Skeeter stared, wide-eyed, at Ianira. He still didn't quite believe it. Ianira approached from the dais, a sharp knife in her hands. Skeeter swallowed hard.

"Do not fear, beloved friend." She cut loose the clinging, confining gauze wrappings, freeing him to stand up and beat his thighs with equally leaden arms to restore circulation. Then he was swept away, buffeted, occasionally kissed—and the kissers were not always female—his back pounded until he was certain the well-wishers would leave bruises the size of dinner plates. He wasn't precisely sure just what the vote to Accept meant.

Apparently Ianira sensed this, as she sensed so much else out of thin air, for she called a halt to the merrymaking and restored order to The Found Ones' chamber.

"Skeeter Jackson, please approach the dais."

He did so slowly, filing down a sudden double line of grinning Found Ones, curiosity and uncertainty wavering within him still. He *hated* not knowing precisely what was about to unfold. He wondered what he should do when he got there? *Show respect*, his mind told him, somewhat dry with disgust that he hadn't thought of it sooner. So when he arrived, he went down on one knee and kissed the hem of her robe. When he dared glance up, her mask was gone and she was actually blushing—furiously.

Regaining her composure quickly, however, she said to him,

"There are things we must explain to you, Skeeter Jackson, for although you are now one of us, it is through accident only. Born an up-timer, you spent formative years of your life down time, with a group of men as harsh as the summer's noonday sun on the marble steps at Ephesus. You have suffered, lived, and learned from every misfortune you have encountered. You might have become a creature like the gems dealer, Goldie Morran, who has no true heart anywhere in her.

"But you did not. You gave to others, not once but many times. Your . . . misadventure . . . down the Porta Romae only cinched your right to hold this honor, Skeeter Jackson. From this day until the end of your life and beyond, you shall be known as a Found One, for although you have been Lost all your life and took great pains to hide it, Marcus was able to discover the truth. You are one of us," she swept the room with one arm, taking in what must have been more than a hundred women, men, and children of all ages, dozens of societies and time periods—some having come through a tourist gate, more through an unstable one.

"You are one of us, Skeeter Jackson, and we are now your Family."

And then, as people filed past, many giving him gifts of welcome—plain, simple gifts made to be cherished over a lifetime: a flower, a handmade handkerchief bearing an embroidered logo which must stand for The Found Ones, a box of food, a new pair of bluejeans—*it* happened. Skeeter Jackson began to cry. It started as a tickle at the back of his throat. Worked its way up to a tight throat, then to wetness welling up in his eyes. Before he knew it, he was crying so hard, each indrawn breath shook his slender frame. Eventually he found himself alone on the dais with Ianira and Marcus and the many, many gifts left for him.

"Why?" Marcus asked quietly.

Ianira rolled her eyes. "Men," she said tiredly. "It is so obvious, Marcus. He has a *family* now."

Skeeter nodded vehemently, still unable to speak. He had a real Clan again! One that accepted him on his own terms, knowing his worst faults, yet took him in anyway and made something of him more than an outcast kid shivering in the Mongolian nights and trying desperately not to waken Yesukai the Valiant, lest he waken the man's formidable temper—and worse punishments.

"I swear," he whispered, voice still choked with tears, "I swear to you, Ianira, Marcus, I will *never* betray your faith. I have a Clan again. And I *never* break faith with the people who are of my Clan. There . . . there were times I believed I was not worthy of finding another to accept me, other than one I adopted from necessity's sake."

"The 'eighty-sixers?" Marcus asked.

Skeeter nodded. "Not that I'll start stealing from them now. I *did* adopt *them*, after all. And . . . and it sounds crazy, but . . . I don't know what to do. I haven't any skills worthy of The Found Ones."

Ianira and Marcus exchanged glances, obviously having given this careful thought. Then Ianira bent close and murmured in his ear. "We have a few ideas you might find . . . intriguing." She then proceeded to describe three of them, just to tantalize his imagination.

Skeeter started; then grinned and began to laugh like a newly freed imp. Not only would he be *useful*, it sounded like *fun*!

"Lady," he shook her hand formally, "you just got yourself a twenty-four-carat deal!"

He had difficulty, still, imagining himself an honest man. But what the hell? Ianira's ideas were fabulous.

An entire new life stretched out before him.

All he had to do was grasp it.

"Yeah," he repeated softly, to himself, "a genuine twenty-four-carat deal."

That said, he dried his face with the heels of his hands and let Marcus and Ianira carry some of his gifts while he carried the lion's share. They escorted him away from the dim-lit Council Chamber (blowing out candles as they went) up to the bright lights and holiday cheer of Commons.

Skeeter Jackson stopped and just *looked*. Today, for the first time in his life, all he saw were happy people making merry during the happiest time of year. "Say, how about we dump these things at my apartment and go celebrate somewhere out there?"

Marcus and Ianira exchanged glances, then smiled.

That was exactly what they did.